First Published 2016.

ISBN: 978-0-9953524-0-7

All characters and events in this publication, other than those clearly in the public domain, are fictitious and any resemblance to real persons, living or dead, are purely coincidental. The moral Right of the author has been asserted.

Cover designed by Brendan Sanders.

www.sevenstonesofpower.com

THE ONYX NECKLACE

ANDY STONE

Northern Wasteland
The Seven Kingdoms
Arachne (Spider Mount)
Scorpio (Scorpian Mount)
Honoin Lel
Avalon
Remidia
Cloiumid Mountain Range
Nostiria
Carolija Island (Isle of Wizards)
Lel Dinion
Remidel
Zenza City
Arlisiac
Cauldron Mountain
City of the Night
Tarrat
Bellarome
King's Rest
Stellerville
Lord's Wait
Entero
Castalia
Kiarome
Sillarome
Darshival
Desert (Disputed Lands)
Southern Wasteland

Prologue: The Beginning of the End

The forest had turned strangely calm, at least compared to the last few days. The morel had been more aggressive in attacking the dryads. There had been no real reason for it, just as there was no real reason for the sudden stop. The dryads had all but been annihilated and another day of attack would more than likely see the end of them.

"What are they waiting for?" Xanthia asked as she stared into the gloom of the forest.

Her white dress, which was synonymous with dryads, had turned almost grey. It was a sign that her strength was waning. It would only be a matter of time before she was overpowered.

The forest was darker than usual. The remaining dryads had dampened their glow, as much as they could without letting it go completely. It had once been their best defence against the morel, who would not step into the light for fear of death. The light also brought power to the dryads. Although they generally lived in peace with the forest, if there was any threat they could be lethal. But something had changed in the last few days. The morel were no longer afraid of the light and if anything it drove them to a frenzy.

The morel had once been elves, but their practice of evil rituals had changed them into wicked creatures. They possessed the same physical features as elves, although their skin was naturally darker. Instead of living in peace with the forest they were like a disease. The morel would have completely destroyed the forest many years ago if it wasn't for the dryads.

At one time the dryads had been akin with the morel. The two races had originated from elves, but unlike the morel the dryads grew closer to the forest. They became more in tune and one with the woods. They felt the forest's very moods and were as much a part of the Eastern Forest as the flowers and trees.

"There is something different about the forest," Xynate, the queen of the dryads, spoke slowly. Her soft blonde hair was covered in dirt. She had been involved in a skirmish with the morel and was lucky to return with her life. "I felt something this morning. I don't know what it is and I can only hope it's a good thing."

"The queen is right, my sister," Xavi, the last male dryad left alive, spoke softly. "It's like the forest has taken a deep breath and is waiting for something to happen."

"It can only be the attack then," Xenia responded. She was the only dryad with black hair. No one knew how it had come to be. All the other dryads had white hair, some with streaks of blonde. "That is what the forest is waiting for, the final attack from the morel. I guess we always knew this day was coming." Her words were ominous.

"Well if this is going to be our final battle with the morel, let's make it a battle to last the ages." As much as Xynate didn't believe Xenia was right it was an appropriate speech.

As one, the remaining dryads intensified their glow and the forest suddenly became alight. Even though it didn't scare the morel anymore, the light did increase their own strength and the strength of the forest around them. They all felt a lot happier and more confident once they were glowing again; there was no faith in the darkness of the forest. The feeling of joy only lasted a moment before they saw what was before them.

Through the trees they could see the morel, standing, waiting for them. It would seem the Xenia was right. It seemed suspicious to the queen that morel had waited for them to glow. Even if they were no longer afraid, it would have been more advantageous for them to attack in the dark. There was something strange about the situation. Even with the newly lit forest the morel didn't make any move to attack. She knew there was something more to come.

Five minutes passed, with no move from the morel, before someone spoke. "Should we attack?" Xavi finally asked.

"We have never attacked unless provoked." The term 'provoked' had been stretched over the years. "They have made no move to attack, so we should make no move ourselves. They outnumber us by so much that I'm not even sure there is an amount to express it. I see no advantage in forcing a battle."

Apart from the four who were talking there were only four other dryads left alive. Although the queen had no idea how many morel were waiting for them, she guessed there was at least one hundred, but more likely closer to one thousand. Despite the morel that they had managed to kill over the past week there would be plenty more.

"The queen is right, it would be suicide to attack now," Xanthia responded.

"Then maybe we should leave. There are plenty of places in the forest we could hide. If they don't want to attack then we shouldn't stay here," Xavi added.

"Then we would just be delaying the inevitable," Xania argued. "I would rather go down fighting now, than wait for another day. That is no way to live the rest of our lives. We are proud beings and if we are going to be annihilated then we should do so in an appropriate manner." There was something about Xania that had made her more aggressive than the other dryads, who were normally peaceful creatures. Some put it down to the colour of her hair.

"That is enough talk of death and dying," a soft female voice came from the forest behind them.

As they turned around they saw a middle-aged woman slowly walking towards them. She had short cut, brown hair and a homely look about her. She wore a dress of brown, but that was all. Although she walked across the forest floor in bare feet, there were no grass or dirt stains. There was a confidence about her that didn't seem to match her appearance as she moved through the trees.

"Who are you?" Xynate asked breathlessly.

"Hush child, there will be time for questions soon enough, but for now I have work to do. There has been a disease in my forest for too long and now it is time to cure it."

She flowed across the forest floor as she made her way towards the morel. The dryads all wanted to call out, to warn her to stay away, but no words came out. All they could do was watch and hope.

The strange woman walked straight up to the first morel without any hint of fear. There was no way she could know what the creatures were. If she did then she wouldn't have been so casual. She walked up and down the line a couple of times and to the dryads surprise the morel made no move to attack. The situation had just become even stranger. From where they stood there didn't seem to be anything restraining the evil creatures.

When she returned to the middle of the group she gently touched one of the morel of the forehead. Instantly the creature collapsed to the ground before bursting into flames. Despite the fire nothing else caught alight. Within a matter of seconds the morel had completely disappeared.

Slowly she stood back to survey the situation. When she was pleased with the result she continued through the morel, touching each of them one by one. Each time they collapsed and burst into flame.

The dryads watched in awe, none of them were prepared to move. Even if they had tried they would have realised they couldn't. Until her job was done she wouldn't allow them to interfere. After two hours had passed she finally returned to the group with a warm smile on her face.

"My children," she started when she returned. "I bask in your glow, but you can save your energy now. Your enemy has been defeated and the forest is free of its taint. You can tell the others to come out from hiding."

The other dryads looked at each other, but the queen stepped forward. It was her duty to protect them and she needed to find out who it was that stood before them. If she had the power to defeat the morel single handed then she didn't know what she could do if she turned aggressive. Despite her fears the queen didn't feel any evil. Although the dryads were very in tune with the forest, and everything in it, she couldn't tell anything about the woman before her.

"We are all that remains," Xynate did her best to keep the sorrow out of her voice.

At first she didn't seem to comprehend what Xynate had told her, but then a look of recognition crossed her face. "So Alaric was right."

At the mention of Alaric, Xynate finally remembered. She had asked him to get help from the Council of Wizards. The woman before them must be one of those wizards. Even though the thought made perfect sense, something was wrong. When she had asked Alaric for the Council's help she had her doubts whether all seven could help in their struggle against the morel. She didn't think just one wizard would be able to do what she had just witnessed.

"Are you one of the Council of Wizards?" she finally asked.

"What?" the woman sounded shocked. "Have I been away from my children for so long that you don't even recognise me anymore?" It was a strange question.

"There is something very familiar about you, but I have to admit that if you are not the help we asked for then I have no idea who you are."

"I am the Wood Sprite Blodwyn and now that I'm back no harm will befall my forest."

Xynate looked at her for a moment. There was something different about her, but there could be no doubt she was the Wood Sprite that had left them so many years ago. She couldn't believe that she had not known straight away. The Wood Sprite and the forest were one, even more than the connection the dryads had with the forest.

"Mistress, I am so sorry we didn't recognise you," Xynate went to one knee in deference and was quickly followed by the others. "Thank you for rescuing us. With you we would have been..."

"Stand my child. It is I who should be apologising to you. I have been away too long. If I had been here then none of this would have happened," Blodwyn spoke softly.

"Where have you been?" Xynate was almost too afraid to ask.

"Come, sit with me and I will tell you everything."

***

The battle had been fierce, but the Alliance was victorious. At the front of the army the battle had been short. The Remidian Army began their attack when word reached Jarwe that there were orglin attacking from the rear. The horn blasts that warned the commanders had also alerted the opposing army. It was exactly what the Dark Knight wanted.

If everything had gone to plan the Alliance would have wiped out the Remidian Army, whilst the orglin took care of the Alliance, but that was not the case. The way the Remidian army attacked seemed very unusual. It was outnumbered at least four to one and it made no sense to force a confrontation.

The soldiers met each other in battle and neither side gave a quarter. Even though they were not truly enemies, both sides were fighting for their lives. It didn't take long for Brielle to realise why the Remidian soldiers were fighting a losing battle. The Dark Knight didn't have enough strength to control the minds of the entire army, but he did have enough to control some of the main commanders. Even though the order to leave the city had come from King Faxon himself, there were those who didn't entirely believe it. The rumours that the dwarf Gilgi was commanding the King had filtered down through the ranks. The order itself wasn't enough to compel the soldiers to leave the safety of the city, but with the added command of their leaders it was.

It wasn't long before the six wizards were able to find the commanders and remove the spell that was controlling their minds. The Dark Knight didn't have the power to keep the spells running. He could only set the idea in their minds and then tie off the spell. He needed all his remaining energy to continue his control of Faxon and destroy the Alliance.

When the commanders of the Remidian army were free of the Dark Knight's spell they surrendered. It only took them a moment to realise what was happening, but when they did they instantly voiced the command. The soldiers didn't wait to drop their weapons and raise their arms over their heads. Although there had been deaths, it could have been a lot worse.

The battle at the other side of the army was a lot more difficult. There was no dissuading the orglin from attacking. The Dark Knight had set them in motion and only the utter annihilation of the Alliance would have stopped them. There were also large creatures, which looked like a cross between a troll and a minotaur. They held huge whips and were striking any orglin that didn't race into the fray. The leathery skinned creatures were unpredictable at the best of times and needed a master with a higher intellect to keep them in line.

Just when it seemed as though the orglin horde was about to overwhelm the Alliance, a horn was sounded from the south. The noise caught everyone by surprise, but there was no time for respite. The orglin, in their frenzy, did not stop their attack. If they had they might have realised that they were doomed to fail.

Finally the Castalial army had reached the Alliance and not a moment too soon. Despite the long march they did not hesitate to join the fray. When the commanders crested a hill and saw the battle enfolding before them, they quickly called their soldiers to attack. Luckily the fury of the charge was as they ran over the hill, or they may have balked at the sight before them. A horde of orglin swarming over the men below would be enough to turn even the staunchest of soldiers.

The large advantage the Castalial soldiers had was that they had been instructed to wear their armour that day as they were getting close to Remidel. Despite the soldier's complaints, the commanders had insisted.

The orglin, equipped only with razor sharp claws and teeth, had a hard time against the steel armour. It wasn't impossible for them to kill the

Castalial soldiers, but it made it very difficult. It was much easier for them to attack the Alliance.

Once the Castalial soldiers had joined the battle it didn't take long for it to be over. There was nothing the beast-masters could do to deter the orglin. Before long they were all slaughtered and all that was left was the job of hunting down the beast-masters. Without the orglin horde they didn't last long.

It was just on dusk when the chaos had finally subsided. The Castalial army joined the fringe of the camp, but until the commanders had met they decided it was best not to assimilate them. Three commanders from the Castalial army, one general and two captains, joined the commanders of the Alliance.

Three additional members to the command group was more than the other armies, but there were a lot more soldiers from Castalia, so there were no complaints.

General Nerva stood over six feet tall and held a commanding presence. He wore a large steel breastplate and helmet with a strong nose guard. Despite the battle he had no blood on him. As general he had commanded and not taken part.

His two captains were not as fortunate. Once the battle had started they were sent into action. Although they both wore armour, scratches from both claws and teeth were prominent amongst the black blood of the orglin. They looked well battle worn.

"General Nerva, you couldn't have arrived at a better time," Jarwe was the first to speak. Despite the fact that the General from Remidia had just commanded the Alliance to attack soldiers from his home kingdom, he seemed in surprisingly high spirits.

"It seems as though there was something at play here. I was expecting we would have reached the army more than two days ago." Nerva paused for a second as he thought. "I had been told of this so called 'prophecy' that has been controlling things and I put it down to superstition, but now... Now I have to believe. There was no reason why we should have reached the rest of the army at the time we did. I can only put it down to fate."

Jarwe couldn't help himself and burst out laughing. The sound brought laughter from the other commanders. The three from Castalia looked at each other, confused at the reaction. They could not see what was so funny.

"I am sorry, general. It's just that you have just voiced something that we have all felt in the past. We can take nothing for granted," Jarwe apologized when he realised that they did not understand his humour.

The other commanders stopped laughing when Jarwe spoke. They too noticed that their reaction had been quite rude. Luckily General Nerva could see the funny side, although he did not think it was appropriate to start laughing. A lot of good men had died and there was no time for mirth.

"What is the situation in the city?" he asked.

Jarwe looked at Sorrell who in turn shook his head. The General from Darshival and Jarwe's second in command, at least until Bern returned, had been trying to gather some information. The commanders were still dazed from the mind-control the Dark Knight had placed over them and the common soldiers did not seem to know anything pertinent. Nerva knew it was not a good sign.

"From the limited information that we have gathered it seems as though a Dark Knight is in control of the city." Jarwe looked toward the group of wizards for confirmation.

The five remaining members of the Council of Wizards stood to one side of the group. They were pretending not to take any notice of what was being said, but it was obvious they heard every word. They had been aloof since Alaric had forced them from their island off the coast of Remidia and brought them into the Alliance. The commanders had hoped for more advice from them, but it had been few and far between.

"There is no doubt that a Dark Knight was controlling the commanders of the Remidian army. We were able to remove his spell and stop him from creating anymore trouble," Gwydion, the eldest and most respected of the wizards, explained.

"It was not as easy as you would think," Brielle added, with a slight amount of distain to her voice.

No one had thought it would be an easy task fighting a Dark Knight, even though they had no idea what was involved. Brielle's comment was unnecessary, but she would not let Gwydion have the only say. She had a sour expression on her normally beautiful face as she waited for a response from the general.

"We appreciate your help," Jarwe started. "I'm sure you saved a lot of deaths, on both sides."

His grateful response did nothing to appease Brielle, but a stern look from Gwydion stopped her from speaking. The aged wizard knew there was no point in enflaming the situation. It had been a tense battle, especially for those at the rear of the army, and any confrontation would be unproductive. There were more important matters to deal with and Gwydion did not what to risk the commanders dismissing them from the conversation.

"Let's not dance around the subject." Sorrell took the chance to bring the conversation back on point. "How are we going to get the Dark Knight out of the city?" The question, although not aimed at anyone, was directed towards the wizards.

"We are here to watch and advise, not to fight your war for you," Althea took her chance to speak. She had been against the decision to leave the island and didn't care who knew. She did not think that the battle with the Evil One involved the council. As far as she was concerned the council were safe on their island and she was quite happy to continue her solitary existence.

Althea's words brought murmurs from the command group, but no one wanted to voice their concerns. There was a mystery about the wizards that made everyone very uncomfortable. They had shut themselves away from the Seven Kingdoms, accept for Eldred, for many years on the Isle of Wizards. The rumours that made it to the mainland were sketchy at best, but they did not paint a friendly picture. Over the years the council were both feared and respected and the end result left the commanders unsure how to treat them.

"That's not good enough," barked Wojtek. Sorrell's advisor was not going to hold on ceremony. "Alaric sent you here to help us and that is what you are going to do."

"And who do you think you are to speak to us in such a manner?" Brielle snapped.

"Enough!" boomed Jarwe. He was the General of the Alliance and it was up to him to take control. "This is exactly what the enemy wants. How are we going to defeat the Dark Knight if we are too busy fighting amongst ourselves?" He let the question float on the air, not really expecting anyone to answer him.

The two looked at each other, but didn't say anything. Neither knew what Jarwe would do if they continued their argument and they weren't about to find out.

"Very good, now let's get down to business. How are we going to defeat the Dark Knight?" Jarwe continued.

"Bern said for us to wait for his return. I think that is our best option," Gwydion voiced his opinion.

"We didn't march all the way from Castalia just to sit at the doorstep of Remidel," General Nerva rebuked the wizard.

"I have to agree with Nerva," Sorrell added. "We have the Dark Knight trapped in the city and last thing we want to do is give him a chance to regroup and escape. I think we need to draw up plans for an assault."

Jarwe did not like that idea. Remidel was his city and he did not want to see it come to any harm. The walls were strong and could withstand days of bombardment. Not only that, but they had no siege engines. Too much time would pass if they attempted to assail the city. In that time there was no telling what mischief the Dark Knight could get up to.

"I don't think it will be necessary to bombard the walls. That will take too much time. We now hold the Remidian Royal Army and I'm sure they will help us. With the spells removed from the commanders minds there is nothing holding them to the Dark Knight. I am still their general and they will have to listen to my command."

It was a much better plan, but it still had its risks. They would have to trust that those still inside the city would not attack them when they approached. Although Jarwe was still the Remidian Army's rightful leader, it had been over a year since anyone had seen him. There was a chance that they would no longer recognise him as their general. Their best chance to gauge their chances for success was to speak with one of the commanders who had led the attack against them.

"Bring Captain Kenyon," he called to one of the nearby lieutenants. "I'm sure he'll be able to give us some more information."

"I wouldn't be so sure. They will still be suffering from the effect of the mind-control," Althea reminded them, her tone a little softer.

They waited in silence until the lieutenant returned with the captain. Despite his large build and strong jaw he looked defeated. It was the only word they could use to describe his appearance. Jarwe had known the captain from his time leading the Remidian Army and he did not look his normal self. He hated to admit it, but he thought Althea was right.

"Captain!" Jarwe saluted as the man approached, hoping that would snap him out of his current state.

"General Jarwe," Kenyon returned the salute, but with much less vigour than it deserved. "I am sorry that we had to fight. I don't know what came over us." Kenyon kept his eyes down as he spoke. He felt great shame for what they had done. There was no good reason why they should have left the city to attack their allies.

"That is alright captain. There was nothing you could do against the Dark Knight's mind-control. We can only be grateful that the wizards realised in time and there weren't too many casualties. This battle could have been a lot worse, especially with the orglin attacking from the rear."

Jarwe's words had their effect on Captain Kenyon. He straightened his shoulders and started to look the part. Whilst Jarwe was in command of the Alliance, Kenyon had been in control of the Remidian Royal Army and he needed to start acting like it. He would be the sub-commander of the Remidian army once it had been assimilated into the Alliance.

"What is it I can do for you general?"

"We need to know what defences are left inside the city walls?" Jarwe came straight to the point.

"Surely you don't mean to attack the city?" Kenyon asked, aghast. "We have surrendered to you; there is no need to attack."

In another situation Jarwe would have laughed at Kenyon's response, but things were too dire for mirth. "Of course not captain, but there is still the matter of the Dark Knight in control of the city and the kingdom. We need to free King Faxon from his yoke. There is no telling what trouble he can still cause if we leave him where he is."

When Kenyon realised what he was planning he visibly relaxed. He scolded himself for thinking that the general was planning on invading the capital. It had been what the Dark Knight, through King Faxon, had been trying to convince them. No one really believed it, but the thought was still in the back of their minds.

"There are a few archers on the walls, but basically I was ordered to take the full army onto the battlefield. I can't believe that I followed such a ridiculous order. There was no chance that we would have survived such a confrontation." Kenyon rubbed his head at the thought.

"Don't be too hard on yourself. There was nothing you could have done," Jarwe reassured him. "So it seems as though our entrance to the city will be relatively painless."

"Getting into the city is only one problem. From there we'll need to infiltrate the palace and even that isn't even close to the difficult part." Sorrell voiced everyone's concerns. "The main question we should be asking is how are we going to defeat a Dark Knight?"

Everyone looked towards the wizards for an answer. Even with the extra soldiers from the Castalial and Remidian armies they could kill the Dark Knight without their help. In open battle there was a chance their numbers could overrun him, but there were only so many that could fit in the palace at any one time. No one really wanted to lead a group of soldiers into the city. Even though they were not a hostile army there was a chance some of the soldiers from the Alliance would take the opportunity to cause problems. There were woman and other spoils for the taking and they couldn't risk any trouble. It would have to be small group they took to defeat the Dark Knight, unless Bern arrived, which they all hoped for.

"We have already said that this is not our battle. You will have to find another way to defeat the Dark Knight," Brielle spoke before any of the other wizards had a chance.

"That is not necessarily true," Minerva spoke for the first time. She didn't agree with what Brielle had been saying. "I think we should discuss this matter further. I take it you're not planning to enter the city right at this very moment?"

"No, we should set camp and let the soldiers rest. It has been a long march and today's battle would have done nothing to ease their fatigue. We'll give Bern and the others another day or two to return and then we have no other choice. We have no word where he is and can ill afford to wait any longer." With Jarwe's words the command group left to go about their business.

Jarwe remained behind and stared at the city. He would dearly love to know what was happening inside the palace and if they had any friends left inside. It was a daunting task to face a Dark Knight and not one he ever thought he would have to do, but that was the job ahead of him and whatever the wizards decided his fate was set.

***

"What was that all about?" Brielle spoke between clenched teeth. Despite the fact that a spell had been cast so no one outside the council could hear what they were saying, she was not going to yell.

"This is not the time for us to sit back and watch. We left the island for a reason and that was to fight." Minerva was not going to back down.

"Minerva is right," Gwydion added. "We have spent too much time away from the rest of the Seven Kingdoms. It is time for us to take a stand. We have sat back and watched for too long now. Our fate is bound to the Seven Kingdoms again and we cannot sit back and let it be destroyed. The final battle is looming and the Alliance will need all its commanders alive if it is going to succeed. If the army fails then we are all doomed."

"You sound like Eldred with all his talk of prophecies. You cannot honestly believe that this is our battle?" Althea came to Brielle's aid.

"Our brother has been right from the start, but we were too proud to listen to him. Our fate is tied in with the Alliance and the Chosen One himself. We have met Alaric and none of us can deny the power that he holds. If he wasn't who he said he is then we would still be sitting on the island completely oblivious," Drake added.

None of the wizards had agreed it was the right decision to leave their home, no one except for Eldred. Eldred was the only member of the council who believed in the prophecy and had spent many years roaming the Seven Kingdoms in search of the Chosen One. Since they had left it was only Althea and Brielle who still didn't think it was their battle to fight.

"So what do you propose we do? Walk in and challenge the Dark Knight to a duel?" Brielle asked.

"We five are of the Council of Wizards. We do not fear the Evil One's slaves," Gwydion barked. "It is true that we have spent too much time away from the Seven Kingdoms, but have we truly forgotten how to fight?"

"I don't know about you Gwydion, but I have been studying the arts of peaceful magic. I follow the healing arts of Topaz and was never designed for battle," Althea argued.

"She is right. I have devoted my life to the peaceful nature of Sapphire and ways of the water. True I am not weak, but the Dark Knights have been trained in pure destruction. How can we compete with such a creature?" Brielle asked.

"There is power in water as there is power in all things. We cannot fear one Dark Knight. Together we have the power to defeat him and together we must," Drake added, raising his voice for effect.

There was a moment of silence as everyone thought on his words. The two had to admit that there was truth to what he said. Once, a long time ago, the council had been a power to be reckoned with. They had grown placid in their isolation, but they could not longer rely on solidarity as a defence.

"You are right," Brielle finally conceded. I have fought the idea for so long that it was ingrained in my very being, but now is the time to stand up and be counted. At one time none could stand before us, but now is the time for us to fight."

"To a vote then. Do we fight the Dark Knight or do we leave the Alliance, and the Seven Kingdoms, to their fate?" Drake asked.

Minerva, Drake and Gwydion instantly raised their right hands. Brielle, despite her revelation, waited a moment before adding her consent. Althea, although she was still not completely convinced, would not be left out. Slowly she raised her hand and the decision to fight was unanimous.

"Very well. We'll leave the commanders to their duty and inform them of our decision in the morning." Gwydion's words were final.

***

Marina trudged through the storm. Her long black hair clung to her deep blue dress. She had walked for more days than she could remember, not really knowing where she was going. All she knew was that there was a destination and she had to reach it. She had no idea how long it had been since she had eaten and yet she did not feel any hunger.

Not too long ago she was a spoilt princess in the Kingdom of Darshival. That seemed like a lifetime ago. When she looked back she did not really know why she had left the safety of her father's palace in Kiarome to travel with Alaric. Sure enough he was good looking, and there had always seemed to be an attraction between them, but that did not seem a good enough reason to leave her life behind. Perhaps she thought that they would return to Kiarome before the final battle. All she knew was that her life had been turned upside down and the person who she had loved had betrayed her.

When he had given her the Sapphire ring she could not have been happier. It was like a part of her had been missing her entire life. Finally she felt complete. She had a man she loved that was a part of her life and that made her happier than she had ever felt, but that did not last long.

When the Dark Knight Argoz had stolen the ring she thought her heart would break. When Alaric said that he would not help her find Sapphire she could not believe what he was saying. There was nothing more important to her in the Seven Kingdoms and she thought the man she loved would move the heavens to return it to her.

She had set out from the Alliance camp outside of Jarrat and tracked the Dark Knight to the Kingdom of Hondin Lel. The Dark Knight had thought he was safe to usurp power in Lel Dinion and rule through the power of King Lisle, but he was sorely mistaken. There was an affinity between Marina and the Sapphire stone that his evil could not break.

As soon as Marina had the stone she took control of the Dark Knight and the kingdom. All she had to do was wait for Alaric to return, which she always knew he would, and then they could be together for all eternity, but she was betrayed again.

Alaric had destroyed the Dark Knight and then stolen the ring from her. She could not believe that the man she had once loved could betray her again. The ring was rightfully hers and yet he would not return it. Now she hated him. There was nothing more she wanted than to regain Sapphire and destroy the wicked man who had taken her from her. That goal was what kept her going. A rage brewed inside her and only retrieving the stone and killing Alaric would sate her desires.

The rain beat down and Marina basked in the storms malevolence. Sapphire controlled water and water was her new friend. In days past she would have run inside when the weather turned bad, but that was in a different life. She didn't feel the cold anymore, not like lesser creatures. The pelting rain seemed to reflect her mood perfectly.

She did not know why, as there had been no sun for days, but she felt she was travelling to the north. As she travelled she felt a sudden urge to travel to her left, which she assumed was west. There was something calling her and she knew she had to follow. A glimmer of hope filled her at the thought of finding Sapphire. Alaric had imprisoned her in the velvet pouch so she could no longer feel her, but she knew that was where she was going.

Before long she came across a small cave cut into the side of a hill. Marina stood at the entrance and thought. The last thing she wanted was to be away from the glorious rain, but there was something, or someone, waiting for her inside. Taking a deep breath, savouring the torrent around her, she stepped inside the cave.

What was waiting for her on the other side was not at all what she was expecting. Instead of being inside a dark, dank, little cave she was in a large ballroom. A multitude of candles in ornately designed candelabra lit the room. The walls were painted white with no other designs and the floor was white marble. At the far end of the room a man sat on a plain white throne. There was another, slightly smaller throne, next to him. The man motioned for her to join him and her legs started to move, as if on their own.

There was something wrong with the man before her, but it certainly wasn't apparent in his facade. Even seated Marina could tell that he stood over six feet tall. Soft blonde hair fell around his beautiful face. A slightly tanned skin showed off his masculine features. He wore a deep blue silk shirt and matching trousers. His feet were bare and they tapped a subtle beat as she approached. Despite his pleasant features Marina knew there was something else to be awed about him.

"Thank you for joining me Marina," his voice was sweet.

The fact that he knew her name should have concerned her, but she was too focused on his beauty to really hear what he was saying. Without waiting for an offer she gently sat down on the throne next him. She did not notice that she was completely dry and her dress was clean of the many days of travel. Small, blue blossoms were intertwined in her hair and she felt very relaxed.

"Thank you for bringing me here," she spoke softly, not wanting to upset him.

"I know what the Cursed One has done to you and I am outraged," his voice remained sweet despite his harsh words. "I am here to help you regain what was taken." Marina's heart lifted at the sound of his words. "Is that something you would like me to do?"

"Yes, very much so," Marina replied without thinking of the consequences. Nothing else mattered to her.

"Good, but I need you do something for me before I can help you."

"What is it? Anything, anything. Just tell me what you need," Marina couldn't get her words out quick enough.

"There is an elf travelling with the Cursed One. She is the key to regaining what was stolen. When the time is right I need you to strike."

The situation was wrong, but Marina didn't care. The man before her was offering everything she wanted and she would do whatever he asked to have Sapphire back in her possession.

"Is the elf dear to him?" She didn't know why she had asked the question.

"More than you will ever know."

"Then I will do as you ask."

Chapter 1: The Duke of Zenza

"What are we doing Asgard? There is no point in just sitting around here. We have done what needed to do and now we should return to the army," Cayley sulked.

"I have asked that for now you call me Bern. It will avoid any unnecessary explanations when we return."

Asgard, who was once known as Heryion, resided in the body of Bern. It was a strong body. Bern had grown up with Alaric in Arsiliac and worked his life on the family farm. Working day in, day out, he had built up a strong physique. That was a bonus for Asgard. A strong body meant it would stand up to what he needed to do.

Along with a strong body Bern had also had a strong mind. At first Asgard wasn't concerned with letting Bern control his own body knowing that when it really mattered he could take control. But that all changed when he found his family in the multitude of small graves outside the walls of Zenza City. Asgard had taken the opportunity to seize control and Bern was happy to let his consciousness slip away. With his family gone he didn't see the point in continuing the inner struggle with what he had come to know as 'the entity'. It was a relief that Bern had given up. No matter how powerful Asgard was he didn't think that he could overpower Bern's mind, at least not completely.

"I know, I know, but we are alone now. No one will hear our true names. I really wish you would call me Esgard. It has been too long since anyone has used my real name," Cayley pouted.

Esgard had assumed the body of the six year old girl Cayley. It would not have been her first choice for a body, especially leading into the Final Battle with the Evil One, but it was the one chosen for her. Surprisingly there was strength in the body that she had not expected and as a six year old she could go unnoticed a lot of the time.

She wore a new, floral dress. When they had revealed themselves to the duke's household and explained who they were, the servants had fussed over her. Although she really didn't need it, it was not long before she had been bathed, had her hair combed and been given a number of new dresses. As much as she did not like someone bathing her, she had to play the part.

"Well don't get into the habit now, Cayley, there is no telling when we might let our real names slip," Bern grumbled. He did not like having to repeat himself so many times.

"Fine!" She continued to pout, but Bern wasn't listening. "So, General Bern, shouldn't we be heading back to the Alliance. I'm sure they will be lost without you." She poked her tongue out at him, but again he wasn't watching.

They had been waiting in Zenza City for a week. The duke had been struggling to recover from the effects of the Dark Knight. Bern needed information but he knew there was no point in rushing the duke. His memory would be sketchy at best and only time would help, if that. Despite Cayley's insistence that they leave he remained firm.

"The duke said he will see us in the morning. There are questions that I need to ask him."

"About the Dark Knight Morgoz? I doubt he would have shared his plans with someone as lowly as the duke. You won't get any useful information from him."

Bern was deep in thought. His meeting with Morgoz had disturbed him. As far as he knew Zargoz was the only Dark Knight left alive, but something had changed and he did not like it.

"That is not what I'm concerned about. Morgoz died at the Cauldron Mountain. I saw it with my own eyes. He should be dead, not still roaming around the Seven Kingdoms causing trouble."

"Maybe you didn't see correctly. Maybe you only thought he was dead?" Cayley tried to make sense of what he was saying.

"No! I killed him myself. He was dead, but it seems that he has been brought back to life."

"That is impossible. No one can come back from the dead or bring someone back from the dead. That goes against the very fibre of being."

Bern shook his head. He knew it was impossible, but he also knew that it had happened.

"Through all the years we have seen I would have thought by now you would know that there is very little that is impossible."

"I know we have seen a lot, but this is beyond that. If people could come back from the dead then they would do so all the time. This is not something that can happen. If Nyrra has found a way to bring his Knights back from the dead then we are all doomed. If we keep killing them then he'll keep bringing them back and we can go on and on until the end of time." Cayley would not be dissuaded.

"I know it doesn't make sense, but it is true nonetheless. I don't think it's as simple as you say. I feel that we have missed some pertinent information and we need to work out what it is before it is too late."

"And you think the duke holds the key?"

"I don't know, but it's the best place to start. He is the only one that has had direct contact with the revived Dark Knight. Hopefully he might be able to shed some light on what is happening. Once we have spoken to him we will move on to the Alliance."

Cayley thought on his words. She still did not believe they were making the right decision. There was a Dark Knight in the palace at Remidel and that was where the Alliance was. They needed to fight the battle right in front of them before worrying about impossibilities. As much as she had faith in Asgard's abilities it was easy enough to make mistakes. It was obvious that he thought he had killed Morgoz, but that simply could not be the case. Until she could prove him wrong she would keep her opinions to herself.

"I think it's time to get some sleep," Bern finally said. "These bodies will need some rest."

"Oh really?" Cayley raised an eyebrow. "Has it been so long since you have controlled a body? Sleep is something for lesser beings. We certainly do not need it."

"Be that as it may, this body is still adjusting to my control and it needs some sleep. Just make sure you don't get up to any mischief," Bern warned.

"What? Me? Never!" She winked at him as she left the room.

It wasn't completely true that Bern's body needed to rest, he just wanted to be left alone. He knew that Cayley would keep pestering him if she stayed. The body would need to rest soon though, at least until it truly fused with Asgard's mind. Once they had left the city he did not think there would be another chance to sleep comfortably before the final battle.

He was sure he was missing something important. He had read the prophecies over and over again. He had the read the ones that no one else had seen and had been destroyed many years ago. He knew things that no one else could possibly know and yet the return of Morgoz was lost to him. It had been a long time since anything had truly surprised him, but this was one of those occasions.

It was late in the night when he finally fell asleep. The answers he was searching for continued to evade him. Cayley was still out wandering the castle. Normally that would have concerned him, but he wanted to try and get some rest.

In the morning he found Cayley sitting, crossed legged, at the foot of his bed. She had a cheeky smile of her face as the sun shone in from a nearby window. He had no idea what time it was, but he didn't think it was too late in the morning.

"I thought you were going to sleep all day," she teased.

"Don't be silly, it's not that late," Bern sounded grumpy.

"Well, you better get up now. The duke is waiting for us."

Bern rubbed the sleep out of his eyes and then dressed in his leather jerkin and trousers. He was not going to stand on ceremony. Once they had spoken with the duke he wanted to be on the road to Remidel. As much as he hated to admit it, Cayley was right. They needed to be with the Alliance to help defeat the Dark Knight.

There was a bowl of water next to his bed. He took the opportunity to splash some on his face and as he did he felt the sharp bristle of a day of growth. Although he could control his facial hair by will alone, he had not yet grown accustomed to Bern's bodily functions. Eventually he would stop his facial hair growing altogether, but in the meantime he would have to consciously keep it clean shaven.

"Seriously?" Cayley asked. "How long have you been in this body?"

"This body is still getting used to me. I'm sure you'll have the same issues when you grow into yours?"

Cayley scrunched up her face and poked out her tongue.

"See. I've never known you to do anything like that before. It seems I'm not the only one who is bound by their body," Bern smiled as he spoke.

Cayley opened her mouth to reply, but then thought better of it. She had to admit that he was right, but she was not going to give him the satisfaction. At times she had played the role of a young girl to further her agenda, but other times the little idiosyncrasies came unbidden.

"I don't think we should keep the duke waiting any longer. The sooner we're done the sooner we can move on to Remidel." Cayley quickly changed the subject.

As soon as they left the room they were met by a group of castle staff. They looked sheepish as Bern and Cayley joined them. Rumours had quickly spread through the castle that the General of the Alliance was staying. No one really believed it was true. The last anyone had heard was that the Alliance was travelling from Castalia to Remidel. They were all in awe when they saw the man of legend walk out into the corridor.

"Would you be so kind as to show us to the duke," Bern spoke with the confidence of a general. It was really unnecessary, but he figured it would give them a good story to tell.

"I will take you," a young man answered.

There were grumbles from the others in the group, mainly because they were not the first ones to speak. Within the duke's household it would be seen as a high honour to escort the esteemed guests. No really questioned why the general had a young girl with him. They were just in awe of the man.

They walked the corridors in silence until they reached the duke's private apartment. Bern did not think it was a good sign in regards to the duke's state of mind. Normally the general would be met in the great hall with a large ceremony, but it seemed as though the duke was not up for such an occasion. Bern was grateful. There was little time and a ceremony would only prove to delay them further.

The young man knocked on the door, nervously, before waiting for a response. Even though the rumours had spread through the castle that the duke had been under the thrall of one of the Evil One's servants, the household was still nervous when approaching him. Not that long ago a wrong word could have sent someone to the dungeons and on some occasions to the gallows.

"Bring them in!" a voice croaked from inside.

The serving man opened the door and offered them entrance before shutting the door behind them. It was not a normal custom, but he did not want to draw any attention to himself.

Bern and Cayley found the duke in his study sitting behind a large mahogany desk. He was not at all what they were expecting. The duke was a middle-aged man with a strong physique, although he slumped over his desk as if he had no energy. His face was drawn and pale and premature streaks of grey filled his dark brown hair. They were all signs of the ordeal from the control of the Dark Knight. In time he would regain his strength, but there was no telling how long that would take. Bern hoped that it wouldn't be long, there was still work for the duke to accomplish before the final battle took place.

"Welcome, please have a seat." The duke didn't stand. "I have organised for some breakfast to be brought here for us."

"Thank you, but we really don't have time to eat," Cayley forgot who she was supposed to be as she spoke.

The duke shot Bern a questioning look. It was surprising enough that the General of the Alliance would bring a girl with him to the meeting, let alone have her answer. Bern had hoped that Cayley would remain silent. There were already enough questions gone unasked without adding more.

"I found my niece outside the city walls. Her mother and father have been killed," Bern spoke the pre-decided lie. "I will be taking her to the capital where she has family."

"Surely it's too dangerous a task to take such a young girl into Remidel. I have heard reports of what has been happening and it cannot be safe. If you leave her here I will make sure she is well looked after. It is the least I can do for everything you have done for me. I don't know what would have happened if you hadn't come along."

"Thank you for the offer, but that is unnecessary." Bern hadn't prepared an excuse. "It is the man who claimed to be your advisor that interests me." Bern took his chance to change the subject. "Can you tell me anything about him?"

The smile that had crept onto his face quickly disappeared at the mention of his advisor. It was something that the duke would rather forget than try and remember. His memory of recent events had been hazy at best. If he had a choice he would simply forget the mayhem he had caused and try to move on. There had been many deaths throughout his duchy and regardless of what the man had done to him it was still his responsibility. If he had been stronger of mind he would have been able to stop what was happening.

"There was nothing you could do." Bern read his mind by the expression on his face. "The man was a Dark Knight and very powerful in the black arts."

Bern's words brought the duke some comfort. The Dark Knights had been a thing of nightmares or tall stories to be told to keep naughty children in check. There had been rumours that the Dark Knights had infiltrated some of the rulers of the Seven Kingdoms, but the duke had just passed them off as idle gossip. If he had believed the stories he might have been better prepared.

"Everything is still a haze in my mind. It might have been a week ago or it could have been a month ago since the man..." the duke could not bring himself to refer to him as a Dark Knight, "came to the city. He used winged words to gain entrance to my castle. At the time it seemed odd to me, but the thought soon left my mind. He told me that the Alliance was storming through the Seven Kingdoms, subjugating each kingdom as it passed. He warned me that I needed to shut down the city or else I would fall under their domination. Again his words seemed wrong. I know the king had trust in the Alliance, but his words sounded so sweet. It was not long before I was willing to believe anything he told me." He paused as he tried to recall what had happened.

There was nothing new to his account. It was the same thing the other Dark Knights had done to control the other rulers, but there was something else Bern needed to know. He knew there was more to the story and he could only hope that the duke was able to recall it.

"What else was there?" Bern tried to coax him.

"I don't know what it is you want from me. Everything after that is a haze. I remember keeping the gates locked even though people were telling me there were troubles outside. My staff implored me to open the gates and let them in. The man refused and I was helpless. Even when he sent my staff to the dungeons there was nothing I could do to stop him. Every fibre in my being was screaming for me to react, but there was nothing I could do."

Cayley shot Bern a worried look. Although she did not know exactly what he was after she could tell the duke was in stress. If Bern pushed too hard then there was a chance his mind would break. There was no telling what the Dark Knight had left behind. Although she would do everything in her power to complete her task, there was no reason to destroy people unnecessarily. She could be cold when she needed to be, but she still felt for the lives of men.

"Did the man say why he was here?" Bern kept pushing. "I mean, all the other Dark Knights took control of the kings and queens of the Seven Kingdoms. With all due respect you are lower ranked than that."

Although it was not meant to be an insult it certainly sounded like one. With any luck the duke was too concerned with his memories to notice. Cayley was the only one who picked up on it and she certainly wasn't about to say anything.

"He said that the Great Lord had great plans for him, but in the meantime he was stay here and make sure we did not join the Alliance." The duke could hardly believe the words as they came out of his mouth. The memory had been buried deep in his subconscious. "Yes, he said soon his brothers would be back and then it would be time to attack." The duke looked hopeful. "Does this mean anything to you?"

Bern thought on his words. They brought more questions than answers, but there was still something nagging at him. There was a vital piece of information that he knew was missing, and he knew it was there somewhere. He had to push the duke further and hope that it was enough to rattle it free.

"Not really, was there anything else. Something, no matter how insignificant," Bern said with a gentle tone. He did not want to push the duke any harder than he had to. The strain on the duke's face was obvious.

"There is nothing else, or at least nothing else I can recall. I don't even know where I found that last memory."

Bern had to wonder if that was something the Dark Knight had wanted the duke to tell him, but that would mean that Morgoz knew he was coming. Again more questions came to mind that he had no answers for.

"I'm sorry that I could not be of any help," the duke sounded dejected again. "I wish I could remember more, but there is nothing that I can recall."

"Thank you duke, you have been very helpful," Bern replied.

"What I can do is offer you some food and drink and the comforts of my household until you are ready to leave," the duke offered.

"Thank you for your kindness, but we need to be leaving now. All we need are a couple of horses and enough food for us to reach Remidel," Bern replied.

Cayley shot him a questioning look. He knew that they really did not need the supplies, but it would be expected of them. If they left the city without them the rumours would be quick to spread. He wasn't sure exactly what they would be, but anything out of the ordinary would not be good. All he could do was shake his head and hope that Cayley did not say anything.

"Of course. Anything that you need," the smile, albeit weak, returned to the duke's face.

"There is one more thing."

"Just ask. I owe you my life and my duchy."

"The Alliance is heading toward the final battle with the Evil One. He has yet to unleash his full army on the Seven Kingdoms. I need you to ready all your soldiers, guards and anyone who can wield a sword, pike, axe and any other form of weapon. The Alliance will need food, cooks, nurses, physicians, blacksmiths and many more in-between. This battle will be greater than anything we have ever known. If we fail then the Seven Kingdoms will fall into eternal darkness. This battle falls on all of us to succeed. Time is short and I know your experience with the Dark Knight has taken a lot of your energy, but now is the time to show your strength. A lot of your duchy is in ruin, but there is still some strength remaining. You must find everyone you can and assemble them here."

"I'm sorry, but I don't understand. I thought the battle had already been fought in Avalon." Even as the words came out of the duke's mouth he knew they were wrong.

"It is true that Avalon is the site for the final battle, but that battle has yet to be fought." Bern thought it only right that he explained things, he felt the duke deserved that much. "We were all misled into believing that the battle was to take place when we took the battlefield, but that was not the case. That time is now approaching and quicker than I would like. There is still much to be done and little time to do it."

"If that is the case then is there any point in gathering my resources?" It didn't make any sense. "There is no time for me to gather my soldiers and then move them to Avalon."

"Don't you worry about that. All you need to concern yourself with is the job I have given you. I'm sorry that I can't give you more information. You need to move now and be prepared to march by the end of the week, at the very latest. Earlier would be better."

The duke opened his mouth to question him further, but then thought better of it. Although he still felt shattered from his experience with the Dark Knight there was a renewed glimmer of hope in his heart.

"I will do as you ask. I will gather all I can and have them ready to march in seven days time."

"Thank you." Bern rose. "We need to leave as soon as possible, if you could relay that to your staff that would be gratefully appreciated."

There was no need for further conversation. As Bern and Cayley rose to leave the room the duke pulled on the red rope next to his desk to summon one of his servants. There was much to be done and he no longer had time to reflect on the past. His first task was to make sure that Bern and Cayley had animals and supplies ready and then he would start gathering his soldiers.

Bern and Cayley quickly made their way to the stables. There was nothing they had brought into the castle that they wanted to take with them. Bern's broadsword was with Perian on the way to Remidel along with the elves and the little band of ex-bandits.

Whatever the duke had said to his staff had worked. Within an hour two horses were saddled and a pack animal had been laden with more than enough food for their journey. Another pack animal had been loaded with a tent and bedding, it was completely unnecessary, but Bern wasn't going to tell them that. He simply thanked them for their assistance before mounting his horse and making his way towards the Eastern gate.

The city seemed to be more vibrant than when they had arrived. The shadow cast by the Dark Knight had already lifted. It was almost as though the people had completely forgotten about their subjugation. The sight brought a warm feeling to Bern's heart, but it only remained there for a moment. He wished that it was all over and these people could get back to their peaceful lives, but that was not the case. The hardship had only just begun. It would not be until the Evil One and his army had been defeated before they could truly be at peace.

"Why do you look so troubled?" Cayley asked as she noticed his malaise.

"I just wish it was all over and these people could go about their lives as normal," Bern replied.

"For the moment they don't look too upset. You should take solace in the fact that today they are happy."

It had not taken long for the information to pass through the city that the duke's advisor was gone and things could get back to normal. That would only last for a short time before the duke's order to ready for battle reached the city. Cayley's words did give Bern a little comfort. For the moment they were happy and that was something.

No one seemed to take any notice of them as they rode through the city. Their anonymity helped speed their journey. Cayley could not understand Bern's reasoning for riding. It would be much easier if they just travelled through the fabric of space to Remidel.

The farms outside of the city walls looked as though they were starting to recover from the effects of the Dark Knight, much the same as those in the city. The main highway was busy with carts bringing in long overdue supplies. If Bern had not known better he would have assumed nothing had happened at all.

Once they had passed through the farmhouses the highway was completely empty. There was no one travelling between Zenza City and the capital, as to be expected. It would be a long time before the highway was back to capacity.

"Surely we can quit this charade and just jump to Remidel," Cayley sounded sour. She was frustrated with their slow pace.

"Now is not the time," Bern snapped. He was deep in thought, trying to remember that vital piece of information. He was not prepared to do anything until he worked out what it was. There was too much at stake to be rushing.

"Surely it is more important to deal with Dargoz. If we wait any longer then we risk many lives," Cayley pushed.

Bern knew that her words made sense, but there was nothing he could do. It would be too suspicious if they arrived ahead of the others, especially without passing them on the road. It was important that everyone still thought he was Bern and travelling wasn't something he could do.

"We will arrive in time. The Alliance is not completely useless. There are a lot of strong leaders and don't forget the Council of Wizards. There are five wizards with the army and Ulman should have returned with Pernian and the others," Bern replied.

Cayley just shook her head and kept riding. It did not matter what Bern said, she was not going to be appeased. Regardless of how she felt she would just have to deal with it. There was nothing she could do without him. If a girl randomly turned up to the army alone she would be sent away. No one would believe that she should be there. Even with Bern it was going to be a push, but they would all have to accept his judgement.

Suddenly Bern reined in his horse. Cayley had travelled a few paces forward before she released. She thought about waiting for him to reach her, but when she saw he wasn't going to move she turned her horse around and went back to him.

"What are you doing now?"

"I know what it is I've missed," Bern blurted the words.

"Well spit it out and we can keep moving," Cayley scolded him. If she had not been so enraged she would have noticed his concern.

"There was a passage from the *Cycle of the Prophecy*. I read it so many years ago I had almost forgotten it. *Only when the Seven have been broken can they be reforged.*"

Cayley thought on his words for a moment before she replied. "That could mean anything. Not to mention that Dargoz is still alive. If that passage had anything to do with the Dark Knights then Dargoz would have to be dead."

"Originally I thought it had to do with the reforging of the Seven Kingdoms so very long ago. It was the next line that never really made any sense to me, but I just put it down to the nature of the prophecies. They were never written in a manner that was easy to read. *If one of the travellers through time shall make one fall then they shall be rewarded with a timely rebirth.*"

"Okay, you might need to explain this to me."

"It seems as though we are referred to in the passage as the 'travellers through time'." Cayley was about to speak, but Bern silenced her with a raised hand. "No, I don't know why that is, it doesn't make any sense to me either. Nevertheless, I was the one who killed Morgoz and it seems as though that is why he has returned before the others."

"So what does that all mean for us?" Cayley asked.

That was a very good question. Bern thought for a moment. The information was one thing, but making sense of it was another. Slowly it dawned on Bern what the passages meant.

"Damn!" he cursed loudly.

"What?" Bern's outburst shocked Cayley.

"We need to get to Remidel before they kill Dargoz," Bern spoke quickly.

"That doesn't make any sense. Why would we want to let him live. Surely it makes more sense to dispose of the Dark Knights before the final battle?" Cayley pushed.

"Don't you see what it means? If we kill Dargoz then Nyrra is free to bring back all his Dark Knights. If we imprison Dargoz then he'll only have Morgoz for the final battle."

His words slowly start to sink in. Bern was right. They couldn't allow Dargoz to die. As much as it pained Cayley it was the right course of action.

"Then what are we waiting for?" Cayley urged.

Without another thought the two suddenly disappeared.

***

"This is getting ridiculous," Pernian grumbled as they stopped for the midday meal.

They had been travelling for five days since they had left Zenza City. Despite pushing hard they had still not reached Remidel. At the pace they were moving it shouldn't have taken more than two days. Something was slowing their journey and it was very frustrating.

"I'm sure there's a good reason why our trip has been delayed," Ulman spoke mysteriously.

Lord Pernian was a young looking elf, with long blonde hair. Despite his youthful appearance, as will all elves, he was much older. Like the other elves in the group he did not show any signs of fatigue from their quickened pace. If the men didn't have horses then there was no chance they could have kept up.

Ulman, the wizard who had joined Bern and the others, did not seem overly concerned about their delayed journey. His composure frustrated Pernian and only proved to increase his foul mood. He was the youngest of the seven wizards and the only one who enjoyed physical combat. He still had chestnut brown hair, even though he had lived for many centuries, and a short, trimmed, beard. It was a simple spell that kept his hair like that and one that he had not had to think about for many years.

"Sometimes I wish the prophecy would just stay out of it," Horace, the leader of the group of ex-bandits from Darshival, voiced his opinion.

"I don't think you really want to fathom the ramifications of that statement," Ulman replied, but did not elaborate.

Before anyone had a chance to speak an elf ran up to the group. It was clear that he had been running hard, but the effects were much less than what they would have been for a man. He panted twice before his breathing returned to normal. He had been scouting ahead whilst they ate.

"What have you found, Belinus?" Pernian asked. There was hope in his voice as Belinus had not been gone long.

"We are about an hour from the city. The Alliance is camped out the front and it doesn't look like it is in any immediate danger," Belunis explained.

"That is the best news I have heard for a long time," Lord Pernian replied. "Eat up, it's time to continue to Remidel," he called out to the others.

Now that they were so close Pernian did not want to waste any more time. It seemed as though the Prophecy was ready for them to reach their destination and he was not going to delay it any further.

As Belunis had said they reached the outskirts of Remidel within the hour and it wasn't long before they arrived at the army's campsite. With the Castalial army joining the Alliance the campsite spread further than the eye could see.

"Lord Pernian, we are glad that you have made it back safely," Orric, the leader and eldest amongst the elves, welcomed him.

Since joining the Alliance Orric had chosen to listen rather than speak. He had lived his life in the elven sanctuary of Eljhem. Even with their solitude he knew that the impending battle with the Evil One was coming and their safe life would be over. Although he knew they would welcome his advice he preferred to let the Prophecy lead them. It gave them a better perspective than if Orric simply told them what they needed to do. Even with all his knowledge of the prophecy there were still many events that were hidden from him. It was for that reason that he remained silent unless it was necessary to speak.

"Is General Bern with you?" Jarwe asked as he looked around for their leader.

"No, he instructed us to leave without him. Something strange was happening in Zenza City. He figured it was better for us to make a start whilst he investigated. I think the entity was involved with that decision so I didn't question it," Pernian explained.

Pernian went on to explain what had happened. He had met Bern and his small group in Quinaliac on the way to Zenza City. The village had been attacked by a horde of orglin and without the aid of his elves, they would have been overrun. The appearance of the serpentant Sidewinder was disturbing, but it was the situation in the duchy capital that concerned them more. Unfortunately Pernian could not give them any real answers to the situation, only that General Bern was taking care of it.

"We thought General Bern would have reached us before we arrived. It took us longer than expected to travel here from Zenza City. We thought that the prophecy was slowing our travel so he could catch up with us, but it seemed as though that was not the case. I have no idea why we were slowed, but we are here now."

"This is indeed disturbing news," Jarwe continued. "I guess there is no reason why we should wait any longer to defeat the Dark Knight."

"I'm not so sure we should rush into action," Sorrell played the devil's advocate. "The wizards have yet to give us their decision. We should wait a little longer. With a little luck Bern will return soon."

Jarwe knew that Sorrell's words made sense, but he also knew they could no longer wait. The wizards had been very conspicuous in their absence. They should have had an answer by now, but none had come.

As soon as the group returned Ulman had made his way to join the other wizards. He could sense that something was happening and they would need his counsel. Jarwe had hoped to speak with him before he left.

"We will give them until morning. If they haven't made a decision by then, we will have to make for the city without them. We cannot give the Dark Knight anymore time to devise another plan," Jarwe commanded.

"So who will you take into the city?" Pernian asked after they had brought him up to date.

"I will take Captain Kenyon and Duke Hadar. We'll also take thirty soldiers from Remidia."

Jarwe had stayed up late with Captain Kenyon trying to devise a plan to gain access to the palace. As much as they hoped the soldiers manning the gate would simply open it when they saw them approaching, they could not rely on it. They had to be prepared for an attack.

The size of the force they took with them was another problem. The last thing they wanted to do was to look like they were an invading army. That would play right into the Dark Knight's lies. On the other hand if they took too few then they risked being captured. Jarwe also didn't know how much action the wizards would take. It was hard enough to convince them to attack the Dark Knight let alone a common soldier.

His words brought a rabble from the rest of the command group. They all wanted to be part of the mission and did not like being left behind.

"Please, I have thought long and hard about this. It is a dangerous task ahead of us and we need to leave our command group behind in case we fail. Sorrell will take command until either Bern or I return." His words silenced the group.

"There is one thing you are forgetting," Hulkan barked.

"And what might that be master dwarf," Jarwe did not sound happy.

Hulkan ignored the jibe. "My brother, or the Dark Knight using his body," he hoped it was the latter at the time of his betrayal "took with him the main component of the dwarven army. Now I don't know about you, but I definitely did not see any dwarves on the battlefield."

Jarwe silently cursed himself for not seeing it himself. They had to assume that the dwarves were still inside the city, waiting to attack. There could be no other explanation. It would not make any sense for the Dark Knight to send them anywhere else.

"Hulkan is right," Jarwe did not apologise for his mistake. "I know in the past there has been tension between you and the Western Dwarven Guild, Hulkan. Those who left with the Dark Knight supported your brother's claim. Do you think they will listen to you once we are inside the city?"

It was a valid question and one Hulkan had been thinking about ever since he had left Castalia. Although he had reconciled with the council, he knew the information would not have reached the dwarves in Remidel. He was sure the Dark Knight would have seen to that, even if the information had reached him before the Alliance arrived.

"I don't have an answer to your question," Hulkan's voice softened. "I would like to think that they would listen to me, but as far as they know Gilgi is still their rightful leader."

It was not the answer anyone was hoping for, but it was honest.

"Very well, I guess we shall just have to hope then. Hulkan, you will come with us. Dorn, you shall assume command of the dwarven army. If we don't return you shall have to wait here for General Bern."

"But what if he doesn't return?" Pernian asked. He was worried that Bern was in trouble as he had yet to reach them. "Should we not march the army to Zenza City to find him?"

"He'll be here. I know he will," Jarwe replied and no one questioned him. "In the morning we will infiltrate the city. For now I think we should all take this opportunity to relax."

Jarwe didn't really believe that anyone would, or even could, relax, but he felt it was the right thing to say. They would all need to be alert come morning, even those who were not entering the city. If he failed in his mission there was no telling what the Dark Knight would throw at them in retaliation.

Chapter 2: Lel Dinion

Alaric sat in his small apartment in the palace at Lel Dinion. He wore a fresh, blood red silk shirt and light brown trousers. He felt that it was a more appropriate dress code for the palace. When he was travelling he had worked out how to magically change his clothes on a whim. I had been a neat trick, albeit completely unnecessary. His clothes never got dirty anymore no matter what the conditions. His blonde hair fell around his shoulders and his green eyes seemed to shine. A cold breeze blew in from the open window, but Alaric no longer felt the temperature.

The events of the day before had been quite disturbing. He had disposed of the Dark Knight without much trouble, but it had been Marina's reaction that concerned him. He knew that she had a link to the Sapphire stone, but he also believed that she would have relinquished it when she had to. He remembered back to the words of Eldred in Arsiliac. He had told him that the stones could take hold of someone. If he had recalled those words he would never have let Marina touch it. There was a time when he cared deeply for her, but that sliver of emotion remained in the back of his mind, a memory.

He broke from his reverie to look at the large, ornately designed, mahogany box that lay on the table in front of him. Inside it held the five *Stones of Power* that he had recovered, all safely hidden in their velvet pouches. He had no idea where the velvet pouches, or even if the material truly was velvet, had come from, but all the stones had one. The material blocked their powers and any affect they would have on the holder.

There were only two stones that were left unfound, the Onyx stone and the Ruby stone. Even as he thought about them he knew that Nyrra would find the Ruby stone before he did. His entire journey had been based around it. IT was the reason he had left Arsiliac, but that now seemed a lifetime ago. He was sent to the Cauldron Mountain with the task to destroy the stone and with it, Nyrra, but that had all been a lie. Not necessarily a lie, but misinformation. Eldred and the others who had sent him on his task had believed that was the reason he had the Ruby stone, but that was just the beginning. It seemed that he was never meant to hold the Ruby stone in his final battle with the Evil One. That meant he only needed to regain the Onyx stone before his final confrontation. The thought both excited him and scared him. So much had happened since he left his quiet little home, but that was the life of someone who was long gone and he would never see it again.

He let his fingers run over the patterns engraved into the top of the box. The thought of opening the lid and checking on its contents crossed his mind, but he decided against it. It had been a long time since he had touched the other stones, but it was not the time or place for reminiscing.

A soft knock on the door broke his concentration. It was only then did he realise that his fingers were on the latch of the box. Even with everything he had learnt it seemed as though his subconscious was still drawn to the stones.

"Come in," he called out, knowing exactly who was on the other side.

An old looking man entered the room, followed by an elf. Eldred looked as though he had aged a lifetime since he had left them at the foot of Mount Scorpio. His once distinguished grey hair had streaks of white through it, as did his long beard. Thick wrinkles lined his face where before there had only been streaks of age. It was not a good sign. Alaric knew his previous facade had been a result of his many years of practising magic, as was his own, which could only mean that Eldred had been under great strain. He was sure with a little concentration Eldred could return to his former appearance, but for some reason he had chosen not to.

In stark contrast to Eldred, Alena held all the beauty that her race afforded her. Her long blonde hair had recently had all the knots and dirt combed out of it that she had compiled from their many days of travel. She looked every bit as beautiful as the first day Alaric had seen her in her home of Elhjem. That too seemed like a lifetime away. At one point in time he had loved her, although he had not had a chance to show it like he had with Marina. He felt that she had loved him too, or maybe still did. In a different life they could have been happy together, but he doubted that would ever happen.

"How are you feeling?" Eldred asked as they walked into the room.

Neither of them took a seat at the table until he offered them one. They moved cautiously, as if any sudden movements might startle him. Something had changed in Alaric since he had suddenly disappeared from Mount Scorpio. It had been such a strange action and it had taken them all by surprise. No one knew where he had been or what he had done, but there was something cold about him that had not been there before. It was as if he had lost all of his emotions. Eldred did not know if it was a good sign or a bad one. Alaric would need all of his strength and emotions if he was going to defeat the Evil One. They were what made him a man, not the monster he was seeking to destroy.

"I am fine thank you," Alaric's response was matter-of-fact. "It is time for me to see King Lisle."

"The King is still recovering from the affects of the Dark Knight," Eldred explained.

There was more to Eldred's words. Although it was true that the king was still suffering, the reason he wanted them to stay in the room was so he could find out where Alaric had been. When he suddenly disappeared he had given them no explanation.

"I have spoken to his servants and we will see him this evening. For now he needs his rest," Eldred continued when Alaric didn't respond.

There was no excuse not to see the King, even if he was still asleep. There was work to be done, but for the moment Alaric was happy to remain in his room. He knew eventually he would have to answer their questions and figured it was best to get it out of the way.

"Where is Richmond?" Alaric asked, seemingly ignoring Eldred's statement.

The Lord of the Bellarome was trying to help restore order to Lel Dinion with the help of the magician Lorio. He had wanted to see Alaric, but Eldred had thought it best if it was just himself and Alena. Until he knew what was happening, he did not want to bombard him with people. There would be plenty of time for that before they left.

"He is trying to help restore order to the palace," Eldred explained. "Luckily the Dark Knight was not here for that long. It should not take too long to bring things together again."

Alaric had deliberately led the conversation away from himself. He knew the conversation would eventually lead back to him, but he needed time to plan how much information he wanted to share.

"That's good. We need to move quickly. Nyrra will be marching his army towards Avalon and if we hope to succeed we can't be late," Alaric added.

Eldred opened his mouth to speak, but then thought better of it. There was something in Alaric's tone that made him believe that he was not just guessing. Somehow he knew what the Evil One was doing. It was just another thing that disturbed the old wizard. Things had been changing so quickly that he wasn't sure he knew Alaric anymore.

"While we are waiting, why don't you tell me what you have been doing since I left you?" Alaric took his chance to lead the conversation further away from his own deeds.

Eldred wished he had composed himself sooner so he could have asked the question first. Although he really wanted to know what Alaric had been doing, he also wanted to tell him their tale. They had been through so much, although he was suspicious that Alaric already knew what had happened. Taking a deep breath he put the thought aside and started to tell his tale.

"When we left you we headed north to *Nordligträ*, although we didn't really know that was our destination. We tried to convince Palen that he needed to lead the Northern Elves to meet the Alliance." Alaric nodded slowly as Eldred spoke. "Unfortunately the Evil One had sent his orglin to attack the *Tree of Life*. Although they told us that they were going to meet up with the Alliance, we believe the elves went to attack the orglin against our instructions."

Eldred paused as he recognised the pensive expression on Alaric's face. There was clearly something that he wanted to say, but he just needed to find the words. Eldred was happy to wait for as long as he needed.

"Palen made the right decision. He could not leave the *Tree of Life* to be destroyed. It is the sacred place of Emerald and if it fell then all vegetation would die. That is one thing that Evil One will do if he succeeds." There was something else that Alaric wasn't telling them. Eldred could see it in his face, but he let it pass. There was much more he wanted to explain.

"From there we crossed over the Cloumid Mountains and came across Khan. If it wasn't for Viper then I believe we would not have survived the journey. He tried to convince Khan to fight on the side of the Alliance. I'm not sure if the dragon really believed him, but it did seem as though Viper was speaking the truth when he said he wasn't an enemy. It wasn't until we reached the castle of Count Kerwin before he showed his true colours. In a mad rage he tried to steal the stones. That was where we last saw him." Eldred skipped over the details as much as he could. He wanted to be finished with his story and ask about to Alaric's journey.

Again Alaric had a pensive expression on his face, but it was clear he wasn't going to speak. Eldred continued to describe their meeting with Khan and then their journey to Lel Dinion.

"Then we arrived here to help free Lisle from Argoz."

Alaric seemed somewhat surprised at some of his words. Eldred had watched him closely for any reaction and in the end he wasn't sure if it was genuine surprise or whether it was for their benefit. He hoped it was the former.

"So where did you go, when you left us?" Eldred started. "It was like you disappeared from the face of the Seven Kingdoms."

Alaric had to laugh. No one expected such a reaction, but they were pleased for the levity.

"You don't know how correct you are," Alaric smiled as he spoke. "I have been travelling through space and time. To worlds that exist between the fabric of this reality."

Eldred had no idea what he was talking about. It was a very mysterious statement that did not make any sense. Just when he thought things were getting back to normal Alaric proved him wrong.

"That doesn't make any sense," Eldred replied. "What are you talking about?"

"I would not have believed it myself if I didn't experience it." Alaric didn't take offence to Eldred's words. "It seemed as though the prophecy had plans for me that we could not imagine. A lot of the worlds I travelled to were either lifeless or had no real relevance to my search, not that I really knew what I was looking for. All I knew what that I would know my destination when I reached it." Alaric paused as he thought what to say next. "I came across a world where the Wood Sprites had been coaxed and imprisoned. Some strange creature was feeding off their power. I don't think I was really meant to travel there, I think the creature had felt my power and drew me towards his world. To cut a long story short I was able to free the Sprites and I believe they have made their way back to the Seven Kingdoms." Alaric was going to skip over that part of his journey, but decided they would be interested.

Alena, although she didn't say anything, was clearly excited at the news. Elves had an affinity with the forests of the world and Wood Sprites were the controlling powers of those forests. It had been a long time since the Wood Sprites had roamed the forests of the Seven Kingdoms, except for Gaius, who they had met to the west of the Cloumid Mountain Range.

"With a little luck Arawn has returned and helped the Elves to secure the *Tree of Life*," Alaric added. "In fact I'm assuming that since we haven't noticed a quick rotting of the trees and flowers that Arawn has succeeded."

"That is great news." Alena couldn't help herself.

"But I was sure the elves needed to join the Alliance. I could feel the prophecy pushing me to make that decision," Eldred said as he rubbed his head.

"Sometimes it's easy to mistake a strong opinion for the tug of the prophecy," Alaric offered.

"I think, after all this time, I've come to recognise the call of the prophecy," Eldred's tone was defensive. He did not like what Alaric was insinuating.

"Be calm Eldred," Alaric soothed. "We all make mistakes and sometimes read the signs wrong. There have been many things that we have expected to be true only to find out they were not."

Eldred had to admit that Alaric was right. There were many times when they thought the prophecy was leading them in one direction only to find out that it was a mistake. Although it brought little comfort to him, he was happy with Alaric's statement.

"Maybe, maybe. Anyway, after we left the Northern Elves, we came across one of the Wood Sprites. I guess that timeline works in with your rescue of them." Alaric didn't think it necessary to explain that Gaius was the one Wood Sprite who had not been taken. "From there we travelled further north until we reached the Dragon's Pass, as you instructed us to." The command seemed like such a long time ago. "It was there that we met Kahn. At first I thought we were all going to die. There is nothing I can do to fight a dragon, especially not one as strong as Khan." Eldred decided it was time to elaborate more on their adventures.

"I feel there is more to this story?" Alaric asked when Eldred paused.

"If it wasn't for Viper I think Khan would have killed us. He was curious to why we were there, but once that curiosity was sated he would have attacked. Viper convinced him not to kill us and to fight on our side in the final battle. I'm not sure Khan was even interested in the battle, but I think Viper piqued his interest. I don't know if the great dragon believed his words, but at least it got us safely through the pass."

Alaric still had a pensive expression on his face. He had known they needed to come to Lel Dinion via the Dragon's Pass, but he had no idea why. Since the death of Raheem and Cain there was only one dragon left in the Seven Kingdoms. The creatures had once been a dominant force, but they were no longer. The Great Dragon War, between the various clans, had killed most of the dragons. The rest were hunted down and destroyed. More from fear and ignorance than any real need. Alaric thought on the future, but he could not see Khan. Whatever the dragon was planning it was blocked from him. He doubted it was a good sign. If Khan was planning to help them then he was sure he would see it. At best he could only hope that Khan remained away from the battlefield. There was no telling what damage a dragon could do.

Viper was another concern. The serpentant had gone from enemy to friend and then back to a potential enemy, but no one could be truly sure either way. He had helped Ra'naroz torture Eldred and Alena in Jarrat, before apparently switching sides. Although they had not spoken of their time in the dungeons Alaric knew it had not been pleasant.

Along with Khan, Alaric had no idea what role, if any, the serpentants would play in the final battle. They were a dangerous unknown. The serpentants held great power, not quite as much as the Dark Knights, but enough to cause trouble. If they chose the side of the Evil One then it could mean disaster for all of them.

Viper had told them that he was on the side of the Alliance, or at least his beliefs lead him in that direction and Alaric was inclined to believe him. Although he could not be completely trusted, he had done nothing since joining them to prove otherwise. His action in the castle of Count Kerwin was puzzling.

Unfortunately, by Viper's own admission, not all of the serpentants shared his beliefs. Their queen had been imprisoned by Nyrra and they believed if they helped the Evil One then he would set her free. Alaric knew that wasn't true, but he couldn't tell them that. They would have to make their own decision on which side they would support, if any.

"Do you know anything about it?" Eldred asked when there was no response from Alaric. He could tell he was thinking intently on his words.

"There are some things that I have come to know over the last few days, but there is nothing I can tell you. I wish there was but their destinies are hidden to me."

"Then what do you know?" Eldred asked, becoming a little frustrated.

"I know the journey of the Alliance and I know their destination. The end result, though, is hidden to me." Alaric didn't elaborate further.

"And what might that be?" Eldred pushed.

"The army moves to Avalon. We were not wrong at the start that was the place for the final battle, it was just the timing was wrong," Alaric explained.

"But the army is in Remidia?" Eldred sounded shocked with the revelation. "It will take months to move it Avalon. You said that time is running out. If that is true then we'll never get the army there in time."

"All in good time Eldred," Alaric returned. "There is information that I can't share, or I risk it not coming to be."

Eldred shook his head. "What sort of answer is that? I have been candid with you all along. You should give me the same courtesy."

Alaric refrained from laughing. There was no room for levity and it would only prove to infuriate Eldred even more.

"There were times when you kept information from me. Information that you didn't think I would understand and you were right. Well... Now it is my turn to keep information from you that you would not understand. Trust me. If there was anything you needed to know I would tell you." There was no hint of arrogance in his tone. It was a statement of fact, nothing more.

Eldred thought about questioning Alaric further, but then decided he was right. They had kept vital information from Alaric to protect him and now it seemed as though he was doing the same. It was frustrating not knowing what was happening, but he had to accept that Alaric knew what he was doing. It still did not make the unknown any easier to deal with.

Alena, on the other hand, seemed to be taking it all in her stride. She listened intently to Alaric's words and didn't seem to think there was anything wrong with them. She had never been too involved with her father's plans. Orric had had many dealings with Eldred, but she was never privy to their discussions. She had always known that one day she would leave Elhjem with the Chosen One and that was all the explanation she needed. It was just another time like that. She knew she would travel again with Alaric and that was all that mattered.

"Very well. What is our next move?" Eldred asked.

"To see Lisle," Alaric stood as he spoke. Eldred had given him just the opportunity to break the conversation and continue with what he needed to do. "Lisle needs to prepare his soldiers for the upcoming battle."

"But..." Eldred was about the question him, but then thought better of it.

Alaric was glad that his old friend was finally learning. There would be no answers, only more questions if he spoke. Time was running short and he had already wasted enough. Although the information Eldred gave him was valuable he could have lived without it.

Eldred pulled on the bellpull by the door before Alaric could leave. He knew that the King would need some time to ready himself for the meeting, but Alaric didn't seem to care.

"Can I help you?" the server asked when he arrived.

"We will see Lisle now," Alaric commanded.

"The King is in his apartment resting. He will not see anyone today," the server spoke with confidence.

"That is not acceptable," Alaric barked. "Run along and tell the King that we will meet him in his apartment."

The server just stared at Alaric. He didn't know what to do. No one had ever asked him to disobey a command from the King. The Master-of-the-House had told everyone that the King was not to be disturbed. He had been instructed by the King himself. Although Alaric's face remained calm, the server could sense it would not remain that way for long.

"I... can't... I... don't..." he stammered.

"You can either run ahead or we will see the King in his bedchamber. Which do you think he would prefer?"

Again the server didn't know how to react. There was something about the man in front of him that bothered him. They had all been told of the special guests of the King, but no one knew who they were.

"You can and you will if you don't want us to see the King in his bed clothes." Alaric didn't give him a chance to stumble his words out. "RUN!" Alaric boomed.

The server quickly jumped into action. If there were any doubts in his mind they were gone at the sound of Alaric's voice. He didn't know what he was going to do when he reached the King's apartment, but he knew that he couldn't stay where he was.

"Do you think that will work?" Eldred asked.

"Doubtful, but there's only one way to find out."

Alaric led them out of the room without elaborating any further. He chose a casual pace to allow the King's staff enough time to prepare for their arrival. He could have simply jumped to the door, but that would have defeated the purpose. It was all about grandeur and the staff appreciating who he was. It was nothing to do with gratifying himself, it was purely to start the rumours through the palace and the city. The citizens needed to know the Chosen One was visiting the King and that his mandate was ultimate. In the end it would help gather the soldiers and people of Hondin Lel.

They were met and the entrance to the King's apartment by the Master-of-the-House himself. Alaric had hoped for such an occurrence. That was the reason he had taken his time. He wanted to make sure there was enough time for information to reach the man.

The Master-of-the-House was an elderly man with tufts of grey hair sparsely set on his bald head. His name was Gavril and he had spent his entire life working in the palace. At a young age he was a scullery boy and then became a pageboy when he came of age. Slowly he had worked his way through the ranks until he became the Master-of-the-House. He knew the entire ins and outs of the palace and he would not be as easily persuaded as the server.

"You cannot enter the king's apartment. He is not well and not up to seeing anyone. Even the queen has been sent away until he is better. She is also recovering from their ordeal."

Gavril stood with his arms across his chest, blocking the door. There was a stern expression on his face, but Alaric didn't care.

"I understand the king is not well and I am here to help him," Alaric kept his voice soft, but firm.

"All the physicians in the palace have seen him and no one can work out how to help. We have called for the physicians from the city to see him. Hopefully someone will have a cure. Until then no one is to see the king." Gavril didn't back down.

"You may as well send them all away. What ails the King is not something that standard medicine can heal," Alaric tried his best to explain.

"Then what exactly do you propose to do?" Gavril raised an eyebrow to accentuate his question.

"I have a few methods that are not what you would call standard medicine. Now if you wouldn't mind I don't have time for mindless conversations," Alaric chose his words carefully.

"If you think this conversation is mindless then you should return to your quarters. We are grateful for what you have done, but our hospitality only goes so far."

Alaric had had enough of placating Gavril. He knew his words wouldn't persuade him and that was why he started to goad the Master-of-the-House. He needed a reason to get angry and show his strength.

"This is your last chance. Open the door and let us in!"

The Master-of-the-House opened his mouth to call for the guards, but no words came out. A look of shock fell on his face as he realised he could no longer move his arms or legs. Alaric had wrapped him up tightly in strings of air and stuffed an air gag in his mouth. Slowly he was lifted until he hung a foot above the ground. If his face could show more surprise then it would have. Alaric wished he had waited for Gavril to call for the guards. It would have given more effect to his show.

"What are you doing?" Eldred sounded shocked.

"We don't have to time to waste any longer," Alaric's gaze didn't leave Gavril as he spoke. "I will see the King know."

Gavril tried to cringe backwards as Alaric approached, but his body wouldn't react. At first he thought Alaric was going to kill him, but then he realised he was simply looking for the key. For a moment he felt relieved before he realised again there was nothing he could do to stop him.

When he found the key Alaric seemingly ignored Gavril as he opened the door. The Master-of-the-House thought he was just going to be left hanging there, but before Alaric entered the King's apartment he let Gavril down and released him from his spell.

"Now run along before I change my mind." Alaric didn't wait for a response before he walked inside. He knew the man would run straight for the guards.

Alena and Eldred entered the room and Alaric shut the door behind them. He would need to create a spell to stop the soldiers from breaking down the door. He didn't want to be disturbed while he was helping the King.

They found King Lisle XII in bed. There was no doubt that he was still suffering from the effects of the Dark Knight. The sheets and thick quilt were pulled up to his chin. His face was pale and although his eyes were open nothing seemed to register. He looked as though he had aged a decade since Alaric had last seen him. Drool ran down the corner of his mouth and had pooled onto his pillow and his once brown hair had turned a silvery grey. It never ceased to amaze Alaric how quickly the Evil One's touch could change someone's appearance. He would be able to help, but the King would never look the same again. Although Alaric had cured the king and queen of the more immediate condition, it was obvious that there was more that he missed.

"What are you going to do Alaric?" Eldred asked.

Despite Alaric's command Eldred wanted to see what they were up against. He delved slowly into Lisle's mind and what he found shocked him. There seemed to be nothing there. It was like his mind had been ripped from his body. Eldred knew that someone had been controlling him, but he couldn't be sure if it was Argoz or Marina. When they were gone they had left nothing behind.

"He's gone Alaric." Eldred could hardly bring himself to speak. "There is nothing left of King Lisle, just an empty shell."

Alaric didn't take any notice of Eldred. He already knew what was wrong with Lisle and how he was going to fix him. The fact that there was nothing in the King's mind made things much easier. It would have been much harder if an aggressive entity had been left behind to try and trap him, although he was also ready for such an occurrence.

When Eldred looked to Alaric he noticed there was something in his right hand. It had not been there before and he wondered where Alaric had taken it from. He held a golden crown with the Opal *Stone of Power* inset at the front. Eldred had not even noticed that Alaric had taken the stone from the chest. There was something very disturbing about it.

The colours in the centre of the stone swirled around as it gave off a gentle, light blue glow. Alaric seemed to ignore the stone, but Alena and Eldred were transfixed by it. Alaric was distracted by the voice inside his head.

"There is nothing you can do for him, let him die. You have more important things to deal with. You don't want to drain your energy on such trifling matters," the male voice was trying to coax him. It was different from the struggles he had with the other stones.

Alaric ignored the voice. He wasn't going to give it the time it wanted. He focused his energy on Lisle and it didn't take him long to realise what Eldred had been talking about. Alone, there was nothing he could have done, but with the aid of the Opal stone he would be able to bring Lisle back. It was impossible to destroy someone's conscious completely.

"Bring him back," Alaric kept his mind's voice matter-of-fact. He wasn't going to get sucked into the stones games. He knew that he could overpower it if he wanted to, but it would be easier if it just did what he asked.

"Who are you to give me orders?" the voice snapped.

"You know exactly who I am and you know exactly what I have to do. You also know that my destiny is not carved in stone. If you don't help me now then I might just decide to change my destiny."

"You wouldn't let this world fall into darkness," the voice scoffed. "That would spell disaster for those you love."

Alaric's mind voice started laughing. "For someone so wise you should know better than to assume anything. I don't need to let the Seven Kingdoms fall into darkness to make you and yours suffer. Now my time is growing short and this conversation is starting to bore me. You know I can compel you to do what I want, so let's just make it easy for both of us."

Alaric's words brought silence inside his head. He knew that the stone was thinking on what he said. It was not at all what it was expecting and it didn't know how to respond. That wasn't exactly what Alaric was aiming for, but it was something. In the end he would get his way, it was just a matter of how.

"Fine, I will let you get away with it this time, but be warned that I will not take such offence in the future. It is true that I will need your help, but remember that you will also need mine if you want to succeed. This relationship goes both ways and you would do well to learn some respect."

Alaric ignored the jibe. The Opal stone was doing what he asked and that was all that mattered. It was better that the stone realised it on its own rather than Alaric forcing his will on it. As much as it was upset it would be worse the other way around.

The light in the stone suddenly blinked out and for a moment Alaric thought the stone had changed its mind. Just when he was about to force his will on it he felt a sudden warmth fill his body. The stone was drawing power from him. Although he didn't think it was trying to control him, he stayed vigilant. As soon as he felt anything untoward he would lash out.

From the outside it didn't look like anything was happening. All Eldred and Alena could do was watch and hope that Lisle was going to get better.

Slowly Lisle lifted his head, before it returned to his pillow. His eyes remained open and lifeless, but it was a sign something was happening. For the first time since his delving in the mind of the king, Eldred felt some hope that Lisle might recover. He had no idea what Alaric was doing, but it was obviously working.

As the process continued Alaric felt the heat in his body increase. The stone was using a great amount of power to reverse the effects of the Dark Knight. Lisle's conscious had been buried deep, but it was still there. It was just a matter of finding it and setting it free.

Sweat appeared on Alaric's brow. It was the first time his body had shown any sign of stress for as long as he could remember. Since he had learned how to regulate his body temperature he had not perspired, except under extreme duress. As much as he didn't think the Opal stone was trying to wear him down he couldn't be sure. As he felt his legs start to wobble he knew it was time to stop things.

"I'm not finished," the voice sounded strained.

Alaric closed his eyes and forced his body to remain calm as he pushed more energy towards the stone.

"I can feel him. I can bring him back."

Alaric had figured the stone would have been able to bring Lisle straight back. The Opal stone had the power over minds and was the reason why Alaric had chosen it over the others. He was sure it was doing all it could, but he couldn't help feeling some distrust.

"There! It is done!" The light in the stone suddenly blinked out.

As soon as the stone had finished Alaric's body returned to normal. The sweat suddenly disappeared and he was no longer shaking. Alaric didn't waste any time in returning the stone to its velvet pouch. Although it seemed to be inactive he didn't want to take any risks.

"What are you doing in my bedroom?" barked Lisle.

A wave of relief washed through Eldred's body.

Chapter 3: Return of the King

The guards banged on the door as they tried to either open it or break it down. The Master-of-the-House had unlocked it as soon as they arrived, but they did not expect the door to remain closed. No matter what they tried it wouldn't budge.

Lisle called out for help when he realised there were three people standing over him. In his shock he failed to recognise them as allies. The fog that had covered his mind was gone and his consciousness had suddenly returned with no memory of what had happened. As far as he knew he had just woken with three intruders in his room.

The guards outside would have doubled their effort to break the door down if they had heard the king, but Alaric had not already placed a spell on the apartment. No sounds from inside would reach those on the outside. He wouldn't release his spells until he was sure that Lisle understood what was happening and did not try to have them arrested.

"Be calm Lisle," Eldred tried to soothe him, although he didn't move any closer. He didn't want to risk frightening him.

"Get out of my bedroom. How dare you wake me from my slumber? I'll have your heads for this!" he boomed.

"Please be calm. You are the King of Hondin Lel and you need to start acting like one," Alaric kept his voice level. "We are not here to hurt you."

Lisle looked from Alaric to Eldred, seemingly ignoring Alena. He knew he had seen the man speaking to him before, but he could not place from where. It was the wizard he recognised first.

"Eldred? What are you doing here? The last time we met you were marching off to your doom. I didn't think I would ever see you again." Lisle sat up and rubbed his head.

Although he had just woken, or had been woken, he didn't think his memory should be so hazy. If Eldred was in the palace then he was sure he should know about it. Even if the wizard had snuck in during the night someone would have advised him. The situation did not make any sense at all.

"That is a long story," Eldred replied.

To everyone's surprise Alaric started to retell the story. He kept the involvement of the Dark Knight and the effects on Lisle to a minimum. There were things that he would need time to accept and Alaric did not have any to waste. When they were done it seemed as though Lisle was beginning to accept things.

"Would you be so kind as to wait out in my sitting room whilst I get changed?" Lisle's voice was weak, almost like he had been defeated.

Despite Alaric glossing over the worst parts of his ordeal, his words still had an effect on the King. It seemed all his strength had returned to him and that was a good sign. Eldred and Alena looked to Alaric to see if they should acquiesce. He simply nodded his head before leaving the room.

They didn't have to wait long before the King arrived. He was dressed in a simple red shirt and brown trousers. At first he had thought of dressing in his regal robes for the occasion, but then decided that it didn't call for it. There was more information he needed from the group and there seemed little point wasting time with ceremony.

"What is that racket outside?" Lisle asked as he entered.

"We may have used a little force to gain entrance. I would say half the palace guards will be trying to get in," Eldred sounded a little sheepish.

"Once I let the spell go the guards will rush into the room. You will need to be quick to send them on their way, so no one ends up dead," by the tone in Alaric's voice it was the guards he was concerned for.

Lisle was still trying to work out how he knew the man before him. There was something familiar about him, but he couldn't put his finger on it. He didn't think he was a noble, at least not one from his kingdom, but there was a power about him he had never seen before. If he didn't already know the rulers of the other kingdoms he would have thought he was one. He had heard that there was a new High Chancellor, but he really didn't think this was him.

"I will make sure that everyone will be kept safe," Lisle assured them.

Alaric raised his arm and flicked his hand, instantly breaking the spell. It was purely a flourish for show and not at all necessary.

As soon as the spell was gone the door smashed open. Alaric had hoped that they would simply open the door, but he was not surprised when they didn't. Lisle was not at all happy, but it did give him a reason to raise his voice.

"What is the meaning of this Gavril?" Lisle boomed when he saw his Master-of-the-House behind the first row of guards.

The sudden release of the door had taken everyone by surprise, but the words of their king shocked them even more. It was not at all what they were expecting. From what Gavril had told them the King was in dire trouble.

"I... I'm... are you alright Sire?" Gavril didn't know what to say.

"Does it look like I'm alright?" Lisle didn't wait for the obvious answer. "I hope you have plans to fix my door. Now if you don't mind I am entertaining guests. I think we might like some tea and something to eat. I believe that is still your command?"

"Yes Sire! I will see it done," Gavril had no idea how to react. "You heard your King. Clean up this mess and have someone replace the door."

"I think we should move to my private office. I think there are going to be a few people moving around in here," Lisle offered, but made no move to rise.

"I think you're right," Alaric said as he stood.

They left the dumbfounded guards milling around the front room. Some made an effort to pick up the splintered wood, whilst the others looked around for something to do in the hope they wouldn't be called out by the king.

Gavril just stood, watched them and rubbed his head. He had no idea what had just happened or even if his memory was serving him correctly. If his memory was right then the King could still be in trouble. Although he sounded in control there was still a chance he was under duress. If he was wrong then there was a good chance he would no longer be Master-of-the-House come nightfall.

"I wouldn't stand there if I was you Gavril," one of the guards barked. "The king has given you an order and by the tone of his voice I would not leave him waiting."

The words were enough to make the decision for him. He had to trust that if the king was in danger then he would have given him a signal. When it was said and done the room was filled with guards trying their best to clean up. If the King was in trouble then help was not far away.

In the end he decided to play it safe. He ordered that no less than a dozen soldiers were to stand guard at the door. Realistically he could have left one hundred guards and they would not have been able to stop Alaric, but it made him feel better. All he could do was hope that his King was in safe hands.

"I don't know how I'm going to explain things to my poor Master-of-the-House. He looked so confused, but I guess that is a problem for another time," Lisle mused when they were all seated.

"The final battle is quickly approaching," Alaric ignored Lisle's comment and came straight to the point.

"This sounds like a familiar tune," Lisle aimed his comment at Eldred.

"We were misled," Eldred started when it was clear that Alaric wasn't about to help him. "The final destination was correct, it was just the timing that was wrong." Eldred repeated what Alaric had told him. There was no other way he could explain things.

"I take it you didn't break into my apartments to discuss the past." Lisle pushed his comment aside. "Why is it that you needed to speak with me so urgently?"

Lisle seemed to forget that if it wasn't for Alaric than he would have lived out the rest of his life as a vegetable and that time would have been very short. Although Alaric picked up on the fact he was too focused on the future to bring up the past.

"Things are different now," Alaric started. "There was no other way we could have come to this point and as much as it seemed like the wrong decision to march everyone to Avalon it was the right thing to do."

Alaric paused as he let his words sink in. As much as he just wanted to cast a spell to help Lisle come around to his way of thinking, he didn't think his mind would survive it. It had already been through a lot and Alaric couldn't risk doing irreparable damage. He also wanted Lisle to come to the realisation on his own. There was no telling what would happen once Alaric had left.

"I agree with you that things are much different. If I hadn't sent any soldiers to the Alliance then I might have been protected against the Dark Knight. There is no telling what mischief he could have caused if you hadn't come along when you did."

Alaric shook his head. It seemed as though everyone saw the underlying comment in Lisle's words except for the King himself. He waited for a moment to see if he realised and only continued when he didn't.

"You see, the point is that I did come along before anything really untoward could happen." Alaric paused and thought for a moment. Although he really didn't want to dwell on the past he had to make a point. "And the bulk of your army returned before it reached Avalon. What was the reason behind that?"

Lisle shifted uncomfortably in his chair. It was obvious that he had not been expecting Alaric's words.

"Why my army had not reached Avalon by the time the Alliance struck I cannot tell you. I dispatched them with more than enough time to make the march. They had only reached half way when I received word that the Evil One's army wasn't there. It was at this point that I decided to have them return home."

Alaric felt there was more to the story, but he was happy to let it pass. Just as he was about to speak again, there came a knock on the door. Everyone expected to see a group of servants on the other side with the tea and food, but instead there was an elderly looking man dressed in a pure white robe.

Lorio was the court magician. Although he did not have the magical capabilities that were inherent of sorcerers he had spent his life studying the craft. Although incantations were not as powerful as the magic that flowed through sorcerers, it was still something. He had been the court magician and Lisle's confidant for nearly thirty years. Hondin Lel was the last kingdom to still keep a magician in court.

Lorio kept a long white beard that was synonymous with magicians. His white hair was trimmed neatly around his shoulders. He looked a lot neater since his return to the palace. Trekking through the sewers, although necessary to save his King, had been a trial. The first thing he had done when the kingdom was safe was to take a bath and scrub away the preserved filth.

"It is good to see you up again, your majesty," Lorio bowed as he spoke.

"Lorio, my old friend. I must apologise for any hardships I have caused you."

"Think nothing of it," Lorio brushed aside the apology, as was to be expected. "I am just glad that you are feeling better."

Standing behind him was Lord Richmond. He was quite happy to remain anonymous while Lorio spoke with the King. Although he had spoken to many kings and queens he was happy to just listen.

Like Lorio he had taken the time to bathe and clean himself when the battle with Argoz and Marina was over. He wore a light brown tunic and matching trousers. His brown hair had been washed and brushed, but it was still longer than when he had left his home of Bellarome.

"Lord Richmond?" The King saw him for the first time. Richmond was surprised that he recognised him. "I believe you had a part to play in my rescue, thank you."

Richmond was taken aback. He was not expecting such a greeting from King Lisle. It was true that he had been involved, but he really didn't think his involvement warranted any mention. In the end he didn't think that his involvement had any real effect on the end result, but he wasn't going to question the King.

"Thank you your majesty," he replied.

"Please, you two, be seated. You are making me very uncomfortable loitering around there," Lisle barked.

Richmond looked to Lorio who didn't know what to think. They had heard the King had recovered, but they really didn't expect it to be true. All they could do was take a seat as they had been commanded.

"Now let's get back to business," Lisle continued.

Before anyone could talk there was another knock on the door.

"What now!" boomed Lisle.

"I'm sorry, your majesty, I have your tea and food," a nervous serving lady poked her head around the door.

"Well come in. Don't leave us waiting," Lisle barked.

His sharp words forced her into action. She pushed the door open and led a group of servers into the room. They fussed around until the table was laden with food. The conversation remained on hold until they were left alone again.

"It seems as though someone doesn't want us to continue our conversation," Lisle looked towards Alaric as he spoke. "Would you like something to eat and drink?" he offered.

"Thank you," Alaric replied. Although he was neither hungry nor thirsty, he felt things would move along faster if he just agreed.

To everyone's surprise the King poured the tea and served the food. Normally a server would have done so, but since Lisle had dismissed them he felt he should do the job.

"Now, let's get back to business."

"You need to gather as many men as you can," Alaric continued. "If the Alliance is going to succeed in Avalon then they will need a lot more soldiers."

Richmond and Lorio had confused expressions on their faces, but neither of them spoke. They had come in halfway through a conversation and didn't want to interrupt. They could only hope that things would make sense soon enough.

"What do you think Lorio? You have been my advisor for many years and I would appreciate your advice."

"I'm sorry, but you will need to bring me up to speed."

Alaric remained quiet and Lisle explained what he had proposed. Time was ticking away, but he could not push any harder.

"That is indeed a very dangerous proposal. If the threat to Hondin Lel is not over then we will leave ourselves open to invasion. If all our soldiers are in Avalon then there will be nothing we can do to defend ourselves." Lorio voiced his thoughts.

Alaric let out a sigh of frustration. "We are just going around in circles. The threat to Hondin Lel is over, for now. The only threat will be if the Alliance fails. If that happens then nothing will be able to defend your walls." Alaric tried to remain calm.

No one responded. Everyone made a sign of sipping on their teas and nibbling their food. There was something in his tone that made them not want to speak.

"I need an answer and I need it now," Alaric said when everyone remained silent.

"I can't do it," Lisle resigned. "I just can't leave my kingdom without any defence."

Alaric shook his head. It was not a surprise, but it was still not the response he was looking for. Despite his rush for time he couldn't leave until Lisle changed his mind.

"Very well," Alaric stood as he spoke. "I shall inform the other rulers that you are willing to let everyone die."

"What? Wait!" Lisle stammered. "Don't be so rash."

Alaric refrained from smiling as he returned to his seat. He had no intention of leaving, but Lisle had taken the bait. It seemed as though his ruse was going to work.

"What have the other rulers done?" Lisle asked when Alaric had returned to his seat.

"Nothing yet, but history will tell us that they will offer whatever they can. King Faxon was the first to gather his soldiers in Remidia. He too has suffered under the thrall of a Dark Knight. Even as we speak Dargoz, the Dark Knight masquerading as the dwarf Gilgi, has control of him and his kingdom. Once he is freed I have no doubt that he will pledge to support all that he has. Queen Oriana was under the thrall of the Dark Knight Na'garoz for a long time. She has suffered the most of all the rulers of the Seven Kingdoms, but I will not go into the details. She will commit all and more to see the end of the Evil One. Entero will fully support the Alliance." Alaric paused as he let the information sink in, but he was not yet finished. "The new High Chancellor will be more than happy to assist even further. He saw firsthand what the Dark Knight Za'aroz did to his predecessor. Castalia has already added a great weight of numbers to the Alliance and it shall do so again. Then there is King Unwin of Darshival. Kiarome was the first city to fall under the control of a Dark Knight. Fenaroz controlled the king until he finally plunged a sword into his back. That was many months ago now. Since Kiarome hasn't been attacked since then, Unwin will know exactly what I'm talking about. And now that only leaves you, who has refused to support the Alliance."

Lisle thought on Alaric's words. He was the only one in the room who didn't realise what Alaric had done. Lorio was about to speak, but a sharp look from Eldred stopped him. Deep down Lorio knew it was the right thing to do. From the start he had been against helping the Alliance, but since the arrival of the Dark Knight he had quickly changed his tune. Now that he had seen what the Evil One was capable of he wanted nothing more than to assist in his destruction.

"Your words make sense. Hondin Lel will not be left behind. My soldiers and my people are the strongest in the Seven Kingdoms. There is no chance the Alliance could prevail without them. It is our duty to see that the Seven Kingdoms are safe for future generations," Lisle sounded very proud of his decision.

If there had been room for levity then Alaric would have laughed, but it was not appropriate. It seemed as though he had achieved his goal and he did not want to do anything to spoil it. King Lisle could still change his mind if he saw through Alaric's ruse.

"Very well. There is not much time remaining. We need to get to work immediately." Alaric stood as spoke.

Before Alaric could say anything more there was a loud knock on the door. The sound took everyone by surprise. The servers would not arrive before they were summoned and the guards had been told specifically not to let anyone else enter.

The door opened with anyone giving them leave. On the other side was the group of bandits that had helped them enter the city. At their head was Hagar, the son of Duke Hadar, from Western Hondin Lel. The young man was the spitting image of his father. He had short cropped hair and thick dwarven beard. His thick upper body had strong set shoulders. He had a concerned expression on his face.

"I am sorry to barge in on you, your majesty," Hagar bowed as he spoke. "There have been some riots outside of the palace. It seems there have been rumours circulating the city that you were murdered by the Chosen One. I'm not sure how it started, but it seems that Argoz had some supporters in the palace. When he was destroyed they still wanted to cause some chaos." It was as if Hagar couldn't get the information out fast enough.

"Calm down Hagar." Lisle didn't sound too worried. It seemed like a strange reaction. "What exactly is happening?"

"It seemed that the Dark Knight had sleeper cells in the city," Vasil stepped forward as he spoke. Lisle had a pensive expression on his face as if he was trying to pick where he knew him. The bandits had been given rooms, clothes and had bathed for the occasion. They looked nothing like the men they had met outside the city. Vasil had short cropped blonde hair. His features were softer than first appearance and he couldn't have been older than his mid-twenties. Eldred thought there was something very strange about him. "I heard rumours before we left the city that the Evil One had agents embedding inside the walls, but I didn't believe it."

"You should have been more careful Wessel," Lorio scolded.

At the sound of his name Lisle suddenly remembered who he was. Wessel was the leader of his spy network. As a child he had grown up on the streets as an urchin before being taken in by the Thieves Guild. He was apt at pick-pocketing and no one suspected a small child. The thieves used him to sneak through cracks in open windows to steal the goodies inside.

It wasn't until he was in his teens before he was finally caught by the local guard, trying to steal a loaf of bread, of all things. He managed to talk his way out of losing his hands by offering to inform them of the thieves, and he was very good at it. It was not long before he had recruited other spies and soon enough he had his own spy network working in and under the city.

Lorio had not used his real name in the city as he wasn't sure if the men with him were also spies. The fact that they were with him in the king's presence was enough to confirm whose side they were on.

"I was out of the city helping you and your friends inside. If it wasn't for me then you would still be looking for a way in." It wasn't exactly true, but he made his point.

"We are getting off point." Lisle looked more comfortable with the revelation of his name. "What is the situation outside in the city?"

"Not good at the moment, but it shouldn't take long to get things under control. I think if you are seen on the palace walls then that would go a long way to easing your citizens' concerns," Wessel suggested.

"We are done here anyway," Alaric said when Lisle looked towards him. "I think it would be a good idea to show the people that you are in fact still alive and well."

Lisle nodded his agreement and stood. "We have a lot of work to do. By the end of the week we shall be ready to march towards Avalon." Lisle seemed suddenly proud of his decision. "What will you do Alaric?"

"We will go to Remidel and meet with the Alliance. I need to speak with the commanders and let them know their next move."

"Very well then. I will have some horses readied for you. You should be on the road before midday," Lisle offered.

"Thank you, but that is unnecessary. Our horses are outside of the city walls," Alaric explained.

Eldred opened his mouth to speak, but then stopped. He really didn't want to know how Alaric knew where the horses were. He doubted they would be travelling by horseback to Remidel, but he figured Lisle didn't need to know that."

"It is a long journey to Remidel. I will have supplies prepared for you," Lisle offered.

"Thank you, but we really need to be moving. We have enough supplies to get us to our destination."

As Alaric made his way out of the room he noticed that Hagar was following. He stopped when they were in the sitting room.

"The King will need help gathering his troops," Alaric said.

"I figured I would be more help coming with you," Hagar replied.

"Thank you, but there will be time for you to join the Alliance. In the meantime you should return to your king. He will need all the help he can get."

Hagar opened his mouth to contest, but Alaric silenced him with a wave of his hand. He had already lost too much time and he wasn't going to waste any more. When Hagar returned he hurried the others out of the King's apartment. Although he was planning on jumping to the horses, he did not want to risk anyone seeing them.

As soon as he was sure they were alone Alaric blinked them out of the palace. One moment they were walking through the palace corridors and the next they were outside the city walls with the horses. The change was so sudden that everyone, except for Alaric, stumbled and fell forward.

"What was that?" Richmond asked after he picked himself up.

Although Richmond had experienced skipping between the fabric of time, he had always been given warning first. The suddenness of Alaric's spell left him dazed and confused.

"I am sorry, but I couldn't wait any longer," there was little emotion in his tone.

"How... did we get out here?" Richmond was still struggling with his new surroundings.

Alaric raised his right hand and clicked his fingers. Instantly Richmond's eyelids fluttered and he collapsed to the ground unconscious.

"Why did you do that?" Alena sounded shocked.

"Richmond was struggling with the effects of travelling. This was a small jump compared to what we are about to do. It is better if he is unconscious for the next trip. When he wakes up, at least for a few hours, he will forget what he has experienced," Alaric explained, his voice emotionless.

Alena took a step back. There was something very disturbing about the tone of his voice. His lack of emotion both disturbed and frightened her. She had heard of people who lacked emotions. Her father had called them psychopaths. They cared not for those they hurt and the only sentence could be death. If Alaric had become a psychopath then all their lives were in danger.

"Don't worry Alena," Alaric read the expression on her face as if he was reading her mind. "You are all safe. My rage is for the Evil One and his minions."

Alena blushed, but Alaric ignored it.

"The jump to Remidel is going to be a lot more confronting for you than anything we have done before. If you like I can knock you out like Richmond," he offered, but there was no compassion in his voice.

"I think I'll be fine," Eldred grumbled. "I have lived around magic for more lifetimes than I can remember. It was the sudden change of scenery that startled me, nothing more." He didn't know why he was defending his reaction, but he felt it was important.

"What about you Alena?"

"I will be fine, thank you." She shied away from the question.

"Very well then, but don't say I didn't warn you," Alaric said as he turned to face the horses.

When it was clear he was done speaking with his companions, Adelanta sidled up next to him. The white elven stallion had missed his rider. There was an affinity between him and Alaric that could not be explained.

Alaric rubbed his nose in what could only be called a sign of affection. Alena was both pleased at his moment of softness and jealous that he hadn't shown her the same.

"The horses will be fine," Alaric turned and spoke. "Now I think it's time to get moving."

"Wait a moment Alaric," Eldred said.

"What?" Alaric tried his best not to sound annoyed.

"You can't just send us to Remidel without telling us what we are jumping into. From all accounts there is a Dark Knight in control of the city."

"I can assure you that it is no rumour either. Dargoz has taken the guise of Gilgi. I'm not sure how long he has been the dwarf, but definitely when he led the Remidian army from the battlefield in Avalon. It seemed as though he was happy with what he had achieved there and decided to cause some mischief in Remidia," Alaric's voice was matter-of-fact.

"That's all well and good, but if he is control of the city then he is in control of the soldiers as well. We can't risk running into danger."

"You just let me worry about that!"

Alaric had a wry smile on his face and he winked at Eldred. It did nothing to ease his nerves, but before he had a chance to speak again Alaric cast his spell and they suddenly disappeared.

Chapter 4: Into the Lion's Den

General Jarwe sat on his horse atop the small hill and watched the sun rise. The wizards had assured them they would tell them their decision that morning. Whatever they decided would be the difference between certain death and a chance of success. Jarwe did not like those odds. At best it was a suicide mission, but there was no other choice. If he didn't lead the way into the city then someone else would and that was not a responsibility he was going to shirk.

The sounds of horse's hooves could be heard behind him, but he didn't take his eyes from the slowly rising sun. Whoever it was would soon make their presence known. If it was an assassin sent to kill him then it would only be shortening the inevitable. They were dark thoughts and he needed to get them out of his mind. The others would be looking to him for strength and that was exactly what he would give them.

"You're up early general." Jarwe recognised the voice as Sorrell.

"Not really in the mood for sleep," Jarwe said as he shifted his eyes towards the city.

"I know what you mean. I'd like to say I wish I was coming with you today, but that would just be a lie."

Jarwe thought about laughing, but decided the situation didn't warrant it. He knew exactly what Sorrell meant. If he had a choice then he would prefer to remain with the army. It had been his decision to lead the group into the city and there was no going back. If he wasn't prepared to go into the lion's den then he couldn't expect others to.

"I couldn't agree with you more. There is death waiting for us inside those walls and all the bravado in the Seven Kingdoms won't change that. If the wizards don't agree to help us then I fear we won't be returning," Jarwe spoke grimly.

"Then you should not go, general. You are the leader of this army and we cannot risk your death," Sorrell protested.

"Would you not go if you were in my position?"

"I guess not."

Jarwe did not feel any better for winning the discussion. All he wanted was for the wizards to arrive and make their decision. Until then he would have no idea if he was going to see the sun set or not. Either way it might be the last sunrise he would ever see.

"Have the men started to assemble?" Jarwe asked, changing the subject. "I want to be on the move as soon as we have an answer from the wizards."

Sorrell knew it was time to leave. General Jarwe needed time to think. He could only hope that his malaise was gone when the others arrived. They would all need to gather strength from their leader if they were going brave the task before them.

When the sun had completely crested the horizon, Jarwe turned his horse around and made his way back towards the campsite. The army was already a hive of activity despite the fact they would not be marching that day.

He found the command group assembled at the front of the army, but there was no sign of the wizards. A great wave of disappointment washed through his body, but he shouldn't have been surprised. The wizards had been aloof ever since they joined the Alliance and he didn't think they would change anytime soon. All of a sudden it seemed as though his fears had come true. They would need to take on the Dark Knight without their aid.

"Have we heard anything from the council?" he asked after the short greetings were done.

"No one has seen them yet this morning, although I must admit we weren't really looking for them," explained Duke Hadar. "We've sent some pages out to try and find them."

The large man looked even fiercer in the morning light. The sun shone off his steel breastplate which had been polished during the night. His bushy beard had been neatly trimmed and his hair cut short.

"You're looking well preened this morning," Hulkan commented, deciding to try and lighten the mood.

Hulkan

himself looked as though he had slept in his leather tunic. His great beard and hair were ruffled and his eyes were slightly bloodshot. There was little doubt he had been drinking. If it was anyone else Jarwe might have berated him, but the dwarf was known for liking a drink and could still function the following day.

"My father always told me. 'Look your best when you go to meet death, otherwise she might not accept you as a lover.'" Hadar's words brought a round of laughter from the small group. Even Jarwe allowed himself a moment of levity.

"Then it looks like my bed will be cold tonight," gruffed Hulkan.

His words brought even more boisterous laughter from the group, drowning out the sound of the horses approaching.

"It is good to see you all in high spirits," Gwydion raised his voice to be heard.

The sound of his voice brought a sudden silence to the group. They had all believed the wizards had forsaken them. Both relief and guilt filled their hearts. Although the day had yet to be won, at least they could start with hope again.

"Gwydion," Jarwe nodded his head in greeting, trying his best to hide his surprise, before he greeted the other five wizards.

"There will be little time for humour once we enter the city. I do hope you all understand the severity of what we are about to do," Gwydion scolded them.

"You don't have to Gwydion. We all know what we face and the dangers before us," Jarwe's voice was solemn. "I assume you have made a decision?"

"We have and do not think this was an easy one," Gwydion started.

Jarwe didn't like the tone of his voice. Suddenly he had a very bad feeling the wizards were not going to assist them.

"Fear not general." Gwydion recognised the expression on his face. "We have decided that we can no longer sit back and observe. There was a time when the council was the greatest weapon the Seven Kingdoms had ever seen and it is time we help everyone remember," pride was thick in his voice.

Not all the wizards seemed happy with the decision, but Jarwe was willing to let that pass. He didn't think they would do anything to hinder them and those who agreed would certainly help.

With their group complete it was time to make their move into the city. Jarwe had finished one task, an important one, but it was by no means the most difficult. It would be no easy task gaining entrance into the city and it would be even harder gaining entrance into the palace. If, and when, they had achieved those goals, their hardships were only just about to begin. Defeating the Dark Knight, even with the aid of the wizards, would not be a simple task. It was true that the wizards had once been a powerful force, but that was many years ago. They had not fought a battle in over a hundred years and Jarwe knew their skills would be rusty.

"Very well, let's be off. We don't want to keep the Dark Knight waiting any longer than we have to," Jarwe tried to sound nonchalant, but failed miserably.

No one paid any attention to his sombre tone. They were all lost in their own thoughts. Although they had known what they were getting themselves into when they had volunteered, they were still on edge. Bravery was much easier on the eve of adventure than when the adventure began. No one would be denied if they no longer wished to participate, but the shame would be too great.

Jarwe lead the way towards the city with Kenyon by his side. The wizards rode in a line behind the leaders with the thirty regular soldiers behind them. Duke Hadar and Hulkan rode at the rear. They thought it best if the soldiers in the city didn't see the dwarf until he was inside. Hadar had decided to come along and keep him company. They hoped all the city soldiers' attention would be focused on the two men at the front of the line.

As they came within range of the archers they all tensed in their saddles as their nerves increased. Although Jarwe thought the wizards could stop any arrows flying in their direction, he couldn't be completely sure. If they needed to save all their energy for the Dark Knight then there was a chance they would let some of the soldiers, maybe even Jarwe himself, fall.

Thankfully they reached the main gate without any hostile activity from the wall. The soldiers just looked happy to watch them approach. In truth they just wanted to know what was happening. There had been no word from the army since it had left the city and surrendered to the Alliance. It was morbid interest more than anything else that stayed their bows.

"Who is in charge of the gates?" Jarwe boomed.

"Who wants to know?" a voice yelled back.

"I am General Jarwe, commander of the Alliance and the Remidian army."

"You might be General of the Alliance, but you are no longer General of the Remidian Army," the voice was matter-of-fact. "The King rescinded your position about a month ago."

Jarwe shot Kenyon a questioning look.

"I am sorry that I didn't mention it earlier. I didn't think that it would come up and I was sure King Faxon would return you to your rightful position once he was free of the Dark Knight's yoke," Kenyon apologised.

"So who is general of the army now?" Jarwe asked through clenched teeth.

"King Faxon named the dwarf Gilgi general of his armies. No one liked the decision, but there was nothing we could do about it."

"Well, I'm sure the Dark Knight doesn't take the battlefield with the army. Who is the field-commander?" Jarwe asked.

"Ah... that would be me general." Kenyon shuffled his feet nervously.

"Well then speak to the man and get him to let us into the city."

"Is that Gerfy?" Kenyon asked, hoping it would be.

"Yes it is?" Gerfy sounded surprised. "And who is this?"

"It is Captain Kenyon. As you know I am field-commander of the Remidian Army and I command you to open the gate."

"You surrendered your position to an invading force. I do not believe that you are still the field-commander."

"Regardless, just open the gate."

There was a moment of silence. It wasn't much of an argument, but it was all he had. Gerfy was right. Since he surrendered to the Alliance he could no longer call himself field-commander. For the moment he would just have to remain the captain of a captured army, at least until it could be assimilated into the Alliance.

"Alright, I guess it couldn't hurt, it's not like you've got an invading force with you," Gerfy conceded.

There could be no doubt that if the King's advisor heard what he had done then he would end up in the dungeons or at worse swinging from the gallows, but he didn't care. He knew something important had happened on the other side of the walls and his curiosity was getting the better of him.

"So tell me what has happened?" Gerfy opened the gate just wide enough to allow the two men to ride in and shut it before the others could enter.

A dozen armed men stood behind Gerfy and didn't look impressed. The gate was not to be opened for anyone, not since the army was let through. The order was meant to prevent their own soldiers from re-entering, no matter what was happening outside, but no really understood the order.

"Speak quickly now or you shall be marched straight to the dungeon." Gerfy tapped the hilt of his sword.

"Those six men and women who rode behind us are the Council of Wizards. Do you think they will appreciate the fact that you have just shut the gate in their faces," Jarwe ignored the threat. He couldn't let Gerfy get the upper hand.

"What... errr... what are you talking about?" Even the soldiers behind him started to shuffle around nervously.

"The Council of Wizards has business in the palace with the King and his advisor. I wouldn't recommend you keeping them waiting outside for much longer, lest they destroy the city gates and come in anyway," Jarwe warned.

"There has been no word sent from the palace," confusion was thick in Gerfy's voice. "If we were to open the gate then we would have been told."

"You are being painful for no reason," Kenyon interrupted. "You know that you and your twelve friends are no match for General Jarwe and myself. If we wanted you dead then you already would be and we can open the gates ourselves."

Gerfy turned around to look at the other guards, but they had already started to move out of the way. It seemed that Kenyon's words had their desired effect.

"Very well, just make sure you fix whenever is wrong in the palace."

Gerfy stood aside. He wasn't going to stand in their way, but he wasn't going to help them either. There was a small voice in the back of his mind absolving him if he was doing the wrong thing. Given the chance he would turn and run, but instead Jarwe and Kenyon dismounted and handed him their reins.

When the gate was opened Jarwe turned back to the guard. "You can come with us to the palace. I believe we shall need your assistance gaining entrance."

"Oh, no!" Gerfy cried. "I can't come with you. I need to guard the gate."

Jarwe wasn't going to let the excuse slide. There were plenty of people to guard the gate and no one from the Alliance was going to approach. They could leave it wide open and the city would be safe.

"It wasn't a question of whether you wanted to or not. You *will* come with us and you *will* get us into the palace. In doing so you will help free your kingdom from the yoke of the Evil One," Jarwe's voice was cold.

"Yes, sir," his voice sounded dejected.

Although Gerfy had never met Jarwe he had heard plenty of stories about him. Even if half of them were true then he was not a man to be toyed with. All he could do was hope that they were doing the right thing and he wouldn't be hanging by a noose come sundown.

As expected the streets of Remidel were empty. No one wanted to be caught out if the invading army decided to attack. If the Alliance was able to breach the walls then being caught on the streets was the best way to end up dead, raped or both. Even though the army had no intention of attacking, the citizens didn't know that.

They rode in silence, not wanting their voices to echo around the empty streets. The sound of their horses' hooves on the cobbled streets would be warning enough for the guards at the palace gates.

They rode in the same pattern as when they approached the city. Gerfy rode at the front with Jarwe and Kenyon, with the wizards and soldiers behind. They wanted it to look like he was an equal not a prisoner, even though that was exactly how he felt.

To everyone's surprise, even Gerfy's, there were no Remidian soldiers guarding the gates into the palace grounds. Instead the walls and gates were guarded by a multitude of dwarves. It seemed that Gilgi didn't trust the soldiers and figured the dwarves would be more reliable.

"Halt!" called one of the six dwarves at the gate.

Jarwe reined in his horse and signalled for the others to do the same. For the moment he would leave Hulkan at the back of the line. He would only call him forward if he couldn't talk their way into the palace.

"We are here to see the King," Jarwe started.

"No you're not," the dwarf retorted. "No one is allowed into the palace until the invading army has been defeated."

"I can vouch for them," Gerfy thought it was time for him to speak. "They are here from the Alliance to treat with the king.

Jarwe instantly wished he hadn't mentioned they were from the Alliance. The dwarves quickly armed themselves, even though they were outnumbered. Those on the parapet wall readied their crossbows and aimed them at the group below.

"What are you doing? How dare you bring these soldiers to the gates of the palace? They should not have even been allowed into the city. Now if you want to keep your heads I suggest you leave immediately."

"Bronn? Is that you?" Hulkan barked as he rode to the front of the line.

The dwarf looked confused when he heard his name. It was the first time he had been placed on the palace gates and he didn't think anyone from the outside would know who he was. The expression was only there for a moment before he recovered and his gruff expression returned.

"Who are you?" Bronn called out as he tried to see the approaching rider.

"Bronn you old dog," Hulkan let out a boisterous laugh. "I thought you had gone to meet Horinga."

"Hulkan? I could have said the same for you. When I heard that you had betrayed your brother I thought he would have had you hung."

Everyone else had gone quiet, intent on listening to their exchange. It was clear that the two dwarves knew each other, but how they felt about each other was a completely different story. Both sides hoped that it was friendship and not animosity.

"You wish. I can still beat you today as I have every other time before this," Hulkan had an evil grin on his face. It looked as though he was ready to strike at any moment.

"As I remember it I gave as good as I got, but if I beat you too many times then I would be sent to council. They wouldn't like the son of their leader being beaten by a common dwarf. But don't think I would go easy on you anymore," Bronn sneered in return.

There was a moment of uncomfortable silence before Hulkan jumped from his saddle. He made a move as if he was going for his axe before he rushed Bronn and picked him in a fierce bear hug. No one knew how to react. Thankfully the archers on the wall refrained from firing. It wasn't until Hulkan let this fellow dwarf down did they see the broad smiles on their faces.

"Bronn was my best friend growing up in Castalia," Hulkan explained. "We had many brawls together and despite what he says I was the victor more often than not."

Bronn playfully punched him in the arm to show his disagreement, it was clear the other dwarves were becoming annoyed.

"You know that your brother will not see you. There is too much bad blood between the two of you. I can have someone ask the question, but I fear I already know the answer," Bronn offered.

"Unfortunately my dear brother is dead," Hulkan started, but didn't get a chance to finish.

"I guess you might wish that to be true. Even brothers can have a reason to hate each other and Horinga knows you two have the best reason, but your brother is still very much alive. I had a meeting with him not two days ago when he placed me in charge of these gates. He told me not to let anyone in under any circumstances. I'm sorry Hulkan, we go back a long way, but I am loyal to your brother and the guild."

"That's not what I mean. The dwarf you had a meeting with is not my brother. My brother was killed a long time ago. In his place is a Dark Knight." Hulkan paused to let the information sink in. "We are here to destroy him and free you and the Kingdom of Remidel from his oppressive rule."

Bronn didn't know what to make of it. As he had only known Gilgi as Hulkan's younger brother, he couldn't gauge if there had been a marked change in his personality.

"I don't know," was all he could say. "We serve Gilgi. Is there any way to prove what you say?"

Hulkan had hoped his old friend would just accept what he had said, but he had to admit it was a fantastic story. He doubted he would believe it himself. Given the history with his brother it would be expected for Hulkan to try and usurp his power.

"The guild removed him from his position. It has reinstated me as leader. I know that I cannot prove it, but you have to believe me. We are here to help and the only way we can do that is if you let us into the palace," Hulkan kept his tone soft, which didn't sound right coming from his mouth.

"You know as well as I do that there is nothing I can do without a formal writ. If they made a new leader then I'm sure they would have given you the appropriate documents."

"There was no time to have the papers drawn up. We had to leave Castalia in a hurry and as I'm sure you can appreciate we don't have time to send for the guild."

It was a plausible excuse, but it still didn't help the situation. If Hulkan was lying then there was no telling what Gilgi would do to him. Bronn couldn't believe his leader was a Dark Knight, although there had been many decisions that seemed off.

Hulkan watched his old friend carefully as he thought on his words. Just when it looked like Bronn had made a decision a queer look came over his face. It was almost like he was searching for something in his mind that had been there one moment and gone the next. Hulkan opened his mouth to speak, but then thought better of it.

Jarwe also noticed the sudden change in Bronn and guessed that one of the wizards had decided things were taking too long. He was grateful for the assistance, but he could only hope that it didn't drain too much of their energy.

"Well," Bronn started, but he wasn't sure if he should continue. Everyone was staring at him in anticipation. "Open the gates!" he called out. Even as the words left his mouth he knew they were not right, but there was nothing he could do to stop them.

"Thank you Bronn, you are doing the right thing," Hulkan spoke softly.

The other dwarves all looked at each other in surprise. As soon as one dwarf regained his senses they all moved into action. The last thing they wanted was the wrath of their leader.

"Thank you," Jarwe spoke softly to no one in particular as he rode through the gates. He wasn't sure which, if any, of the wizards had helped, but felt it an appropriate response.

When they were all inside the palace grounds they dismounted and allowed the dwarves to take their horses to the stables. Jarwe was surprised to see that there were no groomsmen or servers in the courtyard. It seemed as though the Dark Knight had removed all the men and women from the palace. It was as if he trusted the dwarves more than Faxon's loyal servants, but he doubted they would be inside cooking and cleaning for him. The dwarves were proud warriors and there would only be so much Dargoz could get them to do.

The palace loomed up in front of them. Built from stone from the Cloumid Mountain Range, it stood three storeys high. Four turrets stood in each corner with a flat roof to allow archers to shoot down at any invaders below.

To everyone's surprise the large mahogany doors were unattended. Normally a least six soldiers would stand guard to make sure no one untoward gained entrance. Jarwe didn't know if it was a good sign or a bad one.

"This doesn't seem right to me," Jarwe mused.

"Nothing about this is right," Hulkan answered. "Were you really expecting anything to be normal?"

"I guess the Dark Knight figures that everyone will be stopped at the main gates so there is no need to arm the front doors," Kenyon mused.

His reasoning made sense and it was enough to urge Jarwe forward, not that they had any other choice. Taking a deep breath he grabbed one of the ornately designed brass handles and gave it a pull. He half expected the doors to be locked, but instead they opened easily.

Jarwe lead them into the large palace foyer. Dark granite pillars broke up the polished marble floors. Along the walls to their left and right were many doors leading off to other places in the palace. At the far end was a wide stairway leading up to the second floor.

Standing in the middle of the foyer was a man dressed in a black silk suit. His dark hair was neatly trimmed and his face had been freshly shaven. There was a blank expression on his face that didn't change with the new arrivals.

"The soldiers can stay outside," there was no emotion in his voice.

Jarwe didn't know what to think. From the man's position he could not have seen the soldiers standing behind them.

"You are expected, but your soldiers are not welcome," he continued when there was no response.

"What do you think?" Jarwe asked no one in particular.

"I don't think we really have a choice. For the moment it seems as though we are welcome, let's not change that," Gwydion kept his voice low, although he knew the retainer would be able to hear eveything.

"I agree. If the Dar... Ah, King wanted us dead then there would be guards waiting for us. I think it would be wise to acquiesce." Hadar quickly corrected himself. Although they all believed the Dark Knight knew that they knew who he was they didn't need to confirm it.

"You stay with the soldiers Kenyon. Give us an hour. If we're not back by then you should return to the Alliance," Jarwe commanded.

"But we could come and rescue you?" Kenyon retorted.

"If we are not back in an hour then we are already dead," Drake's voice was ominously cold. It was a statement of fact, nothing more, nothing less.

Kenyon nodded before leaving and closing the large door behind him. The sound of them closing echoed through the foyer and sent a chill down Jarwe's spine. It reminded him of a closing casket, maybe his own.

For a moment everyone stood where they were. No one knew what to do, so they waited in silence for retainer to speak again.

"I don't think the king would like to be kept waiting," he said

Without waiting for a response the retainer turned and made his way up the stairs. Jarwe looked at the others, but no one wanted to speak. There was no other choice but to follow him.

In the middle of the stairs was a large black carpet runner. It had clearly been replaced recently. Before it had been red, as was common for palaces, but the Dark Knight had changed it to black. It was a subtle change, but obvious to everyone as they walked up the stairs. They all walked on the marble sides to avoid the carpet. There seemed to be something evil about it and no one wanted to touch it.

The retainer did not wait for them at the top of the stairs but instead opened the doors leading into the throne room.

Once they were at the top of the stairs there was no avoiding the black carpet. It spread out in a T to the left and the right and short of a great leap there was no way to cross without touching it. Jarwe wanted to pause and access the situation, but he knew that wasn't an option. The others would be looking to him for strength and he could not falter over silly fancies.

The grand throne room was completely empty apart from the new arrivals and the king. Faxon was sitting at the far end of the room on one of the large golden thrones. The throne next to him, reserved for Queen Demelza, was empty. In fact the queen had been unseen since the arrival of Gilgi. There had been a rumour that she had run away with a minor noble, but there had been no proof.

The throne room had been stripped bare of all its tapestries and paintings. There were no chairs, which normally lined the area in front of the throne. It reminded Jarwe of a disease. He looked around for the Dark Knight, but there was no sign of the dwarf. Jarwe thought it was quite strange.

"General Jarwe, the traitor!" Faxon boomed from his throne.

It was not at all what they were expecting. All the other leaders who had been controlled by a Dark Knight had lost their strength, both mentally and physically. It seemed that Faxon had lost neither. For a moment a terrible thought entered Jarwe's mind. It was possible that the Dark Knight had ditched the body of Gilgi and taken over the king's, but until he could confirm he was right, he was not about to believe his fears.

"Your majesty," Jarwe bowed in deference. The act gave him time to think, as well as being appropriate.

"Get up!" Faxon barked. "Deference from a traitor is no deference at all."

Jarwe rose abruptly. The situation was nothing like he had imagined. He had been expecting the Dark Knight, at least in Gilgi's form, to be in control. It would then be up to the council to destroy him. He thought his only job was to see them safely inside the palace.

"So what do you have to say for yourself?" Faxon asked.

"I'm not sure what you mean?" Jarwe replied.

"My son, your prince, commanded you to leave the Alliance and return home with the Remidian Army, but instead you decided to remain. Not only that but you also convince some of my loyal soldiers to revolt with you and now you think you can just waltz into my throne room and all will be forgiven?"

Jarwe still couldn't figure out what was happening. If he had been expecting the verbal attack from Faxon then he could have prepared his answers. He never thought that his King would call him a traitor and ask him to defend his actions. He looked around at the others, but no one wanted to speak. The six wizards were looking nervously around the throne room. It looked as though they were waiting for something to happen. Jarwe wasn't sure he wanted to know what it was. The others kept their heads low, avoiding eye contact with anyone.

"I am not a traitor," Jarwe began. "Prince Hawthorne was duped by a Dark Knight," he thought about mentioning Gilgi, but decided against it. "You put me in command of the Remidian Army and I was placed in command of the Alliance. We were sent with the charge of fighting the Evil One's army and that is exactly what we are doing and that is what we'll continue to do until the Evil One himself has been defeated."

King Faxon made a sign of thinking. He had been expecting Jarwe's answer and had planned for it.

"That would sound fair to a lesser man, but I know of your betrayal. It was a trick of the Evil One to have us gather our forces in the east. You should have brought the army home with Prince Hawthorne. Now you will be sentenced to death."

Jarwe should not have been so surprised with Faxon's response. He was clearly under the thrall of the Dark Knight and his words were not his own, but there was something even stranger about the situation. The fact that the Dark Knight was yet to show himself was the most disturbing fact of all.

"I know you are not yourself, your majesty. You have been deceived by a Dark Knight. The dwarf you think you know as Gilgi is in fact Dargoz."

Faxon burst out laughing, the noise echoing around the throne room. Again it was not the reaction that anyone expected.

"Gilgi told me you would say that. Of course an agent of Evil would try and place the blame onto someone else. It is you that has invaded my kingdom. It is you who threatens everything that we believe in."

"This is getting us nowhere," Jarwe said to the wizards. "Is there anything you can do to remove the spell on his mind?"

All the wizards turned to Drake. He was a follower of Opal and all things to do with the mind. They knew Drake was going to delve into the king's mind when they entered the throne room, with or without the presence of the Dark Knight.

"There is nothing that I can find, at least there is nothing on the surface. I don't want to delve too deeply. There is no telling what sort of traps the Dark Knight might have left for me."

"So are you saying this really is Faxon I am speaking with?" Jarwe sounded amazed.

"I can't be sure of anything. Dargoz was the Dark Knight who was best at controlling peoples' minds. I dare not delve too far. There are too many risks to both Faxon and myself."

"I can assure you that there is nothing wrong with my mind. I am in full control of all my senses."

"Then where is everyone?" Jarwe asked. "If we are the traitors that you believe us to be, I would have thought you would have soldiers lining the walls. No, I don't believe that everything is as you say." Jarwe took a step forward, not really knowing what he was going to do. He stopped before he over committed himself.

"Very good general," a voice came from behind the throne. Everyone waited until the dwarf appeared, although everyone knew who it was. "It seems that you are smarter than I gave you credit for."

No one knew if he had been behind the throne the entire time or whether he had crept in the through the back door. Either way, the Dark Knight had finally shown himself and the true trial had just begun.

Chapter 5: Wolf in Dwarf's Clothing

Dargoz moved around to the front of the king's throne before sitting down on the queen's. He looked quite ridiculous with his feet more than a foot from the floor. He wore a blood red, silken robe; nothing about his dress or his demeanour suggested he was ready for battle. If the Dark Knight was trying to confuse them, he was doing a good job.

"Dargoz!" Gwydion stepped forward. "We meet again."

The Dark Knight peered at the wizard. It was obvious he knew who he was, but couldn't place him. Suddenly a knowing expression crossed his face.

"You are one of the wizards. I didn't think you were going to crawl out from whatever rock you have been hiding under." He paused and looked at the other five wizards. A concerned expression crossed his face before it was quickly replaced by an evil grin. "I count only six. There is one of you missing. Does that mean there is dissention within the council?" The question didn't require an answer and Dargoz wasn't about to wait for one. "Maybe with all seven you might have been able to defeat me, but with just six... I don't think so."

"You overestimate your own abilities, but then I guess the cursed were always deluded," Gwydion spoke sharply. He wasn't going to let Dargoz win the verbal battle. They would need every advantage they could get, even if it was a small one. "Any one of us could defeat you. You would be wise to watch your tongue."

Dargoz burst out laughing, which in turn caused Faxon to do the same. "If you truly believed that then I would already be dead. I don't even think you believe that all six of you are a match for my powers. I believe there is something else you want. Now it is time that you stop wasting my time and let me know what it is."

"Leave now!" Gwydion blurted. "Leave now and we won't kill you." There was no way Dargoz was going to accept the offer, but Gwydion thought he should try. If there was any chance they could achieve their goal without fighting then it was worth it.

"No, I don't believe that is the reason you are here."

"We are here to kill you!" Jarwe stepped forward and then instantly wished he hadn't.

The Dark Knight had no plans to exchange words with the general. The man was no threat and therefore not worth his time. He lifted Jarwe up with a subtle spell and wrapped him up in air. Jarwe could neither move nor speak. It was a simple spell and certainly didn't leave an opening for one of the wizards to attack.

"Some people are just so rude," Dargoz sounded bored. "Now what do you think I should do with him?" Slowly Jarwe's neck started to turn. No matter what he tried there was nothing he could do to stop it. Dargoz twisted his neck around until it was about to snap. "Should I just snap his neck and be done with it?"

"You are proving nothing. This is a spell that any novice could achieve in their first week of training," Gwydion scoffed. "Now if you would stop messing about, we can get down to business."

"Fine, if this man's life means so little to you."

Dargoz made a twisting motion with his left hand, just for show. A snarl crossed his face when he realised his spell had been blocked. He looked to the group of wizards, but he couldn't tell which one of them had created it. In the end he figured it was just as easy to release his own spell instead of wasting energy unravelling it.

Without a wasting a moment Dargoz released his current spell before creating another and sending Jarwe flying across the room. Before he crashed into the wall he was stopped and gently lowered to the floor.

"What is the next parlour trick you would like to show us?" Gwydion mocked.

"I would watch your mouth old man. I have been around a lot longer than you and I have more *tricks* than you can possibly imagine. Now let's start again. What is it that I can do for you?"

Jarwe caught his breath at the back of the room. The shock of being so close to death and being able to do nothing about it had him rattled. He had faced death many times, but he had always felt in control of his own destiny.

The Dark Knight seemed to ignore him now he was released and the sudden anonymity gave him a chance to survey the situation. The king remained seated, although he had lost all of his fire from before. A glazed expression was now on his face and it didn't look like he was following the conversation at all. It made Jarwe believe that it was the Dark Knight controlling his king and not that he had been duped.

Hadar and Hulkan remained safely behind the six wizards. They didn't look as though they wanted to get involved in the discussion. There was nothing they could do and it was best if they stayed out of it.

"Since you were expecting us I would have figured you would have soldiers here," Gwydion continued. "Even you could not be so arrogant as to believe that you would be a match for the six of us."

"Well let's put that theory to the test."

Dargoz didn't waste any time in releasing his next spell. Slowly Brielle felt pressure on her throat. The pressure increased until she had to gasp to draw in air. Just before her windpipe had been cut off altogether, she managed to hold the spell. Although she couldn't dispel the attack, she could stop it from getting any worse.

The wizards knew the attack was coming, but they thought it would be directed at Gwydion. Although Brielle was never in any real danger it did come as a surprise. A second longer and Dargoz would have been able to complete his grip and she would have been dead.

Dargoz suddenly burst out laughing when he felt a spell hit him. No one except for Drake, who had cast the spell, noticed anything. He had hoped that whilst Dargoz was distracted with his attack on Brielle he could cut him off from the energy around him. Dargoz had to protect himself. He was not so arrogant as to not expect an attack from at least one of the wizards. As soon as he felt it coming, he swatted it away like he was swatting a fly.

"Do you think me that arrogant that I would not be expecting an attack," he held his grip on Brielle as he spoke. Her face was starting to turn red and despite her small gasps for air her lungs were not getting enough to sustain her life. If the spell wasn't broken soon then she would die. "I would have thought you would have tried something with a little more effort. I think it is the six of you who are suffering from arrogance."

When he finished speaking he suddenly ducked his head as a whip of air passed over him. If he had not noticed the spell coming then the wind would have taken his head clean off.

"Now that is better, but unfortunately not good enough," Dargoz scoffed.

Noticing that Dargoz was completely distracted with the wizards Jarwe slowly started to inch his way around the wall. The last thing he wanted to do was draw attention to himself so he moved as slowly as he could in stages when he was sure the Dark Knight was busy. Hulkan and Hadar seemed so focused on the scene before them that they didn't even realise he was still there. He had no idea what he would do if he managed to get close enough to strike, but he did know that he could not just stand and watch.

Suddenly the throne room started to shake as Dargoz prepared his next spell. He had released Brielle from his grip so he could focus his attack on all six of them. The rumbling started and stopped as the wizards tried to counter his spell. They didn't know exactly what he was doing, which made it much harder to counter. Whatever they were doing, it worked and slowly the rumbling stopped.

"Hmm, I see that the old tricks aren't going to do the job. Let me see if I can come up with something new for you."

Dargoz raised both his arms out in front of him. As he did, flames suddenly shot up from the floor. The first blaze narrowly missed engulfing Gwydion. Everyone could feel the intense heat as the fires shot from random places on the ground. The only sign of where the fire was going to come from was a slight reddening on the carpet.

The wizards started dancing around the throne room as they avoided the fire bursts. On more than one occasion the fringe of either a dress, robe, or some trousers were singed, but each time the wizard was able to extinguish the flame before it caused any damage.

Each time one of the wizards thought they could end the spell they had to jump out of the way of another blast. Although the fire seemed random, it did seem to target those trying to stop Dargoz. The Dark Knight had created the spell to follow anyone who tried to use magic against them. It was effective enough to keep them busy whilst he planned his next attack.

As the wizards dodged for their lives Dargoz raised his right hand. A bolt of blue light shot out towards Minerva, struck her on the chest and sent her flying across the room. Luckily all the wizards had cast a protection spell. The blue light would have certainly killed anyone who wasn't protected. In the end all she received was a nasty blow to her ribs and back. The air was knocked from her lungs and she instantly dropped to her knees, gasping for breath. Hadar thought about coming to her aid, but he didn't want to draw attention to himself. All he could do was hope that she would recover in time to protect herself from his next attack.

Dargoz had not been expecting the wizards to be able to block his attack and moved his attention to Ulman. Another blue light came, this time from his left hand. Ulman was able to dive out of the way as the light was about to hit him and a flame was about to engulf him. The light exploded against the far wall, but when it disappeared it left no damage.

With his attention on Ulman the other wizards tried to formulate their own attacks. When they realised that the flames were attracted to their magic it was easy enough to avoid them.

Although Dargoz was confident, he knew that the wizards would not be easy to kill. The blue light attack was certainly not the strongest he had, but it should have done more damage. If he was going to kill the wizards then he would have to let his fire spell go. He would need all his strength.

When the flames disappeared, the wizards were able to go on the attack. Althea was the first one to regain her composure and raised both hands out in front of her. A yellow light shot out from both palms.

At the last moment Dargoz dived out of the way. The yellow light struck the queen's throne and in a flash it was gone. Everyone expected a reaction from Faxon, but the King didn't even seem to notice. All that remained of his wife's throne was a wisp of smoke.

With the sway of battle starting to lean in their favour, Drake continued the attack. With Althea's initial attack it gave Drake more time to draw in more energy. His spell was going to be much more powerful and since they had already started to destroy pieces of the throne room, he didn't think there would be any problem in destroying a little more.

Suddenly the carpet ripped and tore in front of the Dark Knight. Chunks of dark granite ripped free and hurled towards him. Dargoz ducked out of the way of the first block, but the second caught him on the shoulder and knocked him off balance. He only had enough time to raise his arms to protect his head as he rolled out of the way.

The Dark Knight cast a spell in defence and the next chunk of granite stopped inches from his face. It floated in the air for a moment before disintegrating into dust. The granite dust slid to the ground like it was being passed through an hour glass.

The wizards kept pressing the Dark Knight. When one attack failed another followed closely behind. The last thing they wanted to do was to let him gain the upper hand again. In turn each of the wizards tried their best to kill him, but just when it seemed they might succeed he was able to defend himself. The only thing they gained was not being attacked in return.

When all the wizards had exhausted their first attack Dargoz stood and raised his arms above his head in a sign of surrender. At first they thought it was a trick, but morbid curiosity made them stop. They all wanted to hear what he had to say.

"It seems that I may have underestimated the six of you," Dargoz didn't sound stressed at all. It was a worrying sign as the wizards were showing signs of fatigue. If the Dark Knight could defend attacks from all six and not be stressed then he was more powerful than they had thought. "But it also seems that you have bitten off more than you can chew. I can feel your strain. With each attach you grow weaker whilst I grow stronger."

The six looked at him in awe. What he was saying was true. Somehow, in his defence, he had grown stronger. It was as if he was feeding on their spells. It should not have been possible. Sure they had all heard of the spell that could feed off others, like a parasite living off its host, but no one had managed to replicate it. When the spells had started killing those who were being drawn upon it had become outlawed over a century ago.

The spell that the Dark Knight had used would have drained any lesser wizards or sorcerers. Gwydion didn't know why he had stopped when he did, but he was grateful. By the time they would have realised what he was doing it would have been too late.

"Surrender to me and I will let you live," Dargoz offered.

"Do you think we would really become your thralls?" Gwydion scoffed, trying his best not to pant. "We know all too well what it means to surrender to the Evil One. We do not intend to be a slave like you are."

Dargoz threw his head back and laughed. "Surely this one doesn't speak for all of you. I am not a slave. I am held in the highest amongst The Chosen. Those who have died need replacing. Bow down to me and you can live forever with the Great Lord. When he defeats the Cursed One we will rule the land and all lands to come."

"Don't think for a moment that any of us would ever listen to what you have to say. Your brothers are dying, one by one, and you will be next. Your *Great Lord* will fail and fall to the Chosen One. It is you who should surrender."

Gwydion knew it wasn't an option, but he thought he should offer it again. He didn't know why Dargoz was stalling. He certainly didn't believe his offer was true. If they surrendered then they would all be dead. There had to be another explanation. The Dark Knight had control of the situation; it didn't make sense for him to delay.

"Very well, but don't say I didn't warn you," Dargoz said with doom in his voice.

Suddenly Gwydion understood what he was doing. Dargoz had drawn in the power from the other wizards during their attack, but he needed time to be able to use it. The reason he had stopped was to prevent himself from drawing in too much power. If he had then he would have burnt out and killed himself.

Drake cried out in pain before collapsing to the ground. His body writhed as Dargoz started draining him of energy. The attack was much more subtle and more deadly than his others. It seemed as though it had been his plan from the start. If he made it look as though he was attempting to kill the wizards then give them a chance to respond, they would never know his plan. It was perfect and they had walked straight into his trap.

Gasps cascaded from the other five as they realised they could no longer feel the energy around them. Dargoz had completely severed their connection and left them helpless. There was nothing they could do to help Drake or defend themselves. It seemed as though the Dark Knight had won and soon enough they would all be dead. There was little doubt he would make them suffer before he killed them.

"You have finally realised what I am capable of." Drake's cries were cut off as Dargoz spoke. He didn't want his gloating to be interrupted. "You should have taken my offer. At least then your deaths might have been painless." No one thought his statement was true.

Next to drop to the floor was Minerva. The Dark Knight was happy to slowly draw the life from each of the wizards one by one. Drake had been drained to point of death. There was nothing more he could do except to writhe on the floor in pain. Dargoz was quite happy to wallow in his misery.

Try as she might Minerva could not reach the energy around her to defend herself. She knew it was still there and she could almost feel it, but whenever she thought she could grasp it another shot of pain ripped through her body. Eventually she gave up. It was all she could do to remain conscious.

The four remaining wizards all wondered who Dargoz was going to attack next. Despite the two on the ground, screaming in pain, they steeled themselves, telling themselves that it would not be as bad. They all knew that it was false bravado.

Gwydion felt a tug at the back of his neck and instantly knew what it was. He was next to be drained and all hope left him. He had thought Dargoz would have left him for last, to gloat over what he had achieved. There was a glimmer of hope that he would be able to break the spell, but soon realised that would not happen.

The next thing he knew he had dropped to his knees. He could feel the life-force being sucked out of his body and the pain was like nothing he had ever felt before. It was like someone was ripping through his insides with a dull knife. He tried his best not to cry out, that would only increase the Dark Knight's pleasure, but he couldn't help himself. There was nothing he could do to stop, or even dampen, the pain.

"What can we do?" Althea asked Brielle and Ulman.

"We can fight!" Ulman boomed, drawing his bastard sword which was sheathed to his back. "I will not stand here and wait to die."

Ulman charged forward, but he could only manage three steps before his legs collapsed from underneath him. He tried to crawl closer to Dargoz, sword still in hand, but the pain overcame him. His sword clattered to the floor that had been ripped up from Drake's earlier attack.

"Do you really think that you could kill me with a sword?" Dargoz laughed. His voice had changed. It was now full of ecstasy.

"I think we should run!"

Brielle turned to flee, but she didn't even get to move her legs before she collapsed. The same pain hit her like the others. She tried to claw her way to the exit, but she could not gather the strength. All she could do was suffer the pain and feel her life being drained from her.

"So, what do you have to say for yourself?" Dargoz asked Althea.

"I have nothing to say to you. Of all the seven you are the most feeble. I would never bow down to you," Althea scoffed.

"Oh I think I can make you bend."

Althea felt pressure on the back of her left knee. At first she pushed the sensation to the back of her mind, but as it increased she tried harder to stop it. Like the others there was nothing she could do to stop the Dark Knight. His attack was not as quick as with the others, but it was just as strong.

Slowly Althea dropped her left leg until her knee touched the ground. When Dargoz was satisfied he moved onto her right knee. He manipulated her body like a rag doll until she was prostrating herself in front of him.

"Enough. I will not be treated like this," she spoke through clenched teeth.

"Would you prefer it if I treated you like the others?"

Suddenly the pain ripped through her body and she cried out. Her body remained prostrated on the floor and there was nothing she could do to move, not that it would have done anything to stop the pain.

Just as suddenly as it came the pain disappeared again. Dargoz released the spell on Althea and let her rise. She looked at the others who still writhed in pain, but there was nothing she could do to help.

"Now we can try this again. Bow down to me and I will let you live."

"I will never bow down to you," Althea spoke through clenched teeth.

"Look at your friends! I can keep this up all day."

To emphasize his point he started to apply pressure to her head. Slowly he clamped down harder and harder until she screamed out. Her hands held her head, but there was nothing she could do to stop the pain. She wanted to claw her brain out, but just as she was about to start scratching, the pain disappeared.

"This is your last chance. Bow down to me like the Great Lord commands and I will spare your life."

Althea spat blood before drawing a deep breath. "You don't have the authority to kill me and you know it. Now do your worse and be damned."

"Very well then. You can watch while I kill your friends. You shall die la..." his last word was cut off as a sword suddenly protruded from his chest.

Throughout the chaos Jarwe had continued to inch his way around the throne room completely unnoticed. Althea had not seen him sneak up behind Dargoz and only realised he was there when she saw the blade.

Instantly, all his spells dissipated.

The wizards on the ground were still suffering the effects and could do nothing to help, but as soon as Althea was released from the spell, she was able to draw in the energy around her. The feeling was glorious and swept away the affects of the Dark Knight.

Dargoz screamed out in anguish. Although the sword wasn't enough to kill him he knew it had sealed his fate. Jarwe had no idea what to do next and he just held the sword with all his might.

The Dark Knight used magic to knock Jarwe backwards, leaving the sword still inside him. He spun around to face his attacker and he was surprised to see Jarwe standing three paces away from him. Being stabbed was the last thing he had expected to happen. The general had no magical powers and should never have been a threat.

"A valiant effort, but fruitless nonetheless," as he spoke the sword slid out from him. Jarwe expected to see a spray of blood, like he had seen so many times before on the battlefield, but there was nothing. The wound had healed and there was no damage to his shirt. "It takes more than a sword to kill me. Now you will feel the full extent of my power."

Jarwe wanted to cringe. He wanted to run away, but his legs would not move. In the face of battle he had always been stalwart, but facing a Dark Knight was something completely different. There was nothing he could do to defend himself. Even in attack he had been completely useless.

"Don't waste your time with him, worry about me!" Althea called from the other side of the room.

Dargoz swung around to see Althea holding a ball of purple light in her hands. She made no move to attack, but her intentions were clear.

"You wouldn't dare. You don't have the authority to kill me," Dargoz sneered.

"You were always over confident," Althea smiled as she spoke.

Without another word Althea hurled the ball of light towards him. Not expecting Althea to actually attack, he had to defend himself. The light struck him with full force on the chest and engulfed him in purple flame. Knowing that the purple light wouldn't kill him she prepared her next attack.

Seeing they had the advantage again Jarwe suddenly burst into action. He snatched up his sword and waited for the purple flames to die down.

The other five wizards were still struggling to get to their feet. Although they could feel the energy around them no one had the energy to channel it. It would take a while for them to recover from the effects of the Dark Knight. They wanted nothing more than to remain on the floor, but they needed to show a united front. If Dargoz thought they were a threat then he could not focus all his energy on Althea.

Suddenly the air started to shimmer. At first no one noticed it, but it became clear to those who weren't focused on the fight. Two figures slowly appeared. One they recognised as Bern, the other, to their surprise, was a small girl.

Althea charged two bolts of lightning in her hands as the flames finally started to fade. The Dark Knight had changed. His face was a mess of burned flesh and the skin had started to peel from his arms. It was time for her to send the finishing blow.

"Stop!" Bern cried when he realised what was happening.

Althea turned just before she released her attack. When she realised who it was she let her arms drop, but kept the lightning crackling in her palms. She didn't know why he called for her to stop, but there was something in his tone that made her listen.

Dargoz moved his attention to the newcomers. He was just as surprised to see a young girl as the others were. There was something odd about the new couple. He could sense a power about them that they should not have.

"Thank the Gods that you haven't killed him," Bern said to the wizards.

There was a sickening cry that was suddenly cut off from the direction of the throne and Bern's heart sunk. Jarwe had used the distraction to sneak up behind Dargoz again. This time he was going to make sure he did the job properly. Jarwe had swung his sword and completely severed the Dark Knight's head.

His head flew through the air after the impact before it rolled to rest at Bern's feet. Jarwe panted for breath from the stress more than any real exhaustion from the effort. A smile crossed his face. He had succeeded.

A cheer came from Hulkan and Hadar who had finally found their voices. They had been too afraid to move when Dargoz was alive, but now that he was dead their strength had returned. They moved to try and support the injured wizards. They could only imagine the pain they had suffered. They looked as though they could barely stand. Whatever strength they had used to face the Dark Knight, it was quickly fading.

Althea stared at the dead body of the Dark Knight and a feeling of dread filled her body. She didn't know why. They had come to destroy him and that was exactly what they had done. There could be no other result and yet she still felt like they had done that wrong thing.

"Are you alright?" Hadar asked, but she didn't notice until he touched her on the shoulder.

"Yes, thank you."

With the battle finally over she let the energy leave her body and a wave of fatigue washed over her. Her legs started to wobble and Hadar placed his arm around her shoulders to steady her. Althea was grateful for the support. The fight with Dargoz had taken a lot from her, not that she should have been surprised. The other wizards were in worse shape, but they had been attacked harder.

"Good job everyone," Gwydion tried his best to sound unaffected, but failed.

Jarwe wiped that dark blood from his blade as he looked down at the limp body of the Dark Knight. When he woke in the morning he had not thought he would survive to see the sun set. Never in his wildest dreams would he have believed that he would have been the one to deliver the killing blow.

For some reason Jarwe couldn't bring himself to look at the others. He couldn't take his eyes from the body. He knew he had done the right thing, but he couldn't help feeling sorry for him. The feeling made no sense, but it was there nevertheless.

"What are you all doing in my throne room?" Faxon barked from his throne.

Everyone had forgotten about the king. The effects of the Dark Knight had completely disappeared when he died. Dargoz had not had to keep a tight hold on Faxon. His disguise had proved well. Faxon had given him the run of the palace almost without any mind-control.

"What is happening here?"

Chapter 6: Victory or Failure

"What have you done!" Bern gasped.

A severed head was always so permanent. A sword through the chest or a broken neck was repairable, but there was nothing to cure a severed head. There was little doubt that the last Dark Knight had been killed and soon they would all be reborn, just like Morgoz had been. The final battle had just become much harder.

"There is nothing we can do about it now," Cayley tried to ease his concerns. "And you can't blame them. We would have done the same thing not a day ago."

"I know. It's our fault, or my fault, that this has happened," Bern resigned. "But there will be time for recriminations later. Now we have more important matters to deal with."

Faxon rose from his throne and took a step forward as he tried to work out the situation before him. The dwarf Gilgi had been killed by the traitor Jarwe, that he knew, or at least he thought he knew. Something had changed within him and he wasn't sure of anything.

When Gilgi and Prince Hawthorne had told him that Jarwe had turned traitor, he had instantly dismissed it. He had known the general for a long time and he was nothing if not loyal to the crown. Whatever the reason he had remained with the Alliance must have been a good one. He could not believe the man had turned traitor.

He couldn't recall what Gilgi had said to change his mind, but it had not taken long before he was convinced. He had signed the death warrant himself, although he could not remember why.

The scene before him should have confirmed the fact, but for some reason he did not feel that way, instead he felt as though a large weight had been lifted from his shoulders. All he needed was for someone to explain to him what had happened and why Gilgi was lying on the ground missing his head.

"Jarwe!" Faxon tried to get the general's attention as he was the only one he recognised.

Slowly Jarwe let his eyes drift from the Dark Knight. For some reason he thought the body would change from that of the dwarf or burst into flame. His death seemed to be a complete let down. The effort that it had taken deserved something more fitting.

"Your majesty." Jarwe suddenly remembered himself and bowed.

"Stand up general. I don't think this is the time to stand on ceremony." Faxon waited for him to rise before he continued. "Would you mind telling me why the leader of the Western Dwarf Guild is lying headless on my throne room floor?"

"There will be time for answers," Bern moved forward. "But as you can see there are some who need rest, or at least to be seated. Is there somewhere a little more comfortable we could go to speak?"

"And who are you to address me in such a manner?" Faxon didn't sound very confident. There was something about the approaching man that oozed confidence. Faxon knew that he was not the most commanding figure in the room and that worried him. He wondered if he was about to share the same fate as Gilgi and thought he should call for his guards, but he stayed his voice.

"My name is Bern and I am the General of the Alliance. Fear not Faxon I am here to help you." Bern instantly picked up on Faxon's tone. "Now if there is somewhere, close, we can go, that would be great."

Normally the King would not stand for such insolence, but there was no one in the room that he needed to prove himself to. He still wanted to know who they all were, but as he looked at the group before him it looked as though most of them were about to collapse. He didn't think he would get any answers if he didn't acquiesce.

"I have a small sitting room behind us." He paused and made a quick count. "I'm not sure it will be able to fit everyone though."

"That's alright," Bern said. "Duke Hadar should see Captain Kenyon and tell him what has happened here. The rest of the Alliance needs to be informed of our victory." Bern chose his words carefully. Although he knew they had not succeeded there was no point telling the others just yet. It would bode better for the other commanders and the rest of the army if they believed they had. In truth they had failed. "Hulkan will need to speak with the rest of the dwarves and try and explain the situation. The rest shall take respite in the sitting room."

Both Hulkan and Hadar thought about protesting, but in the end they realised that Bern was right. With the Dark Knight dead they would need to be on the move again. There was still plenty of work to be done.

As soon as they left, Faxon led the others though a small door at the back of the room. Jarwe walked a step behind the king and the six wizards paired up and supported themselves through the door. Bern and Cayley were happy to follow behind. Bern thought about dismissing the little girl, but he did not think that would get him anywhere.

The wizards were happy for the opportunity to sit and didn't wait to be offered a seat. The sitting room was less formal than Bern had expected. He thought there would have been a central table with chairs around it, but instead it was set more like a lounge room. Armchairs and couches were scattered around the edge of the room with coffee tables in-between. Many colourful tapestries hung on the wall. Jarwe was happy to see that the room had not been touched by the Dark Knight like the rest of the palace. He was grateful to be able to sit in a comfortable arm chair.

Although he had not taken much part in the battle with the Dark Knight he felt exhausted.

Faxon tugged on a bell pull next to the armchair he sat in. He wanted to order some refreshments before they started, what he was sure, would be a long and arduous conversation.

After a few minutes had passed and no one had come, Faxon pulled again. This time he gave it three sharp rings to indicate his displeasure.

"I am sorry. I don't know what my staff are doing. It should not take this long to be served."

Jarwe was about to speak when the door opened. They were all surprised to see the suited man who had met them at the front door. The dull expression on his face had been replaced by one of pure confusion. He didn't even look as though he knew where he was.

"Balfour!" Faxon snapped. "What are you doing here? And why hasn't a server come to assist us?"

Balfour was Faxon's Master-of-the-House and had been for the past ten years. If anyone was to know what was happening in the palace, it would be him. That was the reason he was the first person Dargoz had controlled. He had used a power compulsion spell and then tied it off. Over time the spell would dissipate on its own, but it would remain long enough for Dargoz to achieve his set goals.

"I'm sorry your majesty. I don't know what is happening. The last thing I remember was the prince returning from the east. You sent me to organise a great feast, then I met someone in the hallway." Balfour scratched his head as he tried to remember. "I think it was a dwarf. No, it definitely was a dwarf, although I couldn't tell you who it was. The next thing I remember I was standing in the foyer and your bell was ringing. When I heard it the second time I figured you wanted me. I didn't see anyone else in the palace. My head is so hazy and I don't know why."

Faxon opened his mouth to speak, but then stopped. Although his memory wasn't as bad as Balfour's it still had gaps. Like Balfour he remembered his son returning home and meeting with Gilgi. From then on everything else seemed to be blurred together. He could remember giving Gilgi control over the palace, but he had no idea why he would do such a thing. Something else was nagging him.

"Where is my son?" he asked, almost afraid of what the answer might be.

"I don't know. I'm sorry, but I can't remember seeing Prince Hawthorne after he returned with the army."

Faxon thought for a moment. The wizards were enjoying the chance to rest and were not really paying attention to the conversation. Jarwe wanted to mention the Dark Knight, but a stern look from Bern kept him quiet.

"Well, it seems you have your work cut out for you. Find my staff and have them send some food and drinks here and then bring me my son."

"Yes, your majesty." Balfour bowed before leaving.

Faxon waited until the door was shut before he spoke again. "Would someone please tell me what is happening here. Nothing makes any sense and my mind is cluttered with random memories."

"Gilgi was a Dark Knight." Bern didn't waste any time. "He placed a compulsion spell on you, that is why you're struggling to remember things. He also cast one on your Master-of-the-House. That spell was more powerful than the one cast on you, so whatever you are feeling he is feeling it ten times worse."

Faxon nodded his head before lowering it. He tried to piece together his memories, but he couldn't. They came to him in no particular order and they didn't make any sense. At one time in his life he would have scoffed at the thought of a Dark Knight, but with what had happened, he could only believe. Before Dargoz, he would have thought his mind was too strong to be controlled by anything, but that simply was not the case. He was not sure if he could continue to rule his kingdom with such shame.

"Don't feel so bad," Bern soothed. "All the other rulers were also controlled by a Dark Knight at some point. There was nothing you could do about it."

Bern's words did make Faxon feel a little better, but he still wished he could remember what he had done. There was a nagging sensation in the back of his mind that something terrible had happened. It wasn't that he had done it himself, but he had known and done nothing to stop it. He could only hope that his son would be able to tell him.

"So can you shed any light on what has been happening here?" Faxon finally asked.

"I'm sorry, but I only arrived right at the end of the battle with the Dark Knight. I have no information of what happened beforehand."

"What about the rest of you?" Faxon snapped without thinking.

"This is the Council of Wizards," Jarwe spoke quickly. The last thing he needed was for his king to upset them, especially since they had just saved the kingdom. "They saved us."

"But it was you who slew the Dark Knight. I saw you remove his head like you were cutting through butter," Faxon returned.

"Thank you, but with all due respect you were somewhat catatonic for most of the battle. I was just able to get into the right place at the right time. It was the wizards who deserve all the credit for the victory."

"Very well, I do apologise," his voice did not sound sincere.

"You would do well to find some respect," Brielle snapped. "I knew your great-grandfather, King Cherles IV, and he had respect for the mystic arts."

"Yes, and as I recall he was betrayed by his court magician to his death. It was my grandfather who had to bury his father who was only forty at the time. He then had the magician executed and outlawed magic in the Kingdom of Remidia. My father relaxed the laws, but we will never have a magician in court in Remidel in my lifetime or that of my son's," barked Faxon, offended at Brielle's outburst.

"One rogue magician does not represent the magic community and definitely not the Council of Wizards. It's attitudes like yours that have dwindled our numbers over the years," Drake continued where Brielle had left off.

"Enough!" boomed Bern. "This conversation is getting us nowhere. We have more important matters to deal with than petty squabbles from the past."

The wizards looked at Bern in shock. There was something different about him, but they could not tell what it was. No one had spoken to them in such a manner. Not even the king.

Bern felt a tingling on the back of his neck and knew that one of the wizards was creating a spell. If he really cared he could have worked out who it was, but he thought it would be better to take whatever they were going to dish out. There was little chance it was going to be a dangerous spell. The situation didn't warrant any great show of power and they all were still suffering from the battle. To block the spell would raise too many questions that he did not want to answer.

Suddenly he felt a band of air whack him on the back of his head. He nodded forwards slightly and rubbed his head in a sign that the spell had worked, but he ignored the wizards and returned his attention to the King.

"Now that the Dark Knight is dead we need..."

Bern was cut short as the door was suddenly pushed open. Balfour rushed into the room panting and it was obvious that he had been running hard.

"You need to come with me," his tone had an urgency that concerned everyone.

"Calm down Balfour. What are you talking about?" Faxon asked.

"I have found Prince Hawthorne."

"And, where is my son? Why is he not with you?" panic started to fill Faxon's voice.

Balfour didn't know what to say. He had rushed to the sitting room and not stopped to think on how he was going to break the news.

"I found the prince in the dungeons," he blurted. "He has his chest wrapped with a bloody bandage. No one could, or would, tell me how long he has been down there. It looks as though he has been tortured on more than one occasion. I don't know how he received his wound, but I was told it was caused by a sword. His breathing is laboured and his skin is deathly pale. I wanted to have him brought to the palace infirmary, but it did not look like he would survive the journey," the words rushed out of his mouth.

Faxon didn't know what to say. The feeling of dread increased tenfold when he heard the information. Although he did not believe that he had sent his son to the dungeons, he knew he had done nothing to stop it. If his son died then he didn't know how he was going to live with himself. His fears were clearly written on his face.

"Althea, you have studied the medicinal arts of Topaz. If anyone can heal him it's you," Bern said.

There was no time for him to mince his words. The look of surprise on the faces of the six wizards was enough to tell him that he had revealed too much. Despite his secrets he knew the life of Prince Hawthorne was more important. His part in the prophecy was not over and he could not risk him dying.

"You seemed to be the quickest to recover." That seemed odd to Bern, but there would be time for questions later. "You need to go with Faxon and do whatever you can to keep him alive."

"I don't..." she started.

"There is no time for you to pout. This is not a request. I know that you are not as weary as the others and you are the most proficient in healing," Bern boomed. Everyone in the room shrank back from his words.

"With all due respect," Gwydion started, his voice weak.

"There is no time for respect or winged words. This is something that has to be done NOW! Faxon, you should go with the wizard and see to your son. There are still things that need to be done, so I need you to leave me in control of the kingdom."

There were gasps around the room, but Faxon moved into action as if he was in a trance. He was still struggling with the fact that Hawthorne was on his death bed. From the account given by Balfour it might already be too late. The words echoed in his mind as he made his way to the door.

"Whatever you need!" he said as he left, not waiting to see if Althea was following.

"Show them to the prince and then return here," Bern said to Balfour who nodded in return.

Althea looked to the others for support, but they gave her none. They all knew he was right. All she could do was stand and follow. She didn't want to risk another berating. Her ego had already been punished enough for one day.

"What do you think you are doing?" Jarwe boomed. "This is exactly the story the Dark Knight was selling. You cannot think to take control of Remidia?" Jarwe could not believe that Bern had just asked, and received, power over the kingdom. It was just unbelievable.

"Relax, there is nothing untoward happening here. We have little time to waste and there is no telling how long the King will be by his son's side," Bern explained.

"King Faxon will do his duty," Jarwe replied. "If he needs to make decisions then that is what he shall do."

Bern shook his head. After everything they had been through he did not think Jarwe would question his motives. It was almost like he believed the Dark Knight's lies.

"You know that I have no desire to rule a kingdom. It took a long time before I was able to accept control of the Alliance." He pulled on Bern's memories to make a convincing argument. "The final battle will be upon us soon and we need to organise the army as soon as possible. There is work to be done and we must do it."

"General Jarwe is right," Drake added. "It is not for you to assume control of Remidia. It will only fuel the lies the Dark Knights have spread. If we need to gain support of the people then this is not the way to go about it."

"You five look as though you are ready to drop." Bern ignored him. He moved to the bell pull and tugged on it hard. He could only hope that the palace staff had started to return to work. "I will have rooms for you. You all need to rest before we speak again."

There were grumbles around the room. The wizards had never been dismissed in such a manner, but they also knew that he was right. They would need rest before they were able to hold a decent conversation. The battle with the Dark Knight had taken more from them than they had expected.

As they stood to leave the room a young serving maid entered. She looked around for a sign of the King and frowned when she could not find one. It was a most unusual situation, but then again there was very little that had not been unusual recently.

"What can I do for you?" she asked.

"While the King is looking after his son he has left me in control of the palace," Bern started. "These five need rooms to relax. See that they are not kept waiting. I am sure there are plenty of free apartments."

She gave him a questioning look. Although Balfour had instructed them that it was back to business as usual he had mentioned the man before her. If he was in control of the palace then she was sure that Balfour would have told them. On the other hand they were in the king's private sitting room and they would not be there if they weren't supposed to be.

"Is this something I should expect from the household staff?" Bern let the question sink in before he continued. "If this is the case then I shall have a serious word with Balfour. Things will have to change when I am in charge, although I don't think Faxon will be too pleased with an idle house."

The serving maid's eyes opened wide in surprise and fear. "Of course, err... my lord. Please follow me. There are two apartments next to each other that will be comfortable for all of you."

She waited for a moment before a stern expression from Bern sent her on her heels. The wizards slowly followed after her. It would not take her long to realise that she would have to slow down for her guests to follow.

"What is going on Bern and who is this girl with you?" Jarwe asked when they were alone.

"There will be time for answers, but now is not that time. I will explain everything when we can all get together. For now we need to get Faxon's house in order." Bern left no room for argument. "It seems as though his staff are returning to work from whatever it was they were doing and that is a start. Hopefully Hulkan will have sorted out what the dwarves are doing and Hadar has returned to the Alliance. You should rejoin the army. They will feel better when they see you."

"That is all well and good, but you are the General of the Alliance. It would be much better for morale if the soldiers and the commanders see you." Jarwe did not want to be dismissed. He wasn't sure what Bern was planning, but he did not think it was good.

"For now you are still in command and it will stay that way. Now if you would please leave I have business to attend to."

Jarwe didn't know what to say. Bern was his commanding officer and in the end he had to listen to his orders. All he could do was stand, shake his head and give Bern a stern look before storming out of the room.

"What are you planning Asgard?" Cayley asked when they were alone.

"Please Cayley," Bern barked.

"Sorry," she pouted. "*Bern*, what are you planning?"

"We need to gather all the soldiers we can get. Although I won't be able to outright order them to join the Alliance, I can set things up so Faxon will not have a choice."

Before Bern could elaborate on his plan the door opened and Balfour entered. He was glad for both the interruption and the return of the Master-of-the-House.

"What can I do for you general?" Althea had given a brief explanation on their way to the dungeons. "I am at your disposal."

"Good, finally things are coming together," Bern started. "First I will need you to gather the commanding officers that remain in the palace or the city. I know most of the soldiers were sent out to fight the Alliance, but I am sure there are still some around."

"Yes, sir!" Balfour saluted and was about to leave.

"That's not all. There needs to be an announcement to the residents of the city that it is safe to walk the streets again. Reinstate the city watch. We need to get the city back into its normal working state."

Balfour seemed to be more comfortable with that command. He had thought that they had replaced one dictator for another, but that did not seem to be the case. It was a good start to bring stability back to the kingdom and Balfour was not going to waste any more time.

"So, now can you tell me what you are planning?" Cayley's voice was firm.

"All in good time my dear."

***

The dungeons were hot and musty and it had been many years since Faxon had been there. He knew that the dungeons were necessary to house the vilest of criminals, but he did not like seeing them in person.

As they rushed through the caverns he couldn't help but notice the condition of the cells. Blood and chunks of meat were strewn around and he gagged each time he looked, but he did not have the time to stop and retch.

Deep down he knew that it wasn't his fault, but he could not help feeling that he could have done better. Those who had created such atrocities had been placed there under his rule. The Dark Knight had not needed to find new men to do his bidding. Although it was nearly impossible to find a non-sadistic dungeon master, if he had taken more time then he might have been able to stem the horror.

Althea followed a step behind the King and Balfour. She used all her self control not to look inside the cells after peering into the first one. She was a healer; that was her main skill and what she enjoyed. She had never had the stomach for torture or the results. After her ordeal with Dargoz she wondered if she was being punished by some mischievous deity.

They found Hawthorne on the second level of the dungeons, laid out on a torture table. There were no infirmaries in the dungeons. Those who were suffering either got better on their own or died. Either way it was nothing to the dungeon masters. The torture table was the only place they could comfortably lay Prince Hawthorne down, even though it was not at all suitable.

The smell in the cell was revolting. The stench of rotten meat and stale blood filled their noses. It was impossible to tell if it was just the cell or if any of it was coming from the prince. The bandage wrapped around his chest was completely soaked with blood and it looked as though it had never been changed.

"Do we know how long he has been here?" Althea asked.

"I do not know. No one has given me any answers and I don't think they will. They all fear for their lives and rightly so," Balfour replied. "Now I should return to General Bern. I think I should keep an eye on him until the King returns."

Faxon did not respond. All he could do was to stare at his son. The prince looked deathly ill. His chest barely rose and fell and his skin was so pale that there didn't look like there was any blood pumping through his body. The king trembled and could not ask the question that plagued him.

Althea walked around the table, but made no move to touch the body. She didn't know how he was still alive. By the look of the bandages it had been a least two days, if not more since he had been placed there.

"There is nothing I can do," Althea sounded defeated.

"You haven't even looked at the wound," Faxon's tone was incredulous.

"I can sense no life left in him. I'm sorry, but he will die shortly."

Her words snapped Faxon out of his malaise. He could not believe that she was willing to give up without trying anything. She was one of the Council of Wizards and apparently the best at healing.

"General Bern told you to keep him alive. He would not have done so if he did not think you could," the words spewed out of his mouth. "What do you think he will do to you if you fail?" He didn't know if Bern would do anything, but the words seemed right.

Althea stood back at the harshness of his words. It was true that there was something disturbing about Bern's new persona, but she didn't think there was anything he could do to punish her. On the other hand there was something very strange about the man and she could not risk the repercussions.

"There is little I can do here. He needs his wounds cleaned and fresh bandages. There is nothing here that I can work with."

"You are a wizard. Surely there is something you could do?"

Althea sighed. She had to try. If she didn't then Faxon would tell Bern and the other wizards and she couldn't risk the repercussions.

Slowly she created a spell to check the wound and instantly she stepped backwards. As she did there came a moan from Hawthorne, but nothing more. Faxon looked at his son and then at Althea in horror.

"What was that?" he gasped.

"That is no ordinary wound." Althea shook her head in disbelief.

"What do you mean?"

Althea didn't know exactly what, she had never come across such a wound in her many years of healing. It was not something the Dark Knight had done, she knew that for sure. His evil would have been the first thing she felt. What was before her was something new and she had no idea what it was.

"I don't know," she gasped.

Faxon's rage subsided and sorrow filled his heart. There was no lie in Althea's voice. If there was nothing she could do then there was nothing anyone could do. He stepped forward to collect his son's body.

"Don't touch him!" she called out.

"If he is going to die then I will give him what comfort I can. I will not leave him to die in the dungeons."

"He is not dead yet," there was a touch of hope to her tone. "There is nothing I can do to heal him, but that was not what Bern asked me to do. He asked me to keep Hawthorne alive." It was obvious that an idea had come to her and that gave Faxon some hope. "He has stayed alive for this long and I should be able to keep him alive for a little longer. With a little luck we should be able to move him into the palace as well. I don't know about you but I've had enough of this cell."

"Do you really think you can?" Hope filled his voice as he retreated to give her room to work.

"Let's just take one thing at a time."

Chapter 7: A Fresh Day

In the morning, the wizards met in the front room of one of their apartments, all except for Althea who stayed with Prince Hawthorne. She refused to leave his side until he was cured. She didn't want to risk tying off her spell and having him die. There was a chance that her own life depended on the prince surviving and she was not going to take any chances.

They had managed to move him into the palace and more comfortable surroundings. Under Althea's instructions they didn't risk removing the bandages. She had a feeling that if the wound was revealed, then his life would be over. Until other options arose she would keep him in the same state as they had found him.

A good night sleep and a hearty breakfast had washed away their fatigue. With their renewed vigour came the memories of the previous day. Of all the disturbing events, there was something that plagued on all their minds.

"Why did Althea not receive the same treatment as the rest of us?" Gwydion finally voiced what they were all thinking as he sipped on his second cup of tea.

The question sat in the air as no one wanted to respond. They all had their own suspicions and none of them were pleasant. If what they thought was true then there was no telling what the repercussions might be.

"There has to be a reason and the only one who can truly answer that is dead. The Dark Knight needed to taunt one of us and it seemed that Althea was his choice," Brielle said.

"That doesn't make any sense," Ulman barked. "There was no reason why he would taunt any of us. He had us." It was not something he wanted to admit openly, but it needed to be said. "All he had to do was finish the job. There has to be another reason."

"Then why don't you give us one?" Drake returned.

"Arguing is not going to get us anywhere," Minerva kept her voice level. "We are all thinking it, but it looks like I'm the only one willing to voice it. Althea is an agent of the Evil One."

Her revelation brought a round of silence. No one wanted to answer her. No one wanted to believe that it was even a possibility, but it was the only thing that made sense.

"I know everything points to that, but there has to be another explanation," Gwydion said.

"If she truly is a servant of Nyrra then why is she trying to save Hawthorne? Wouldn't it make sense for her just to let him die?" Brielle returned.

"It would make perfect sense for her to save Hawthorne. If we suspect her then that would throw us off the scent," Drake said.

"So that gives us nothing," Gwydion sighed.

"Surely we would know," Brielle argued. "Surely she could not have worshipped the Evil One on Ĉarolija. We would have all felt the evil radiating from her." Brielle and Althea were close friends and she could not believe what they were saying. Even though the thought had crossed her mind she had dismissed it as soon as it had come. "I have spent many hours with Althea and she has done nothing to make me believe she is evil."

"Maybe you are too close to this," Minerva offered.

"And maybe you are all too far away," Brielle snapped back.

"We are the Council of Wizards," Gwydion reminded them. "We keep our cool when everyone else loses theirs. This is no way for us to react. We can work this out without raising our voices."

"Oh you'd like that wouldn't you," Brielle was not going to be appeased. "If you hadn't noticed we are no longer on our little island. The Seven Kingdoms has changed and we don't have to time to meditate on these questions."

"Please, Brielle, this is getting us nowhere," Drake tried to soothe her. "If Althea is an agent of evil then we need to work out what to do with her."

"How can we make a decision without solid evidence?" Ulman asked. "Would any of us like to be convicted of such a heinous crime without sufficient evidence?"

"And how do you expect us to find more evidence?" Minerva asked the rhetorical question. "It's not like we can just skip back to the island. I don't know about the rest of you, but it will be a long time before I could make that sort of jump."

The wizards all looked inside themselves and shook their heads. Returning home to check through her possessions was not an option.

"If she is truly an agent of evil then she must have something with her to prove it," Ulman suggested.

"Would you?" Gwydion asked. "I know I would leave nothing to chance once we left the island."

"I am sure the Evil One will want to keep an eye on her," Drake disagreed. "In my studies I have come across items called 'orbs of distance'. They are artefacts of the ancient world and were used to communicate across the Seven Kingdoms. Nyrra used them to relay orders to his commanders across the various battlefronts. I'm not sure how many were ever made, but I feel there were at least fourteen."

"So you think Nyrra would give one to Althea so they could communicate with each other?" Gwydion asked. "It will definitively give us an answer if she had one."

"But if she doesn't then we are back to square one. I think we need another plan before we start going through her possessions," Minerva added.

"If she has anything hidden then I'm sure she would have a powerful spell protecting it," Ulman suggested. "Maybe we don't even need to find anything. If there is a protection spell, we know something is suspicious."

"Don't be a fool Ulman. You might not have anything worth protecting in your packs, but I know I have a spell to stop any curious fingers. If this is something we are going to do then we need to be very careful. If indeed she is an agent of evil then there is no telling what kind of traps she has waiting for us," said Minerva.

"So you really plan on doing this?" Brielle sounded aghast. "Well let's get it over with."

There didn't seem to be any other option. The longer they stayed and discussed the matter, the more chance there was of Althea returning. They needed to leave and return without her knowledge. If she was an agent of the Evil One then they didn't want her to know they were onto her. Worse still if she wasn't.

"Very well," Gwydion conceded. "Let's go."

Just as they were about to leave the room Balfour entered. He did not look happy.

"The general has asked for you to join him in the sitting room," he didn't offer any pleasantries.

"I'm afraid that we have things to do," Brielle scoffed. "We will not have time for him today."

"I used the term 'asked' as a sign of respect, but the general was quite insistent that you join him. He was quite forceful," Balfour explained.

"You can tell the 'general' that we don't take orders. We will come and see him only when we have finished our business," Althea was not going to be dissuaded.

"Very well," Balfour did not sound at all interested. "But it will be you who explains it to the general when you arrive."

The Master-of-the-House turned and left the room, not waiting for a response. He was not at all impressed with his new master. If it had been King Faxon who had given him the command then he would have fought harder to get them to acquiesce. For General Bern he was not going to risk his life to order the Council of Wizards to do anything. He knew how dangerous they could be.

Drake shrugged his shoulders at Ulman before they both burst out laughing.

"Oh come on you two, it isn't that funny," Minerva scolded them.

They had found the situation quite amusing and Minerva's words only fuelled their mirth. Their laughter died down to muffled chuckles and it wasn't until they were out in the corridor that they regained their composure.

The palace was alive with activity. It had not taken long for Balfour to restore the household staff to their former positions. As soon as he was able to briefly explain what had happened, they were all happy to return.

Outside the palace walls the city was also starting to come to life again. A small garrison of soldiers had been brought back inside the walls to keep the peace. A number of announcements had also been made throughout the city, indicating that it was safe to walk the streets again. Like within the palace the citizens were given little information on what had transpired.

The wizards kept their heads held high and ignored the looks as they rode past. Although they didn't think anyone would recognise them, they didn't want to risk it. The last thing they needed was for a group of people to stop them and ask questions. They needed to reach the campsite, check Althea's possessions and return before she left Hawthorne's side. Any delay would certainly put them at risk.

When they were outside the city they rode directly towards their own campsite. The last thing they needed was to be stopped by one or more of the commanders. If they thought the citizens would be bad the commanders would be ten times worse.

Their camp was towards the northern end of the Alliance. They had managed to segregate themselves from the rest of the army, giving them some anonymity. If anyone went to enter their small campsite they would simply find a reason to walk away. It was a simple spell, but effective against anyone who didn't use magic.

As soon as they were inside, their voices would not reach anyone else. It was another simple spell. No matter how loud they yelled no one would hear them.

They found Althea's possessions, as expected, stacked neatly inside her tent. At first glance there did not seem to be anything unusual about them, but the wizards knew better. A magical trap would not be obvious, at least not until you were caught in it.

As they travelled through the city they had decided that Brielle should be the one to search for the spell. She protested vehemently, but the others insisted. Even though she was the best choice, she did not know why she should have to put herself at risk. She also knew better than to go against the rest of the council.

From outside Althea's tent nothing seemed out of the ordinary, even to those searching for spells. She nervously opened the flap as the others watched from a safe distance. Suddenly she felt like a fish being pushed onto a hook.

Like with all of wizard's tents Althea's was larger than those throughout the rest of the camp. The wizards liked their little luxuries and although they were few and far between, their tents were one they would not live without. There was clear headroom for them to stand comfortably and move around.

At the far end of the tent was her bedroll with a set a drawers and a mirror to one side. On the left was a small table and chair. She imagined at some stage there would be books and papers on the table, but it seemed as though they had yet to be unpacked. It was the bags on the opposite side of the tent that piqued Brielle's attention.

As she took a step further into the tent a feeling of 'wrongness' entered her body. She knew instantly there was magic in the air, but she wasn't sure exactly what it was. It didn't look, or feel, as though there was anything protecting her possessions, so she looked around one more time before leaving. If there were traps set then she was not going to be the only one caught in them.

"Well?" Ulman asked.

"There is definitely something there, but I can't work out what it is," she replied.

"You didn't spend much time in there," Drake snapped. "Are you sure there is nothing you could find?"

Brielle opened her mouth to berate him, but instead took a deep breath. "There was nothing protecting her bags. Whatever she has set is much more subtle. There is definitely something there, but it will take time to work out what it is. I think we are better off if we all make the effort, it will make things happen a lot quicker." Although it was not her only motive, it did make sense.

Gwydion was the first to agree and stepped inside the tent. They needed to prove either way if she was an agent of evil. Like Brielle he felt the wrongness of the tent, as did the others as they followed behind.

The tent was crowded with all five of the wizards inside, but there was no other way they could all work on the spell. From outside the tent there was no indication of what was happening.

It was not an easy situation to work in. They all tried their best to move around each other to gain a different perspective. On the surface everything looked normal and no one without the power within them would notice anything at all, but the sight before the wizards was much more disturbing. After an hour they all left to discuss what, if anything, they had discovered.

"This isn't looking good for our sister," Ulman started.

"We found nothing!" Brielle exclaimed.

"That is exactly my point. She is trying very hard to hide something. If you want to go through my tent you will find some very simple spells, but we found nothing inside hers," Ulman explained.

"This is getting us nowhere," Minerva interrupted them. "There is only one way we're going to work out what Althea is up to and that is to ask her."

"No!" Gwydion started. "Ulman is right. The tent is too... tidy. It is like no one has stayed there. I think she has masked it with a cloaking spell. It's a risk, but I think I can break it."

No one said anything. They all knew the risks involved in trying to break a spell that could not be seen. If Gwydion was right then it should be simple enough, but if he was wrong then there was a good chance the spell he created would consume him. Either way he had to take the risk. If Althea was an agent of evil then they would need to know.

"You should all step back, just in case I'm wrong," Gwydion said as he stepped back inside the tent.

Once he was inside, Gwydion closed his eyes. He wanted to get a fresh perspective. With no one else in the tent he was hoping to find what he was looking for.

The wrongness washed over him as he tried to delve into the hidden spell. Each time he thought he knew where it was it slipped away. There was nothing for it; all he could do was take the risk that could potentially cost him his life.

A cloaking spell was fairly common, but there were many variations. Although it wasn't imperative that Gwydion new the exact spell to break, it would certainly help. The main problem would be any traps Althea had left. That was what he had to be careful of. There were common traps left on cloaking spells and if he was right then he would be able to sever them without injuring himself. If she had left anything stronger then Althea would not have been able fight the Dark Knight, he was sure of that.

Gwydion started by dispelling any traps he could think of. As he didn't know which traps were actually there he had no idea if what he was doing was actually working. All he could do was hope that he could think of everything Althea might have used. The only sign that he was not doing anything wrong was the fact that he was still alive.

When he was satisfied that he had done everything he could to prepare himself, he started working on breaking the cloaking spell. A bead of sweat, from both exertion and stress, appeared on his brow.

It took Gwydion five minutes to carefully piece together the weaves of his spell. When he finally released it the sudden change in the room knocked him to the ground. His head swam from the effect, and he felt as though he was going to retch. It took him a moment to settle himself before he returned to his feet.

His head was still swimming and he had to sit before he could take in the scene around him. He thought about calling out to the others, but he needed to gain his composure. As he looked around the tent he panted for breath and wiped the sweat from his face.

The peaceful scenery that had been there before was completely gone. The bedroll was unmade, with undergarments strewn across it.

Normally one of the servers would have cleaned the tent, but since it looked neat and tidy there was nothing for them to do.

It was the table that drew his attention. There were a number of books and leaves of paper scattered around, but that wasn't what took his attention. Sitting in the middle was what he had hoped he would not see. A small white orb sat neatly and proudly amongst the mess. There was no doubt it was one of the orbs Drake had told them about. There could be little doubt that she was indeed an agent of the Evil One.

Taking a deep breath he called out for the others to join him. Despite the fact that he wanted to rise he didn't think his body was able. The spells had taken more from him than he expected. He had not fully recovered from the previous day's trials and he felt exhausted. As the tent started to fill he straightened his back and steeled himself. Even seated he was not going to let the others see his weakness. He made a sign of looking at the orb, hoping that was the reason they would think he was seated.

"Oh my!" Brielle was the first to speak when she saw it.

"It is as I feared," Drake barked. "That is an orb of distance."

"There could be another reason why she has one." Brielle would not give up on her friend. "There is only one way to prove for sure. Someone has to use the orb and see if the Evil One is on the other side."

"Don't be stupid Brielle," Drake barked. "Just to touch the orb is to risk being enthralled by the Evil One. That might be the very way Althea was turned. To actually use the orb would be complete folly."

"Surely between the five of us we can work out how to use it without being trapped," Brielle pushed.

"And how much time do you think we have to study it?" Minerva added.

Drake had to admit that he would dearly love the opportunity to study the orb. He had read many accounts of what they could do, but had never seen one in person. He also knew that Minerva was right. It could take months, even years before he could even feel safe to touch it. They just did not have to time to test Brielle's theory.

"And do you think you have the strength for a battle of wills with the Evil One?" Ulman asked, his deep voice accentuated inside the tent. "Look at Gwydion. He can barely sit up straight."

Gwydion started at the sound of his name. He didn't realise he had slumped over the table. Instantly he propped himself up as best he could, but he didn't think he could remain there for much longer.

"Come on Gwydion," Minerva said. "I have some potions in my tent that should pick you up. If we are going to confront Althea then we will need you with us."

Ulman and Drake had to help Gwydion to his feet. The strain of the spell was taking its toll and it seemed as though it was not getting any better. The two wizards had to assist him to Minerva's tent. His legs felt weak and he knew he wouldn't make it on his own.

They sat him on the ground as Minerva searched her things for a potion. It didn't take her long to return and as soon as the sticky liquid hit his stomach, Gwydion felt rejuvenated. He knew it was only masking his fatigue, but it would be enough to get him through the day.

"What's our next move?" Brielle asked him as he returned to his feet.

"I guess we go and confront Althea," he replied.

There were no arguments from the others. Brielle cast a spell over Althea's tent to keep anyone from entering. With the orb inside it was too dangerous to leave unprotected.

They made their way straight for the palace. Again they rode with their heads up, not making any eye contact with anyone. The guards posted at the gates knew who they were and didn't try and hinder their progress.

When they reached the palace they weren't so lucky. Bern had sent soldiers to man the gates with specific instructions to watch for the return of the wizards. He was not at all pleased that they refused his summons and he wasn't going to let them return without seeing him.

"The general insists that you see him straight away," one of the guards said.

"We don't have time for the general. We have more important matters to deal with," Brielle sounded sullen.

"I am sorry, but he was very specific." The soldier placed his hand on the hilt of his sword.

"Do you know who we are?" Brielle snapped. The others seemed happy for her to take the lead. "Do you really think those swords will stop us?"

"We know who you are," the soldier didn't sound impressed. "We have also been told that you have been through quite an ordeal and would struggle to stop us if we detained you."

Brielle was about to unleash another tirade, but Gwydion stepped in front of her. "Of course we will see the general. Brielle did not mean any offence."

Brielle was about to shift her rage to Gwydion, but a clamed hand on her shoulder from Drake stopped her. Nothing would be gained by arguing in front of the palace. They would have to placate the general for a short time before they approached Althea. If they didn't then they risked Bern hunting them down and interrupting their interrogation.

The soldiers filed in around the wizards before ushering them inside the palace. Although they had agreed to come along peacefully Bern was not taking any risks. He wanted to see all five of them and did not want to risk losing anyone in the palace. The soldiers didn't want to know what would happen if even one of the wizards disappeared on them.

They found Bern in the King's sitting room. He had a pile of papers in front of him and looked deep in thought when they arrived. He didn't look up as they were ushered in and it wasn't until the soldiers had left did he say anything.

The strange young girl who had appeared with him in the throne room sat at his side. None of the five knew who the girl was or why she was still sitting with the general. Her hair had been put in braids and she played with them as if they annoyed her. She wore a simple yellow dress and again she did not look comfortable wearing it.

"I see you are not used to complying with orders," Bern started. "But I guess I should not have been surprised. However you will need to learn if we are going to win this war." Bern made a sign of stacking the papers in front of him. "Please have a seat."

None of the wizards knew how to react. They had been expecting him to rant and rave, but his words were calm and precise.

"Why have you summoned us?" Minerva asked softly before Brielle had a chance to snap. Hostility would get them nowhere and would only delay their escape.

"There is something that has been nagging at me since I returned. There was an exchange that didn't make any sense between Althea and the Dark Knight. Could you shed some light?"

The wizards looked at each other with confused expressions on their faces. They had not expected such a response. It seemed that he was more intuitive than they gave him credit.

"Don't just stand there. Have a seat and let's discuss matters," Bern added when there was no response.

The wizards all found a seat, if only to give them more time to think. Once they were all seated they looked towards Gwydion to continue the conversation.

"What do you mean general?" Gwydion started.

"I was hoping you could tell me," Bern added.

It was a game of cat and mouse. Neither side wanted to be the first to offer any information. It was as if the first to offer anything would lose the game. It seemed that Bern was not going to offer anything further and they were not sure if they should do the same.

"I don't know what you are talking about general," Gwydion feigned ignorance.

"Don't be so obtuse Gwydion. I could see the expression on your face when Bern asked the question. You know exactly what he's talking about and you know much more," Cayley snapped. Her words were so harsh that Gwydion didn't know how to respond.

"Anyway, what would a little girl know about such matters," Minerva cooed towards her, which only proved to frustrate Cayley even more.

She opened her mouth to speak, but Bern cut in before she had a chance. No matter what he said to her he could not get her to play with the other children in the palace. He couldn't really blame her. If he was in her situation he would certainly not like being treated like a child, but there had to be a reason why the prophecy had chosen such a body for her.

"Don't deflect the question," Bern kept his voice level, unfazed by Minerva's avoidance. "This is not the time for riddles and half-truths. The Seven Kingdoms hang in the balance and you have information that I need to know."

The wizards all looked to Gwydion. It would be his decision if he revealed anything. As much as the eldest of the wizards didn't want the responsibility he knew it would come down to him. He sighed before he started.

"We believe that Althea could be an agent of the Evil One," Gwydion sounded sad as he spoke.

"That is what I was afraid of. Her conversation with the Dark Knight just wasn't right," Bern returned. "Do you have any proof?"

"We found an orb of distance in her room, now I don't expect you to know what that is..." Gwydion started.

"You didn't touch it!" it was the first time emotion had crept into Bern's voice.

"No, we didn't touch it," Gwydion replied quickly.

"Good. They are dangerous artefacts now," Bern replied, his voice returning to normal.

"You know about the orbs?" Gwydion raised an eyebrow.

"They used to be a very important method of relaying messages across the Seven Kingdoms. Now the only ones that remain have been corrupted by Nyrra's evil. It makes sense how she could have turned. He somehow managed to imbibe the orbs with his evil and to touch one unawares is to be ensnared in his trap. As soon as she touched it she would have been instantly turned. I take it you have no idea how long it has been since she first touched the orb?"

"No. Why?" Gwydion asked.

"It could have given us a guide as to how deep Nyrra has ingrained himself," Bern explained.

"How do you know so much about such things?" Brielle couldn't help herself. "I wouldn't have thought information on ancient artefacts would be too prevalent in rural Remidia?"

"That is of no consequence." Bern kept his face calm, even though he knew he had made a mistake. He had revealed too much information to those who might be able to figure out who he really was. "What we need to do is work out is what to do about Althea."

"We will not condemn our sister without speaking with her first. I am sure there is more to this situation than what we have assumed," Gwydion snapped.

"Be calm, I will stay my judgement until after we have spoken with her," Bern replied.

"You dare to presume to sit in judgement on one of the Council of Wizards?" Brielle couldn't control herself as she voiced the opinion of the others. "*We* will decide the fate of our sister after *we* have spoken to her. You are the General of the Alliance and that is it. You presume too much if you believe you have dominion over us."

Bern slammed his right first down on the coffee table next to him. A cup of water splashed once before toppling over. He didn't seem to notice or care.

"I have had just about enough of your sullen behaviour. You march around like spoilt children, expecting everyone to bow to your whim. It is time you learnt some respect!" he boomed.

Bern felt a spell being created, but not who was creating it. If he had not been so enraged he might have accepted the clips behind his ear like he had done before, but he was in no mood. The look of surprise on Drake's face showed him who it was.

"With what you have all seen since you left your little island I would have thought you would appreciate the gravity of the situation? Even the dullest of children would realise what is happening." Bern was deliberately trying to be offensive. "In the end it will be paramount that all seven of you are standing in that last battle and that is exactly what I intend to achieve."

Again the wizards were dumbfounded. They had no idea how to react, especially Drake. He wanted to mention the fact that his spell had been blocked, but he didn't know how Bern would react. The last thing he wanted to do was to enrage the general further.

"If Althea is indeed an agent of evil then there will only be six of us standing beside you at the last battle, that is assuming that Eldred is still alive," Gwydion kept his voice calm.

"I would not be so quick to write your sister out of the picture. I am still hopeful that she can be brought back."

"I think we are all missing the point," Ulman spoke for the first time. "If Althea is working for the Evil One then Prince Hawthorne's life is at great risk. Don't you all remember that we sent her into the dungeons to keep him alive?"

"She would not dare to let the prince die. I was quite specific on that matter. If she is an agent of evil then keeping the prince alive would be a great way to put us off her scent. I doubt she would risk being discovered by killing Hawthorne," Bern replied.

"Either way I think we should be leaving now," Gwydion stood as he spoke. "The longer we leave Althea with Hawthorne the greater the risk to his life."

"Sit down Gwydion!" The words came unbidden. Bern had a strange feeling that they needed to remain where they were.

Gwydion did as he was commanded, although he did not know why. "Is there a reason why you want to waste our time?"

"Yes, but why that is I don't know. All I know is that we have to remain here, for now."

"Very well, what would you like to discuss why we wait?" Gwydion asked, not happy with Bern's response.

"There was something else strange that happened in the throne room," Minerva jumped in before Bern had a chance to reply. "When Jarwe severed the head of the Dark Knight you said something. Now what was it? Ah, yes, that's right. You said 'what have you done'. Why would you say that?"

Bern had to resist the urge to look at Cayley. He had hoped no one had noticed his comment in the throne room. He had also wanted to speak with Cayley about what they should do if the Dark Knight was killed. It was going to be very hard to claim he was still the farmer who had been raised to general with the information he had.

"There is a passage in the prophecy, Alaric told me before he left," he hoped that was a good enough excuse to avoid any further questions. "It seems as though we were set up here. Nyrra wanted us to kill the Dark Knight."

"That makes no sense," Gwydion started when he thought Bern had finished. "Why would the Evil One want to kill his most dangerous soldiers? We all know the prophecies are difficult to read the best of times. Surely you have misinterpreted it."

"I'm afraid not. It stated in the prophecy, in its own roundabout way, that when the seven Dark Knights had been killed then Nyrra could bring them all back to life."

"What?" the word resonated from all the wizards.

"That is impossible," Drake said. "It is one of the first things that we learn, and that is that death is final. There is no way to bring anyone back from the dead and believe me when I say that many have tried over the years."

Bern looked at Cayley and raised an eyebrow but she shook her head. They had never technically died themselves so they had not technically been brought back. He had to admit that they'd had exactly the same reaction when Bern had made the connection, but it didn't change the fact that it was true.

"I guess the prophecy has decided to make an exception in this case. I have no idea how he is going to do it, but I have seen proof. Morgoz was in Zenza City."

"That doesn't prove anything," Gwydion pushed.

"Alaric assures me that Morgoz died in the Cauldron Mountain." Bern wanted to tell them that he was there and there was no doubt that Morgoz had died, but he couldn't reveal too much. "And I don't think he would lie about such a thing."

"Lying and not knowing are two different things. I can't believe that the Evil One has found a way bring someone back from the dead. If he has then we may as well give up now. As soon as we kill someone, or something, from his army then he could just bring them back to life," Ulman sounded resigned.

"I don't think it is that easy. For some reason the prophecy wants Nyrra to have his Dark Knights at the Final Battle. I don't believe that he can just randomly bring anyone back to life. I don't even know if he is the one bringing them back or if the prophecy is doing it for him," Bern tried his best to explain something he really didn't understand himself.

As he spoke the air towards the back of the sitting room started to shimmer. The wizards all looked at each other in surprise. There was no sensation of magic being used. Whoever had created such a spell had managed to mask it. Fear and confusion crossed their faces as they waited to see what was about to happen.

The wizards all relaxed when they recognised Eldred first, and then Alaric, Alena and Richmond. For a moment some of them had thought it was the Evil One himself and silently chided themselves for thinking it.

"Alaric!" Bern exclaimed, suddenly understanding why they needed to stay. "You couldn't have arrived at a better time."

Chapter 8: Together Again

"We have made a mistake," Bern said after giving Alaric a brief description of their last conversation.

"Don't worry too much about it," Alaric offered. "There was nothing you could do about it. It seems the prophecy wants Nyrra to have his Dark Knights at the final battle. One way or another Dargoz was going to end up dead."

His words brought some relief to the others. It was more so the confidence in his voice than the words themselves.

"We have much to do before the final battle," Alaric continued without waiting for a response. "Have the command group brought to the palace. What I have to say affects them as well and I don't want to have to repeat myself."

No one really knew who he was speaking to or who was supposed to react. Alaric didn't really look at anyone as he spoke, but it was clear that he expected it to be done.

"There is more that you need to know," Minerva was the first to break the silence.

Alaric looked at her, as if seeing the wizards for the first time. At first he had a confused expression on his face before it changed to recognition.

"Yes, I have been a little too focused on certain issues. I can sense there is something very wrong here, I would like you to explain to me what that is." Alaric looked towards Gwydion for an answer.

Gwydion looked towards Eldred. He was the only wizard who really knew Alaric, but Gwydion suspected he didn't know him so well anymore. There was something different about him from when they had met at the Isle of Wizards and it was obvious to everyone. Gwydion knew he would have to be careful.

"The prince is on his death bed. It seems as though Dargoz took great pleasure in torturing him," Gwydion started. "We sent Althea to try and heal him, but that was before we suspected her of being an agent of the Evil One." Once he started the words flowed from him. They couldn't get out of his mouth quick enough. When he was finished he took a deep breath.

"Well it looks as though we have another job to do. In the meantime, Richmond, can you see that the horses are properly cared for? I think the stable-hands were a little shocked at the way we arrived."

"Of course," Richmond was keen to leave. He could feel the tension from the wizards. He didn't like to think what could happen if it suddenly broke.

"Alena, I'm sure your father would love to see you. While you are there could you have the command group assemble the army and then meet us in the throne room in the morning?"

Alena nodded and left just as quickly as Richmond.

"Now, where can we find Hawthorne and the naughty Althea?" Alaric asked, apparently unconcerned with the gravity of the situation.

Bern led them through the corridors, with Cayley by his side. Alaric had seemingly ignored the little girl and didn't seem to take any notice of her as they walked. Gwydion watched him closely and couldn't work out if it was a good sign or a bad one.

They found Hawthorne in a private room in the palace infirmary. The smell they were met with could only be described as death. Althea looked drawn and stained as she sat on the right side of his bed. Faxon sat on the other side and didn't look much better.

The blood soaked bandage was still wrapped around his torso. Althea had not wanted to remove it and the surgeons were too afraid to go against her will. His skin was white and his breath was slow and laboured. If it wasn't for the occasional rise and fall of his chest everyone would have assumed he was dead.

"There is nothing I can do," Althea's voice was weak. "Can I let him die now?"

"I think she is right," Faxon choked out the words. "I can't bear to see him like this anymore. Please! Let him die."

"Don't despair," Alaric spoke softly as he walked around the room.

He had to admit that Althea had done a good job keeping him alive. Even without seeing the wound he knew that Hawthorne would have died without her help. He doubted any of the other wizards could have done such a good job. He had to wonder about her motives. There was no way he could deny the evidence against her, but that was beside the point. He could only fix one problem at a time.

"You have done all you can for him Althea," he said before turning to the others. "Take her to a room to rest and make sure she is not disturbed."

They could all read between the lines. When he said that she should not be disturbed he really meant to not let her out of their sight. There would always be one of the wizards by her side. At least until Alaric was ready to see her.

Bern and Cayley remained with Alaric. It took an effort, but eventually the wizards were able to usher Faxon from the room. It wasn't that he needed the space, but what he was about to do would raise questions and he really didn't want to waste time answering them.

"Do you think you can help him?" Bern sounded unsure.

"Of course," Alaric replied.

Suddenly a large chest appeared next to Alaric, bobbing gently in the air.

"What's that?" Cayley asked.

"My little box of tricks," Alaric said as he smiled at her.

It was the first time that he had acknowledged Cayley and he didn't at all seem concerned that she was there.

The chest opened without Alaric touching it and a gold sceptre floated out. The Topaz *Stone of Power* sat at the top and glowed softly. It moved through the air until it reached Alaric's right hand. Without skipping a beat he lowered the sceptre until it touched the bandages on Hawthorne's chest. Instantly the sceptre bounced backwards, refusing to touch them.

"What was that?" asked Bern in surprise.

"Needless to say it was not the reaction I was expecting," Alaric looked questioningly at the sceptre as if he was expecting a response. "I think we need to do remove the bandages. Would you do the honours Cayley?"

Bern and Cayley looked at each other in surprise. No one had mentioned her name since they arrived.

"I'll do it," Bern stepped forward.

"If I remember correctly Cayley was better at these types of things," Alaric said as he motioned for Bern to stop.

They couldn't argue with his logic. Cayley had always been better at healing, although removing bandages didn't seem like a serious job. Cayley stepped forward and Bern had to slide over a chair for her to stand on so she could reach. She was about to touch them when she suddenly felt a wave of evil wash over her.

"There is something not right here," Cayley gasped.

"There is a lot that is not right here, but Alaric will fix it," Bern replied.

"No! That's not what I mean. There is something evil about the bandages, or maybe it's the blood. Whatever it is I'm not sure I want to touch it. In fact I'm not sure I could touch it even if I wanted to," Cayley explained.

Alaric looked at them pensively and hummed softly. It was something unexpected, but he was certainly not about to give up. Whether it was the Dark Knight or Althea who had placed the spell, he was sure he could unravel it without killing the prince. Slowly he delved into the spell to try and work out exactly what it was and what affect it would have on Hawthorne if he removed it.

Althea's spell was easy to find and was not connected to the evil imbibed in the bandage. When that spell was gone he didn't think Hawthorne would be far behind if he couldn't cure him. The first thing he needed to do was to get the bandage from his chest.

"I think I have it. When I am finished you will have to remove the bandage quickly. Once I start we will have little time if we are going to succeed."

Alaric closed his eyes and felt the energy rush into him. The feeling was euphoric, but there was no time to bask in its majesty. He let the sceptre slip from his hand and it floated lovingly beside him. When he was comfortable with the amount of power he held, he started the spell. Instantly he felt the evil retract away, but as he reached out with his spell the evil struck at him like a viper attack. Alaric stumbled backwards, but caught himself before he fell.

Pain coursed through his body as the evil tried to penetrate him. The surprise of the attack was the only advantage the evil had. Alaric calmed himself and the pain disappeared. The evil snapped at him, but couldn't get any further. It was the attack that Alaric had been planning for. He had drawn it away from the bandage and now all he had to do was dispel it.

The trap had been set. Alaric drew in more energy and the evil shrunk back. It had thought it could overpower him, but that was all he needed to get it away from Hawthorne. When he was sure the evil was completely free he blinked it out of existence.

When Alaric opened his eyes the bandage had been removed. The sword wound was a gaping hole. Whoever had bandaged him had made no attempt to close the wound. The edges had turned black and smelled of death. His chest had stopped rising and falling and his lips had turned blue.

The sceptre returned to his hand and Alaric placed the Topaz stone on the wound. Its yellow glow intensified until it enveloped Hawthorne completely. Slowly the wound started to close and the smell disappeared. The blackness faded until it was completely gone and the colour started to return to his face. Suddenly he sucked in a lungful of air.

Hawthorne sat bolt upright and his eyes opened. The movement surprised everyone except Alaric. It was just the reaction he was looking for.

"Thank you!" Alaric spoke softly as the sceptre floated back to the chest. The yellow light blinked out as the lid shut and the chest disappeared.

"What is happening?" Hawthorne asked as he looked around nervously.

"It's alright now Hawthorne. You are safe," Alaric said.

"The last thing I remember was being in the dungeon." Hawthorne pushed himself from the bed and stood with a start. "I have to see my father. Gilgi is a Dark Knight and he is in danger."

"Calm down Hawthorne," Bern said. "The Dark Knight is dead. Your father and the kingdom are safe, for now."

"I think your father would like to see you," Alaric said. "I'm sure he's not too far away."

"Yes, of course," Hawthorn rubbed his head as he left the room.

"Are you sure he should be walking around?" Cayley asked. "Not more than five minutes ago he was on his death bed. I have some experience with healing, but I have never seen such a transformation."

"I would be prepared to see a lot of things you have never seen before," Alaric replied.

"I think it's time for you to give us some answers," Bern snapped.

Alaric looked at his old friend, as if seeing him for the first time. A sad expression crossed his face, but only for second before it returned to its cold countenance.

"So you finally got rid of my old friend, Heryion. Or should I call you Asgard?" Alaric asked, his voice void of emotion.

"I don't think this is the place for such a conversation, should we return to the sitting room?" Although all three had blocked the smell of the dungeons, Bern wanted time to think and the walk would do just that. "And we agreed that it is best to still call me Bern and Esgard, Cayley. We need to avoid any unnecessary questions for the moment and the Alliance needs its general back in command."

"Very well," Alaric agreed.

Without a second thought Alaric blinked them out of the infirmary and back to the sitting room. Although Bern and Cayley could travel through the fabric of time, the suddenness of Alaric's spell took their breath away.

"What was that?" Bern gasped.

"I'm sorry," Alaric apologised. "I thought you would have been used to travelling."

"We are, but not so suddenly," Cayley replied.

"When did you learn to do that?" Bern asked.

"I've learnt a lot over the last few weeks. That is just a small taste of what I can do now, but there is little time to discuss such things."

Bern thought for a moment. As much as he wanted to push Alaric further he decided against it.

"I'm sorry about Bern," he started slowly, trying to gauge a response on Alaric's face, but he gave none. "We were outside Zenza City and we found his wife and children in shallow graves. It was at that point that Bern completely gave control of his body to me. I needed control of his body, but I didn't mean for him to leave altogether."

"I always knew that Bern was never going to make it to the final battle. I think I knew even back when we left Arsiliac, but I didn't want to believe it. At least he is with his family again."

It was not the response that they had been expecting. Alaric had just lost his best friend and companion and there seemed to be little reaction.

"What is going on with you?" Bern asked. "Something has changed within you and I think we need to know what it is."

"A lot has changed within me. I travelled through times and worlds. In the end a hundred life-times worth of knowledge was unlocked in my mind."

Bern didn't know how to respond. It didn't seem as though Alaric wanted to elaborate and he didn't think that anything he said could make him. Normally a simple spell would have compelled the information, but he knew there was no chance of that working.

"We have some disturbing news," Bern decided to change the subject. "As I'm sure you already know, Nyrra needed all his Dark Knights dead before he could bring them back to life. We tried to get here in time to stop the others from killing Dargoz, but we were too late."

"I wouldn't be too concerned," Alaric recognised the tone in Bern's voice. "There was nothing you could have done. The prophecy wanted Nyrra to have his Dark Knights at the final battle and that is exactly the way things are going to play out."

"So if you know the prophecy then you know the result?" Cayley asked, dubious at his comment.

"If only that was the case. I know many things, but the result is and will forever be clouded until it happens. There are still things we have to do and still things that will affect the final battle."

"And would you mind telling us what they are?" Cayley asked.

"I would love to, but it doesn't work like that. I will set you all on the right path, but you will still have to make it there on your own."

"Surely you could tell us? You know how close we are to the prophecy," Cayley replied.

Alaric ignored her.

"We should go and see Althea."

Without waiting for a response Alaric blinked them out of the room and into the apartment where Althea was resting. Drake sat up with a start when they suddenly appeared without warning.

"What are you doing here?" Drake stammered before regaining his composure.

"We're here to see Althea," Alaric said.

"She's in the bedroom resting. She's had a long and hard ordeal and I don't think we should interrogate her just yet. There's no telling what might happen in her current state. Despite what she may or may not have done we don't want her dead."

"That's alright. I have no intention of killing her. I think you should get Althea while Bern finds the other wizards. I'm sure you'll all want to be here for this."

There was no room for arguments. Even Bern wasn't going to argue with him. Instead he just opened the door and walked outside. He didn't have to move far to find the other five wizards loitering in the corridor, as if waiting for something to happen.

"Alaric is inside. He wants you to join us." Bern didn't wait for a response before returning to the room. If something was about to happen then he didn't want to miss it.

Drake was helping Althea into the front room. She didn't look happy at being raised and even less when she saw Alaric.

"What is the meaning of this?" She snapped.

"Please, be seated," Alaric offered. "We have much to discuss."

The wizards all looked for somewhere to sit whilst Alaric, Cayley and Bern remained standing. If anyone had walked in, they would have been completely confused. It looked as though the three were about to scold the seven wizards.

"Surely this could wait until morning. I'm sure after a good sleep I will be feeling better," Althea snapped.

"It will all come to bear," Alaric assured her. "All you need to do is sit back and relax."

Althea was dubious, but the other wizards assured her that it was all going to be okay. She slowly started to relax, but that only lasted a moment before she felt Alaric attempting to probe her mind. Instantly she sent up a block with all the strength she could muster. Alaric let himself retreat and waited for her response.

"What do you think you are doing?" she asked aghast. "What do you all think you are doing?" she then asked the six wizards.

"Be calm Althea," Alaric said. "We know that you have been interacting with Nyrra. We need to know what you have been talking about, what information you have given him and what he's instructed you to do."

"You dare accuse me of betraying everything I believe in. And you six are just going to sit there and let him say these offensive things?"

"Be calm Althea," Gwydion barked. "We found the orb in your tent. We know you have been using it."

"And how would you know what I have been using?" Althea snapped. "I found that orb and I have been studying it, but I have not used it. I would not be so silly as to touch such an artefact without knowing exactly what it does."

The wizards retreated for a moment, unsure of their original suspicions. It would make sense that she studied the orb before trying to use it, that's what they would all do. They would give her the benefit of the doubt until they could prove it conclusively. Alaric was not going to be so forgiving.

The lie was something that Nyrra had placed in her mind. If she was ever to be questioned, then her mind would fight vehemently to prove her innocence. Even if she wanted to confess, the words would not leave her mouth.

"We know that is not true, but I assume you already know that. You are under that thrall of the Evil One, but we can fix that. If you help me then there will be less pain for you. Either way I will get the information I need and you will soon be free," Alaric told her.

"I will not be treated..." suddenly she was silenced and her eyes rolled back in her head.

"What do you want?" her voice, although still keeping some of its femininity, was harsh and guttural. "This one is mine. Although I should have guessed that it would only be a matter of time before she was discovered. These miserable creatures can never be trusted. They are too weak-minded to be of any real use."

"I don't have time to bandy words with a simple shell. You are not Nyrra, just a remnant of his consciousness that he implanted here."

"That is what you think. This one is mine and it will die before it lets you get rid of me."

Suddenly Althea cried out in pain. No one knew what Alaric had done, but Ulman jumped to his feet.

"Stop Alaric! You are going to kill her."

Alaric didn't reply, but his response was clear. Ulman was forcibly seated again and when he opened his mouth to protest no words came out. It was clear that Alaric would not let anyone interfere and there was nothing they could do about it.

"It's alright," Eldred spoke softly. "I'm sure he knows what he's doing."

"How can you be so sure?" Brielle asked, but her words fell on deaf ears.

"Tell me what you wanted Althea to do for you?" Alaric asked.

The voice coming from Althea burst out laughing. It was a rough noise and sent shivers down the wizards' spines. There was something very unnatural about it.

"You can't give me orders. I'll see her dead before you get your answers."

"We'll see about that."

There was a moment of silence as Alaric made a sign of preparing his next spell. He wanted the phantom Nyrra to believe he didn't have the power to succeed. It would lead it into a false sense of security and hopefully make Alaric's next move easier on Althea.

"Tell me what I want to know!" Alaric commanded.

There was another scream of pain from Althea, this time in her own voice.

"She was simply there to watch and report the movements of the council and any other information I might find useful," the voice was strained as Alaric forced the words from it. "When you reached the final battle she was to create mayhem in the lines behind the soldiers. At least until she was killed by her own allies." The phantom strained to keep the words inside, but there was nothing it could do. "She was a mere puppet, but a useful one."

"And what information have you gathered from her?"

"Very little," her face contorted as the phantom spoke. "She was not very forthcoming, but at least she did what I told her to do."

There was a short pause and Althea cried out in pain again. The sound made the others, even Bern and Cayley, cringe. There was no reaction from her body, but they could tell she was in great pain. If there was anything they could do to help her or stop Alaric they would, but they knew anything they tried would be fruitless.

"There really has been little information," the voice was strained again. "She has given me the movements of the Alliance and now I know that you have returned. The time for the Final Battle and your destruction is soon. I am done with this ant and now it will die."

Althea's body started convulsing violently and foam appeared in the corner of her mouth. The wizards all jumped to their feet and the air suddenly electrified as they all drew in energy.

"Be calm," Alaric snapped. "And sit down."

The wizards all did as they were told and reluctantly let the energy release as they sat. There was no nonsense in Alaric's tone and it commanded respect. Whatever he was planning they would have to trust that he wasn't going to let her die.

Alaric delved into Althea's mind. The phantom that Nyrra had placed was deep in her subconscious. Even for Alaric it would be no easy task to remove.

"Help me," Althea's mind-voice was weak. It was obvious that the phantom was trying to take complete control.

"Where is it?" Alaric asked.

"It is deep in my subconscious. When it knew you were coming it hid. Please, you have to get rid of it. There is nothing I can do."

"There is a lot you can do. The more you can do to help me the less painful it will be for you."

"I... can't. It's too strong. I've tried to fight it ever since it invaded my mind, but there is nothing I can do."

"You are one of the seven and you are just going to give up? That doesn't sound right to me. Either way I am going to get rid of this phantom. If you don't help then it will mean more pain for you."

"What do you want me to do?" her voice was weak.

"You need to bring the phantom up from your subconscious. If I delve too deep into your mind it will result in pain. Remember it's your mind. You control it. You might not be able to get rid of it, but you can certainly push it around."

Alaric felt her agreement even though she didn't voice it. He remained where he was as Althea searched through her subconscious. There was nothing he could do until the two surfaced.

In what could have been minutes or days before Alaric felt something happen. All of a sudden he felt two presences around him. One was pure evil and the other was filled with fear. There was no doubt which one was which.

"I think it's time for you to go," Alaric said.

"Give it your best shot, but know that Althea is coming with me."

That was the last thing the phantom ever said. Alaric simply removed it from her mind.

"Thank you!" the soft voice came as Alaric returned his consciousness to his own body.

As expected he found Althea slumped in her chair. Her eyes were closed and her breathing laboured. The other wizards watched her closely, but no one made a move to help. They weren't sure exactly what Alaric had done or was still doing and they didn't want to do anything to hinder him.

"The phantom Nyrra is gone, but she is still very weak. The phantom, I believe, has been in her mind for a long time. The best way I can explain it is that it has become part of her psyche. When I took it away her body and mind went into shock," Alaric explained.

"Well, are you going to do something about it?" Brielle asked in surprise.

"Of course I am. I just thought you would like to know what is happening," Alaric sounded confused.

When he finished speaking he walked to where Althea was seated. The chest appeared again, floating next to him. Alaric kept his eyes on her as the lid popped open. A thin gold crown with the Opal *Stone of Power* in the centre floated obediently towards his left hand. A gentle swirl of colours emanated from the stone.

Slowly Alaric placed the stone on Althea's forehead. The stone started to glow more intensely and the swirling colour covered her head. Only a second passed before she slowly opened her eyes. Alaric withdrew the crown and let it float back into the chest.

"What... What happened?" Althea asked in a weak voice.

"All in good time," Alaric replied.

When he was sure that her mind had been healed the sceptre floated from the chest. A soft yellow light came from the Topaz stone. Alaric touched the stone to Althea's chest and let the light encase her completely.

Suddenly Althea felt a warmth fill her body. At first it made her shiver, but then she felt the fatigue wash away. The feeling was exhilarating and she bathed in its glory. When Alaric removed the stone and the light faded away she returned to normal. It was like the extremes her body had been through had never happened.

"This is amazing," she gasped as she sat up. "It's like the trials of the last few days have completely gone."

"The *Stones of Power* can do things that you couldn't even imagine. Unlike the potions that you like to use you are completely refreshed. Now I will do the same for the rest of you."

"I don't think it is necessary." Gwydion was not so sure. There seemed to be something very unnatural about the stones. "We will recover in a few days."

"You don't have a few days," Alaric said has he moved closer. "Now please, don't make me hold you down like children."

There was no mirth in his threat and with what they had seen they knew he was capable of following through.

Alaric repeated the process with the other wizards who had battled with Dargoz, as Eldred didn't need any healing. When he was done he let the sceptre float back into the chest before the lid shut and it disappeared. The wizards had no idea how Alaric had achieved such a feat.

"Would somebody please tell me what is happening? It feels as though I have woken from a strange dream," Althea asked.

"You have been in the thrall of the Evil One," Gwydion started when it was obvious Alaric wasn't going to elaborate. "You found an orb of distance and when you touched it the Evil One placed some king of mind control in your head."

"But I found that orb over a century ago!" Althea was shocked.

"The phantom Nyrra had buried itself deep in your mind," Alaric said. "I wouldn't be surprised if it had been there from the moment you touched the orb."

"I... can't believe it. I have been under his thrall for so long. My memory is so sketchy. I have no idea what I might have done to betray us."

"It's alright now. It is gone and it won't come back. That said I wouldn't be touching the orb again anytime soon."

"What should we do with it then?" Gwydion asked.

"Bern can deal with it," Alaric said.

"Surely the Evil One will be able to take control of the general," Drake said, aghast. "Wouldn't it be better if you removed it?"

"Don't worry about Bern. He will be able to take the orb," Alaric reassured them.

"What is that supposed to mean?" Drake wasn't about to let it go.

"There is no time for pointless conversation." Alaric wasn't going to elaborate. He knew that Asgard wanted to keep their identities secret from the others and he wasn't about to change things. He would be leaving again soon and Bern would be left to lead the army and he didn't want to do anything to risk that. "It is time for us to join the rest of the army."

Chapter 9: Training

Alaric gave them no warning as he blinked them out of the room. A moment later they appeared in front of the army. Those who had been seated didn't have time to change their position and thumped unceremoniously onto the ground. If anyone had been assembled they would have burst out laughing, at least after the initial shock.

It wasn't long before Jarwe arrived with the rest of the command group. As usual Alaric had timed things to perfection. With each act there become fewer doubts about his connection to the prophecy.

"General Bern!" Sorrell was the first to speak. "It's so good to have you back."

For a moment Alaric felt a little jealous, they all seemed more excited to see Bern than himself. He knew that his old friend, or at least the body of it, was their general, but he was their Chosen One. He quickly shook the feeling off. It had been a long time since he had felt such emotion and he didn't like it. He had become cold and unfeeling for a reason and that's how he was going to defeat the Evil One.

"It seems as though you have done well enough without me," Bern replied.

"Only just," Jarwe spoke under his breath.

"What?" Bern asked.

"Ah..." Jarwe had not realised he had voiced his thought. "It is good to have you back with us Bern. You can lead us towards the final battle."

"I am not sure..." Bern started, but was cut off by Alaric.

"Your general has returned and he will lead you into the final battle." There was something in his tone that belied the truth, but only Bern caught it. "And that battle is approaching ever quicker. At the end of the week the army must be assembled and ready for war."

"Then the battle will take place in Remidia?" Jarwe sounded surprised. "So everything we have done so far has been for nothing?" The words blurted from his mouth and he instantly wished he had kept it shut.

"The battle will not be fought in Remidia," Alaric stepped forward as he made his announcement. A few mouths opened to make greetings, but Alaric ignored them. "The battle will, as it has always been foretold, take place in Avalon."

"That is impossible," Sorrell burst out, unable to contain himself. "It will take us months to move the army to Avalon. We have just set up camp. It will nearly take a week for the tail of the army to be packed and ready to move. With all due respect it is not that easy to move an army this size, especially one that has almost instantly doubled in size. The Castalial army has only just started to assimilate itself into the Alliance."

"Well you can stop that right away. When the army starts to move it do so in its individual armies," Alaric explained.

"What?" the question was echoed around the command group.

"What have we been doing all this time then?" Jarwe asked the rhetorical question before Alaric had a chance to respond. "The Alliance is one army now, and no longer an "alliance" as its name might suggest."

"I still see the banners of the various kingdoms," Alaric made a show of looking about the army as he spoke, "still flying throughout the campsite. Not only from the five kingdoms, but don't forget the dwarves and elves who do not show standards. Yes, we are one army, but the soldiers still know where they came from. When we march on Avalon we shall do so as one and as seven."

"The five kingdoms keep their own identity, but what of the elves. There are two tribes of elves in this army. Do we not count as separate forces?" Kilean asked, taking offence at what Alaric was implying.

"The elves will fight as one and there will be one more tribe with you," Alaric said.

"Who?" Kilean's voice was echoed by Orric and Pernian.

The three elves all believed their numbers were final. The only tribe left was the Northern Elves and it had been clear a long time ago that they wanted nothing to do with the war.

"They are right," Eldred said. "We asked the Northern Elves to join the Alliance, but it seems as though they have decided not to. They would have been here by now if they had."

"We are getting ahead of ourselves. All I will say for now is that the Northern Elves will be with us at the final battle," Alaric was not going to elaborate further.

"That is unacceptable," Orric boomed. He had assumed command, as the eldest, over both elven tribes. Kilean had been happy to let him do so as long as he could be part of the decision making. "I can sense a deep change in you Alaric, but that does not give you the right to treat us like children."

Alaric thought about creating a spell to silence the elf, but decided it would be too offensive. Although he didn't think Orric would try and take his elves away from the Alliance, he did deserve respect. That respect would only get him so far. Alaric was not about to reveal any information he didn't want to.

"All will be revealed, Lord Orric, but now is not the time. I have little time before I have to be on the move again and there are more important matters for me to deal with."

"What do you mean you will be on the move again?" Jarwe asked, aghast. "You're not coming with us to the final battle."

"You must travel to the five kingdoms," Alaric addressed the seven wizards, completely ignoring Jarwe's question. "And also to *Nordligträ* and the Cloumid Mountains."

At the sound of his home Dorn's attention was suddenly piqued. With the elves arguing with Alaric he had let his mind drift away. He had no interest in their petty disputes. Since he had brought the dwarves back to the army from the city, their numbers rivalled those of the elves, that was one thing that made him happy.

"As much as I would love to return home, the guild has already made it known that they won't assist. Besides myself there were very few who supported the idea of a 'final battle!'" Dorn explained.

"Be that as it may, it will be your job to convince them. You are cousin to the king. He will listen to you," Alaric explained.

"And I will also help," Hulkan added.

"No Hulkan. There are still able dwarves in Castalia. You will return home and gather all you can," Alaric said.

"The council has committed all the forces they were prepared to," Hulkan retorted.

"Be that as it may, you will go to Castalia and gather as many dwarves as you can." Alaric returned his attention to the wizards. "You will need to go with a representative to each of the five kingdoms, to *Nordligträ* and to the Cloumid Mountains. One to each."

"To what end?" Gwydion asked. "You taught us the lost art of travelling, and we are grateful for that, but it would take all our energy to travel to the locations and then to Avalon. Whatever troops we could add to the Alliance would never reach the final battle in time and we would be too weak to fight. I assume you need us to fight?"

"That is why I am here and if you would all stop asking questions I will explain what needs to be done," Alaric's voice was firm. "As I'm sure you all know there is more than one way to travel through the fabric of space and time. The way I taught you is the easiest and safest for a small amount of people to travel long distances. What I do is much more complicated and much more efficient, but I doubt any of you would have the strength to use it." There was no disrespect in his tone, it was matter-of-fact. If he had paused for long enough one of them would have said something. "A gateway is the best way to move large numbers over large distances."

"I have heard of gateways," Gwydion confirmed.

"I have read a text that claimed they were possible, but nothing ever happened when I tried," Minerva added.

"Well they are possible and with a little training you will be able to create one large enough to move the soldiers to Avalon," Alaric continued. "Now, I must warn you all that these gateways can be very dangerous. In essence a gateway is ripping through the fabric of time to create a pathway between two places. Anyone standing in the place where you create a gateway will be severed. Watch!"

Alaric pointed to a nearby tree. Slowly a small coloured speck of light could be seen to the bottom right, about two feet from the trunk. A triangle spread from the speck until it created a rectangle of multi-coloured light, three paces wide and four paces high. The light then passed through the tree, cutting straight through it. Slowly the tree creaked before collapsing to the ground leaving wisps of smoke. The colours then began to swirl wildly in the centre of the rectangle.

"So now we just walk through it I suppose?" Drake didn't sound certain.

"Not if you value your life," Alaric warned. A rock suddenly appeared in his right hand and he hurled it at the gateway. As soon as it hit the light it sizzled into ash. "Nothing will pass through the gateway in its current form and anything or anyone who tries will be flash fried. You saw what it did to that rock and I'm sure you could imagine what it would do to flesh and bone?" He let the question float over them before he continued. "Now creating this side of the gateway is the easy part." The seven wizards had all watched Alaric carefully as he had created the gateway in a vain attempt to work out what he was doing. No one could even guess at how he had created it. If that was the easy part then they didn't think they had a chance of recreating it in its entirety. "You need to choose your destination on the other side. The safest way is to know your end location like the back of your hand. Now if you would look over there?"

Alaric pointed to a vacant place about ten paces behind them. Slowly a similar light started to coalesce and it wasn't long before another shimmering window of light appeared with the exact measurements of the first one. Slowly it started to shimmer and bubble as the light started to disappear. Soon they could see an image of their backs through the gateway. When they turned around they could see that the original gateway had also changed and they could clearly see the ground on the other side.

"Now, if you would, someone can walk through," Alaric said.

The wizards all looked at each other, none of them wanted to be the first. It was Jarwe who finally stepped forward. He stopped when he reached the gateway. The image before him shimmered like he was looking through a window of silvery water. When he had volunteered he thought it was a good idea, but now faced with the prospect he wasn't so sure.

"Don't worry general. You'll be fine." Alaric tried to reassure him.

Jarwe took a deep breath and then stepped into the gateway. A cold sensation filled his body and he shivered. When his foot hit the ground he had come out through the other side. He stumbled as the scenery around him suddenly changed. Although he was expecting it, it still unsettled him.

"That was amazing!" Jarwe gasped when he returned to the others. "It was like walking through icy water, but that sensation was only there for a moment. It was like walking through a door from one room to another."

Hearing the words from Jarwe and realising that nothing had happened to him the others were all keen to try the gateway. Alaric thought about stopping them, but then decided to let them go. The wizards would get a better understanding once they had used it.

"Just make sure you don't come in from the side. They are safe from the front and from behind. The sides, however, are as sharp as a razor," Alaric warned.

When they had all had their turn at walking through the gateway Alaric closed it. He didn't want to risk someone walking by and cutting themselves in half.

"Now unfortunately we don't have the time to travel to all the locations that you will need to create gateways to, so you will have to be careful, or lucky might be a more apt description."

No one really liked what they were hearing. Alaric had explained very little to them and that worried everyone. "Now I will teach you how to create a gateway," he addressed the seven wizards. "The rest of you should start preparing the army to move. For now, the best thing to do is to separate the Alliance into its individual components. In the morning I will create a gateway to Avalon in the field to the north of the city gate, it will be the safest place. You will need to set some guards on the city side to make sure no citizens accidently wander into the gateway, although I doubt they will want to get that close to the army," Alaric explained. "The elves will need to be ready to march first, then the Enteroite army, followed by Remidia, Castalia, Darshival, Hondin Lel and finally the dwarves."

There was a murmur around the commanders. They didn't not know why Alaric had chosen the order and felt it was a slight against them.

"That is all," Alaric snapped when no one moved. "I don't know about you, but I definitely do not want to be late to the final battle."

His words brought action from the command group. They all looked nervously at each other before hurrying back towards the rest of the army. No one wanted to be last in case Alaric decided to berate them further. Bern and Cayley remained with Alaric and the wizards. They figured that their part was still yet to be played.

"Now, let's see if you can follow this weave," Alaric said.

This time he created the spell much slower, making sure the wizards could follow it. A small spark of light appeared a pace from where they were standing. Just like the first gateway it burst into life, although much slower. It was not an easy spell to learn, but he hoped the seven wizards, with their many years of experience, would quickly work it out. After he had created the first gateway he moved on to the second. The second gateway was the same spell, the only difference was choosing the location. Although his second gateway was not far away, it would have to be in a location that could not be seen. If the location was not right then there was no telling what could happen. If a gateway was opened at the edge of a cliff then anyone walking through would plummet to their death.

When he was happy with what he had done he extinguished the two gateways. Soon there would be a flurry them and one more would just add to the confusion.

Minerva was the first to try. She felt confident that she had followed what Alaric had done, but she was mistaken. She was able to create the small dot of light, but when she tried to extend it, it fizzled out. Alaric's heart sunk. She had been so close and yet she had been unable to complete the spell.

One way or another they all failed at their first attempt. Gwydion's gateway zigzagged out from the dot and collapsed before it had a chance of finishing. Even though it was far from the neat rectangle Alaric had created he was sure if he had managed to complete it, the gateway would have worked.

"That is not a bad start," Alaric said after an hour, even though no one had managed to successfully complete the spell. "Maybe if you watch me again it might help. I can see that you are all getting close."

Alaric created another gateway, again a lot slower than before. Time was getting away from them and they all needed to be gone in the morning, but the chances of that happening didn't look good. He thought they would have figured out the spell a lot quicker, but they had not even begun to work out the second gateway.

"If you think of it as like sliding open a window it might make things easier." Since Alaric had never been taught how to make the spell he had no idea how to teach the others. The spell was as natural to him as breathing. "Creating the spark is the hardest part."

"I know we must seem like novices compared to you, *Chosen One*," Drake replied "but this is something we weren't even sure was possible before today."

"I'm sorry if I offended you, but we don't have time for excuses. Now try it again. This time do as I suggest."

Drake suddenly regretted speaking. He knew he would be the first one to try again. The small spark of light appeared two paces from the group. They had all mastered that part of the spell. Just as Drake was about to try and open the gateway he remembered what Alaric had told them. Although it didn't make sense to him he knew he had to try.

Slowly he thought about sliding open a window and as he did, the gateway slowly started to open. Taking a deep breath he calmed himself as excitement filled him. He knew he had to concentrate if he was going to complete the spell. As he came close to finishing he could feel the threads starting to waver. It was always at this point that the gateway had collapsed, but he had never held it for so long.

"Just tie it off there, it is big enough," Alaric called out.

Drake fumbled to try and take control of the spell and just when he thought it was going to collapse again, he managed to tie it off. When he looked out he could see a full gateway before him. Even though it was only four feet high and three feet wide it was complete.

"Well done," relief was thick in Alaric's voice. "Now you need to create another one over there." Alaric pointed to where he had created his gateway. "You won't be able to make it any larger than this one, so don't try. In fact you need to make it exactly same size. If you make it any smaller then whoever walks through will risk losing an arm, leg or a head," Alaric warned.

Drake had been so relieved that he had finally been able to finish the spell that he wasn't really excited about starting again. Slowly he started the spell and tried to replicate it.

"Stop!" Alaric cried out and the spell fizzled out.

"What?" Drake sounded annoyed. "I was doing exactly what I did the first time."

"But your location was off by a good pace," Alaric said. "Creating the gateway is the same, but the location is the most important part. When you create a gateway on the other side you need to be precise. If you are out by just inches it could have disastrous consequences."

"I understand."

Drake concentrated on the exact location where Alaric had created his second gateway. There was a burn scar on the ground to give him something to aim for. When he was confident he started the spell again. He followed the same steps as he had before and the gateway appeared with much less effort. When he was done he looked pleased with what he had created.

"Well done. Now extinguish your gateways and let's see if everyone else can do the same," Alaric's tone was matter-of-fact.

After the gateways disappeared, Drake explained to the others exactly what he had done. He wanted the other six to achieve what he had been able to do.

Alaric stood and watched the wizards, one by one, step forward to create their own. With a little effort they all succeeded at their first attempt.

"Now comes the truly difficult part. You need to be able to create the gateway to a location you can't see. For now I would say the easiest task would be to open a gateway in the front room of your houses on Ĉarolija Island. Remember to be very careful if you don't want to damage anything."

Brielle was the first to try. She had been the most confident and proficient and the others were all happy to let her make the first attempt. She was quickly able to create the first gateway, in the same place as all the others. She made it the same measurements as the one Alaric had created and he realised he would have to get that idea out of their heads. It would be very easy for them to get in the habit of creating one size of gateway. The ones they would need to create for the army would need to be much larger.

Brielle thought about the exact location she wanted the second gateway to appear. She had to admit that without seeing the exact location it was a lot harder. When she was finally happy that the gateway would open where she wanted, she created the spell. Slowly the mirrored surface of the first gateway rippled with the image of Brielle's front room.

"May I go through?" Brielle asked softly. She dearly wanted to visit her home again as well as wanting to see what she had created.

"Are you sure that it is safe to pass through your gateway?" Alaric asked.

Brielle had taken a step forward, but stopped at the sound of his words. She was sure that she had created the spell properly. There was no doubt that the image on the gateway was her front room. There looked as though there was enough space for her and all the others to comfortably walk through. Alaric knew the answer to his question, but he wanted all the wizards to think about what they were doing.

"Yes, I am sure it is safe to walk through," Brielle replied. As she passed though she gasped as she realised what she had done. A small table that sat in the middle of the room had been completely severed in two.

"That is one of the reasons I said you needed to be careful," she jumped at Alaric's voice behind her. "If there had been a person sitting at that table there is a good chance they would have lost an arm or two."

"That would be unfortunate, but I don't envisage how I could possibly know if there was someone sitting there. I know this area very well and I still managed to destroy my table. How are we supposed to do this when we have no idea where we are creating the gateway?" she snapped, more upset with herself than Alaric.

"Just bear in mind what has happened here," Alaric warned as he stepped back through.

Brielle took a deep sniff of her home. There was a musty smell in the air, but underneath she recognised the scent. She wanted nothing more than to walk from room to room and even walk out into what she imagined would be a warm day. It seemed like a lifetime since she had been able to smell the salty sea air, but she knew she had to get back to the others.

Ulman was the next to attempt the gateway. Although they were all instructed to create the second one in the front room he decided, after hearing of Brielle's mistake, to create his outside the front of his house. When he had completed both spells he looked as though he was very proud. They could all see the front of his house shimmering in the gateway.

"I don't think that is the front room of your house?" Alaric said.

"I thought it would be safer to create the gateway out the front. Less chance of severing anything," he replied.

"Then you should go and see what you have achieved," Alaric replied. His tone gave nothing away.

On the other side Ulman closed his eyes and breathed in the salty air. He had missed the smell of the island. When he opened his eyes he could see the front door of his house beckoning to him. He wanted nothing more than to open it and walk inside, but a voice from behind stopped him.

"I think you should turn around," Alaric said.

When he turned around his heart sank. In his haste to create the gateway he had forgotten about the palm tree which stood at the front. The gateway had sliced through it and the tree had fallen to one side.

"Damn!" he cursed.

"Listen and learn," Alaric said as he turned his back to Remidia.

Althea and Eldred were the only two wizards who managed to create the second gateway without causing any damage.

"Now you will need to work together. One will explain a location that is common to them and then each of you will create a gateway to that location," Alaric explained.

"May we have a short break," Gwydion asked. "It has been a long session and I'm sure everyone would be better for a rest."

Alaric sighed. There was no time to waste. "What do you tell a novice or an apprentice if they ask for a break?"

Gwydion lowered his head in shame. He had trained many wizards over the years and if any of them had asked for respite he would have worked them harder. The question didn't need answering and it was clear to Alaric that he understood.

"You have until tomorrow morning to get this right and I am sure that you will want to get some sleep."

The rest of the afternoon was spent creating more and more gateways. It wasn't until the sun had all but set before Alaric let them rest.

"There is one more thing that you need to learn," Alaric said as the wizards slumped to the ground. They were exhausted, but Alaric didn't ease up on them. Their exhaustion was nothing compared to what they would endure in the final battle. "The gateways you have created are fine for one person or a small group to travel through, but what you will need to create will be much larger. You will have to move a lot of soldiers through to Avalon in a short space of time. Now watch what I do and see if you can replicate it."

Alaric started with the same small spark that all the other gateways had. When he opened the gateway it stretched much higher and wider than the first one. He stretched it until it was ten feet tall and twenty feet wide.

"Something else you need to remember is that your gateway needs to be at least half as high as it is wide. That is the first mistake you could make on your own. To move the army the gateway would not need to be that high, so you would be inclined just to make it wide. As soon as you stretch it past the point of half its height it will snap and that is not a pleasant feeling. You will have to make the decision yourself how large you make each gateway, depending on how many forces you can gather," Alaric explained.

The sun had set when they finally finished. To the east the city lights had been lit and to the west the campfires burned brightly. The seven wizards were all exhausted when Alaric finally said they could rest for the night. None of them looked as though they would be able to make it back to their campsite, by magic or by foot.

"One more thing before you go," Alaric said.

The wizards all moaned and Alaric let himself chuckle at his little ruse. It was the first time Bern had seen him show any real sign of humour since he had arrived. He thought it was a good thing, a sign that there was still some emotion left inside.

The wizards were all relieved when they saw the strange chest floating beside him. They had all thought Alaric was going to send them back to the camp to sleep off the day's exhaustion. That's what they would have done to any apprentice, even if they had the ability to heal with the Topaz stone. This situation was different though. They were heading towards the battle to end all battles and Alaric needed them refreshed, as much as they could be.

When Alaric was finished healing them, they felt as if they had just risen from the most relaxing sleep. They felt like they could easily continue their training, but that was not what Alaric had in mind.

"Remember that there are many hard days ahead of us. Take this opportunity to get a good night sleep. There is no telling when you will get another chance," Alaric commanded.

The wizards looked at each before making their way back to their camp. No one wanted to argue with him, there was no telling what he would do if they did.

"What do you want us to do?" Bern said when the wizards were out of earshot. He didn't sound pleased. There didn't seem to be any reason why Bern and Cayley had to stay and watch them all day.

"In the morning it will be up to you to move the Alliance into position in Avalon," Alaric replied, apparently not hearing the tone. "I figured that you would know how to create a gateway, but if I was wrong then watching the others would certainly help you I obviously couldn't say anything in front of them. You are right that we need to keep up the illusion that you are still Bern, with a strange entity that comes out on special occasions."

"So if I have to create a gateway to move the army won't it be obvious that I am not who I say I am?" As much as he felt somewhat offended he had to admit to himself that it had been a long time since he had created one. Without watching the wizards fail and succeed he wasn't sure he would have been able to do it.

"That is fine. I will create the gateway at this end. The wizards will be off around the Seven Kingdoms so they won't be around to witness you changing its location for each army in Avalon. The soldiers will just think it is part of the spell I created and if anyone asks that is the excuse you can use," Alaric explained.

"So what is the plan?" Bern asked.

"First you will lead the elves through. They will line up on the western side of Avalon, close to the forest. That is where they will be most comfortable and where they can do the most damage. Pernian will assume command of them, when they are there and Orric will take command when he arrives with the Northern Elves. Next to them will be the Hondin Lel army. Captain Achim will take control until Lord Hadar returns with the rest of the army. I know he hasn't been privy to the command group, but he is the highest ranked officer from Hondin Lel. All he needs to do is assemble that army in Avalon. There will be no battle until Hadar arrives." Alaric paused for a moment, wondering if he had given away too much information, but then he remembered who he was speaking with. "Next in line will be the Remidians. General Jarwe will be in command until Prince Hawthorne arrives. At that point Jarwe will resume his command of the Alliance."

"And what might I be doing then?" Bern asked. "I thought you wanted me to lead the army into the final battle?"

"You will be there at the start, but you and I know that you won't be there at the end. You both have always known the role you will play," Alaric calmly replied.

"The Castalial army, being the largest, will take up position in the centre. Corporal Horace will lead them to Avalon whilst Captain Elyas will try and convince the High Chancellor to commit more troops. Even with all we have done for the new High Chancellor, I am not confident on that mission." Bern hoped he would say more, but Alaric was not about to elaborate. "Next will be Darshival. General Sorrell will lead the troops, as he will during the final battle. Lord Richmond will gather more soldiers in Darshival. Next will be Entero led by Captain Gaël. Duke Xavier will lead the army and will be pivotal in gathering more Enteroite soldiers. Lastly, the dwarves. Bronn will lead them to Avalon while Hulkan goes to Castalia and Dorn to the Cloumid Mountain. When they arrive at the battlefield then Hulkan will assume command."

"It seems like you have it all planned," Bern replied. "And what would you have us do?"

"You are still recognised as the commander of the Alliance. Everyone will feel more confident if the command comes from you," Alaric explained.

Bern wasn't sure if his words were true or whether Alaric was just placating him. Moving the army from point A to point B seemed like a waste of his and Cayley's time. He had to admit that Alaric did have a point. While he was still parading as Bern then he would have to act like it, and that meant leading the army.

"What are you going to do?" Cayley asked.

"All in good time," Alaric replied. "Now you need to prepare your army. I need to go and speak with Faxon and Hawthorne."

Alaric didn't wait for a response before he blinked away. Bern and Cayley just looked at each other, neither knowing what to say. The time was approaching and they knew things were going to change, they had just not expected things to change so much.

***

King Faxon and Prince Hawthorne were eating alone in the prince's apartments. Faxon's face was drawn, but he was looking a lot better. The strength had returned to his features and before long he would return to normal. Hawthorne, who had suffered a much worse ordeal, looked as though he had not suffered at all. They both looked up in surprise when they noticed Alaric.

"How dare you..." Faxon boomed before fading away when he realised who it was. "Sorry Alaric, you startled me."

"That's alright. I came to discuss the Remidian effort for the Alliance," Alaric skipped over the formalities. "In the morning you need to send out a decree that all soldiers and able bodied men will be conscripted to the Alliance."

"Please Alaric, give us time. We have been under the yoke of the Evil One for a long time and we would like to have some family time."

"There is no time for that," Alaric returned. "The final battle approaches and you need to do your part."

"We have done our part," Hawthorne added his voice to his father's argument. "We have suffered for our part."

"And you will suffer even more if the Alliance fails," Alaric snapped before Hawthorne could continue. "The fight has only just begun and your true role has only just started."

"What does that even mean?" Hawthorn asked.

"You will lead the Remidian army in the final battle, but for now you have to gather as many soldiers as you can. First you will empty the capital and then you have to move onto Zenza City. The duke is gathering as many men as he can as we speak. When they see their prince arrive it will do wonders for their morale. They have seen the devastation of the Evil One and a lot of residents have lost their homes. When they see you they will be heartened."

Hawthorne liked what he was hearing, but Faxon was not so pleased. There was a sour expression on his face and it was clear that he was about to voice his concerns.

"I would have thought it made more sense for the king to lead the soldiers?" he barked. "I know it has been a long time since I have seen battle, but I have not forgotten. If this is the final battle then I will not be left behind like a milk maid."

Alaric was surprised at Faxon's words. He had thought he would have problems convincing the King to empty his lands of soldiers, but he had not expected his reaction. Hawthorne had always been at the front of the Remidian army, with Jarwe in command of the Alliance. It had been a long time since anything had come as a surprise to Alaric and he wasn't sure what to do about it.

"Very well. You can take charge of gathering the soldiers from Remidel and Hawthorne can leave in the morning." Alaric had to think quickly. A wrong decision would mean the death of them all.

"That is not for you to decide," Faxon retorted.

"Father! Remember who you are speaking to. If the prophecy wants me to lead the soldiers then there is nothing we can do to change that," Hawthorne replied. "You know that to be true. Even if we decided to go against the Chosen One's wishes when we reached the battle the prophecy would force its hand."

Alaric left them to their thoughts. He had achieved what he wanted to and there was no reason to stay any longer. In the morning they would do as he commanded and then he would need to complete his own journey. He could feel the prophecy pulling him to the north. He was yet to know exactly where he had to go and that meant it was not yet to time to leave. In the morning he was sure the prophecy would reveal the location he needed to travel and at the end would be the Onyx stone.

Chapter 10: On the Road

The commanders and the wizards had gathered half an hour before dawn, but there was no sign of Alaric. Although he had not specified a time for their meeting, they had all assumed he would want them to be on the move at first light. Orric had already had the elves assembled where Alaric had instructed.

It wasn't until the sun crested the horizon did Alaric appear. He didn't apologise or even look abashed. Their looks of displeasure simply washed over him.

"I see you are all here, that is good," he started, enflaming their mood. "Now it is time for you to start moving the elves to the battlefield Pernian."

"With all due respect Alaric I thought I was the one leading the elves," Orric said with confusion on his face. It was obvious that it wasn't just what he thought. He was attuned with the prophecy and he knew that it was his destiny to lead them. He ran his hand through his greying hair as he waited for Alaric's response.

"Yes, I should have known you would feel the tug of the prophecy. You will be there to lead the elves into the final battle, but in the meantime you must travel to *Nordligträ* and rally the Northern Elves. They must be there to fight alongside you. The elves must be as one when the time comes."

"Are you sure that is a good idea?" Kilean asked. "There is bad blood between us. I'm sure our brethren have never forgiven us for leaving."

"I wouldn't be so sure Kilean. A lot of time has passed since you left, but that is beside the point. The Northern Elves must be there at the end and that is all that matters." It was obvious that Alaric was done with the conversation. "Brielle, you will go with Orric. You spent your life following the works of Emerald and you will be able to reassure the elves that they are doing the right thing."

No one seemed pleased with his words, but there was no point in trying to discuss it. They were all keen to be on the move, but they all wanted to move on to Avalon. That was where the final battle was going to take place and that's where they would be the most use.

"Now comes the tricky part," Alaric continued when no one else spoke. "Eldred, Alena and Richmond, you were the last three to be at *Nordligträ*. Who thinks they could explain a safe location to Brielle?"

"I could," Eldred said. "But would it not be easier if I took Orric there? I have already spoken with the council and Palen trusts me."

Alaric shook his head. "If only it was that easy. With all due respect Eldred, if you had been able to convince Palen to join us then he would be here now."

"But that was because the *Tree of Life* was under attack. I'm sure under different circumstances they would have been here."

"Be that as it may Brielle must go with Orric. Now if you could explain a safe location for them to travel to."

"I don't really know of any safe places," Eldred had to admit. "I guess the forest floor might be a good place, but there is no telling if any of the elves might be walking past."

"Yes, there is always a chance that someone could walk into the gateway if you are not careful. There is one more part to you training that I didn't mention yesterday." The wizards didn't like the sound of what they were hearing. "I'm sure you all felt something when you created the second gateway. It is that feeling that you need to be aware of. When you create the second gateway and there is potential danger you will notice a slight change."

"Why didn't you tell us this yesterday," Brielle snapped.

"Because it was a distraction you didn't need. Before you create a gateway to your final location I want you aim it at the heart of the army."

Brielle opened her mouth, but then stopped. Instead she created a gateway five paces from where the stood. When it was completed she focused her attention on the army. Just when she was about to create the second gateway she felt what Alaric was talking about. She could feel the people standing around, there was no where she could put it without risking someone's life. She knew that she could still create the gateway, but every fibre in her body was telling her not too.

"Now that is an extreme situation, but you know the difference."

Brielle simply nodded her head.

"Eldred, would you please explain a safe enough location for Brielle to go?"

Eldred thought for a moment. He figured the forest floor in front of the main building would be the best place.

When Brielle was comfortable with his explanation she prepared herself. She concentrated on her spell and when she was comfortable that everything was safe she created the second gateway.

Brielle didn't wait for Orric to step through. He looked at Pernian and something passed between them before he followed after her. When he was safely on the other side the gateway blinked out.

Alaric breathed a sigh of relief. He wasn't sure things were going to start so smoothly, but they were on the move at long last.

"Next will be Eldred. You will travel alone to Jarrat." Eldred's face dropped at his words. "I know you have suffered a terrible experience there, but you will also know the city better than anyone else. Captain Gaël is the highest ranked soldier in the Enteroite army and he will be needed to assemble the army in Avalon. You must find Duke Xavier. He will be required to lead the army into the final battle. Hopefully the queen will have recovered by now and between the two of them they will realise that our need is greater than theirs."

Eldred nodded his head. It wasn't just the return to Jarrat that upset him. He had been the only wizard to follow the prophecy from the start. He had been the only one who had truly seen the threat from the north and had been the only one to do anything about it. Although he knew he had an important mission and was the only wizard who could be trusted by himself, he would have thought he could have stayed to find out what the others were doing. There was nothing he could do. If he complained then he would just look as though he was pouting and that would be no example to set for the others. He had been given a mission and he would take the challenge head on.

"Yes, Alaric, I will do what needs to be done. By the end of the week I will have the rest of the Enteroite army on the field in Avalon," Eldred's voice was firm.

Like Brielle he tried to create the second gateway in the middle of the army and he too was shocked at the sensation he felt. There was little chance he could mistake that for a safe place. When he was confident he knew where he was going he walked through his gateway before it blinked away.

"We are moving along nicely," Alaric commented, almost to himself, as he looked at the sun. "Minerva, it will be your job to take Captain Elyas to see the High Chancellor. Although Linus has only been in the position for a short time I am sure he will help."

"I am not so confident," Elyas said. "He has already committed half the army and from what I heard, the Grand Cathedral was up in arms. I don't think it will be so easy for him to commit the rest of our forces. The conclave will not allow it."

Alaric had to admit that Elyas was right, but that was irrelevant to the fact that they needed all their soldiers.

"Tell Linus that, as is true in ancient law in Castalia, he has the final say on troop movements in time of war. Regardless of what the conclave decides it is completely up to him." Alaric wasn't sure where the information had come from, but he knew it to be true.

"I don't know if he will want to go against the conclave, not this early in his rule. There has been more than one High Chancellor, erm, disappear when he upset them. Now of course there are no official records kept of such an act, but it is still widely known to be true."

"Then you will do everything in your power to convince them otherwise. If we do not have the full support of the Grand Cathedral then we will lose the final battle and everything will be lost."

Alaric's words quickly silenced any thought of continuing the conversation. There was little time and Alaric had already indulged the captain too much. Everyone would want to voice their concerns that their respective leaders would not give anymore soldiers and there simply was not enough time. Bern needed to start the elves moving across to Avalon.

"You also need to take Hulkan to the guild," Alaric continued talking to Minerva. "I feel that you will be needed to help Elyas with the High Chancellor, so you should drop Hulkan off first."

Minerva nodded her head. She recognised his tone and knew there was no room for questions. She had watched the other wizards carefully and knew what she had to do. Despite watching the reaction of the others she was still surprised when she tried to create the gateway in the middle of the army. She silently chided herself as she created a gateway into the foyer of the Western Dwarven Guild. Hulkan and Elyas quickly followed after her and the gateway blinked away.

Alaric let out a sigh of relief. He hoped those still left to travel would not question him so much.

"Ulman, you must go to Kiarome with Lord Richmond," Alaric said.

"Of course," Ulman barked. He was about to open a gateway when Richmond stepped forward.

"I know we are pressed for time Alaric, but what should I tell Unwin about his daughter. I am sure the conversation will come up no matter what I do to try and avoid it."

"Tell him as little as possible. If he asks then just say she is well and with the army. She sends her regards and will be home as soon as the final battle is over. That should give him enough motivation to give us all of his support," Alaric replied.

As much as Richmond did not want to lie to his king, he had to admit it was the best course of action. If Unwin was to find out that Marina was missing and the circumstances behind it, then there was little chance he would supply more troops. All he could do was hope that Unwin wouldn't be able to see through his lie.

"Very well. I will do my best."

Richmond explained the best place for Ulman to transport them. The palace gardens seemed to be the easiest to explain and there was enough room to find a safe place.

Ulman was grateful that Alaric had told him to try the army before creating his true destination gateway. As soon as he found the place in the gardens he felt the strange sensation that something was wrong. It wasn't as strong as it was with the army, but he knew there were people nearby. It took him three more tries before he found a suitable location. As soon as he did he didn't waste any time in passing through into the palace of Kiarome. Richmond hurried after him and then the gateway disappeared.

Alaric looked over his shoulder back towards the city, as if he was waiting for someone, but no one knew who it might be.

"Althea, you will go to Lel Dinion with Duke Hadar."

Althea did not look happy. Alaric found it quite odd as Hondin Lel had been her kingdom of birth. The small town she was from no longer existed, but that didn't mean anything. It was the very reason he had chosen Althea to travel to Lel Dinion.

"Is there something wrong?" Alaric asked.

"I have a long history with the rulers of Hondin Lel. King Lisle XII's great-grandfather exiled me from Lel Dinion and the kingdom and I haven't been welcomed back since. I think you should find someone else to go with Hadar," she said.

Alaric really wanted to know what had gone wrong. Normally he would have the answers somewhere in his memories, but there was nothing. In the end he knew there was no time for explanations. All he could do was reassure her that it was the right thing to do. Whatever had happened in the past would not affect what she needed to achieve. If it did then the prophecy would have chosen one of the other wizards to make the journey.

"You will be alright," Alaric reassured her. "There is nothing for it. Whatever the differences are between you and the Kingdom of Hondin Lel you must fix them and move on."

Althea was about to speak again, but she was silenced by a hand on her shoulder from Gwydion. All she could do was nod her head.

It had been a long time since Althea had been in the palace or the city in general and she needed Hadar to explain what he thought would be a safe location. After she had tested her skills in the army she started her gateway.

"There are too many people in the throne room." It was a lie, but a convincing one.

She rejected the next three locations that he suggested until he came up with one outside the palace grounds. She didn't think just appearing in the palace would do her any good. Lisle would need some warning that she was coming, but she didn't think the others would understand.

"There is a house not too far away from the palace. I know the owner and she will not mind us suddenly appearing," Hadar explained.

Althea wanted to question his reasoning, but decided it would be better just to create the gateway before Alaric said anything. She didn't think it would be long before he realised what she was doing. They both walked through the gateway and then it was gone.

"I'm sorry I'm late," the voice came from behind Alaric.

They had all been focused on Althea's gateway and no one had noticed Prince Hawthorne riding up on them. He dismounted and puffed as he approached. It was obvious that he had been riding hard.

"Better late than never," Alaric greeted him. "Now it is time for you to leave, Drake. You will go with Hawthorne to Zenza City. Hopefully the duke will have gathered together everyone he can. You should have the easiest job of all."

That didn't make Drake feel any better. Something didn't seem right to him and he had a bad feeling things weren't going to be as easy as Alaric suggested.

Hawthorne explained the royal apartments with great detail. No one would be there, but Drake still had to test the army like the others. When he knew what he was supposed to feel he created the gateway in the front room. Hawthorne didn't waste any time following him.

Gwydion was the last wizard and knew exactly where he was going. He would have to travel to the Cloumid Mountains with Dorn. He had the most difficult of all the locations. He would have to create a gateway in the heart of the mountain. That was where the dwarves kept their homes. Although he felt he was up to the challenge, he was not looking forward to it.

"Gwydion and Dorn, you are the last to leave. You have a week to convince the dwarves under the mountain that they should join their brothers from Castalia. If I could give you more advice on how to achieve such a goal I would, but it is not my place."

"It has been a long time since I have been home," Dorn said. "I am not sure I'm going to be able to explain a safe place for Gwydion to open a gateway."

"And this is where it becomes a little tricky." Alaric didn't elaborate until Gwydion had tried creating a gateway in the middle of the army. "Creating a gateway into a mountain is just as dangerous as casting it into a group of people. If your gateway opens up in the mountain you will walk straight into a wall of rock where you will be encased." Alaric paused to let the information sink in. "Use all of your senses when creating your second gateway or it will be a very short mission for you."

Dorn did his best to describe the place he had once called home. It was a small house, cut into the heart of the mountain. Dorn had little doubt that it would be someone else's home by now. The other dwarves had not agreed with his decision to leave with Eldred and they would not have kept it vacant on his account.

"Are you sure this is a good idea?" Gwydion asked when Dorn had finished. His account had taken nearly half an hour, but the wizard was still unsure of its exact location. "I don't want to risk walking us into the mountain. From what you explained to us that would be fatal."

"Just try and open your gateway," Alaric finally said.

When Gwydion attempted the gateway into the mountain he was nearly knocked off his feet. He knew instantly that the gateway would have opened into a wall of rock. In the end he really didn't think he needed the test to realise the dangers ahead. There was no chance he would have opened the second gateway with the feeling of dread that came with it.

It took him another three tries before he finally found the location. He thought it was good training., each time he failed he knew he was getting closer.

Dorn shot Alaric a hopeful look before following Gwydion into the gateway. He had no idea what sort of reception he would receive on the other side. When he left, his parents had disowned him and the council vowed if he should ever return then he would be put to death. Despite all that, he was confident he could convince them all to lend their support to the Alliance.

The rest of the command group looked around nervously when the gateway disappeared. It was mid-morning and they knew that time was getting away from them. It was now their turn to achieve whatever Alaric had planned for them. They all hoped it wouldn't be too taxing.

"Bern, it is time to open the gateway to Avalon," Alaric addressed the general.

Alaric looked back towards the city. The elves had assembled, as he had requested and it looked as though they were more than ready to leave. That was a promising sign, although he wasn't sure they would be so keen when they saw what they were about to walk through.

"Pernian, I think you should prepare the elves for what is to come. It will come as a shock," Alaric suggested.

Pernian nodded his agreement before he ran towards them. He had grown used to the strange multicoloured lights of the gateways, but he wasn't prepared for Alaric's next move.

No one really noticed the small dot of light a dozen paces in front of the left flank of elves. Without warning the gateway suddenly burst into life and even Bern had to admit he was impressed. The gateway was twenty paces high and forty paces wide and appeared in a split second. The elves at the front of the line, including Pernian, shrunk back in horror at the mass of multicoloured lights in front of them. No matter what Pernian had said there was no preparing them for the giant gateway looming before them. Slowly the colours started to swirl and then there was the image of a field before them. The sky was blue and there was a forest off to the left.

"When you are finished with the elves the gateway on the other side will shift to the next location," Alaric said for the benefit of the others.

When the elves had all passed through, it would be up to Bern to move the gateway on the other side and he wasn't looking forward to it. The gateway was larger than any he had ever seen before. He couldn't believe the ease at which Alaric had created it. His powers had grown beyond anything he could have imagined. He wanted nothing more than to question him further, but he knew there wasn't time.

"I will be going now," Alaric continued, not giving anyone a chance to respond. "Alena will be coming with me."

The mention of her name suddenly brought her attention away from the gateway. She thought that when Alaric had left she would join the rest of the elves and prepare for the final battle. Her heart lifted when he said she would be joining him. She loved him and thought he felt the same, but since his return he had been so cold. Although there was no time for a relationship her heart filled with hope again.

"Where are you going?" Bern asked just as it looked like Alaric was about disappear.

"I am going to find the last piece of the puzzle," Alaric said and then the two were gone.

Bern looked at Cayley and sighed. It wasn't even close to the answer he was looking for. He quickly remembered himself and didn't think it was a good idea to draw any more attention to the little girl.

After the initial shock, Pernian had started moving the elves through the gateway. Bern was grateful for that. There was still one thing he had left to do, he needed to keep the rest of the command group busy so he could find time to speak with Cayley.

"Now it is time to ready everyone to move through the gateway. You will move through in individual armies," Bern started in a commanding voice. The soldiers stiffened in response. They had all listened intently to Alaric's speeches and now they were itching to move into action. "The next army to go through the gateway will be the Hondin Lel army. Captain Achim." Bern called.

"Yes, general!" Captain Achim spoke with a gruff voice. He was a young looking man, but was thirty years of age. The clean shaven look did nothing to help. If Bern didn't know any better he would have thought he was only just twenty. He was also concerned with Alaric's choice, but there was nothing he could do about it.

"Have the Hondin Lel army form up behind the elves. You will be next through the gateway." He paused. "Make sure you wait for the scenery to change. You will be travelling to a different location in Avalon. That way you will be able to freely set up your army."

"Yes, sir!" Achim saluted and turned to return to the army. His heart was filled with pride and he almost didn't hear what Bern said next.

"Wait, captain! There is more that you need to do." Bern waited for him to turn around before he continued. "You will need to take supplies with you. You will need enough to survive for seven days until the battle starts. You will need to march through the night, but you can rest once you've made camp on the other side."

"Yes sir!" Achim saluted again, but waited before he turned back.

"Get to it captain!" Bern boomed, although there was no malice to his tone.

Bern shook his head and smiled. If Achim survived the final battle then he would certainly climb the ranks of the Hondin Lel army. Even though there were not many soldiers with him they would all tell the story of who led them through the gateway.

"With a little luck the Hondin Lel army should be through by first light tomorrow. Then you will need to follow with the Remidian army," Bern explained to Jarwe. "Take whatever supplies you need."

"Yes, general," Jarwe's voice was a lot calmer than Achim's. "I will have my men start building defences as soon as we arrive. There is enough wood left to build some small forts and to be able to spike the dikes."

"There will be no defences," Bern replied to shock of the others.

"You can't be serious?" Jarwe asked, aghast. "We need defences, if only to protect our supplies. If the Dark Knights' soldiers break our lines then they could reach the camp and destroy everything."

"If the enemy breaks our lines then there will be no need for supplies," Bern's words lowered the heads of the other commanders. "This will be an all out attack from both sides. There will be no need for defences. Have your soldiers ready for battle by the end of the week. That's all you need to do."

Jarwe was the only commander who didn't lower his gaze when Bern spoke. He didn't like what he was hearing, but it made sense to him. All along, deep down, he knew it was not going to be an extended battle. Even when he was having the defences built in Avalon the first time he knew it wasn't right.

"Then that is what we shall do," Jarwe saluted as he replied. "Is there anything else you need from me, general?"

Bern thought about explaining that once the full army was assembled he would be taking command of the Alliance again, but Alaric had specifically told him not to. Again it didn't make sense to Bern.

"No, general. Good luck and I will see you on the other side." Bern returned the salute.

Bern looked to the others and noticed their heads were still lowered. "Who died?" he asked no one in particular.

Slowly they all brought their eyes up to meet his and suddenly felt very foolish. It was like they had already been defeated. If it continued any longer then Bern would have to discipline all of them and that was something he did not want to do.

"Now this is where things will start to get difficult. Corporal Horace will need to send through the Castalial army after Jarwe. Being that it is the largest army, and at the back of the Alliance, it will not be an easy task."

"Why don't we leave the Castalial army until last?" asked Sorrell and instantly wished he hadn't.

"That would make sense and I only wish it was that easy, but it is the Castalial army that needs to go next. To try and change the prophecy would be to cause destruction for us all," Bern's tone was sombre. "The army needs to be ready to follow after Remidia. I'm estimating it will take a full two days for the Castalial army to march through the gateway and then it needs time to set itself on the other side. If it had been my decision I would have sent it through first." He really wouldn't have, but it seemed like something a general would say. "After the Castalial soldiers have made it to Avalon then General Sorrell will lead the Darshivallian army through and last will be the dwarves, led by Bronn." Bern rushed through the command, he had other things to do and he needed everyone doing their job. "Faxon will have more supplies brought in from the city to ensure that everyone is well fed when the battle starts. Now it is time to get to work." Bern dismissed them all.

When they were alone Bern looked down at Cayley. She had a wry smile on her face. It was the first time he had really noticed her that day. Her hair was in pigtails and she wore a light blue, floral dress. It wasn't the most suitable of outfits, but he had to admit that she did look cute.

"Don't look at me like that," she pouted. "The palace women love fussing over me. I could overpower them, but that would give away my true identity. I hope you appreciate what I have to go through."

Bern couldn't help but smile, which made Cayley even madder. She wanted to scream, but that would only add to her girlish facade.

"So what do you want to talk to me about?" she asked when he didn't respond.

"This whole situation just doesn't feel right," Bern started. He looked around to make sure no one could hear them. "Alaric was so sure, but I don't know. I would have thought being this close to the end that it would all come to me."

"I know what you mean. I am the same. If I try to look forward it is like there is a fog covering my thoughts. At this point I would have thought everything, except for the result, would have been revealed to me," Cayley agreed.

"I guess we have no choice, but to follow Alaric's instructions," Bern shook his head. "I think we should go and see Faxon. He will want to know what is happening and we need to confirm that he will supply the rest of the army."

Cayley simply nodded.

They decided it was best if they rode into the city instead of just jumping to their desired location. Although they had suddenly appeared into the throne room when they were battling the Dark Knight, no one had mentioned it. The longer they could keep the army believing that Bern was still in command, the better.

They found the King in the Great Dining Hall. They had converted it into a makeshift throne room while the main throne room was being repaired. Faxon sat on a high backed chair. It looked as though all his strength had returned, but the multitude of ministers and functionaries around him, vying for his attention, were doing their best to drain it. When he saw Bern arrive he waved for the others to let him through. Some of the functionaries moved, but the ministers remained, pretending not to notice.

"Get out of the way!" Faxon boomed.

The ministers quickly moved aside. Bern and Cayley made their way to the makeshift throne, making sure they didn't make eye contact with anyone.

"What can I do for you?" Faxon asked.

Bern looked around the room. He had hoped for some privacy, but it didn't look like that would be the case.

"I just wanted to let you know the Remidian army will be going through the gateway tomorrow."

Rumours of the gateway had rushed through the city and into the palace. Those who had nothing better to do, and some who did, had rushed to the top of the walls to see great wall of coloured light. If Alaric had not ordered the main gates shut then people would have rushed out to see what was happening.

"That is good to know. I only wish that I could go with them," Faxon sighed "but it seems as though the kingdom would fall apart without me." It looked as though he was truly disappointed. "In the light of day I released that my bravado was out of place. This is a battle that my son must win for his kingdom."

"I understand," Bern replied.

"I feel that is not the only reason why you have come here," Faxon continued.

"The armies of the Seven Kingdoms are moving to Avalon to prepare for the final battle and they are going to start running low on supplies. We need all you can spare and probably more."

"You will have all that we have to offer."

His words brought more noise from the crowd.

"But your majesty," a voice came. "Our supplies are already low. The last harvest was not as fruitful as we would have hoped and it has been months since there has been any trade. If we give anything away then our citizens will starve."

"And if we don't, and the army starves, then we will all soon be dead. I am King and I have made my decision. This is not open for debate," Faxon boomed so there could be no doubting his command. "Is there anything else I can help you with?"

Bern was surprised that Faxon had agreed so easily. He had been expecting a lengthy debate.

"No, that is it. Thank you," he replied.

"Good. The city's soldiers will be ready to march in the morning," Faxon added.

Bern had forgotten all about the extra soldiers that Alaric had petitioned from the king. He had been so distracted by what he didn't know that he forgot what he did. At least Faxon knew what had to be done.

"Great, but make sure they all know to walk around the gateway. If anyone tries to pass through the sides then they will be burnt to ash, or worse, sliced in two." Bern warned.

"Of course, thank you," Faxon said. "I don't mean to be rude, but if you are done than I will need to get back to business. If you are raiding our supplies then I believe I have my work cut out for me."

"Thank you King Faxon, I hope I will see you again when this is all over." He knew he would never see Faxon again, but it seemed like the most appropriate thing to say.

"The Master-of-Stores is waiting for you outside the palace. He will help you with everything you need."

It took the rest of the day to work out the supplies with the Master-of-Stores. Even though Faxon had instructed him to give Bern whatever was asked for, the man was not willing to make life easy. He knew they were leaving the city destitute and he wasn't happy with the idea. When it was all said and done it was his job to make sure the people of Remidel were well fed.

The sun was almost set when they returned to the army. The elves were just finishing their march through the gateway and Pernian saw the two and gave a short salute before disappearing. Bern wasn't completely sure if the Master-of-Stores would supply everything he had asked for, but there was no more time for him continue the discussion. He needed to be back in time to move the second gateway before the Hondin Lel army started passing through.

Captain Achim had the army assembled and ready to march. Bern had told him to wait, but not for how long and he looked around nervously for a sign that he should start sending his soldiers through. He would lead the march and make sure everything was safe on the other side. The sun had long set in Avalon and the gateway was now pitch black; it did nothing to ease his nerves.

It was the moment Bern was not looking forward to. He had watched the seven wizards and Alaric carefully, but he had not been given a chance to practice.

"Do you want me to do it?" Cayley asked. "I'm pretty sure I know what needs to be done."

"Pretty sure isn't enough." He spoke more to himself than Cayley. "I'll do it."

Removing the gateway in Avalon was easy. He took his time and felt the threads of the spell. The next location was thick in his mind. Even if he had never been to Avalon he would have known exactly where to create the next gateway. He had to admit, the prophecy did come in handy sometimes.

"Move your soldiers through," Bern called out to Achim.

The captain looked around nervously, not realising it was Bern who had made the command. In the dimming light he couldn't see Bern standing on the hill where the command group had assembled. Slowly he took a step forward and issued the command for the rest of the Hondin Lel army to follow.

"What do we do now?" Cayley asked.

"We wait and watch and make sure the army makes it to Avalon on time."

***

The Remidel soldiers arrived in the morning, just as Faxon had promised. To Bern's surprise there were also citizens from the city, crudely dressed in whatever would pass as armour and armed with a variety of makeshift weapons. Whatever spare weapons the army had were kept for the soldiers. Bern couldn't understand why Alaric had asked for regular citizens to be added to the army. He knew that it was their fight too, but untrained soldiers would only get in the way on the battlefield.

Bern and Cayley remained on the hill for as long as they could and watched the progress of the army. They only came down to eat and occasionally sleep so not to look suspicious. With their plan in motion there was little else for them to do.

"This has to be the most bored I have been in a long time," Cayley commented on day three as the Castalial army started to move through the gateway.

Bern had hoped they would have started as soon as the Remidel army had finished, but it had taken longer for them to assemble than he had expected. He could only hope that they were still on time. If any were late arriving in Avalon then everything would be lost.

"All in good time. I'm sure you will look back on this moment and wish you were still here," there was no humour in his voice.

Cayley just shook her head on watched on.

On the morning of the seventh day Bronn had his dwarves lined up and ready to go. On the other side the final battle was waiting. Bern didn't know if it was minutes or hours away, but he knew it was close.

When the last of the dwarves made it through Bern looked around the landscape. Not that long ago there were lush fields with a sparse scattering of oak and ash trees. Then the army moved in and there were soldiers as far as the eye could see. All that was left made Bern sad. The ground had been trampled to dust and the trees had been chopped down for firewood. The scene before him reminded him of what the Seven Kingdoms would look like if Nyrra won.

"It's not over yet," Cayley said, reading the expression on his face.

"No, not yet. Let's get this over with," Bern said as he stepped through the gateway.

Chapter 11: *Nordligträ*

Orric shivered when he stepped out of the other side of the gateway. He had not been sure what to expect, but it was a strange feeling. One moment he was standing in a field outside of Remidel and the next he was deep in the Northern Forest. The thick smell of pine trees in the air made him feel better. As he looked towards Brielle, it didn't look as though she had been affected at all. He had lived a long life but he could have lived it without experiencing a gateway.

They came out on the forest floor only half a league from the village. Brielle would have much rather they landed in the village itself, but Orric had insisted it would be better if they arrived on foot. If she had thought about it at the time she would have asked for horses, but it was too late for that.

"It has been a long time since I have walked through these woods," Orric said as they walked towards *Nordligträ.*

Despite the fact that the elves had been living in their makeshift village, Orric knew they would be back in the rightful home.

Brielle remained silent and kept her head forward. It was obvious that she wasn't interested in making conversation, but Orric continued.

"It has been too long since I've been inside a forest. Elves were not meant for the outside world, but this war affects us all." He didn't seem to mind that Brielle didn't respond. He knew there would be elves nearby and he felt the conversation would ease their entrance. If they knew he was a fellow elf then there was less chance they would be hostile. "I wish I could stay here for longer, but I know that will not be the case. When this is all over I think I would like to come and see the *Tree of Life* one more time. I have never felt such peace as when I was near the tree."

Brielle quickened her pace. She didn't want to talk and hoped that she could remain a step ahead of Orric, but despite his age he was still an elf and quite easily kept pace. There was a lot going through her mind and his words were distracting her. She had a bad feeling that there was something evil in the forest and the last thing she wanted was to be caught in a trap.

Despite her concerns and Orric's constant banter they reached the village without seeing anyone. That concerned Orric more than if they had been taken prisoner. If everything was fine then there should have been an armed escort to take them to the village. Although it had been a long time since he had been in *Nordligträ* some things never changed.

The village seemed to be completely empty, another sign that things weren't right. Many of the huts on the forest floor had been destroyed and the forest floor was strewn with broken timbers and belongings. At least Orric would have thought the elves would have started cleaning their village. It looked no better than the makeshift village they had been living in before they had returned home.

"Something isn't right," Orric whispered, almost only to himself.

"Don't you think I know that," Brielle snapped. It was the first time she had spoken since they had arrived. "I've been trying to work out what it is, but your incessant chatter has been distracting me."

Orric found it odd to be spoken to in such a manner. Not since he was a child had anyone used such a tone with him. He was about to say something when he heard movement behind them. Orric's shoulders stiffened, but Brielle didn't seem concerned. A stifled cry from behind indicated why she had stayed so calm.

When he looked around he saw a tired looking elf with a contorted expression on his face. Brielle had him wrapped up in weaves of air. No matter what he tried he could no longer move the rest of his body. Eventually his face relaxed and he spoke.

"What are you doing here?" his voice was strained.

"Let him go," Orric barked. "He is not our enemy."

"Then what was he doing sneaking up behind us with that spear?" Brielle asked as she pointed to the spear lying on the ground.

"Well?" Orric raised an eyebrow.

It took a moment for the trapped elf to realise that Orric was also an elf.

"I am sorry, I meant no disrespect." Although he didn't know who Orric was, an elf showing such signs of age was due his respect.

"Then why were you trying to kill us?" Brielle returned.

Although Orric hadn't seen the elf stalking up behind them, he knew that Brielle had. If she claimed he had been about to kill them then he would have to take it as fact.

"I thought you might have been agents of the Evil One. His creatures have been plaguing us recently and we have only just been able to return home."

"Then why were we able to get so close?" Orric asked before Brielle had a chance.

"Our numbers have dwindled. If you weren't making so much noise then there is a good chance you would have made it to the centre of *Nordligträ* before you were noticed, although if you had I'm not sure you would have survived."

Orric knew it was a wise decision to arrive outside the village and to make noise on the way in. In the end it might have saved their lives. He wondered if it was the prophecy or his own intuition, either way it had worked.

"I am Orric and this is Brielle, of the wizard's council," Orric introduced them. He didn't think there was any point in continuing their line of conversation. "I think you can let him go now Brielle."

Brielle didn't look happy, but she knew he was right. The elf knew they weren't there to cause trouble. He would also no longer be a threat and even if he was it wouldn't take long for her to wrap him up again.

"I am Iago," the elf replied when he could move again.

"Who is leading now?" Orric asked. "The last time I was here it was Cibran, but unfortunately I think he might have died a few years ago."

"Palen is now the ruling member of the council," Iago stated. He was about to say something else, but then stopped. "I guess you will want to go and see him. I take it you didn't travel such a distance to speak with me."

"If you could take us to see Palen we would greatly appreciate it," Orric added.

Iago led them through the village. Brielle kept her head straight, but Orric looked around at the rudimentary huts built around the bases of the trees. Made from mud and wood the makeshift houses had been built recently. It seemed as though they had already started to rebuild their village.

Iago led them to a small clearing that had had a large platform to one side. Orric knew exactly what was waiting for them at the top, as the building had been there for many centuries. The branches above them intertwined, creating a ceiling over them.

Iago walked onto the platform and signalled for the others to do the same. When they were all safely aboard he pulled a lever, slowly lifting them into the trees.

When they reached the top they saw that the branches overhead had created a perfect roof. It looked as though even the strongest tempest wouldn't breach its protection, but that was not what gained their attention. After so many years Orric was still amazed at the intricate building across from them. The facade was build from timber, but it was not pine. Orric knew that it had been a gift from the *Tree of Life* and no building would ever look the same.

It was similar to the building the council used in their makeshift village and the same of a dozen others around the forest. Whenever the elves needed refuge there would always be a building they could retreat to that could not be penetrated by their enemies.

The area in front of the building was completely empty. From memory Orric thought there had always been guards at the front of the council building, not that there was ever any real chance for trouble. It was a tradition that had never been broken and Orric didn't think it was a good sign.

Iago walked them to door, but made no move to open it. There was something unsettling about the elf's demeanour. It was almost like he was afraid to open it.

"I will leave you here." Iago inclined his head slightly before returning to the platform.

They walked into a small entrance room which had a long hallway on the far side. There was no one to greet them and Orric wasn't sure what they should do. Brielle didn't seem to want to wait and walked towards the large double doors at the end of the room. She didn't know why, but she knew it was the right way to go.

The room on the other side took up half the building. It was painted completely white, a contrast to the rest of the decor. A floating globe of light lit the room from just under the ceiling in the middle. On the other side of the room was a small dais with a larger and higher one behind it. A small rectangular table with high backed chairs adorned the smaller dais. On the larger dais sat twelve vacant thrones. Two elves sat at the table and looked somewhat out of place.

It took Orric a moment, but he recognised the two as Palen and Kyrene. Their son, Palentonal, had travelled with Alaric to the City of Night. He was poisoned in a battle with a Dark Knight and died in Bellarome. They were the two highest members of the council in *Nordligträ*.

"You are Orric of Elhjem," Kyrene said, then looked across to Brielle. "But I don't recognise you."

A scowl crossed Brielle's face. "I am the wizard Brielle. I have studied the world of Emerald for more years than I can count, so I am quite familiar with you and your home, even if I haven't been here for many years."

A thoughtful expression crossed Kyrene's face, as if she was trying to place Brielle from somewhere. In the end she decided that she had no idea who the woman was, except by reputation. She then looked at Orric with a concerned expression on her face. Orric's letter had been one of the main reasons her son had left, or at least that's what she told herself, to his death. Orric could feel her stare and suddenly felt uncomfortable.

"And what make you think you can just walk into *Nordligträ*, Orric?" Kylene snapped. It was obvious to all that she had not forgiven him.

"I am truly sorry for what happened to Palentonal, but it was necessary to save us all. If it wasn't for him then Nyrra would have taken the Ruby stone from Alaric and we would all be his slaves now." Orric didn't know if that was true, but he spoke as if he did.

"And where is the Ruby stone now?" Kyrene asked. "If it was still in the possession of your Chosen One then wouldn't this mess be over?"

Orric was taken aback. He knew Eldred had been through *Nordligträ*, but he didn't think he would have told them the Ruby stone was missing.

"You look surprised. You think we are ignorant here in the north?"

"Of course not," Orric said as he regained his composure. "It just seemed like an odd statement."

"This is getting us nowhere," Brielle cut in before Kyrene had a chance to continue.

"With all due respect," Palen spoke for the first time "you are not on your island now, Wizard. This is our land and you will show us respect."

Brielle opened her mouth and then stopped. Arguing would get them nowhere and although she wanted to give the elf a piece of her mind she decided against it. Although there was something peaceful about being in *Nordligträ* there was also something unsettling about it. Brielle wanted nothing more than to create a gateway and leave.

"She is right," a voice came from the back of the room. A robed and hooded figure stepped out. Although the hanging globe sufficiently lit the room, there seemed to be a shadow around the figure. "This conversation is getting us nowhere," the voice was like ice. Orric had a bad feeling he knew who, or at least what, was speaking. "You have come here to take the elves to Avalon. Am I wrong?" The question was rhetorical, but the hooded figure waited for a response.

"You know that is why we are here. We are on the cusp of the final battle and we need everyone if we are going to defeat the *Evil One*," Orric replied. He wanted to bait the stranger into revealing his true identity.

"The *Great Lord* will prevail no matter what you do. His army is far greater than yours, not only in number, but in strength. These elves are joining the winning side."

"Is this true?" Orric asked, knowing there must be mind control involved. He hoped Brielle was working on something to remove the spell.

"We have suffered enough," Kyrene said. "The *Tree of Life* was nearly destroyed by a horde of orglin. What Na'garoz says is true. We will stay out of the final battle and in return the Great Lord will spare us his wrath."

As much as Orric was glad to know who stood before him, it didn't make the situation any easier. The last thing they had expected, or been prepared for, was to run into a Dark Knight. Six wizards had been afraid to face one between them and he didn't think Brielle would be much of a match by herself.

"So what is it that you want?" Orric asked. "I assume we would already be dead if you didn't want anything."

"I don't want anything from you. It will be up to the elves to decide what they want to do with you. I only came here to give them the Great Lord's offer. Now it is time for me to head east for the final battle. It will be fun destroying you."

Na'garoz didn't wait for a response before he disappeared. Orric was both relieved and surprised at the move. He was sure it would be easier for Brielle to act with him gone.

"Now you will be imprisoned here for the remainder of your lives," Palen stood as he spoke.

The double doors opened and a dozen armed elves entered the room. Orric looked at Brielle for answers, but the confused expression on her face showed that he would get nothing. The elves approached nervously, but when there was no sign of retaliation they steeled themselves.

"Are you going to do something?" Orric spoke through clenched teeth.

"Not yet," Brielle replied. She had already created a small spell so no one else could hear her words. "Just go along with it."

Orric didn't know what she was talking about, but there was really nothing he could do against a dozen guards. They were led out onto the platform. Only three of the elves could go down with them, but there were another six elves waiting for them at the bottom. Orric thought he might be able to overpower the three in a rush, but those thoughts were dashed when they landed.

They were marched to a nearby hut where they were bustled inside. No one spoke as the door was shut and bolted behind them.

The hut was one room, with no windows. There was a single bed and a small table and chair. It was obviously not designed for two people. Orric was surprised they were allowed to remain together. If it had been his decision he would have kept them separate, but nothing about their situation really made any sense.

"What was that all about?" Orric finally asked when Brielle didn't say anything. All she did was sit on the chair and stare at the wall.

"I thought Na'garoz had put a compulsion spell on them, but I couldn't sense anything," she sounded confused.

"That can't be right!" Orric gasped.

If what Brielle had said was true, then there could be no other explanation. Orric didn't even want to consider what that meant. He could also not believe that Brielle was going to be happy to sit out the final battle in an elven prison.

"I need to think on this," Brielle replied, not taking her eyes from the wall. "This is not at all what I expected. I need to make sure that I haven't missed anything."

Orric didn't like her response, but there was nothing he could do about it. Brielle was deep in thought and he didn't want to do anything to distract her. Instead he paced around the small room.

"Sit on the bed," Brielle snapped. "You're making me dizzy."

Orric didn't want to sit, but he did as he was told. Being confined frustrated him. He thought after a short discussion with the council they would have been on the move to Avalon. There was no good reason why they should remain in *Nordligträ*, at least not one he could see.

It was late in the day, or at least Orric assumed it was, when Brielle finally spoke. "It makes no sense. Na'garoz created no spells. I have scanned and found nothing. It seems that he managed to convince Palen and Kyrene that it is in their best interest to remain behind."

"That has to be impossible. I know the council doesn't believe in the prophecy, but surely they could not believe a Dark Knight, not without magical persuasion. There has to be something you can do?"

Brielle continued to think. His words made sense, but if there was a spell then the Dark Knight would have had to bury it deep for her not to be able to find it. There was no telling how long he had been there, but she didn't think it was long. Eldred had been in Nordligträ and he would have known if there had been a Dark Knight present.

Orric waited patiently for an answer. He lay back against the wall as he sat on the bed. The lumpy mattress didn't feel too comfortable and he doubted either of them would get any real sleep, not that he wanted to. He wanted to break out of the cell and go and speak with Palen and Kyrene.

"I think it's time to eat something," Brielle suddenly said after another long silence.

"I'm not sure if you've noticed, but there isn't any food in here and it doesn't seem like the elves are all that keen to see us. I have a feeling their plan is to just leave us here to rot," Orric replied.

Brielle just shook her head as she created a gateway. When the gateway coalesced Orric could see the front of a wooden building and sand on the ground. There was a smell of salt water in the air, which was much more pleasant than the stale smell of the cell. Orric took a deep breath of the sea air, a smell that was very foreign to him.

"You wait here. We need someone to remain in case they come for us. If the cell is completely empty then it will do nothing for our cause," Brielle explained before she stepped through the gateway.

The last thing Orric wanted was to be left behind, but Brielle had already closed the gateway before he had a chance to follow. The salt air disappeared and the stuffiness quickly returned. Orric wanted nothing more than to step outside and breathe in the fresh forest air. He was not used to being confined and did not like it at all.

Without any light from outside it was impossible to tell what time it actually was. They had already burned through three candles, but he didn't know how long each one took. If no one came they only had four more candles left. Orric thought about sitting in the dark, but he didn't like that idea. If Brielle could create gateways whenever she wanted then she could go and get more candles.

It didn't take long for Brielle to return. Orric could see the fading light through the gateway and figured if it was dusk on the Isle of Wizards then it would have to be past nightfall in *Nordligträ.* She brought with her a platter of cold meat and fruit, which was more than enough to fill their stomachs.

"What do we do now?" Orric asked when they had finished eating.

"It's time to get some sleep," Brielle returned.

"You can't be serious!" Orric gasped. "How do you expect us to sleep like this?"

"I know it doesn't make much sense, but we both know well enough by now that the prophecy doesn't always make sense. It seems it wants us to remain here until morning and that's what we shall do."

"But you can get us out of here?" Orric asked.

"Of course I can. A simple locked door can't restrain me. I would have thought the Dark Knight would have at least created a spell if he wanted us to remain trapped."

"Maybe he knows there is nothing he can really do to prevent us from reaching the final battle?" Orric suggested.

"That could be the case, but I think there is another reason. The more I think about it the more I believe that he is too weak to create any decent spells. It may very well be the result of his reincarnation. I will need to study this and I cannot do it here. I will retire to my home and you can have the bed to yourself."

"I don't want to stay here. This is no place for me to spend the night. At least take me with you. We can both return in the morning," Orric snapped.

"Someone needs to stay here and since you can't create a gateway that needs to be you."

She wasn't going to wait for Orric to continue. She knew it would be a difficult night for him, as it would be for her if she had decided to stay. The small cell was claustrophobic and made her very uncomfortable. She didn't think she would sleep at all, not that she would get much sleep anyway. Although she didn't think she would find the answers in one night, she had to try.

"I will see you in the morning at first light," she replied

Again Brielle didn't wait for a response before creating a gateway and disappearing through it. Orric jumped to his feet, but it was too late to do anything. The gateway closed and with it the smell of fresh sea air. He collapsed back on the bed and dropped his head into his hands.

At some point Orric had managed to fall asleep. He didn't realise until he was woken suddenly by the sound of the door being opened. The candle had burned out and there was no telling what time it was. The cell was pitch black.

When the door was pulled open a light shone in and Orric had to cover his eyes.

"Who's there?" he barked.

"Be calm Master Orric I am not here to hurt you," the male voice was soft. "Where is the wizard?" he asked, but didn't sound surprised.

"She had business to attend to," Orric replied. He tried to look towards the elf, but the light was too bright.

"I'm sorry," the elf replied as he closed the shutters of his lantern. "I am Edvin."

Edvin had a look of age on his face, but with no signs of aging. His hair was blonde and tied in a tail behind him. He wore a light brown shirt and trousers. There was also a concerned expression on his face.

"Something tells me you are not here to let me go," Orric's tone was suspicious.

"It looks as though you don't need my help," Edvin said as he sat on the chair. "But I am not here to discuss that."

"Then what are you doing here?" Orric returned quickly. "Your council has made it quite clear that we are to remain here until we have lost the final battle."

Edvin sighed. "That is true, but we are not all in agreement. We know that a Dark Knight is behind the decision to have you confined. What we don't know is why they could possibly agree with anything that *creature* has told them."

"So what do you want from me?" Orric decided to remain hostile until he knew what Edvin wanted.

"We want your help. I will tell you what happened and hopefully it will all start to make sense."

Orric made himself as comfortable as he could on the lumpy bed as Edvin prepared to tell his tale.

"Now let me be clear from the start, we were never planning to join the Alliance and fight in the final battle." Edvin began. "Just when we were about to change our mind the Evil One sent horde after horde of orglin against the *Tree of Life*. We could not leave her to suffer and die. That would be the end of our world regardless of the result of the final battle."

"I know the importance of the *Tree of Life*," Orric interrupted.

"Of course, I'm sorry," Edvin remained meek. "Even after throwing all our forces against the orglin, it looked as though we were going to fail. Then something amazing happened." Edvin paused, as if he still couldn't believe it himself. "The Wood Sprites are back!"

A glimmer of hope crossed Orric's face, but he quickly hid his emotions. "I must admit that I did feel something not that long ago. I'm sure if I was in my home I would have known what it was, but being so far from a true forest I didn't."

"Of course, Lord Orric." There was nothing patronising in his voice. "Without the aid of Arawn I have no doubt the *Tree of Life* would no longer be here. If I didn't see it with my own eyes I doubt I would have believed it myself." He recognised the suspicion on Orric's face. "But it is true. The Wood Sprite, no doubt with the aid of the *Tree of Life*, destroyed the remaining orglin. When the battle was over and it was clear that the tree was safe we returned home thinking everything was over, but that wasn't the case. It wasn't long before more orglin came, this time to attack the village. They came in small numbers, but enough to cause trouble. It wasn't until the Dark Knight came two days ago that the attacks stopped. He assured the council that they would not return if we stayed away from the final battle."

Orric slowly nodded his head. It was finally starting to make sense. Although he could certainly understand their point-of-view there was no way he would believe anything a Dark Knight told him. If it was his elves then he would fight to the end.

"I know what you are thinking and some of us are thinking the same thing. There is no way we can trust the words of a Dark Knight, but what else are we to do. If we leave then the orglin will destroy *Nordligträ*."

"I don't think the Evil One would risk leaving any of his minions behind. He knows, as we do, that he will need every last creature under his control if he has any chance of winning the final battle. This is clearly an attempt to stop you from joining us in Avalon."

"I have to agree with you Orric. This is exactly what it is, but it seems as though Kyrene and Palen don't want to listen. I am sure if we had a full council it would vote the right way, but this is all we have," Edvin sighed again.

Orric took a chance to think as Edvin stared into the lantern light. He wasn't quite sure if he was thinking or waiting for a response. In the end Orric knew that he had to break the silence.

"Brielle will return in the morning and then you can come and get us. We will speak with the council and make sure they see reason," Orric said.

"I won't be able to get you in the morning. There will be different guards posted on your door and I won't be able to get through. I'm sure the wizard will be able to get you out. There is nothing magical stopping you from leaving."

Orric cursed silently to himself. If the wizard had not wanted the comforts of her own bed then they could have walked out of the cell. In the end he would have to suffer until she returned.

"Very well, we will wait until the morning. Meet us at the platform at the bottom of the council building."

"I will be there waiting for you," Edvin stood and walked out. There was no reason for him to remain and the longer he was there the greater the risk of the council finding out.

With the lantern gone the room returned to complete darkness, but Orric remained seated. Things were starting to make sense, but he felt there was still something missing. Again he fell asleep without realising it.

"I thought you would be ready to go!" Brielle spoke a little too loudly.

Orric suddenly sat upright. His eyes were blurry and for a moment he didn't know where he was. Brielle had lit a candle and the light hurt his eyes. It took him a moment, but when he recovered he retold the story he had heard.

"That makes a little more sense, I suppose," Brielle replied.

She had brought food back with her as she didn't think the elves were going to bring any. It did seem as though they were going to be left to starve to death. That was just another piece of the puzzle that didn't make any sense.

"Did you find anything?" Orric asked as he ate.

"Nothing. There are a lot of ancient texts on the island. I thought I knew which one to look in, but it seemed I was wrong. I wish there was more time, but of course there isn't."

"Do you have a plan?" Orric asked when he finished his breakfast.

"Not really. I thought I would let you lead, since they are your race." Orric didn't like the tone in her voice.

"Well, let's get this over and done with. Shall you create a gateway to the platform?" Orric stood as he spoke.

"No, I thought we would just walk out the front door," Brielle smiled for the first time since they had arrived.

There was a soft click, the lock was released and the door swung open. Orric expected the guards to run in to see what had happened, but there was no movement. When they walked out the guards didn't even seem to notice them at all. It was only then that Orric realised that Brielle had created a spell to make them oblivious to their presence.

They met Edvin at the base of the tree leading up to the council building. He was dressed in a leaf green robe that looked somewhat officious.

"Kyrene and Palen are waiting up top. They have no idea you are coming so be prepared."

Orric didn't quite know what that meant, but he chose not to ask. Edvin ushered them onto the platform and then joined them for the slow ascent. When they reached the top the area in front of the building was again empty. Orric breathed a sigh of relief, although he was sure Brielle would have pacified any guards.

Kyrene and Palen looked annoyed when they saw them arrive.

"This was not at all what we thought when you said you needed to meet with us this morning," Palen addressed Edvin. "I would have thought treason was the last thing on your mind."

"Treason is exactly what I'm trying to avoid," Edvin returned. "Never in our long history have we ever bent over for the Lord of all Evil and now is not the time to start. We need to fight."

"We have already lost so much," Palen blurted.

"Our son has died and now we know why. Your Chosen One left him to die in the Land of Night. He would still be alive, but he was betrayed and for what. The Dark Knight told us everything. We are still chasing the final battle and it has all been for nothing," Kyrene sobbed.

"It has all not been for nothing," Orric barked "and no one left him to die alone. Alaric had to go onto the Cauldron Mountain to destroy the Ruby Stone, or at least that is what we believed. We were all duped by the prophecy, but that still doesn't mean it wasn't meant to happen. Because it happened it will lead to our success. Remember that my daughter was taken and tortured."

"But your daughter is still alive. I would give anything and suffer anything to have our son back," Kyrene returned.

"This is getting us nowhere," Edvin interrupted. He knew that they needed to vent, but time was getting away from them. They needed to change their decision and they needed to do it quickly. "We have all grieved for Palentonal as we have for all those who have died after him. You are not the only ones who have lost children in the battle with the Evil One. Will you let all their loses be for nothing?"

"We will not and that is why we have made this decision. We will protect the remaining elves who live in *Nordligträ* and *Nordligträ* itself. This is the right decision," Palen stood firm.

"If the Evil One wins then there will be nothing left for you here. The Dark Knight is lying. Surely you can see that?" Orric pushed.

"Don't you think we know that?" Kyrene snapped. "We know that the Evil One would never hold to such a bargain, but that is not the reason we agreed to the pact. We did so, because of a vision. I have seen our doom if we follow you into battle."

Orric opened his mouth to reply, but shut it again. He wasn't sure how to respond. They had all been following something they couldn't explain and he didn't know how he could try and refute Kyrene's vision.

"Close your eyes and relax," Brielle spoke for the first time.

"What is this witch saying?" Palen barked.

"Be quiet Palen," Edvin raised his voice for the first time. "We may have a difference of opinion, but we can all still show respect to our guests."

"Our prisoners, don't you mean? And don't think I have forgotten the manner of their arrival. When this is over I think you might be joining our *visitors* in a cell," Palen sneered.

"Be quiet," Brielle snapped.

Palen opened his mouth, but no words came out. It wasn't the tone of her voice, but the fact that his wife sat next to him with her eyes closed. There was a strange expression on her face, halfway between pain and joy. Palen didn't know what Brielle was doing, but he knew she was doing something. He had some rudimentary knowledge of magic, but he knew he was no match for a fully trained wizard, let alone one of the council.

"That was no vision you had. The images were magically placed in your mind," Brielle said as Kyrene opened her eyes.

"But my vision was before the Dark Knight arrived," Kyrene refuted.

"The vision has been here for a long time. I doubt Na'garoz could have summoned the power to create such a vision, at least not without you knowing."

"But we haven't been infiltrated by a Dark Knight before," Palen protested.

"Although it is most likely a Dark Knight who implanted it, there are other creatures capable of such acts," Brielle explained.

"The snake!" Kyrene gasped. "It must have been the snake that came with Eldred. I knew there was something wrong with that situation. So you are in league with them?" Kyrene yelled.

"I am sure it has been there for longer than that, but I can't be certain. All I can tell you is that it is gone and you will no longer have them," Brielle did her best to reassure her.

"Please!" Edvin barked. "You are the only remaining members of the Council and you need to start acting like it. We have to join the final battle. If we remain here then all is lost, even if the Alliance wins."

Kyrene calmed herself and looked at Palen. The anger in his face was gone and there was a look of resignation. He knew they had done the wrong thing. Their motives had been selfish and the Dark Knight was just an excuse to do what they wanted. They never really believed they would be safe from the Evil One's destruction.

"You are right," Palen finally spoke. "We cannot remain here any longer."

"But it is too late," Kyrene sobbed. "All the signs point to the final battle in mere days not the months it will take for us to travel to Avalon."

"There are ways," Brielle replied, not willing to give anything away. "How long will it take to have your elves ready to move?"

"We have a lot of scouts checking the forest for orglin. It will take at least a week if not longer," Palen said.

"Two days at most," Edvin added. "When you arrived I sent out messengers to have the scouts return."

"Very well. In two days I will open a gateway to Avalon and we shall meet the final battle head on."

Chapter 12: Castalia

Minerva stepped through the gateway and landed in the chapel of the God King Ruby. She figured of all the chapels around the outside of the courtyard, it was the most likely to be empty. Although she wasn't worried about her reception by the High Chancellor, she didn't want to the gateway to announce their arrival.

The chapel had a large pitched roof with red glass allowing the light to give a soft ruby hue to the main room. The mahogany used to build the chapel had been brought in from Northern Entero. Simple pews lined the hall leading up to a small altar and simple lectern.

It was clear that it had been a long time since anyone had made an offering to the God of chaos and mayhem. A thick layer of dust covered everything and no footprints had disturbed it before them.

Minerva led the way to the door, but paused before opening it. She had been right that the chapel would be vacant, but there was something she had not thought about. If there was anyone on the other side then they would assume the two were worshippers of Ruby and therefore agents of the Evil One. A long time ago that would not be the case, but in recent years anyone associated with the God King Ruby would be considered an enemy.

Slowly she opened the door a crack to see outside, hoping that no one would notice her. Outside there were people moving throughout the courtyard, but no one seemed to take any notice of Minerva. When she was confident they would remain unseen she signalled for Elyas to move quickly behind her.

When they moved outside no one paid them any attention. Despite their dress they were just another pair of worshippers and no one cared which chapel they had either come from or were going to. It was common practice to avoid fights between the different faiths.

Minerva and Elyas made their way quickly to the steps of the Grand Cathedral. It was only when they diverted from the main gates between the city and the chapel square that anyone took any notice of them.

"And just where do you think you are going?" one of the guards barked, not recognising the armour Elyas wore.

The polished steel breastplate had the large yellow sun of the regular Castalial army. The three yellow lines on his shoulders represented his rank as captain. Their attention had been on Minerva who walked with more purpose and they assumed Elyas was just her private security.

"We are here to see the High Chancellor. It is urgent that we see him," Minerva said.

"Everyone is here to see the High Chancellor on urgent business. That is why the Grand Cathedral has been closed."

"That is not a good enough excuse private," Elyas spoke for the first time and for the first time the guard saw his armour. "We need to speak with the High Chancellor and we need to speak with him now."

"I'm sorry captain, but your rank is not high enough to countermand the High Chancellor's order."

"This is getting us nowhere," Minerva snapped.

One moment they were standing out the front arguing with the guard and the next they were standing in the main foyer of the Grand Cathedral. Elyas stumbled forward and nearly fell over. He had no idea what had happened and the sudden change in scenery made him nauseated.

The cool marble was a complete change from the heat outside. The sandstone seemed to reflect the hot, desert sun and made the courtyard even hotter. Elyas had almost forgotten how hot it could be in Castalia. If he had thought about it before they left Remidia he might have chosen a different outfit.

"What was that?" Elyas gasped when he recovered.

"That is another form of travelling, not really suited for long distances. Speaking of which, I don't know about you but I don't feel like trekking up the stairs."

"I thought the reason we arrived in the chapel of Ruby was so we would be less conspicuous. Suddenly arriving somewhere upstairs would ruin that." Although his words made sense he really didn't want to go through the experience again. He didn't think his stomach was up to it.

"Very well," Minerva said as she started to climb the stairs in front of her.

The large stairs from the foyer led straight up to the first level. The first two levels were kept for the public to visit with the sitting priests and other members of the clergy. Not surprisingly the hallways were empty. With the main doors shut there was no other way for people to enter the Grand Cathedral. There were side doors and other ways for the clergy to come and go, but people knew not to try those. Anyone who did would be sent straight to the dungeons by the guards on duty.

The soldiers patrolling the hallways didn't take any notice of Elyas and Minerva. They figured if they were walking through the Grand Cathedral then they were meant to be there.

They passed the guards and walked through the next two levels without really being noticed. The next three levels were the residences of the clergy, but it was the sixth level where the main chapel was that they hoped to find the High Chancellor. If he was anywhere above, in his private chambers, then it would be more difficult to gain entrance, at least without Minerva's magic.

When they reached the large wooden doors leading into the chapel they found it blocked by a dozen guards. Elyas had a bad feeling they were not going to be admitted.

"I am Minerva of the Council of Wizards and this is Captain Elyas, he is the commander of the Castalial army within the Alliance," Minerva started before the guards could speak. "We are here to speak with the High Chancellor. He knows who we are, although we are not expected. It is imperative that we speak with him immediately."

The guards looked at each other nervously. It had not at all been what they were expecting and no one knew what to say. Eventually one of the guards steadied himself and spoke.

"I am sorry, but no one is allowed into the chapel now that the High Chancellor had started mass and I'm not sure that you would want to. The chapel is at capacity, as it has been since he has starting taking mass again. The Grand Cathedral has been closed to keep the corridors clear. In fact, how did you get inside?"

"I'm a wizard, it takes more than locked doors to keep me out," Minerva snapped.

At the sound of a threat the soldiers placed hands on their hilts, but refrained from drawing their swords. They weren't quite sure what Minerva was insinuating and they weren't sure they could do anything to stop her. The last thing they wanted was to make a scene during mass and they hoped Minerva would do the same.

"We will wait for the end of mass," Elyas said, easing their nerves.

Castalia was still his home and he had a great respect for the High Chancellor. The last thing he wanted to do was interrupt his mass. He couldn't remember the last time he had attended. Tiberius' predecessor rarely preformed mass and had not done so in over a year. He wished they had arrived earlier, he would have loved to listen to the new High Chancellor speak.

"There is an antechamber over there." The guard pointed to a door about ten paces along the corridor. "You can wait there until the service is over."

Elyas was surprised to get such a response. He thought that Minerva had done something to keep them from being sent to the dungeons and he couldn't help but smile as they walked towards the antechamber.

The room was small, but comfortable. They waited in silence for almost two hours before there was a knock on the door. Elyas had wanted to speak with Minerva, but it was clear that she did not want to say anything. There was a concerned expression on her face and he could only assume she was thinking of her impending meeting.

"The mass is finished," the guard said. "The High Chancellor will see you in his private office."

Although the High Chancellor assured the guards that they were no threat there was still an escort of a dozen guards to lead them up the stairs. They walked through the High Chancellors personal chapel and then up another flight where they found Tiberius waiting for them. He was dressed in a yellow robe, which he wore when he was performing mass.

"Topaz is my favourite of the Seven God Kings," Tiberius started when they arrived, as if he needed to explain his garb. "There is something about his healing nature that really sings to me."

"I know what you mean," Minerva agreed, although just to be polite. She had chosen to study the works of Sapphire.

Minerva had been born in Castalia during a time of drought. Being half in the desert the city had struggled. She had always had an affinity with water, even though she didn't know what it was. She could feel the water flowing through the aquifers under the city, even when the levels were dangerously low. It was only a matter of time before her training as a wizard led her towards the teachings of Sapphire. It was that affinity that gave her the position on the council.

"So I am assuming that the final battle has yet to be fought," Tiberius continued. "I think you should bring me up to speed."

"We reached Remidel with just enough time to help the Alliance from an attack of orglin. They came at the rear whilst it was battling Remidian soldiers from the front," Elyas started.

"Remidian soldiers?" Tiberius gasped. "What was Faxon thinking? To meet the Alliance on an open battlefield is suicide, not to mention the loss of soldiers on both sides."

"It was not Faxon making the decisions. He was under the thrall of a Dark Knight," Elyas continued. "Luckily the wizards were able to defeat Dargoz before things got out of control. Faxon is now free and the Alliance is starting to move to Avalon."

"Then the final battle is nearly upon us. A few months, I would assume, to move the army to Avalon?" Tiberius didn't sound so sure of his words.

"The final battle is no more than a week away," Elyas said.

"That doesn't make any sense. Even if you flogged a dozen horses to death, per man, there is no chance of travelling from Remidia to Avalon in a week."

"Please," Minerva spoke for the first time. "Let me explain." She briefly explained the nature of the gateways and Alaric's arrival. "We have come here via one of those gateways because we need your help," Minerva continued.

"I'm not sure what I can do to help you further. I have already committed more soldiers than I should have. Ever since the army left I have been inundated by councillors insisting that I bring at least half the soldiers back."

"You are the High Chancellor. You rule Castalia. You can decide what to do with your soldiers," Minerva pushed.

Tiberius let out a wry laugh, but there was no humour in it. "I would have believed that at one time too, but that is simply not the case. I have only been the High Chancellor for a short period and the decisions I've made have already upset the people in positions of power in the city."

"This war will not wait for someone who wants to feel self-important," Minerva did her best to keep her tone level. "You are the High Chancellor and your edict rules Castalia. If you command it then it will happen."

Tiberius shook his head. Minerva was right, but he still wasn't sure he could empty the city of soldiers. He would still need some to keep Castalia in check. Even though the roads had been closed there were still many foreigners in the city. Although they had arrived with peaceful intentions after a few ales things inevitably changed.

"I will see what I can do," Tiberius resigned.

"That's not good enough. There is no time to see what you can do. We have to have the army in Avalon by the end of the week. It will take that long just to assemble them. We need to move now if we have any chance of success," Minerva pushed as she raised her voice.

Tiberius knew she was right, but he had no idea what he could do. He doubted another decree to empty the garrison would be taken seriously, at least not after days of baulking the command. Their excuse would be simply that they did not believe the order could be true and that would be a reasonable enough assumption. He wasn't sure he would believe it even after writing it himself.

"I think you are fighting a lost cause. I could not possibly give you all of my soldiers. The city watch is stretched enough as it is. I know there is no threat from the other kingdoms, but there are still matters within the city that need to be taken care of. I fear by the time my order is taken seriously the final battle will be over," Tiberius replied.

"All you have to do is write the order. I will see to the rest."

"Oh, that is all I have to do," Tiberius' mocked. "I have a kingdom I have to make sure survives through the final battle. Now I know that we need to win the final battle first, I'm not an idiot, but it will all be for nothing if Castalia is in ruins when it is all over."

"I think you are being a little melodramatic," Minerva said.

"The High Chancellor makes a very good point," Elyas wasn't going to let his ruler and spiritual leader be bullied by a wizard. If he was fighting for the survival of Castalia then he needed to make sure Castalia was still standing when they were done. "If what the High Chancellor says is true, and there is no reason to doubt his holiness, if we empty the city of soldiers then it would only be a matter of time before there was a coup. Many people of power in the city have their own personal security and if enough of them got together they could easily overrun the Grand Cathedral."

Minerva had to admit they were right. She wished Alaric had given her more information. All she had been told was to go to Castalia and secure all the soldiers for the final battle. Tiberius had already given the Alliance half their regular soldiers, more than any of the other kingdoms. She knew the other kingdoms would commit more soldiers, but they didn't have the threat of revolution.

"I know you have already given more than you should, but we still need more. I would not ask if the situation wasn't dire. I know you cannot commit all your soldiers, but we need as many as you can give."

Tiberius thought again. Her soft words were having an effect on him. He sighed once before speaking again. "I will give what I can, but that is something that you will need to work out with the Ministry of War and the Ministry of Defence. They were both put out with my original edict and they will be the ones who will tell you want we can give. I wish I could tell you more, but I am new to the role and there have been many jobs for me to get my head around. The most important are the services I have been performing. Word has gotten around the city of the final battle and people need spiritual guidance. That is how I will help."

Minerva couldn't help but scoff, but thankfully the other two didn't notice. There was much more he could do. Prayer was not going to win the final battle, but she was not about to say anything. The High Chancellor had pledged his support again and she could not ask for any more than that. There would still be an uphill battle convincing the councillors to commit more soldiers, but that was a battle she was going to win.

"Here," Tiberius handed Minerva a sheet of paper. He had scribbled down his orders and signed it at the bottom.

Minerva read the letter before handing it back to Tiberius to place the seal of the High Chancellor next to his signature. Without that the councillors would never agree to the order, and even with it there was no guarantee. With the final battle only a week away they could easily baulk until it was too late.

"Thank you High Chancellor. Hopefully the next time we meet the battle will be won," Minerva stood as she spoke. There was no time for any further pleasantries. The day was already starting to creep away from them. It was early afternoon and they would need to speak with the council before nightfall.

Tiberius stood and nodded. He understood their urgency and he needed to prepare himself for the evening mass. It was time to preach about the God King Sapphire, one he was not too familiar with. He would need to do some research before it was time to speak.

"How are we going to get there?" Elyas asked.

To anyone else it would have sounded like an odd question, by Minerva knew exactly what he was talking about. Travelling would be the quickest way, no doubt about it, but there were only so many times she could jump through the fabric of time without wearing herself out. Another option was a gateway, but she doubted she would be able to find a safe location. In the end there was only one choice.

"We will have to go by foot. The High Chancellor's letter gives us free movement throughout the city. Hopefully we can make it to the councillors before nightfall. I really don't want to waste another day."

They rushed through the Grand Cathedral, but no one seemed to take any notice of them. Elyas wondered if Minerva had created some kind of spell to keep them incognito, but there was no time to ask. Once they were out of the Grand Cathedral, however, it was a different story. The courtyard was already filling up with people waiting to gain entrance for the evening service. Elyas did a quick count and found there were fifty soldiers guarding the front door and even they looked nervous.

Minerva did her best to push her way through the crowd. Even though they were leaving and not arriving people didn't want to get out of their way. Elyas thought about drawing his sword, but he didn't want to risk inciting a riot. Instead they just did they best to work their way to the city gate.

When they reached the gate they found it shut. The guards had realised all too late that too many people were in the courtyard. Another crowd, just as big if not bigger, had formed outside. Elyas didn't need the guards to tell him that they were not getting out.

"Is there any other way we can leave the grounds?" Elyas asked one of the guards."

"I'm afraid not captain. I couldn't let my own mother in or out of the Grand Cathedral at the moment. I hope things calm down soon. If this continues for much longer then I don't think the gates will hold. I have petitioned the city watch for more guards, but they have refused so far."

"What do we do?" Elyas asked as they moved away from the gate.

"Something isn't right in the city and I don't think we can remain here for the rest of the day. I will have to transport us to the other side. From there I can only hope we can move around unimpeded," Minerva replied.

Elyas quickly closed his eyes in anticipation of the spell. The last time he was taken by surprise and the sudden change in environment almost made him vomit. He figured if his eyes were closed it would help. When he opened them again he found that they were still in the courtyard of the Grand Cathedral.

"Why are we still here?" he asked, surprised.

"I sense something is wrong in the city. I'm not sure what it is, but I just had a very bad feeling," there was uncertainty in her voice.

"Well, standing here isn't going to give us any answers," it was false bravado. If Minerva was concerned then something was seriously wrong.

"I guess you're right. We have to make it to the council chambers before they leave for the day. Just be wary that something isn't right. You will know more than I will."

Without warning Minerva transported them to the other side of the wall. Bile started to rise in Elyas' stomach and his head started to spin. It was all he could do to keep from vomiting. Minerva was already half way along the street before she realised he hadn't moved.

"What are you doing?" she called back.

"Nothing." Elyas swallowed hard before following after.

They only managed to round two corners before they ran into a crowd of people. There were all standing around a man who had propped himself up on an upturned crate. There was no room for them to pass and Elyas turned to walk away, but Minerva stayed where she was. There was something wrong with the situation and she wanted to know what it was.

"Don't be sucked in," Elyas said. "You will find many of these groups around the city. Someone always likes to believe they are the true High Chancellor or a prophet of some description. It won't be long before the city watch will break them up."

"Be quiet!" Minerva snapped.

Although they were a good distance from the preacher they could hear his words as if he was standing in front of them. It was a simple spell and didn't take much energy to create.

"The Seven Kingdoms is coming to an end," the preacher started his rhetoric again. "The final battle is nigh and what does the High Chancellor do? He locks himself inside the Grand Cathedral and doesn't let anyone in, that's what he does." Although it was a distortion of the truth the crowd all murmured their agreement. "The Dark Lord will soon destroy the army of the Alliance and the Seven Kingdoms will be covered in darkness." Minerva didn't like what she was hearing. The reference to 'The Dark Lord' was out of place. "We cannot allow this treachery to go unpunished. We deserve the respect of our holy leader and not to be shut out of the Grand Cathedral."

"I don't like this one little bit," Minerva said as she turned to Elyas. "I think we should make our way to see the councillors now."

Elyas led them through the streets. The council building was to the north of the city, close to the second wall. They ran into another two mobs and had to backtrack around them. Those who moved around the city, not taking part or listening to the preachers, looked worried. There was a feeling of dread in the air that didn't make Minerva feel any better. She quickened her step and forced Elyas to move quicker.

When they finally reached the council chambers there was a large sign over the door with a deep X carved into it, indicating that the building was closed. It was still an hour before sunset and Minerva thought they were still in time. It didn't make any sense to her.

"Have you ever known the building to be shut this early?" Minerva asked.

"I have never known it to be shut, even through the night there is generally someone here, even if it's just the cleaners. Something certainly isn't right," Elyas returned.

"What do we do now?" Minerva sounded dejected.

Elyas was surprised at the question. As far as he knew he was just there to assist the wizard and he had no idea how to answer her.

In the end Elyas finally made a decision. "There is a tavern near here, the Sleeping Lady, I have heard it is where the councillors go to drink when they finish work. There is a good chance that's where some of them will be. There are also some rooms at the back, so I guess that would be a good place for us to spend the night."

Minerva nodded and followed Elyas towards the tavern. She felt a little better knowing there was a chance of meeting the councillors that night. There was still a lot to get done and if they lost a day she wasn't sure if they would complete everything. She had been given the largest task to achieve. Not only did she have to move the Castalial army to the battlefield she would also have to move the dwarven army as well. She shook her head at the thought.

When they reached the tavern nothing could be heard coming from inside. Even at the early hour they still expected to hear something. When they entered the main bar they found it was completely empty. A lazy looking barmaid leaned against the bar and looked like she was about to fall asleep. She didn't even seem tp notice them.

"Excuse me!" Minerva's tone was terse.

"Hah!" she looked up slowly. "Ah, sorry what can I get you?"

"Some information would be nice," Minerva snapped.

"I will have an ale and maybe some cool wine for my friend," Elyas smiled.

He knew if they wanted information from the barmaid then they would need to order something and leave more coin than the cost. He placed a Castalial gold mark on the bar and her eyes opened wide.

"You keep the rest," Elyas whispered. Even though the tavern was empty, if the owner was within earshot then most of the change would end up in his pocket.

She smiled and nodded before rushing to get their drinks.

"I could have got the information from her without wasting our coin," Minerva said.

"I know, so could I, but I figured this was the nicer way to do it. If things don't pick up here then she might be out of a job soon and that mark will help her survive for a few months."

Minerva shook her head, but didn't say anything. The information better be worth the price.

"Why is the council building shut?" Elyas asked when the barmaid returned.

"It started happening a few days ago. The streets started filling with prophets shouting about the end of the Seven Kingdoms. It was around the same time that people stopped coming here. If this continues much longer I'll be out of job for sure."

Elyas thought for a moment before continuing. "What is the council doing? I would have thought with the final battle around the corner the war and defence councils would be busy making plans."

The barmaid looked confused then understood what Elyas was saying. "Surely you don't believe the prophets. They have always been shouting about the end of the Seven Kingdoms. Just because there are a few more it doesn't make it real."

With all that had happened Elyas was surprised that there were still people who believed the final battle was a myth and the Evil One was just a story to scare children. Elyas was about to explain her mistake, but Minerva grabbed his arm and shook her head. It was better for her to remain ignorant. Telling her the truth would do nothing but upset her.

"Of course," Elyas said as he faked a laugh. "But do you know what is happening at the council building. I believe this is where some of the members usually come after work?"

"I don't know this for sure, but the rumour is that a man came to visit about a week ago. He put it in their heads that the end was coming and they should shut their doors and pray. I wouldn't have believed it myself, but two days ago the council shut their doors and haven't been seen since."

They were not the words Elyas wanted to hear. If the council had shut their doors then there was little chance of securing more troops. He needed to speak with Minerva in private to work out their next move.

"I can smell something cooking out the back," Elyas changed the subject. "Will you bring a plate out when it is ready and another round of drinks?" Elyas dropped another coin on the table, this time only enough to pay for their food and drink.

They made their way into the dining room and Minerva kept quiet until they were seated. She kept her voice low so the barmaid couldn't hear what she said.

"So, what do you think of that?"

"It does seem odd. Something certainly isn't right," Elyas responded. He opened his mouth to elaborate when the sound of the main door opening silenced him.

Despite the heat, a man came in wearing a thick robe with the hood covering his head. A chill swept into the tavern with him and a sudden feeling of dread filled both Minerva and Elyas. They were transfixed on his every movement, the barmaid, on the other hand, didn't even seem to notice. The man slowly made his way into the dining room and sat at their table without saying a word.

"I have been expecting you," his voice was rasped. "I would have liked another day or two, but never mind. The Great Lord sent me to sow discord in the Kingdom of Castalia and that is what I have done."

"Which one of the Evil One's filth are you?" Minerva asked when she realised what was sitting before them.

"I am known as Fenaroz and soon enough I will be standing over your rotting corpse and it will be you who is the filth," Fenaroz kept his voice emotionless. If Minerva's slight had got to him then he didn't show it. "Now I didn't come here to trade insults."

"And what is it that you came here to do?" Minerva snapped.

"I came here to... warn you." He chose his words carefully. "The Great Lord will succeed and all who oppose him will die. It is not too late to gain his favour. If you remain here and lend no more support to the enemy then he will let you live. You can remain here for the rest of your miserable lives and he will do nothing to harm you. If you do not then before long this city will be nothing but rubble and all in it will be dead."

Minerva shook her head. If she did not know any better it would sound like a fair deal, but she knew that Nyrra and his Dark Knights could not be trusted. It was obviously the last efforts of a desperate man.

"There is no need to make your decision tonight," Fenaroz continued before Minerva had a chance to speak. "Think about it, sleep on it. I think you will realise there is no other option." He stood to leave. "Oh and I think you'll find it quite impossible to gather anymore soldiers, so think about that too."

The Dark Knight left before anyone could speak. The bar maid walked over with their food and didn't seem to notice that he had even been there. She placed the food in front of them and then left when it was obvious they wanted to be left alone.

"At least things are starting to make sense now. It seems the Dark Knight has been busy. I wish we had known not to kill Dargoz. If we had kept him prisoner then things would be so much easier," Minerva mused.

"I guess there is no way to know now," Elyas replied.

"What?" Minerva had not known she had spoken aloud. "Yes, I guess you're right. We need to focus on what we can fix. The Dark Knight has definitely made things hard for us, but that is only another challenge." Minerva thought for a moment as she picked at her food. "Maybe this is a good thing," her words surprised Elyas and he choked on his food.

"What do you mean 'a good thing'? There is no way this can be good for us. There is no telling where the councillors will be and we need to assemble at least half of them to get what we need," Elyas explained.

"With the letter from the High Chancellor maybe we can just go to the commanders and requisition their soldiers. If the councillors are not around to try and countermand the High Chancellor's order then we should be able to get the soldiers we need."

There was logic to Minerva's idea, but Elyas was still unsure. If he was the Dark Knight then he would plan for the High Chancellor stepping in, but there were also other issues.

"We need the counsellors to expedite matters. If we had a month or two then your plan would work, but we have a week and we have already lost a day," Elyas replied.

Minerva lowered her head. She knew he was right, but it certainly didn't make things any easier. For all they knew the council had disbanded and scattered themselves throughout the city. If that was the case then it was a lost cause and the final battle would be lost.

"I guess there is nothing for it then," Minerva conceded. "We need to find the councillors, wherever they might be. But now I think we should get some sleep. There is little more we can do tonight."

Elyas suddenly realised how tired he was. It was still early, but it seemed like such a long time since he had managed to get a good night sleep. He was certainly looking forward to sleeping in a bed again.

When they had finished eating Elyas ordered them two rooms for the night. Although Elyas was used to sleeping in the same room or barracks as other people it was obvious that Minerva wanted to sleep alone. It didn't make any difference to him, they had been given more than enough coin to afford it.

Although it was still early, Elyas fell asleep as soon as his head hit the pillow and he didn't stir until the sun shone through the window in the morning. It took a moment for him to wake fully, his head felt heavy and he thought he may have been drugged the night before. He looked around his room, but nothing was missing. He shook his head slowly, dismissing the idea.

When he opened the door he found Minerva waiting for him outside. It looked as though she was about to knock. It seemed to be too much of a coincidence, but Elyas pushed it aside. There were more important matters to deal with.

"Good morning Elyas, I trust you slept well," she greeted him with a smile.

"I did, thank you." His suspicions continued, but he did feel refreshed. Even if he had been drugged there were no adverse affects. "Do you think we have time for breakfast?" he realised how hungry he was, "or should we start the search."

"I think we have time to eat," there was something strange to her voice, but he was so hungry he decided to let it pass.

When they had finished eating, they both stood from the table. Just like the night before, the dining room was completely empty and the same barmaid served them breakfast. She looked like she wanted some conversation, but it was obvious the two guests didn't want to speak. Elyas was too hungry for anything except eating. When he was done he noticed for the first time that Minerva seemed very pleased with herself.

"Are you going to tell me?" Elyas asked as they walked out.

"What?" she sounded defensive and held her hand in front of her chest.

"You look like you have done something and you are very pleased with yourself."

"Well, I guess I am. When you went to sleep last night I decided to do a little investigating. I managed to find one of the councillors and with a little... persuasion he agreed to meet with us this morning in his office. Hopefully there will be enough councillors for us to get the result we want."

Elyas shook his head. He knew there was more to the story, but he didn't have the heart to ask. All that really mattered was the fact that she had located them and they were willing to discuss matters. Things looked a lot brighter than they had the day before.

When they reached the council building the sign out the front still showed that it was closed, but that was how Minerva had wanted it. If the sign wasn't up then there was no telling how many people would try and see the councillors and she couldn't risk any delay.

The War Council was on the second floor, past the Defence Council. It seemed as though Minerva had only wanted members of the War Council in their meeting as the first floor was completely empty. Elyas thought it was odd. If they were going to get the soldiers they needed then the Defence Council would have to get involved. He hoped that Minerva knew what she was doing.

Five councilmen waited for them in the foyer on the second floor. None of them looked happy. The councillor who had gathered the others had a confused expression on his face. It was almost like he didn't know what was happening.

"Why have you gathered us here?" one of them barked.

"We have closed the building for a reason and don't need to be dragged in here by some witch," another added.

The tone and the words irritated Minerva and she wasn't going to allow such disrespect. "You will watch your tone when you speak with me." She raised her arms and the room suddenly darkened. "I am Minerva of the Council of Wizards and you will treat me as such. It would not be too hard for me to have you replaced on the council with someone more respectful."

It was an idle threat, but the councillors didn't know that. Her anger was real and that was enough to bring them into line.

"Sorry, my lady. I am Councillor Drusus, what is it that we can do for you?"

"Be quiet Drusus," a dark haired councillor snapped. "I am Egnatius and we have been warned that you would be coming. We were told that we should not speak with you, but it seems as though you were able to convince Drusus otherwise. If we had known it was you we were meeting then we would not have come."

"What are you talking about?" Elyas spoke for the first time. "Who have you been speaking to and why would you refuse to see us."

Their reaction showed they had only just realised he was there. Although he was not dressed in his armour that day it was clear he was a resident of Castalia. It took a moment before they recognised exactly who he was.

"What are you doing here captain? You are supposed to be leading the Castalial army in the Alliance," Egnatius snapped.

"I am here on the behest of the Alliance." Elyas didn't miss a beat. "But I will let Minerva explain it to you. Now I am sure there are better places to discuss such important matters."

"Let's move into the boardroom," Drusus suggested.

They walked to the boardroom in silence. Everyone could feel the tension and it didn't seem the change in environment would doing anything to ease it.

"So what is it you came here to ask us?" Egnatius snapped.

"I think you should answer our questions first," Elyas' voice was firm. If they were going to succeed then they would need the upper hand. "Why is it that you feel you can close the council. We are on the verge of war. This is the time that the War Council and Defence Council should be at its busiest."

"What makes you think you can come in here and bark questions at us, captain. We are the ones who..."

"This!" Minerva yelled as she slammed the High Chancellor's order on the table.

When it was clear Minerva was not going elaborate, Egnatius picked up the sheaf and read it. When he was done he passed the paper across for the other councillors to read.

"So, it seems as though you have friends in high places. Very well, we will answer your question first, but then you will answer mine." Egnatius had lost none of his spite. "We have been advised that the end is nigh. There is little we can do here now. That is why we decided to shut the building. If the world is going to end then we are going spend time with our loved ones. If Drusus wasn't so insistent then we would not have come today."

"I am afraid to say that you have been duped by one of the Evil One's Dark Knights." The mention of the Dark Knight sent shivers down their spines. "It is true that the final battle is nigh, but it's not even close to being lost. That is the reason we have been sent here. We need more troops. As you can see we have the blessing of the High Chancellor and if we had more time then we would simply gather the soldiers ourselves."

"What makes you think we believe your story? The man who you 'claim' is a Dark Knight was quite believable. He knew things. Some of those things had already been sent via messenger. If you listen to the many prophets around the city they are confirming the rest."

"Those prophets are just puppets, either willing or unbeknownst of the Evil One. They have been sent to cause dissent amongst the people and it seems as though they are doing a good job."

"Either way, we have already given more troops than we could afford. The new High Chancellor does not know what it means to run a kingdom, otherwise he would not have committed so many." Egnatius was not going to be swayed so easily, but the other four looked ready to turn.

"The darkness can be very persuasive when you are standing on the precipice, but the last thing you want to do is jump off. There are tough days ahead of us, but surrender is not an option," Minerva urged.

"Be that as it may we have made our decision. I don't know what you want us to do." Egnatius remained firm.

"Be quiet Egnatius," Drusus boomed. "You are under arrest for being a traitor." He stood as he made the accusation.

"What are you talking about? I am no traitor. This is an outrage," Egnatius spluttered.

"We always suspected you were an agent of evil," the councillor named Ovidius spoke for the first time.His voice was firm and Minerva noticed that he had a strong build. There was little doubt that he had spent time in the field and was not just a bureaucrat. "We couldn't move when the council voted to leave, but now there can be no doubt. For now you will spend the night in the dungeons and tomorrow you will face judgement."

Minerva and Elyas watched on, not really sure what was happening. The entire situation had suddenly changed and all they could do was sit and watch.

"I will not go quietly," Egnatius kicked his chair back as he stood and drew his rapier.

No one had noticed that Egnatius was the only one who had brought a weapon to their meeting; even Elyas had decided to go unarmed. Egnatius backed away from the table to give himself a chance to strike. When he realised no one else was armed he decided to go on the offensive.

Just as he was about to bring his sword down on Drusus, he froze mid strike. The rapier stopped inches from Drusus' face. The man raised an arm to try and defend himself and it took him a few seconds to realise he was still alive.

"What happened?" he asked, his voice shaken.

"I told you, I am a wizard. One armed man is no match for me, even one who has sworn himself to the Evil One," Minerva said.

Slowly Egnatius' fingers released their grip on the sword, one by one, until it dropped to the floor. Drusus quickly picked it up. He wasn't sure what was about to happen, but he wanted to be ready to attack.

"I think you should take him down to the dungeons now and then we can finish our meeting."

Egnatius stumbled forward and nearly skewered himself on the rapier. The movement was so sudden that Drusus didn't know what to do. When he settled himself he held the blade firmly towards the traitor.

"Are you doing to come quietly?" he asked.

"I don't think so," Egnatius said as he suddenly lunged forward onto the blade.

The movement caught everyone by surprise and for a moment everyone in the room froze. When Drusus composed himself he pulled the blade from Egnatius' chest. Blood spurted from the wound and he collapsed to the ground.

"I guess he didn't want to be questioned," Minerva said. "Now we should get down to business."

"We have to get rid of the body. We can't just leave him here," Drusus said.

"There will be time for that later. We have more important matters to take care of first. Is there somewhere else we can have this meeting?" Minerva asked.

"We can use my office," Ovidius said.

The office was much smaller than the boardroom, but it accommodated the six of them nicely. The other two councillors introduced themselves as Aelius and Brutus. Aelius was the youngest, he had been a member for only a year and looked to be in his early thirties. Brutus looked as though he had seen action in the field. There were two long scars running down each cheek.

"So what is it you want from us?" Drusus asked.

There were so many questions that Minerva wanted to ask. They had walked into something they had not been expecting, but there was no time. They had caught an agent of evil, unbeknownst to them, and there had to be more to it. She quickly put the thought out of her mind and got down to business.

"We need more soldiers for the battle in Avalon," she blurted out.

"But..." Aelius called out, but settled himself before he continued. "We have already given so many soldiers to the Alliance. We cannot offer you anymore. The streets are filled with tension and it is all we can do to keep the people from rioting. The gates to the Grand Cathedral are closing earlier and earlier and yet the people remain. They do not want to be sent away. There are more and more fights breaking out every hour. There is nothing more we can do to help."

"That is not true," Elyas said. "There are enough soldiers in the city watch to take care of the city. It is the Dark Knight who has caused this chaos. Now that he has gone you should be able to get things under control."

"I just don't know," Drusus added.

"Know this," Minerva almost hissed her response. "If you don't give us more troops then it won't matter what happens back here. When the Evil One overruns us how long do you think it will take for him to reach Castalia? Whatever the Dark Knight has promised you is surely a lie."

There was silence around the room as the councillors thought on her words. They knew she was right, but they also knew that they could not give anymore soldiers. They were between a rock and a hard place.

"I don't know what you want us to do. Is seems as though we are damned if we do and damned if we don't," Brutus added.

"No Brutus, you will only be damned if you don't. Yes, it will be difficult for a week or two to control the city, but the only other option doesn't bear thinking about," Elyas returned.

The conversation went back and forth in a similar manner for the next hour. Each time Elyas and Minerva thought they were coming around, one of the councillors would come up with a better excuse to keep the soldiers in the city.

"We can't just keep sitting here talking," Minerva finally changed the subject.

"What do you propose?" Drusus didn't sound convinced.

"This." Minerva pulled the paper from her pocket and slammed it down on the table. "The High Chancellor has instructed you all to listen to us and support us in whatever way you can."

"That's where we differ in opinion. We will certainly support you in whatever way we can, but it is up to us in which way we help," Aelius said, rather pleased with himself.

"Well that can be taken two ways, but we are not here to debate the wording of the High Chancellor's commands. We all know what he means and why he gave us this letter. If you refuse to help us then we will be forced to go back and see him. What do you think he will say?" Elyas threatened.

"You won't get back inside the Grand Cathedral. I doubt even we could get inside at the moment," Brutus said.

Minerva simply raised an eyebrow and that was all that they needed to understand what she meant.

"You have us in a corner now don't you?" Drusus asked.

"Not at all. We are on the same side and working towards the same goal. I was born in Castalia and would hate to see such a magnificent city fall, but there is only one choice to make here. You need to keep the bare minimum of soldiers or even create a militia group to keep the citizens in check," Minerva said.

"If you round up all the prophets that should also help," Elyas added.

"You know as well as I do that if we imprison the prophets that would only make things worse," Brutus replied.

"Not if you announce martial law until the final battle is over. That should keep everyone in check and it allows greater flexibility in giving powers to the militia," Elyas pushed.

"They are right," Drusus conceded. "We have no choice."

"So what does that mean?" Elyas said.

"You will have your soldiers," Brutus knew Drusus was right. "As many as we can get."

"You have four days. The soldiers need to be assembled outside the Southern Gate of the outer city. From there I will create a gateway to Avalon and we shall meet the Evil One's army head on," Minerva stood, it was clear that she wanted to leave. They had achieved their result and staying could only make things worse.

"What do we do now?" Elyas asked as they walked back to the inn.

"I think we need to get something to eat. I don't know about you but I am hungry," Minerva replied.

"That's not what I mean."

"After lunch we shall go and check on Hulkan. Hopefully by now he has gathered together the dwarves and we can start to move them across to Avalon."

Chapter 13: The Dwarves

Hulkan held himself up against the front of the guild house when Minerva and Elyas disappeared back through the gateway. Taking a deep breath he heaved up his stomach. It wasn't a common sight to see a dwarf vomiting outside the guild, but it wasn't so rare that he felt self-conscious about it. He knew he was going to regret the barrel of rum he had found the night before, but that had not stopped him sharing it with his fellow dwarves. It had been a long time since he had been able to have his fill of alcohol and he certainly wasn't going to let it slip.

Wiping his mouth on his sleeve he stood up straight. Suddenly he felt much better. He wasn't looking forward to going inside and thought he might try and empty his stomach again just to stall the inevitable, but he knew he didn't have time to waste. He would only have a day or two at best to convince the rest of the council that all the able dwarves would be needed on the battlefield. He wished he had longer, but Minerva would also have to transport the Castalial army and she could not do both at the same time.

Taking a deep breath Hulkan readied himself for what was before him. He knew his sudden arrival would come as a shock and he was hoping he could use that to his advantage. He needed the upper hand from the start to achieve his goal.

He was met inside by a young pair of dwarves casually holding spears. It was obvious they were not expecting any trouble. In fact it looked as though they were not expecting anyone at all. They jumped to attention when Hulkan entered.

"What? Who? No one is supposed to be here today," one of the dwarves stammered.

"Be off with you before we call for reinforcements," the other one added, gripping his spear.

"Get out of my way the both of you," Hulkan moved forward, but stopped before he was stabbed. "Do you know who I am?"

The two dwarves looked at each other, but it was clear they didn't. If they had then they would not dare point their weapons at him. Although he was no longer their leader he still deserved their respect. He would have to teach them a lesson, but it would have to wait.

"The Guild is in session and they do not wish to be disturbed. Be on your way or you will spend some time in the dungeons," one of the guards threatened.

There were three small cells underneath the guild building. Hardly what one would call a dungeon, but it made their point.

"I think it will be you who will be spending time in the cells. Now, I don't have time to waste.," Hulkan tapped the hilt of his axe, more out of frustration than any real threat.

"Take your hand off your axe," the first guard sounded nervous and strengthened his grip on his spear. Hulkan knew he could beat both the guards, but the risk of killing one of them was too great.

"I am Hulkan. Now I think you should lower your spears before I do something about them," he barked.

The two guards looked at each other. It was clear that neither of them knew what to do.

"I don't know you, I will go and ask the other members of the guild hall if they do," one guard said, keeping his spear level.

"Do that and you will spend time in the cells. Let me by and nothing will happen. If I am not who I say I am then the guild members will let you know."

His words made the guards think, but they were not going to let him pass so easily.

"Very well, but leave your axe here."

Hulkan knew that it was a fair trade off and that the guard wouldn't let him in with it. It was a simple solution and he didn't need his weapon in the guild meeting, or at least he hoped he wouldn't.

"Very well," Hulkan said as he unlashed his axe and handed it over.

If they had bothered to check him further they would have found two daggers hidden in his leather jerkin, but they figured the axe was a good enough sign of faith. When they had it, they both stepped aside to let him though.

Hulkan kept his head high and eyes forward as he passed the two guards. He needed to look the part if he was going to convince them of the truth.

Without knocking, Hulkan pushed the door open to the guild chambers.

"What is the meaning of this?" an old dwarf barked before he saw who it was. "Hulkan, I am sorry, what, I mean..."

"Be calm Agmundr it is just me. I have known you since I was a child and you were one of most trusted advisors when I was in command."

"You charge in here like you are our leader, but that vote went to me," Brac didn't sound happy.

"And you would not be in that position if it wasn't for me," Hulkan snapped.

"Enough the both of you," Ilar, Hulkan's father and chairman of the council, said. "You have only just left, what brings you back here?"

"I have come here because the last battle is looming and we need to do our part," Hulkan started as he took a seat.

"You know we have given all we can. That was the council's decision when I was made leader," Brac retorted.

"That was then and things have changed," Hulkan barked. "We need every dwarf that can hold an axe, anything less will mean the death of us all."

"You can't be serious?" Stirg, the youngest member asked. He was so young that his dark brown beard had not yet fully grown. It was strange for someone so young to be a guildmaster, but his father had died and as his son it was his right to take the position.

"I can and I am. The final battle with the Evil One is less than a week away and the dwarves will not be left behind. The elves have committed themselves entirely. Would you have it said that the dwarves of the Western Dwarf Guild were too afraid to join the fray?" Hulkan let his words settle over the guild. "This is the time for the dwarves to prove that we are the strongest of the three races."

"That is a fine speech, but..." Stirg started, but was cut off by Brac.

"I am the leader of the guild now and I have already made my decision. You were given command of the dwarves in Remidel and we continue our support to the Alliance, but that is it."

"I know what you said and I know what the guild decided, but that is not enough," Hulkan pushed.

"But you said the battle will start in less than a week? How are we to get our dwarves to Avalon in that time? It's impossible," Agmundr added.

"Don't you worry about that," Hulkan replied. "Transportation is all taken care of. All we need to do is assemble outside the guild hall in two days time."

"Two days!" Agmundr asked. "That is not enough time to."

"Be quiet Agmundr," Brac snapped. "Unless you are going to say something positive, stay out of things. I am the leader of the guild and I will decide what is best for us."

"Then maybe we made the decision too quickly," Stirg commented.

There were murmurs around the table, but no one added their voice to his words. Hulkan wanted to speak, but he didn't think it would do anything to help.

"It is too late, the decision has been made and it can't be changed. Now I think this meeting is..."

"That is not true," Ilar boomed. "In times of extreme duress or the inability of the leader to rule, it is possible for the council to take over for a time. When the danger or incapacitation is over a new decision is made on who will be the new leader."

"Are you threatening us?" Brac boomed, although the comment was directed at him personally.

"He is not threatening anyone, he is merely stating what we already know," Agmundr agreed.

"Hulkan is right. The final battle is nigh and we need to be there. If you will not lead us, then vote for Hulkan to," Ilar said.

"You are only saying this because he is your son," Brac accused.

"How dare you say such a thing to me?" Ilar slammed his fists on the table as he pushed himself to his feet. "I have been on this council longer than anyone in this room and not once have I ever let my personal life cloud my judgement."

"But you are no longer on the council. Your opinion and you vote means nothing." Brac knew he had support on the council and he wasn't going to be dissuaded.

"Ilar is right, it is time for us to vote," Stirg added.

"Then call the rest of the council if you must, but I know we will get the same result." A smug expression crossed Brac's face.

"There is no time for that. We will vote now," Ilar stated.

"Impossible," Brac boomed. "We cannot vote on the leader of the guild without all the council members present. I will not hear of such rubbish happening under my rule.'"

"Under normal conditions I would agree with you Brac, with these are extenuating circumstances and it is permitted in the guild rules to hold a 'flash' vote if the need requires it, and I believe it does," Ilar explained. "As chairman of the guild I call upon you all to vote now."

The vote went quickly and Hulkan won almost unanimously.

"Very well. There is obviously nothing I can say to convince you otherwise," Brac stood when the decision had been made, "but I don't have to take part in it."

"That is where you are wrong. You will be joining us on the battlefield like everyone else," Hulkan commanded.

Brac looked as though he was going to say something, but decided against it. Instead he got up and stormed out of the guild hall.

"Don't worry about him," Stirg said. "I'm sure he'll calm down when he's had a chance to think." Hulkan wasn't so sure, but there was no chance to discuss it further.

"Well I think our business is done here," Ilar said. "Let's go and tell the dwarves that we have a war to prepare for."

With the meeting over they all left the guild hall. Hulkan collected his axe from the relieved guards on the way out. As much as his time was short, Hulkan was glad to be home. When they were outside he took a deep breath of the warm desert air.

"What will you do know?" Ilar asked as they walked away.

"I guess I should go and see mother. I didn't get a chance last time I was here and I may never return."

"Your mother is in the city today. She will be home tonight. You should come around for dinner. After your return we had a house prepared for you. We figured even though you were no longer our leader you did deserve somewhere to live. If we had known you were going to be leader again it would have been a lot nicer."

"That's okay, I won't be staying long. As long as there is a bed I'll be fine."

Hulkan could think of nothing better than a hot bath and a good sleep. Since he had achieved what he wanted, his hangover was starting to catch up with him. He either needed sleep or to start drinking again. He knew what he wanted, but he didn't think it was appropriate.

"Have someone run a bath for me." He ordered his father like a servant, but it was to be expected in his position. "I need some time to think."

Ilar knew his son had been drinking the night before, but didn't say anything about it. With the final battle looming he didn't want to waste time with recriminations. It wasn't all that out of place for a dwarf to be suffering the effects of overindulgence.

Hulkan spent the rest of the day doing his best to relax. After a soak in a hot bath and good sleep he found himself at a loose end. It was still an hour before nightfall and he didn't think his mother would be home so he decided to go for a walk.

The dwarven village was on the southern side of Castalia. It was still within the walls of the city, but the dwarves treated it like their own land. If anyone who wasn't a dwarf wanted to enter then they would need permission, generally from one of the guildmasters.

There was a cool a breeze blowing through the air. Hulkan knew it was an omen, he just didn't know if it was good or bad. When the sun went down Castalia could get very cold, but there was rarely a cool breeze during the day.

Hulkan shrugged off the feeling as he walked through the town. There were few dwarves on the street, as he expected. Those who were not in the army would be working the mines, or inside preparing the evening meals.

As he walked he had no idea where he was going, he was just happy to be home. He wished that it was all over and he was home for good, but the hardest part of his mission was yet to come. He knew there was a good chance that it would be the last time he walked through the streets of Castalia, but the thought didn't make him sad. If anything it made him more determined to survive.

Before he knew what he was doing he arrived at the house he had grown up in. He looked at the wooden door and thought about knocking. It had been so long since he had seen his mother he didn't know what he was going to say. As much as Ilar had avoided the conversation, they would both want to know what happened to Gilgi. He wasn't sure what he was going to tell them. He wasn't sure how much he really knew.

Taking a deep breath he knocked on the door and waited for someone to answer.

An elderly looking female dwarf with long blonde hair opened the door. Hulkan stayed where he was and watched the surprised reaction on her face. It was obvious that Ilar had not told her that her first born had returned home.

"Hulkan?" her voice was choked and tears started to well in her eyes. "What...? What are you doing here?"

"I am only here for a day or two," Hulkan replied, still standing out the front. He didn't want to move before his mother did.

"Come here!" she rushed towards him. Tears streamed down her face as she gripped him in a fierce embrace.

Hulkan placed his arms around his mother and let his head rest against her shoulder. He thought about letting a tear out himself, but he didn't think that was appropriate.

"When you father said there was going to be a guest for dinner I didn't for a moment think it would be you," she said when she finally let go. "Come inside."

Hulkan followed her inside as she wiped her tears away with the sleeve of her shirt.

"Gulla, is that Hulkan?" Ilar called from inside.

"Yes, dear," she called back.

"Bring him into the sitting room."

Ilar was sitting in their small sitting room. There were four armchairs, each with their own side table and a coffee table in the middle.

"I thought you might like a drink before dinner," Ilar started as his son sat down. He filled a mug before he spoke again. "Or are you still struggling from last night?" he said as he raised his left eyebrow.

"Give me that," Hulkan's voice was gruff as he snatched up the mug and took a long draught. "It'll be a cold day in Nostiria when I refuse a drink."

His words brought boisterous laughter from all three. Dwarves were renowned for their ability to drink. Given a chance, and with nothing better to do, they could go on for days.

"And where is my other son?" Gulla said when the laughter subsided.

Hulkan looked at his father. He had no idea what he had told her about Gilgi and he didn't give him any sign.

"I'm afraid that Gilgi is dead." Hulkan didn't know how he could break the news. In the end he figured there was no way to dance around the subject.

"Did you kill him?" Gulla remained strangely calm.

"No," Hulkan didn't sound offended. He knew that if he had remained in Castalia that Gilgi would have eventually killed him. It was common when someone created a coup that the old leader would end up dead. "He was killed by a Dark Knight. The Dark Knight then took his facade and had been using his body to control the army." Hulkan went on to briefly explain what had happened in Remidel. Both his parents listened intently, too stunned to ask any questions.

"Does the Evil One have no morals?" Ilar boomed when Hulkan was done. "What right does he had to kill my son and usurp his body."

"Be calm Ilar, our son is dead and there is nothing we can do about. Yelling and screaming is going to achieve nothing."

"At least we know it wasn't Gilgi who betrayed us by taking our army away from the Alliance. Despite all that he did to me he was still my brother," Hulkan let the thought drift away.

Gulla quickly changed the subject. She knew that she only had a short time with her one remaining son and she didn't want to spend that time in mourning. They spent the rest of the evening drinking, eating and talking about better times. Hulkan enjoyed himself and for a moment forgot about the battle quickly approaching.

He left late in the night, or possibly very early in the morning, and stumbled his way back to his home. It would be the last time he got to drink before the final battle and he certainly was not going to miss out. In the morning he would assist with gathering the dwarves and then the following day they would step through the gateway to Avalon. He would need all his senses if he was going to lead his dwarves to victory.

***

The dwarves were all assembled and ready to march by mid-morning. Hulkan stood at the front of the line with the rest of the council, his father by his side. Only Ilar and Stirg were remaining behind and administer those who were either too young or too old to wield an axe.

Hulkan looked up towards the cloudless sky. The sun was already halfway to its pinnacle. Minerva was late and Hulkan didn't think that was a good sign. Time was getting away from them and they needed to get to Avalon.

Just when Hulkan was about to call the dwarves to return to their homes, the air in front of him started to shimmer. Minerva appeared looking tired, another sign that Hulkan didn't like.

"Are you alright?" Hulkan asked. "You're late and it looks like you haven't slept for a few days."

"It's a long story, but I'll keep it short. We found an agent of the Evil One in the War Council. We managed to root him out before he could do any more damage, but that was just the start. Whenever it seemed we were getting somewhere another agent reared its head. Hopefully we have them under control now," Minerva's voice sounded strained. "But enough of that. We need to get you on the other side of the Seven Kingdoms."

Without waiting for Hulkan to respond she opened a gateway five paces from where they stood. If he had not warned the dwarves of what was coming then they would just have to deal with it. The dwarves at the front of the line shrunk away from the wall of coloured light. Nothing could have prepared them for the gateway.

Slowly, as the lights coalesced, they could see a vision of Avalon on the other side. At the edge of the gateway they could see the rest of the dwarven army and the reality of what they were about to do set in.

"Move out!" Hulkan boomed before anyone had a chance to turn and run.

The front line started moving without question. Their leader had spoken and they acted at once. If he had waited a moment longer then those at the back would have rethought their decision. Death waited for them on the other side and there was nothing they could do to prolong it.

Hulkan stood firm as he watched his fellow dwarves march towards their doom. Whenever he made eye contact he nodded his head in approval. It was all he could do to stop himself from ordering them back home. Even though every young dwarf, both male and female, were given an axe when they came of age, he knew very few had ever received any training. Those who had would have forgotten most of what they had learned. If any came close to combat then they would surely die. Even knowing this Hulkan had to send them to their deaths.

When the last dwarf passed through, Hulkan turned to Minerva. "I will see you on the battlefield." He didn't wait for a response before stepping through the gateway himself. As soon as he was in Avalon Minerva closed the gateway.

***

Dorn and Gwydion stepped through the gateway and onto the snowy ground at the foot of the Cloumid Mountains. Dorn had tried to insist that it would be quicker if they opened the gateway in the city square inside the mountain, but Gwydion had told him it was impossible. He had tried, but the feeling of dread had almost overwhelmed him. There was no way he could open a gateway inside the mountain.

"Where is the entrance to the dwarven city?" Gwydion asked as he looked up and down the mountain range. Dorn had explained the location to him and he was sure he opened the gateway exactly where he was supposed to, but there was no sign of any entrance.

Dorn looked at the mountain in front of them and shook his head. The entrance was there somewhere; he knew that to be true, despite being away from his home for so many years. The problem was the snow underfoot. There was no telling how deep it went, but he was sure it was covering the entrance. That in itself was a disturbing sign. In the snow season there was always someone stationed to keep the snow from covering it up.

"It's here somewhere. It's just buried under who knows how much snow," Dorn explained.

"So what do you suggest?" Gwydion didn't sound happy.

"Couldn't you melt the snow so we can find the entrance?" Dorn asked.

"That's an interesting thought and quite possible if we knew where the entrance was, but I'm not going to waste my energy melting snow up and down the Cloumid Mountain range. When this is all over I still need to have the strength to fight in the final battle. If the Dark Knights have indeed returned then there is no telling what might happen," Gwydion explained.

Dorn shook his head. He looked at the mountain range, but there was nothing he recognised.

"Then I guess we should start digging," Dorn said as he marched towards the foot of the mountain.

"Are you sure there is nothing that can narrow down the location?" Gwydion asked, the thought of digging randomly through the snow didn't excite him.

Dorn took another look at the mountains. Everything looked the same, there were no obvious landmarks. All they could do was start digging.

"There is nothing I recognise," Dorn said.

Taking a deep breath Dorn dropped to his knees. If they were going to have to dig out half the mountainside then they would have to start somewhere. Taking two big handfuls he dug into the snow and threw it out behind him.

"Careful!" Gwydion barked.

"Sorry!" Dorn didn't realise the wizard was walking up behind him. A cheeky grin crossed his face and he could only imagine what he would have looked like being struck with snow.

Before Gwydion had a chance to say anything there was some movement a couple of paces to their left. At first the snow started to pulsate, but then a hand shot up. Dorn jumped to his feet and placed a hand on the hilt of his axe. There was no telling who or what was coming up.

Slowly the snow started getting sucked down to create a small hole. It wasn't until a snow covered head popped out before Dorn relaxed. The dwarf looked at the two and a big smile crossed his face. If it wasn't for the snow, Dorn would have recognised him as his life-long friend, Arnór.

"You look like you could use a mug of ale in front of a hot fire," he said jovially as he shook the snow from his beard and hair.

Dorn suddenly realised that snow and the general cold was starting to get to him and he had started to shiver. He pushed the feeling aside as he realised who was standing before them.

"Arnór? What are you doing here?"

"I live here, but more to the point, what are *you* doing here?"

"There will be time for that later, but for now I think we should go inside," Dorn said as he looked to the sky. The clouds were dark and it looked as though they would break any minute.

Arnór thought for a moment. There was a strange expression on his face that Dorn didn't think was a good sign. It was only there for a moment before it changed back to being friendly.

"Come inside and I'll explain everything."

Arnór disappeared back into the hole and entered the mountain. Dorn didn't bother looking at Gwydion before following.

The entrance to the mountain was a large double door made from thick mahogany with iron strapping. There was nothing ornate about the design. It was obvious it had been built solely to keep out enemies. For a dwarven door it was quite large, although the snow had only been dug out enough for Arnór to climb out. The hole between the bottom of the snow and the top of the door was only just large enough for Gwydion to crawl through. He thought about casting a spell to remove more of the snow, but in the end he decided not to waste his energy. If he looked like an idiot for a moment then that was a sacrifice he would have to make.

Sliding down on his backside Gwydion made his way into the mountain where the other two were waiting for him. The foyer was large enough to fit two wagons side-by-side and another dozen or so men or dwarves. The mountain was the major trading point between the dwarfs, Remidia, Castalia and Entero. Mostly Remidian traders came through since that side of the mountain was in their kingdom. The other two kingdoms would be taxed at the borders, but sometimes it was worth the merchants' long journey.

The entrance was designed to be small so neither side would have the space to fight. The dwarves didn't want to risk anyone trying to steal the valuable gemstones and ores they were trading. It was also dimly lit by two torches hanging from sconces on the wall as there were no traders due anytime soon.

When Gwydion arrived Arnór picked up one of the torches and passed the other one to Dorn. There were other unlit torches around the foyer, but Gwydion didn't bother taking one. There would be enough light from the two torches for them all to see and if not he could simply create a small ball of light for himself.

They walked through the smooth cut walls of the mountain corridor leading towards the city. The floor sloped gently upwards with iron tracks running up the centre to guide the wagons. For the first fifteen minutes there was no deviation to their path, but then it started to open up. The main corridor tripled in width and doubled in height. It was the start of the main city tunnel and was designed to be more formal than the one they had been in. There were two tunnels, one to the left and one to the right. Just like the one they were in they were much higher and wider. They were the two major conduits from the mines to the Remidian side of the border. Dorn was surprised that he didn't see anyone around. Although there was no one at the bottom to trade with there were many storerooms off the side. He would have thought there would be someone moving either gems or ore into one of them.

"Something doesn't feel right?" Dorn said as they continued. "I think you should tell me what's happening."

Arnór ignored him and kept moving, making Dorn even more suspicious. They only took another couple of paces before Dorn stopped and signalled for Gwydion to do the same.

"Stop!" Dorn kept his voice as level as he could. He didn't want his voice resonating through the tunnels. "Something isn't right here and I want to know what it is."

"When we reach the crossroads we'll take the path to the lower city. There is a small house on the outskirts where we can talk and you can dry off," Arnór spoke between clenched teeth.

There was enough tone in his voice for Dorn to realise that it was not the time to ask questions. He could only hope that he could trust his old friend and Arnór wasn't leading them into a trap. As much as it was odd that they were going into the lower city, he had to trust he was leading them in the right direction.

The change in direction in the main corridor was called the 'crossroads,' even though there were only two paths, one lead upwards and one down. The lower city was reserved for the dwarves of lesser standing than those who occupied the upper. It was rougher and dirtier than its higher counterpart and it mainly housed the mining dwarves and their families. It also contained those too ill, feeble or poor to look after themselves. There were many taverns which were filled most nights, but that also led to brawling in the streets. At certain times of the day the lower city could be quite dangerous.

It wasn't long before the corridor ended and they entered the lower city. Dorn felt a rush of relief, it was good to be home, but it was also a concern that Arnór had brought them there. It seemed as though their first stop would have been the ruling council, if not the King of the Mountain.

The marketplace, which was the start of the city, was strangely vacant. In fact there were no dwarves to be seen at all. A chill ran down Dorn's spine. He looked at Arnór, but his friend didn't give anything away. He led them to the left side of the marketplace where there was a tavern. The buildings around the edge of the market were built from a mixture of stone and wood. It was a deliberate contrast so the city wouldn't be the same as the mountain they lived in.

The tavern was completely empty, not even a tavern wench to run the bar. A fire crackled against one of the walls and it looked as though it was about to burn out. Dorn looked around nervously, but if there was no one around then there was no one to attack them. Arnór pointed for them to take a seat at the table in front of the fire while he walked around the back of the bar and poured three mugs of ale.

"Thank you, but it is a little early in the day and we have a lot to do," Gwydion said when Arnór placed a mug in front of him.

"I don't think you'll be getting too much done, at least not today." Arnór took a drink when he finished talking.

"What is going on?" Dorn asked. "None of this is making any sense. Where is everyone? Why did you bring us here?"

"I brought you here because it isn't safe for you in the upper city, at least not at the moment." Arnór decided to answer the last question first.

"I know my parents didn't appreciate it when I left and the council was also upset, but that was a long time ago."

"Oh, that, that isn't why you're in danger," Arnór continued. "There is more I need to tell you in regards to that, but there will be time for that later." Dorn didn't like what he was hearing, but he kept his mouth shut. "A strange man arrived here about a week or two ago. At first we thought he was a trader, but he managed gain entrance into the upper city. From there he talked his way into the council and had them order both gates shut. We were to completely shut off the outside world."

"Why would the council agree to such a thing? Surely they know that the stores of food would only last so long. We need the Seven Kingdoms to survive," Dorn sounded aghast.

"I know, but he was very convincing. He told us the final battle was approaching and it looked as though the Evil One was going to win. He told us that if we remained where we were then we would be safe when the "Great Lord" ruled."

"That sounds like the talk of an agent of the Evil One," Gwydion added. "How could you be duped by such a man?"

"I can't say for sure as I don't sit on the council and wasn't privy to their meeting, but the man did make an announcement to the upper city and he sounded very convincing." The expression on his face showed that there was something he was leaving out.

"What is it?" Gwydion asked.

"I don't know, well not exactly. When the man was speaking I felt... the only way I can explain it is euphoric. Not only that, but there seemed to be a haze over the rest of the crowd. It was one of the strangest things I have experienced. All I can remember is leaving the square thinking that it was a fantastic idea."

"Now you don't think so?" Dorn asked before Gwydion had a chance to speak.

"For the first few days I did, but then something changed within me and suddenly it didn't make as much sense. As you said, we can't stay hidden in the mountain for too long. We need to trade for food and other items to survive, but that wasn't it. Two days ago I heard a rumour that you were returning. Apparently you were not to be admitted at any cost. I know your leaving was strained, but this order seemed a little excessive."

"I guess my father was involved in that decision?" Dorn sounded sour.

Dorn's parents were both part of the council of the Cloumid Dwarven Guild. When he told them he was leaving they were less than impressed. In the end they disowned him and told him he was never welcome to return.

"I am afraid your parents are both dead," it was clear in his tone that he wanted to avoid the subject.

Dorn was about to speak, but Gwydion cut him short. "I am sorry for your loss Dorn, but now is not the time. Please, continue your story."

Arnór was grateful for the change of subject. "For some reason I knew I had to come and get you, regardless of the orders. There is something very wrong here, but I don't know what it is. I can only hope that you can shed some light."

"I think I know who it is, or at least..." Gwydion was interrupted before he could finish his statement.

They had been so engrossed in their conversation that they had not noticed the man enter the room.

"I was wondering when the light would dawn on you." His voice was deep and hoarse. It was a strange tone for the arrogance it held.

The man wore a thin black cloak with the hood drawn over his head. An odd smell wafted from his direction. "It was not that long ago that we met in the throne room of the palace in Remidel."

"Dargoz!" Gwydion still gasped even though he knew the Dark Knight was due to come back to life.

Dorn jumped to his feet. He didn't hesitate in drawing his axe, not that he really knew what he was going to do with it.

"Be calm dwarf. I didn't come here to fight with you."

"Then why have you come here?" Gwydion asked.

"I have come to give you a message from my master." It sounded as though Dargoz was struggling to speak. Gwydion slowly drew in the energy around him, trying his best not to alert Dark Knight, but he failed. "There is no need for that wizard. You know what happened last time and that was with five of your friends and even then you were no match for me." Gwydion let the energy slip away, even though he knew there was something amiss. "As I said I am not here to fight you. The Great Lord will crush your Chosen One and the rest of his army. When you think about it, you know what I say is the truth."

"Enough of your lies, get to the point," Gwydion snapped.

"Stay here and the Great Lord will have mercy on you. There is no benefit for the Great Lord to clear out the entire mountain. Plus he will need someone to mine the stone for his great castles. He has decided that the dwarves shall get this job," his words sounded sickly sweet. Gwydion was waiting for that subtle feeling that he was using magic, but none came. "Even you can stay here if you want, wizard, although I have no idea why the Great Lord would want to keep you alive."

"Be off with you, filth," Gwydion snapped. "Another word of this and we will see who walks out of here alive." There was something about the Dark Knight's stance that made Gwydion believe he might actually win.

"Very well, I have said all that I have come here to say. Heed my words or the next time we shall meet will be in Avalon and you will not leave that confrontation alive."

Dargoz spun around and stumbled slightly as he left the tavern. There was definitely something not right about the Dark Knight, but Gwydion couldn't put his finger on it. Now that he knew what was happening he had to do something about it.

"We need to go and speak with the council," Gwydion said when Dargoz had left.

"I don't think that is a good idea," Arnór said. "The council were quite emphatic that if anyone was to let you into the city they would be put to death, shortly after you."

"Then what do you propose we do? There has to be a reason why you let us in?" Dorn asked.

"There is a house in the lower city that you can stay in for now. I still have friends in the upper city. If I can gather enough support then we can get you an audience with the council without you being arrested," Arnór explained.

"They haven't condemned me," Gwydion returned. "We don't have time to wait. I must speak with them now."

"Arnór is right," Dorn conceded. "The council will not be bullied. If Dargoz is leaving then maybe some of his black magic will dissipate. Either way we will have a greater chance if we wait, but we cannot wait too long," he turned to Arnór. "It has to be done in the morning, so whatever it is you have to do you must do it quickly."

"Of course." Arnór stood and motioned for the others to follow.

Both the dwarves had finished their ales, but Gwydion's had remained untouched. Even after the confrontation with the Dark Knight, which rattled his nerves, he couldn't bring himself to drink. There was much to be done and he didn't want to risk clouding his judgement. Just because the Dark Knight said he was leaving, it didn't mean it was true.

"Why is the market empty?" Dorn asked.

"The council ordered everyone to remain inside. The mines have also been closed. It seems they have taken the news about the final battle badly. It's like they have just given up," Arnór explained.

"That is another reason why we need to move quickly," Dorn said. "Are you sure you will have everyone you need by the morning?"

"I have some friends on the council and others in high standing. We have already spoken and are ready to speak with the others. Your arrival will help with our cause, but you need to do what I say."

Arnór left them in a small house which had clearly been vacant for some time. A fine layer of dust covered the floor and the furniture. Despite the dust, there was quite a homely feeling about the house once the candles had been lit.

Before they could settle into a conversation the door opened and young dwarf entered carrying a basket of food. Dorn and Gwydion were sitting around the small dining table and they didn't really take much notice her.

"I know you've been gone for long time, but I would have thought you would have recognised me," she scolded with a playful tone.

Dorn looked at her properly for the first time. The confusion was clearly written on his face as he tried to place her. She was a young dwarf and could not have been more than eighteen years old. It had been at least six years since Dorn had left his home, but suddenly his expression changed as he recognised who she was.

"Little Eydís?" Dorn sounded shocked. "Is that really you?"

"Well I'm not that little anymore," she blushed as she spoke.

"Well it looks as though you have plenty to catch up on and I have work to do," Gwydion stood as he spoke.

"You can't go outside," Dorn and Eydís said at the same time.

"Well, yes and no. Don't worry, I'm not going into the dwarven city. I am going home. There is something very disturbing about the Dark Knight and I need to do some research. I'll be back come morning." That was all the explanation Gwydion gave before he opened a gateway and the smell of sea air filled the room.

"Wait!" Dorn called before Gwydion stepped through. "You couldn't open a gateway when we came here. How are you going to make it back?"

"Now that I've been here I will be able to create one right where this one is, just remember where it is." Gwydion smiled briefly before he left.

"What was that?" Eydís voice was breathless.

Dorn had forgotten how confronting gateways could be if someone wasn't used to them. He could tell by her tone that it had come as a shock. Slowly he explained to her what it was, but she didn't seem happy with it.

The two ate and talked for the rest of the day. Eydís told him all that had happened, that she knew, in the mountain since he had left and Dorn told her about the outside world and all his adventures. She listened in awe and had to stop him every now and then to repeat what he had said. It wasn't until late in the evening that the conversation of his parents came up.

"As you know your father and mother were not happy when you left. They thought you would take your father's position on the council when he retired," Eydís started.

"I had quite the argument before I left, but there was nothing I could do to make myself stay, even if I had wanted to. They told me that I would never be welcome back under the mountain, but I knew they didn't mean it," Dorn explained.

"And you were right," Eydís voice sounded sad. "King Ashnar decreed what your parents had threatened you with not a week after you left. Since you left in such a manner you were never allowed to return. Your father protested. He was quite adamant that the rest of the council would have his back, but that was simply not the case. The council stood behind the King's judgement and your parents were sent to the cells. They stayed there for a year and a day before they were finally given a chance for reprieve. They were told that if they disowned you then they could return to their home. Of course they did not and even when they were sentenced to death they would not speak against you."

Dorn stood up, violently pushing his chair backward and slamming his fist down on the table. "What was Ashnar thinking?"

"Be calm, there is nothing you can do about it tonight," Eydís placed her hand on his. It was clear that he wasn't thinking straight and she didn't want him rushing into anything.

"You are right," Dorn said as he paced around the room. "I guess I should probably be getting to bed."

"That sounds like an interesting idea," there was a playful tone to her voice that Dorn completely missed.

"Will I see you in the morning?" he asked.

"Maybe, if you play your cards right," her voice was soft and sensuous.

"Good, I hope to see you then," Dorn said as he made his way to the bedroom.

It wasn't until late in the night when Dorn woke that he realised what she was insinuating. He cursed himself before falling back to sleep.

Gwydion was waiting for him in the dining room when he rose that morning.

"Arnór is outside with a small group of dwarves. I was just coming to wake you."

"I guess there is no time for breakfast then?" It was a rhetorical question.

Dorn collected his axe and made his way out of the house. He wasn't sure if carrying a weapon was the right decision, but if things turned nasty he didn't want to be unarmed. When he saw the group of dwarves waiting, all armed, he decided that he had made the right decision.

"Hello Dorn, this is Baldur, Valdis, Rut and Noskar They are all Guildmasters," Arnór introduced them all.

Dorn's heart sunk. When Arnór had told him there was support on the council he expected more guildmasters to be present. There were fifty guildmasters sitting on the council, one to represent each hold of around ten smaller villages and towns throughout the Cloumid Mountain Range. He really didn't know what four members of the council were going to do against the other forty six and King Ashnar himself.

"Let's get moving. We have already lost a day and can ill afford to lose any more time," Gwydion didn't seem too worried about their lack of support.

Like the day before the lower city was completely vacant. Dorn felt nervous walking through the empty streets and the market. He felt as though there were many eyes watching him from the shadows.

The upper city was a stark contrast to its lower, poorer counterpart. Unlike the lower city where the buildings were roughly built from cheap wood and stone and the streets were dirty more often than not, the buildings in the upper city were built from mahogany and stone covered in gold leaf. Some were made from deep, black granite and others from sandstone brought in from Castalia. All in all it was very impressive, but Dorn didn't notice any of it. He was focused on the palace at the far end of the city, raised on a platform ledge. Stairs led up from both sides, wide enough for three people abreast.

Arnór led them through the city. Although it wasn't completely empty, there were fewer dwarves than there should have been. They all stared at the group as they walked by, mainly because of Gwydion. It has been a long time since there had been anyone of 'normal' size in the mountain and it was a strange sight to be seen.

In front of the palace was a large meeting square where the rest of the council was assembled. Only fifteen members had come for the meeting, but they still outnumbered those on their side. A dais had been raised so they were able to sit and still look down at the partitioners. A higher, but smaller stage had been build behind for King Ashnar to sit on. A throne had also been brought out so he would look the part.

"Dorn!" King Ashnar boomed when he saw the group arrive. "I never thought we would see you here again. Did you not get the message that you are no longer welcome?"

"With deference, King Ashnar," Dorn bowed as he spoke. "Your feelings for me need to be put aside. The final battle looms and if I survive then you can do what you want with me."

Ashnar was taken aback by Dorn's candour. It was the last thing he was expecting the dwarf to say, but that only lasted a moment before he composed himself.

"This final battle that you speak of is nothing to do with the guild. We have been safe under the mountain for centuries and we shall remain that way."

"That is not exactly true, your majesty," Arnór spoke on behalf of the guildmasters. "There have been increased attacks from the goblins on the outer villages."

"Then that is even more reason to bolster our own defences and leave this so called 'final battle" to the outside world," the guildmaster named Dagur spoke. He sat in the middle of the dais and had been given the role of speaker for the meeting. "We have been assured that the Evil One has no plans for the mountain."

"And you believe the Lord of all Lies?" Gwydion asked, his voice booming around the square. "What do you think the Evil One will do if he defeats the Alliance? He will fill your halls with goblins. It will be their domain."

"And what would a wizard know of such things?" Dagur returned. "Goblins have been trying to take our halls for centuries and we have always defeated them. This is not our battle, nor will it ever be."

"And what shall we do when the outside world has been destroyed?" Arnór asked before Gwydion had a chance to respond. When there was no response to his question he continued. "I'll tell you what will happen. Our source of food will soon run dry and force us from the mountain. Even, on the very off chance, that the Evil One lets us live here, as soon as you set foot outside he will kill you all."

"When has the outside world ever really cared about us dwarves under the mountain?" Dagur asked, but didn't wait for a response. "When the mines came under attack no one came to our aid. Even when we were forced to shut down our trade route with Hondin Lel no one came to our aid and now you would have us stand up and save them from destruction."

"It is that destruction that will be the end of us all. If we don't go to save the outside world we go to save ourselves," Arnór continued.

"What would you have us do?" Dagur asked.

"It is time for us to make a stand. To join with others and fight," Valdis added her voice.

"She is right," Baldur added. "It is time for us to fight."

Dorn watched the other guildmasters closely and he could see that they were starting to turn. "Put it to a vote!" he called out, hoping he hadn't called it too early.

"Very well, I think we can assume the four of you are voting for war," Dagur said.

"But we don't have everyone here?" the guildmaster, Horan, who was sitting next to Dagur complained. "A vote of this magnitude needs the full council."

"It will take days to gather everyone together and we don't have the time. We need the decision made now so we can start gathering everyone together," Dorn snapped. "The final battle is in six days time and we need to be ready to fight."

"Then it is a moot point," Horan said, sounding somewhat relieved. "We cannot possibly gather our army together and move it to Avalon in six days. There is no reason to take this any further."

"Don't you worry about that," Gwydion said. "Have your soldiers and anyone with a will to fight here in five days and I will make sure they make it to Avalon in time."

"How..." Horan started, but was interrupted.

"We vote now and then we will worry about how things are going to work," Dagur said.

The vote didn't take long. To the surprise of everyone the council voted with eleven agreeing to go to war and only four voting against, the rest abstained. Dorn felt a wave of relief wash over him.

"Enough of this," boomed Ashnar. "I will not agree to lead my dwarves to their doom. This battle of yours is folly and nothing to do with us. Guards!" Dorn hadn't noticed that a dozen of Ashnar's personal guards had assembled behind them. "Arrest the traitors."

The guards, all armed with pikes, lowered their weapons and stepped forward. They circled the group below the dais, but made no further advance. In fact they stood motionless, caught in a spell Gwydion had cast.

"We are not going anywhere," Gwydion growled. "The council has voted and the guild will be going to war."

"How dare you come into my city and bark orders at me," Ashnar didn't seem to notice what had happened to his guards. "We will remain here and that is final!"

Chapter 14: Entero

Eldred stepped through his gateway and onto the field outside the castle in Jarrat. The makeshift prison the Alliance had created had been removed, but the ground was still scarred. Although he knew it was impossible he thought he could still smell the charred bodies of the orglin that had been burned after the short, but intense battle.

Looking towards the castle he shuddered. The last time he had been there he had spent months in the dungeon being tortured by Viper and the Dark Knight Na'garoz. It was an experience he certainly didn't want to relive, but he had been instructed to return and that was what he must do.

The city was a hive of activity, which came as a surprise to Eldred. He had expected everyone to be locked up inside awaiting the final battle, but it looked as though it was business as usual. The trade routes with the other Kingdoms had remained shut, but that seemed to be the only affect the Evil One was having on Jarrat.

Shrugging his shoulders he pushed away the thoughts of torture and started on his way. He joined the road and followed the crowd making its way slowly towards the castle.

No one seemed to take any notice of Eldred, they were all concentrating on the castle in front of them. He was quite happy with his anonymity. The sun was shining and all in all it was a pleasant day for a walk. It wasn't until he reached the gate that he became concerned. The progression had slowed and the guards were checking everyone as they tried to gain entrance. Most were allowed through, but there were still some who were turned away. Eldred tried to keep his head down and walk though with the group ahead of him.

"Lord Eldred!" Eldred froze when he heard his name. He wasn't sure if it was good sign or a bad one. "We have been expecting you."

He didn't know how to respond. He looked at the head guard, but he didn't recognise him. There was no way he should have known he was coming. Something was terribly wrong.

"How did you know I was coming?" was all he could say.

"There is someone waiting for you in the guardhouse."

Eldred took a closer look at the guard and noticed there was a glazed expression on his face. Everything inside of him was telling him that he shouldn't go inside, but he really wanted to know who wanted to see him.

"Well let's not keep him waiting then," Eldred said as he started to move.

As he continued to the gatehouse he hoped that someone was going to call him to a halt, but no words came. When he opened the door and saw a solitary figure sitting at a small table, he quickly drew in the energy around him.

"Be calm wizard. I mean you no harm," the voice was hoarse, but there could be no doubt who it was.

"What are you doing here, Na'garoz?"

He had not completely believed that the Dark Knights had returned, but there was no doubt it was true. What the Dark Knight was now doing in Jarrat was a completely different riddle. Eldred didn't think he would survive a one on one battle, but Na'garoz made no move to attack. Despite his words Eldred held the energy within and stayed prepared.

"I am here to give you an offer from my master. The Great Lord offers you amnesty. Stay here in Jarrat for the final battle and he will leave this land for you to rule. I don't know why he is offering such a deal since we are going to crush you anyway, but I would suggest you take it."

"Give me one reason why I shouldn't kill you right now?" Eldred fingered the hilt of his sword to accentuate his point.

"You know as well as I do that you are no match for me. The only reason you are not already dead is because the Great Lord told me not to kill you. If it was up to me I would be roasting your dead corpse tonight." There was no lie to his threat.

"Very well, you can go back to your 'Great Lord' and tell him that I will gladly watch as the Chosen One kills him and the Alliance destroys his army of filth. You should be thankful that I don't kill you now," Eldred snarled.

"So be it, then you will die with the rest of your worthless kin, but don't think it will be so easy convincing the others here. Remember that Oriana spent a lot of time with my brother. He broke her and she will not want to suffer the same way again." With that Na'garoz stood and left.

There was something very odd about his manner and it looked as though he stumbled slightly as he walked. Eldred wondered if it had all been a bluff and whether he should have just tried to kill him.

There was no time for him to remain in the guardhouse thinking on it. He needed to get inside the castle and speak with Queen Oriana and Duke Xarles. They were the two he would need to convince to send the remainder of the Enteroite army to Avalon. He knew it was not going to be easy, but he had convinced many others to do much harder tasks.

When he returned to the gate the guard didn't look like he recognised him. It was obvious that the Dark Knight had placed a spell on him, which had now dissipated.

"Where do you think you're going?" he sounded confused.

"I have important business in the castle. I must see Queen Oriana immediately," Eldred commanded.

"And who are you to think you can see our Queen," he said, his confidence returning.

"I am Eldred, one of the seven wizards on the Council of Wizards. I don't have time to be standing here talking with the likes of you."

The guard took a step back. It was not the answer he had been expecting. The old man standing before him didn't look like a thing of legend, but his tone certainly did.

"What are you doing there Leofric? You're holding up the line. Either let him in or send him on his way," the head of the guard called out.

Leofric thought for a moment. He really shouldn't let the man pass, but if he was indeed a wizard then he didn't want to face the repercussions. In the end he decided it was safer just to let him through. If he wasn't who he said he was, then the soldiers at the castle would stop him.

"Move along and be quick about it. There are more people with pressing business waiting to get in."

Eldred simply smiled and nodded before walking through. He cringed as walked through the castle grounds, remembering his last visit. No matter what he tried that memory kept coming back to him.

There were a dozen soldiers standing in front of the large double doors to the castle. They didn't really seem to notice him until he approached.

"The castle is shut to visitors," one of the guards spoke calmly.

"I have come with a message for Queen Oriana from the Alliance. It is urgent that I speak with her," Eldred replied.

Although he couldn't fault the guards for doing their job the delays were becoming frustrating. He wanted nothing more than to cast a spell and walk past them, but he knew that wasn't the right thing to do.

"I have important business with the Queen. I am Eldred and have come with a message from the Alliance. Time is short and I don't have any to waste," he came straight to the point.

"We've received no notice that there would be an emissary from the Alliance arriving today," the guard returned.

Eldred sighed. "Of course there was no..."

"Eldred?" a familiar voice came from behind.

Eldred spun around as his heart started to pound. At first he thought Na'garoz had returned, but when he saw the short cropped brown hair, he instantly recognised Duke Xarles. The man wore a deep red doublet with gold trim and matching hose. Eldred thought he looked like the perfect Queen's consort, but he kept that to himself. The Duke had played a pivotal role in the liberation of Jarrat from the hand of the Dark Knight Ra'naroz and Eldred had a suspicion it wasn't just for the love of his Kingdom.

"What are you doing here? I thought you would be on your way to Avalon."

The guards watched them without moving. The one who had spoken suddenly didn't look so sure of himself.

"I don't think this is the right setting for such a conversation."

"Of course," Xarles said as he looked at the guards, as if seeing them for the first time. "Come inside. I am sure Queen Oriana will be pleased to see you."

Eldred was glad to hear that the Queen was up and about. When they had left she was in a catatonic state. Alaric had said he would return and make her better, but there had been no confirmation that he had.

"The queen is feeling better?" Eldred asked as they walked through the hall.

The castle seemed to be running as normal, as if the Evil One's touch had never been there. Functionaries and nobles moved through the corridors taking little notice of them. It helped Eldred relax as he made his way to the Queen's office.

"She has her moments, as to be expected, but I think she is recovering. I don't know what the Chosen One did to her, but it seems to be working."

"That is good news."

There were two soldiers standing guard outside the queen's office. Concern crossed their faces when they saw Eldred approach, but it softened when they saw Xarles.

"Good morning Duke. Is the Queen expecting you?" one asked.

"Not this early, but I have important information for her," Xarles replied.

"Very good." The soldiers stepped aside and let the two men enter.

Inside the small, simple office the Queen was sitting at her desk at the far side of the room. Her long brown hair was tied up in a bun and she looked more aged than last time he saw her. She wore a simple black velvet dress. Her crown sat on a small side table to the side of the room and she looked up and smiled when she saw Xarles enter.

"My saviour, I am glad to see you this morning. These mundane papers are starting to pile up and really don't have the energy today," she spoke softly and didn't seem to notice Eldred.

"That's okay, my queen, there is plenty of time for that. We have a visitor," Xarles kept his voice soft, as if he was speaking to a child.

Oriana looked at Eldred, seeing him for the first time. There was a strange expression on her face, as if she was trying to place where she had seen him before.

"I don't think I am up for visitors today," she looked down at her papers and started to flick through them as she spoke.

Xarles gently pulled Eldred to the side of the room. Oriana didn't seem to notice, she was more concerned with shuffling the papers in front of her.

"Every now and then she slips back into a malaise, not that anyone could blame her. I don't think we can push her any further," Xarles said apologetically.

"I understand your concern, but we don't have time to wait. The final battle is mere days away and we need to move now. We need to get all of Entero's soldiers to Avalon." Eldred held his hand up stopping Xarles from asking the obvious question. "The same way I arrived here from Remidia; in a matter of moments. I will create what is called a gateway between here and Avalon. The soldiers will step through the gateway on the field outside the castle and then step out onto the fields of Avalon. All I need is for the queen to approve the movement. Or..." Eldred let his thought float away.

"I think we should discuss this somewhere else. The Queen needs to rest," Xarles said. "We are going to leave you now, your majesty." Queen Oriana didn't look up. She stared at the papers on her desk, but didn't look as though she knew what she was doing.

Xarles led Eldred from the office. "Have Maria come and take Queen Oriana to her apartment." He said as he walked through the door.

The soldiers knew exactly what he meant. As much as they tried to keep her condition a secret it was widely known throughout the castle. At least, as far as Xarles knew, the rumours had not reached the city and he wanted it to remain that way. He hoped she would be completely recovered before that happened.

Xarles led them down the corridor until they reached his personal offices. Since the Dark Knight had left the castle, the duke had been promoted to the queen's personal assistant.

"What can we do?" Eldred asked.

"There is not much we can do. There are limited resources left in Jarrat and there isn't enough time to go to the outer provinces."

Eldred thought for a moment. He could create a gateway to anywhere if he needed, but he wasn't sure that would gain much. Alaric seemed confident that the gateway wouldn't use a lot of his energy, but that was just creating one. If he had to create multiple gateways then he wasn't sure what would happen. He would need as much strength as he could muster for the final battle.

"Not only that, but I'm not authorised to make such a decision," Xarles continued.

"Surely you have been given power to make the decisions when the queen is not feeling well." Eldred put her condition as delicately as possible.

"It never really came up. When she is in her malaise she is in no position to bestow that power upon me and when she is well no one wants to bring it up. It seems that when she is her normal self she doesn't seem to remember her malaise, it's almost like they never happen."

"So what happens when she is unfit to rule?" Eldred asked.

"There are enough loyal ministers to keep the Kingdom running. It's just what you are asking is too big for anyone to accept on her behalf. Only Queen Oriana can make such a decision," Xarles insisted.

Eldred sighed. He knew that Xarles was right, but that didn't make things any easier. There was no time to wait for the queen to recover and he wasn't sure what he could do to help. There were a few spells and some potions he could create, but there was no guarantee they would work. In the end he decided that there was nothing else for it. If he failed then he would be no worse position than if he never tried.

"I will need some things from your medical stores," Eldred said as he started to write down some ingredients.

"What are you doing?" Xarles asked.

"I am going to try and help Oriana. Hopefully I can make a potion to wake her from her malaise. We don't have time to wait for her to get better. If we send out messengers today there's a chance we can get soldiers from the outer regions in time."

Xarles thought for a moment as Eldred continued to write. There was something in his tone that made him nervous. Queen Oriana was certainly improving every day and he wasn't sure if he wanted the wizard to risk anything. If he made her worse, then Xarles didn't think he could live with himself.

"There, see that everything is brought to Oriana's apartments. I will mix the remedies there," Eldred stated when he had finished his list.

"I'm not sure about this. Alaric said that it would take time for her to fully recover. I don't think we should take any more risks. She is our sovereign and we would be lost without her," Xarles spoke with no confidence.

As soon as he started Eldred seemed to loom over him, even though he was still seated. There was something very imposing about the wizard that made Xarles wish he had kept his mouth shut.

"Who do you take me for?" Eldred asked. "I am a wizard not a potion maker. I know the right herbs to use. I can't guarantee that I will make her better, but it definitely won't make her worse. Now if you have had enough of wasting my time I would appreciate it if you got me what I need."

Xarles apologised and jumped to his feet. It had been a long time since anyone had spoken to him in such a manner and it certainly had its affect. Eldred couldn't help but snigger when Xarles had left the room. There was a certain pleasure he, as his six brethren, took in dressing down the nobility. Xarles didn't really deserve it, but he did need something to get him moving.

Eldred waited a moment before he slowly made his way to Queen Oriana's apartments. He knew that there was little chance of him gaining entrance without the Duke, so there was no reason to hurry. When he reached the front door he was met by two soldiers who did not look pleased to see him.

"The Queen is not feeling well and even if she was I doubt she would want to see the likes of you," one soldier sneered.

"I would be very careful how you speak to me if I was you." Eldred was in no mood to be disrespected. He had hoped Xarles would already be there. Originally he had planned on waiting for the Duke, but the soldier's tone had changed his mind.

Shock was clear on both the soldier's faces as they suddenly slid away from the door. No matter what they did there was nothing they could do to stop it. In fact that was all the movement they could do. Eldred had wrapped them up in air and would not let them move again until he was sure they weren't going to alert the rest of the castle guard.

"I am not here to hurt you or the queen, but I have no time for this. My name is Eldred." The expression changed on their faces, as Eldred released their heads. "Now, if I let you go are you going to remain here or are you going to run off to get more soldiers?"

"No sir, if we had known it was you we would never have tried to stop you," fear was thick in his voice, but Eldred wasn't convinced.

"Now I can't let the Queen's apartment go unguarded, and I can't risk you running off to get help. So here's what we'll do. I'll let you go and if you leave your post before Xarles arrives I will turn you both into frogs."

The two solders breathed in deeply when they were released. Both were shaking and trying their best not to show it. Even if they had thought about lying to Eldred before they definitely wouldn't do it now.

"We will remain here," both soldiers said at once.

"Good," Eldred replied as he opened the door and entered.

The front room was dark. The curtains were drawn and no candles were lit. There was also a subtle smell of incense burning in the air. Something didn't seem right. It was as if the air was too thick.

"Is that you Xarles?" a weak voice came from the next room.

Eldred walked into the sitting room where he found the queen sitting in a chair. A small fire had been lit and gave the only light. The thick curtains had been drawn and like the front room, no candles had been lit. Eldred took a moment to see if there had been any spells left on the room. There was no telling what traps the Dark Knight had left behind for him, but there didn't seem to be anything.

"No, it is me, Eldred," Eldred kept his voice low as he took a seat near her.

"Oh!" she sounded disappointed. "Where is Xarles?"

"He will be here shortly," Eldred reassured her.

"Would you be so kind as to throw another log on the fire? It is bitterly cold today."

Eldred thought, if he wasn't able to control his own temperature, that if it was any hotter he would start sweating. Despite the heat he did as he was asked and placed a small log on the fire.

"Is Xarles here?" she asked again.

"He will be here shortly. What I want you to do is relax now. I need to find out what is wrong with you," Eldred kept his voice soothing, so as not to upset her.

Oriana didn't seem to hear what he said. She stared into the fire and watched the flames lick the wood.

Eldred closed his eyes and drew in the energy around him. He thought he would feel the taint of the Evil One, but there was nothing. Although the room itself was stuffy, there was no sign of evil. That was not what Eldred was hoping for. If there was evil in the room then there was a good chance he could get rid of it quickly. That would have been the simplest and quickest solution.

Eldred moved until he was squatting next to Oriana and placed his hand on the side of her head. She didn't even seem to notice his touch. He let the energy flow into her mind as he delved for the possible cause of her condition. He searched and searched, but there didn't seem to be anything wrong with her, at least nothing he could find. Sighing deeply he let the energy leave his body and he returned to his chair.

"Did you fix her?" Eldred jumped as he heard the voice from behind.

"No, unfortunately not," Eldred replied. "It looks like I have my work cut out for me."

Xarles was followed into the room by a number of official looking men. It seemed when he went for the supplies the alchemists wanted to take the opportunity to meet the wizard. It was the last thing Eldred wanted.

"Set everything up in the dining room, and make sure there is plenty of light," Eldred ordered.

Eldred took one last look at Oriana before he made his way to the dining room. All the vials of liquid, herbs, alchemist tubes and beakers had been spread across the dining room table. Nothing was labelled and although he could decipher the herbs, the liquids were another story. He thought those standing around the table had done it deliberately. It would give them an excuse to stay and 'help'.

"First I need some ground hogroot, penilia and some distilled elm nectar." Eldred figured if they were going to be there he may as well put them to use.

The alchemists looked at each other. There were three mortar and pestles as well as a coal burner. The elm nectar had already been distilled and there was no time to use the burner. If anything needed heating Eldred would use magic to do so, but he wasn't about to let the others know that. If they thought they were just going to stand back and watch they were sorely mistaken.

"Hurry up, I don't have all day," Eldred boomed when no one moved.

All six alchemists moved into action, even though there were only jobs for two of them. The two who grabbed the mortar and pestles first quickly started grinding the herbs. The other four looked around nervously for something to do.

With each potion Eldred mixed there came failure. Xarles watched him carefully and watched the reaction, if any, that came from the queen. It was late in the day when he had finally had enough.

"She has drunk enough for one day Eldred," Xarles spoke firmly, which brought murmured sounds of concern from the alchemists.

"But there has been no change in her condition," Eldred sounded exhausted.

"Even if there is a miraculous change there is not enough time to get anything done today," Xarles retorted.

Eldred let his head rest on the palms of his hands as he thought on what to do next. He had already gone through all the remedies he thought might work and even tried some random ones. There was nothing else he could do, but he wasn't about to give up. He needed to convince Xarles to move into action.

"Clear this mess up," Eldred barked at the alchemists. "And be quick about it."

The six men quickly moved into action as Eldred and Xarles watched on. Eldred made a point not to make eye contact with Xarles in case he took it as a chance to speak. What he had to say did not need repeating throughout the castle. It wasn't until they were alone before Eldred took a seat at the freshly cleared table.

"It is time for you to stand up and be counted. Not that long ago you led a band of rebels when it was for the good of the Kingdom. Now it is time for you to do what you know is right again," Eldred urged him.

Xarles had remained standing when Eldred started speaking. There was something very uncomfortable about the situation and standing made him feel a little better.

"You know there is nothing I can do. Even if I made the decision no one would listen to me. Only a direct order from Queen Oriana herself would achieve what you wanted."

Xarles spoke the truth and Eldred knew it. As much as he wanted the duke to make a stand, there was really nothing he could do. In fact there would be a risk that things would be worse. With the queen in her current state an order of such a magnitude could cause a revolt.

Eldred had thought long and hard about what he was going to say next, but in the end he decided he had no choice.

"There was a Dark Knight at the gate. He was waiting for me." A look of horror crossed Xarles' face and he had to sit down. "Do you know if he was in the castle?"

"I don't know." Xarles looked around nervously.

"Don't worry, he's gone now," Eldred tried to reassure him. "I just need to know if he saw Oriana. He might have done something to deteriorate her condition."

"I can assure you that no Dark Knight has seen Queen Oriana," Xarles sounded defensive, almost shocked at what Eldred was insinuating. "No one gets past the guard." Even as the words came out of his mouth he realised how futile they were. "There have been very few moments that she has been out of my sight. If a Dark Knight has been here I am sure I would know."

Eldred let the conversation go. He really didn't think Na'garoz had done anything further to Oriana. Whatever was wrong with her was still the effect of Ra'naroz's spell. There was nothing he could do except wait until morning.

"Fine, I suppose I could use some rest now," Eldred conceded. "I guess I will need a room for the night."

Xarles thought for a moment. Ever since the Dark Knight had been found and removed from power, the castle had been overrun with dignitaries and potential new politicians. There wasn't a spare apartment or room in the castle. If Xarles had been given notice of Eldred's arrival then he could have made a room available for him, but it was too late in the day.

"I'm sorry, but there is nowhere for you to stay tonight. All the rooms are taken," Xarles apologised.

Eldred sighed again. It had been a long day and he wanted nothing more than to eat a decent meal and crawl into bed, but there was also something nagging the back of his mind. There was something very strange about the meeting with Na'garoz and he wanted to check the tomes he had at home on the Isle of Wizards. With the new knowledge of gateways it would be easy for him to go home and then return in the morning.

They ate supper in the queen's dining room. There seemed little point in moving and Xarles, especially after hearing about the Dark Knight, didn't want to leave her alone. When he was done Eldred created a gateway to his home and stepped through. The subtle smell of sea air remained after the gateway had closed.

In the morning Eldred returned at first light. He created a gateway straight into Oriana's dining room where he found Xarles sitting down with her eating breakfast. Neither seemed too surprised when Eldred suddenly appeared.

"Eldred!" Queen Oriana said. "What a pleasure to see you this morning. Xarles has told me that you have important business you wish to discuss."

Eldred looked at the two in shock, both from the fact that neither seemed startled at his sudden appearance and Oriana seemed to be her normal self. Whatever had afflicted her the day before was completely gone.

It made no sense but there was no time to try and figure it out. He just had to push it to the back of his mind and move on.

"That's right. The final battle is approaching quickly and we need all your soldiers." There was no point wasting time. There was no telling how long Oriana would remain in her current state and he couldn't risk losing another day.

"That is indeed a big ask." Oriana pushed aside her breakfast and gave Eldred her full attention. "I don't need to tell you the affect the Evil One has had on my Kingdom. We gave the Alliance all the soldiers we could spare when they left Jarrat. I'm not sure what else you want. If we give you more then we will leave ourselves defenceless."

"I understand your concern," Eldred started, "but you must understand that there is nothing for you to defend against. The Evil One is moving all his forces to Avalon, as are the other Kingdoms. If the Alliance fails, then nothing will stop the Evil One from covering the Seven Kingdoms in darkness."

"What do you think?" Oriana asked Xarles.

"Everything inside me is telling me that we cannot leave ourselves defenceless, but I know that Eldred is right. We have to do what we can to defeat the Evil One and if that means emptying our lands of soldiers then that is what we have to do."

"You speak wise words," Oriana almost cooed at Xarles and Eldred knew there was something between them. "You will have my support, but I fear that there is not enough time to gather enough soldiers to make it worthwhile."

"I have thought on this and if you send your quickest riders this morning you can have the soldiers here in five days. It is then that we need to move to Avalon."

"Even an official letter from the queen will not force the nobles into action. They will not like losing all their soldiers and they will send emissaries back here to question the order," Xarles added.

"Then give them no choice," Eldred returned.

"I have never ruled with an iron fist," Oriana said.

"Now is not the time for a feathered touch. You are their Queen and they will listen to what you say. If not then they will feel your wrath. I'm sure there are many who would love a castle and a region to rule," Eldred continued.

"I'm assuming you have something in mind?" Oriana asked.

"Well I've never known a noble who wouldn't jump to action when their personal coffers were at risk. If you tell them that for every soldier that isn't in Jarrat in five days time you will tax them one thousand gold crowns."

"That will bankrupt some of the poorer nobles," she used to term 'poor' loosely.

"Then I am sure they will send their soldiers. When it is said and done it won't matter how much coin they have left. The Evil One will certainly not barter for anyone's lives. Make sure you put that in your missive."

"Very well I will have the letters drawn up after breakfast," Oriana said.

"There is no time to wait. Call for the scribes now and have the messengers in the saddle ready to ride."

Oriana wasn't overly happy with the way Eldred was speaking to her. She was the Queen of Entero not some scullery maid. She took one look in his eyes and realised that she might as well have been a scullery maid for all Eldred cared. He was a wizard and didn't really care for titles.

"Very well, Xarles would you see that is gets done," Oriana said.

"If you pen something now I will make sure the scribes copy it word for word and then you can give it the royal seal," Xarles replied, getting to his feet.

Eldred relaxed for the first time. All he could do was hope that Oriana was able to write the letter and then seal the copies before she slipped back into her malaise. Either way he needed to be back in Avalon in five days and if he had soldiers with him the all the better.

Chapter 15: Darshival

Richmond stepped through the gateway and came out into the palace gardens. It wasn't home, but it felt close to it. When they had last left Kiarome he didn't think he would ever return to his home kingdom and that was true for his friend and advisor Tancred. The thought of his childhood friend brought a tear to his eyes, which he quickly wiped away. There was no time for foolishness. He could grieve for his friend when the final battle had been fought and won.

Ulman followed Richmond through before closing the gateway behind them. He looked around the garden to see if anyone had noticed their arrival, but the garden was surprisingly empty. Ulman didn't think it was a good sign, although he couldn't work out what it meant.

Richmond didn't seem to notice that anything was wrong. He was more concerned about entering the palace and speaking with King Unwin. Despite the uncomfortable conversation about asking for more soldiers, he knew the king would want to know about his daughter. He really didn't know how much he should tell Unwin about what Marina had been doing. She had left without saying goodbye and if he knew the whole truth then there would be little chance of gaining his support and that was the most important thing. He could deal with Unwin's wrath after the final battle had been won. That was the thought he kept running through his mind. Nothing else mattered except winning.

The soldiers looked as though they were waiting for them to arrive. Richmond was so caught up in his own mind that he didn't notice, but Ulman was instantly put on edge. A feeling of dread came over him.

"Lord Richmond and Lord Ulman, we have been given orders for you to see King Unwin immediately," one of the guards said in an officious tone.

"Very good," Richmond said. He was about to walk past the soldiers when Ulman restrained him.

"How did you know we were coming?" Ulman asked the soldier.

"We were instructed by the king's master-of-the-house. He didn't tell us why, but he said you would be here today and you would need to see King Unwin straight away."

There was something amiss in the guard's tone. Richmond picked up on it when he realised why Ulman had stopped him. The situation was not at all as it should be and if they weren't careful could be walking into a trap.

"Give us a moment," Richmond said.

"But King Unwin is insistent that you meet him straight away," the guard pushed.

"He can wait a few more minutes," Ulman said as they walked out of earshot.

"What do you think this means?" Richmond asked.

"I don't know, but there is a suspicion that the Dark Knights have been brought back to life. If a Dark Knight has infiltrated the palace then this might be a very short visit."

Richmond's heart sank. He remembered the last time he was in Kiarome and the state of King Unwin. He couldn't believe that he had been ensnared again.

"So what do we do?" Richmond replied.

"I don't think we have a choice. We have to see what the situation is in the palace. That is what we came here to do and waiting isn't going to do anything to help us."

"What if there is a Dark Knight there?" Richmond's tried his best to remain calm, but his tone belied him.

"Then we will cross that bridge when we come to it."

Ulman had no idea what he would do if he had to face a Dark Knight. The battle they had in Remidia was still thick in his mind. They had struggled to defeat one with all seven of them. He didn't think there was much chance of him winning one on one. The large claymore he wore strapped to his back felt extra heavy. It always made him feel more comfortable when he wore his large sword, but on this occasion it made him feel very self-conscious.

"Okay," Richmond said as they approached the guards. "We can find our own way," he added when it looked as though they were going to provide an armed escort.

"Of course, Lord Richmond," the guard sounded confused.

The corridors of the palace were strangely empty. It did nothing to calm their nerves. At first they dragged their feet, but with no one around, there was nothing to hinder their pace. Their anxiety was at a peak when they reached the doors to the throne room. Whatever was waiting for them on the other side was not going to be good.

For some reason there were no soldiers standing guard. Richmond placed his hand on the door handle, but stopped before he opened it. Everything inside him was telling him to turn and run, but he knew that wasn't an option. Taking a deep breath he pushed the door open and walked inside.

Ulman instantly filled himself with energy when he saw the robed figure standing next to King Unwin. The king sat on his throne and didn't look as though he was suffering any affects from the Dark Knight, but it was hard to tell.

"Relax, Lord Ulman," the Dark Knight spoke a slow drawl from under the hood of his robe. "I am not here to fight with you."

"Then what are you doing here?" Ulman wanted nothing more than to unstrap his claymore and strike him down.

"I am here to give you a message from the Great Lord. Now, I think this is better done in privacy, if you don't mind King Unwin?"

Unwin dismissed him with a wave of his hand. It was the first time Richmond noticed the scowl on his face. Whatever had happened before they arrived had not put the King in a good mood. Richmond could certainly understand his distaste for the Dark Knights.

Richmond looked at Unwin who in turn shrugged his shoulders. It was not the response they had been expecting, but there was nothing else they could do. Although they both knew they could not trust a Dark Knight, they still had to listen to what he had to say. At worst they might get an insight into what Nyrra was planning.

The Dark Knight led them to a small antechamber at the back of the throne room. Only a small table at the back decorated it, it seemed somewhat appropriate for their meeting with the Dark Knight.

"Be quick about it," Ulman barked. "We don't have time to waste with the likes of you." He wanted nothing more than to peer through the hood and work out which Dark Knight had come back to life.

"It's okay, I won't be staying here any longer than I have too. The Great Lord petitioned me to give you his offer, although I can't for the life of me work out why."

"Get on with it," Ulman barked again. His nerves were starting to get to him.

"Very well, the Great Lord has generously offered to spare your lives if you remain here for the duration of the final battle."

"And why would he do that?" Richmond almost couldn't believe the words that came out of his mouth. There was something different about the Dark Knight. He didn't command the usual fear that was synonymous with his kind.

"I have no idea. We will crush you in Avalon regardless of who will be there, but that is the offer he's giving and I would suggest you take it. He doesn't make offers lightly. Stay here and he will leave Kiarome for you to rule, or live out your pitiful lives if that's what you choose."

"If that is all, you can leave now," Ulman said.

"Don't think that I want to stay a moment longer," the Dark Knight went to step forward, but stopped. "I think you will have some explaining to do with King Unwin. I mentioned to him the fun I had with his daughter and I don't think he was overly impressed.

"Argoz!" Ulman whispered.

"That's right. Now it is time for me to leave."

The Dark Knight walked past the two and left through the door. Ulman thought it was odd. He was expecting Argoz to simply disappear. If what Argoz had said was true, then they would have a hard time convincing Unwin to offer more soldiers.

"Tell me, Lord Richmond, where is my daughter?" Unwin's voice was deathly calm when they returned.

Richmond cringed at the sound of the question he had been dreading. Instantly he thought about lying, but if Unwin caught him then it would be the dungeons for both of them.

"She was duped by the Dark Knight Argoz," Richmond bent the truth, but only a little. "He lured her to Lel Dinion and enslaved her. The Chosen One tried to free her, but her mind had been damaged too much. There was nothing he could do. Once Alaric had killed the Dark Knight she fled the city."

"And why did you not go after her?" Unwin cut in.

"You know as well as I do that if I had a choice then I would have brought the princess back here, but that is not my mission. We had to leave for Remidia without delay."

"And you claim that you freed Marina from the Dark Knight, but that is not the story that has been relayed to me," Unwin returned.

"And why would you believe a Dark Knight, Unwin?" Ulman's voice boomed around the throne room. "They are renowned for lying and there is no good reason why Argoz would tell you the truth."

"You will address me as King Unwin or your majesty in my throne room, wizard," he almost spat the last. "Your kind has also been known to manipulate the truth. Why should I believe anything you say?"

"Because I am not here to trick you. I am here to help you and everyone else in your kingdom." Ulman did his best to remain calm. The initial shock of facing a Dark Knight again had passed and he had no problem standing up to the king. "If there was anything we could have done for Marina then we would have, but there just wasn't the time." Ulman was just guessing from what Richmond had said. He really had no idea what had happened to her. "I am sorry, but when this mess is all over I promise that we will do everything we can to see her returned to you."

Unwin didn't look as though he was interested in Ulman's words, but a confused expression crossed his face. He wasn't so sure of himself anymore. He knew the Dark Knight's could not be trusted, but that wasn't his only source of information.

"A number of messengers have returned from Lel Dinion to tell me pretty much the same story. I would never believe the words of a Dark Knight, but I cannot ignore the same story over and over again."

"And do you not think that those messengers are agents of the Evil One?" Richmond asked before Ulman had a chance to speak. "I was there in the throne room of Lel Dinion when Alaric defeated Argoz. I was also there to see Marina attack the Chosen One. She was not herself, your majesty, something had changed inside her. She was wearing the Sapphire ring of power and when Alaric took it from her she lost her mind. I don't know where she went, but as Ulman said, we will do everything we can to see her returned to you."

"That is a promise that I will keep you to Lord Richmond. If she is not then you will spend the rest of your life in my dungeons," Unwin threatened.

It wasn't much, but Richmond felt as though they were slowly starting to get somewhere. As much as the king wanted to believe that he and his daughter had been betrayed, he knew it wasn't true. The Dark Knight was definitely lying, but he still wasn't sure if Richmond and Ulman were telling the truth.

"That sounds like a fair deal," Richmond kept the conversation moving. "But you will have to do something for us."

"You dare come in here making demands of me, after everything you have done?" Unwin couldn't believe what he was hearing.

"Under normal circumstances I wouldn't ask, but we all know these are not normal times. We need all your soldiers, including your personal guard," Richmond came straight to the point. "The final battle is in mere days and we are still outnumbered."

"Ha! I've heard that story before. Whilst the last final battle was supposed to take place I was under the thrall of another Dark Knight. Now you want me to leave myself open to attack again. I think not."

It wasn't the way Richmond had wanted things to happen, but it was certainly a response he was expecting. There was little chance Unwin was just going to offer up the rest of his soldiers without some serious convincing.

"You are right. The first battle was a ruse by the Evil One and this is exactly what he wanted. He wanted to sow distrust throughout the Seven Kingdoms and it looks as though that is just what he has done." Ulman tried his best to impart some wisdom.

It was funny how Ulman had come full circle. When the Alliance had stood on the battlefield in Avalon the first time he had been on his island oblivious to the outside world. Now he believed with his entire being that the Nyrra was a true threat and he would not rest until he achieved his goal.

"That is easy for you to say, but I still need to look after my people. I cannot empty my kingdom of soldiers."

"Normally I would agree with you, your majesty, but this is an unusual and extremely dangerous situation. I will be sending all my soldiers from Bellarome," Richmond tried to reassure him.

Unwin remained quiet. For the first time his mind was starting to change. As much as Richmond had left his home, the king knew that he still cared for his people. He couldn't imagine he would leave his people to suffer, but that still didn't mean that he was right. For many years Entero had been trying to steal into his kingdom. If he sent all his soldiers north then his borders would remain undefended and open to invasion.

"All the kingdoms need to fight together," Richmond continued, as if reading Unwin's mind. "If but one kingdom fails then the Evil One will win and it won't matter who rules when the battle is over. The Evil One will leave no one alive to reap the rewards of any treachery."

"I will need to speak with my advisors. Your words make sense, but there is still much that needs to be discussed. I cannot make a decision like this lightly," Unwin replied.

"I understand, but there is no time. We need to send riders to Sillarome and the surrounding villages to gather as many soldiers as we can. In five days we need to start moving the men to Avalon. I will travel to Bellarome and have my soldiers and any man willing to hold a sword ready to march," Richmond replied.

Unwin shook his head. The words the Dark Knight whispered in his ear still resonated with him, but he knew they were false. If the Dark Knight was so keen on him leaving his soldiers in Kiarome then there must be truth to Richmond's words. Despite everything, he knew it to be true.

"Very well," Unwin said finally. "You shall have your soldiers. Let it not be said that Darshival was not there at the final battle. We will see the job done, but be warned, if my daughter is not returned to me then you will feel the hangman's noose around neck."

"Thank you, your majesty," Richmond said as he bowed slightly. "Would you be so kind as to have a room prepared for Ulman while he stays here? I will be leaving for Bellarome right away."

"Don't worry about me. I will be returning to the Wizard's Isle. There was something very disturbing about our meeting with Argoz and I want to check through my books. I will return tomorrow and help organise the troops," Ulman replied.

Richmond had hoped that Ulman would transport him straight to Bellarome, but it seemed he had different plans. As much as he didn't like walking through a gateway, he really didn't want to have to ride all the way. It was a three day ride at best, but he only had two. He would have to ride through the night if he was going to return home in time to have his soldiers ready.

Unwin stood and Richmond and Ulman waited for him to leave before they spoke.

"I will come and get you in six days. Hopefully by then I will have all the soldiers from here in Avalon. Be ready for me when I arrive."

Ulman didn't wait for Richmond to respond before he opened a gateway to the Wizard's Isle. The smell of salt air filled the throne room and Ulman took a deep breath before stepping through.

Richmond looked around nervously, but the room was completely empty. He took a moment to remember where he was. There was a very good chance that he would never see the royal throne room of Darshival again. The thought made him sad, but he only allowed himself a moment before he moved off.

The corridors were still empty, which made his progress all the easier as he rushed out of the palace and towards the stables. If he was going to make to Bellarome in time he would need a good horse. He wished he had asked King Unwin to send word that he was coming.

"Get me the fastest horse in the stables, boy!" Richmond barked at the stableboy when he arrived.

"I'm sorry, but we haven't been told that anyone would be riding today. None of the horses are ready." The boy looked at Richmond nervously. He didn't recognise the man and he certainly didn't look like a noble. He was dressed in a rough leather tunic that looked as though it hadn't been cleaned for weeks. His leather trousers seemed to be in much the same condition.

"I don't care what you've been told boy. I am Lord Richmond and I don't like to be kept waiting," he boomed.

The boy clearly recognised the name if he didn't recognise the face, but that only added to his confusion. If there was a noble coming to borrow a horse then he was sure he would have been told.

"Of course not, me lord, but I wasn't told of your arrival, so I can't give you a horse." The stableboy decided to stand firm on his beliefs.

"Where is your master, boy? I am sure he will love to hear how you treat the nobles of this land," Richmond gave him a stern look.

"My master is in town buying supplies. You see there is nothing I can do to help you. I'm not authorised to give out horses." The stableboy thought he had won.

"That was not the wisest of things to say, boy." Richmond tapped the hilt of his sword. "Now if I was a common thief I would know that you were here alone." Richmond waited for the information to sink in. The look of horror that eventually crossed the stableboy's face showed he understood. "Now I think you should go and get me that horse." The stableboy turned to run. "And if it isn't the fastest horse in the stable then King Unwin will hear about it."

It seemed like hours, but was only a few minutes, before the stableboy returned. The horse was saddled and ready to go. It looked like a sturdy beast and Richmond could only hope that it could keep a strong pace. He had no possessions to take with him, which would aid his journey. A small pouch of coins was all he had to get supplies.

"Thank you," Richmond said as he mounted.

As he kicked the flanks of his horse he tossed the stableboy a silver half crown. He knew the master would give him a beating for letting Richmond take a horse and it was a small gesture of compensation.

There were no problems leaving the palace and entering the city. The guards assumed that someone leaving the palace was allowed entrance.

In stark comparison to the palace, the city was abuzz with people. It was like nothing had ever happened and they were not on the verge of war. Richmond took solace as he slowly made his way through the streets, that at least the people of Kiarome seemed untouched from the effects of the Evil One. He hoped they could remain that way during and after the final battle.

The ride through the city was painfully slow and Richmond's nerves grew with every passing minute. He wanted nothing more than to yell out to everyone to get out of his way, but he didn't want to draw that much attention to himself. There was no telling where the Dark Knight was, or where any agents of the Evil One were hiding. He couldn't risk being captured. He needed to leave the city without anyone knowing who he was or where he was going. It was all going smoothly until he reached the city gates.

"Dismount!" barked the guard.

"I am in a terrible hurry..." was all Richmond was able to say.

"Dismount now or we will drag you from the saddle and send you to the dungeons," the guard levelled his pike at Richmond to accentuate his point.

There was nothing for it. It seemed as though he was going to have to try and talk his way out of the city. He only hoped that he didn't have to reveal too much to the guard. The least amount of people who knew was and what he was doing the better.

"I have urgent business in Lord's Rest," Richmond said when he was dismounted.

"You should know that no one is allowed out of the city without King Unwin's specific permission. Do you have the appropriate papers?" he asked, already knowing the answer.

"No I do not." Richmond wished he had taken the time to change, at least until he had left the city. A noble, dressed in such finery, would have a much easier time. In his current guise he looked just like everyone else trying to pass through the gates, if there was anyone. For the first time he realised there was no one else either coming or going. "But do you think I would be here if I wasn't supposed to be. King Unwin is busy gathering troops for the final battle. I am going to Lord's Rest to help his cause."

"If you were here on king's business then you would have the appropriate paperwork," the guard sounded disinterested.

It seemed there was no way he was going get out of the city without revealing his true identity. He reached into the top pocket of his tunic, which instantly put the guards on edge. What he retrieved made the guards relax for a moment before they tensed again.

Richmond produced his ring that carried the family crest. He knew the guards would recognise it, unlike the stableboy.

"I am Lord Richmond and I am on royal business. Now we could wait for you to send a runner to see the king, but I think we both know what the result would be." Richmond raised a questioning eyebrow.

"Of course, my lord, I'm sorry to have delayed you," the guard did his best not to stammer.

"And be sure that you don't mention this to anyone," Richmond looked around at all the soldiers as he spoke. "I know how you soldiers like to gossip, but be assured that if my movements are made known there will be dire consequences."

As soon as he was back in the saddle Richmond kicked the flanks of his horse and urged it into a gallop. The sun was already high in the sky and he had hoped to already be at Lord's Rest. He needed to stop in the village to eat and get supplies; he also needed to purchase a new horse. Pushing hard he had hoped to be in Stellerville before nightfall, but now there was no chance of that happening.

Despite the chill in the air it didn't take long for Richmond to become covered in sweat. All he could think about was the final battle and the lack of time to gather all of his soldiers.

He could feel that his horse was on its last legs when he reined into Lord's Rest. Both rider and beast were covered in sweat and looked as though they were ready to drop. Only one of them had come to the end of their journey, whilst the other had to soldier on.

Richmond reined in at the inn's stables and almost fell from the saddle. He looked around, but there was no one to be seen. With the city being shut off, there was really no reason for the stable to be manned. Richmond tied the horse to a post and slowly made his way inside the inn.

The inside was much the same as outside. Richmond recognised the man sitting at a table as Onfré. He had run the inn for many years and had recently been given ownership after the death of Emil. Onfré didn't even seem to notice Richmond's arrival.

"Excuse me," Richmond's voice was weak.

"Huh," Onfré sounded like he was deep in thought. "Oh, I'm sorry. I wasn't expecting anyone." Onfré stood and walked towards his guest. It wasn't until he was closer before he realised it was Lord Richmond. "I am truly sorry, Lord Richmond. If I had known you were coming I would have been better prepared."

The inn was dimly lit and it was obvious that no one had been there for a while. Since the death of Emil and the battle in Kiarome there had been few visitors to Lord's Rest. The affect of the Evil One was clear. If Richmond had time he would have done something to help, but he really needed to keep moving.

"I am not here to stay. I have to be on the move again, but I do need some supplies and a new horse."

"Of course, I will have something made for you and a pack of food to take with you. I have sent the stableboy home for the night though and all our horses have all been stabled. I'm assuming you are heading towards Kiarome?" The words came out quicker than Onfré had planned.

"No, I am travelling to Bellarome." Richmond decided to trust the innkeeper.

"Then you better get a room for the night. It'll be dark soon and you can't travel through the forest at night," Onfré sounded hopeful.

"I can't stay. I need to be on the road as soon as possible. I would have liked to have been through the forest before nightfall, but that won't be the case."

One thing that Onfré didn't know was that the forest had been emptied of a good number of bandits. There would still be some around, but Richmond hoped his journey would remain unhindered. The tough part would be riding in the darkness of the forest. He would not be able to push his horse quicker than a walk and even that was dangerous, but there was no other choice. He couldn't afford to lose a night to sleep, not until he reached Bellarome.

"As you say, my lord. I will send for the stableboy to ready a horse for you and have something prepared for you to eat," Onfré said as he shot Richmond a questioning look.

Richmond took a number of coins from his money pouch. His funds were running low and he still needed to buy food and new horses when he reached Stellerville and King's Wait. He tossed a gold crown and a silver crown to Onfré who in turn shot him another questioning look.

"One of the king's horses is in the stable. If you have it returned to Kiarome you will be handsomely rewarded," Richmond explained. "But I would wait a week or two," he added quickly.

"I guess I don't have much of a choice," Onfré sounded disappointed as he stashed the coins in his pocket.

Richmond sat in the dining room and waited. It seemed like most of his day had been wasted. It wasn't long before Onfré came in with a plate of sandwiches. Since there was no one coming into the tavern for meals anymore Onfré had not had anyone work the kitchens. Sandwiches were the best he could manage, but Richmond didn't care. He was just happy to have something in his stomach.

When he was finished eating Onfré returned with a small pack of food. Richmond had not expected much and he was grateful for what he had been given.

"Your horse is ready. I fear it is not in the same category as the one you brought from the capital, but it will get you safely home," Onfré said.

"Thank you," Richmond said as he stood.

He wanted nothing more than to retire for the evening, but sleep was still a long way away. The horse was waiting for him out the front of the inn with a young stableboy holding the reins. He didn't look happy at being called in at such an hour. Richmond ignored him as he took the reins and mounted.

The sun was starting to set as Richmond made his way out of the village. There was little point in pushing the horse for the short ride to the forest. He would need the animal to have all its senses to survive the ride. Clouds covered the moon and it looked as though there would be no moonlight to aid their journey.

Richmond's eyelids were drooping when they reached the edge of the forest. His horse became skittish and jerked him fully awake. She was not happy with the trees looming before her. At night the forest seemed even darker.

"Be calm," Richmond whispered in her ear and stroked her mane.

His soothing words and soft touch seemed to have its affect and the mare returned to her steady walk as it passed into the forest. Even though the temperature was slightly warmer, Richmond still felt a chill and wrapped himself in the thick cloak Onfré had given him.

The trip through the forest was like a dream. In the pitch black Richmond couldn't see anything around him. He didn't know if was asleep or awake or somewhere in-between. Once she was into the forest the horse seemed a lot more comfortable and was happy to work her way through the darkness.

The sun was creeping over the horizon when Richmond approached the village of Stellerville. He tried his best to keep his eyes open, but it was a losing battle. As he rode towards the stables he found the streets were empty. He could only hope that there was someone working the stables. The thought of pushing his horse through to King's Rest crossed his mind, but she had been walking all night and he doubted she would be able to keep the pace.

Luckily he didn't have to wait long. The horse master wasn't interested in doing a trade and Richmond was forced to give his name again. With so many people knowing who he was and where he was going, he decided that secrecy was futile.

On his new horse he quickly raced out of town, the speed jolting him fully awake. He wasn't sure if he had managed to get any sleep through the forest, but he definitely needed some. The only problem was that he wasn't sure when he would get any. At best it would be dusk when he reached his home and then he would have to start gathering his soldiers. There would be little time for anything else. On the other hand he couldn't risk burning himself out before the final battle.

Richmond stopped briefly in King's Wait to change horses again and have something to eat. His fatigue had sapped his appetite, but he knew he needed food. If he didn't then he wouldn't have the energy to complete his task.

The sun was slowly starting to set when the city of Bellarome came into view. Richmond thought it was the most beautiful sight he had ever seen. He wanted nothing more than to pretend that he had returned for good.

Richmond was met at the gates by a number of guards. He hoped to either recognise them or have them recognise him. The guards were men he didn't recognise and in his current state there was little chance they would know who he was. His face was drawn and his eyes drooped. Dirt and dust from the road was stuck to the sweat on his face. He doubted even his own parents would recognise him in his current state.

"I am Lord Richmond," he tried to keep his voice strong despite the overwhelming fatigue.

"Ha," laughed the head guard. "Lord Richmond is dead!"

It was not the response he was expecting.

"So if Lord Richmond is dead then who is in charge of the city?" Richmond thought he'd try and gather some information first.

"Lord Bernhald," the guard replied.

Richmond cursed to himself. Of all the people who could have made a play for his lordship, it had to be him. Richmond had imprisoned the man five years ago for trying to assassinate him and gain control of the city. It seemed as though he had managed to achieve his goal. Even though Richmond was not really dead he had somehow made the citizens of Bellarome believe he was. Lord Bernald would certainly not give up power easily.

"Is Captain Reinhard around?" Richmond asked. If he was going to claim his right then he would need friends.

"Reinhard has been imprisoned as a conspirator," the guard didn't sound happy. "Anyone who was loyal to our old lord has been imprisoned. There is a completely new hierarchy now. Some of us lowly guards were lucky to keep our jobs."

Things were going from bad to worse as a wave of fatigue washed over Richmond. He desperately needed sleep and nearly fell from the saddle. If he was going to achieve his goals then he would have to take a risk. As he pulled his signet ring out of his pocket he hoped he had read the situation properly. In his current state he wasn't sure if he was thinking correctly, but there was nothing for it. He tossed the ring at the guard who caught it.

"Guards!" the head guard boomed when he realised what he was holding. The other guards quickly levelled their weapons at Richmond and his horse. "So you are the one who killed our lord," there was spite in his voice. "You will not see the sun set if I have anything to do with it."

The adrenaline pumping through Richmond's body jolted him awake. "I am not the man who killed Richmond, because Richmond is still alive. I am Lord Richmond and I am certainly not dead, at least not yet. I am still the rightful ruler of Bellarome and if we had time I would send you to Kiarome for reinforcements. Are you still loyal to your rightful lord?" Richmond's voice certainly sounded commanding.

The head guard looked around at the other three guards. They were all loyal to Lord Richmond, or would be if they believed he was still alive. The situation had completely changed and even if Richmond was who he said he was they didn't know what they could do. Lord Bernhald was in command of the city now and all the soldiers.

"So if you are Richmond what do you propose we do?" the guard asked, a little perplexed.

"First you can tell me your name."

"I am Private Cord," he replied in an officious tone. He thought about saluting, but decided against it.

"I guess if we are going to do this then I'm going to need to wash. A change of clothes would be nice, but that might be asking too much."

"My home is nearby," Cord replied. "I can't help you with the clothes, but you can wash up. If you are indeed Lord Richmond then you will look more the part with that dirt off your face."

A wave of relief washed over Richmond and his head started to spin. He knew as soon as the adrenaline had worn off the fatigue would wash over him again, but there was still so much he had to do.

"Lead the way," Richmond said.

"You three stay here and if anyone asks tell them that I was feeling unwell," Cord said to the other three guards.

The three guards all nodded their agreement and Cord started walking into the city. Richmond followed on the back of his horse. It would have looked less conspicuous if he had dismounted, but he wasn't sure he would be able to walk.

"Do you trust them?" Richmond asked, keeping his voice as low as possible.

"With my life," Cord replied. "Let's keep the discussion to a minimum. For now I'm going on faith, I don't completely believe you are our Lord Richmond."

Richmond shook his head, but kept silent.

It wasn't long before they arrived at Cord's house. Slowly Richmond dismounted and nearly fell as his feet touched the ground.

"Are you alright?" Richmond didn't even realise that Cord had moved to his side.

"I will be. I've been riding non-stop from Kiarome and haven't had a chance to sleep," Richmond explained.

"Then let's get you inside before anyone realises."

Although the streets weren't completely deserted there were very few people about. Richmond doubted anyone, even his closest friends, would recognise him in his current state, but he was grateful for the assistance.

"Lili!" Cord called out when they were inside. "I'm home."

"What are doing back so early?" his wife called back from somewhere towards the back of the house.

"Come here," he barked back.

"Who in the God Kings' name is this?" she asked when she saw her husband almost completely holding up a bedraggled stanger.

"This is Lord Richmond," Cord said.

Lili burst out laughing. "Everyone knows that Lord Richmond is dead. Now stop joking around and tell what you are doing here and who this vagabond is."

"I can assure you that I am Lord Richmond," he did his best to sound officious. "I have been in the saddle for a long time and need to clean myself."

"Go and run him a bath," Cord barked.

"There is no hot water. It will take time to heat enough for a bath," Lili complained.

"I didn't ask for an excuse," Cord scowled at his wife.

"That will be fine," Richmond said as he wobbled on his feet. He wanted nothing more than to be seated, but he wouldn't until he was offered. "I just need to wash my face and hair. That should be enough for people to recognise me again."

"I will bring some warm water in for you, err, lord. Please have a seat," Lili offered.

Richmond collapsed into an armchair, his head swimming. As much as he wanted to keep his eyes open and discuss options with Cord, it just wasn't going to happen. Richmond was fast asleep before Lili could return with the hot water.

Richmon

d had no idea what time it was or where he was when he woke. The last thing he could remember was approaching Bellarome. As he looked around the room a dull light started to shine through the window. Slowly the memories of arriving at Bellarome and the guard taking him to his home came back to him.

It wasn't until he was up did he realise someone had stripped him down to his underwear. He looked around and found his dirty riding clothes folded on the back of a chair. When he was dressed he realised that he had completely lost the night. Time was getting away from him and he had achieved very little. With Bernhald usurping his position it was going to be hard to gather his soldiers before the end of the final battle let alone the start.

"Hello!" he called out.

Before long he heard movement from the back of the house and soon he could hear footsteps. Richmond stretched as he waited. Sleeping on the small couch and days in the saddle had created stiffness like nothing he had ever felt before.

"Lord Richmond," the soft woman's voice seemed different to that of Lili's the night before. "My husband will return shortly. Would you like something to eat while you wait?"

His stomach rumbled his response and he followed Lili into the small dining room. It wasn't until he was seated did he realise that his face and hair had been cleaned, as well as the rest of his body. Lili or Cord must have done it whilst he slept. As much as he was grateful to be clean again, he was a little uncomfortable about the way they had gone about it.

Neither Lili nor Richmond spoke as he ate a light breakfast of dried wheat and milk. It wasn't much of a breakfast, but Richmond was just happy to be eating something. Cord returned not long after they had finished looking as tired as Richmond had the night before. There was a broad smile on his face.

"Good morning, Lord Richmond," he greeted. "You're looking a lot like your normal self today." It seemed as though the guard had some good news and couldn't keep the smile from his face. "I have managed to find some soldiers around the city still loyal to your rule. We will be able to free those who have been imprisoned and then take back the city."

Things seemed to be improving. There was no time to lose and they needed to make their secret assault as soon as possible.

"I take it you have a plan?" Richmond asked.

"Of course," Cord replied. "There are half a dozen soldiers waiting outside. They will escort you into the castle. I will take another small contingent into the dungeons and rescue the imprisoned soldiers. If Bernhald relinquishes power then all well and good. If not we will arrive just in time to stop any unreasonable bloodshed."

It seemed like a very risky plan, but Richmond had to agree. If Bernhald heard that the prisoners had been released then he would have time to barricade himself inside the castle. It wouldn't keep him from being executed, but it could delay Richmond enough to stop him reaching Avalon with his soldiers.

"Let's get moving then," Richmond ordered.

Outside were six soldiers waiting for them. They were all dressed in armour sporting Richmond's family crest. He wasn't sure if it was a good idea for them to show their true colours so early, but he was glad to know they were on his side. Although he didn't recognise any of them, they looked as though they were seasoned soldiers.

The streets weren't as busy as Richmond had expected for the time of day, but he was grateful that no one was hindering their pace. They walked with a purpose, but not too quickly. They didn't want to look too conspicuous.

The doors into the castle, as expected, were guarded by four soldiers. Richmond was surprised that with everything going on there weren't more, but he doubted Bernhald would expect Richmond to be returning. Again he was grateful for small mercies.

"Where do you think you're going?" one of the guards asked, obviously not taking any notice of their armour.

"We are going to see Lord Bernhald," one of his soldiers replied.

"I don't think..." before he could finish Richmond and his soldiers had drawn their swords.

"Take them to the guard house," Richmond commanded.

It was the first part of their plan. Two of Richmond's soldiers would stand guard and make sure no one else entered the castle, not that they were expecting anyone. Their plan revolved around secrecy and that's the only way it was going to work. Even with the soldiers from the dungeons they would be seriously outnumbered.

Richmond walked through the corridors of his home with his head held high. The last thing he was going to do was sneak around like a criminal. He was the Lord of Bellarome and that's exactly how he was going to act.

They found Lord Bernald sitting comfortably in Richmond's throne room. Surprisingly there were no soldiers on the door, it seemed as though Bernald believed his own lies that Richmond was truly dead. His councillors milled around him and he looked as though he was the king-of-the-castle. Richmond recognised most of the men in the room and they were certainly not those he would have in positions of power.

No one seemed to notice the five men when they entered, which was exactly what Richmond was hoping for. Even the soldiers, standing at the back of the throne room, didn't seem bothered. As much as Richmond wanted to call Bernald out for being a traitor and usurper, he needed to give Cord time to free the prisoners. Seconds could be the difference between failure and success.

"What do you think you are doing?" Richmond boomed when the waiting became too much for him.

"Who are you?" Bernhald tried to see through the crowd at who had spoken in such a tone.

His councillors all quickly moved aside. They could sense the mood in the room and didn't want to be between their lord and the newcomer. When they saw the four soldiers they moved even further to the side, if they could, they would have left altogether.

"I am the man who you claimed has died to steal my city and lands," Richmond boomed. "Do you deny the lies you have spoken?"

"Richmond?" he sounded truly surprised. "Thank the Gods you are still alive. We were all so saddened when we heard the news of your death." Bernhald signalled to the soldiers at the back of the room, but kept his tone sincere. "It truly broke my heart when I heard. It was a small mercy when the people of Bellarome decided to make me their lord."

Richmond noticed that two of Bernhald's soldiers had disappeared out the back of the throne room. It seemed as though the new lord was also playing for time. Although he had four more soldiers than Richmond, he didn't want to take any chances. Little did he know that Richmond also had reinforcements on the way and was quite happy to play the same game.

"If you think for a moment that I believe your lies then you are a bigger fool than I took you for. You set the lie in place and it looks like you believed you would get away with it."

"Leave us!" Bernhald boomed to the councillors, who in turn ran for the door. He waited for them to be alone before he spoke again. "It is irrelevant what you think. When the war is over the Great Lord will reward me for what I have done here. Your death will please him and will be the final nail in the Alliance's coffin."

Finally it all started to make sense. Richmond had always known there was something off about Bernhald, that was the main reason he had put him in prison, but he had no idea he was an agent of the Evil One. His decision to have Bernhald executed had just been made easier.

"I should have known. All this time you have been working for the enemy. Anyway, better late than never."

As if on cue both the front and back doors opened and Richmond's soldiers rushed inside. The look of horror on Bernhald's face was a small comfort. It was obvious he had not been expecting Richmond to have any reinforcements.

"Kill them all," Bernhald commanded.

The battle was short, but aggressive. Despite spending the last month in the dungeons the soldiers on Richmond's side fought like they had just left the training ground. Bernhad's soldiers fought strongly, but there was no continuity in their tactics. They were like berserkers and Richmond wondered if they were under some kind of spell. The thought was only there for a moment before he needed to defend himself.

They were outnumbered two to one, but their skill with the sword far surpassed their enemy. Within fifteen minutes the battle was over and all of Bernhald's soldiers lay dead on the throne room floor. All of Richmond's soldiers had survived and Bernhald looked on in horror at his impending doom.

"This is what happens to those who follow the Evil One," Richmond said as his soldier's encircled the throne. "You can tell him that, like you, he has already failed."

"Of course, I will take whatever message you like to him," Bernhald whimpered, not understanding what Richmond had meant. "I really did think you had been killed. If I knew you were alive then I would never have taken over."

As much as Richmond wanted to make him suffer he had already lost too much time. Taking another step forward Richmond quickly ran him through. The look of surprise widened on his face as if he really believed Richmond was going to let him go. A pang of sorrow hit Richmond as the limp body of Lord Bernhald slid to the floor. He had hoped the Evil One's touch would have stayed away from his home, but he knew that would never be the case. At least he was able to remove the threat before he was able to do too much damage.

"What now, Lord Richmond?" Captain Reinhard said as he saluted.

"Now we prepare for the true battle, the final battle!"

Chapter 16: Hondin Lel

Hadar stepped through the gateway and into a back alley. As much as Althea had wanted to go straight to the palace, Hadar had insisted they walk through the city. King Lisle had been imprisoned in his own mind by the Dark Knight Argoz and Hadar wasn't sure if he would cope with more magic. Althea followed closely behind and scrunched up her nose. It was not the most pleasant of locations for them to step into.

"Hurry up," she snapped. "This place stinks."

Hadar ignored her and made his way out of the alley and onto the streets of Lel Dinion. The streets were strangely empty and Hadar thought they could have appeared anywhere and not be noticed. He knew the affect the Dark Knight and Marina would have had on the city, but since his death and her disappearance he would have thought things would be getting back to normal. In the end he decided it was too much to hope for with the final battle looming.

The journey to the palace gates was quick with no one to block their path. Althea's mood didn't seem to change and it was obvious to Hadar that she just wanted to jump them to the palace, but needed to comserve her energy. There was no telling what she would have to do before the final battle and she couldn't waste it on a whim.

Hadar couldn't help thinking about the state of King Lisle and Queen Mara. Richmond had told him that they had been under the guile of not only the Dark Knight, but also Marina. When he had first been told he couldn't believe it, but he knew it was true. He had no idea what the princess had done and he knew her father would not be happy. It would also make it difficult to gather the soldiers required if Lisle didn't want to join forces with Unwin.

That was the smallest problem they faced. When Alaric had left the King and queen they were still suffering the effects of their ordeal. Alaric had done all that he could with the time he had and there was no guarantee they would have recovered. If they were still incapacitated there was no telling who was in charge of the kingdom, but Hadar doubted they would give them what they needed.

A hundred different thoughts ran through Hadar's mind as they approached the palace and Althea seemed oblivious to them all. She marched towards the gates like a woman possessed. If she had concerns about their mission she didn't show any.

"I am Althea of the Wizard's Council and I am here to speak with King Lisle," she announced when they arrived. She didn't wait for the guards to question who they were and why they were there.

"Of course, come right through," the guards stumbled, not really knowing what to say.

Hadar was both surprised and pleased with the results. It didn't seem as though anyone was allowed into the palace, not that there was anyone trying to. Either way he was just happy that they had not been delayed. There was not a lot of time left before the final battle and they needed to start gathering soldiers. His son, Hagar, had been sent home by Alaric to gather all the soldiers from his duchy. With a little luck they would already be in the city.

The guard hadn't said the King was indisposed, which Hadar thought was a promising sign. He was sure they would have said something if Lisle was suffering, at least he hoped they would.

The palace grounds, albeit not a hive of activity, had a few people moving around. No one really took any notice of them and Hadar also saw that as promising. It seemed as though it was business as usual.

No one stopped them until they reached the throne room. Although they didn't know if King Lisle would be there they figured it was the best place to start. Two soldiers were standing guard when they arrived.

"The throne room is closed." The guard didn't seem to care.

"Where is King Lisle?" Althea asked in a terse tone.

The question and the tone forced the guards to take notice. They looked at Althea and tried to place who she was, but neither recognised her. They didn't even bother looking at Hadar.

"Who do you think you are to demand to see the king?"

"I am Althea." She paused for a moment. "And this is Duke Hadar and if you don't know who we are then I'd suggest applying for a new job." Althea spoke like she was lecturing a child. "I don't think King Lisle would appreciate it if he heard you kept us waiting."

The guard was not going to be persuaded as easily as the one at the gate. He clearly recognised Duke Hadar's name and the man himself when he bothered to look, but he didn't recognise Althea.

"The King is in a meeting at the moment and I don't think he wants to be disturbed," he replied.

"I think he will be more upset if he doesn't meet with us," Althea continued.

"We have an important message from the Alliance. He needs to hear the information straight away," Hadar spoke for the first time.

"Of course, Duke Hadar, he is in his war council," the guard said.

Althea huffed before turning and walking away. Hadar shook his head before following after. He didn't think she knew where she was going and was proven right when she turned right instead of left at the end of the hallway.

"You need to change your attitude when you speak with the King," Hadar warned.

"I have spoken to kings and queens since well before your great-grandparents were born," Althea's tone still sounded like a petulant child.

She certainly didn't sound like a great wizard of legend. "I think I know what I am doing."

"Be that as it may, I think you would be better to let me do the talking. I have known Lisle for a long time and considering how sensitive these matters are it would be best for me to speak with him," Hadar insisted, seemingly unfazed by her demeanour.

"Do whatever you think is best. I certainly don't care," her tone belied her words.

Hadar had been told that Althea had been controlled by the Evil One and he could certainly understand her foul mood, but that was still no excuse. What they were working towards was much more important than her bruised ego.

When they arrived outside the King's war chamber there were two soldiers standing guard. When they saw them approach they both straightened, but relaxed when they recognised Hadar. They didn't seem to notice Althea at all, which did nothing for her mood.

"Is King Lisle inside?" Hadar asked.

"Yes, Duke Hadar," one of the soldiers replied. "I'm sure he'll be pleased to see you."

Hadar didn't know what to think. He didn't think it was a good sign, but there was only one way to find out. One of the soldiers opened the door and Hadar led Althea into the room.

King Lisle was sitting at the head of his large war table. Hadar recognised the man next to him as the court magician, Lorio, but he didn't recognise the other two men. All four looked up when they entered. Lisle smiled when he saw Hadar, but that quickly changed when he saw Althea.

"Sorry to interrupt you your majesty," Hadar started. "This is Althea, one of the wizards from the Council of Wizards."

"Yes, I know who she is." His comment caught them both by surprise. "What I don't know is why you thought to bring her here?"

"I'm afraid I don't think we have met," Althea sounded confused, "and yet you sound as though you know me."

"No, we have not met, but that doesn't mean I don't know who you are," Lisle sneered as he spoke. "You knew and betrayed my great-grandfather. I am surprised you don't remember, but I guess my kingdom doesn't rate very high on your list."

"I have no idea what you are talking about. I have never betrayed your kingdom or any of your ancestors," Althea snapped.

"Lorio, would be so kind as to explain?" Lisle was fuming.

Hadar had never heard of anything between Althea and the kingdom. He was sure if something so terrible had happened it would be well known. Despite the rush for time Hadar really wanted to hear what Lorio had to say.

"You were visiting from Jarrat, or at least that was the excuse you gave the court," Lorio started. "You came here professing to have great information for us, but instead it was in fact misinformation. You claimed that King Ulrich III was amassing an army at Bellarome to invade our South-Eastern border. We took you on your word and sent an army to defend our villages. But it was not from Darshival the threat was coming from, it was from Entero. We lost many when the soldiers from Jarrat attacked our virtually defenceless villages. If it wasn't for the valiant effort of Hadar's great-grandfather Halaar, then we might very well be sitting in Entero not Hondin Lel." Hadar remembered the battles his ancestors had fought against the Enteroite invasion, but he had never heard anything about Althea being involved. "The records of your betrayal were sealed so the royal family of Hondin Lel could keep their respect, but the information has still been passed down through the generations." Lorio finished.

"So tell me," Lisle started before Althea had a chance to defend herself, "why should I not call for the hangman to ready his noose?"

Althea took a moment to think. It was such a long time ago that she had completely forgotten about it. Eventually the memory returned and she slowly shook her head.

"Not that I need to explain myself to you, but it was not my intention to betray you. I was also betrayed. It was the King of Entero who told me of Ulrich's plan to attack. Little did I know what he had planned and if I had then I would have warned you. It was for this reason that I left the mainland for the Isle of Wizards. With all the deceit and violence in the Seven Kingdoms I just didn't want to get involved."

"Then why didn't you tell anyone?" Lisle asked.

"When I found out what had happened it was too late. What do you think would have happened to me once I had returned to Lel Dinion?" Althea returned.

Hadar was happy with Althea's excuse and there was little time to waste continuing the conversation. There was no real way to tell what had actually happened, it was so long ago, and her response seemed genuine enough.

"I think there will time for this after we have won the final battle," Hadar said before Lisle had a chance to speak.

"As usual you are right Duke Hadar," Lisle replied. "We have been discussing plans to move our army to Avalon." That was just what Hadar wanted to hear. He had been concerned about the stories he had heard around the Alliance and presumed Lisle would be more confrontational to the idea. "Now let me introduce you to Vasil and Bion."

"Nice to meet you." Hadar nodded. "I hope this doesn't sound rude, but who are they?"

"They are from the thieves' guild," Lisle almost cooed as he spoke.

"And my next question is what are they doing here and not suffering in the dungeons?" Hadar sounded confused.

"Normally that would be the case, although normally we wouldn't be seen in the palace," Vasil said. There was something strange about his words, but Hadar let it pass. "The final battle affects us all, wouldn't you agree Duke Hadar?"

"Of course it does, but that still doesn't explain things," Hadar replied.

"We helped Eldred and the others gain entrance to the palace," Vasil suddenly felt ashamed at his words and his face started to turn red.

"That's alright Vasil. I'm not that ignorant to believe that the guild wouldn't have ways into my palace," Lisle reassured him.

"Thank you, your majesty. Of course we had heard rumours of the final battle, but when you are part of the guild all you really care about is where your next meal is coming from. It wasn't until I saw with my own eyes what was happening did I realise that we could no longer remain hidden in the bowels of Lel Dinion," Vasil continued.

"But what can a gang of criminals do to help?" Hadar asked and instantly wished he hadn't.

"You would be surprised what it takes for someone to live on the streets," Vasil sounded defensive. "I know we are not a group of trained soldiers, but we can hold our own. Either way this is our battle too and we will not be left behind."

Once the shock had subsided Hadar was filled with a warm pride. Even the bottom feeders of the city were prepared to fight for the survival of all and he couldn't help but smile. He remembered the group of bandits that had joined them from Darshival and the role they had already played. He thought the thieves might be just what the Alliance needed. Despite everything seemingly going their way, he had a bad feeling that something was still wrong.

"I look forward to fighting beside you," Hadar said. "Is the army ready to march?"

"We have gathered the soldiers from the city and the thieves' guild are almost ready, but we haven't heard from your son," Lisle explained. "He left when the Chosen One was here to gather soldiers from the outer regions. He was supposed to send word as soon as he reached your home, but nothing has come," Lisle sounded concerned. "We sent riders two days ago, but they haven't returned."

Hadar knew something was wrong when he had walked into the room. The sick feeling in his stomach had only grown, even with the good news. The first thing he wanted to do was rush home and make sure his family was alright, but he had to think about what was best for the Alliance. He quickly decided that finding out what was happening with his son *was* the best thing.

"Althea and I will go home and see what had happened. Have the army ready to march in five days. Assemble them outside of the city and we will do the rest," Hadar announced.

The use of the pronoun did nothing to improve Althea's mood. It was bad enough that she had to transport Hadar to Lel Dinion. Now it seemed as though he felt he could give her orders as well, and she wasn't going take it lightly. He would learn some respect before the day was out.

"We were charged with coming to Lel Dinion to collect Lisle's soldiers and that is exactly what we are going to do. I am not here to create gateways at a whim because you feel an urge to go home," Althea's tone was terse.

"We are here to gather soldiers for the Alliance and that is exactly what I am suggesting. If you don't want to assist me then I am sure King Lisle will supply with the horses I need, although I fear that will take too long." Hadar was not going to let her speak down to him. There was too much at stake. "I am sure the rest of the Council of Wizards will think highly of you when I tell them what you have done."

Althea was taken aback. She had not expected him to speak to her in such a manner. His reaction was not at all what she was expecting, but she had to admit he was right. She had a lot to make up for and being stubborn was not the way to go about it.

"Very well. I will take you home, but don't think I will be taking you around the countryside. Bear in mind that getting you to the final battle is only the start. I will still need the energy to fight," Althea warned.

"We will do whatever we need to do to get the army to Avalon," Hadar pushed. "But I will not push any further than we need to."

Althea was about to speak again, when Lisle cut in. "We all have jobs to do and sitting here isn't going to get them done."

Hadar led Althea out of the war room. The last thing he wanted was further conversation with her. All he wanted was for her to open a gateway to his home.

"So where do you want this gateway to open?" Althea asked abruptly.

Hadar explained the field out the front of his castle like he had just been out for a walk. He had spent many hours there and he figured it was the closest and safest place. He could have explained any room in the castle, but he didn't want to waste time if Althea couldn't open the gateway there.

As soon as Althea had completed the gateway, Hadar didn't hesitate to walk through. He was so close to being home. It was only going to be for a short time, but it was better than nothing. He missed his wife and his children and despite the impending doom, he couldn't wait to see them.

The air was crisp and there was still the residue from the morning frost on the ground. The morning cloud cover had passed and the sun was high in the sky. Everything reminded him of better days and he stopped to take a deep breath.

"There is no time for that," Althea snapped when she walked through. "You wanted me to create a gateway because there was no time, now I think you should act like it."

The wizard was really starting to get on his nerves, but he had to admit she was right. There was no time for him to bask in the glory of his homeland. Letting the air out of his lungs he started walking towards his castle.

The guards at the gate seemed surprised to see their duke return. He was the last person they expected to see approaching and with a woman as well. They quickly overcame their surprise, stood up straight and saluted. Hadar returned their salute, but didn't stop to speak with them.

The courtyard was strangely empty. Although Hadar wasn't expecting it to be very busy, he thought there would be people around. He looked at the barracks on either side of the courtyard, but he couldn't see anyone inside. The feeling of dread increased and he quickened his pace.

The solid oak doors, strapped with iron, were unattended. Hadar never had the front doors unguarded and he didn't think his sons would do anything different. Slowly he opened the door and peered inside. He felt as though a trap was waiting for him, but there was no one on the other side.

The large entrance foyer, with marble and granite pillars, was also completely empty. Hadar couldn't help but think that something was wrong. There should have been a functionary or two moving around on their daily business. He walked up the black stone stairs at back of the foyer. He was sure he would find his son in his conference room on the second level.

Like everywhere else the second floor was also empty. Hadar led Althea to the conference room where he paused with his hand on the door. He wasn't sure he wanted to see what was on the other side. Althea stood at his side and waited.

Taking a deep breath he turned the handle and pushed the door open. Sitting at the head of the large mahogany table was a robed figure. The hood completely obscured his face. To his left sat his eldest son, Hagar and to the right sat his wife, Pelagia. Hadar remained calm as the dread inside him intensified.

"You were the last person I would have thought to see here," the hooded figured spoke to Althea. His voice was hoarse and harsh.

"And I should not be surprised to see you here. I should have known that your Great Lord would have his servants do his dirty work for him. What I don't understand is why everyone is still alive," Althea replied as calmly as she could.

"Who is that?" Hadar asked.

"That is the Dark Knight Ra'naroz, returned from the grave. When I heard that the filth was coming back I didn't believe it, but it seems as though it is true."

At the sound of the Dark Knight's name Hadar's hand went to the hilt of his sword, but he stayed from drawing it. He knew there was no chance that he could strike down a Dark Knight.

"So, I take it you haven't come here for the lifestyle?" Althea returned her attention to the Dark Knight, seemingly unfazed. "What is it that you want?"

"Straight to the point," Ra'naroz started. "I guess I shouldn't have expected anything less. I still don't know why the Great Lord chose you over the other six. I guess it's because you're so malleable and gullible."

"I would be very careful if I were you. I may have been bewitched before, but I have all my senses now. Don't think I won't end you. I doubt your master will bring you back a second time," Althea raged.

"Be calm, I'm not here to fight you or you would already be dead." Something in his tone made Hadar sceptical. "I am here to give you a message."

"You must listen to him father. His words make sense," Hagar interrupted.

"Be quiet son," Hadar barked.

"You would do well to listen to your son, he gives you sage advice," Ra'naroz warned.

"This conversation is already boring me. I don't know about you but we have work to do," Althea said.

"Very well," Ra'naroz started. "The Great Lord is offering you amnesty."

"Don't be stupid," Althea interrupted. "If that is all you have to say you can just leave now."

"I will leave, but you will hear me out first," Ra'naroz's tone turned dark. "If it was up to me I would just kill you on the battlefield, but the Great Lord has different ideas. He says that if you remain here and take no more soldiers to Avalon, then he will leave you this land when he has won. If I were you, I would suggest you take the offer. I doubt he will offer anything like this again."

"I think it is time you left," Hadar sneered.

"Please father, take the time to think about it," Hagar said.

"Be quiet. There is no bargaining with the Evil One. If he wins the final battle he will rape the land of everything pure. Leave now, I won't say it again. If you stay I will have your head on a pole in my courtyard."

"I am not here to fight with you and I have done what I came here to do. You can do what you want with my lord's offer. Personally I would prefer to kill you on the battlefield." With that Ra'naroz stood up and left the room.

When he was sure the Dark Knight was gone Hadar looked at his son. He couldn't believe what Hagar had said. He had been raised to distrust anything related to the Evil One. There was no way he should have believed what Ra'naroz had promised them.

"What were you thinking?" Hadar asked. "Why did you even let him into our home?"

"Be calm Hadar," Althea said, her voice soothing for the first time. "We all know how persuasive Dark Knight's can be. I don't even think you could have resisted him."

Althea walked over to Hagar and took a careful look at him before placing her hands on his face. Hagar didn't know what she was doing, but was too surprised to do anything about it. All he could do was remain seated and wait for her to finish. The expression on her face when she retreated didn't look good.

"What is it?" Hadar asked when she didn't say anything.

"I thought the Dark Knight would have clouded your son's mind, but there is nothing there. It seems as though he just let Ra'naroz in."

"He came under a flag of truce with an important message for you. He seemed to know that you would be here. When I heard his offer I knew you would want to hear it," Hagar sounded excited. "Didn't you hear what he was offering? He said we could wait out the final battle and survive."

"I know what words came out of his mouth, but I do not for one moment believe it is true. There is no chance the Evil One would leave us alive if he wins the final battle and I for one want to go down fighting, not cowering in my castle," Hadar rebuked.

"Be calm, my husband," Pelagia spoke softly. "He is only thinking about the lives of your people."

Hadar opened his mouth, but then shut it. He knew she was right and he would probably have done the same thing in Hagar's position, but that didn't change the fact. They had lost valuable days in preparation and nothing was going to get it back. He needed to focus on the future.

"Very well. There will be time to discuss this when the final battle has been fought and won. Now we need to get our soldiers together. Please tell me that you have done something right," Hadar continued, not really easing up on his son.

"I sent riders out to all our lands to gather as many as we can. It was after that that I told those soldiers to remain where they were, pending further commands."

Hadar looked at Althea. He knew what she had told him, but the quickest way to get all their soldiers together would be to use gateways, but she promptly shook her head.

"With confirmation that the Dark Knight's have returned I will need all my energy for the final battle. There is something else though. There was something strange about Ra'naroz," Althea said.

"Of course there was something strange about him. He's a Dark Knight. Everything about him is strange," Hadar dismissed the comment.

"Hadar," snapped his wife. "That is no way to speak to a lady. Especially one of Althea's standing." She blushed as soon as she finished speaking.

A smile curled on Althea's lips for a second before she regained her composure. It had been such a long time since anyone had treated her with deference that she had almost forgotten how good it felt.

"There was something very strange about Ra'naoz, both in appearance and the tone of his voice. I'm not sure what it is, but I need to go home and check through my library. I feel there is something very important that will be vital to us winning the final battle," she explained.

"What does that mean?" Hadar sounded genuinely confused.

"It means that on the morning of the fifth day I will return and you will need to be ready," Althea said. "If you are not then the Gods will need to have mercy on us all."

Althea didn't wait for a response from Hadar, it would only prove to delay her further. She wanted nothing more than to be away from him. There was something about him that disturbed her. He didn't cower before her like he should, but she didn't think that was it. There was something else, but she couldn't put her finger on it and there was no time to give it more thought. There was a more important puzzle that needed solving.

Pelagia and Hagar both gasped as one as Althea created the gateway. They gasped even louder when she walked through and disappeared on the other side. They had never, like most people, seen anything like it.

"What was that?" Hagar asked when he had regained his composure.

"That is a gateway and that is how we are going to get the army to Avalon in time for the final battle. Now we need to get word out to those soldiers waiting for orders. We have no time to waste."

***

Vasil and Bion walked through the streets of Lel Dinion as if they were free men. Neither could remember that last time they had walked around in broad daylight without feeling that every eye was watching them. There was a new life dawning for them and the final battle was a way to get them out of the sewers. The entire guild wasn't in complete agreement and that's what they needed to change. A meeting had been arranged in the Bad Duck, a tavern well known for being frequented by the guild.

Inside, the tavern was almost empty. Two men and a woman sat around a table and a few small groups were scattered around the large bar room. It was the two men and a woman that caught Vasil's attention. They were dressed in filthy rags. There was no chance they were trying to hide their allegiances.

"Thank you for coming," Vasil started. "Kore, Leander and Lorise." He nodded at each of them in turn. "I thought there would be more."

"I don't know what you mean, m'lord," Lorise accentuated her drawl to make her point. "We are here to serve you."

"Enough of that," Bion barked. "This is serious business."

"Of course, we didn't mean to offend your lordships," Kore added.

Vasil shook his head. He knew they would get some grief for their current attire, but there was no time for such foolery. "You've had your fun, but this is serious."

"How can we take you seriously dressed like that?" Leander asked.

"And would you like me to speak with the King of our land dressed in my usual stinking clothes?" Vasil let the rhetorical question sink in before he continued. "We took a big risk and we did so for everyone. I think you would do well to remember that."

"Very well," Larise's voice returned to normal. "We came here to listen to what you had to say, so let's hear it."

There was nothing friendly in anyone's tone, not that Vasil expected there to be. Even within the Thieves' Guild there were many factions. When Vasil had made the decision to speak with Lisle he knew that was only the first battle he would have to fight, but he knew he was doing the right thing. He had seen the affects of the Evil One on his beloved city and could not sit idly by and let someone else decide their fate.

"The final battle with the Lord of all Evil is coming and we need to be counted. We have lived our lives under the streets of Lel Dinion, but if the Alliance loses then there will be no safety for any of us," Vasil started.

"The Lord of Evil has done nothing to me. One might say he is more on our side than those you propose we fight with," Leander retorted.

"It is true that those above us have done little to help us over the years, but do not for a moment suggest that we worship the Evil One," Vasil did his best to keep the anger out of his voice, but failed miserably.

"That is not what Leander is suggesting," Kore calmly replied. "We are not suggesting that we should join the enemy, but we don't see why should care for those who never really cared for us?"

"You need to get that thought out of your head. We are not fighting for them, we are fighting for our own survival. This is a fight that affects us all and I for one will not hide in the sewers whilst someone else decides my fate," Vasil pushed. "That said, the King has promised a pardon for anyone who fights and their family. This is a chance to get out of the sewers and make a better life."

He could tell that his words were starting to have their affect. The fact that only three 'leaders', as much as anyone in the guild could be called a leader, had turned up, was a fair indication of how the guild felt. If he could get through to the three before him and, along with the three others that he already had, it would be enough to mobilize the guild.

"That is all well and good, but we don't have any trained soldiers. What use are we going to be on the battlefield?" Larise asked.

"If this was going to be a standard battle, then I would agree with you, but we will be fighting the Evil One's army, made up of a myriad of creatures. I can guarantee they will not fight like trained soldiers. We have lived a much tougher life than the soldiers we will be fighting with and that might just be the edge that we need," Vasil explained.

"I don't know," Kore mused.

"Vasil is right," Larise's tone had changed completely. "We will show everyone what it means to live in the underbelly of Lel Dinion."

Larise's words brought a cheer from the rest of the patrons. Vasil turned around and realised that the other guild leaders were standing behind them. It seemed that he had more support than he had originally thought. He had to admit to himself that if had known they were all there he might not have pushed so hard, but in the end he had succeeded and they would be counted in the final battle.

Chapter 17: Remidia

Hawthorne stepped through the gateway, walked straight into a chair and stumbled over. The heavy curtains remained drawn over the windows, as was custom when they were not in use. As he knocked over the chair he disturbed the thick dust which made him cough and sneeze. The last time he was there the rooms had been cleaned and prepared for him. He stumbled around until he was able to push himself up.

Drake came through with more aplomb. Realising the other side of the gateway was almost pitch black, he had created a small ball of light. He saw Hawthorne get to his feet and stifled the urge to laugh.

"You could have made that before I walked into the chair," Hawthorne point to the light.

"Let's get moving," Drake brushed the conversation aside. "We have little time for small talk."

Hawthorne wasn't sure if he was deliberately being rude or if he was just trying to show his dominance. Either way he was right. There was little time and none to waste. Bern had told Hawthorne that he had left instructions for the Duke of Zenza to gather soldiers together for the final battle, but Hawthorne could feel something nagging at him

He led the way out of the royal apartments. The corridors were full of people moving around, but no one seemed to notice where they had come from. Hawthorne felt a little put out that no one recognised their prince, but everyone looked too busy to take much notice. At least it would give them a chance to find the duke without being waylaid.

They found the duke in his throne room and he didn't look surprised at the new arrivals. As soon as he saw Hawthorne he got down from his throne and bowed deeply.

"Prince Hawthorne, it is a pleasure to receive you. If you had given me more notice I would have had the royal apartments made ready for you," Duke Hamnet greeted them. "It has been such a long time since anyone has visited us from Remidel. How is your father?"

There was something very strange about Duke Hamnet's tone. It was almost as if nothing had, and was, happening and it was just a normal visit by Hawthorne. He couldn't believe the man could simply push aside all that had happened and pretend that nothing was wrong.

"Thank you Hamnet," he replied slowly. "But these are not times to be talking of simple comforts."

"Of course, your majesty, I didn't mean to imply anything," Hamnet almost stumbled over his words. "I know we have important business to discuss, but I didn't want to seem rude."

Hawthorne visibly relaxed. He was glad the duke was simply holding on ceremony, regardless of the fact there was no time for it. Even when he had returned home there had been too much happening to be treated with such reverence and he had to admit that he liked it.

"Is there somewhere more private we can talk?" Hawthorne said when he realised a crowd had started to gather. There was really no need for privacy, but Hawthorne couldn't help thinking there were still traitors in the estate.

"Of course," Hamnet said. "We can retire to my sitting room. I will have some food and drink brought for us."

Hawthorne suddenly realised he was hungry. In his rush to the palace he had not eaten that day. He decided there would be no harm in enjoying a good meal whilst they discussed business. The crowd seemed disappointed that Hawthorne was leaving as he followed Hamnet out the back of the throne room.

"General Bern told me that he ordered you to gather as many soldiers as you could. How have you gone with that task?" Hawthorne came straight to the point once they were alone.

"I have sent out riders, but it is a difficult task. The Evil One has ravaged these lands. Those who are still alive are afraid to leave their homes."

It was a reasonable excuse, but not one that Hawthorne wanted to hear. The city would provide sanctuary for those left behind and there would be a risk to their homes, but those homes could be rebuilt.

"I appreciate what you have all been through, but it is no different to the other kingdoms. If we all don't work together then it won't matter who stays behind, we'll all be dead," Hawthorne replied, a little firmer than he had intended.

Hamnet thought for a moment. He had hoped his words would make sense to Hawthorne. There was something else that he had hoped not to mention, but there didn't seem to be any other option.

"There was something the Dark Knight told me before he left. At the time it didn't seem to make any sense, but the more I thought on it the more it did," Hamnet started.

"You should know after everything that has happened not to listen to a Dark Knight," Hawthorne couldn't believe what he was hearing.

"Let him speak," Drake spoke for the first time.

"I know Dark Knight's can't be trusted, but there was something about his words that made me listen."

"You were under the thrall of the Dark Knight, anything he told you would make sense."

"Please Hawthorne." Drake could see that there was something more in Hamnet's eyes.

"Most of the time, when I was under the power of the Dark Knight, I was in a haze," Hamnet sounded ashamed. "This story has stayed in my mind. I can't say whether he twisted my mind to make it seem better, but all I know is that I have to tell you want he said." Hamnet paused, waiting for a response, but none came. "He said that he had a message from his 'Great Lord'. He said that if we remain in Remidia then he would spare our lives when he wins the final battle."

"Is that it?" Hawthorne asked when he didn't continue.

"There is more. He said that he didn't know why the Great Lord was offering such a deal and if it was up to him then he would just kill us all and be done with it."

Hawthorne looked to Drake for a response. Of all the messages the Dark Knight could have left behind, an offer of amnesty was the last thing they were expecting. There had to be more to it.

"He must have known there was no chance we would accept such a bogus offer," Drake mused. "I wish he was here so I could question him further." No one believed that was actually true. "Is there anything else you can remember?"

"No, that is it. Everything else is clouded or gone completely," Hamnet said.

Drake didn't know what to think. There was no chance that they would remain behind and the Dark Knight would have known that. Even the Evil One couldn't believe that they would accept such an offer. If nothing else it might have been a tactic to delay them and if Hamnet hadn't achieved the task Bern had left for him, it might just have worked.

"So what do we do now?" Hamnet asked.

"We continue as planned. We need to gather all our soldiers and have them ready to move. In five days we will transport them to Avalon in time to face the Evil One," Hawthorne commanded. "Where are all your soldiers now?"

"Most are outside the city helping clean up from the affects of the Dark Knight," he sounded embarrassed. "My city has been in disrepair and I am trying to make it up to my citizens."

"I understand and feel for you, but there will be time to rebuild when the final battle is over. You need to rally your troops and have them prepared," Hawthorne replied.

"You said 'most' of your soldiers. Where are the rest?" Drake asked.

"I sent half a battalion to Quinaliac. It was there they fought a tough battle with a horde of orglin. I wanted to make sure they were not left open to another attack," Hamnet sounded defensive.

"We need everyone." Hawthorne paused as he thought. "I know they have been through tough times. Arsiliac has been destroyed and Quinaliac was lucky not to suffer the same fate." He thought further. "It seems that everything is in order here. I think if they see their prince it will give them the motivation to continue the fight."

"I think that is a good idea," Drake agreed.

"Have a horse saddled for me right away," Hawthorne commanded.

"Relax!" Drake said as Hamnet was about rush into action. "I will create a gateway there. We don't have the time to be riding back and forth and Hamnet's time will be better spent organising the soldiers back here."

"Thank you," Hawthorne replied.

Drake didn't waste any time in creating the gateway. Hamnet shrunk back away from the sudden door of coloured light and fell off the back of his chair. Despite the severity of the situation Hawthorne couldn't help but laugh. He remembered seeing the gateway for the first time, but his reaction was nothing like the duke's.

"I think you should explain this to your soldiers so they don't get a fright when we move to Avalon," Hawthorne suggested as Hamnet picked himself up from the ground.

"Yes, err, sorry about that," Hamnet looked around nervously as he stumbled over his words.

"Don't worry, it happens," Drake said before he stepped through the gateway.

"Remember that we need the army ready to move in five days. There is no leeway on that," Hawthorne said before following Drake through.

The gateway opened on the outskirts of Quinaliac. It wasn't until he closed the gateway that Drake realised that he didn't really know where he was. All he knew was that he needed to reach Quinaliac and the gateway seemed to find its own location. If he had more time he would study the phenomena, but that would have to wait.

The village before them was not at all like Hawthorne remembered. It had been many years since he had been to the village, but it was obvious there had been a battle there recently. Fences had been ripped down and there were scratches against the wooden buildings, some of which had been destroyed by the rampaging horde.

Drake didn't seem to take any notice of the apparent carnage and made his way towards the centre of town. He figured that would be the best place to start looking for survivors. According to Bern, many of the citizens of Quinaliac and Arsiliac had returned once he had entered the city.

"Halt!" a commanding voice came from behind them. It was obvious that it came from a soldier. "Where do you think you're going?"

They both stopped and turned around. An armoured soldier with five other armed men stood before them. The five men stood behind the soldier, but looked as though they were prepared to fight.

"Prince Hawthorne," the soldier gasped. "I am sorry. We had no idea you were coming, if we had we..."

"That is alright," Hawthorne said, stopping the soldier from stammering. "Who is in command here?"

"That would be Fayne," the soldier replied.

Hawthorne thought for a moment, but he didn't recognise the name. "I don't believe I know him."

"He is, or was, the owner of the inn. Ever since the battle with the orglin it seems the villagers have made him some kind of minor noble. Luckily he was here and had fought the orglin once before. His knowledge of their battle tactics was invaluable."

There was something in the soldier's tone that made Hawthorne nervous. He had come up against self made nobles before and they were never easy to deal with. Most of the time they were arrested and brought to Remidel for the King's justice but sometimes, when the citizens supported them, bloodshed would ensure. If that was the case in Quinaliac then they would be out of luck. There was definitely no time to depose a false noble.

"What is this man like?" Hawthorne asked as they walked.

"As far as a nobleman goes I don't think he's really fitting the role. I would almost hazard a guess that he would much prefer to go back to being the innkeeper."

That was promising. If he didn't want the job then there was a good chance he would agree to whatever Hawthorne told him. That was the best case scenario and one he was hoping to be true. Ever since he stepped through the gateway he had a feeling that something bad was going to happen.

The soldiers took them to the village inn. Even if they were calling him a lord, Fayne was not about to give up his home. Two soldiers stood at the front, which Hawthorne didn't take to be a good sign. If Fayne truly didn't want to be a noble then there would be no reason for his inn to be guarded.

"Is Earl Fayne expecting you," one of the guards asked.

"This is Prince Hawthorne you dolt," the soldier returned. "He doesn't need to be announced."

"The earl is in a meeting. I will check to see if he will receive you," the other guard said.

Hawthorne was starting to get irritated, but he thought it would be quicker just to let the soldier go. If he returned and still refused them entrance then he would do something about it.

"The earl will see you now," the guard said.

The inn was completely empty except for two men sitting on the far side. One was completely robed in black with the hood covering his face. The other was clearly Fayne, even though he wasn't dressed like a nobleman. It was the hooded man that sent a chill down Hawthorne's spine, he knew that was the source of his dread.

"Earl? Fayne I believe," Hawthorne greeted.

"Just Fayne, your majesty. I have no intention of being anything more than an innkeeper." Fayne was about to rise, but stopped at a motion from the robed figure.

"What are you doing here, Morgoz?" Drake asked. "I thought you would be too busy preparing for your death?"

Hawthorne's hand went to the hilt of his sword, but he stopped himself from drawing it. He knew there was nothing he could do against a Dark Knight. The last time he had faced one it had nearly cost him his life, if it hadn't been for for Alaric then it would have. When Dargoz had died he thought he had seen the last of the Dark Knights, but when he heard that they were returning he couldn't believe it.

"I came here to give you a message," Morgoz replied.

"We have already heard your message and we are certainly not interested," Drake replied as he drew in the energy around him.

"You can relax," Morgoz replied. "I am not here to hurt you."

"Well, I can't offer you the same deal," Drake snapped.

When the words were out of his mouth he unleashed a fire ball at the Dark Knight. At the last minute Morgoz rolled out of the way and the ball of fire hit the wall leaving only a small scar. Instead of continuing the attack Drake prepared to defend himself. He knew he only had one chance to kill Morgoz and now he would have to suffer the consequences. There was little chance he would leave the confrontation alive.

When it was obvious there would be no further attack, Morgoz picked himself up and returned to his chair. He made no move to attack Drake and didn't look too fazed by his attempt to kill him.

"I told you that I am not here to fight you, as much as it would give me great pleasure to destroy you. The Great Lord didn't believe that passing on a message through the Duke of Zenza was suitable enough. He wanted me to come here and give you the message in person. He felt that you would take his offer more seriously that way," Morgoz spoke plainly.

"Then you can go back to your Great Lord and tell him he was mistaken. We are not interested in anything you have to say," Drake replied.

"Be that as it may I will give you the offer again. The Great Lord pledges that if you remain here once the final battle is over he will grant you amnesty. You can have these lands to rule and he will leave you be."

"We heard the offer the first time and rejected it," Drake continued. "Now you hear it for yourself. We will meet you and defeat you in Avalon. If you have nothing better to say then you can leave and be grateful I am letting you do that."

"Think about it wizard. It is not only your life at stake. I would think the little prince would be grateful for an opportunity to save his people, well at least some of them anyway," Morgoz said as he stood.

Drake couldn't be sure, but he thought the Dark Knight stumbled as he stood. There was something very strange about the whole encounter.

There were a lot of things that didn't make any sense, none more than the fact that Morgoz didn't try and kill them.

"It seems the people of your village look to you for instruction now Fayne," Hawthorne started when Morgoz was gone. Even though he was their prince he wasn't sure they would listen to his orders. "What do you think of the Dark Knight's offer?"

Fayne was taken aback by the question. He thought with the arrival of Prince Hawthorne all decisions would be deferred to him. Something seemed a little odd in the question, but he took it on face value. If it was some kind of trap then he was happy to walk straight into it. He had nothing to hide.

"These people have been through a lot and some have lost everything. I'm sure you would have heard that Arsiliac was razed to the ground. If there is a chance for peace then I think we should jump on it," Fayne replied.

"That is exactly what I thought you would say, but there is only one way to gain peace," Hawthorne let his words sink in. "The Evil One cannot be trusted. If he wins the last battle then we are all doomed, no matter what promises he might make. The only way to achieve peace is if we all stand together and fight him."

Hawthorne could see that his words were making sense. He knew that Fayne would want to take the deal from Morgoz, but now he couldn't think of anything worse.

"You're right," Fayne agreed. "We will join you in Avalon. How long do we have to prepare?"

"The final battle is in seven days time, but don't worry, we can get you there in time," Hawthorne explained. "How long do you think it will take to have your soldiers, and anyone else who can fight, ready to leave?"

"I don't think it will take too long. I am sure most of those who are able to hold a weapon will be keen," Fayne was starting to become excited. "There are some soldiers scouting through the forest to make sure there are no orglin still around. They should be back by nightfall. Although we have found no sign of them we don't go into the forest at night."

"So should we move them to Zenza City tonight or in the morning?" Hawthorne asked Drake.

"I'm afraid you are going to have to make your own way to Zenza City. There is enough time for you to journey there, even if some of you are on foot. There was something very strange about our meeting with Morgoz and I need to go home and do some research. I have a feeling there is some information that we have all missed; something that will be vital in the final battle."

Hawthorne had a disappointed expression on his face, but it was only there for a moment. Not that long ago he had been prepared to ride hard to Quinaliac and bring the soldiers back without Drake's help, but the gateway had saved him a day.

"Very well. We will march in the morning!" Hawthorne announced.

"Then I will see you in five days," Drake said as he created a gateway and disappeared.

"I guess we have work to do," Hawthorne said as he smiled towards Fayne. "In five days we will be on the battlefield in Avalon and then it will be the final battle."

***

King Faxon stood on his balcony and looked down on the monstrous gateway outside his city. A few months ago he would not have thought such a thing was possible. Although he had supported the Alliance, almost from the start, he always had his doubts on the validity of the prophecy. When he had heard that there was no battle initially in Avalon, he thought everything was over. Even when he was beguiled by the Dark Knight Dargoz he had not believed what was coming.

At first he had wanted to march with his soldiers on the army of darkness, but then he knew he had to stay behind. Looking at the last of the soldiers passing through the gateway and on to Avalon, he wasn't sure if he had made the right decision. He knew he couldn't lead the army, that was up to his son, but that didn't mean he couldn't take part.

The strength that the Dark Knight had drained from his body had returned and he gripped the hilt of his sword. It had been a long time since he had been in battle and he had to admit to himself that he had not kept up with his training. The more his hand strengthened on the hilt, the more he knew he was doing the right thing.

No one questioned him when he wore his armour that day. No one questioned him when he asked for his horse to be saddled. The Remidian army was marching through the gateway and everyone thought he was just going to watch them go through. When it was said and done it was good for morale, but no one noticed that he chosen his battle armour and not his ceremonial armour. He put it down to the fact that everyone was excited with the army on the move. In a few days that excitement would change to terror. Terror at not knowing their own fate and that was something Faxon was not going to do. If he was going to die then he would die in battle, not hiding in his castle.

There were still soldiers moving out of the city and Faxon didn't think it would be hard for him to slip into the crowd. Once he had his helmet on with the visor down no one would know who he was. No one would be expecting the king, so he doubted anyone would put two and two together. Until he reached the stables he would keep his helmet under his arm. Moving through the palace he would need everyone to know who he was, and when he reached the stables it would be the only way he would get his horse.

Taking a deep breath Faxon wondered if he would ever smell his home again. He didn't think he was going to return from the final battle. He didn't know if he was just being silly or whether it was providence. Strangely there was no fear in his heart and only a modicum of sorrow. He had lived a good life and he had ruled well, or at least he thought he had. If he didn't make it back then he knew his son would be a strong and fair ruler.

It took him a moment to get his feet to start moving, but once they did he moved like a man on a mission. The look of determination on his face stopped anyone from trying to stop and speak with him. Anyone with important business knew it could wait. Wherever Faxon was going he didn't need to be interrupted.

When he reached the stables his horse had been saddled and was ready for him to ride out. He would wait until he was out of the palace before he donned his helmet, it would make it easier to get through the gate if they knew who he was.

As he rode through the streets of Remidel with the visor down, crowds of people cheered him on. They didn't know, under all that armour, it was their King riding past. All they knew was that the soldier was heading to the final battle to save their lives and that was worth celebrating. It wouldn't be long before they were all huddled in their homes praying that the Alliance was successful.

When he reached the soldiers outside the city he saw that they had almost completely gone through the gateway. The cheering crowd had kept his nerves at bay, but being out in the open they crept back in. He slowly made his way to the back of the group and dismounted. There were a few soldiers with horses, but no one else was mounted and he didn't want to look conspicuous.

From the other side of the gateway Faxon could see the fields of Avalon. Most of the view was of the soldiers who had already passed through and his heart started to race. There was no way for him to back out. If he tried to leave without lifting his visor he would be brought back and he couldn't let anyone know he had been too afraid to face the final battle. There was nothing for it. When he reached the front of the line he simply followed the other soldiers through to the other side.

Chapter 18: Spider Mountain

Alaric landed them at the foot of Mount Arachnid. He wore his usual black leather jerkin, coat and trousers, which suited the light snow falling around them. A chill wind blew, but Alaric didn't seem to notice the cold. Alena, other the other hand, pulled the bearskin jacket close around her. She didn't know where Alaric had found it, but she was grateful for the extra warmth.

Although the gateways didn't take as much energy, Alaric preferred jumping through the fabric of time. He had grown quickly in the past few weeks and knew he had the energy to jump without weakening himself for the final battle with Nyrra.

For the first time he looked at the mountain looming up before them. The snow had covered most of it leaving only twenty paces from the bottom still visible. When the mountain was completely covered there would be little chance of them finding the entrance they were looking for. Although Alaric didn't know exactly where it was, he knew they would have to climb to find it.

"Alaric?" Alena asked softly.

"Later, we need to get moving. I have a feeling this weather is only going to get worse. If we aren't inside the mountain before the entrance is snowed over I doubt we will be able to find it," he explained as he started up the mountain.

The base of the mountain was a gentle slope and Alaric wove his way through the many spruce trees as he carefully made his way up.

Alena followed quickly behind. There were many questions she wanted to ask, but it was obvious that he didn't want to speak. The further they climbed they steeper it became and in some places the mountain became sheer. Alaric thought about scaling it, but instead decided it was best to walk around. Wherever the entrance was, he figured it would have to be easily accessible.

To make matters worse the snow had started to pile up on the ground slowing their journey. In some places it came half way up their calves and it was beginning to fall more heavily. It would not be long before it was impossible for them to move.

"Do you have any idea where we are going?" Alena asked when Alaric stopped.

"We are close, very close." It looked like Alaric was listening for something.

Alena took the chance to take a deep breath. The fresh mountain air was very refreshing. Each time she entered a forest and then had to leave it made her sad. It was not natural for an elf to spend that much time outside of a forest. Even the coldness didn't really bother her as long as she was surrounded by trees.

"We need to be careful when we enter. It has been a long time since anyone from the outside has entered Mount Arachnid. There is no telling what will be waiting for us on the inside, but if Nyrra knows we are coming then I can only imagine it won't be pleasant."

"Do you think he knows?" Alena sounded worried for the first time.

"He knows, I am sure of that. What I don't know is whether he would waste his creatures trying to stop me or whether he is just moving them all to Avalon."

His words did nothing to ease her tension. She knew that he had changed, that he had grown in power, but she didn't think he could take on a horde of orglin or whatever else the Evil One had in store for them.

When Alaric was sure he knew where they were going, he started off again without saying a word. If Alena was looking for reassurance she wasn't about to get it. She had known Alaric had turned cold since he had left, but she had hoped being alone with him would make him open up to her. She loved him. She had loved him from the first day they had met. She had been told from a young age that she would fall in love with the Chosen One, but until they met she wouldn't believe it.

It wasn't long before Alaric came to an opening in the mountain. The hole was half covered with snow and Alaric knew that it would only be a matter of minutes before it was completely hidden. Alaric scooped out enough snow so they could walk into the mountain. Alena thought it was odd that he didn't use his new found skills to clear the entrance, but she didn't say anything.

Alaric created a small ball of light when they were inside. A small cave was the entrance point into the mountain and there were many scratches on the walls and some dried wood on the ground. Whatever the cave had been originally used for, it had not been used for many years. Dust covered the floor and cobwebs filled the corners.

"Do you think we could have a small fire?" Alena chattered her words. The snow had covered her and the cold had penetrated the thick bear skin.

"You can leave the bear skin here," Alaric spoke over his shoulder as he surveyed the cave.

Before Alena could question him, she felt a warmth fill her body. The sudden feeling took her breath away. When she recovered she realised that not only was she completely dry, but she was also warmed right through. She might have just been for a walk through a summer garden opposed to trekking through the snow.

"Okay, this is definitely where we are supposed to be," Alaric said. "I don't like these scratches on the wall, though it looks like either orglin or goblins." He was so mater-of-fact that Alena didn't know what to think.

"Wait!" Alena said as Alaric started towards the tunnel at the back of the cave.

"What is it?" his voice was oddly soft, not at all what she was expecting.

"Don't you think we should be more careful? If these scratches have been made from evil creatures then we could be walking into a trap."

"Some of these scratches look relatively fresh." He pointed to accentuate his point. "I have no doubt that we are walking into a trap."

Alena opened her mouth, but couldn't think of any way to respond. Although she had come to accept the unexpected from him, she had no idea he would say that. If they were walking into a trap then it would make sense to run in the opposite direction. His calm attitude did nothing to ease her concerns.

"Why are we continuing then?" she finally asked.

"Because this is the way we are supposed to go. I thought you would have realised that by now. There is no other way we can get to our destination so there is no point in trying to fight it."

Alaric didn't wait for a response from Alena. Whatever she had to say would prove nothing more than to waste time. There was no way he could answer her questions in a way she would understand, and he really didn't want to try. Alena shook her head and followed after him.

Alaric had to duck his head slightly to stop it from scrapping across the roof of the cave. Two thoughts entered his mind. Either the tunnel had been built by dwarves or dug out by less than savoury creatures. Either way he was sure it had been created many years ago and whoever or whatever had made it was surely long gone and posed no threat. It was their descendants that worried him. He knew they were walking into a trap, he just didn't know what.

It wasn't long before the tunnel increased in size, both in height and width. Alena quickened her step so she could walk next to Alaric. She thought about asking another question, but there was no telling how far her voice would carry throughout the mountain.

After the tunnel had sloped upwards for an hour they came out into a large cavern. Alaric increased the intensity of his globe of light so they could clearly see everything around them. Alena shrunk back, expecting to see all number of creatures hiding in the shadows, but there was nothing there. She wished he would just tell her what they were walking into. At least then she wouldn't be so on edge.

Alaric walked around the cavern. It looked as though it was a natural formation, which led him to believe that dwarves had nothing to do with the tunnel. The air felt stale and stagnate, if anything had lived in the cavern it hadn't for a long time. It was not what Alaric was looking for. Like Alena he just wanted to find out what it was they were walking into.

"What is this place?" Alena asked when Alaric made no move to continue.

"It looks like it's just a cavern. It may have been used for something a long time ago, but I can't imagine what." Alaric knew if he really tried he could imagine, if not remember, what it was, but he had a bad feeling that he really didn't want to know. For a moment he regretted coming to the mountain. Something terrible had happened there many years ago and he really wanted to leave.

"Which way should we go?" Alena tried to sound upbeat.

There were four exits leading out of the cavern, not including the one they had come through. Alena looked at all of them, but there was nothing telling her which way she should go. She had always thought she was in tune with the prophecy, but it seemed as though she was wrong. If it was that important she was sure she would feel the familiar tug.

"That way." Alaric pointed to the tunnel at the far end of the cavern. He didn't know why and he knew he didn't have to. All he needed to know was that it was the right way to go.

Alena didn't wait for Alaric. It was clear that he wasn't going to provide any further information. She didn't stop until she reached the entrance to the tunnel. That was where her bravado ended. There was no telling what they would find and she certainly didn't want to be in the lead.

Alaric smiled as he walked past and the small globe of light dimmed before following after him. It was the first sign of emotion he had shown in a long time. She hoped that maybe the old Alaric was still in there somewhere.

The tunnel was larger than the one they had arrived through. Again it was impossible to tell if it had been built or if it was natural, although he had a feeling it had been made for some purpose. The further they travelled into the mountain the closer they came to springing their trap. Whoever, or whatever, it was that was waiting for them wasn't far away. Under normal circumstances Alaric's heart would be pumping faster and his nerves would be on edge, but he didn't feel any of it.

There was something else in the back of Alaric's mind besides the impending doom. There was something very familiar about the mountain, although he knew he had never been there before. He had a lot of memories and knowledge that weren't his own, but this feeling was something different. It felt homely. The thought filled his mind until he heard movement ahead and his attention was brought back around.

"I think we should stay here," Alaric said as he stopped.

"What is it?" Alena said breathlessly. Her heart was racing and her legs started to shake. She couldn't remember the last time she had been so scared. She wanted to grab Alaric and hold him tight.

"It's alright," Alaric put a comforting hand on her shoulder which made her jump in surprise. He suppressed the urge to laugh. "I think you should take a few steps back."

Alena did as she was told even as Alaric put gentle pressure on her shoulder. She didn't want him to stop touching her, but she knew she had to do what he said. There was no telling what was coming for them and she didn't want to do anything to hinder him.

At first the sound of footsteps could be heard, but soon there came unworldly shrieks. Whatever was coming for them had caught their scent and was in a fury. Alaric shuffled back before he drew his sword. His nerves were starting to show and he gripped the hilt firmly and took a fighting stance.

Alena could hardly contain herself as the shrieks and rushing footsteps became closer. She wanted to turn and run, but she knew her legs would not carry her.

Slowly Alaric let the light flicker out and for a moment they were left in complete darkness. Alena wanted to scream and she opened her mouth, but nothing came out. She had no idea what Alaric was thinking. Whatever was coming for them was used to the dark and would only prove to be an advantage for them.

Shortly after the white light had disappeared Alaric's sword started to glow red. Alena started to relax, slightly as the light slowly intensified until the entire tunnel glowed. A deep red Finally it seemed as though Alaric had a plan, even if Alena had no idea what it was.

The swarm came about ten paces in front of them and Alaric wasn't surprised to see goblins pour around the corner. All the remaining orglin would be at the final battle and Nyrra would have a hard time getting the goblins to leave their mountain homes. There would be some at the final battle, but they would be less than happy about being out in the open.

At first they were in a frenzy, but when they hit the red light they came to an abrupt halt. The goblins behind the corner kept rushing forward into the ones that had stopped. The screams continued, but Alena didn't know if it was from glee or fear. Either way Alaric was prepared to strike if they reached him.

The goblins at the front of the line looked genuinely scared as they were pushed closer to Alaric. They had no idea who the man was. At first they thought they were going to taste man flesh, something they had not had in years, but now they feared for their lives. One man shouldn't have been able to stop a swarm of goblins, but he did.

Suddenly Alaric heard a squeak from Alena as she grabbed him from behind. As he turned around he saw another swarm creeping up. It seemed the frontal attack was only a ruse and the true trap was coming from behind. The goblins stopped when they realised they had been seen.

"Okay, let's go!" Alaric said in a guttural language that Alena couldn't understand. Alaric wasn't even sure it was a language, but he knew the goblins understood.

Alena was too afraid to ask what he had said. It was not a feeling she was accustomed to. She wasn't a helpless woman; she was a she-elf and a trained warrior, but nothing could get rid of the terror she felt. Surrounded by swarms of goblins even the most stalwart of generals would feel terrified, but that thought did nothing to reassure her. Only Alaric could stand before them and not feel fear.

The goblins looked at each other, but didn't know what to do. They smelled the two as soon as they entered the cavern and knew they could easily overwhelm them, but the man before them didn't cower in fear like they had expected. Not only that, but he spoke words they could understand.

"I think your King will want to see me. I'm assuming his master sent you after me," Alaric said when no one responded to him.

"We did smells you," one of the goblins said in a guttural tone. "No one sents us to finds you."

"Either way, take me to your king." Alaric waved his sword menacingly towards the goblins.

"Put its away and we will takes you," the goblin said.

Alaric made a flourish with his sword before sheathing it. As soon as he did the red light disappeared and his little white light returned. Alena had no idea what was happening, but it seemed as though Alaric had succeeded and that was a good thing. Again she wanted to ask him, but was too afraid to speak.

Alaric didn't look worried as he followed the first swarm. Alena kept looking over her shoulder to make sure the goblins behind them kept their distance. She had no idea what Alaric had said or what he had planned, but she felt extremely nervous. If they decided to rush an attack there was nothing she could do to stop them.

The next problem was the smell coming from the filthy creatures. The closest she could equate it to was a mix between a pig sty and vomit. Alaric didn't seem to take any notice, but then nothing seemed to faze him. It was all Alena could do to keep the contents of her stomach inside. To add to her misery the temperature started to rise and the air became thick the further they walked into the mountain. Eventually the feeling overwhelmed her and she vomited as she walked.

"Stop!" Alaric called out in the guttural half-language. "What's wrong?"

Alena lurched again before wiping her mouth with the back of her sleeve and gasping for breath. "The stench is just too much."

Alaric smiled. "I'm sorry. I didn't even notice."

Alena felt a tickle at the back of her neck. Suddenly the smell of filth disappeared and the scent of sweet cherry blossoms filled her nose. The sickness in her stomach settled and she felt a as good as she could ever remember. A feeling of bliss filled her body and she wished that she could remain that way forever. Even the feeling of pure dread had left her.

"Don't worry, it will all work out," Alaric said to try and comfort her.

When Alaric started moving the swarms moved with him. The sea of evil and filth kept pace with every step he took. Although she could not be positive, Alena felt that Alaric was somehow controlling them. The thought made her feel even better.

After an hour they suddenly came out into a massive cavern. If it wasn't for Alaric's spell Alena thought she would have fallen over at the sight before her. She had been scared when the swarm came around the corner, but nothing could have prepared her for what she saw. The cavern was filled with goblins, thousands upon thousands of goblins. Although Alaric seemed confident, she really didn't know what chance they would have if they decided to attack.

The goblins spread out and kept a small circle around the two as they all walked forward. In the middle of the cavern was a large stone throne and on it sat a large fat goblin with a crude stone crown on its head.

"So you are the Cursed One," the Goblin King spoke in the same guttural tone as the others, but there was no hiss to his words.

Alena stood and watched, unable to understand the strange growling language. In the end she wasn't sure if she really wanted to know what they were talking about.

"So your master told you I was coming?" Alaric asked.

"I have no master, but yes the Great Lord visited me and told me you would come here searching for a treasure."

That gave Alaric the answer he was looking for. If the goblins had the Onyx Stone then Nyrra would have taken it. That meant the stone was still somewhere in the mountain. He would still have to find it, but that would be a problem after he had finished with goblins.

"I find it quite amusing that he knew I would be here, but he didn't think enough of you to give you reinforcements," Alaric pushed.

"Look around you. I have gathered all the goblins in this mountain and they will end you. There is nowhere for you to run." Drool appeared in the corner of his mouth.

Alaric wanted nothing more than to destroy the king and his filthy race, but there was information he needed. He would have to be careful. It was obvious that the Goblin King was getting ready to give the order to attack.

"You think that this is your mountain, but that isn't the case," Alaric started, not really sure where he was going. "But you can't possibly know everything. If you did then you would have found my treasure and given it to your master."

"This is my mountain. There is no one and nothing here that I don't know about," the Goblin King growled.

Alaric laughed. "Is that what you think? I wouldn't be here if there wasn't something for me to find and it seems as though you have no idea where it is." Alaric was trying to goad him, but there was a good chance the Goblin King didn't have the answers he was looking for.

"Don't push me, Cursed One. Look around you. There is nowhere for you to go. You are my prisoner to do with as I wish."

Alaric had thought the king would have been easier to crack. He had no idea what Nyrra had told him, but he should have realised it would be no easy task.

"Alaric!" Alena's voice was soft.

"What is it?" Alaric whispered.

"Look!"

The goblins were edging closer to them. Whatever was holding them at bay, be it the Goblin King or a spell from Alaric, was starting to waver. The feeling of contentment left Alena and her fear had returned. She thought that Alaric's magic must have been waning, but nothing from his facade suggested it.

"It's alright," Alaric assured her again. "Everything is under control. I doubt I will get any more information out of this one. I doubt he knows anything outside of this cavern."

"Talk to me, not to her," the king snapped. "Or I will have you skinned alive for your insolence."

"So your master didn't tell you about me?" Alaric asked.

"He told me enough, and if you refer to him as 'my master' again I will have my goblins tear you limb from limb. He told me that you were coming here and he told me not to let you leave and you can be sure that is exactly what we are going to do. You have breathed your last breaths and soon you will be dead."

Suddenly the Goblin King started choking and gasping for air. It wasn't something Alaric had planned on doing, but he didn't like the sound of the threat. If there was any chance, and he really didn't think there was, of gaining information, then the Goblin King needed to believe his life was in danger.

"I would think twice before you threaten me. Obviously *your master* didn't tell you who I was and what I can do. If he did then you certainly wouldn't be speaking to me in such a manner. He told you that I was coming here in search of a treasure. The treasure is a necklace with an onyx stone. If you truly know every inch of this mountain then you will know where it is."

Alaric only released his magical grip on the goblin's throat enough for it to speak again.

"I don't know what you are talking about. If I knew of this treasure then I would have given it to the Great Lord."

Throughout the conversation the goblins edged ever closer and Alaric knew that his time was up. There was nothing he could get from the Goblin King and the longer he waited the greater the risk of being overrun by the swarm.

"Whatever you do," Alaric said to Alena. "Stay exactly where you are. If you move I won't be able to protect you."

Alena didn't know what he was talking about, but she assumed it wasn't an attack from the goblins. If she remained where she was when they attacked then she would be quickly overrun. Whatever Alaric was about to do she knew only one thing, she would remain exactly where she was until told otherwise.

Alaric completely released his grip on the king. He thought about taking one of the stones from the chest, which still floated invisibly next to him, but decided that he didn't need their help. Although he would have the stones with him for his final battle with Nyrra he couldn't rely on their power. If they found a chance to overpower him he wouldn't be surprised if they did.

Without warning the entire swarm of goblins, including the king, burst into flame. Alena knew why Alaric had told her to stay where she was. The entire cavern was on fire, except for a small ring around Alaric. The fire burned so hot that the thick stone walls started to melt.

Alena couldn't believe what she was seeing. She would not have thought the pure destruction was possible, even by the Evil One himself. Alena didn't know what she was more afraid of, the goblins or the fiery maelstrom before her.

The cavern burned intensely for a minute before the flames completely disappeared. Nothing at all remained of the goblins, not even ash. The fire had burned so hot it had completely disintegrated them. If she hadn't seen them with her own eyes she would never have believed the goblins had been there. All she could do was stand and stare at Alaric. She opened her mouth to speak, but was cut off by a voice from above them.

"Those goblins have been a problem for a long time. I never thought to try what you just did," a man said from a platform high in the cavern.

With the crowd of goblins it had been hard to see around the cavern, but at the far end there was a large opening leading out. Many paths led up and around the edge of the cavern with many exits at random places. The new arrival stood at the highest platform to the left of where they stood.

Alena jumped at the sudden sound, but Alaric didn't seem fazed. He simply looked at the man. He looked to be middle-aged with wispy grey hair and dressed in a simple white robe. It was impossible to gauge any other features from the distance, but it was obvious this was the man that Alaric was looking for.

"It's a little hard to speak to each other at this distance," Alaric's voice carried without him having to raise it.

"I wouldn't have thought there would be any issue," the voice came from across the cavern in front of them.

Alaric remained where he was and Alena couldn't move even if she wanted to. One moment the man was standing above them and the next he was walking towards them. There was no doubt that magic was involved. It was just whether it was good or evil.

"There is no need to extend our voices when we can speak face to face," Alaric said.

There was something very familiar about the man, but Alaric couldn't work out what it was. It was a strange feeling. Ever since he had reached the mountain his destiny had been clouded, something that hadn't happened in a long time. Alaric could see that the man's skin was strangely tanned for someone who lived under the mountain.

"I guess you are right," the man said when he reached them.

"I am..." Alaric started.

"I know who you are and who your friend is," he interrupted. "There will be time for proper introductions, but now is not that time. There are more, and much more deadly, evil creatures in this mountain than just the goblins and that spell of yours will be a nice little beacon for them. When they come I would want to be anywhere but here."

As much as Alaric wanted to ask his name, he had to agree that he was right. When he entered the mountain he knew he would be confronting the goblins or orglin. He also knew they weren't the only evil residing there. As much as he knew he could defeat whatever it was coming for them it would be much easier to just leave. It also didn't look as though their new friend was keen on staying.

"Where should we go?" Alaric asked.

"Back to my home. We will be safe there. "My name is Darius."

Chapter 19: Darius

They followed Darius out of the cavern and Alena instantly felt more comfortable. Something about it didn't feel right to her and she had little doubt in Darius' words. If there was evil in the mountain it would be drawn to the cavern, with or without Alaric's spell. There was no doubt why the goblins had chosen it for their home. She never expected to return to Mount Arachnid, but if she did she would never use that entrance again.

They walked in a straight line for about an hour. There was no way the mountain was that large and Alaric could feel the magic each time Darius changed their course. The magic was so subtle that Alena didn't notice anything, but after a while she realised that something wasn't natural. If they had been walking in a straight line they would have been out of the mountain.

"Wouldn't it be easier just to transport us to your home?" Alaric asked eventually.

"Yes and no. I would ask you this question. Would it not have been easier for you if you had just *arrived* at my home? As much as it is nice to have that cavern finally cleared of goblins, I'm sure it would have been a lot easier for you?" Darius asked.

Alaric thought for a moment and then the answer came to him. He knew that he had to come to Mount Arachnid and he knew there was something inside for him. At first he just thought that the prophecy didn't want him to know where to find it, but now he knew it was something else. Even as he tried to find the location there was nothing there. Something magical was blocking his abilities and he could only assume it was doing the same to Darius.

"So you can see why I needed to create this little labyrinth to keep everyone out," Darius continued when he knew Alaric had come to the realisation. "There is no chance of anyone finding their way without my help."

Alaric doubted that was true. He could feel the magic around him and he was sure, with enough time, he could work out the right combination.

"There are over a billion different combinations," Darius said, as if reading his mind. "Each time you take a wrong turn you are either lost in the mountain forever or you go back to the start. There are no clues or tricks, nothing that would help you pick my lock, as it might be."

Alaric let the thought drift away. If what Darius said was true then he could go mad trying to figure out the different combinations.

"What it is blocking the location of your home? It would have to be powerful indeed for me not to feel it," Alaric asked.

"I thought you would have known?" Darius sounded genuinely surprised.

Alaric shook his head. "The *Rock of Ages*?" It was a question, but he already knew the answer. It would make sense for the Onyx stone to be there. It was the most sacred place for rock and stone and that was the power possessed by the Onyx stone.

They walked the rest of the way in silence. Like Alena earlier in the day Alaric had a lot of questions, but it was neither the time nor the place to ask them. They would both have to wait until they reached Darius' home before they would speak again.

Suddenly there was a break in the corridor ahead of them. A large door was cut into the stone and they were finally able to stop. Darius made a flourish with his right hand, more for Alena's benefit than any real necessity, and they watched the door slowly grind open. The stone was more than three inches thick and Alena didn't think it could possibly be opened by strength alone.

The opposite side was nothing at all what they were expecting. Instead of cold stone, the walls were made from a rich oak with the floors a smooth marble. The entrance had a large ceiling, at least ten paces high, and had many tapestries along the walls. Alaric had to wonder at why he had such a large and ornamented foyer. He couldn't imagine Darius would have many visitors.

Darius led them through a door and into a smaller sitting room where he offered them a seat. He was about to sit himself when a thought came to him.

"Can I get you something to eat?" he asked Alena.

Alena had no idea what time it was, but she knew she was hungry. "Yes, please," she replied.

Darius turned and left the room. As soon as the door was shut it was opened again and he returned with a platter of fresh cheese, bread and fruits.

"Sorry it's not more, but I figure there will be time for feasting later," Darius said as he placed the platter down on the table.

Alaric picked at the food, but it was out of politeness not hunger. Darius didn't really expect Alaric to eat anything, but it would have been rude if he had just placed the platter in front of Alena. In the end there was more than enough food for all three of them.

"So you are Alaric and Alena," it wasn't a question. "I should have known you would end up with an elf."

It was an odd way to start the conversation. If Alena wasn't too busy eating, then she might have taken offence. Alaric didn't know how to respond. Darius obviously knew more about him than the other way around and he didn't like it. Although everything about Darius indicated he was a friend that could easily change.

"I'm not sure I know what you mean," Alaric said.

Darius laughed before answering. "I am sorry. I thought you would have been told more about me."

"I'm not sure why," Alaric replied, still confused. "Until today I didn't even know I was coming here and I had no idea who I would be meeting."

A look of knowing crossed Darius' face as he realised what had happened, or what had not happened. It suddenly made sense why Alaric didn't know who he was and Darius wasn't sure he wanted to be the one to break it to him.

"I would have thought the council would have told you about your heritage when they found you," Darius said.

"I have only just recently met the Council of Wizards and they certainly didn't find me. I found them," Alaric was trying to work out what Darius was saying.

"Was it not the Council of Wizards who found you as a baby?" Darius asked.

"No! I was found by the wizard Eldred and then given to a family in Arsiliac."

"That was not right," Darius said, sounding a little upset. "You were supposed to be left with the council. They were supposed to train you."

"And what do you have to do with this?" Alena asked. She suddenly wished she hadn't when both men looked at her. "That is what we want to know," Alena continued when no one spoke. "None of this makes sense. You know who we are and you're talking like we should know who you are. I think you should just tell us."

"She is a feisty one," Darius smiled, trying to be playful, but failing miserably. "I'm sorry, but there is no easy way to say this... I am your father Alaric." He paused and waited for a response. There was a look of horror on Alena's face, but Alaric's remained blank.

"I don't understand," Alena said. "Why would you just leave him in the forest for anyone to find?"

"I didn't leave him anywhere. I gave him to Eldred, one of the wizards on the council. He was supposed to take Alaric to the Isle of Wizards to train him."

"Eldred never took him to the Isle of Wizards. He grew up in a small village in Remidia," Alena continued when Alaric remained silent.

"Do you have the Onyx stone?" Alaric finally asked, seemingly ignoring the conversation.

"Unfortunately no," Darius replied sounding genuine. "I have known for a long time that it is in the mountain and I have searched for it for more hours than I can remember. Sometimes I feel as though I have searched every inch of this mountain, but I have yet to find any trace of it."

Alaric watched Darius carefully, not that he really thought he would keep the stone from him. There was no deceit on his face or in his voice, but Alaric could not believe that the stone had evaded him for so long. There had to be another reason.

"I was drawn here," Alaric said. "I didn't come here to find my long lost family; I came here to find the Onyx stone." It was almost like Alaric was talking to himself, trying to figure out what he was missing. "It has to be here somewhere."

"If it was here I think I would have known. I figured that you would be able to feel it once you were in the mountain," Darius said.

"That is why it has to be here somewhere," Alaric replied. "Where is the *Rock of Ages*?"

"It is in a large cavern in the middle of my home, but there is nothing else there. Trust me, I have spent a lot of time with the rock," Darius replied.

Alaric didn't respond. It was the only answer. The Onyx stone had to be around the *Rock of Ages*. It was the only explanation. If it wasn't then he had no idea what he was going to do.

Darius led Alaric down a small corridor; Alena followed them closely, not wanting to be left behind. Again Alaric could feel the magic changing their actual position in the mountain. It didn't seem as though the *Rock of Ages* was in the middle of Darius' home, but he couldn't be sure. There was no telling how large his actual home was and the magic shrouding its location presumably came from the rock.

This time Darius led them through a normal oak door. Alena thought there would be another magical entrance, but that wasn't the case. The room containing the *Rock of Ages* was like a large cavern. The walls and ceiling were rough, grey stone. Only the floor looked as though it had been cut and polished. The rock itself was black, but not granite and stood twenty feet high. It was ten feet thick at the base and tapered to four feet at its top. Alaric didn't know what it was made of. It was like nothing he had ever seen before. He could feel the magic flowing from the rock. He had been to many magical places before, but there was something different about the rock. It felt, familiar. Alaric took a step forward, but Darius grabbed his arm and stopped him.

"Be careful how close you get," Darius warned. "You can feel the magic radiating from it. That intensifies the closer you get and if you are not careful it can burn you out. I nearly learnt that the hard way."

Alaric brushed aside his hand and took another step forward. Alena tried to rush forward to stop him, but Darius grabbed her with both hands and pulled her back. He was surprisingly strong.

Alaric walked carefully towards the *Rock of Ages*, but he wasn't worried about being consumed. He could feel the immense power around him and it was glorious. If there was ever a place in the Seven Kingdoms that would ever feel like home, this was it. He clearly understood why Darius had made his home here.

The air around the rock seemed to blur and waver the closer Alaric came. The feeling was euphoric, but that wasn't why he was drawn in. There was something more about the rock that was calling to him. He reached out but stopped just before he touched it. When he was sure he knew what to do, he continued. Instead of hitting hard rock, his hands passed through the black stone. A moment later he pulled them out and he was holding a golden necklace with an onyx stone set at the bottom.

"Well, I'll be..." Darius gasped. "It was here all along."

Alaric walked away from the rock and back to the other two, keeping his eye on the stone. Of all the *Stones of Power* the Onyx stone had more of an effect on him.

"It is about time," the deep male voice resonated in his head. "I have been trapped here for longer than I can remember. I would have called out to you, but the rock kept me prisoner."

"As far as prisons go I can think of worse ones," Alaric said with his mind voice. His offhand comment was met with silence. "Either way you are free and there is work for us to do."

"What are you doing?" Darius asked.

His words brought Alaric back to reality and only then did he realise he was wearing the necklace. He had no intention of doing so and had no recollection of doing it. It should have been a warning sign for him, but he wasn't about to take it off. Nothing in the world felt more natural to him.

"I think you should take that off," Darius said.

"Would you like to wear it?" he asked.

Darius had to admit it was something he had been longing for, but the tone in Alaric's voice made him believe it wasn't truly and option. There was a strange look on his face and he could swear there was a black tinge to his green eyes. There was something very disturbing about him and Darius knew he had to get him away from the *Rock of Ages*.

"Let's go back inside," Darius suggested.

Alena nodded her agreement, but Alaric didn't move. He stayed where he was until the others had left before finally moving after them.

"Don't trust them," the voice was smooth. "They will try and trick you. They will betray you in the end."

"Don't try and play those games with me, I have heard it all before," Alaric spoke softly, but firmly in his mind. "There is something different about you, but don't think for a minute that I won't put you in the box."

His head became quiet. Alaric knew that the voice was sulking, but it was better than the alternative. He now had the six stones that he needed for the final battle, but there was still time before he needed to be in

Nostiria to fight Nyrra. He had just found his father, but he knew there was more to the story. He wasn't sure if it was pertinent to his battle, but he had to find out.

Darius brought them back to the sitting room. Alena sat down, but the two men remained standing. Darius had to admit that the necklace did look good around his neck, but he couldn't relax until it was put away. Darius pulled a velvet pouch. It was f of the same design as the other pouches, and he tossed it on the table.

"I think it would be best if you put that away. I know a lot more about that stone than you, and I think we need some privacy."

"Don't do it," the voice whispered and even inside his head it was hard for Alaric to hear. "He will tell you lies."

As much as Alaric didn't want to put the stone away he knew it was the right thing to do. When he picked up the velvet pouch the voice screamed inside his head. Not that long ago the noise would have made him cringe, but there was no outward sign of what was going on inside his head.

Alaric paused before he lifted the necklace over his head. It felt good around his neck. It felt like it was supposed to be there and he didn't know how he had lived without it. If it wasn't for the screaming in his head he might have changed his mind. He wanted nothing more than to remove the noise and the only way to do that was to put the necklace in the velvet pouch. As soon as he did the screaming disappeared.

"What was that all about?" Darius asked.

"What do you mean?" Alaric sounded genuinely confused.

"The screaming in your head," he said as he looked at Alena. "I'm surprised you couldn't hear it."

"How? Something is definitely not adding up here," Alaric changed his tact. "I think it is about time you tell us some more about yourself."

"I see this Eldred really didn't tell you much," Darius continued. "I think this story is best served over some good wine."

Alaric didn't really feel like drinking, but Alena's face lit up and he couldn't do anything to change that. He still loved her, but there was nothing he could do to show it. He had to keep his emotions in check. When the time came for the final battle he couldn't let his feelings get in the way of what he had to do. With what was before them he didn't know if he could bring himself to break her heart.

Darius returned shortly with two large crystal carafes, each filled with a deep red liquid. He placed them on the table where three golden goblets had suddenly appeared. Although it was completely unnecessary, Darius poured the wine. He did it purely to try and make Alena more comfortable. Although she had been around magic for a long time it could still be disconcerting.

"To long lost family!" Darius proposed a toast.

Alena joined in the toast, but Alaric didn't look interested. She shot him a look which made him at least half raise his glass before taking a drink. There wasn't much time before the final battle, but Alena was going to enjoy as much of it as she could. They had found the last *Stone of Power*, assuming that Alaric was right and Nyrra had the Ruby Stone.

"So who are you?" Alaric asked when he lowered his goblet.

"That is a very good question," Darius took a drink as he pondered how he was going to answer. "I am one of the original wizards created to wield the Onyx stone."

Alaric thought for a moment. "But the name Darius is not synonymous with one of the seven wizards?"

"No, I guess it's not. I have had so many names over the years it is hard to remember them all."

"But why?" Alena asked, engrossed in the conversation.

"When Nyrra betrayed us and we were forced to imprison him in the Northern Wasteland, we other six were not held in high esteem. Eventually the Seven Kingdoms turned on us and attempted to hunt us down."

"But I thought you had all been killed?" Alaric said.

"That was the common story, but no, we are all alive. Or at least I believe we all are. We cut contact shortly after the hunt for us began."

"So then you can all help us with the final battle?" Alena sounded excited.

"Calm down, it's not that simple," Darius said. "I draw my power from the *Rock of Ages*. Outside this mountain I doubt I would have the power to blow out a candle. I can't speak for my brothers and sisters, but I feel confident that they are in the same situation."

"Then how can Nyrra still have all of his power, if not more?" Alaric asked. It was strange for him to be asking questions again. There was something about the mountain that clouded his knowledge. He was sure if they were anywhere else the answers would just come to him.

"Your guess is probably as good as mine, but if I was to hazard one I would say his rage has given him strength. His pure malevolence has kept his ability to draw on the energy around him. The Ruby stone is filled with rage and that is his strength. I have come to peace with my life and that is why my power has waned and I wouldn't have it any other way. If I had a choice I would not travel with you to fight Nyrra."

His words made sense, but Alaric wasn't sure he was correct. There had to be something else, but in the end it was irrelevant to their situation so he pushed it to the back of his mind.

"Why would you say that?" Alena asked, aghast.

"When it is said and done Nyrra is my brother and I will not kill my brother. I know he has done wrong in the past, and will continue to do so if he succeeds in the final battle, but that still doesn't change anything.

Maybe if we had treated him differently those many years ago things might be different now."

"You know that isn't true," Alaric said. "Nyrra is pure evil and now that I have found out he is my uncle it means absolutely nothing to me. Even if I found out *he* was my father it would not change my mind. The only way the Seven Kingdoms will be safe is if Nyrra is dead."

"I know," Darius conceded "but it still doesn't mean I have to be involved. Either way it's a moot point. There is nothing I can do to help you now."

Darius watched Alaric carefully. He wondered if his son would attack him if he thought it would help him achieve his goal.

"Tell me about Alaric's mother?" Alena asked when she finished her goblet.

Darius poured her another drink. It was a much more pleasant topic of discussion, but he wasn't sure Alaric would see it that way. It was obvious that Eldred had told him nothing of his past and that was a problem.

"His mother," Darius deliberately addressed Alena even though it seemed that Alaric was also interested, "was an elf named Caitria. She knew as much as I did that our lives were destined to meet."

"You used the past tense," Alaric's voice was quiet. "Does that mean she is dead?" He almost couldn't bring himself to ask.

Alena felt a sudden burst of sorrow. It was the first real sign of emotion, even though his face didn't show anything, he had shown for a long time. It was just unfortunate it was deep sadness. She wanted to hold him close, but she couldn't bring herself to move.

"I'm afraid so. She died shortly after your birth. We both knew that our time together would be short, but it was our destiny. I did love her, or at least I think I did," Darius stared at the wall behind them as he thought back on his time with Caitria. "Either way we both knew that she would not survive long after the birth of our child. I knew that I couldn't raise you, that wasn't my job. That is why I gave you to Eldred for the council to raise."

"Well maybe you should have taken more care," Alaric snapped. "Don't get me wrong. Eldred gave me to a loving couple, but I certainly didn't get the training that I needed."

"It looks as though you have done alright." Darius raised an eyebrow.

"I came close to dying on a number of occasions. I would put it down to luck more than anything else."

"It is luck that keeps us alive, my son," Darius did his best to lighten the conversation.

"You said Caitria was an elf," Alena spoke before Alaric had a chance. "I didn't think any of the Northern Elves came this far north?"

"Normally they don't. Caitria left her home in *Nordligträ* one morning and started walking. Originally she was out on a hunt, but that soon changed. Before she knew what had happened the sun was setting and she was nowhere near home. It wasn't that she was scared, she had not travelled far enough north to be afraid of the forest, but her heart was heavy. Instead of turning around in the morning she kept going. She was able to hunt for food, and water was easy for her to find. At night she slept in the trees to avoid any nasty creatures on the forest floor. She didn't know where she was going, she just followed a feeling. I met her at the foot of this mountain looking tired and wane. There was a glazed look in her eyes. I offered to take her to the safety of my home, but for some reason she wouldn't set foot into the mountain. I knew of a safe place not too far away. There was a grove with a small brook running through it and it was surprisingly peaceful. I made trips back and forth from here bringing whatever supplies we needed. We remained living in the grove for twelve months. When you were born, Caitria had a sudden urge to return home where I knew I would not be welcome, so I decided to stay here. I met Eldred at the foot of the mountain and explained to him where Caitria had gone and that is all I can tell you."

"So there is a chance she is still alive?" Alaric asked, somewhat hopeful.

"I don't know for sure that she is dead, but in my heart I know it is true," Darius sounded sad again.

Alaric let his head drop. It had been a surprisingly emotional day and not at all what he had been expecting. He thought he would have found the Onyx stone and be gone, not that he was in any hurry.

"I am sorry," Alena offered both Alaric and Darius her sympathies. "It has been a surprisingly long day. I think I might get some sleep." Alena felt suddenly very tired. "Is there somewhere I can lay down?"

Darius half led and half carried Alena to a room where there was a large double sized bed. She didn't know if it was the wine or just the excitement of the day, but all of a sudden she felt extremely fatigued. As soon as her head hit the pillow she drifted off to sleep.

"That wasn't very nice," Alaric said when Darius returned.

"It is getting late and she needs to sleep before the final battle," Darius said.

"We have six more days before the final battle begins."

"You have less than one," Darius said. "I would have thought you would have felt the flow of time. I don't know if it is the mountain itself or the *Rock of Ages*, but time moves differently in here. Some days can last for years and some years can last for days. I don't know if it evens out over time, but that's the way it is."

Alaric should have known. The prophecy affected time when it needed to and it seemed as though it was doing it again. He had hoped that he would have more time with Alena before the end. He truly loved her and that's why he had brought her with him, at least that's what he told himself.

"I guess I shouldn't be surprised. There is little for me to do now before the final battle and it doesn't look like the prophecy wants to give me any time to relax," Alaric mused.

"I guess not, but we still have tonight," Darius poured them both another goblet of wine and raised his own.

Alaric followed suit before he downed half his goblet. It really didn't matter how much he drank he would not get intoxicated, but the rich red wine did taste nice. It had been a long time since he had tasted anything. Since he no longer needed food to sustain himself he had virtually stopped eating and drinking. For the moment he could relax, if only for a short time.

"Tell me about the Onyx stone?" Alaric asked.

"There is not that much to tell. The Onyx stone draws on the power of the earth and rocks. I would say it is one of the more powerful stones, but then again I might be biased."

"That's not what I mean," Alaric said.

"I'm sorry, I don't think I understand what you are getting at," Darius looked and sounded genuinely confused.

"What is the secret of the Onyx stone, and all the seven *Stones of Power* for that matter?" Alaric pushed.

"I'm afraid that I still don't know what you are talking about. There are no secrets to the stones. They are simply powerful talismans."

Alaric watched him closely, but there seemed to be no deceit in his face. If he was trying to hide the truth then he was doing a very good job.

"What about the voices in my head?" He wasn't sure if he should mention them or not, but since Darius had already heard the voice he didn't think it would matter. "Each time I pick up a different stone there is a different voice in my head. Why?"

Darius thought for a moment. He remembered the voice when Alaric had worn the necklace, but it seemed like such a long time ago. As much as he tried he couldn't make out what the voice sounded like or even what it said to Alaric. It was very frustrating and eventually he stopped trying.

"I think I know what you're asking, but I have no answer for you. It's almost as if the memory has been ripped from my mind. Whenever I think I'm getting close the answer slips away."

Alaric thought for a moment. He knew the information was definitely there, but he wouldn't be able to get it without help. If Darius was not who he said he was then it was a big risk showing him the other stones, but there was no other option. He had a good feeling about him and he believed that they were truly related.

Suddenly the chest appeared on the table in front of them. Darius didn't seem at all surprised and Alaric didn't pay him much attention. He would have been disappointed if Darius didn't know about the chest. What he wouldn't know was what it contained.

Alaric carefully opened the lid so Darius couldn't see what was inside. He pulled out the velvet pouch that contained the opal crown and slowly released it from its prison. Once it was free there was no noise inside his head. Those stones he had already conversed with knew better.

"What are you planning on doing with that?" Darius asked suspiciously.

"There is something blocking your memory. I am going to use the Opal stone to remove it," Alaric said.

"There is nothing blocking my mind," Darius replied defensively. "If there was I would certainly have known about it and removed it years ago."

Alaric ignored his father's words. He knew there was something wrong. There was information inside his head that Alaric needed to know. The riddle of the stones had plagued him for a while now, taking up too much of his spare time, but no realistic answer had ever come to him.

Taking a deep breath Alaric closed his eyes and started the spell. At first Darius tried to resist, but when he realised he wasn't strong enough to keep Alaric and the Opal stone out, he relaxed. Whatever Alaric was planning would only be worse if he struggled and he really didn't think his son was going to do anything to harm him.

It didn't take long for Alaric to find what he was looking for and instantly his conscious shrunk back. He had delved into the depths of minds twisted by the Evil One's creatures, but it was nothing like what he came up against inside Darius' mind. It was like a stone wall at least a mile thick, although that wasn't even close to what it was.

"I think I might need your help on this," Alaric spoke to the voice that he knew was nearby.

"Maybe, but do you think there are some things you weren't supposed to know?" the voice remained soft.

Alaric wasn't about to give up. The Opal stone was there to work for him and if he was going to succeed in the final battle he needed to force his will on it.

"Very well, but don't say I didn't warn you." The voice knew what he was thinking.

Alaric thought about shaking his head, but in his current form it was futile. Focusing on the barrier in front of him Alaric forced his will and the will of the Opal stone onto it. He needed the break through whatever it was that was blocking Darius' memory.

After about five minutes Alaric's consciousness retired to his body. It was not a move he had made and the shock made him gasp for breath. His body felt like someone had swapped his blood for ice water and he shivered uncontrollably.

"Are you alright?" Darius asked at the sudden change.

"I don't know what it is inside your mind, but I have never come across anything like it," Alaric replied aghast.

"Is it dangerous?" Darius sounded concerned, but not scared.

"I don't know. I have no idea what it is, but it does seem that it has been there for a long time. If it was dangerous I guess you would have known about it by now," Alaric tried his best to reassure him. "Whatever it is it's blocking your memory of the stones."

There was nothing more Alaric could do, or was willing to try. The way he was pushed out of Darius' mind was aggressive and he didn't know what would happen if he tried again. One thing he knew for sure was that he couldn't break through.

"I guess some things weren't meant to be known." Darius tried to lighten the subject.

Alaric shook his head as he replaced the opal crown. The answer was so close and yet it might have been worlds away. There was nothing more he could do. Just as he was about speak again the door opened and Alena entered.

"What time is it?" she asked sleepily.

"That is a very good question," Alaric said as a sudden feeling of restlessness came over him.

"I feel like I have slept for days," Alena replied.

"The mountain will have that affect," Darius smiled. "I think you should have something to eat before you leave."

"Thank you," Alena said. "So where do we go now?" Alena asked, not realising the shift of time.

"We go to the Cauldron Mountain to meet Nyrra," Alaric explained. "The final battle is about to begin."

"What!" she almost squealed with surprise. "How *long* was I asleep?"

"It's alright. Time passes differently here. I think it is due to the *Rock of Ages*, but don't quote me on that," Darius said as a plate of bacon, eggs and crusty bread appeared in his hand. He placed it down in front of Alena who didn't care where it had come from. She was ravenously hungry and she was used to food and drink suddenly appearing from nowhere. "It seems our time together is to be short. I wish we could have spent more time getting to know each other." He smiled sweetly at Alena.

"We shall return when it is all over," Alena believed her words regardless of how futile they were.

Both Darius and Alaric let the comment drift away. Neither of them truly knew what was going to happen, so there seemed little point in bringing her down. They waited for her to finish her meal before they both stood.

"Thank you for your help," Alaric said.

"If there was something more I could do to help I would. As much as I wish my brother would change I know you are doing what you think is right. I hope to see you again one day."

"Are you ready?" Alaric turned to Alena.

Alena stood and moved towards Darius. He was a little taken aback until she wrapped her arms around him. It was certainly not what he was expecting, but he placed his arms around her and returned the embrace.

When they were finished Alena walked over to Alaric and held his hand. It was completely pointless in the spell he was about to create, but if it made Alena feel better then Alaric wasn't about to say anything. It may very well be the last time they touched and he was grateful for the contact. He wished they could spend more time in the seclusion of the mountain. Taking another, unnecessary, deep breath Alaric transported them out of the mountain.

Chapter 20: On the Eve of Battle

Jarwe sat on the back of his horse, Madra, on the hill which had been come to be known as Victory Hill. It overlooked the central point of the army where the Castalial army was mustering. It was the best vantage point for the entire army, even though he could only just see the Remidian and Darshivallian solders on either side. He had no idea how Alaric expected him to lead an army of such magnitude. Once the battle started there was little he could do. There would be no time to run messages up and down the battle front.

It was the morning of the day before the final battle and there had been no sign of any of the other armies. He had expected to see gateways pop up since sunrise, but there had been none. Nothing had happened since the one bringing the last of the soldiers from the Alliance to Avalon had closed.

General Bern and Cayley, the strange little girl who never left his side, stood next to him. The light breeze didn't seem to have any effect on the blonde pigtails that she had insisted on wearing. They stared out over the soldiers seemingly unconcerned that there was no sign of the other armies. It did little to ease Jarwe's nerves, but at least it was something. Bern, or the entity inside him as it was known within the army, seemed to know things were about to happen before they did. If he didn't look concerned then it seemed everything was going to plan.

Jarwe rubbed his face and the stubble was sharp. He had stopped shaving three days ago. His head had a fine coating of brown hair and he figured that if he survived he could clean himself up afterwards. Normally he would shave his head and face before a battle, but this was something different. He felt that it was neither necessary nor appropriate.

As he looked out over the battlefield there was still no sign of the opposing army. Jarwe thought back to the first time he lead the army in Avalon and what had happened. It had all been a ruse, a distraction to keep the Alliance from its main goal. Jarwe had to wonder if this was just another trick by the Evil One. There was a possibility that he was ravaging the other five kingdoms as they waited.

"Don't worry," Cayley said, as if she was reading his mind. "Nyrra will be here. His army will appear and the battle will ensue. There will be no waiting."

"What do you mean?" Jarwe asked, not taking his eyes from the field.

Just when he thought he had come to terms with Bern and the strange entity that came and went; Cayley appeared. There was no doubt that she was more than the little girl she appeared to be. There was definitely more to her, but there was no time for explanations, not that she would tell him anyway.

"Nyrra's army will be here in the morning, mid-morning," Bern added. "I'm not sure exactly how he plans on bringing them here, but they will come all at once. This battle is going to quick and brutal. We need to make sure the army is prepared. Nyrra will work on 'shock and awe' tactics. This battle will be done, one way or another, by nightfall tomorrow night."

Bern's words did nothing to reassure Jarwe's nerves and if anything it gave him more to worry about. It seemed as though there was going to be a surprise attack, even though they knew the army was coming. Deep down he really hoped it was a ruse. With everything that had happened and everything he had seen he didn't know if he wanted to fight another battle with the Evil One. By all accounts there were creatures coming that made the orglin seem like puppy dogs.

Before Jarwe could speak a rider approached them. "General Bern," the soldier saluted from horseback. "The elves have started arriving from *Nordligträ*. They should be through and settled by midday."

"Good news. Has there been any sign of the other armies?" Jarwe asked.

"Not yet general."

"Have Brielle meet us here when she has finished. There is a transport ground she can use to create a gateway here from the battle ground," Bern explained.

The soldier saluted again before riding off to the western side of the Alliance. After seeing the gateways and passing through them the soldiers didn't seem to have a problem with them. If Bern said the wizard could create a gateway in the valley behind them then that is what they would do.

Bern had set up the valley so each wizard would have their own place to create a gateway for the command ground. When they tried to create the second gateway there would be nowhere else they could place it. It was an ingenious way to someone creating a gateway in front of another.

The gateways would be the best way to relay information around the field. It was much better than semaphore and quicker than messenger. Jarwe had no idea how he would manage the entire army without them, presuming all the wizards arrived on time. The more time that passed the more Jarwe wasn't convinced that was going to happen.

"You should go and get something to eat. That should take your mind off things, at least for a little while," Cayley suggested.

Jarwe had not had the stomach to eat breakfast and he still didn't think he could eat. Waiting for the gateways to open and the soldiers to fill the Alliance had his nerves on edge. He didn't think he would be able to eat until the rest of the soldiers had arrived, at the very least.

"I will be fine, thank you," Jarwe replied.

Cayley looked at Bern, but he didn't seem to notice. She couldn't blame Jarwe, but she was concerned. As much as she didn't need food to sustain herself, she knew that he did. He would be no good in the morning if he didn't eat something. Either way she wasn't going to push it, but if he didn't eat the evening meal it would be a different story.

By midday they had word that two more armies had started to make their journey through their gateway to Avalon, the Remidian and the dwarven. Despite the fact the elven army had finished their arrival there had been no sign of Brielle. Jarwe thought about sending a rider, but then decided against it. The last thing he wanted was to show the rest of the army that the wizards were already not listening to his commands.

"Surely the Evil One would have his army here by now if he was going to attack tomorrow?" Jarwe said.

"You should know by now that it doesn't take long to move an army half way across the Seven Kingdoms."

There was a crackle of grass being singed behind them as the first gateway opened in the transport ground. They all turned around expecting to see Brielle step through, but it was Drake, followed by Prince Hawthorne.

"It's good to see you my prince and you Drake," Jarwe greeted them as he dismounted. He legs nearly collapsed under him as he had grown used to being in the saddle. It was clear that everyone saw, but he simply ignored them. "I wasn't sure if you were going to make it when there was no sign of you this morning."

"We were always coming. It just took a little longer than we thought to be ready to move," Hawthorne replied, his tone matching Jarwe's humour. "What is the situation here?"

"We are simply waiting for tomorrow to come," Jarwe said. "And for the other armies to arrive."

"I saw the gateway open for the Enteroite army before we left."

"So the western side of the army is almost complete?" Jarwe mused.

"It does seem that way," Hawthorne seemed a little confused with the small talk.

"What plans do you have for us?" Drake asked, looking around to see who was in earshot. There was something about his stance that made Jarwe think he wanted to be elsewhere.

"Not much until the rest of the armies arrive," Jarwe replied.

When he finished speaking there was another crackle from behind them and two gateways appeared at the same time. Through one came Brielle and Orric and through the other came Dorn and Gwydion. It had taken less time than Jarwe had expected for the dwarves to arrive from under the mountain.

"Good afternoon," Jarwe greeted the newcomers.

"We should retire to the command tent," Bern spoke for the first time. "This is no place for a meeting."

"But shouldn't we wait for..." Jarwe said, but didn't get to finish.

"We can catch the others up later, but there is no more time for waiting," Bern said.

Bern led them down to the command tent where they were met with a table laden with food. At first Jarwe wanted to protest. He was pretty sure the rest of the army wasn't eating so well, but it could very well be one of his last meals. The sight of food had suddenly made him ravenously hungry.

They all sat and started eating, except for Cayley and Bern who only made a show of it. Jarwe looked at Bern, hoping that he would start the conversation, but he simply shook his head. He would not be around in the morning when the battle would start. Regardless of what had happened in the past, Jarwe was the General of the Alliance and he needed to take control.

"The battle will start in the morning," Jarwe started, a little unsure of himself. "The army will arrive from nowhere and will attack as soon as they get here. We believe the Dark Knights will find a way to transport them here."

"It is interesting that you say that," Drake said.

"Yes, indeed," Brielle added.

"What are you talking about?" Bern asked.

"There was something very odd about our meeting with the Dark Knight Za'aroz," Brielle continued. "I couldn't put my finger on it at the time and when I returned home to study it I found nothing, but there was definitely something amiss."

"I have to agree. As much as I didn't expect a warm welcome, I didn't think the king under the mountain would try and imprison us," Drake started. "He will never forget what happened next. Just as the soldiers were about to try and remove us from the square, the rest of the council members arrived. They voted to join the Alliance and there was nothing Ashnar could do to stop them. Dorn was pardoned and given control of the army."

Bern noticed there was a strange expression on Drake's face when he finished his story.

"What is it, Drake?" he asked.

"Oh, nothing," Drake lied.

"There is no time for this Drake. You found something and I have a feeling it is very important," Bern snapped

A smile appeared on his face and he looked like a child who had been caught stealing cookies. Bern shook his head. They were on the brink of the biggest battle the Seven Kingdoms had ever seen and the wizards were acting like spoilt children.

"I knew there was a passage in one of my tomes about the Dark Knights return, not that it's written outright mind you. It seems that if someone is to be brought back from death it takes time for them to fully recover. It seems as though we could have killed them all and been done with it," Drake sounded disappointed with his last comment.

"Did it say how long it would take for them to recover?" Bern asked.

"No, but by the state of Morgoz I wouldn't think it would be long," Drake replied.

"By the looks of Za'aroz I would doubt he will be back to full strength by now. Thinking back I would have thought Orric could have killed him, no offence," Brielle added.

Dark Knights, at full strength, would have been Nyrra's major card to play. Now he might drain them just getting his army to the battlefield," Bern mused. "This is a promising sign, but we shouldn't get ahead of ourselves. This could just be another ruse from the enemy to lull us into a false sense of security."

"So what do we do?" Orric asked. At first he looked at Bern, but then looked across to Jarwe.

"We plan for the worst and hope for the best," Jarwe replied, but he really didn't know what the worst would be. He had fought and won many battles but the one they would fight in the morning would be like nothing he had seen before. He wished that Bern would stay in command.

"And what exactly does that mean?" Dorn asked. He would be sharing the command of the dwarven army with Hulkan and needed as much information as he could get.

"We have to prepare the soldiers for what will come," Bern said. "The Evil One's army will arrive all of a sudden and it will come as a shock to them. Each army will have to fight its own individual battle. The evil creatures will not wait for our soldiers to gather their wits. They will charge as soon as they arrive and we need to be ready for that."

"How can we prepare the soldiers if we don't know what's coming?" Jarwe had to ask the question.

Bern knew it was coming, but he didn't know the answer. He thought he would know which evil creatures Nyrra would throw at which army, but nothing came to him.

"The soldiers get their strength from their leaders," Bern replied. "Whether they know what is coming or not is irrelevant."

Jarwe lowered his head in shame. He knew how to lead an army and he couldn't believe he had asked the question. There was too much self-doubt happening. If he didn't believe in his own abilities then how could the rest of the army.

"You are right," Jarwe said. Before he had a chance to continue the tent flap opened.

To everyone's surprise they saw Eldred and Duke Xarles enter. No one had expected them until mid-afternoon and no one thought it was a good sign. If he had already finished moving the Enteroite army to Avalon then they didn't receive all the soldiers they were hoping for.

"What went wrong?" Jarwe asked.

"Nothing, why?" Eldred sounded genuinely confused.

"You came here awfully quickly," Jarwe continued. "That must mean there are not many soldiers coming from Entero?"

"We got as many as we could in the time given to us. The soldiers are moving into place as we speak," Eldred replied.

Jarwe shot Bern a confused expression, but he didn't respond. "Isn't it too dangerous to leave a gateway unattended?"

"I set guards around it to make sure no one walks into it by mistake. I will close it when I return," Eldred said.

During the final battle the gateways between the armies and the command site would need to remain open. The ones used to bring the armies to Avalon were just on a grander scale. Each took the same amount of energy to keep open once they had been created. The other wizards looked a little abashed about not thinking of it themselves. They had all remained until the gateways were ready to be closed.

"So it is just the eastern side of the army that we are waiting on now," Hawthorne changed the subject.

"They are all supposed to be here by now," Orric replied. "I fear that something is wrong. We might need to prepare for the fact that they are not going to be here in time."

"There is still time," Jarwe said, more to convince himself than the others. "As long as the armies are all here by morning and the soldiers are ready to fight that is all that matters."

"Jarwe is right and don't think anyone is getting any sleep tonight." Orric agreed.

"But Minerva is still a worry," Drake added. "She had two armies to bring across and we still haven't seen her."

"She can create two gateways to bring them here," Eldred returned.

"That's if she realises that she can," Brielle said. "As much as it cringes me to say I didn't realise I could create two at once. I thought when I created a second gateway the first would collapse on itself."

"We can tell her when she creates her first gateway, here if she hasn't worked it out for herself," Eldred said.

Bern shook his head. Sometimes the obvious wasn't easy for some people to see. Eldred had spent enough time in the Seven Kingdoms to know how things worked, but it seemed the other wizards had not. At least they weren't at each other's throats, which he thought they would be.

Next to arrive was Ulman and Lord Richmond. Just like all the other wizards, accept for Eldred, Ulman had not realised he could create two gateways at once. A rider had to be sent to explain when word reached them of his arrival. It seemed as though Eldred was going to be the only one who had worked it out for himself. They weren't to be blamed, really. Alaric should have explained things better. Bern would have, but that would have given too much away and he still needed his anonymity.

"It seems as though the Evil One has a long reach," Richmond started to explain why they were late. "Bellarome and Sillarome had both been taken over by an agent of evil. Although we know we need every solider here, we had to leave some behind to clean up the mess. The Evil One is clever."

"We had to do the same thing," Dorn admitted. "The outer villages were being attacked by swarms of goblins. It seem the Evil One couldn't bring the goblins out of the mountain to fight his final battle," Dorn explained. "But we do estimate that another three thousand dwarves have been added to the Alliance."

Jarwe took a moment to smile. They had thought they would be lucky to get another thousand soldiers from the mountain. It looked like things were finally starting to turn around.

"How many soldiers have the rest of you brought?" Jarwe asked, happy with the change of topic.

"There were not many left in Remidia," Hawthorne was the first to answer. "Maybe another thousand at best from the Duchy of Zenza. There had been another orglin attack on Quinaliac, but when we checked the forest there was no sign of the Evil One's agents so we took all the soldiers we could gather."

"Unfortunately we couldn't get as many soldiers as we would have liked," Xarles said. "We put as much pressure on our minor nobles to supply us, but the distance was an issue. We managed another two thousand five hundred, plus maybe a few late comers. Most of our soldiers went with the Alliance when it left Jarrat." It almost sounded like Xarles was apologising.

"It's hard to know exactly, but we estimated about another seven thousand soldiers from Darshival," Richmond continued.

"There were only a hundred, give or take a few, left from *Nordligträ*. The battle with the orglin over the *Tree of Life* took its toll. There are only the too old and too young to fight remaining in the village," Orric explained.

It wasn't much, but they weren't expecting many from *Nordligträ*. All they really knew was that the elves needed to take their place in the final battle if they had any chance of success. It was the army with the least amount of soldiers, but they would not let the Alliance down.

"Then all we can do now is wait for those to arrive from Castalia and Hondin Lel," Jarwe resigned.

Before anyone else had a chance to speak the tent flap opened and Duke Hadar entered. Everyone looked for Althea, but she wasn't with him. They had left a message for her and Minerva to create another gateway and meet them at the command tent. There was no reason why she shouldn't be there.

"Good afternoon to you all," Hadar greeted them, a slight puff to his voice.

"Where is Althea?" Gwydion asked.

"She wanted to remain with the army."

"Did you get the message about being able to create two gateways at once?" Brielle asked.

"Yes, but she said there was something wrong, maybe unstable is a better word, about her gateway. She didn't want to leave it alone in case it collapsed in on itself," Hadar explained as best he could.

"We've never had problems with a gateway," Eldred said, not that they had much experience. "Do you think a Dark Knight might be involved?"

"Or maybe she is still playing for the other side," Drake suggested.

"How can you even suggest such a thing," Brielle snapped.

"How could we have thought such a thing in the first place and then find out it was true?" Gwydion asked the rhetorical question.

"She said she would be here as soon as the army has completed its journey," Hadar boomed, instantly silencing the wizards. "We had a nasty meeting with a Dark Knight and Althea seemed to be shaken by it, but she is certainly no traitor. If she was then we would have no soldiers passing through at all. Instead we have almost fifteen thousand soldiers from Hondin Lel."

That was the best news Jarwe had heard all day. The Hondin Lel soldiers, except for the few Hadar had brought with him, had not yet joined the Alliance. It was obvious that the Evil One had played a part in delaying them, but no one really knew what it was.

"Then it's just a matter of waiting for Minerva to bring the remainder of the Western Dwarf Guild army and the Castalial army," Jarwe sounded hopeful.

The group remained in the command tent for the rest of the afternoon. They sat in hope that Minerva would arrive, but there was no sign of her. When the sun was starting to set they decided that it was time to go and see to their respective armies. Only Jarwe, Bern and Cayley remained.

"What are we going to do if Minerva doesn't make it?" Jarwe asked the question that had plagued him for the last two hours.

"She'll be here and she will bring with her the rest of the Castalial army, or at least as many soldiers as she can get," Cayley tried to reassure him.

"That's just it. There's not that much time for her to move such an army here," Jarwe returned. "And she still has to bring the dwarves as well."

As if answering his concerns the tent flap opened and Hulkan hurried into the tent. Everyone hoped to see Minerva and Captain Elyas follow him, but they were nowhere to be seen.

"Thank the God's you are here," Jarwe said, only slightly relieved.

"Things didn't quite go to plan. The Evil One has agents all over Castalia. It took Minerva a long time to root them out," Hulkan explained as he picked at the leftover food on the table. He looked for some ale or wine, but Jarwe had instructed that there was too be no alcohol for anyone. Hulkan was about to ask, but he knew what the response was going to be.

"So has she started to bring across the soldiers from Castalia?" Jarwe asked, hopefully.

"Not yet. The messenger told Minerva that she could create more than one gateway, but she already had the army line up behind the dwarven army," Hulkan explained. "She passed back through the gateway to Castalia so she can move both at the same time, although it shouldn't take too long for the dwarves to pass through, they are all keen for battle," pride filled his voice.

"Very well," Jarwe said. "You should go and prepare the dwarves for what is before us in the morning." Jarwe briefly explained what they had already discussed earlier in the day. "Have a messenger go to Castalia and have Elyas and Minerva meet us here as soon as they can."

Hulkan nodded his agreement as he grabbed a cold haunch of lamb. He wished he could enjoy what was more than likely going to be his last meal, but there was too much to be done. He left the tent as quickly as he had arrived. He had no idea how he was going to prepare his fellow dwarves for what they were about to witness.

"So it looks as though we have an army," Jarwe sat back and did his best to relax for the first time that day.

"I have a bad feeling things aren't over yet," Cayley said and Jarwe sat back upright.

"What do you mean?"

Before Cayley had a chance to reply the tent flap hurriedly opened and a red faced messenger rushed in. He took two gasps for breath before he settled himself.

"General Jarwe," he panted as he spoke. "Fighting has broken out in Castalia. It seems that a group of rebels has started attacking the city since most of the soldiers are assembled to travel here."

"So what is happening? Has Minerva started moving the soldiers yet?" Jarwe asked quickly, hardly believing what he was hearing.

"Minerva has created the gateway, but the soldiers have refused to move through whilst the city is under attack. There is nothing Elyas can do to get them to move. Normally he would threaten to imprison those who disobeyed his orders, but that would only be a false threat."

"Thank you," Bern said. "You can go now."

"What do we do now?" Jarwe asked.

"Now we prepare for tomorrow morning. There is nothing more we can do here. We can't send any soldiers to Castalia to help and we can't force the soldiers to come here, not by tomorrow morning anyway. Whatever will be will be," Cayley said.

Jarwe looked at Bern, not happy with the response he had been given. He had no idea who the girl was and her cryptic answers were grating on him. The expression on Bern's face didn't fill him with any confidence.

"We must trust that the prophecy will lead us to victory and the Castalial soldiers will arrive on time. For now you should try and get some rest. In the morning you will have to lead the entire army to victory."

"And where are you going?" Jarwe asked.

"We are going to Nostiria to help Alaric with his final battle with Nyrra. We have been waiting a long time to finish our allotted task. It has been a long time coming," Bern explained without really explaining anything.

"I don't suppose you're going to tell me what that task is?" Jarwe asked.

"All in good time," Bern replied as he led Cayley from the tent.

Chapter 21: The Elven War

Orric stood next to Pernian and watched the sun rise, he wondered if it was going to be the last sunrise he would ever see. He took a deep breath, inhaling the fresh Avalon air. A thin film of dew covered the grass. There had threatened to be a frost overnight, but thankfully it had stayed away.

"Do we have any idea when this battle is going to start?" Pernian asked.

Orric ignored the question as the obvious 'no' was not a response that needed to be made. He looked back at the army of elves behind him. They had no idea what was about to happen, but they stood strong. He didn't know how long that would last if the opposing army didn't arrive soon.

Kilean and Palen rode up to meet them. The other two leaders of the different elven clans had agreed to meet at dawn. It had been over a century since the related clans had been together. Those from *Nordligträ* did not feel comfortable around Kilean's elves. They remembered the stories of the elves who had disappeared with their favoured treasure. Orric had assured the two leaders that they would be given equal respect, but he was in command with Pernian second. They would both have to listen to orders and act when they were given.

"The elves are ready," Palen said before Kilean had a chance.

"Very well, I don't think it will be long now. Has there been any sign of Brielle?"

"She is on her way from the transport ground now," Kilean answered.

Orric had spent the night preparing what he was going to say to the elves. He knew he needed a commanding speech to prepare everyone for the horror that would befall them. Most of the elves would never leave Avalon.

"Good morning," Brielle said when she arrived.

Orric and the others greeted her before he turned to face the army. "My fellow elves," he started. Brielle had created a spell so Orric's voice would carry across the army of elves without him having to yell. "Yesterday we stood divided, but today fight as one. The Evil One plans to enslave and destroy us, but we won't let that happen." Orric paused as a cheer passed over the elves. The sound echoed to the east as the other leaders started their speeches. "Whenever and however the evil arrives we will defeat it. We will not give in to our baser instincts to run in fear. No matter what terror appears on the other side of the battlefield we will stand together and we shall fight. If only one of us survives this day then it will be a success, but let's not give the Evil One the satisfaction of our deaths. We shall defeat him and his minions and save the Seven Kingdoms for all time." The end of his speech brought another cheer from the elves before him.

When he was done he turned and faced the battlefield. The sun had completely bridged the horizon and Orric knew that the battle was almost upon them.

Without knowing what the enemy was going to throw at them made it very difficult to make any plans. Orric had decided to bring the archers to the front of the line. Those with horses, not many at all, were next in line with those on foot behind. Once the archers had loosed their arrows, the cavalry would join the battle. If it wasn't conducive for horses then the archers would take up their swords and join the fray.

Suddenly the air became electric and small crackles of lightning skirted the space no more than a thousand feet in front of them. It seemed the Evil One's army was going to appear closer than they expected. The archers would have a chance to get two, maybe three shots off before they would have to switch. According to Bern the army would charge as soon as it hit the battlefield. There was no reason to think otherwise.

Dark storm clouds roiled across the sky behind the flashing air and lightning started to shoot down. The ground, at least a league if not more behind the expected field of battle, exploded with a deafening crack of thunder. Orric wanted to turn around, but he wasn't sure what he would see. The elves who had cheered and stood stalwartly during Orric's speech, started to waver. The final battle was coming and if the display before them was anything to go by it wasn't going to be pretty.

"Messenger!" Brielle called out.

A messenger ran up beside her and she passed on a message to give to the other wizards. At the transport ground behind Command Hill there would be messengers waiting to travel to all the armies. Brielle was sure the weather wasn't natural and if the storm hit during the battle, as was the most likely scenario, then it would surely hinder the Alliance. There was no telling what they would face once the Dark Knight's arrived, but she thought they should fight what was in front of them.

Not long after the messenger left another messenger arrived. It seemed that all the wizards had the same idea.

They had all agreed that they needed to do something to stop the approaching weather. If the Dark Knights were controlling it then it would be a good use of their power. If it was Nyrra then they would have to be prepared for an attack from the Dark Knights.

Brielle waved her arms in front of her before she let them return to her side. That was the only sign that she was doing something. Although the dark clouds didn't disappear they slowed their advance and the lightning stopped. It seemed that the final battle had already started and it was the wizards who got to fight first.

"Archers, ready!" Pernian called over his shoulder.

The small bolts of electricity intensified before there was a loud ripping sound, as if the fabric of reality itself was being torn apart. Suddenly a massive gateway opened in front of them. It was twice the size of any gateway the wizards or Bern had created. At first it bubbled a deep red and purple before it finally coalesced. The scene before them made all the elves take a step back, even Orric wanted to turn and run. Before anyone had a chance to react a sea of orglin came pouring out.

"Orric!" Pernian said softly.

There was no response from the ancient elf. It had been the moment he had been prepared for as long as he could remember and he didn't know what to do. He heard Pernian's words, but all he could do was look at the orglin storming towards them.

"Orric!" Pernian spoke louder as the orglin came closer and closer.

"Archers!" Orric quickly regained his senses. "Fire!"

Orric's words, still affected by Brielle's spell, carried throughout the army. It was much better than the normal flag semaphore that armies used in battle. All the elves would get the command as soon as Orric spoke it, which was why Pernian didn't voice the command himself.

After the command was given the sound of bow strings snapping could be heard. As the arrows arced towards the approaching orglin it was as if time itself stopped. No one expected the arrows to hit their targets. Everyone was just waiting for the Dark Knights to create their spells and swallow them up.

"Draw your bows," Orric boomed. He didn't need to look behind to know they were all waiting. "We are at war, not in the training field."

The arrows dipped towards the orglin that ran at full pace, not concerned with the approaching death from above. The arrows fell and to everyone's surprise hit their targets. Orglin scattered to the ground. Those that weren't hit didn't care for their fallen comrades. They just continued on the path that was set for them. They would feast on flesh and those that died would be one less orglin to fight with.

Seeing the arrows hit their mark spurred the elves on to loose another round. That was all they would get to fire as the orglin had already covered half the distance.

Pernian was the first to draw his sword. Although the cavalry had been brought forward, it was only to be used if Nyrra sent something other than orglin at them. The elven horses, although strong and brave in battle, would be no match for the ferocity of the orglin.

"Bows down," Orric commanded. "Swords up. Horses to the rear. Charge on my command."

The elves on horseback moved out of the way as best they could to allow those on foot room to charge. It gave them something to focus on and not let the fear take control.

"Let's show the Evil One what elves are made of," Orric said. "CHARGE!"

Pernian led the charge. It had been decided the night before that he would not remain with Orric. The command was for one elf only. Kilean and Palen had retreated with the others on horseback, leaving Orric alone with Brielle. He couldn't believe the orglin were still pouring out of the gateway. At first he thought they were outnumbered two to one, but as they kept coming he thought it was closer to four.

Pernian charged with his fellow elves. He didn't know if they were from Elhjem, *Nordligträ* or the South, but it didn't matter. They were all elves and they were all fighting for the survival of the Seven Kingdoms and everything in-between. He gripped the hilt of his sword with all his might, but he knew he would need soft hands when it came to battle. If he kept his current grip then he would be too stiff to fight effectively.

The orglin weren't perturbed by the charging elves, brandishing their swords. They had been whipped into a frenzy by their masters before they passed through the gateway and nothing would stop them. The horde moved almost as one in the race to kill and feed.

Pernian only slightly slowed his pace to balance himself for the attack. As the horde swarmed around him, he slashed out with his sword. He cut down orglin left and right as he pushed forward.

The orglin threw themselves against the elves with no care for their own wellbeing. Space was the biggest issue for the elves after the initial strike. Pernian managed to clear a small space in front of him, but that didn't last long. The orglin didn't care for the standards of battle. Shortly after Pernian stopped his advance the orglin forced him backwards. Although the ever piling bodies of dead orglin slowed their advance, it did nothing to stop their ferocity.

Orric watched the fight in horror. The orglin had no care for themselves or the elves. It seemed for every orglin the elves cut down another three would take its place. The most disturbing thing was that every elf who fell to an orglin they were instantly swarmed and ripped apart. The orglin that were cut down straight away busied themselves gorging on the corpses. The sight made his stomach churn.

"Is there any sign of the Dark Knights?" Orric asked Brielle to take his mind from the battlefield.

"Nothing. There's no way to know who is controlling the weather, but we have slowed its advance. The storm will come eventually, but we will hold it for as long as we can," Brielle explained.

Orric did his best to think. The scene before him was caught in his mind and made cognitive thinking difficult, but he was in charge of the army. There were still elves waiting for commands. He had sent two thousand elves in the first wave, but there was little doubt they were fighting at least ten thousand orglin, and more were still pouring through the gateway. Orric wondered if they would ever stop. If they didn't then it would only be a matter of time before they were completely overrun.

"Is there anything you can do to close that gateway? If we can close it down that will stop the flow of the enemy, at least for a short time." Orric asked.

"No," was her initial reaction, but only because she hadn't thought about it. The spell to hold back the storm was taking a lot of her energy, but there was still more she could do. Orric was right. If she could close the gateway then it would give them some respite from the orglin.

She looked at the gateway and realised straight away it was nothing like what they had created. The gateway itself was pure malevolence. If anyone, from their side, tried to pass through it they would be consumed. As much as it was a good idea, her first answer was right. She had no idea how to close or even destroy the gateway. "There is nothing I can do to get rid of it," her second response was more controlled.

Orric knew that was going to be the response, but he had to ask. The dead bodies were starting to pile up. The only good thing was that it proved to help the elves and hinder the orglin's advance. Then, to Orric's horror, the orglin started devouring their own kind. He didn't know what was worse, being on the battlefield or watching everything unfold from his vantage point. He shook off the feeling of disgust and prepared to give his next order.

"Front line pull back, second line advance," Orric boomed.

The break in the battle was the perfect time to relieve the elves who had charged in first. Although the thick leathery skin of the orglin didn't stop the blades from slicing through, it did threaten to blunt the elven steel. Not everyone would have a chance to have their swords sharpened, but there were blacksmiths ready and waiting.

After the second line there was one more line of infantry of nine hundred elves before the three hundred on horse. Orric did his best to try and count the elves as they came back, but it was a futile task. From the two thousand that charged in the first line only an estimated five hundred had returned. If Orric knew the exact number he may have lost all hope as the orglin continued to pour from the gateway.

It didn't take long for the gorging orglin to eat through their fallen comrades. As soon as the ground was clear the battle continued. The orglin which had just feasted had lost interest in fighting and were quickly cut down by the advancing elves, keen for battle.

"Where is Pernian?" Orric asked as a returning elf walked past towards the makeshift smithy.

"Last I saw him he was at the front of the line. I haven't seen him return, but there are so many coming and going it's hard to know for sure."

Orric nodded and let the elf continue on. He would have to be quick if he was to have his sword resharpened. There would be little chance for rest, but the elves would take all they could get. There was no telling when they would be called back into battle.

A bad feeling passed over Orric as he thought Pernian must be dead. He was at the front of the line of attack and he had not returned with the rest of them. There could be no other explanation.

In fact Pernian was still fighting at the front. He had been slashing at two orglin when the command came in from Orric. Each time he tried to retreat more and more orglin came to kill him. Even when the second line caught up with him there didn't seem to be a chance for him to retreat. With each slash he could feel his blade losing its keenness. When he first started attacking his sword cut through the orglin like he was cutting through butter, but as the battle wore on he had to put in more and more effort just to break the leathery skin.

Pernian didn't advance when the second line closed in around him. The orglin pushed forward with as much ferocity as the first ones through the gateway. The second line of elves tried to push them back, but to no avail. The orglin had covered half the distance from where the battle first started to where Orric stood. If things continued as they were it wouldn't be long before he would have to order a retreat. If that happened, he didn't like their chances of success.

Orric watched the gateway closely. He couldn't believe there were so many orglin. It was like the Evil One had a never ending supply. Eventually the flow stopped and for a brief moment Orric thought they were going to win Then, with horror, Orric watched those who had been pushing the orglin through the gateway pass through themselves.

Five giants, each brandishing a massive cudgel in one hand and a fierce looking whip in the other, stood at least twenty feet high. As they lumbered after the frenzied orglin more than one of them was crushed under their mighty feet.

"What are we going to do about those?" Orric asked in awe.

Brielle changed her view from the storm to the gateway and gasped when she saw them. "I thought all the giants had died out centuries ago."

"Do you have any idea on how we can kill them?" Orric asked.

"Leave them to me," Brielle said with a hint of sorrow in her voice.

Brielle focused her attention on the middle giant. Taking a deep breath she reached out and shot a fire ball from both palms. The ball of flame shot over the battlefield. Both sides were so busy with their attack that they didn't notice the fiery death above them. The giant continued to push the orglin forward oblivious to what was coming towards him.

The fireball struck the giant on its thick steel breastplate. The flames should have consumed him, but instead they fizzled, splashed fire and then disappeared. The giant didn't even look like he noticed.

"That certainly wasn't supposed to happen," Brielle said.

Brielle created another fireball and threw it at one of the other giants, but the result was the same. She didn't think it was a Dark Knight blocking her spell. If it was, then the fireball wouldn't have hit its target. There was something about the armour that was saving the giants from her attacks.

"There is nothing I can do to stop them. Your elves will have to kill them," Brielle explained.

Orric shook his head. He had no idea how they were going to kill the giants. One swing with the cudgel would smash a skull to pieces.

"What are we going to do about those... things?" Kilean had ridden up to get some advice from Orric.

Before Orric had a chance to respond, a messenger came through the gateway from the transport ground. He rushed to join the others.

"Jarwe said that you need to take the giants out at the legs. Their skin is tough, but you should be able to hack away. They are slow, but very powerful. Quick slash and move tactics should see them come down. Once they are on the ground it shouldn't be too hard to finish them off," the messenger explained.

The messenger waited for a response, but none came. Orric was grateful for the information, but he was too busy for pleasantries. His eyes didn't leave the battlefield even as the vital information was being relayed to him. The orglin horde was slowly dwindling, but so were the elves. The fact that there had still been no word from Pernian worried him even more.

Pernian still fought on at the front of the line. The sword he had brought into battle was completely blunt, so he had picked up two more from his fallen comrades. The one he held was a little heavier than his own, but the blade was still nice and sharp. He continued hacking away at the orglin as they rushed toward him. His brown leather jerkin was soaked with their dark black oily blood. It was all he could do to keep his hand from slipping on the hilt of his new sword.

There was no time for anyone to look up and see the giants slowly lumbering towards them. The orglin kept coming and coming. Pernian wanted nothing more than to retreat and gauge the situation, but he wasn't about to back out of the fight.

Orric watched as the orglin were slowly whittled away. He had no idea how many were left when he called for the third line to relieve the second. With a little luck the third line would not suffer as many casualties. Brielle had to let the spell drop that made his voice carry, so Orric had to pass the command through the line.

The third line ran in to attack with a renewed vigour. The orglin had almost been completely defeated and the flow of enemies through the gateway had ceased with the giants. The battle had lasted a little over two hours, but it seemed as though it was coming to an end. It had not been the ordeal everyone had expected, but no one was going to complain.

The second line was reluctant to withdraw. They could sense that the battle was almost over and wanted to remain on the battlefield for the winning stroke. As the third line reached them they slowly started to back away.

"Have you seen Pernian?" Orric asked each elf as they passed him.

The answers were all very similar. Some said they had seen him fight at the front of the line, but no one could confirm if he was still alive. No one had seen Pernian return with the second line of elves. There was a chance he was still alive, but Orric wished that he could see him with his own eyes.

"It looks like we might not be needed in the end," Kilean sounded relieved.

It did look that way. The third line would finish off the orglin and the giants, hopefully with minimal casualties. Orric couldn't believe that was all the Evil One was going to throw at them, but nothing more came through the gateway. Although he was a good distance away from it he could see there was nothing waiting on the other side. For a moment he let his heart lift at the thought the war could be over.

As the morning continued the third line whittled away the last of the orglin. Even when the elves finally outnumbered them, the orglin didn't stop their advance. Pernian was now onto his sixth sword. He had lost count of how many orglin he had killed, but he guessed it was in the hundreds. His arms and legs ached with every new swing and with each one he thought it would be his last.

Finally, when the orglin had either been killed or gone past him, he came upon one of the giants. He stared at it in disbelief. Even though the creature was ten paces away it still seemed to loom above him.

"Lord Pernian!" a voice came from beside him. "Lord Orric said we should use speed and stay low. The giants are powerful, but slow."

Pernian looked over as he recognised the voice and saw Darziel, his old friend from Elhjem, standing next to him. It was clear he had come with the third line. There was little blood on his tunic and he looked fresh.

Pernian couldn't imagine what he looked like to Darziel. He was completely covered in the thick black blood of the orglin and he felt as though he could collapse at any moment, but there was still a job to be done. He simply nodded his head and prepared to attack as the giant approached.

Adrenaline pumped through Pernian's body and for a moment he felt as though he was complete. His strength had returned and he steadied himself as the giant closed in.

The giant didn't see any danger in the small elves before him, he just swung his massive cudgel thinking to sweep them aside. Darziel and Pernian were prepared for the attack and they ducked and rolled to either side, avoiding being trampled to death. The giant continued forward, not seeming to care if he killed them or not.

The two elves jumped back to their feet, swords still in hands. It seemed the giants were going to be easier to kill than they originally thought. They quickly caught up with it and as one they drew back their swords and brought them down on the giant's immense calves. Instead of hacking into the thick flesh, as they expected, the blades bounced back with a jarring twang. Pernian looked at Darziel who shrugged his shoulders.

The attack gained the giant's attention. It turned around and cracked its whip at Darziel who was only just able to move out of the way. There was little doubt the evil looking whip would strip the flesh to the bone. Pernian swung his sword, but he had to duck and roll out of the way of the cudgel before he had a chance to strike out again.

Pernian slashed at the giants legs as best he could and Darziel did the same, but with little effect. Eventually Pernian managed to only make a small cut

"This is getting us nowhere," Darziel puffed. "I'm going to try something different."

Darziel ducked under the attack from the whip and instead of rolling out of the way he moved in and drove his sword into the giant's thigh. Despite his effort the blade only sunk in three inches and didn't seem to hinder it at all. The giant moved quicker than either elf had expected and swung down with his cudgel. Before Pernian could call out, Darziel was struck across the side of his head. The blow smashed his skull and sent him flying across the field, killing him instantly.

Pernian pushed aside the sorrow at watching the death of his old friend. Seeing the blade enter the giant's thigh gave him an idea. Slashing and hacking was getting them nowhere. Darziel's attack was the only thing that had seemed to work. He quickly rolled under a backhanded swing from the giant and came to his feet behind the great beast. He quickly plunged his sword into the back of its knee. He pushed with all his strength until the blade popped out the other side. The giant stumbled and fell with an almighty cry of pain and anguish.

There was no chance of retrieving his blade as the giant struggled to regain its composure. Its right knee was ruined, but it was still trying to return to its feet. Pernian looked around for another sword, but there was nothing he could see amongst the carnage. Before he had a chance to make his decision a band of elves rushed up towards him, their focus on the giant.

The elves jumped on the reeling giant and started stabbing with all their strength. Pernian had to turn away as the creature slowly died. He couldn't imagine the pain it felt as each blade pierced its thick skin. The dull rumble that came from its mouth was full of pain. Pernian knew that the creature was evil and they were fighting the final battle, but he still didn't have to like it. When he turned around the giant had stopped moving and the elves were looking towards the gateway.

As he looked around he saw the other four giants had suffered the same fate. For a moment he felt a rush of joy through his body when he realised nothing more was coming through the gateway.

"That's it," one of the elves cried. "They're all dead."

"We've won!" another called out from somewhere behind them.

It seemed like they had won, there could be no other explanation. Relief washed over him and his legs started to wobble. Without warning his body gave way and he collapsed to his knees. There was time for him to weaken and he could finally allow his body to relax.

The cheering elves suddenly went silent when the gateway started to waver. Slowly at first the image on the other side started to fade before the gateway collapsed on itself. The scene on the other side was not at all what they were expecting and sent terror running down their spines.

Blocked by the original gateway, a second gateway stood two hundred paces away. Standing in front of it was an army of minotaurs. Orric looked on in horror. Just when he thought the battle might have been over, a fresh one was about to start. The storm that had been raging behind them and slowly growing nearer was now over the gateway. It wouldn't be long before they were fighting in the maelstrom.

"Bring up the horses," Orric commanded at the top of his voice, but without the spell it didn't carry as far as he wanted. "I need to you to enhance my voice again," Orric said.

Brielle had forgotten she had released the spell to create the fireballs and cast it again. The spell did nothing to drain her energy and as long as she didn't do anything else she could keep it up whilst holding back the storm.

After Orric had issued his command a messenger came from the transport ground. The message was a little too late in explaining there was a surprise waiting behind the first gateway. At least Orric now knew he was not alone. It seemed the other armies were facing the same problems.

"Horses to the front," Orric didn't waste any time.

The minotaurs stood ten feet tall and the elves on foot would be no match for them. They held wicked looking axes and small shields. Orric had heard stories from the past of the ferocious minotaurs with the body of a man, a very large man, and the head of a bull. They were capable fighters and their size made it hard for the elves to fight on foot. There was no doubt that it was time for the mounted elves to get into the battle.

From the distance it was hard to tell how many there were, but Orric estimated there could be no more than five hundred, which still outnumbered their cavalry.

"Is there anything you can do to help?" Orric asked Brielle as the cavalry slowly made their way towards the battlefield.

The storm was almost upon them and Brielle had to intensify her effort to keep it at bay. There was nothing she could do to help the elves in their attack. Her silence was all the answer that Orric needed.

Palen and Kilean led the way, slowly, onto the battlefield. There were two reasons for their pace. The first was to allow those on foot to retreat without fear of being trampled and the second was that the minotaurs had yet to advance. Neither wanted to join the battle quicker than they had to and it wasn't until they were past the pile of dead orglin before they started their charge.

Palen was grateful for his elven horse. The white stallion kept his nerve as they slowly approached yet another horror. He didn't think a normal horse would be so stalwart. There was no telling what was happening on the other battlefields, but if theirs was anything to go by it would be mayhem.

"Hold strong!" Palen called out as the rain started to fall.

The elves kept a steady pace as the minotaurs approached. Orric watched on, not really knowing what else he could do. Even though he was in command, he really felt useless. Although their battle with orglin was a success he wasn't so sure what the result with the minotaurs would be.

The minotaurs charged in with no care for the advancing elves. Palen braced himself for the first attack, one hand on the reins of his horse, Alto, and the other brandishing his sword. For the most part the grip on the reins was just for balance. He would have to rely on Alto to know where to move in battle, which he was more than capable of doing.

Alto trembled slightly as the minotaurs advanced. He had never seen a creature like it and the stallion knew it wanted to kill him. If it wasn't for the strength of his rider he would have turned and run, but there was job to be done and he wasn't about to back away.

The minotaurs moved to crash into the approaching animals, but the horses were smarter than that. As the minotaurs dropped their shoulders the horses shifted their run so they didn't collide with the great beasts. At worst they would only receive a glancing blow. Palen slashed out at the minotaur as he rode past, dealing a vicious cut to the side of its face. The blow didn't seem to have much of an affect and the minotaur kept running towards the next elf. It dropped its shoulder hoping to connect with the next horse, but again the elven horse dodged the advance as the elf slashed out. The minotaur was caught in the same place that Pernian had struck. Half its face sid off as it crashed to the ground, dead.

After the initial charge both sides settled into a more conventional battle. The minotaurs had lost more than the elves at the start, but their ferocity with their axes gave them a distinct advantage. The horses and elves moved as one, but the minotaurs didn't care who they attacked. The elves quickly learned if they didn't defend their horses, the minotaurs would hack them down. Once the elves were on the ground they were no match for them. Unlike the orglin the minotaurs had no intention of stopping to feed. The bloodlust was upon them and only complete annihilation would sate them.

Kilean ducked under the razor sharp axe of one of the minotaurs. His horse, Saltar, shifted before he had a chance to make his own attack. If he didn't, then Kilean would have been hacked by a minotaur on his left flank. Saltar jumped forward to avoid an attack from behind by another beast. Kilean kept his head low and randomly slashed out left and right. All he knew was that if it wasn't for Saltar he would already be dead.

When Kilean finally recovered and looked up, all he saw were minotaurs all around him. Saltar danced backwards as a minotaur approached, but only managed a pace before he backed into another. Kilean looked around quickly and realised he was boxed in, but the minotaurs made no move to attack him. He waved his sword as menacingly as he could, but he knew it was futile. He couldn't imagine why they were waiting. He looked around again to see if there was help nearby, but he couldn't see anything but a sea of monsters.

Slowly the one in front of him stood aside, but before Saltar could make a dash for freedom it was replaced by a larger minotaur with tufts of grey through it bull's head hair. There was something different about it.

"Your kind has fought well," its voice was deep and guttural, "but now it is all over." It almost sounded as if it was an apology.

Kilean steadied himself and prepared for the attack. Before he had a chance to move he felt an axe sink deep into his back, severing his spine. His body went numb from his neck down as the minotaur in front approached, brandishing his axe for the final blow. A strange smile crossed Kilean's face which caused the monster to stop. He didn't know why, but he finally felt at peace. As he slid from the saddle his sight grew dark and he slipped into the sweet embrace of death.

Orric watched on in horror as elf after elf was hacked down. It seemed that for every minotaur they killed two elves were slain. If the elves on horseback couldn't defeat them he thought there was little hope for those on foot.

"Brielle! You have to do something," Orric called out.

Although the rain was falling on the battlefield it was not nearly as intense as it could be. Brielle had fought hard to keep the maelstrom at bay, but she knew Orric was right. The elves were losing and if the cavalry all died there would be no hope for anyone. Slowly she released the spell holding back the storm and the rain started to pour down. Lightning crackled in the sky and booms of thunder resonated around the battlefield. The elven horses, which had been stalwart throughout the battle finally lost their nerve. They whinnied, jumped and reared in terror.

Slowly fireballs started to descend from the sky. At first Orric thought the Dark Knights had arrived, but when he saw the fireballs hit the minotaurs he knew he was wrong. Brielle had finally joined the battle and she certainly didn't let him down. Not every fireball hit its target. Some crashed into the earth creating small explosions and some hit the elves. The spell was very complex and there was nothing she could do to aim them all in the right place. If she thought there was another spell that would be as effective she would have used it, but nothing crossed her mind.

After five minutes, the fireballs stopped falling and the rain stopped. Brielle dropped to her knees and panted for breath. There was no doubt that someone had broken her spell, but with it came a break in the weather. The clouds quickly parted and the sun shone down on the battlefield. No one really knew what to make of the situation, but it was the elves who recovered first. Amongst the burning corpses of minotaurs, elves and horses the battle continued.

Brielle's spell had certainly turned the tide and Orric watched on as the elves finished the job. The minotaurs were in disarray with the their numbers decimated by the firestorm and it was certainly not something they had expected. When they stormed the battlefield there was no thought of failure. The horses moved around the corpses giving their riders the perfect opportunity to slay the large beasts.

Before long the battle was over. Only a dozen elves remained on horseback, but that was all they needed. It had been a brutal battle, but they were victorious, despite the sadness of their losses. When the elves realised all the minotaurs were gone a cheer arose from the field.

Like the first gateway, when the orglin had been annihilated, the second gateway started to crumble. What they saw on the other side sent fear racing through their hearts. When the gateway was gone they could see an even larger gateway a hundred paces behind it. It spanned as far as the eye could see, and Orric assumed the full length of the battlefield. The land in front of it was a sea of evil creatures. Orric looked out and saw more orglin than had poured through the first gateway. There were more minotaurs, giants and many other evil creatures. Orric's heart sank. The battle was truly over, but not in the manner they had hoped for. He didn't know how the rest of the Alliance was fairing, but there was no chance the elves would survive.

Suddenly a large ear-piercing screech came from the west. A shiver ran through Orric's body and his heart sank even further.

"What new hell is this?" he asked no one in particular.

Chapter 22: Back to *Crenallous*

Alaric and Alena suddenly appeared in the top chamber of the Cauldron Mountain, the Mountain of Fire, *Crenallous*. The temperature was considerably hotter than in the Spider Mountain, not that Alaric noticed, but a bead of sweat had appeared on Alena's brow.

The room glowed a soft red from the hole in the middle. Alaric walked over and looked down. The lava had risen since he was last there, but Alaric didn't know if that was a good sign or not. It didn't look like it would be long before the mountain erupted and he certainly didn't want to be there when it did.

"It looks like we're the first ones here," Alena voiced the obvious to break the silence.

"It was always going to be that way. It couldn't have happened any other way," Alaric didn't take his eyes from the lava as he spoke.

Alena shook her head at his response. It really told her nothing, not that she really knew what she was looking for.

"How long until Nyrra gets here?" She looked around nervously at the mention of his name as if that was enough to make him appear.

"Not long now."

Alaric walked away from the 'cauldron' to the edge of the room and looked out over the western side of the kingdom. It would not be long before the final battle would begin and he no idea what the result would be. One thing he did know, if he failed against Nyrra then it wouldn't matter if the Alliance was successful or not. Nyrra would certainly see them all destroyed once he was finished with Alaric.

His words weren't what Alena was looking for. She wanted reassurance, not non-committal comments. She knew that he would be there soon, otherwise what were they doing there? Either way it was just an opening question. What she really wanted to know was what her part was. There didn't seem much she could do against the Evil One, but there had to be a reason why Alaric had brought her with him.

Alaric remembered the first and last time he had been in the top chamber. The first time was when he was to face the Evil One and what he thought was the final battle. He had felt so much more nervous back then. His heart raced and adrenaline pumped through his body. It seemed like a lifetime ago. This time he was completely calm. Dark clouds started to roll across to the west and it looked like a storm was brewing. Alaric knew that it was a sign the final battle was about to begin.

"What am I doing here?" Alena finally asked.

"What do you mean?" Alaric sounded genuinely surprised as he returned his attention back to the cavern.

"I mean, what part do *I* have to play in your battle with Nyrra?" she said, again looking around nervously at the mention of his name.

It was a very good question, Alaric thought. He really had no idea and had not given it much thought. All he knew was that Alena needed to be there with him. Whatever was going to happen was going to happen. He had done everything that he could to get them there in good order. He wished he knew the result, but it had yet to be written.

"I know that I have received a lot of information over the past few weeks, knowledge that no one should have, but the battle has always been hidden to me. Nyrra has the same problem. Neither of the prophecies give any more than the locations of the final battles, here and Avalon," Alaric explained as best he could.

His words brought little comfort to her. She had a nagging feeling that she was not going to leave the mountain and that made her feel sick to the stomach. Her legs started to shake with nerves and she didn't know if the waiting was going to be worse than the battle itself.

Alaric slowly walked over and placed his arms around her, kissing her forehead. At first he felt her trembling, but it soon subsided. He had loved her once, he knew that and the feeling was still somewhere deep inside him, but if he was going to succeed then he couldn't allow himself any luxuries. He knew at some stage he would have to choose between Alena and the rest of the Seven Kingdoms and if he let his love come to the surface he would condemn the world. He would gladly give his own life for hers, but he didn't think that would be an option.

"This is a lovely sight," the sweet voice came from the opposite side of the cavern.

Alaric had felt the sudden shift in energy, but he didn't want to let the embrace go. There was something very soothing about being in her arms and he wanted Nyrra to think he was emotional. That would give him the advantage. He took a moment to soak up the majesty of Alena before he gently pushed her away and turned to face his nemesis.

Nyrra had chosen a much more pleasant facade than Alaric had been expecting. Before him stood a man six foot tall with flowing blonde hair half-way down his back. His face was thin with a strong jaw and deep blue eyes. The black velvet shirt was half unbuttoned revealing a thick muscular chest and the top of his abdominals. Alena's jaw dropped open at the sight. If she didn't know he was the Evil One she would have found him very attractive. There was a wicked smile on his face, as if he knew something they did not and there was a good chance that he did.

Alena backed away from Alaric, but not from fear. She thought terror would have ripped through her body at the sight of the Evil One, but it didn't. Although she felt much safer when she was close to Alaric, she did not want to be near him when the final battle started.

"Don't be afraid of me child," Nyrra cooed when he saw the movement. "You will be with me soon enough. I will make sure you survive."

"I don't think you will have much say in the matter. The Chosen One has come here to destroy you. The prophecy has told us of his victory. There is nothing you can do here, but die," even Alena was surprised at the strength in her voice, but it didn't have the desired effect.

Nyrra burst out laughing before he spoke. "She is certainly is a feisty one you've found there, but no, the prophecy has not given you the result and if it did it would not be set in stone. You see the prophecies have always just been a guide, as I'm sure you know by now," Nyrra turned to Alaric. "The future is not written and only time will tell who will be victorious."

Alaric was surprised that Nyrra didn't call himself the victor. It was the first time he had had ever heard him speak of Alaric having a chance to succeed. It was small, but it was something.

"Of course, that being said, we all know what the result will be." Alaric couldn't help himself but smile. It seemed Nyrra had also picked up what he had said. "And now I think it is time to give you one more chance to bow down to me. I have nothing against you Alaric and I would be more than happy to have you serve at my right hand. I will even let you keep that she-elf for a pet." Nyrra raised an eyebrow at the expression.

Alaric let the smile drop from his face, although it took a great deal of effort. It seemed as though his plan was already working. Nyrra was trying to use Alena to sway Alaric and that was exactly what he wanted.

"Do you honestly think that I would believe anything you say? What would your seven slaves, who you promised the Seven Kingdoms, do if you made me your favourite? No, there is nothing you can say that would make me take your offer," Alaric spoke calmly. He had betrayed his false emotions early and if he overplayed it then Nyrra would get suspicious.

"That is not true. I could create a spell that would tether our life-spirit together. You know this to be true," Nyrra said.

Alaric thought for a moment. The spell was somewhere in the back of his memories. The process had been outlawed many centuries ago. It was true that if they were tethered and Alaric died then Nyrra would follow shortly after, but that was simply not enough to convince him. There was more to the spell and that was the reason it had been banned.

"It is true that if you tethered our life-force we would be bound, but who would control the leash?" Alaric asked calmly. When the spell was created there was always a master and a slave. If Nyrra was the master even Alaric, with all his new found power, wouldn't be able to break it. He would live, but he would live as a slave for the rest of his life.

"I would, of course, but I could think of worse ways to spend eternity. I am very generous to those who serve me loyally," Nyrra continued.

"I have witnessed your generosity. In fact I have killed those you have claimed to have protected. All your Dark Knights have died and will die again. Why would I want to follow their fate?" Alaric asked. He wanted nothing more than to start the battle with Nyrra, but he knew the time wasn't right. For the moment they would both have to continue the conversation.

"Be that as it may, there could never have been any other ending for them. It is not possible to bring something back to life until it has died. They have all been brought back and they will lead my armies to victory in Avalon." He thought for a moment before he returned his attention to Alena. "What about you?" he asked, but Alena remained silent. "Surely you have a say in this matter. Wouldn't you prefer to be my slave's lover in a life of luxury rather than in the pits of fire that awaits you if he fails, and he will fail?"

"I will happily die before I would ever suggest joining you," Alena spat on the ground when she finished speaking. "I will join my ancestors in the afterlife. Only you and yours will burn in the *Pit of Eternal Fire*."

Nyrra burst out laughing again. It was both at her words and her tenacity. It had been a long time since anyone without any real power had spoken to him in such a manner. He wanted nothing more than to crush her like a bug, but he knew Alaric wouldn't let him. It was not yet time for them to start fighting, he knew that, but it didn't mean he had to put up with her insolence.

"I would watch your tone," Nyrra snapped. "Remember that I could kill you with a snap of my fingers. My patience will only last so long."

Alena shrunk back at the venom in his tone. With his appearance and the tone of their conversation she had almost forgotten who he really was. A sudden chill passed through her body and she wished she was still wearing the thick cloak. She took another step backwards, but she didn't want to distance herself too far from Alaric. There was no telling what the Evil One would do if he saw the opportunity to attack her.

"She has nothing to do with this, leave her alone," Alaric let the fake emotion back into his voice. Nyrra was making it all too easy for him.

"Then why did you bring her here. You know as well as I do that she is as much to do with this as we are," Nyrra snarled.

"You know as well as I do that she has to be here." Alaric paused as a thought came to him. "Now that I think about it, there is someone missing."

"All in good time." A wicked smile crossed his face. "The battle is not due to start yet and unlike you I am not about to show all my cards."

Alaric looked around the cavern, but there was no sign of anyone else. He remembered back to a passage in the *Prophecy of the Stone.*

And the two shall finally meet
in the mountain of fire
The hero of light shall meet
the hero of night
But alone they will not be
Each shall have another
a softer life the share their fate
And the fate of the world

Alena was always going to be there at the end with Alaric, he knew that even before he read that passage, but the other was complete surprise to him. He could not imagine who or what would be 'a softer life' to Nyrra. There was nothing soft in his world.

It was true that he really didn't know why Alena was there. He had pondered the idea many times since he realised what was coming, and nothing had come to him. There didn't seem to be any good reason why she should be in the cavern with them. The battle was always to be between Nyrra and Alaric, but he would try and use her as best he could.

"Of course!" Nyrra blurted as if he had just realised something so obvious. "How can you believe anything I say in such a bare environment? Let me show you just one of the lives you could be living."

Alaric prepared himself for the spell to come. That last thing he wanted to do was to get caught off guard, even though he didn't think Nyrra was planning to attack him.

The air wavered and slowly the cavern disappeared. Marble columns sprouted from the floor, covered with ivy. The walls turned into a white plaster and the floor turned a rich mahogany. Alena found that she was no longer standing, but instead she lay across a white sofa. Her clothes changed in front of her eyes until she was wearing a soft, silken dress. A cool breeze blew in from somewhere to counter the heat from the mountain. At first the situation seemed wrong to Alena, but as she relaxed back into the sofa nothing felt more right.

Alaric stood on the opposite side of the room and watched. The silk dress was sheer, almost see-through. His eyes were transfixed on her breasts. The fake reality was almost perfect, or it would have been at one stage in his life. It was something he had dreamed about as a younger man, but that life was long gone. Either way it was Alena that Nyrra was trying to entice, but Alaric had to play the game. The Evil One would be expecting him to react and that was exactly what he was going to do.

"What are you doing standing there?" Alena cooed. "Come and sit with me my love." Her voice was sweet and belied the situation. It was clear she had been caught in Nyrra's spell.

At any time Alaric could break the spell, but for some reason he didn't. He didn't think the final battle had started, but this could still be Nyrra's first attack. Whatever he was trying to do Alaric was going to play along until he knew what it was.

Alaric slowly walked across and sat down next to Alena. She instantly wrapped him up in her arms and nuzzled into his neck. She felt warm and soft to his touch. The feeling was familiar and pleasant, but he pushed it aside. He couldn't let his feelings for Alena resurface, no matter what happened.

"Let's get something to eat," Alena suggested and she clapped her hands.

A group of scantily clad serving women entered the room carrying silver trays laden with fruits, cheeses and cold meat. Alaric had to admit that in another life he could have enjoyed it, but he knew that was never going to be his life. Even if he defeated Nyrra he could never return to such a lifestyle.

As much as Alena knew there was something wrong she couldn't help but hope that everything was real. It was what she had dreamed about ever since she had first met Alaric. She pushed aside the bad feeling in the back of her mind and lost herself in the warmth of his embrace. She picked up a bunch of grapes and started feeding herself and then Alaric one at a time.

"Ah!" Alena said as she heard little footsteps approach. "Here are the children."

Alaric almost started choking at the mention of children. Nyrra had definitely gone all out with his illusion. He held his breath when he saw a boy of six and a girl of four come running up to them. They jumped onto Alena and she held them close before sitting up. They all joyfully picked at the platters in front of them.

The illusion was becoming too real for Alaric's liking and Alena was slipping further and further into it. She played with the children as if they were really her own and nothing was out of the ordinary. He wasn't sure if her mind could handle much more of it. If her conscious fractured completely and she believed the illusion was real, there was no telling what would happen when it was broken.

Taking one last look at his children, or at least Nyrra's reality of them, he looked up for Nyrra. There were a number of functionaries in the room and he knew Nyrra would be one of them.

"A very nice trick, but you will have to do better than that," Alaric said to a young man, dressed in a loose fitting cloth pants. He didn't look out of place, but Alaric knew it was Nyrra.

"I don't know what you are implying," he feigned innocence. "It seems as though she is enjoying herself. This is a reality I could create for you if you would only bow down before me."

"This is nothing like what the world will be if you succeed. It is a nice fantasy, but it will never come true," Alaric returned. "Now shall I dispel it or will you."

"Very well," Nyrra replied and the scenery around them slowly changed back to the cavern.

Alaric breathed a sigh of relief. He didn't think a sudden change would have done anything to help Alena's psyche. He didn't think Nyrra was doing him any favours, but he was grateful nonetheless.

"What happened?" Alena sounded confused.

"That was a glimpse of what your life could be if Alaric bends his knee. There need not be a final battle. We can sort this out now and be done with it."

Alena looked around the cavern, the confused expression only grew on her face. The memory of the cool room, with her... children was still in her mind. It was such a beautiful memory and definitely the life she wanted for herself, but she knew it wasn't true and could never be true, or at least not while Nyrra was still alive. The memory of their fake children stuck in her mind. She had never thought about having children with Alaric, there had never been any time, but it was something that she wanted. After seeing them she didn't know how she could go back. Even with that thought in her mind there was no way she could live in luxury when the rest of the Seven Kingdoms was suffering. In the end she knew there was no choice.

When she looked at Nyrra she realised they were both watching her intently, waiting for her response. There was a strange expression on Alaric's face, as if he really didn't know what she was going to say. Alena thought for a moment and tried to work out if Alaric was trying to tell her something. There was a chance he would take Nyrra's reality. That thought only lasted a moment before she shook her head, removing it forever.

"It was a nice fantasy, but that's all it was. There is no truth in it. There is no life for us under your subjugation. Our utopia will only come with your death," Alena sneered.

"Maybe I have been a little too appeasing, maybe if I changed into something a little more terrifying you might take my offer more seriously," Nyrra growled as he spoke.

The air around Nyrra started to shift as his face and body started to change. The handsome face started to smudge with blackness. Soon enough a horrifying facade replaced the handsome, more pleasant one. Two thick ram's horns protruded from a black, leathery scalp. His face had the same black skin with deep red eyes and razor sharp teeth. His nose was little more than two small holes above his mouth and his ears were much the same. He wore no shirt. Thick muscles covered his front and two black wings spread out behind him. Thankfully, Alena thought, he wore pants, but that didn't stop her from shrinking away from him.

"What do you think now?" Nyrra's voice was deep and rasping. "I have been very generous in my offer so far, but it seems as though you might need to see what life will be like when I kill your Chosen One."

Before Alaric could react, the scenery around them changed again. The already hot temperature of the cavern increased considerably. Instantly Alena felt sweat appear on her brow followed quickly by the rest of her body. Flames appeared around the edge of the small room she was standing in, but there was no one else with her and that didn't seem right. She couldn't remember how she came to be in such a place. The heat was searing into her body and she could feel her skin start to burn.

"This is what it will be like to live in my world," Nyrra's voice boomed from above her. She looked up and saw two large red eyes looking down on her. "I will keep you alive so I can make you suffer day after day, and just when you think I will take your life I will make you suffer more. Take my offer and this will be just a memory, not your reality."

"Enough," Alaric's voice boomed over Nyrra's and the fiery room suddenly disappeared.

Alena stumbled forward at the sudden change, but steadied herself before she fell. Both memories, the good and the terrible, were still thick in her mind. She knew, now, that they were both fantasies, but they seemed so real. Even though there were no scars on her arms, but she could still feel the intense heat burning into her flesh.

"Now you can make a much more informed decision. I am sure Alaric will bend to your will if you decide that you wanted to live out the rest of your life in luxury," Nyrra spoke softly as his facade changed back to the original, more appealing look.

Alena looked towards Alaric to see what he thought, but he just stared at Nyrra. It was almost like he was deliberately trying to avoid the unasked question. In truth he really didn't want to sway Alena's decision one way or another. He didn't know what she was about to say, or why, but he knew that it would have a great affect on the outcome of the final battle.

"There is nothing you can say or offer me to betray everyone I have even known and loved. Alaric will kill you Nyrra and for that fact alone I don't need to take your offer seriously," Alena did her best to sound stalwart. The comfort she had felt when Nyrra had first arrived was completely gone. He was evil and even with the change in his facade she should have realised it from the start. There was nothing she could do if Alaric failed and she didn't think she would want to continue living anyway.

"Very well, it is a life of suffering you have chosen," Nyrra sneered as he spoke.

"We have heard your offer and we have rejected it now it is time for you to reveal who we are missing, or are you going to risk the wrath of the prophecy?" Alaric sounded hopeful with the question.

The sound of soft footsteps could be heard behind them. "Ah! Here we are." Both Alaric and Alena looked around to see who it was.

Behind them were the stairs leading up from the last chamber. At first they could see no one and Alaric thought it was an illusion created by Nyrra to distract them, but then he saw a mop of jet black hair. At first it was impossible to tell if it was a man or a woman as the hair was drabbed over its face, but soon enough the deep blue dress gave away the gender.

It took Alaric a moment to realise who it was, but when he did his heart sank. He didn't need to see the face to know it was Marina. Even after the last time they had met he couldn't believe she would have turned to the Evil One, but it seemed as though she had. There was no chance Nyrra would risk bringing someone to the final battle he would have to control magically, it would be too big a risk.

The connection between the Sapphire stone and Marina was unmistakable, but Alaric found it hard to believe she would turn to evil purely because he wouldn't let her have it. She slowly climbed the stairs and then walked over to stand next to Nyrra. Her feet were bare and except for the blue dress the only other adornment was a gold necklace encrusted with sapphires. She pushed aside her hair and looked up at Alaric. Her face had been painted white with large black circles around her eyes. Blue lipstick accentuated her lips. All in all she certainly looked like a creature of evil.

"Shall we begin?" Nyrra asked with an evil grin on his face.

Chapter 23: The Dwarven War

Dorn felt a lot better when Hulkan finally arrived. The sun had just risen and although word had come late in the night that the dwarves had started to come through from Castalia, he had yet to see any real proof. It wasn't until his old friend walked up next to him that he was able to relax. Although he had only known Hulkan for a relatively short period of time he felt comfortable referring to him as an 'old friend'. It would not be long before the final battle started and he couldn't think of anyone else he would want by his side.

Hulkan walked up to Dorn full of confidence. There had been problems in Castalia and for a moment he wasn't sure they were going to make it in time. It was late in the evening when they finally started to make their way through the gateway. Luckily there was only a small number left to join the rest of the dwarven army in Avalon. He didn't know how the Castalial army was going to make it in time. Minerva had been told that she could create more than one gateway at a time, which would help, but he heard that another fight had started. When the last of the dwarves had passed through the gateway and Minerva had closed it, no one could tell him if the Castalial army had started moving through. Hulkan didn't know what would happen if they didn't make the battlefield in time. It was the largest army and would take the centre position. Whatever was happening on the other side of the battlefield wasn't really his concern. All he had to worry about was the battle in front of him. Once he had won that then he could worry about the others, if they even needed worrying about.

"It's good to see you again," Dorn greeted him.

"And you too," Hulkan agreed.

Hulkan looked out over the empty field in front of them where the battle was going to take place. Behind them the dwarves lined up, waiting for instructions. Hulkan and Dorn stood atop a small hill where they could watch what was happening. To the east, if they looked hard enough, they could just see the tip of the Cauldron Mountain, but neither of them wanted to be reminded of what was to occur there.

They were waiting for Gwydion to join them before they made any real decisions regarding the army. As much as Hulkan knew the decision was up to him, he wanted the advice of the wizard. He was itching to storm the battlefield with his fellow dwarves, but he knew his place was on the hill.

"What do you think the Evil One will throw at us?" Dorn asked, if for no other reason than to cut through the silence. Even the dwarves assembled behind them seemed to make no discernible noise.

"Everything he has," Hulkan answered without really thinking. He kept his vision on the field in front of him as if he looked away disaster would ensue.

Dorn opened his mouth to ask the question again, but stopped when he saw the expression on Hulkan's face. Thinking back he didn't think he had ever seen the dwarf take anything so seriously. Even when they were fighting the Evil One's agents he always seemed to have an air of humour about him. It seemed as though the enormity of their situation had finally caught up with him.

"Good morning, and what a lovely morning it is," Gwydion sounded a little too blasé for Dorn's liking. It *was* a beautiful morning, the sun was shining and there was a subtle cool breeze, but that was nothing compared to what was ahead of them. "I know we are heading towards the last fight of our time, maybe of all time, but that is no reason to ignore such a beautiful day. It may very well be the last one we have."

There was something very profound and yet disturbing about his attitude. Dorn looked to Hulkan for assistance, but it didn't even look as though he heard a word Gwydion said. Dorn didn't know if he should be concerned or not. The final battle would be upon them soon and Hulkan would need all his faculties if they had any chance of victory.

"Do you have any idea how long we have before the final battle will begin?" Hulkan asked, moving his gaze to Gwydion.

"Your guess is as good as mine, but I don't think it will be much longer. By the look of those clouds to the north there is a storm is coming. At a guess I would say the battle will start when the clouds reach us."

Hulkan turned around to face the dwarves. It was time for one final speech before the final battle started. Gwydion created a spell to carry his voice throughout the army.

"Dwarves from the desert and under the mountain," Hulkan started as best he could. "We stand here together, united, united with one goal. To destroy the Evil One and all his minions," he raised his voice at the last and waited as a cheer arose from the dwarves. "The halls of Horinga are waiting for us. For those of us who don't make it there will be meat and mead on the tables lined up for as far as the eye can see." His words brought another round of cheers even though he spoke of their death. "Horinga will feast us tonight, but let us make him wait a little longer. We are here to send the minions of the Evil One to the pit of fire where they will burn, over and over again. It will be a sad night in the Halls of Horinga, for we will see this day out." The end of his speech brought an even greater roar from the army. With that he returned his sight to the battlefield.

Suddenly the air started to crackle in front of them. At first Hulkan thought it was from the approaching storm, but when he saw the little bolts of electricity rip through the air about a thousand feet in front of them, he knew it was something else. They all knew it would not be long before the final battle was about to start.

The dark storm clouds roiled across the sky behind the crackling air. Lightning started to strike the ground, exploding grass and dirt alike.

Gwydion didn't like the look of the clouds. There was something disturbing about them.

"Messenger!" Gwydion called out at the top of his voice, as if the storm was already upon them.

A messenger ran up to the top of the hill. There were another five waiting behind him. They would come up in order and relay the messages to Jarwe.

It wasn't long after the first messenger passed through the gateway before another returned. Gwydion wasn't sure if it was a good sign, but he was going to wait and see before passing judgement.

"It is agreed by all wizards that the storm coming is not natural. It is not known if it is the Dark Knights or the Evil One himself who is controlling the weather, but it needs to be stopped before reaching the battle," the messenger sounded nervous, but he still managed to finish his speech.

Gwydion turned back towards the storm. It was a relatively simple spell to hold it at bay, but it would still require more energy than what he had hoped to use at the start of the battle. There was no telling what the Dark Knights would throw at them once the final battle had begun. There was also the threat of the serpentants, which they had avoided talking about. Viper had said they would be there, but he didn't know which side his brothers would be fighting on. Since none had turned up so far, he could only assume they had sided with the Evil One. It would be another battle only the wizards could fight and he wasn't sure they were strong enough for both.

Raising his arms was the only sign that Gwydion was doing anything about the storm. The dark storm clouds remained in the sky, but their advance had slowed to a crawl. The final battle had begun, if it was only a subtle start. Soon enough it would be time for physical battle and that would be remembered in the stories as the commencement of the final battle.

"What's the plan?" the voice came from behind them.

Everyone looked around to see Brac and Arnór come marching up the hill. Hulkan was beginning to regret putting him in charge of the Western Dwarf Guild army under his overall command. Hulkan had thought the promotion would have improved his disposition, but that didn't seem to be the case. His tone was filled with spite, as if the wait was Hulkan's fault.

"It looks like the enemy will be here soon," Hulkan ignored the jibe and spoke as if he had not even noticed it. "Bring the front line up. I want them to see what is happening and hopefully it will not be such a shock."

"What shall we tell them is coming?" Arnór asked, a little confused.

"Their worst nightmares," was all Hulkan said.

Arnór looked at Dorn who just did his best to smile in return. There was no telling what was waiting for them and Hulkan's description was the most apt.

Suddenly the sound of a huge tear resonated throughout the air as the small bolts of electricity intensified. A gateway scarred across the battlefield in front of them. The dwarves marching towards their starting position stopped at the sight before them. It was larger than any gateway they had seen before and it bubbled a deep red and purple. When it finally coalesced, a sea of orglin rushed out onto the field before them.

None of the dwarves knew what to do. They had been expecting something terrible, but the sight before them was something more and they had no idea how to react. Everyone was waiting for instructions from Hulkan, but he didn't know what to do. He watched in horror as the orglin poured out of the gateway. It would not be long before they reached his position if he didn't order the attack.

"I don't want to overstep things, but I think we need to attack now," Dorn kept his voice low so no one else could hear him.

His words brought Hulkan out of his reverie and the fear that rushed through his body suddenly disappeared. He had been given a job and that was to lead his fellow dwarves to victory.

"Hold your line!" Hulkan called out. "Ready your weapons."

Axes were drawn almost as one at Hulkan's command. Dorn breathed a sigh of relief. The battle was far from over, but it was a start.

Hulkan wanted to wait until the last minute. He wanted to be able to gauge the numbers of the enemy before he committed the front line into action, but there wasn't the time. The orglin had made it almost half way across the battlefield and there didn't look to be any end to their numbers. If Hulkan didn't act soon they would be overrun before he made his command.

"Charge!" his voice boomed, even without the assistance of Gwydion's spell.

Instantly the dwarves in the front line moved into action. They charged as fast as their little legs could carry them. If they had been on top of the hill and seen what was coming towards them they might have paused, but they had no idea of the numbers swarming through the gateway.

The two armies crashed together with a loud bang. The dwarves seemed almost as chaotic as the orglin in their attack. On average the orglin stood about five feet high and the height of the dwarves seemed to work against them. As a matter of necessity they were used to attacking upwards. The orglin van jumped as they approached the dwarves, sailing over the top of them. If it wasn't for the gravity of the situation Hulkan would have burst out laughing.

The first line of attack for the dwarves was made up of those from the Cloumid Mountains. At first there was discord with the decision, but when Dorn explained that they were the stronger dwarves it made them feel better. They were led by Arnór on the battlefield. Dorn had tried to keep him behind, but he would have none of it. He had worked hard to get them out of the mountain range and he wasn't going to sit back and spectate.

Arnór wielded his axe with impunity. The orglin were not much different from the goblins that had infected the Cloumid Mountains since before he was born. The thick leathery skin was no match for with the double bladed war axe. It cut through skin and bone with ease.

The orglin seemed confused with the height of their attackers. The dwarves fought with a ferocity they had never seen before. Before they had a chance to attack they were hacked down from below. The dwarves pushed forward without a thought for their own safety. Heads and limbs of the orglin flew all over the place.

Hulkan and Dorn couldn't be prouder as they watched the slaughter before them. For every dwarf that fell hundreds of orglin were taken with him. Even with those odds, Hulkan wasn't sure they were going to win. The orglin still streamed through the gateway and didn't look like it was stopping anytime soon.

"Is there any way we can shut this gateway?" Hulkan asked, more of an afterthought than anything else. "Or even reduce the size of it? If we can stem the flow it will make life a lot easier on our dwarves."

"That was one thing about gateways that Alaric didn't tell us about. I agree that it would be very handy right about now, but even if I could I'm sure it wouldn't take long before it was opened again," Gwydion explained.

"Is it the Dark Knights?" Dorn asked.

"I really don't know. I have been searching for them, but I have yet to find any sign. If it was a Dark Knight who created the gateway, he has masked it very well," Gwydion continued.

Hulkan and Dorn both returned their attention to the battlefield as the orglin continued to race through the gateway. The dwarves had managed to push them back to the middle of the battlefield, but they could go no further. The battle had reached its peak. As the bodies piled up, the area for movement became less and less.

"First line fall back," Hulkan called out. With the aid of Gwydion's spell his voice carried to the army on the battlefield.

Slowly the first line started to pull back as the second line started its march forward. It moved slower, as directed, than the first charge. The last thing they wanted was dwarves running into each other and stumbling all over the place. Dorn had moved into action, taking command of the second line. As much as Hulkan wanted to join his friend he knew he had to remain on the hill.

What happened next surprised, horrified and yet pleased him. The orglin didn't seem worried about harrying the dwarves as they retreated. With the area opening up in front of them they dived on the corpses, not caring if they were dwarf or orglin. As the orglin devoured them Hulkan felt the bile rise in the back of his throat and he had to force it back down.

The break in the battle gave the dwarves time to swap the first line with the second and prepare for the battle. Hulkan looked at the gateway in hope that the swarm of orglin had stopped coming through, but that was not the case. Their progression had slowed with the gorging orglin blocking their path, but it continued nevertheless.

Arnór panted as he made his way to the top of the hill as quickly as he could. He had sheathed his axe, but had not had the time clean the black oily blood from it. His tempered steel breastplate was also stained with blood, but beside the odd scratch it was relatively unscathed. At least he had wiped the blood from his face, even though there were still traces in his thick, red beard. Hulkan had to admit that he was relieved to see him approach.

"How goes it on the front?" Hulkan asked without taking his eyes from the gateway. It felt like if he shifted his gaze some new horror would befall them.

"All things considered, not too bad. The orglin have no idea how to fight. I doubt they have even heard what a dwarf is. At first they were looking to attack well over our heads. Even when they realised the battle was coming from below them they didn't really know what to do. For every dwarf that fell I would estimate a hundred, if not close to a thousand, orglin fell to his blade," it was obvious in his voice that he was tired, but he wasn't going to let that stop him. He looked as though he was ready to storm the battlefield again.

"Go and get some rest," Hulkan said. "There is no telling when you will need to take the battlefield again."

"I will take it now if you command it," Arnór actually sounded eagre.

Hulkan had to laugh. There was nothing really humorous in the statement, but it still lightened his mood, if only for a moment.

"In good time Arnór. I'm sure your axe could use a trip to the smithy."

Arnór looked at his blade and realised that Hulkan was right. The blade was starting to look dull and if he wanted to kill more orglin he would need it sharpened.

The dwarves waited for the orglin to finish eating the dead, some being physically sick, before the battle continued. As disgusting as it was the piles of dead bodies were making it difficult to fight and the orglin were doing them a favour.

With the feeding over the orglin pushed on with as much ferocity as before. More and more orglin poured through the gateway and Hulkan wasn't sure if it was ever going to end. When he saw that the last of the orglin had passed through he breathed a sigh of relief. It seemed as though the Evil One's supply was not endless.

His relief last only a moment before he saw the creatures that were driving the orglin forward. Four giants, each brandishing massive cudgels in one hand and a wicked looking whip in the other, lumbered after the frenzied orglin. Any orglin that didn't rush forward fast enough was crushed under their mighty feet or slashed to death by their whips.

"What are they?" Hulkan gasped.

"They are giants from the far north, further than the Northern Wasteland, if you can believe such a place exists," Gwydion explained. "At one time, many centuries ago, it was said that they walked in the Seven Kingdoms and lived at peace with the other residents, although I do find that very hard to believe."

"How do we kill them?" as much as Hulkan was interested in what Gwydion was saying, there was little time for a history lesson.

"It is said that giants cannot be touched by magic. At a guess I would say my brothers and sisters are finding that out right about now, assuming they are also facing giants that is," Gwydion didn't seem overly concerned. "Their strength is surpassed by very few creatures in this world, but they are exceptionally slow and stupid."

"I still..." before Hulkan could finish his statement a messenger came running up the hill.

"Jarwe said that you need to attack the giants at the legs." Hulkan hoped there was more to the message because that was a fairly obvious statement. The dwarves would have to stand on each other's shoulders if they wanted to attack any higher. "They are slow, but very powerful and their skin is very thick. Tell your dwarves to be careful not to get their axes stuck in the legs. Once they are on the ground it shouldn't be too hard to finish them off."

The messenger didn't wait for a response. Even if Hulkan had a question there was no more information to give. The dwarf returned his attention to the battlefield. It was clear to the messenger that his job was done and he returned down the hill to wait with the others in case he was needed again.

The orglin were still thick on the battlefield and Hulkan doubted that anyone would have noticed the giants. He didn't want to distract them whilst they were deep in battle, timing was everything.

Dorn took a deep breath as he brandished his axe. He was at the front of the line of dwarves, from both guilds, and watched as the orglin gorged themselves. The sight was disgusting, but it gave them time to ready themselves for their next advance. Dorn waited until the last minute before he called for the attack. He didn't want to divert the orglin from feeding.

The adrenaline pumped through Dorn's body as he hacked at the first orglin he came across. He could have stayed on the hill with Hulkan and no one would have thought twice, but he knew his place was on the battlefield. He had not followed the Chosen One and then the Alliance all around the Seven Kingdoms to sit out the final battle.

The first orglin were easy to kill. They were still busy feasting to worry about the attacking dwarves. Once they were past the line of dead bodies the intensity increased. With every orglin Dorn hacked to death another two seemed to take its place. The dwarves were well outnumbered, but that didn't seem to make any difference. In fact Dorn couldn't believe how easy they were dealing with the Evil One's army and wondered if the other armies were having such a good time.

As the orglin horde started to diminish Hulkan barked out his next command. His voice sailed over the battlefield. At first no one really knew what he was talking about and no one wanted to take their eyes from the orglin, but as the giants approached there was no doubting the orders.

Dorn was the first past the orglin to attack the giants. There were still orglin behind him and if he had pulled his dwarves back then they could have destroyed them completely, but Dorn didn't want to wait. The giants didn't even seem to notice him. It seemed the short statured nature of the dwarves was going to continue to be an advantage.

With the words of Hulkan echoing in his mind he swung his axe, but not with full force. If he embedded his weapon in the giant's leg then he would be left defenceless and that would mean his life. He felt the blade dig in and pulled back quickly. At first the giant looked confused at the sudden pain in its leg. The creature slowly turned around, but even then he couldn't find the source of its pain. It wasn't until it looked down until it saw the dwarf preparing for a second strike.

More dwarves came to help Dorn fight the giants. The battle with the orglin was almost over and those at the front of the battlefield didn't want to miss out on the glory of killing such a mighty beast.

As Dorn moved in for his next attack another dwarf hacked at the giant's right knee from behind. Although the blow was not enough to cripple the great beast, it was enough to drop it to one knee. As it came down it brought the cudgel around to balance itself and knocked Dorn in the chest as he advanced. Although it was only a glancing blow it was enough to send Dorn flying across the battlefield, leaving a dint in his breastplate. As he came to his feet he felt a pain rip through his chest and he knew that at least one of his ribs had been broken. His only option was to cut the straps and remove his breastplate. Without his armour he would be completely open to attack, but with it on he couldn't breathe.

Turning around Dorn gripped the handle of his axe and prepared to continue his attack. What he saw sent a wave of relief through his body and he nearly collapsed as the adrenaline left his body. A group of dwarves had swarmed the giant and were currently on top of it hacking with all their strength. The giant tried to lift its cudgel, but with each cut its strength waned.

As Dorn looked around the battlefield he saw the other three giants being overrun by a group of dwarves and that was the last of the battle. The orglin had all been slaughtered, the giants were all but dead and nothing more was coming through the gateway.

"We've won!" a cry came from deep within the dwarven army. "The final battle is over and we have won."

A cheer arose over the battlefield, but Dorn didn't make a sound. On face value it did seem as though the final battle was over, but he knew it couldn't be that easy. The Evil One had not brought his army into the Seven Kingdoms to be defeated so easily.

"Stand your ground!" Dorn called and instantly wished he hadn't. Pain ripped through his chest and he dropped to one knee.

"Are you alright Dorn?" a nearby dwarf asked him.

"I'll be fine," a great cough and then groan belied his statement.

"Looks like we should get you back to camp, the battle is over and you are in no state..." Suddenly there was a crackle in the air in front of them.

It didn't take long for the battlefield to become silent as the gateway started to crack. Within a matter of moments it shattered like a piece of glass. When the coloured shards hit the ground they disappeared. On the other side of the gateway was a slightly smaller one about three hundred paces behind it. The second gateway had been completely blocked by the first one. Dorn felt a drop of rain on his head as the enormity of the situation sunk in.

With the first gateway down, the creatures waiting in surprise moved into action. They looked like giant lizards covered in plate armour with a pointed head. Even from a distance it looked as though they stood roughly the same height as the dwarves. Their short stature had been an advantage against the orglin and the giants, but it would do nothing against their new adversaries.

"What is the name of Horinga are they?" Hulkan gasped.

"They are called scartlers and they are from the Southern Wasteland," was all Gwydion replied.

"We need to get you to the med-tent," the dwarf said to Dorn as the first drop of rain hit his head.

Dorn looked to the sky. The storm clouds were overhead and it looked as though they were about to break. If the new arrivals weren't bad enough it looked as though they would be fighting in the torrent that

Gwydion had been trying to keep at bay. Instead of acknowledging the request he gripped the handle of his axe with all his strength, ignoring the pain ripping through his chest.

"Now is not the time for bravery. All you will achieve is your own death," the voice came from behind him but the fierce pain blocked it to a whisper. It wasn't until the dwarf grabbed his shoulder and started to pull him back did he realise the futility of his bravado. He dropped his axe as the pain became too much for him and he dropped himself to one knee, gasping for breath. "I need help here!" the dwarf called out even as the scartlers made their advance.

"Third line!" Hulkan boomed at the top of his voice and with the aid of Gwydion's spell it thundered across the battlefield.

It was the moment he had been dreading. At first he thought it was a wise move putting Brac in command of the last line of dwarves, but when it came time for action he wasn't so sure. The dwarf had been against the war with the Evil One from the start and now was his chance to prove his treachery.

"The second line needs help, charge!"

To his surprise and relief he saw Brac lead the third and last line of dwarves onto the battlefield. When they were gone the first line started to ready themselves again.

The start of the battle had gone so well and there had been few dwarven casualties, but Hulkan didn't think that was going to remain. The scartlers looked like they were ready for destruction. If they poured through the gateway like the orglin had then had no idea how they were going to survive. Slowly he tapped the hilt of his axe, both with anticipation and an urge to take the battlefield.

Hulkan held his breath as the scartlers crashed into the dwarves. At first it seemed like things were going better than expected. The scartlers ran forward, but didn't have the mobility to move when it came to attack. The dwarves at the front of the line were able to simply sidestep them before severing the creatures' heads.

When the initial charge came to an end the scartlers settled into their attack. The dwarves fought hard, but the giant lizard like creatures were up to the challenge. It didn't take the dwarves long to realise that the only way to kill the lizard-like creatures was to hack their heads off at the necks or with a lucky strike to the head. Attacking the hard plates on the scartlers back was a waste of time and proved nothing more than to dull their blades.

Although the number of scartlers were nowhere near that of the orglin, they were much more efficient. As the rain fell down they snapped at the dwarves with their razor sharp teeth and whipped at them with the thick tails. As soon as the teeth clamped down on the dwarves they would tear through flesh and bone. Whoever had been caught was soon dead.

"We're not going to last at this rate," Hulkan said to Gwydion. Although the scartlers had stopped coming through the gateway Hulkan estimated there were outnumbered at least two to one. To make matters worse for every scartler killed at least two dwarves were slain. "Is there anything you can do?"

Gwydion had been busy fighting the storm and had only vaguely been paying attention to the newcomers. With the appearance of the second gateway the pressure of the storm had intensified. The rain fell and it only continued to increase with each passing moment. He knew Hulkan was right. If he didn't do anything to help then the scartlers would eventually overrun them. Even with the first line ready to march again there was little chance they could survive the onslaught.

Taking a deep breath Gwydion let go of the spell holding back the storm. As he did the rain increased in intensity, but it only proved to hinder the enemy. The scartlers were from the Southern Wasteland where it was lucky if it rained once a year. They fought on warm sand and the pouring rain quickly turned the soft dirt to mud. Their movements slowed in both their march and their attack. Gwydion couldn't believe his luck, but his job was not finished. Even with their movement hindered they were still a formidable enemy.

Hulkan turned around as he heard footsteps from behind him. Relief washed over him when he saw Dorn approach. The dwarf had his shirt and armour off and his ribs were heavily bandaged. He looked a little worse for wear, but he was still alive.

"Good to see you Dorn," Hulkan said with as much enthusiasm as he could muster.

"I wish I could say the same for you. I was just getting started when that giant hit me with his cudgel. I would much rather be out there taking on those lizard creatures," Dorn groaned with the pain from his ribs.

Gwydion ignored the banter and started his spell, but then a thought came to him. He could use the storm to his advantage. Creating lightning when the sky was clear was a tough challenge, but it was a lot easier than anything else he could think of.

It was not long after Gwydion had created his spell before the first bolt of lightning crashed into the sea of scartlers. Gwydion made sure to aim the lightning back from the battlefront so he didn't risk hitting any of the dwarves. As much as he tried to aim the lightning when it appeared in the sky, it would crackle down on its own course. As the first bolt of lightning exploded into the ground it threw dirt and scartlers into the air.

Hulkan watched on in hope as lightning bolt after lightning bolt struck. Each attack killed at least one of the evil creatures and sometimes two or three. It soon dawned on him that even with Gwydion's help there were still too many for the dwarves to overcome them. He would need to order the first line back into the fray if they had any chance of success. To make matters worse he could see that Brac had made his way to the back of the line and was doing his best to avoid any battles. That was not at all what a leader should be doing and with Dorn returned there was no one in command.

"Brac!" Hulkan called out, but Gwydion had to let the spell go to concentrate on his own attack.

"What is it?" Dorn asked.

"Brac is at the back of the line and it doesn't look like he is interested in leading the army. Look!" He pointed to the two flanks. "He should be replenishing the flanks from behind the middle. If this keeps up we will be slaughtered in a matter of minutes."

"What do you suggest? I would gladly take the battlefield again, but I feel that I would be less than useless." Dorn held his chest as if he needed to accentuate the fact.

"It is time for you to lead from the hill," Hulkan said as he unlooped his axe and held it firmly in his right hand. "It's time for me to take the field."

Dorn was about to open his voice to protest, but he knew Hulkan was right. He always knew that he would finish the battle in command of the army, he just didn't realise it. He wished that he could storm the battlefield with Hulkan, but he knew he couldn't At least there was something useful for him to do, although he wasn't sure there was much left to command.

"Follow me, our brothers need help," Hulkan commanded the remaining dwarves to follow him onto the battlefield. "Secure the flanks," he barked. "And try and hold the scartlers back. Don't allow their advance. Give Gwydion time to destroy them." To accentuate his point another explosion could be heard in front of them.

Hulkan hoped that everyone had heard what he said, but with the storm raging around him he couldn't be sure. The dwarves moved off to the left and right. As he moved forward he came up to Brac.

"What are you doing back here?" Hulkan yelled over the tumult.

"To make sure no one breaks from the line," Brac sneered.

If Hulkan didn't know the dwarf better it might have sounded like a reasonable plan, but he knew that wasn't the case. He had watched the entire battle from the hill and no one looked like breaking the line and retreating, no matter what the Evil One threw at them.

"To the front of the line," Hulkan yelled at the top of his voice, making sure the dwarves around him heard. "We will bring this battle to the Evil One."

Hulkan almost had to push Brac through the army to reach the front of the line and he would if he needed to. He wasn't going to let the dwarf remain at the back. When they reached the front Hulkan made sure they were fighting side-by-side. With the threat of being eaten alive Brac actually sprang into action.

"Just try and hold them," Hulkan said as Brac severed the head of a Scartler.

"If I'm here then I will kill anything that wants to kill me."

Hulkan had to admit he was right. There was more chance they would die if they didn't take their chance to kill. It was at that point he realised the lightning had stopped shooting from above. The line of scartlers had reached the line of dwarves and Gwydion didn't want to risk anymore lives.

"Push hard!" Hulkan commanded. "We're nearly there."

The words of their commander brought a renewed vigour through the ranks. Those who had been doing their best to hold the scartlers at bay went on the attack. Gwydion had decimated their numbers, but the creatures at the front of the line had no idea what had happened behind them. All they were concerned about was the battle in front.

The dwarves pushed harder and harder as they knew the battle was almost done. Hulkan chopped the head off a nearby scartler before rushing forward. He took a dozen steps before he realised there were just dwarves around him, no scartlers. Even with his small stature he knew the scartlers were all dead.

Hulkan wanted to let out a cheer, but after the first battle he kept his mouth shut, as did the rest of the dwarves. On the surface it seemed like they final battle was over, but Hulkan had a bad feeling that wasn't going to be the case.

Dorn watched on from the vantage point of the small hill. Even as the rain pelted down he could see everything that was happening on the battlefield. When the last of the scartlers had been taken care of a feeling of hope flooded his body. The storm clouds broke and the sky was suddenly clear, but it was only there for a moment. Like the first gateway the second started to shimmer as soon as the last scartler had stopped breathing. Within a matter of seconds the gateway cracked and then shattered to the ground. What was waiting for them on the other side was worse than anything Dorn could have imagined. A sea of evil creatures filled the space in front of the gateway. There were more orglin, minotaurs and scartlers as well as a myriad of other evil creatures. No matter what advantages the dwarves had started with they were now completely gone. Even with the aid of Gwydion's magic he didn't think they would stand a chance. To make matters worse he saw a cloaked figure standing at the front of the mass of evil. Even from the distance he knew it was the Dark Knight Dargoz.

Suddenly there was a loud ear-piercing screech from the west. A shiver ran through Hulkan's body as he looked to see what it was. Before he had a chance to see anything he felt a searing pain in his back and he stumbled forward. At first he had no idea what it was, but as he stumbled to his knees the realisation came over him. With all his energy he turned around to see the sneering expression on Brac's face. As much as he didn't think he was going to make it through the final battle, he had no idea this would be his end.

Chapter 24: The Sapphire Queen

Marina walked slowly and deliberately until she was standing next to Nyrra. Alaric wanted nothing more than to strike out. He had spent a lot of time with Marina and although he didn't truly love her he had felt very close to her. They had spent more than one night together and Alaric found it hard to believe that she could have changed so quickly. If Alaric himself had not hardened, he knew he would have felt sad, but he had no time for emotions. Emotions would be the end of him.

Slowly he felt something in the back of his mind twinge and he instantly knew what it was. Alaric still had the chest nearby and it seemed as though Marina was the first to realise it, or at least she was the first to try and open it. The Sapphire stone was inside and it was drawing her in. Ever since she had touched the Sapphire stone she could think of nothing else. Alaric didn't know exactly what her relationship to the stone was, but he knew it was extremely powerful.

There was no way she would be able to break his spell, but the fact that she knew the chest's location was in itself very disturbing. Even Nyrra by himself wouldn't be able to open it. Only with the aid of the Ruby stone would he even come close. Even so Alaric felt nervous with the new development and he needed to start the conversation again to keep his mind off it.

"So what is this all about?" He asked. As much as she really didn't matter to him anymore, he still needed Nyrra to believe she did. "What is she doing here?"

"Don't listen to him," Marina spoke between strands of wet, black hair. Alaric could only just see her eyes through it and although they were a deep blue he thought they burned like fire. "He doesn't care about me. If he did then he would never have taken her away from me."

"Be quiet now," Nyrra hissed at Marina. "This is not your time to speak." Marina didn't seem to care about the tone of his voice. All she was concentrating on was the invisible chest with the Sapphire stone inside. "Does it surprise you that I have such a pet at my side? I would have thought you would have been prepared for such an occurrence. You could only dream about what we have been doing." Nyrra reached out and gently flicked her hair in a strangely playful manner.

Alaric took a menacing step forward before he controlled himself. An angry sneer crossed his face, or at least the best he could do. By the large smile on Nyrra's face his reaction had worked. It was almost too easy, but the last thing he wanted was to become overconfident. He couldn't fall into the same trap.

Alena's reaction was just as intense. She gasped in horror and covered her mouth before she could say anything. It was obvious that Nyrra was looking for a shocked response from both of them and she stopped herself before she gave away too much. It was Alaric's battle and she didn't want to get in the way.

"Make the most of your glory, it will be all for naught when I stand over your corpse," Alaric spoke between clenched teeth to accentuate his point.

Nyrra burst out laughing, seeing the humour in Alaric's threat. "I think you might find that it will be me standing over your corpse when this is all said and done. And when I have finished with you I will take your she-elf into my bed and have my pleasure with her."

As much as Alaric had steeled himself, the last threat did hit a nerve. He did not want the image of Nyrra raping Alena inside his mind, but there was little he could do about it. The thought made him want to strike out, but that was what the Evil One wanted.

"And she will enjoy it like nothing she has ever experienced before. All those nights she has laid with you will seem like a distant past."

Alena couldn't believe what she was hearing and before she knew it she had her bow drawn and aimed at the Evil One. Loosing the arrow she prayed it would hit its mark and to her surprise it did, piercing the Evil One's chest. Nyrra looked down at the arrow in surprise as dark red blood started to bubble from the wound. He had been so focused on Alaric that he had not thought to see what Alena was doing.

Alena could hardly breathe as she watched him. She had done it. She had killed the Evil One. But then Nyrra started to laugh. It had just been a masquerade for her benefit. She should have known that a mere arrow could not have killed him. He simply pulled the arrow from his chest and let it drop to the ground. The blood that had seeped from the wound disappeared, along with the wound itself. Alena dropped her bow, realising that it was no use.

"There is still fire in this one, Alaric," Nyrra continued. "I think I'm going to like breaking her."

Alaric knew he could no longer remain calm. Alena had struck out and that was exactly what Nyrra was expecting. With a flick of his wrist Alaric shot a small ball of brilliant white light at Nyrra. Of course, as he expected from the start, the light only reached half the distance before it disappeared. Alaric started to pant, as if the effort had exerted him.

"I see there is fire in you too. For a moment I thought your heart had turned to ice," Nyrra sneered. "But I guess that can wait."

"I want her back," Marina said. "I have waited this long and you said if I came with you that I would get her back."

"All in good time my pretty," Nyrra stroked her hair in a gentle, yet condescending manner. "Let me discard of Alaric first and then you can have whatever you want."

Alaric thought about offering her the stone, but he still wasn't sure he could trust her. If he gave it to her and she still fought on the side of evil then he didn't think he could win. He needed all the stones he had if he was going to defeat Nyrra, but he could offer it to her when the battle was over.

"You know Nyrra is the father of all lies," Alaric said as softly as he could. "He will never free you from his yoke and he will never give you the Sapphire stone. If I didn't need it to defeat him I would give it to you now, but when it is all over you can have it."

"And why should I trust anything you say?" Marina sneered and flicked her dark hair back so he could see her. Her face was covered in thick, white makeup with black circles painted around her eyes and blood red lips. She looked like something out of a child's horror story. As much as he would have liked to believe Nyrra had chosen her façade he knew it was all her doing. Something had broken inside her and he didn't know if there was any way to fix it. "You were the one that took her from me in the first place. If it wasn't for you she would be with me now and I would have nothing to do with this. No, nothing you can say will convince me that you are anything but the enemy."

Even though Alaric knew she was gone, he needed to know for certain. Slowly he started to delve into her mind. If Nyrra had planted anything he would be able to remove it. Even if Nyrra had done something he would able to cure her of it, but there was still no guarantee that she would return to him.

"You will find nothing there," Nyrra laughed as he spoke. "I have done nothing to alter her mind. Everything you see before you is what you have done. She came looking for me, not the other way around, and when she found me she knew exactly what she had to do."

"What is he talking about?" Alena asked, almost too afraid to speak.

"Marina is linked to the Sapphire stone. I'm not exactly sure why, but her connection is unmistakable. I guess this is the affect that Eldred warned me about in the beginning. The stones all tried to get the better of me. The voices in my head were very persistent, but I was strong enough to overcome them. It seems Marina wasn't strong enough."

"Is that what you think?" Marina sneered again. "You think that *She* has tried to take over my mind? You would be greatly mistaken. We are of one mind. When you reveal Her to me you will find out for yourself. You should have just given Her to me when you had the chance."

There was something in her threat that made Alaric take note. He had never really believed Marina's mind had been taken over by the Sapphire stone, but it had definitely tainted it. Marina was obsessed, there was no other word for it, but that was the least of Alaric's concerns. Nyrra was his prime target and Marina, like Alena, was just a distraction, one that he wished was not there. Either way the die had been cast and there was nothing he could do to change it.

"So are you going to let her do all the talking for you?" Alaric returned his attention to Nyrra. He had to try and keep his attention focused on the Evil One. With every distraction there was no telling what he was plotting. "I thought this battle was supposed to be between you and me?"

"If that was the case then you wouldn't have brought your she-elf along. If I didn't know any better I would think that you want the girls to fight your battle for you."

Alaric fingered the hilt of his sword. There had been too much talk, he knew that, but he didn't know whose advantage it was to keep the conversation going. Nyrra didn't seem to be in any hurry to attack and neither did he.

"You seem to be enjoying yourself," Alaric thought he'd push a little harder. "I thought you would have wanted to finish this as soon as you could?"

"You know as well as I do that the time isn't right," Nyrra shook his head in disgust. "The battle to the west has only just started and as much as it makes no real deference, we still need to let it play out. At least as long as it's supposed to. We all know the one who wins here will finish off the losers respective armies."

Alaric knew he was right, but that still made the battle in Avalon vitally important to the Seven Kingdoms. If the Alliance was completely destroyed before Alaric had finished with Nyrra then it would not bode well for the Seven Kingdoms. If the Evil One's army had a chance to leave the battleground then it would be very difficult for Alaric to chase them all down. It was at that point that Alaric realised he had already drawn his sword. He didn't know when or why, but he was certainly ready for a fight.

"I must admit that is a bold move." Nyrra looked surprised. "I guess we need to do something to pass the time."

Nyrra made the motion of drawing a sword and when he was finished he held a large broadsword of fire in his right hand. It was much thicker, but only slightly longer, than the slender elven sword Alaric had. The size made little difference. Each would use not only physical strength, but magical strength as well. Suddenly Alaric's sword also burst into flame. It was purely for show and would have no lasting effect, but he felt he needed to do something to show that he could.

With his sword ablaze Alaric didn't waste any time moving in to attack. Marina instantly moved back, out of the way, not wanting to get slashed by an errant swing. She also wanted to try and stay out of Alaric's field of vision. If there was a chance for her to attack then it would be best if it was unexpected.

Alena moved to the side so she could get a better view of the fight. If there was a chance to help Alaric then she would, but she really didn't think that was going to happen. Whatever the two were planning it would be far greater than anything she was capable of.

Alaric didn't wait for Nyrra to prepare himself. As soon as his blade was lit he went on the attack. He didn't call on any of the techniques he had learned over the last year and his attack was that of brute strength, more to alleviate his frustration than anything else. Nyrra easily defended against the wild attack, although he was forced to take a number of steps back.

When Alaric had finished with his manic first attack it was time for Nyrra to go on the offensive. At first he had been quite happy to defend whatever Alaric had in store for him, knowing that it would not be the end of the final battle, but with his unorthodox attack he could see a chance of being killed and that was not something he could accept.

Nyrra's attack was much more fluid than Alaric's. Despite the size of his fire sword he moved it as if it was nothing but a rapier. Alaric moved with the flows of Nyrra's attack. It had been a long time since he had fought someone with the same skills. From his added memories he had always been a swordmaster. The memories of him training at Elhjem seemed like a lifetime ago.

Nyrra went on the attack for a good ten minutes before Alaric finally managed to gain the advantage. This time his attack was more controlled and he switched through the different flows like they were one move. Nyrra had to admit he was impressed. If the final battle was just the skill with the sword he knew that Alaric would soon have the better of him, he was grateful this was just the beginning.

Alena watched in awe, unable to move. As far as she knew the final battle between good and evil was taking place before her and the result would forge the future of the Seven Kingdoms for years to come. As the battle continued and the two fiery swords hit each other, she felt the temperature in the cavern double. Sweat poured down her face and if she was in another situation she would have stripped down to her undergarments. She seemed to be the only one made uncomfortable by the sudden rise in temperature.

Taking a look at the bow on the ground before her she wondered if she could be of any assistance to Alaric. Before she bent over to pick it up she saw something move behind them. With the scene before her she had almost completely forgotten about Marina. The evil woman had positioned herself behind Alaric and Nyrra as they moved back and forth. She made sure she stayed between them and Alena. It didn't make any sense.

As Alaric slashed at Nyrra and drove him back across the cavern, Marina stepped out from where she had been hiding. Alena stared at her, wondering what it was she had been planning. Before Alena had a chance to move Marina pushed out at the air in front of her. Whether it was the enormity of the situation or pure surprise, Alena didn't move as a bolt of pure blue light shot from Marina's hand towards her.

Alaric noticed the attack too late to do anything about it as Nyrra used the distraction to strike out. At the last minute Alaric blocked his attack before taking a number of steps backwards.

"Alena!" Alaric cried out as the light was about to hit her. As much as he had steeled his heart from loving her he still didn't want to see her die.

Alena closed her eyes and prepared for the inevitable as the light approached. The light only took a second to cover the distance, but it seemed like a lifetime. When nothing happened she slowly opened her eyes and realised that the light had disappeared. She looked towards Alaric, but his attention had only been diverted for a moment before it returned to Nyrra. It wasn't until he heard her move behind him that he realised she was still alive. He had no idea what had happened. He had not stopped the light and he couldn't imagine why Nyrra would want to keep her alive. There had to be another answer to the riddle. He could tell by Nyrra's expression that he didn't know what had happened either.

"It's not possible," Marina screeched. "She should be dead. You told me that I could kill her.

Nyrra didn't know how to respond. Marina's attack on Alena was supposed to be successful, albeit not so early in the battle. It was destined to be a turning point. Alaric would crumble at the loss of the she-elf he loved. Despite the setback Nyrra knew that there would be changes to the prophecy and things certainly weren't over, but that still didn't explain what had stopped the attack.

"Did you think we would not be here?" Alaric instantly recognised the voice. It was that of his old friend Bern, the body used by Asgard.

Alena spun around and Marina and Nyrra looked past Alaric to see who it was. Marina recognised Bern, but she had no idea who the little girl was at his side. Of all the people Alena had thought to see, Bern was not one of them. She would have thought he would be leading the Alliance in Avalon.

"I know you," Marina said. "You are Bern."

"This body is that of Bern, but what is inside is completely different," Nyrra could see through the façade. "And it looks like you have brought your little friend. When last we met I wasn't sure if you would ever find each other."

Bern moved forward until he was standing between Alena and the others. There was little point in the move, but it made Alena feel safer.

"This is Asgard and his little friend is Esgard," Nyrra explained. "And they have no business being here, but that's never stopped them before." Nyrra turned to face Asgard. "You know this isn't your battle to fight. This fight is between Alaric and me. This has nothing to do with either of you."

Alaric was relieved that Asgard and Esgard had finally arrived. He thought they would be there shortly after him, but with every passing minute he wasn't sure they were going to make it. He had found as many passages in the prophecy stating they would be there as he had found with them being absent.

"Well we are here now," Esgard marched up in her plain black dress. It was a big difference to the floral ones she had been wearing around the army. Her blonde hair had been tied up in a bun, as if she was trying to look older than her façade. In the army she had played the good girl and let Asgard take control, but that was only because no one knew who they were. In the cavern their façades meant nothing.

Bern had chosen to wear a simple leather jerkin and trousers. There was no particular reason for the dress it just felt appropriate. In the end they could have both been naked and it would have made no difference.

"And maybe you should just turn around and go back to where you came from," Nyrra sneered.

Alaric slowly inched his way to the side so he wasn't standing between them. The distraction gave him a chance to prepare his next attack. He had extinguished his sword and sheathed it. He didn't want anything to bring the attention back to him.

"You would like that wouldn't you?" Esgard continued. "Is that maybe because you are afraid?"

Nyrra burst out laughing. "I will show you how afraid I am."

The taunt coming from the little girl had more of an effect than if it had come from Asgard. It had all been planned before they arrived. Asgard would announce their arrival and then Esgard would try and provoke him. Their main goal was to try and get him to reveal the Ruby stone, which was still hidden to them. They were also hoping that when he revealed his stone, Alaric would reveal the other six. Only then would the battle truly begin, as far as they were concerned.

Nyrra didn't waste any time in creating his spell. Suddenly a number of small tornados appeared around the edge of the cavern. They spun around picking up rocks and ripping boulders from the walls before hurling them around. The rocks hurtled through the air in no particular order and Esgard and Asgard simply stood where they were and watched them fly. Alena had to duck out of the way more than once to avoid being struck. She could only assume the others were using magic to to.

Alena ducked and wove her way over to where Alaric was standing. She noticed that he too was not fazed by the flying boulders and figured it would be the safest place to be. The attacks weren't aimed at him and he would easily be able to deflect anything.

At first the attack seemed to be very innocuous, but as it continued it became more apparent. When rocks and boulders flew across the cavern they ended up back in one of the tornados. Within a matter of seconds they spat the rock out in two or three pieces. The rocks flew back and forth across the cavern getting smaller and smaller with each pass.

Only Alena seemed to be concerned with the attack as she huddled behind Alaric. The Chosen One stood his ground as the small rocks flew past him. Occasionally a rock would graze across him either ripping his clothes or cutting his skin. As soon as a rip or cut appeared, they instantly disappeared. Alaric didn't seem at all concerned. Even though the attack was aimed at Asgard and Esgard, everyone in the cavern was in danger of being struck.

Asgard and Esgard remained where they were and seemed about as concerned as Alaric. Unlike him they magically defended themselves. Each time a rock or stone came close it would bounce off an invisible barrier before dropping to the floor. It was a fruitless exercise, but Nyrra wasn't about to stop.

Soon the cavern was a sea of stones flying back and forth. Alaric remained standing where he was. Cloth and blood flung from his body as the small stones ripped through him.

"Enough of this!" Alaric finally boomed and as he did the rocks suddenly stopped flying around the cavern. They all stopped in midair for a second before dropping to the ground. The tornados remained for a little longer, but one by one Alaric extinguished them. He had hoped either Asgard or Esgard would have broken the spell, but he couldn't wait forever. In the back of his mind he knew the final battle in Avalon had started. "This is getting us nowhere."

"Quite right you are, but it is a spot of fun. I wouldn't have thought you would be so keen to die," Nyrra had a strangely playful tone.

"Look around you uncle, there is nothing for you here. Marina isn't up to the challenge. I could take on the both you by myself." Alaric didn't know why he called Nyrra 'uncle' but it seemed appropriate.

"The death is and always has been yours. The fighting has started to the west and there is very little time left for you."

Alaric paused and waited to see if anyone else had anything to say. He knew what he wanted to say, but he wasn't sure if he should. When no one else spoke he sighed before continuing.

"Very well. I have an offer for *you* uncle. Return to the Northern Wastelands, take your armies with you and swear to never return. Do this and I will grant you your life. You can live the remainder of your life to the north and leave the Seven Kingdom's in peace."

Nyrra burst out laughing, but Alena cut in before he had a chance to speak. "You can't be serious Alaric," she was almost pleading with him. "He cannot be trusted. Even if he was to accept your offer there is nothing stopping him returning one day, and if you are not here who will stop him then?"

"She is right," Asgard tried his best to sound like Alaric's old friend Bern. "There is no offer you can make that we can trust he will keep." There was more to Asgard's reasoning, but he wasn't going to let it be known.

"There is one thing," Alaric said softly. "There is a passage in the prophecy that speaks of an offer that I am to make to Nyrra. Although as usual it was very obscure and gave no answer, but I think I still understand its meaning.

An offer shall be made
But none shall trust
Who shall make
And who shall receive
The words are true
And trust is given
Blood of my blood
Is the key to all
And then break the trust
An impossible task

"That doesn't mean anything," Esgard said.

"On face value no, but if you read between the lines and know a thing or two," Alaric replied.

"Well don't be so elusive and tell us what it means?" Alena snapped at him, although she didn't know where she gained the confidence to speak.

"If Nyrra agrees to go into the Northern Wasteland with his army then I can seal him there with my blood," Alaric started.

"That seems a little too easy," Alena replied, worried at what he was implying.

"The seal that was created the first time was always doomed to break. With my blood it will last forever," Alaric replied.

"Why don't you tell them how much blood the seal will need?" Nyrra sneered, clearly already knowing.

"What is he talking about?" Alena asked.

"It would need all my blood," Alaric resigned.

"And what of the Ruby stone?" Esgard asked, not overly concerned that the deed would cost Alaric his life.

"Irrelevant to the offer. If Nyrra takes the Ruby stone into the wasteland he cannot use it to return the Seven Kingdoms. In fact if he has it in the north then it can never be used to destroy the Seven Kingdoms again," Alaric explained.

"That is not acceptable," Asgard said.

"It is the offer that I have given and I will stand by it," Alaric replied, not backing down. "What do say you uncle? Will you accept my offer and live out your days in the north?"

Nyrra burst out laughing. He had already made his decision before the offer was given. There was nothing that would make him go back to the wasteland.

"Why would I accept your offer? You will be dead soon and the Seven Kingdoms will be mine. There is nothing you can offer me to make me change my mind."

"Very well then," Alaric didn't sound at all surprised with Nyrra's response. "I think it might be time to get things started."

"Right you are. It's now time to for you to die."

When Nyrra finished speaking the two suddenly disappeared. Shock was clearly written on everyone's face. No one had expected that to happen and no one knew what it meant.

Chapter 25: Enteroite Army

Duke Xarles, or Commander X as he was now known, stood on a small hill and looked out over the field before him. The grey of dawn was upon them, but the sun had yet to bridge the horizon. Xarles hoped that it never would. If it didn't then the day couldn't start and the final battle would never come. He knew his logic was flawed, but it still gave him some kind of hope.

When he had woken the day before he had no idea he would be leading his fellow Enteroites into battle against the Evil One. After he had helped to free Queen Oriana from the grips of the Dark Knight, he thought his role in the battle with the Evil One was finished. The Alliance had moved on and things were seemingly getting back to normal. When Eldred told him that he needed to be in Avalon to lead the Enteroite army he knew it was his destiny. Even when he believed his role was over he knew it wasn't.

Even though he had been told that he would not be fighting he had chosen to wear his steel breastplate and greaves. The queen had wanted to give him some royal armour to wear, but there had been no time and Xarles preferred to wear the eagle and fox of his family crest. He tapped the hilt of his sword, which he wore at his side. He didn't know what would be worse. Taking part in the final battle or watching it unfold before him.

It wasn't until Eldred was standing next to him before he realised the wizard was there. He had been so deep in thought that the surprise was clearly visible across his face.

"Something I should know about?" Eldred asked, trying to lighten the situation.

"Not really, just wondering when this battle is going to start," Xarles replied as he returned his attention to the field.

The Enteroite army had assembled behind him, but he couldn't bring himself to look. It would be the last time a lot of them would be seen alive. The army would look to Xarles for support and for the moment he didn't have the heart to give it. He knew he would need to address them soon, but he just wanted a few more moments to himself.

"Soon enough, soon enough," was all Eldred said.

Xarles was happy enough with the response and was glad that he didn't continue the conversation. It seemed Eldred was also happy enough with some silent time. There was a cool breeze as the sun slowly started its ascent above the horizon. With it Xarles' heart started to pump faster.

"I don't like the look of those clouds," Xarles pointed to the far north.

"They look like they're too far away to be of any concern to us," Eldred only gave them a glancing look. "You need to focus on the task in front of you. It will not be long before the army of the Evil One takes the battlefield."

"I take it they will arrive in much the same fashion as we did?" It seemed to make sense to Xarles.

"If I was to take a guess I would say yes, but the Evil One has many tricks. The Dark Knights have returned and there is no telling what they capable of now," Eldred explained. "Whatever Nyrra has in store for us you can be sure that his army will arrive in a hurry."

There had to be some magic involved. The field before them was still completely empty and the battle was due to start at any minute. It was time for him to address his soldiers and bring them hope of success.

"My fellow Enteroites," Xarles started with the aid of the voice carrying spell from Eldred. "We have travelled across the Seven Kingdoms to come here to Avalon to fight the Evil One." Xarles paused as a cheer arose across the army. "Some of you have travelled with the Alliance and some of you helped us to defeat the Dark Knight in Jarrat. Either way we have all been involved with this fight for a long time." He didn't bother excluding those from the outer regions who had really done nothing. "The Evil One thought we would cower behind our walls. He thought our queen could be made a thrall, but we never gave up. Now our land and our queen are free and soon we shall do the same for the rest of the Seven Kingdoms." Another cheer moved across the army. "Do not fear this day, for fear is the greatest weapon of our enemy. At the end of the day we shall stand victorious on the field of battle and we will go down in history as the army that saved the Seven Kingdoms from disaster." His last words brought and even louder cheer from the soldiers.

When he was finished Xarles turned back to face the battlefield. From behind the hill the army couldn't see what was happening. All they knew was what they had been told and that the enemy had yet to arrive. Xarles had deliberately kept the army from seeing the field before them. He didn't know what the enemy had in store and when it came he didn't want his soldiers baulking.

Suddenly Xarles felt the hair on the back of his neck stand on end. There was a strange electricity in the air and he knew it wouldn't be long before the Evil One's army joined them on the battlefield. Slowly crackles of lightning appeared about five hundred paces in front of them.

"Ready the first line!" Xarles boomed, louder than he intended.

Eldred watched and waited. As he looked at the sky he realised that the storm was moving a lot quicker than it should. The realisation dawned on him that the storm wasn't natural. If it had just been over his side of the battlefield he was sure he would be able to stop it, but as he looked to the east and the west he realised it spanned the entire length.

"Messenger!" he called out as loud as he could.

A young man ran up the hill as soon as he heard Eldred's voice. He was the first messenger of the day and was keen to do his duty. Eldred told him what he wanted relayed to the other wizards and he was quickly off to the transport ground.

Not long after the messenger left another ran up the hill. Eldred was pleased that the other wizards had come to the same conclusion. It had been a long time since they had all worked in unison and that was an achievement in itself. One of Eldred's greatest fears about the final battle was the Council. He knew they would all have to work together and that was something they had not been able to achieve in the past. It seemed as though everyone had their mind set on victory and that was a good thing.

The spell was a relatively simple one to keep the storm at bay, although it certainly required a group effort. Despite the ease of the spell it would consume much more energy than Eldred had wanted to use so early in the battle.

At a guess Eldred thought the storm was created by the Dark Knights. Nyrra would be off somewhere in *Crenallous* fighting the Chosen One. He would need all his strength if he had any chance of beating Alaric. If it was the Dark Knights who created the spell then Eldred didn't think they would be able to put up much of a fight elsewhere, at least that's what he was hoping.

Suddenly a loud ripping sound could be heard across the battlefield. Xarles held his breath as he waited for what was to come. A beam of bright light spread across the air in front of them and suddenly a giant gateway appeared. At first it bubbled a deep red and purple before it coalesced and a sea of orglin poured out.

Xarles had been expecting Nyrra to bring an army of evil, but he couldn't have imagined the scene before him. The gateway spanned the full width of the battlefield.

"I don't want to be rude, but I think it might be time to voice some commands," Eldred kept his voice low.

Xarles shook himself from his reverie. Eldred was right. They were standing at the front of the army and would be the first to be killed by the orglin. Without instruction they would remain where they were.

The infantry was brought to the front of the line with the archers staggered through the ranks. The cavalry was further back, but enough room had been left between the soldiers to bring them forward. It wasn't the most ideal of situations, but it was the best they could do. The fact that Xarles had limited military experience gave him an advantage with the unorthodox setup.

"Archers! Draw your bows." The orglin were out of range, but that wouldn't last long. "Cavalry to the front."

The Enteroite horses, unlike the elven ones, were trained for battle. Not only that, but they also wore armour protecting their necks and the top of their legs. Even the thick leather armour designed more for glancing blows, would provide good protection against the orglin. They were much better suited than the infantry to take the brunt of the first attack.

When the orglin were halfway across the battlefield Xarles called for the archers to loose their arrows. Almost as one the twang of bowstrings snapping back into place could be heard. No one waited to wonder where their arrows were headed. They had been given an order and that's what they were going to do.

"Nock and fire again," Xarles commanded as the first rain of arrows nearly reached their pinnacle. At the rate the orglin were charging forward he didn't think they would have time for a third volley.

Eldred watched the arrows arc in the air. Even when he suggested the archers stay near the front of the army he had his doubts on their effectiveness. If the Dark Knights had created the storm then they would be around to stop the arrows from hitting their targets. It wasn't until the first arrow struck before Eldred relaxed, if only slightly. The first volley of arrows flew into the advancing orglin killing more than Xarles thought they would. The orglin ran in a close pack not really giving the arrows much chance to miss.

The orglin running behind the front rows didn't care that their brethren had been mown down by a hail of arrows, nor that the archers had launched another attack. The arrows flighted through the air like the first volley and Eldred held his breath. Just because the first volley hit its mark didn't mean the second would. It was a tense wait as the arrows made their way down toward the storming orglin.

"Cavalry to the front!" Xarles repeated his previous command. He wasn't going to wait to see what happened with the second volley. He needed the cavalry onto the battlefield. "Shortbow behind." The longbow archers had done their job and would not be effective once the cavalry hit the fray. The shortbow archers would be able to pick off the orglin that made it past the initial charge. "Charge!" Xarles called. "Shortbow take the field."

The order was all the soldiers needed to kick their horses into action. It had been the moment they had been waiting for and the waiting had been excruciating. Once they were over the hill they could see the mass of evil before them, but they didn't falter.

The well trained horses charged toward the orglin without a care for their own safety. They had been in battle before and they knew if there was danger then their rider would look out for them. They could sense the feelings of the soldiers and knew they were charging towards something important. Although they didn't know the full extent of what was before them, the horses knew they couldn't falter.

The orglin didn't seem bothered about the charging cavalry. The horses would trample over them, but they didn't care. The bloodlust was overcoming them and all they could think of was gorging on their victims. Even when the horses crashed into the front line of orglin the evil creatures behind didn't halt their advance.

The horses charged into the sea of orglin for as far as they could before they finally had to slow to a stop. Any orglin caught under hoof were instantly crushed to death. Those caught by a flank were sent flying through the air. Xarles watched on from the hill and was pleased with the instant success. It had worked out better than he had thought and initially Eldred had not liked the idea. The orglin didn't really seem to know what to do. With the thick leather armour protecting the front of the horses they couldn't gauge an attack. Any orglin trying to attack from the side were quickly hacked away by the soldiers.

If the orglin that managed to pass by the horses had turned around they would have had a better chance of attacking the horses' unprotected rear, but instead they continued their charge. It was as if they were trying to get to someone on the other side of the battlefield, but all they were running towards was more death.

The shortbow archers had moved into position and were waiting for the orglin to come into range. At first there was shock at the swarm racing towards them, but some stern words from Xarles pushed them further onto the battlefield. Their tentativeness did nothing to reassure the nerves of the soldiers still waiting for the order to attack.

The archers took their time and waited for the orglin to come into range before they fired and each orglin received at least half a dozen arrows. Even though they were a well trained unit it was impossible for one archer to shoot at one orglin. Even though the archers all wore armour and had a short sword, none them wanted to engage in hand-to-hand combat.

After the initial charge of the cavalry the orglin were forced to stay and fight. They could do nothing with a frontal assault and even in the bloodlust they knew they had to fight. Eventually the orglin stopped breaking the lines and the archers were able to relax.

"Is there anything we can do about that gateway?" Xarles asked, not really expecting a positive response.

Eldred looked at the gateway. He had been concentrating on the storm and hadn't really thought about it. Although Alaric had not explained to them how they could break the gateway spell he was sure it was possible. Before he tried anything he realised it would be a moot point.

"Even if I did shut down that gateway I'm sure whoever created it would just make another one. At best it might give us a few seconds of respite, but I doubt even that," Eldred explained.

He didn't think it was even worth spending the energy to see if he actually *could* destroy it. He was sure there would be a way, but he couldn't waste his energy trying. There was no telling what the Evil One had in store for them.

Xarles knew that would be the case. He asked the question more to make conversation than anything else. The nerves were starting to get to him. Although the cavalry was doing a great job there seemed to be an endless supply of orglin. When one of the horses went down the sight was enough to make him gag. When the horse fell to the ground an orglin ripped out the back of its hind leg. The sound of the horse screaming resonated above the din of battle. With the horse down a number of orglin swarmed on top and started gorging.

"It looks like the cavalry are starting to tire," Eldred said as another horse was being dragged down. "I think you should consider sending in the first line of infantry."

Xarles looked out on the battlefield with fresh eyes. If he had thought the cavalry needed replacing he would have already made the command, but he couldn't dismiss Eldred's warning. He looked around and saw horse after horse being swallowed up by the ravaging orglin. He couldn't tell if they were starting to waver, but he knew it was time to send in the infantry.

"Infantry, first line!" Xarles called. "Time to relieve the cavalry. Controlled march to the front line. Cavalry, start your retreat." Eldred's spell carried his words to the battlefield.

The cavalry that were surrounded by orglin did their best to back out of the fray. The horses deftly made their way around the orglin corpses and remains of the soldiers and horses. Despite the fact they still wanted to fight and help the others they had been given the command.

Another ten horses and soldiers were taken down before the cavalry was in full retreat. At first they backed out slowly, but when they realised the orglin weren't interested in giving chase they quickened their retreat. Xarles felt the bile rise in the back of his throat as he watched the orglin and it was all he could do to stop himself from vomiting. The feeding frenzy was like nothing he had ever seen before. On the plus side it distracted them and gave the cavalry time to leave the battlefield and the infantry to move into place.

"Longbow!" Xarles called out after swallowing hard. He saw an opportunity to send a volley of arrows into the horde before they finished dining on their own kind. "Move up and fire."

The scene before the archers took them by surprise, some were even shocked at the orglin's feeding frenzy, but that didn't stop them from moving forward. When the orglin were in range, and far enough away from the approaching infantry, they all fired. It wasn't quite as poetic as the first volley, but it was just as effective. The arrows arced through the air, passing over the heads of the infantry, before landing deep in the horde of orglin.

The dead orglin were quickly consumed by those around them. The new death did nothing to hurry those at the front of the line.

Xarles had expected to only get one volley from the archers, but the orglin had yet to finish their gorging. When the second volley was in the air the orglin at the front were ready to continue their attack.

The orglin swarm had bunched up tight since those at the front had stopped. Those at the front were pushed forward into the oncoming soldiers and the infantry had no problems disposing of them. It seemed that they needed momentum to gain any real advantage.

Xarles breathed a sigh of relief when he saw the sea of orglin finally come to an end. There were still thousands to defeat, but that would just be a matter of time. All in all he couldn't believe how easy it had been. There was still another line of infantry waiting to take the battlefield. He thought about sending them in to finish them off, but decided to keep them back. There were more than enough soldiers on the battlefield to get the job done.

The sigh of relief quickly turned to a gasp of horror when he saw what came out through the next gateway.

Even from the distance Xarles could tell the creatures stood at least twenty feet tall. In one hand they held a massive cudgel and in the other a menacing looking whip. Ten giants spread across the battlefield. Every now and then they would crack their whips to keep the orglin moving forward. If any of them fell behind they would get struck by the mighty cudgels.

"What in the name of the God's are they?" Xarles finally asked.

"They are giants," Eldred replied, just as breathlessly. He had heard of giants, but he didn't think they still existed. "I don't know much more about them."

Xarles didn't like the sound of that. The giants looked as though they would be difficult to take down. Even on horseback they would loom over the soldiers and Xarles didn't think anyone could stand up to an attack by the cudgel.

"Is there anything you can do to help?" Xarles asked.

"I'll certainly try," Eldred replied.

The wizard had already started preparing the spell he was going to use, but he needed to be careful that he didn't take too much energy away from the storm. It was important he kept the rain from the battlefield. If not he would have already fired his first attack.

Xarles felt something electric in the air and then suddenly the earth exploded around one of the giants. When the dust settled the great creature was still moving forward. It didn't look as though Eldred's attack had done anything.

Eldred was unperturbed by the failure of his attack and readied the second. He never thought his first attack would finish the job, although it would have been nice. A moment later the earth exploded around the same giant. This time Eldred expected to the see the giant stumble through the dirt and rubble and fall to the ground, but it didn't. The giant marched through, seemingly unconcerned with the explosions around it.

"Was that supposed to happen?" Xarles asked.

"Not at all," Eldred looked confused. He thought about making another attack, but if the first two failed, and not only failed, but didn't seem to have any affect at all, he didn't think it was worth wasting his energy. "It seems as though I won't be any help with the giants."

The steady stream of orglin was slowly coming to an end and Xarles would need to make a decision on how to attack. He thought the cavalry would be best suited, even though the giants would still tower above them.

"What should..." before Xarles could finish, a messenger raced up from the transport ground.

"General Xarles, General Jarwe said that you should keep your attack low. The giants are strong, but very slow. Don't stay too close. One strike with either the whip or the cudgel will see you dead."

The messenger waited for a response, but when it was clear none was coming he returned down the hill. Normally Xarles would have felt rude for not responding, but he was too focused on the battlefield. The orglin were nearly completely dead and the giants were getting much closer.

"Shortbow!" Xarles called out.

"I don't think they will do any good," Eldred said before he could voice the command. "The giants have thick, leathery skin as good as any armour. From the distance the archers could get the arrows would, at best, break the skin, but even that would be unlikely. The infantry will need to finish the job."

Xarles knew Eldred was right. He had hoped to use the archers to bring down the giants. That would limit the casualties. Even the steel armour would be no protection against the heavy cudgels and he wouldn't be surprised if the whips would slash tight through it. Taking a deep breath Xarles voiced the command.

None of the soldiers had the chance to look up and see what was coming. Those who weren't already engaged with one or more of the orglin took a moment to look further down the battlefield. Some were distracted enough to get quickly overrun. Xarles cringed as he knew his words had caused their death, but there was nothing else he could do.

As much as some of the soldiers wanted to turn and run they knew it wasn't an option. They had thought the orglin was going to be worst of it, but they were sorely mistaken. Even with their superior numbers they didn't know how they were going to defeat the giants.

A few soldiers tried to take on the giants and bathe themselves in glory, but they soon found out it was futile. Even with the slash and run tactics the giants were no fools. They slashed with their whips and thumped with the cudgels.

"What are they doing?" Xarles asked.

"It's alright," Eldred replied. "Just watch."

Despite wanting to do more there was nothing Xarles could do but watch. It was up to the soldiers of Entero to defeat the giants.

With no orglin to push forward the giants concentrated on the soldiers gathering all around them. Every time a soldier would come close, the giants would strike out. At first the soldiers either backed away or were killed instantly.

"This is never going to work," Xarles sighed.

Eldred was starting to believe the same, but he still had faith. The soldiers encircled the great beasts and one after the other dashed in to strike. The giants lashed out with their whips and struck out with their cudgels, but their reaction time was slow. When it was clear the giants could no longer attack, a group of soldiers would dash in and hack at their legs. It was obvious that they would need to bring them down in order to finish them off.

One by one the giants fell. Once they were on the ground there was little they could do. The soldiers swarmed around them and began stabbing with their short swords. Before long all the giants lay dead. A great cheer arose from the army and the cry of 'We've won' was echoed around the battlefield.

Eldred watched the scene with a stern expression. Something just didn't seem right. A full rank of infantry stood behind them, ready for battle. He couldn't believe the final battle was over without the need for them.

"It's over," Xarles could hardly bring himself to speak and his words could hardly be heard.

As soon as the words had left his mouth the gateway started to crack with a loud boom. The sound brought silence to the battlefield. The soldiers behind the hill had started to move forward at the sounds of victory, but they stopped with the new noise. With a crash the gateway shattered to the ground and disappeared. What was waiting for them on the other side made Xarles' heart sink.

Large creatures standing at least ten feet tall waited for them. Some were made of clay, some of wood and some of stone. They all looked as though they were made of piles of stones joined together to make a creature with arms, legs, a body and a head. Xarles had absolutely no idea what they were.

"What are they?" he asked breathlessly.

Eldred couldn't believe what he was seeing. If he thought giants had died out a long time ago, he had doubted the creatures before him had even existed. The stories he had heard seemed so unreal and they had been long gone from the Seven Kingdoms when Eldred was born.

"They are golems," Eldred said. "I thought they were just stories to frighten small children. I can't believe they are still around."

Xarles didn't like what he was hearing. There had been few casualties against the orglin, but the giants had made up for it. Xarles estimated that half the soldiers from the first line of infantry had been killed. He had no idea how he was going to defeat the golems, especially the stone ones. To make matters worse he could see drops of rain fall on the soldiers. It seemed the storm wasn't far away.

"What should I do?" Xarles asked, fear thick in his voice.

The gateway was another hundred paces away from the front of the infantry. The soldiers stood where they were, unsure what they should do. For a brief moment they had thought they had won and then a new enemy had appeared.

"Bring the soldiers back," Eldred said. "Bring the second infantry and the shortbow archers to the front. Have the cavalry ready to charge."

"What can the archers do against, *those*?" Xarles asked.

"Just do it!" Eldred commanded.

The tone in Eldred's voice pushed Xarles into action. The initial shock of the golems had stayed with him and if it wasn't for Eldred he would have remained transfixed with fear.

Xarles' command boomed throughout the army and everyone jumped into action. The soldiers on the battlefield were more than happy to retreat. They had no idea what they would do against the golems. As they started their return the golems started their slow and deliberate charge. The creatures had been just as surprised when the first gateway disappeared. It wasn't until Xarles' words echoed across the battlefield before they remembered what they were there to do.

The second line of infantry and the shortbow archers moved up together. The soldiers started to baulk when they saw what was approaching them. Even the archers, who had seen the orglin, slowed their advance.

"Shoot at the wooden golems," Xarles repeated Eldred's command. "Infantry, target the clay golems." Xarles turned to Eldred. "What about the stone golems?"

"I'll take care of those," Eldred said. "The storm is almost upon us and I doubt we'll be able to hold it for much longer." There was another reason why Eldred wanted the storm to come, but he didn't want to voice his suggestion. There was a chance the rain would hinder the golems, especially the ones made out of clay.

As Eldred released his spell the rain started to pour down. At first it came over the golems and then over the soldiers. It wasn't long before the ground became soft and muddy under foot, which proved to slow their advance. When the soldiers were in place the archers readied themselves to attack.

When the golems were in range the archers fired their first volley. As the arrows arched towards their target they suddenly burst into flame. At first the archers thought it was the Evil One hindering their attack, but when the arrows hit their mark and the wooden golems burst into flame they knew it was Eldred.

The pelting rain slowed their approach. The clay golems were having the worst of it. The rain started to soak in and make their clay layer slippery and start to melt. For a moment Xarles thought they would melt away before they reached the soldiers, but soon enough he knew that wasn't going to happen.

The stone golems were having a hard time moving through the ever softening ground. Their pure weight pushed them into the mud, further slowing their advance. Again hope filled Xarles that they wouldn't reach the battlefront. He had no idea what the soldiers could do against pure stone and could only hope Eldred had something planned.

At first Eldred concentrated on the wooden golems, making sure each arrow that hit its target burst into flame. When he saw the stone golems approach he knew he had been focusing on the wrong type. Although the wooden golem would be harder for the soldiers to take down, they were nothing compared to the stone ones.

The soldiers hacked at the clay golems, taking chunks from their bodies, arms and legs. The creatures moved slowly, but powerfully. Anyone struck by a flailing arm or leg was sent flying across the battlefield. Those who weren't killed instantly were in no position to continue fighting. All they could do was drag themselves backwards, if they still had use of their arms, and hope to stay out of harm's way.

The stone golems plodded through the mud. When they reached the battlefront they all lurched into the action. The infantry who tried to attack the stone golems quickly realised what a futile effort it was. Their swords just skidded off the stone sending sparks flying into the air.

Eldred concentrated on his spell. The arrows still flew at the wooden golems, but he could do more. He should have started with the stone golems, but nothing could change that. Suddenly the ground started to explode around them. Dirt and stone flew into the air as the golems exploded with the ground around them. Any soldiers caught too close were also exploded into the air.

"What are you doing?" Xarles asked incredulously. "You're killing soldiers."

"There is nothing I can do about it," Eldred's voice was strained. Sweat poured down his face and he almost wished the storm would reach them to quell his heat. "If I don't destroy those golems they will kill everyone."

Xarles wasn't happy, but he knew Eldred was right. The soldiers would be dead soon if Eldred didn't cast his spells. With each exploding stone golem, two or three soldiers went with it. No one had worked out to stay away from them in the heat of the battle.

Like the stone golems, any of the soldiers that came too close to a wooden one were engulfed in flame. And like Eldred, there was little the archers could do about it. If they waited too long then the golems would take more lives. All the soldiers wanted to do was attack without thought for their own lives.

Golems exploded across the battlefield as the battle continued. Eldred could feel the energy draining from his body, but there was nothing he could do. If he stopped the spell then the golems would overrun the soldiers.

Despite the efforts of Eldred and the soldiers, the golems were slowly eating into their ranks. At the rate they were going the soldiers wouldn't be able to survive the onslaught.

"Cavalry!" Xarles spoke normally, but then had to repeat the command at the top of his voice when he realised Eldred had dropped the spell. "Reinforce the infantry. Attack the clay golems and try to stay as far away from the others as possible."

The cavalry had reformed when the first rank of infantry had returned and they were ready to get back in the battle. They could see the evil creatures getting the best of the infantry and shifted uneasily in their saddles. They wanted to charge out and help, but could do nothing until the command was given. As soon as the words came out of Xarles' mouth the horses were kicked into action.

When the cavalry was halfway to the front the rain started to pour down around them. Eventually they had to slow to a walk. The muddy ground under hoof was making their advance slow and awkward, but when they reached the battlefront they moved straight into action. The addition of horse and rider seemed to confuse the golems. They didn't know what to make of their new enemies as stone and wood continued to explode around them. The horses seemed to take it all in their stride, even if they had never seen anything like it before. All they knew was that there was a new enemy and it needed to be destroyed.

From horseback it was much easier to fight the clay golems. Even in the mud the horses were able to remain stable as they moved around to give their rider the optimum chance for attack. The golems were not as sure-of-foot and struggled to keep up with the horses.

Slowly hope returned to Xarles' heart. The infantry from the second line had almost been completely decimated, but the cavalry had turned the tide of the battle. He looked at Eldred who was at the point of collapse. He wanted to ask a question, but he didn't want to distract him. There were still golems to kill and he didn't want to risk anything.

One by one the golems fell to sword, flaming arrow or exploding ground. Xarles had the first line of infantry prepared to march, just in case something else came through the gateway, but he hoped they wouldn't be needed. Slowly the golems were finally finished. Xarles could almost not believe what he was seeing. Nothing more came through the gateway and all the golems were dead.

"Is that it?" Xarles could hardly bring himself to ask the question.

"I hope so," Eldred said as he dropped to one knee. His was voice weak.

Xarles wanted to help the wizard, but he couldn't take his eyes from the battlefield. The final battle seemed to be over. They had taken a lot of casualties, but it had been worth it. If it was truly over then they had just saved the Seven Kingdoms, assuming the other six armies had been successful.

Suddenly a cheer arose from the army when nothing happened. It seemed as though they too were confident the battle was over. Then the gateway started to shimmer. Before it completely disappeared and what was waiting for them on the other side sent a chill down Xarles' spine. The final battle was far from over and the advantage had just shifted towards the Evil One. At the same time the storm clouds suddenly dissipated and the rain stopped.

Xarles could hardly believe what he was seeing. A sea of evil creatures stood on the far side of the battlefield. More orglin stood with golems, scartlers and minotaurs, as well as an array of creatures Xarles couldn't even begin to describe. He looked for support from Eldred, who had returned to his feet, with a look of complete disbelief on his face. Xarles had no idea what they were going to do. There were monsters as far as the eye could see with an even larger gateway behind them. Even at the distance he could tell there were more creatures than what they had already fought.

Eldred's gaze was transfixed on the creature standing at the front of the army. He knew, without any doubt, it was the Dark Knight Na'garoz. If the Dark Knight attacked there was nothing he could do. The battle with the golems had drained him of his energy. It was all he could do to keep from collapsing to the ground and if he didn't think it would have a negative effect on the soldiers, he would have.

Suddenly there was an ear piercing screech from the west. Eldred couldn't imagine what it could be, although the noise did sound somewhat familiar. Whatever it was it wouldn't be long before they found out. Either way, he didn't think they would live long enough to really care.

Chapter 26: Gone

"Where have they gone?" Alena asked when Alaric and Nyrra suddenly disappeared. Although she didn't want to draw attention to herself she had to ask the question. Even without Alaric by her side she felt more comfortable with Nyrra out of the room. If Asgard and Esgard left it would be a completely different story. Without them there would be nothing she could do to defend herself against Marina.

"I have no idea," Asgard could hardly believe the words as they came out of his mouth. It had been the last thing he was expecting and he didn't think it was a good sign. They had held the advantage against the Evil One and only Nyrra would want to change the location of the final battle. "But I don't think it's a good sign."

"Don't be too quick to see the downside. Until we know what's happened let's assume that Alaric knows what he's doing." Esgard did her best to try and reassure them both."

"I wouldn't be so sure if I were you," Marina sneered from the other side of the room. "Nyrra was well prepared for this battle. If he has taken Alaric somewhere you can be sure that only one will be returning, and I doubt it will be who you're hoping for."

Alena shrunk away from her viscous words. There was something very disturbing at the ease Marina could say such a thing. Although she had never met the woman, Alaric had spoken fondly of her. He had glossed over their time together, but she could tell that Marina was special to him, or at least she had been before his emotions had turned to stone.

"What happened to you Marina?" Alena couldn't believe the words had come from her mouth. All she wanted to do was find somewhere to hide, but the words came unbidden. "You were once a Princess of Darshival, beloved by thousands. How could you turn to the Evil One?"

Marina turned her attention to Alena. "So you are the she-elf I have been hearing about. You know even when I bedded down with Alaric I knew he wasn't really there. I should never have trusted him with Her. Deep down I always knew he was going to betray me. I wonder what he would do if a killed you right now." An evil smile crossed her face at the thought and Alena backed away.

"There will be none of that," Esgard stepped forward as she spoke. It seemed like such a strange comment coming from such a small girl. Marina raised an eyebrow before she remembered that the little girl Cayley was just a façade. "The final battle is between Alaric and Nyrra, not you two."

"If only we knew where they were," Asgard spoke under his breath.

***

The room was dark as Alaric opened his eyes. At first he didn't know where he was, but that quickly changed as he felt the soft pillow under his head. He reached over, but there was no one sleeping next to him. Alena must have risen early that morning, but he couldn't think why. There was nothing that needed her attention at such an hour of the day.

Before Alaric could think any further his bedroom door opened and a sliver of lantern light entered the room. Alaric covered his eyes, despite the dim light, and saw a young pageboy enter. Even in the dark Alaric could see a nervous expression on his face.

"What is it?" Alaric barked, a little harsher than he intended.

"The traveller has arrived," the boy stammered.

"Traveller?"

"The one you said you were expecting last night. You said that you wanted to be woken as soon as he arrived," the boy sounded confused.

The vague memory of the night before returned. He remembered something about someone coming to see him, but he couldn't remember who it was or what they wanted. As much as he didn't want to leave the comfort of his bed he knew he had to rise. Whoever was waiting would have to have important information or when Alaric returned to bed the newcomer would be going to the dungeons.

Alaric quickly dressed himself in a loose fitting red shirt and deep blue silk trousers. He didn't know why he chose those clothes, but they seemed to be appropriate enough. He slipped on a pair a blue suede shoes and then followed the pageboy out of his room.

There were a few people moving throughout the palace, a sign that morning was approaching. The kitchens would be busy preparing the morning meal and making preparations for the rest of the day. The walls were bare stone as the tapestries were being cleaned, for some reason that escaped Alaric. The sconces were fully lit with torches in preparation for his meeting.

The pageboy led him to his private meeting room, opposed to his formal one. Alaric was curious as to who he was meeting. Normally his private meeting room was kept for his close personal friends, like King Hawthorne of Remidia. If he was expecting anyone like that he would surely remember.

The pageboy opened the door without knocking and Alaric entered. There were two people sitting on the far side of the room around a small side table. He recognised the first instantly as his wife, Queen Alena. The thought seemed odd inside his mind, but he pushed it aside and soaked in her beauty. She wore a sheer, white silk dress and white slippers. A beautiful gold necklace fell down around her soft neck ending in a large cut ruby. The man sitting opposite her was someone he had never seen before and yet he was strangely familiar.

"Ah, Alaric, nice of you to join us," the man welcomed him.

Alaric took the third seat around the table as a steaming cup of tea was placed in front of him. Nothing seemed out of the ordinary as the sun streamed into the room from a nearby window. Alaric looked outside and gauged it to be a about mid-morning and even that didn't seem out of place.

"I was wondering how long it would take for you to get here," Alaric said, still not truly knowing who he was.

"How has everything been going here?" the man asked.

Alaric stood and walked to the window. He didn't know why, but it seemed appropriate as he looked out over his kingdom. The last battle was over and Alaric had made Avalon his kingdom to rule. It seemed the most logical choice. Stone was brought from the Cloumid Mountains, along with marble and granite to build his castle. The dwarves had worked tirelessly to get the job done. The rest of his city was built around him. As he looked down, the people on the streets made a point not to look up at him. They moved around with a nervous quickness, as if at any time someone would attack them. It certainly should have seemed odd, but again it didn't. If he had won the final battle then everyone should feel safe, especially in his own kingdom.

"Everything is well," the words came from his mouth without any real control. "The people are under control now. It was hard at first, but a few public beatings and hangings put them in line."

Alena smiled seductively at her husband. Alaric thought she was the most beautiful thing in the world. He couldn't imagine what his life would be like without her. Conceding the final battle to Nyrra was the best decision he had ever made. It was the only thing he could have done to save the Seven Kingdoms, or at least one. There was no doubt Nyrra would have killed Alena if Alaric had decided to continue his attack.

He knew the rest of the Seven Kingdoms had been systematically destroyed. As soon as Alaric had conceded defeat Nyrra was free to take the battlefield. The armies of the Seven Kingdoms had been on top and close to winning and if Nyrra had not been free to help his minions he was sure the Alliance would have won.

Nyrra bathed in the blood of the Seven Kingdom's armies that day. There was more death than he could have ever hoped for. It had been the day he had been waiting for ever since he had been trapped in the Northern Wasteland and it exceeded all his expectations. Even thinking about it sent a shock of elation through his body.

Once the army had been defeated it was only a matter of time before the rest of the Seven Kingdoms fell. At first Nyrra had promised Alaric that he would leave the rest of the Seven Kingdoms and he would remain in Nostiria, but that didn't last long. As soon as Nyrra settled himself he unleashed his evil leaving only Avalon untouched. For the moment he didn't need to destroy Alaric, but his time would come.

Alaric took one more look out over his kingdom before returning to the others. He had made the right decision, he knew there could have been no other option. It was all about Alena. She had survived and so did he. They had their own little kingdom and that was enough to live their lives. It wouldn't be long before they would start having children.

"I couldn't think of a better way to live out the rest of our lives," Alaric said. "How are things in the rest of the Seven Kingdoms?"

"I have nearly cleaned up all the rebels. I don't think there is much left for me to do," Nyrra replied.

Alaric watched him carefully. Nyrra had chosen a strangely plain façade. His dark brown hair was cut short around his strong yet strangely plain face. It was not at all what Alaric would have thought he would have chosen to look like. He wore a simple leather tunic and trousers. It looked like something he would wear if he was trying to travel incognito, but everyone knew he was the true master and the disguise was completely unnecessary. Alaric thought it was very interesting.

"It won't be long now before the other six kingdoms are completely under my rule," Nyrra said.

That was what Alaric was waiting for. Although Nyrra didn't realise it, the threat was there. Alaric had known from the start that once Nyrra was done with the other kingdoms he would be drawn to Avalon. He wanted to return to the window to see if there was an army waiting for him, but he resisted. If there was there was little he could do about it. He was not allowed to have an army of his own, that was one of the conditions Nyrra had placed on him. It was as much for his own safety as anything else. They both knew it wouldn't be long before someone would try and assassinate him if they were allowed to bear arms.

"And then what will you do?" Alaric asked, hinting at the questions true meaning.

"Then it will be time for me to return to Nostiria and rule from there," Nyrra didn't fall for the trap.

"Then it is finally all over?" Alaric asked.

"Now, come now my love," Alena interrupted. "Surely there is something more pleasant we can discuss. Nyrra won't be here for long and we don't want his visit to be all about business."

The light in the room was starting to dim as night approached. The situation should have seemed strange to Alaric, but as Alena held his hand and led him towards their bedroom nothing seemed out of place. All he could think about was climbing into bed with his wife.

As soon as they were in bed Alena lifted Alaric's nightshirt over his head and ran her hand over his muscular torso. Her soft hands made his skin tingle. It was a feeling that he hadn't felt in a long time and he liked it.

Alena wore a very sheer, white nightdress that left nothing to the imagination. Alaric stroked her hair gently before running his fingers down her body. It seemed a lifetime ago since they had been intimate with each other.

Closing his eyes Alaric kissed her passionately on the lips. Whatever had seemed wrong with the situation before was completely gone. He lost himself in Alena and she in him. For a time he forgot all his worries and all that mattered was his wife.

Before Alaric knew what was happening the sun was shining through an open window. As he sat up he saw Alena sitting on the other side of the bedroom. In her arms was a baby suckling at her breast. Instantly he knew it was their son. The memory of making the baby was still thick in his mind, as if it was only yesterday.

"How is he today?" Alaric asked.

"He's very content." Alena smiled as she watched her son feeding.

Alaric stayed in bed and watched the pair lovingly. He didn't think he could be happier if he tried. It had always been his dream to have a son and at one point in his life he never thought it was going to happen. When he started the final battle and a few weeks prior he never thought he could be this happy. In fact he didn't think he would live long enough to lament his choices. When he had decided to concede the battle to Nyrra he thought he was doing the wrong thing, but that couldn't have been further from the truth.

It was true that Nyrra had decimated the other kingdoms and no one dare leave Avalon anymore. The other kingdoms were overrun with evil creatures. At first Alaric wasn't sure Nyrra would keep his word and make sure none of that evil reached Avalon, but it was true. Anyone walking along the border, as long as they stayed on the right side, was completely safe. Anyone who stepped over, if only for a minute, was never seen again.

Suddenly there came a knock on the door before Alaric could say anything else. The pageboy entered and looked very familiar, which seemed odd although it shouldn't. He had a nervous expression and tried his best to avoid shaking, although he failed miserably.

"There is a visitor to see you," he stammered.

"I'm not expecting anyone today," Alaric replied, but even as the words left his mouth he knew they weren't right.

"Don't be silly," Alena giggled. "You know who is here."

Alaric shook his head as he walked through the hallways. It seemed as though the tapestries were being cleaned again and the stone walls were completely blank. It seemed strange, he could have sworn they had only recently been cleaned, but he let it pass.

He found Alena and Nyrra waiting for him in his private meeting room. They were sitting around a small side table sipping tea. There was a cup and a chair waiting for Alaric. The situation seemed odd, but he sat down nonetheless.

"How is everyone, your majesty," Nyrra asked.

"Everything is just perfect. My son is a strong boy and will be a fine ruler when the time is right." Nyrra shifted uncomfortably at Alaric's words and he wondered what he had said to gain such a reaction. "The kingdom is well and prospering." That was true in some regard. The people had grown used to how things were since the final battle had been lost. People were still nervous around Alaric though. He had made a deal with the Evil One and therefore must be evil by association. Those who worked in the palace did so in fear, but the rest of the city had realised that life wasn't so bad. A small village had popped up outside the city walls, which Alaric thought was a good sign of things to come. "And how are things with you?" Alaric asked, changing the subject slightly.

"As too be expected. The world outside of your little, so called, paradise is mine. The pain and the suffering is constant, as it should be. Those who survived the initial cleansing wished they had not," a broad smile crossed his face.

Alaric knew his words should have made him angry, but they did nothing to alter his mood. In fact it didn't seem all that out of the ordinary.

"None have crossed your borders?" Nyrra asked.

"Not that I know. It is common law that anyone who crosses our borders are to be executed at once." The law had been extremely unpopular, but those who openly opposed the king would at best end up in the dungeons, at worst, the gibbet.

"Very good, I see that things are working out nicely," Nyrra's smile turned to a sneer.

"What do you mean by that?" Alaric asked.

"Now, now, there is no need for that," Alena cooed. "We are all friends here and anyway, I think it might be time for bed." Alena said as they made their way back to the royal apartments. "What a lovely day it was today," Alena commented in an offhand manner.

"Yes, my dear," Alaric said as he stroked her hair in bed.

Alena wore a sheer red silk nightgown and Alaric was already completely naked. Alena rubbed her hands all over his body and Alaric couldn't remember a time he had been happier. Conceding the final battle to Nyrra had been the best thing he had ever done. Before another thought could enter his mind he felt Alena's soft lips press against his.

"There'll be time for thinking later," Alena whispered seductively into his ear as her hand made its way down his stomach.

Alaric looked out on the crowd with a large smile on his face. It was his son's sixteenth birthday and his great hall was filled with people. He sat at the head table with Alena, his son on her right and Nyrra on his left. No one seated in the crowd looked up at them, but Alaric didn't notice. He didn't care. It was a momentous day in the life of his son and nothing could dampen his spirits. It only seemed like yesterday that he was a baby and now he was a man.

"Isn't this everything you hoped for?" Alena said.

"I couldn't think of anything else I would want," Alaric replied.

"This is indeed a momentous occasion," Nyrra said. "Did you ever think you would live long enough to see your son turn into a man?"

It was a strange question. At one time he would never have thought to see such an occasion, but ever since he had conceded the final battle there really could be no other result. If he wasn't around for his son's sixteenth birthday then what was the point of it all? He knew it was a pertinent question, but he couldn't work out why. In the end he didn't know how to answer it and just decided to ignore it.

"How are things with your kingdom?" The Seven Kingdoms were no more. There was only the Kingdom of Avalon and Nyrra's kingdom, which was now a wasteland of total destruction.

"Everything has been cleared out nicely. There is little for me to do now," Nyrra replied.

Alaric couldn't work out why Nyrra had been so keen to leave the Northern Wasteland if all he wanted was another wasteland. He could have remained where he was and everyone would have been happy.

"But enough about me, how are things here?" Nyrra asked.

If Alaric had bothered looking out over his citizens he would have realised things weren't well. The people before him were so afraid to look up they almost pushed their faces into the food before them. It wasn't Nyrra they were afraid to make eye contact with, but Alaric himself. They had grown used to the so called Evil One, but knew that as long as they stayed within their borders they were safe from his retribution. It was Alaric who they were afraid of. He would fly into rages for no reason and have people executed without trial.

"Things have never been better. The kingdom is expanding nicely."

That was true in itself. Anyone who could leave the city headed for safe haven in the countryside. If there was an option everyone would leave the city, but then that would give Alaric an excuse to enter the villages and towns. Those in the city feared for their lives, and those of others.

"Very good. That is what I want to hear. You are grateful for the choice you have made and the life I have given you," Nyrra smiled.

A strange expression crossed Alaric's face. The comment from Nyrra didn't make any sense.

"Do you think we should have another baby?" Alena cooed in his ear.

Alaric looked over and saw her naked body in the moonlight. The sight made his heart beat faster and he already knew what she wanted.

"Your son will need brothers and sisters to help him rule your kingdom."

Alaric pulled her close and kissed her lips. The feeling of her soft skin against his made his heart beat even faster. There was no arguing with her now and he had to admit a large family did seem like a good idea. It didn't take long for Alaric to get lost in her embrace and become incapable of disagreeing with her.

The smell of fire filled his nose. It was a strange sensation and yet not to be unexpected. He stood at his bedroom window and looked at the streets below. Buildings were on fire and orglin ran through the streets. Alaric knew his sons were leading the soldiers against the horde of evil creatures, but there was little they could do.

"Do you think they will be alright?" fear filled Alena's voice.

"It's over," Alaric didn't sound at all concerned as he watched the horror unfold before him.

Fireballs flew down from the sky as Alaric's sons tried to counter the onslaught. At first they tried to avoid any magic that would damage the city, but as the orglin continued to pour through the gates and storm the walls, they knew there was little point. When the city had been built the walls were an aesthetic choice and gave no real defence. With the final battle over there seemed no real need for strong defences.

"This isn't right," Nyrra said. He couldn't believe what he was seeing.

"Was there any doubt that this was always going to be the end result if I conceded to you," Alaric said.

Nyrra looked at him in surprise. For some reason he was dressed differently. Instead of his bedclothes he wore a thick, black, leather jerkin with black leather trousers and a long black leather coat. There was something about his tone and dress that belied the situation and Nyrra didn't feel right. The entire situation didn't seem right. Alena was on the floor weeping, which was about the only thing that made sense.

"This still shouldn't be happening," Nyrra watched the mayhem below. Normally the destruction would have led to a feeling of elation, but instead it just confused him. "This is your fantasy, we're inside your head."

Alaric burst out laughing. It had been the moment he had been waiting for. His ruse had worked. Nyrra believed everything he did and thought that he was running the fantasy

"That is where you are wrong. This is your fantasy and we are inside your head. In your mind this is what would happen if I conceded defeat to you. As you can see it would only be a matter of time before you betrayed me," Alaric's voice was even.

"This is impossible," Nyrra sounded worried for the first time. "You're not strong enough to control my mind. This is what I do, not you."

"I think you should run away now before I trap you here forever," the threat was there, but Alaric didn't think he could carry it out.

Even though he didn't think Alaric was capable of trapping him inside he own mind he didn't want to take the risk. Without a second thought Nyrra disappeared, leaving Alaric alone.

Alaric looked around the room. He had to admit that it was a nice fantasy for a while and if he was a different man he might have accepted it, but his life was completely different now and he no longer had the same dreams he once had.

The scene only remained for a brief moment before it faded to black. Alaric knew it was time to move on as the final battle between him and Nyrra continued. So far he was happy with its progression, but there was still a lot to come.

Chapter 27: Hondin Lel Battle

Duke Hadar looked out over the dark battlefield. It wouldn't be long before the sun rose over the horizon and then it wouldn't be long before the final battle would begin. He had no idea what was coming, but he had his doubts whether they could stand up to the Evil One's army. Of course he had kept his fears to himself. As the leader of the Hondin Lel army it would do nothing for morale if he voiced his concerns. The soldiers would be looking to him for strength and that's exactly what he was going to give them.

Hadar changed his view as he heard footsteps approach from behind. He knew it was Althea and his eldest son Hagar. They had said they would meet him at dawn and despite them being a little early, he was glad they had arrived.

At first Hadar didn't think they were going to make the battlefield in time. Althea had brought Hadar to Avalon two days before the army was ready to march, but with the Dark Knight feeding misinformation throughout Hondin Lel, Hadar doubted half the soldiers would arrive. He was grateful to be proven wrong and a huge weight was lifted off his shoulders when he saw the soldiers start marching through the gateway.

"Any movement?" Hagar asked.

"Nothing yet," Hadar replied.

It was a rhetorical question. One thing they all knew was that the sun would be up before the final battle began. It just seemed like the most logical way for Hagar to start a conversation with his father.

"The army is ready to move up when you give the command," Hagar continued.

Like the other armies Hadar had set himself up on a small hill to get a better view of the battle. The Hondin Lel army would be spread out around him when the time was right.

"We'll wait for the sun to rise. We don't want the soldiers running into each other," Hadar replied.

"Who do you want to line up first?"

"I have no idea," Hadar seemed a little irate with the question. They had no idea what they were about to face and therefore Hadar had no idea whether he should move up the archers, the infantry or the cavalry. "Do you know what is coming for us?" He asked Althea. The wizard had already told him she had no idea what the Evil One was going to unleash, but he didn't believe her. Althea had been very unhelpful from the start and he wouldn't be surprised if she was keeping secrets again.

"There is nothing more I can tell you," Althea kept up her standoffish attitude, which did nothing to change Hadar's opinion of her.

Althea didn't like the large man from Hondin Lel. He gave her no respect and that was unforgivable. She wanted nothing more than to wrap him up in strands of air, have him bend over and spank his behind. Maybe then he would give her the respect she deserved. If it was up to her she would, but the others had told her not to and they were right. There was no telling what the Evil One would throw at them and if the Dark Knights were there she would need all her strength to fight them.

Hadar wanted to push her further, but as the sun started to crest the horizon he decided against it. It was time to get the army moving into position. He had decided to place the first line of infantry at the front with the longbow archers behind. Having no idea where the enemy was coming from meant he had no idea where to place the archers or even if they were going to be of any use. The sudden realisation of the gateways had changed everything. Nyrra could literally place his army anywhere. If everyone had not been so sure that the battlefield was right in front of them, Hadar would have had his doubts. If he was Nyrra he would bring his army to the rear or to one of the flanks. If his army suddenly appeared at their rear Hadar thought they would lose half their numbers before they even realised what was happening. The thought kept racing over and over in his mind.

"Where do you think the Evil One's army is?" Hadar asked.

"No idea," Althea replied tersely. "You know as much as I do."

"Do you know when the army is going to get here? I'm assuming by gateway since there is no sign of them on the horizon?" Hadar ignored the tone in her voice and continued his questions.

"You know as well as I do that we have no idea how they are going to get here." Althea paused for a moment. "But yes if I was to have a guess, I would assume they will be using a gateway or another form of travelling."

Hadar was happy enough with that response. There was no telling when the Evil One was going to bring his army, but they would be arriving soon. From some reason that made Hadar feel better, even though it should have terrified him. There was no telling the horror that would befall them and yet he felt calm. He didn't know if that was a good sign or a bad one and he had completely lost his senses.

"Move up the infantry and the longbow!" Hadar boomed, even though Althea had created a spell to carry his voice. "First line only, cavalry behind. Shortbow with the second and third line."

The soldiers behind the cavalry would not be able to see the battlefield. Hondin Lel was renowned for its archers, only bested by the elves. Unfortunately Hadar didn't know how useful they were going to be. He had a feeling that the cavalry was the best option, but besides the dwarves, which had none, the Hondin Lel army had the least amount of horses. Whatever the Evil One sent at them he would need to use the infantry first.

When the soldiers were in place and the sun had bridged the horizon Hadar prepared himself to address the army. It had been the moment he had been dreading. He had no idea what words he could use to motivate the soldiers against the horrors they were about to face, but that was exactly what he had to do.

"Soldiers of Hondin Lel," Hadar started. "We have come here at last to Avalon to face the Evil One's army in the final battle. He has tried his best to keep us from reaching Avalon more than any of the other armies." Hadar didn't know if that was technically true, but it really didn't matter. He paused for a moment giving the soldiers a chance to come to the revelation on their own. "That means he is more afraid of us than any of the other kingdoms," his words brought a cheer from the soldiers. "The Evil One knows how strong and brave the Hondin Lel army is and he fears us." Another cheer came from the soldiers. "Whatever the Evil One has in store for us we will stand strong. We will not falter and we shall be... VICTORIOUS!"

"I don't like the look of those clouds," Hagar pointed to the horizon when Hadar had finished his speech.

"I'm sure they're fine," Althea brushed them aside.

"But they are moving very quickly," Hagar continued.

Something in his tone made Althea look up again. She had seen the storm clouds, but at that distance took little notice. She figured the battle would be well and truly over before the storm hit, but taking a second look she knew she was wrong. The storm was moving too quickly for it to be natural. A thought crossed her mind and she called for a messenger.

"Tell the others that the storm isn't natural and we need to stop it hitting the battlefield. Whether it is the Dark Knights or Nyrra himself, we can't allow him the advantage," Althea ordered and the messenger instantly ran into action.

It wasn't long before another messenger returned telling her exactly what she had relayed to the others. Althea dismissed the messenger before he could finish what he was saying. Hagar shook his head at the messenger's expression and the man returned to the transport ground.

Suddenly there was electricity in the air and Hadar felt the hair stand up on the back of his neck. He hoped that it was from Althea trying to hold back the storm, but he knew that wasn't the case. The final battle was only moments away. Whatever the Evil One had in store, they would soon find out. As much as he wanted to spend more time with his son, it was time for Hagar to join the army. His son had wanted to join the first wave of infantry, but Hadar, despite his pride, insisted that he join the cavalry. Hagar was a master horseman and it was a much better place for him. With a little luck he wouldn't need to use the cavalry, but he knew that was just wishful thinking.

Suddenly a loud tearing sound could be heard throughout the battlefield. Hadar held his breath as he waited for what was to come. Before long a beam of bright light opened up and spread across the sky about two hundred paces from the front of the line of infantry. A moment later a giant gateway appeared. At first it bubbled a sickly red and purple colour before it coalesced. Before anyone could see what was on the other side a horde of orglin poured through.

Hadar didn't know what to think. No matter what had gone through his head, he never imagined the force before him. His shock only lasted a second, even though it seemed like hours, before he moved into action.

"Archers! Fire one volley into the enemy and then infantry start your march." Although he really didn't think the arrows would hit their mark, he had to try. If the Dark Knights were there to create the gateway then he was sure they would stop the arrows.

Either way the few thousand arrows in the air would do little to stem the flow of orglin. Already Hadar estimated there were over ten thousand of the evil creatures on the battlefield and it didn't look like that number was going to decrease any time soon.

Hadar held his breath as the arrows reached their peak and started their decent. Just before the arrows hit, Hadar let out his breath and to his surprise the arrows hit their target. He looked at Althea who also had a surprised expression on her face. If Hadar had any idea the arrows would work he would have the archers send in another volley, but it was too late. As soon as the arrows had left their bows the infantry started their charge. If the longbow archers fired again then they would risk their own numbers.

With the order given the soldiers charged forward without a thought for their own safety. They wore breast plates and helmets, but nothing to protect their arms and legs. What they lacked in defence they made up for in speed and manoeuvrability. Hadar could only hope he had made the right decision sending them in before the cavalry.

The infantry charged into the oncoming orglin leading with their shields opposed to their short swords. At the pace they were charging the swords would easily pass through the orglin, but the risk of their swords coming loose was too great. It was a common tactic practised on the training field and they used it well. Levelling their shields high they were able to crush the heads of the orglin that had no idea what they were racing into.

After the initial charge the battle continued. The soldiers slashed out at the orglin as they tried to swarm over the top of them. Their thick leathery skin was no match for the freshly sharpened blades of the infantry. The soldiers slashed with their swords and used their off hand to block any attacks with their shields.

Hadar watched from atop the small hill with pride at what he saw. The soldiers fought bravely and to his reckoning, not that he could see the entire battlefield, he estimated that only a dozen soldiers had fallen to the hundreds of orglin. The only problem Hadar could see was the superior numbers of the orglin pushing the infantry ever backwards. It was a slow decline, but eventually the battle would reach the rest of the army and if that happened, it would be chaos.

It didn't take long to for Hadar to realise his best course of action. The longbowmen were still standing at the front of the line with full quivers. They could easily step up and shoot arrows into the belly of the orglin army. The risk would be if any of the orglin broke the line of soldiers, but it was one Hadar was willing to take.

"Archers!" he called out. "To the front. Fire at will into the middle of the opposing army."

At first the archers didn't know what to make of the command. It had never been done before and even though they were standing at the front of the army they thought their day was done. Hadar had to repeat the command before the longbowmen started moving forward. No one was in any hurry to approach the battlefront, but no one lingered either.

"We need to stop the flow of orglin through that gateway," Hadar mused aloud, almost to himself. "Is there anything you can do to help?" Hadar almost cringed at asking Althea for help.

Althea, despite being busy with the spell holding back the storm, had been thinking the same thing. She had tried to delve into the spell, but had come up with nothing. Alaric had certainly taught them how to create a gateway, but had said nothing about dispelling one. Althea thought it would be a handy thing to know, if it was even possible. Most spells could be unravelled.

"There is nothing I can do to close the gateway," it was the most pleasant Althea had sounded all day.

"Is there anything you can do to help?" Hadar asked, his voice gruffer than he meant.

"Don't you think that if I could I would have by now," Althea snapped. Hadar wasn't sure the question was quite as rhetorical as it sounded. "If you would kindly hold back the storm I would be glad to attack the orglin."

"Okay, no need to be snide," Hadar barked before returning his attention to the battlefield. He didn't know why he had been stuck with Althea and wished he had another wizard by his side.

The longbow archers had moved as far as they could dare, with the front line only a dozen paces from the battle. There was no need to wait for the command to draw and shoot. Being so close to the action, something they had never experienced before, they didn't want to risk being overrun. A lot of the longbowmen had only defended castles and cities from atop a wall or turret. Now they could hear the screams of dying men and the screeches of dying orglin and some vomited before they could settle themselves to shoot.

The arrows flew into the middle of the attacking orglin army. Like the first volley, Hadar didn't think the arrows were going to hit their mark, but as more and more orglin fell he knew he was wrong. Either the Dark Knights were not on the battlefield or they just didn't care about the orglin. Hadar seriously thought it was the latter. He doubted very much that Nyrra would go to all that effort, he assumed it must have taken a great effort, to bring his Dark Knights back from the dead just to leave them out of the final battle. Whatever they had in store he knew it would not be pleasant.

With each volley more and more orglin fell. To Hadar's disgust the orglin behind those being cut down stopped to gorge on their fallen comrades. The orglin pushing up from behind were more concerned about fighting over the corpses than the slowly approaching army.

The Hondin Lel infantry continued to push forward and drive the enemy. It seemed as though Hadar's plan was going to work. Despite their initial fear, the longbowmen followed after the infantry after each volley.

As the battle continued the infantry found the thick, leathery skin of the orglin wasn't as easy to penetrate as it had been at the start. With each attack the skins slowly started to dull their blades until all they could do was hack wildly. As the archers started to run out of arrows, the orglin became more focused on their attack. Hadar had been so focused on his successes that he hadn't noticed the decrease in the rate of orglin being killed by the soldiers. Not only that but the orglin were starting to get the better of the infantry. The orglin, after realising scratching the steel armour wasn't doing anything, would jump on the soldiers and pull their helmets off. With the soldiers' heads exposed the orglin didn't hesitate to scratch with their sharp claws or sink their teeth into the soldiers' faces.

"I think you need to do something," Althea suggested.

Hadar only just heard her voice and if he had known what she had said he would have ignored her anyway. He could see what was happening on the battlefield and he knew instantly what he had done wrong. By moving the longbowmen in behind the infantry he had cut off the soldiers' retreat. Even if he wanted to use the cavalry there was no way they would get through in time. It would be up to the second line of infantry to relieve the first, but that was not going to be a quick solution.

"Archers!" Hadar boomed. "Retreat." It was the first command he had to give as more and more soldiers fell to the gruesome orglin. "Second line of infantry, ready your march!"

All Hadar could do was watch as the archers slowly retreated. The second line of infantry made their way through the horses as the first line was slowly being devoured by the orglin. At least the breastplates were slowing down the advance. The orglin had to crack open the shells as if they were eating oysters. The thought of devouring the fleshy goodness inside was overwhelming and even with the looming death before them they couldn't help themselves. Although it was a disgusting sight Hadar was grateful for small mercies.

"First line, drawback!" Hadar was relieved to bark the command as the second line had finally made its way through the archers. "Second line, push forward."

With the orglin furiously trying to devour the fallen, the retreat of the first line was smoother than Hadar had anticipated. The orglin stopped not only to eat the fallen soldiers but also their own kind. Those pushing up from behind were delayed by their gorging brethren.

When the second line reached the battlefront the orglin didn't get up from their feeding frenzy. Soldiers walked from body to body stabbing any orglin that were still alive. It wasn't until they had walked through the piles of dead bodies and feeding orglin before the battle started again.

The first line of infantry was quick to make their way to the makeshift smithies to have their swords resharpened and the dints hammered out of their shields. Despite the ever creeping fatigue they wanted to be ready if they were called into action again. They would have some time to rest as there was still the cavalry and the third line of infantry to go before they would be needed again.

The longbowmen returned quickly to the camp and scrounged around for any remaining arrows they could find. The arrows used by the longbowmen and the shortbowmen were too different to be used together. The longbow used an arrow that was a full two inches longer than that of the shortbow and with larger flights. The shortbow arrows were designed for accuracy opposed to distance. The shortbowmen stood amongst the horses of the cavalry. Hadar had yet to decide what to do with them.

The second line of soldiers was excited to join the fray. Although they had been marshalled behind the cavalry they had been told what the first line was doing. They had also been told how to manage the orglin.

Hadar thought about bringing up the shortbowmen just in case some of the orglin broke through, but as the battle continued it didn't look like it was going to happen. As the infantry engaged the orglin, the flow started to slow. Hadar held his breath as the last of the orglin swarmed through the gateway. For a moment he thought it was all over before the giants came lumbering through. Hadar had never seen anything like them before in his life. In one hand they carried a vicious looking whip which they cracked at the orglin to push them forward and with their other they had a massive cudgel. They used the cudgel to smash any orglin that decided to fall behind.

"What in the name of the God Kings are those?" Hadar asked breathlessly.

"They are giants," Althea sounded disinterested in his question. "It doesn't surprise me that Nyrra would need them to whip the orglin forward. Those pitiful creatures wouldn't have the courage to fight on their own."

"If you knew they were coming then a little warning would have been nice." Hadar took his attention away from the battlefield to face her. "What are we supposed to do against that?"

"There's nothing I can do to help. Giants are immune to magic. What you need to do..."

Before Althea could finish talking a messenger ran up to meet them. "General Jarwe said you need to stay low and fast. The giants are strong, but slow. Stay away from the whips and cudgels. Those whips can cut through steel and I don't think you need to be told what those cudgels will do."

"Thank you," Hadar said before returning his attention back the battlefield.

The messenger waited a second to see if there was anything else before returning to the transport ground to wait with the other messengers.

Hadar opened his mouth to bark the command when Althea interrupted him. "I wouldn't say anything yet. There are still a lot of orglin to be taken care of and you don't want to distract your soldiers. The thought of those giants would be enough to send the bravest man screaming.

Hadar had to admit she was right, but it didn't make things any easier for him. Even with the advice from Jarwe he didn't know how the soldiers were going to kill the giants. He could see eight stretched out across the length of the battlefield. If the creatures could push forward tens of thousands of orglin there was no telling what they were capable of. There was a chance the eight giants could destroy the entire army of men.

One-by-one the orglin died. With freshly sharpened swords the second line were making short work of them, but Hadar still didn't think they could do much against the giants. He wanted to send in the cavalry, but he couldn't go against the advice of Jarwe. Although Hadar had no idea where Jarwe got the idea from, the man was still General of the Alliance and that meant Hadar had to listen to him.

"Third line!" Hadar boomed as the second line neared the giants.

"What are you doing?" Althea asked.

"I'm not risking anything. Nothing else is coming through the gateway now. I'm going to end this and end it quickly."

Althea didn't think it was going to be the end, but she didn't voice her suspicions. She had spent time under the thrall of the Evil One and she knew he had many more wicked creatures under his command. Although she had no idea what the six other armies were facing and there was no sign of anything else coming through the gateway, she knew the battle wasn't over.

The third line charged forward, knowing the dangers of the giants, without a care for their own safety. The second line had almost completely finished with the orglin and were about to join them. Hadar couldn't wait any longer and made the command explaining how they should fight. Only those who weren't engaged with the enemy looked up, even though the others wanted to. No one could believe what they had heard, but they weren't going to be distracted so easily.

At first Hadar thought it was a good idea, but then he realised it wasn't. The two ranks of soldiers worked independently of each other, but being mixed together no one knew whose orders were meant for whom.

As the second line and third line soldiers joined the battle, there was little communication between the two groups. The soldiers didn't know if they were attacking the giants or distracting them whilst other soldiers attacked. In the confusion soldiers were crushed by the mighty cudgels and the attacks were ineffective.

"You have to do something," Althea snapped in horror as she watched the massacre in front of him.

Hadar shook his head. It had been one bad mistake after another and it cost good men their lives. He had been so blind in thinking their mere numbers would take the final blow that he had not thought of the repercussions.

"Hadar!" Althea barked.

"Second line! Retreat!" Hadar commanded.

The soldiers from the second line did as they were commanded leaving the third line to battle with the giants. With just the one rank of soldiers fighting the battle became much smoother. A number of soldiers would distract the giant whilst the others came in from behind slashing at their mighty legs.

One by one the giants fell until the soldiers were left alone on the battlefield. When the soldiers realised the enemy army was dead, cheers of victory arose through the infantry. The final battle was over and Hadar let out a cheer, but Althea remained calm.

"Be prepared!" was all she said.

Hadar let his cheer die away. "What?" he asked as the comment sunk in. "What do you mean 'be prepared'?"

Before Althea had a chance to answer a loud crack echoed around the battlefield. At first Hadar thought it was thunder booming in the distance, but when he saw a crack appear in the gateway before it shattered like a pane of glass, he knew what it was.

For a moment Hadar thought it was the end of the Evil One's affect, but then his heart sunk when he saw what was on the other side.

Creatures, even hunched over as they were, stood over eight feet tall. Pale and wart covered skin was clothed only by filthy fur loin cloths. Hadar hated to think what creature could be found to make such clothing, but there was little time to ponder. They carried cruel looking weapons which included cudgels, rusted war axes and rusted swords. Hadar could only guess where they had found such weapons and who had died to supply them. Although Hadar had never seen the creatures in the flesh he had seen their images in books and on tapestries. They were ogres.

"Third line! Slowly give ground," Hadar commanded. He needed time to think with the new enemy before him. For a moment he had thought they had won, but that was quickly ripped from him. The ogres moved a lot slower as they loped towards the infantry. As the front ogres saw the dead bodies in front of them, drool started to drip from their open mouths. Like the orglin they looked as though they were more interested in feeding than fighting.

"Finally we're getting some luck," Hadar said aloud, although he only meant it for himself.

"I wouldn't speak so soon," Althea said as ogres still lumbered through the gateway. "They will only be distracted as long as they are feeding."

As soon as the ogres from behind caught up with the rest, they started fighting over the dead bodies. They didn't care what they were going to eat and Hadar wondered if they would feast on their own like the orglin had. If Hadar could move the archers forward in time there was a chance they could kill the feeding ogres. This would give the others more to feed on and so on and so forth.

"Archers!" Hadar called out. Both the shortbow and the longbow archers knew the command was for both groups.

"I don't think that's a good idea," Althea said before Hadar could continue with his command. "The ogres will eat most things, but never one of their own," she added as if reading his mind. "You are better to send the cavalry in now."

Hadar had been warned that Althea had been in the thrall of the Evil One and to wary of her. Even though Alaric had assured them that she was cured, the others weren't so sure. Hadar had a tough decision to make. If Althea was still an agent of the Evil One then there was a good chance he was sending his cavalry to their death, but if she was right and he ignored her then he would be sending a lot of good men to their deaths.

"Their skins are thicker than the orglin. The shortbow might have a chance if they get close enough, but the longbow will be almost useless. It would take a lucky arrow to bring an ogre down in one shot. You have to trust me on this one, I know what I'm talking about."

There was no more time for Hadar to ponder his decision. The ogres had almost finished their gorging and would soon be looking for more bodies to eat. The infantry had slowly started making their way back.

"Stand down," Hadar finally finished his command. "Cavalry to the front and infantry return." As he finished speaking he noticed the rain had started to fall on the heads of the ogres. It was only gentle at first, but he knew it wouldn't be long before the storm hit.

"It looks like you can release your spell now," Hadar mentioned casually as the cavalry made their way towards the battlefield. "The storm is about to hit."

Althea had been so busy concentrating on the battle she had almost forgotten about the storm. As she looked up she saw a bolt of lightning crack behind the gateway. The dark storm clouds had now covered the battlefield and the rain had started to fall.

"Is there anything you can do to help with the ogres?"

The thought had never even entered her mind. She had been busy holding back the storm and increasing the range of Hadar's voice. She didn't think that would be her complete role in the final battle, but she had not thought of doing anything else since.

She looked at the ogres as they slowly loped towards the cavalry. Although they weren't fast they moved quicker than the giants and had just as much strength. She couldn't do what she wanted at the front of the battle in case she hit it one of the soldiers.

As Althea started to create her spell the cavalry started their charge. At first they weren't sure how to approach the ogres, but when there was no command from Hadar they decided to charge. The sudden change in pace took the ogres by surprise and they didn't have enough time to set up any defences. The horses charged at their foe without a thought for their own safety and despite their momentum, they couldn't knock the ogres to the ground. More than one horse stumbled and fell, throwing their riders towards the approaching beasts. It didn't take long for the ogres to tear apart any riders separated from their horses.

The charge had been a complete failure and despite not giving the order himself Hadar had to feel responsible for yet another bad decision. If there was someone else to take over his command he would have surrendered it already. He could only hope that Althea could stem the carnage.

When Althea released her spell a beam of bright white light, about two feet thick, shot down from the sky and exploded into the centre of the opposing army. A moment later arms, legs, heads and a number of other ogre body parts flew into the air.

After the first explosion a number of other explosions happened across the battlefield. Althea made sure to keep the beams of light as far back from the main battlefront as she could, but as she continued, controlling the direction of the light became harder and harder. She didn't know if it was her strength starting to wane or if there was a Dark Knight moving its direction, but after a smaller beam of light landed in a group of cavalry she knew it was time to stop. She had killed a lot of ogres, but that still didn't make her feel any better.

"I think that is all I can do," she puffed, the strain of the day was starting to show.

"Thank you," Hadar replied, which surprised her.

The cavalry was fighting bravely, but by Hadar's estimate they would not be able to defeat the ogres. Even though the ogres had stopped coming through the gateway, they still outnumbered the cavalry. Not only that but it seemed that for every ogre they killed at least five soldiers died. He wanted to send in the archers to try and kill a few more, but he had to trust Althea. Even though the cavalry were struggling against the ogres, he had to admit she was right. He could see how hard it was for the soldiers to break their skin, even with a freshly sharpened sword. He didn't think the arrows would do much good either. On the other hand he wasn't sure how much use the infantry would be. The first and second ranks had time to have their swords resharpened and the third ranks' blades would still be sharp, but he didn't know if that was going to be enough to win.

"Infantry!" Hadar called but didn't specify the rank. "Is this the last of them?" Hadar spoke softly, almost to himself.

"I don't know. What I do know is if you don't defeat the ogres then it doesn't matter what is coming next, we'll already be dead," Althea offered.

Hadar knew she was right. If the ogres manage, and it seemed as though they would, to break through the cavalry it would only be a matter of time before the infantry fell and then everyone else.

"Charge in. Kill those ogres!" It was the only real command he could give. The rest would be up to them.

The infantry charged forward without a care for which rank they belonged to. They could tell by the tone in Hadar's voice that this was a last ditch effort to win the final battle. The battle was going to be a free for all and the last army standing would be victorious.

The introduction of the infantry, although a last effort, was in fact a master stroke. The ogres were focused on the battle on horseback and they didn't think to look down at the new arrivals. The soldiers were able to hack at their legs, severing hamstrings and Achilles tendons alike as well as smashing their knees. With the attack coming from below distracting the ogres, the cavalry were able to get freer movement and hack at them from the top.

The combination of high-low attacking worked better than Hadar could have imagined.

The numbers were still in the favour of the enemy, even with the addition of the infantry Hadar estimated that the ogres had superior numbers, but the army was starting to even the ledger. Soon enough the deaths were one-for-one and then slowly the ogres started to fall. It wasn't long before all the ogres lay dead on the ground.

Hadar couldn't believe it. Not that long ago he thought they would all soon be dead, but as the battle continued he knew they were going to be victorious.

"Thank you Althea," Hadar said as the last of the ogres was slain. "I couldn't have done this without you."

For a moment Althea was going to take the compliment, but then a bad feeling came over her. "I don't think this is over yet."

Suddenly a cheer arose from the army when they realised the ogres were all dead and nothing more was coming through the gateway. They had lost a lot of men, but those who remained were glad it was all over. The elation only lasted for a moment before a loud crack indicated that the gateway was breaking, just like the first one.

As the gateway shattered and disappeared, the storm clouds suddenly disappeared and the sun shone down on the battlefield. Again Hadar thought it was a good sign, but only for a moment. A sea of orglin with ogres, golems, scartlers and minotaurs, as well as a number of other evil creatures stood in front of an even bigger gateway.

"What do we do know?" Hadar gasped.

Althea didn't hear him. She recognised the figure, even from such a distance, standing at the front of the army. The Dark Knight Ra'naroz smirked at her. The battle with the storm and ogres had drained a lot of her energy and she knew she didn't have the strength to fight a Dark Knight.

Before anyone could move and ear piercing screech came from the west. Hadar couldn't imagine what new horror was approaching them. If he had the heart to continue he would have called the remaining soldiers to attack, but with what was waiting before them there was little point. There was nothing they could do except wait to be killed or enslaved.

Chapter 28: Deep Inside

A large, evil smile crossed Nyrra's face as he sat on his throne out the front of his fortress at the foot of the Cauldron Mountain. He laughed as he thought of the mountain by that name. *Crenallous* was its real name. Cauldron Mountain was what the weak little creatures had named it. He understood the reasoning as a fireball fired into the air and lava ran down its sides. The top of *Crenallous* had split open to mark his victory against the Cursed One. The lava poured down on all sides except for the one where the City of Night stood. The lava then entered the giant moat around the city. When Alaric had first been there he had thought at one time there are been water in the great canyon, but he was wrong.

Looking out of the courtyard he saw his seven Dark Knights standing in front of a small group of orglin. The orglin were all foaming at the mouth waiting for what was about to happen. Nyrra had to admit to himself that he was also excited to start the day's executions. It was his favourite part of the day.

"Bring in the first victim," Nyrra commanded.

A door at the back of the courtyard opened and two orglin dragged a young man towards the gibbet. It pleaded and begged for its life. That brought another smile to Nyrra's face and he had to stop himself from drooling. It didn't really matter if he did, but he didn't want to show the seven his elation. When it was really said and done he didn't trust his seven chosen followers. He knew, given half a chance, they would try and kill him and take his power. That was something he would never let happen.

"Please, please!" the man begged as the noose was placed over his head and he was drawn up by his arms. If that was all that was going to happen to him the he might have been happy to die, but the rumours had reached those in the prisons of what happened when they were brought in front of the Evil One. "I don't want to die, let me go. I will follow you. I will do whatever you want me to."

It was the ogre standing next to the gibbet holding a viscous looking whip that scared the man the most. Tears streamed down the man's cheeks

Nyrra burst out laughing. "I know you will, but right now I want you to scream."

That was all the command the ogre needed to draw back the cruel whip and strike it against the man's back. As much as it wanted not to scream there was nothing it could do to stop. Nyrra continued to smile in pure pleasure at the sight.

"Please," the man begged again. "I will do anything to help you. I know where there are more people you could find. I could help you find them. Please!"

"You see," Nyrra turned his attention to the cage to his left. It was larger than it needed to be and had once housed one of the great dragons. The dragons were all dead now, but the cage still served its purpose. The man in the cage was hunched down in one of the corners. "They will do whatever I want them to do. They will even betray their own for some relief." Nyrra signalled to the ogre before continuing his rhetoric. "Listen to the beautiful music they make," Nyrra referred to the screams of the man as the ogre continued to whip it. Alaric did his best to block out the sound by covering his ears with his hands. The chains he wore made it difficult and he had to lower his head so his hands would reach. "Whip him harder, make him scream louder," Nyrra ordered. "You see," Nyrra said as the ogre did as it was commanded. "There is nothing you can do to block out the music. It will echo through the heavens."

Blood flew as the whip connected again and again. The shirt it wore was tattered at the back a fell down from its arms. The screams continued as the ogre relentlessly continued the torture. The evil creature could do it all day and didn't care if it lived or died. That was exactly what Nyrra wanted.

Soon enough the screaming stopped and the man lost consciousness. It wasn't dead, but it was no longer any use. He signalled for the man to be killed. The trapdoor under it opened and the ogre produced a wicked looking knife. It was almost as long as a sword and he cut the rope tied to its arms. As soon as they were severed the man dropped through the trapdoor, instantly breaking its neck.

Nyrra relaxed back on his mighty stone throne. It was only at the point of death did his realise he was sitting on the very edge. Letting out a deep breath, he didn't even know he was holding, he continued to relax. It was all a game and he had already won, but he wasn't about to stop playing.

"Bring out the next one!" Nyrra yelled.

The ogre removed the noose with one hand whilst holding onto the new victim with his other. Once it was free of its bond the ogre took a big bite out of its head, crunching through skull and brain. It would have preferred to eat the entire body, but it knew that it had to share. Without waiting it threw the dead body into the crowd of orglin. Instantly they swarmed on it and started tearing it apart. The sight was enough to make the bile rise in the back of Alaric's throat, but he wasn't going to give Nyrra the satisfaction of watching him vomit. He swallowed hard and waited for the next victim to be brought forward.

Alaric's heart sank when he saw the next victim being half dragged forward. He still wore his armour that had rusted since the final battle had been fought and lost. Alaric tried to look into Prince Hawthorne's eyes, but there didn't seem to be any life left in them. Whatever had happened he had been broken.

"This one is special?" Nyrra noticed the expression on Alaric's face. "Yes, no? I think yes is the answer."

When Hawthorne was lined up on the gibbet the ogre placed the noose around his neck before ripping his breastplate from his body. The force dislocated Hawthorne's left shoulder, but he still didn't cry out. Alaric wondered if there was any life left in him at all.

"What is your name?" Nyrra asked when he had been strung up ready to be whipped.

When no answer came Hawthorne's body suddenly went stiff. Veins started to pop on his forehead and his face started turning red. It was obvious he was in pain, but there was nothing he could do to move.

"That is Prince Hawthorne," Alaric finally cried out and his body went limp on the gibbet.

It took Nyrra a moment to recognise the name and realise his importance, or at least his former importance. With Nyrra's victory there were no longer any kings, queens, princes or princesses left in the Seven Kingdoms. In fact there were no more Seven Kingdoms. Nyrra was the only ruler and there was only one kingdom.

"He doesn't look too princely to me. Let's see if we can do something about that," Nyrra grinned evilly. "There's no point trying to break an already broken man."

Slowly the light returned to Hawthorne's eyes and his body stiffened. The strength returned to his body, but Nyrra didn't fix the dislocated shoulder and a shot of pain ripped through him. Hawthorne simply let out a groan at the pain before he realised where he was and shut his mouth. He bit down on the pain and waited for more.

"So you are Prince Hawthorne from the former Kingdom of Remidia?" Nyrra asked.

"I am Prince Hawthorne of the Kingdom of Remidia. There are still Remidians out there and they will fight you until the end," Hawthorne's voice was hard as steel.

Nyrra burst out laughing again. "Now this is what I'm talking about. This is a man I can break."

"Do your worst," Hawthorne barked before spitting towards the Evil One. "No matter what you do, you will not break me."

Nyrra laughed his evil laugh again. "Well let's see about that." Nyrra nodded to the ogre.

The ogre didn't wait to lash Hawthorne across his back. Despite trying to be strong Hawthorne buckled slightly at the knees and he let out a groan before he steadied himself.

"That is a little taste of what will happen to you, but it could all end now."

"It will end when it ends. I will never bow down to you," Hawthorne's voice was strong.

"We'll see about that," Nyrra replied as the ogre whipped him again.

This time Hawthorne's knees buckled a little further and his groan was a little louder, but again he quickly recovered. He knew it would only be a matter of time before the pain became too great for him to remain standing, but he would not give up. He wouldn't betray his people and give satisfaction to the Evil One.

"Enough of this," Alaric's voice was weak.

"Be quiet you," Nyrra said and Alaric found that no words would come out.

The ogre whipped Hawthorne until he could no longer stand before it stopped again. With the respite he was slowly able to return to his feet, but his legs still shook. He wanted it to be over, but he wasn't going to ask Nyrra to take his life. If he did he would have failed.

"You are strong, there is no doubt about that, but let's see what you have to say about this," Nyrra said as he signalled to the back of the courtyard.

Hawthorne tried to turn around, but couldn't see who or what it was. As soon as the gate opened to the cells he heard a deep scream. Although he didn't know who it was he knew it was a woman. She was dragged to the front of the gibbet so Hawthorne could watch what was about to happen to her.

"Tell me where you are from?" Nyrra spoke softly to the sobbing girl.

"Zenza City!" she wailed.

Hawthorne's eyes widened at her response. It was exactly the reaction Nyrra was waiting for. It would not be long before he broke the prince and the Cursed One would see exactly what he was capable of, if he didn't already know.

"One of your subjects I believe?" It was a rhetorical question. "Tell your prince to bow down to me and I will let you go."

"Please, your majesty, do what he says. Set your people free. We don't deserve this," she wept and pleaded.

Hawthorne felt sorrow for the poor woman in front of him. In the end there was nothing he could do for her. Even if he bowed down to the Evil One he doubted Nyrra would be true to his word. All he wanted was for him to break and that was the one thing he couldn't do.

"Be brave my child," Hawthorne said. "It will all be over soon."

A look of hope crossed her face when Hawthorne started talking, but it turned to horror when she understood what he meant. There was going to be no salvation from him. She looked towards the cage and Alaric. If anyone could save her it would be him.

"Please! Alaric! Save me! Save us all!"

There was no response. It looked as though he was in a catatonic sate. He sat hunched over his knees and gently rocked back and forth, staring off at nothing. There was nothing he could do to help. Her fate was up to the Evil One.

"Please. I will do anything you want. Please!"

Nyrra nodded to one of his Dark Knights who let six orglin scramble forward. The woman wanted to run away, but she was too scared to move. The orglin didn't waste any time when they reached her. They all jumped on her in unison and started tearing her apart. They ripped at her arms and legs, tearing flesh from bone before they started to devour her. In a matter a minutes there were only bones, blood and shredded clothes remaining of what was once a beautiful lady.

Hawthorne wanted to be sick. Even seeing the battle between the Alliance and the Evil One's army couldn't have prepared him for the scene in front of him. No matter the emotions rushing through his body he couldn't give in. He had already come to terms with his death and he wasn't going to go back on it.

"My people would rather die than be subjugated by you," Hawthorne spat when he finished speaking.

"Well let's just see how many share your feelings," Nyrra sneered.

Another woman was brought out and asked the same question as the first. She pleaded with Hawthorne, but he simply told her to be brave for her kingdom before she was ripped to pieces. After she had been devoured, a man was brought out and given the same treatment. Hawthorne had no idea how many citizens of Remidia had been captured, but he thought the process could go on for days if Nyrra decided to keep him alive for that long.

"Very well," Hawthorne said before the next victim was brought out. "What is it you want?" he kept his teeth clenched and his voice was like steel.

"You see, it's only a matter of time before they break," Nyrra said to Alaric. The ogre knew it was time to continue the torture and gave Hawthorne three more quick lashes. Hawthorne's legs collapsed underneath him and a fresh bolt of pain ripped through his dislocated shoulder. With a great effort he returned to his feet. "I want you to tell me that you will be my slave. I want you to tell me that you with serve me for the rest of your pitiful life, no matter what I want you to do."

"I will do what you say," Hawthorne finally resigned. No matter what he had said at the start he couldn't stand and watch Remidian after Remidian beg for their lives, only to be ripped apart by hungry orglin. He knew Nyrra would continue until they were all dead unless he surrendered and then he would still die. At least he could save some of his fellow Remidians' lives.

"Only a matter of time," Nyrra said to himself and smiled again. He had thought the prince would have held out for longer, but it didn't worry him. Now it was time to work on Alaric again. "Bring him down and give him the whip."

"What?" Hawthorne said as the ogre took him down from the gibbet.

"You will whip the next victim or I will make you watch when I have my orglin have their way with your former citizens."

Hawthorne knew he didn't have a choice. He wished his right shoulder had been dislocated too, then he wouldn't be able to use the whip.

"Bring out our special guest," Nyrra commanded to no one in particular. "You might want to pay attention to this one," he said to Alaric.

Alaric was still curled up in a ball and he didn't want to move. As much as Nyrra liked seeing Alaric in such a state he certainly didn't want him to miss what he had in store. As the door to the cells opened Alaric looked up and his heart dropped.

The she-elf stood tall as she was led, not dragged, to the gibbet. Alaric had thought she was already dead, but he couldn't remember why. Unlike the other prisoners she was dressed in a clean linen shirt and pants of a deep green. Her soft blonde hair fell in ringlets around her shoulders and looked as though it had recently been washed. The entire situation didn't seem right at all, but Alaric couldn't work out why.

Alena kept her head held high as she was tied to the gibbet like those before her. She didn't seem worried about the blood that stained her bare feet. She looked directly at Nyrra, with no fear on her face.

"What is it you want from me?" Alena asked.

"I want nothing from you. What I want is from your friend," Nyrra sneered at her. "You can begin now."

Hawthorne looked at Alena's back. It was going to be hard enough torturing someone he didn't know. He had no idea how he was going to do it to someone he cared deeply for.

"I won't do it," Hawthorne stood firm, although he didn't know what was going to happen. He knew Alena was going to be whipped, but he would rather die than do it himself.

"Oh, I see what the problems is," Nyrra sounded genuinely surprised, but Hawthorne knew it was sarcasm. "That is much too pretty a shirt to ruin with whipping and blood. Let's just get rid of that."

"What?" Hawthorne gasped.

The ogre knew exactly what Nyrra meant. The creature moved forward until it was standing behind Alena. She could feel the hot, stale breath of the creature on the back of her neck and it made her cringe. Before Hawthorne really knew what was happening the ogre ripped the shirt from her back, exposing her naked back to Hawthorne and her breasts to

Nyrra and Alaric. The sight brought Alaric to his feet, but there was nothing he could do to change it.

"Now whip her," Nyrra commanded. "Or you will watch her being ravaged by orglin after orglin."

Hawthorne felt the bile rise up in the back of his throat, but he doubted he would be true to his word He had seen the orglin and they were more about feeding than gratifying themselves. When he didn't respond one of the nasty creatures started moving towards her. It soon became apparent that Nyrra was going to follow through and Hawthorne couldn't let that happen.

"Fine!" Hawthorne yelled out as he brought the whip back.

He flicked the whip at Alena as softly as he could without making it too obvious, but unfortunately Nyrra didn't fall for it. Alena screamed out in pain, continuing the ruse, but Nyrra was having none of it. He had seen torture too many times to be tricked.

"Whip her like you mean it or I will let my orglin have their way with her whilst you watch and believe me it won't be pretty."

The orglin continued towards Alena and looked genuinely disappointed as Hawthorne whipped her again. This time the crack of the whip drew blood and Alena screamed again, only this time it wasn't fake. The sight pleased Nyrra, but it was not going to be enough.

"Did I say stop?" Nyrra asked. "Don't think my orglin mind the state of their prey. Continue until there is no longer any skin on her back."

"I'm sorry," Hawthorne whispered as he started again.

Tears rolled down his face as he continued to whip her. With each strike her blood splattered back onto him. Alena screamed and moaned with each cut and there was nothing either of them could do to stop it. What Nyrra had in mind if he did would be much worse. He could only hope that she would die soon and he could stop torturing her. That was the only thought that kept him going.

All Alaric could do was stand and watch the horror before him. That was what Nyrra had planned. He didn't care for the two in front of him, he only cared for the man caged to his right.

"You see?" he asked. "This is what is in store for you."

"Don't be so sure," Alaric's voice had changed. It was as hard as stone and not at all what Nyrra had been expecting.

"We've had enough of you," the voice came from beyond the gibbet. Nyrra looked in surprise. "It is our time now."

The gibbet had completely disappeared along with Hawthorne and Alena. There was no sign it had even existed. Nyrra didn't know what was happening. The voice came from one of his chosen seven, but he wasn't sure exactly which one. Whoever it was they were about to get a lesson in pain.

"You have served our purpose and now it is time to go," Dargoz's voice was dripping with arrogance.

"And what makes you think you can defeat me. I am your lord and don't you ever forget it," Nyrra boomed.

He reached out with the power around him to strike down Za'aroz, but nothing happened. He couldn't even draw on the evil around him. When he looked at the Dark Knight again he realised he held the Emerald stone in his right hand. Nyrra had captured all the stones from the Cursed One during the final battle. He knew that was true although the memory was already starting to fade. He didn't know why he had given Za'aroz the Emerald stone or Na'garoz the Topaz stone, but at least he still had the Ruby stone. He looked into his top pocket.

"Looking for something?" Dargoz asked as the realisation struck him.

The Dark Knight was standing in the middle of the line of chosen. Nyrra couldn't believe what he held in his right hand. How could he get the Ruby Stone? It didn't make any sense. Even if he gave six of his chosen the other stones there was no way he would relinquish the Ruby stone.

"What is going on here?" Nyrra gasped.

"This is what is waiting for you," Alaric spoke nonchalantly.

Somehow the Cursed One had escaped from his cage. Nyrra had no idea what was happening. He was no longer dressed in the tattered rags Nyrra had left him in. He wore black leather trousers, a black leather jerkin and a long black coat. There was no longer fear on his face and his expression was stone cold.

"You can't do this. I control your mind now. This is what will happen if you refuse my offer and I defeat you," Nyrra still sounded confused.

"This is your fantasy," Alaric replied. "We are in your head and this is what will happen to you."

As if in answer to his statement beams of light shot towards Nyrra from the stones. The Dark Knights, his Chosen, had turned on him. That couldn't be right. Alaric had to be distorting his truth, but that was impossible. Even if he was right and they were in his head the Cursed One was not strong enough.

The lights stopped before they hit him, but it took more energy than Nyrra thought. He knew what would happen if he was killed in his own mind. His body wouldn't die, but he would never return to the real world. That was one of the ways he was hoping to trap Alaric.

"How have you done this?" he panted.

"You are not as strong as you think you are," Alaric replied. "I could keep you here if I wanted to, but that is not the way things are meant to end."

Nyrra tried to leave, but he couldn't change anything. If they were truly inside his mind then he should be able to leave whenever he wanted. The situation continued to confuse him.

"But don't think I will make it that easy for you," Alaric sneered.

As Alaric disappeared the beams of light shot from the stones again. Although Nyrra knew his fate wasn't over he dived out of the way. In doing so he only managed to avoid the first attack. When he returned to his feet he was struck first by the red light from the Ruby stone. A great pain ripped through his body, which was followed by more pain as the other lights struck him. He wished it would all be over as he was struck again by another round of lights.

Chapter 29: Remidia Battle

Prince Hawthorne stood in the dark and looked out at where the final battle would soon take place for his Remidian soldiers. When he set off from Remidel with his father to meet the elves at Elhjem, which seemed a lifetime ago, he did not believe he would be standing where he was. They had sent General Jarwe with the Remidian army to Avalon to fight on their behalf, but so much had changed since then and he had travelled so far. He had been challenged by the Dark Knights and only just survived. Despite everything he had been through, he knew the battle was the greatest test he would ever face.

As the grey of dawn approached he heard the sound of footsteps. He wished he could remain in his reverie, but he knew he had to focus. He didn't need to turn around to know it was Captain Kenyon and the wizard Drake. It was a sign that the final battle was about to start, although Hawthorne hoped it would at least wait for the sun to break the horizon.

"Your majesty," Kenyon greeted. When he received no response he continued. "The army has moved up into place, but now they want to know what is happening."

The army had been told to assemble behind the prince, but in no particular order. No one knew if the cavalry or the infantry should be in front. The archers wanted to move forward, but couldn't go against the current orders. They all knew the final battle was close and they didn't want to be left in a rabble when it began.

Hawthorne continued to stare out at the battlefield. He wanted to look to the east to see if the sun had started to rise, but he didn't want move his line of sight. If Nyrra's army arrived he wanted to make sure he had as much time to prepare as he could.

"There is little we can do until we know what we are up against," Hawthorne finally replied. "What would you have me do?" He asked the question to both Kenyon and Drake, not really caring for a response.

"Make a command of some description. The men need to know what they're doing and they need a lift in morale," Kenyon urged.

Hawthorne knew he was right, but that still didn't make it any easier. He had no idea which rank he should use first. He turned around and looked at his army. The infantry had managed to make their way to the front, although the cavalry also looked keen for battle. The archers seemed lost between the two, but they were still ready for action.

"We still have time," Hawthorne replied. "The Evil One's army hasn't even reached the battlefield." As soon as the words came out of his mouth he knew they were wrong. He looked over and saw the sun peak above the horizon.

"I have a feeling they will use a gateway, or something similar, to get here in a hurry," Drake voiced what they were all thinking. "He will want to try and take us by surprise. If we don't get ready that's exactly what he'll do."

"So what do you propose we get ready for?" Hawthorne asked. "If I knew what was coming then I could get my army in order."

Drake opened his mouth and then shut it again. He didn't like the way Hawthorne was speaking to him, but he had to admit he was right. Until they knew what the Evil One was going to throw at them there was very little they could do. Despite that, Hawthorne still needed to make a decision. He couldn't leave the army as it was when the Evil One's army appeared.

"I'm sorry, but I can't help you with that one, but it doesn't change the fact that Captain Kenyon is right. You need to make a decision and you need to make it now," Drake finished.

Hawthorne let his shoulders drop if only for a second. The severity of the decision was weighing on him, but he couldn't shirk his responsibilities. It was his decision to be made and he would have to make it. The infantry had stronger numbers than the cavalry, so he decided it would be best if he placed the first rank of infantry at the front of the line.

"Keep the infantry at the front, but move the second and third line back. Leave room for the cavalry to come forward if needed. Also have the longbow archers move in behind. Hopefully we can use them at some stage," Hawthorne did his best to sound commanding.

Captain Kenyon gave him a quick salute before returning to the army to give the commands. He much preferred to be busy than to be standing around waiting. He had no idea how Hawthorne seemed to remain so calm. If he was in the same position he would be going out of his mind.

"Is there anything else you can think of?" Hawthorne asked Drake.

"Sorry, what do you mean?" he asked, only half paying attention.

"You have been involved in this for a lot longer than I have. You have read all the prophecies. Surely there is something you can tell me about what is to come?" Hawthorne asked.

His words gained Drake's full attention. In theory he was right, Drake should have spent more time reading the prophecies, but that had never happened. Only Eldred had dedicated his life to the prophecies. In hindsight he should have listened to Eldred's warnings and he might have had an answer for Hawthorne. Instead they would be going in blind.

"There is nothing more I know, otherwise I would have already told you. There is as much at stake in this battle for me as there is for you. If we fail then we are all dead or we will become slaves of the Evil One."

As the sun continued to rise over the horizon Hawthorne returned his attention to the battlefield. He wondered where the Evil One's army was. He thought the battle would start when the sun rose, but there was still no sign of them. What concerned him were the dark storm clouds gathering to the north. Rain would certainly not help their cause.

"Is there anything you can do about that?" Hawthorne asked.

"It will be well into the afternoon before that storm reaches us. If we are still battling by then I will do something about it," Drake replied, not really taking any notice. All he wanted to do was save his energy for what was to come. The Dark Knights had returned and he was sure he would have to do battle with one, at least one.

Hawthorne shook his head, but he didn't push any further. There was something very disconcerting about the clouds, but he had to trust Drake's judgement. As the wizard had said "there was as much at stake for him as there was for everyone else". If there was an issue with the storm then he had to believe that Drake would have already fixed it.

Kenyon returned to Hawthorne after he had relayed the order to the troops. Drake had created a spell to carry the prince's voice throughout the army, but Hawthorne wanted to use Kenyon as much as possible. On the battlefield the soldiers would need to look to him for any additional instructions that Hawthorne couldn't give himself.

"The army is ready," Kenyon stated the obvious to break the silence.

Hawthorne didn't reply. He simply turned around to face the army and took a step forward. It was the moment he had been waiting for. He knew the final battle was close and the time was right to make his address.

"My fellow Remidians," Hawthorne started and silence fell over the army. "Our journey has been long and for some of us this is not the first time we have stood on this battlefield waiting for the Evil One. The first time was a ruse, but let's not take that for granted. We are on the brink of the final battle, but fear not." Hawthorne paused for affect. "It is the Evil One who should be afraid. We are not going to let him, nor his army, leave this battlefield alive." His words finally brought a raucous cheer from the soldiers. "His army will be here soon and they will come as if from nowhere and no matter what he throws at us we will stand strong. We will not turn and run no matter what fear we feel." Hawthorne felt he was losing the soldiers with his last comment. "Today we will show the Evil One what it means to be Remidian. We will send him back to the pits of fire." Another cheer arose from the army as Hawthorne turned back to the battlefield. He didn't want to risk saying the wrong thing and dropping their morale.

"Those clouds look ominous," Kenyon said.

Drake looked up again. The clouds had almost doubled the distance since Hawthorne had first pointed them out. Hawthorne also noticed and realised that they were certainly not natural. They both called for a messenger at the same time, but only one arrived. Drake explained what he wanted to relay to the other wizards and the messenger disappeared through the small gateway behind them.

Almost as soon as the messenger left another one came running through the gateway. When he reached them he relayed the exact same information as Drake had just given. Drake didn't bother responding and the messenger returned to the transport ground. He had already begun preparing the spell and released it as soon as the messenger left.

Suddenly the air was filled with electricity and the hair on the back of Hawthorne's neck stood on end. At first he thought it was from Drake's spell, but he soon realised his mistake. A strip of brilliant light appeared in the middle of the battlefield. Before Hawthorne could say anything the light ripped across the sky as a gateway started to appear. When it was finished it bubbled a deep red and purple. For a moment Hawthorne hoped that was all that was going to happen, but slowly the swirling bubbling colours coalesced and the scene before him was enough to make his heart drop. He didn't even see the barren mountain range in the background. All he could see was a sea of orglin come pouring through the gateway.

"Infantry!" Hawthorne called out, as if in a dream. "First rank only. Charge!"

The soldiers didn't wait to jump into action at the command of their prince. It didn't matter what was coming through the gateway. Most of them had fought orglin before and knew what to expect. Even with the superior numbers rushing through, the soldiers were not perturbed.

"Do you think you should use the archers as well?" Drake asked as he watched the two armies race towards each other. The decision would have to be made soon if the archers were going to be effective.

"The infantry will be fine," Hawthorne replied, calm after the initial shock. "The thick armour of our soldiers will be impossible for the orglin to penetrate. To use the archers would only prove to waste our arrows and there is no telling what else the Evil One will throw at us."

After the battle with the orglin at Jarrat, Hawthorne had learnt a few things about fighting them. He knew that the breastplates, thigh protectors, arm guards and helmets would be almost impenetrable to them. It would be difficult for any of the soldiers to be taken down, but Hawthorne knew he couldn't be over confident.

The infantry charged towards the orglin, although their advance, with the extra armour, was slow. The soldiers had slowed to a walk by the time the two armies met. Charging into the oncoming enemy was not their style. They all carried half-broad shields that were hard to control at a charge, but by placing their full weight behind them they would be able to block the first onslaught.

The orglin threw themselves against the infantry. At first the line of soldiers was able to repel them, but as more and more swarmed through they had to lower their shields and prepare to attack.

The orglin continued to hurl themselves against the infantry without a care for their own lives. They had been whipped into a frenzy and only cared about death. They wanted to feed and they didn't care how it happened. What they didn't realise was that they couldn't open the hardened steel armour like they could with the soft flesh within.

King Faxon sat on his horse toward the front of the line of cavalry. It was by pure chance that he was in a position to watch the battle unfold as no one knew he was there. He had managed to keep his identity secret by wearing his helmet whenever he was outside and eating his meals alone in his tent. If anyone had realised who he was, there was no chance he would be allowed to fight. If he was there would be a guard of soldiers around him protecting him. More than likely he would be forced to stand with his son in command of the army and that was not the way things were supposed to happen.

The soldiers made quick work of the orglin as they continued to throw themselves against the infantry. At first their swords sheared through the thick leathery skin with no problems, but as they continued their blades started to dull. Those at the very front of the line slowly gave those behind a chance to move up.

Hawthorne watched the battle intently and quickly realised what was happening. The first line was working well together, but it would only be a matter of time before their swords became useless and the orglin would break through.

"Second line!" Hawthorne boomed, still not wanting to use the cavalry. "Ready to the front."

From his position he could see the soldiers that had started at the front of the line continue to make their way back. Normally they would look to collect a sword from a fallen comrade when their own became blunt, but there simply weren't enough to make it worthwhile. The orglin had managed to take down some of the soldiers, but not many.

Before Hawthorne gave the command for the second rank to relieve the first, he looked towards the gateway. The battle had been raging for what he estimated to be an hour and he hoped they had stemmed the tide of orglin, but that was not the case. The battlefield behind the front still teemed with the evil creatures and there didn't look to be any end in sight. Orglin still poured through the gateway, if only slightly slower than from the start.

Hawthorne cursed to himself, louder than he had planned, when he realised that there was a chance Nyrra had an almost unlimited supply. Even if it was one death to a thousand orglin they would eventually be overrun.

"What is it?" Drake asked as he watched the battle.

"There seems to be a never ending supply of orglin coming through that gateway. Is there anything you can do to stop them?" Hawthorne asked, hopefully.

Drake looked at the gateway. It had never crossed his mind to try and close it and he silently chided himself. If he had closed the gateway at the start then the final battle might well be over. That thought gave him the answer to the question. Even if he knew how to unravel the spell used to create a gateway whoever, or whatever, had created it in the first place would just do so again. It was more important for him to keep the storm at bay.

"I don't think there is anything I can do to close it," Drake replied, keeping his suspicions to himself.

Hawthorne didn't respond. Deep down he knew that was going to be the answer and he had already planned his next move.

"First line, start your retreat," he boomed, even though Drake's spell made his voice carry throughout the battlefield. "Second line, start your advance."

The soldiers waiting for the command were quick to march towards the battlefront. As much as they wanted to charge forward they didn't want to get caught up in the retreating army.

What happened next made the bile rise in the back of Hawthorne's throat. As the first rank of soldiers made their retreat the orglin horde stopped to fill on their fallen brethren. Hawthorne knew to expect the worst from the enemy, but he couldn't have imagined what he saw before him. The orglin feasted on the dead with no impunity. It was even worse when they came across the dead soldiers and Hawthorne had to watch them being torn apart.

The pause in the battle gave the soldiers a chance to change position without the risk of attack. All the retreating soldiers relaxed their weapons, but kept a wary eye on the feasting orglin.

The second rank of infantry didn't wait to start their attack once they were through the first line. As much as it would help clear the battlefield if the orglin were left to feast, they didn't want to give them a chance to regroup. The second wave crashed into the gorging orglin adding them to the ever growing pile of corpses before they started to climb over the dead to get to the rest.

Hawthorne instantly saw the mistake, but could do nothing about it. He couldn't leave those at the front out by themselves. In the end it might have been kinder. The pile of dead made it hard for the armour wearing soldiers to reach the battle on the other side. The orglin had more freedom of movement and could easily traverse the ever growing pile of dead.

The first rank of soldiers suffered few casualties, but the second rank, only just taking the battlefield, had already suffered more. Hawthorne knew he had made a mistake that had cost good men their lives.

"I think you should pull your men back," Drake voiced what he was already thinking.

"Second rank, pull back behind the line of bodies," Hawthorne called out.

Those already over had little chance of survival. The orglin might have stopped to feast before, but they had no intention of letting the slow moving infantry get away.

As much as the sight sickened Hawthorne he had to admit that it was a good thing. The orglin would decimate the dead until there was nothing blocking the charge of the soldiers. At the rate the orglin were devouring the corpses he didn't think they would have to wait too much longer.

"Stay strong," Hawthorne ordered. "Ready for the attack. When the feeding is over charge forward."

There was nothing else they could do except wait. Hawthorne didn't know what was harder, watching the battle or waiting for it to restart.

After what seemed like an age the orglin had finally cleared the piles of dead. The soldiers didn't wait to make their charge when the orglin started advancing. The two armies met with a crash that erupted around the battlefield. Only with the new sound did Hawthorne realise how quiet it had been.

With the barrier of dead bodies removed the second rank became just as effective as the first. The orglin hurled themselves against the armoured men and were simply cut down. The field-commanders had watched the first rank closely and had realised that the soldiers at the front would soon lose the keenness of their blades. They ordered them to attack and then retreat allowing those behind with fresh blades to join the battle.

The soldiers pushed into the forever swarming horde. With each orglin that died it seemed another dozen rushed through the gateway. Hawthorne didn't think his army would last long. Eventually their swords would dull to a point where they couldn't be resharpened and then the orglin would be able to tear them apart.

Just when Hawthorne was about to give up hope the orglin finally stopped rushing through the gateway. It seemed as though the Evil One didn't have a never ending supply of the evil creatures. Hope returned to Hawthorne's heart that the final battle would soon be over and they would be victorious.

"It's over," Hawthorne spoke under his breath.

"Not yet!" Drake pointed to the gateway as six monstrous creatures lumbered through.

"Giants!" Hawthorne gasped.

"What did you say?" Drake asked in surprise.

"They're giants," Hawthorne replied.

"How do you know that?" Drake asked, for no real reason.

"Their gigantic size for starters and the patching tufts of hair around their body. One thing to note is that large cudgels in their right hands. You'll never see a giant out without one. The large whips in their left hands are something new though." Hawthorne recognised the confused expression on Drake's face. "I have read a book or two in my days," Hawthorne explained.

The information he gave wasn't exactly true, but Drake knew it wasn't time for a lecture. All that mattered was that there were giants on the battlefield and they would have to be stopped. Even though there were only six they could easily take down the entire army.

"Cavalry!" Hawthorne called out. "Ready to charge!"

There was still plenty of time before the giants would reach the soldiers, but he wanted the cavalry to be ready. He didn't know how he was going to get the infantry out of the way of the horses, it would just have to play out for itself.

Faxon felt a rush of adrenaline shoot through his body as he heard his son's command. It had been the moment he had been waiting for. He sat straighter in the saddle before he let his shoulders sink when he saw the giants lumbering towards them. Although he had never had a chance to see one in person, he knew exactly what they were. As he watched the gigantic creatures he remembered something from his past. Not only had he seen pictures of giants in his studies, but he had also studied the campaigns from many years ago in which the Remidian soldiers had fought against them. King Kinborough had sent in his cavalry to attack a small group of raiding giants. The men and horses were cut down leaving none alive. A young squire, whose name was lost with the ages, eventually realised the giants were extremely powerful and strong, but very slow. They also seemed to have a problem attacking anything low down, as he saw when an unhorsed soldier did his best to attack on foot.

If it was just the one account Faxon would not have been so worried with the command, but he remembered reading another. It was in a tome written in a time that was not recorded, but many years before the first Faxon had read on the topic. The creatures the men rode were different to the current day horses, but the result was still the same. Those who rode were smashed and killed, whilst those on foot were able to dash and slash their way to victory.

He wanted nothing more than to ride to the front of the line of cavalry and reveal himself, but he knew that wasn't an option. He had made the decision to join the army and to do so incognito. It was Hawthorne's lot to command and he had to trust his son was going to do the right thing.

Before the cavalry moved into action a messenger rushed up from the transport ground. Hawthorne really didn't want to be disturbed. He knew something important was about to happen with the giants taking the battlefield. If they were able to destroy them they might just win the final battle and that was something he did not want to miss.

"Your majesty," the messenger bowed slightly as time would allow, "there is an urgent message from General Jarwe."

"What is it?" Hawthorne snapped, not taking his eyes from the battlefield.

The cavalry started their march towards the front of the line. The horses wanted to charge in, sensing the impending battle, but their riders restrained them. A charge would do more harm than good.

"Stop the horses," the messenger gasped. "The general said you need to use the infantry against the giants. The soldiers need to stay low and move quickly. The giants are very powerful, but very slow. This attack will confuse them and hopefully reduce the casualties."

The messenger waited for a response from Hawthorne, but he was too focused on his advancing army. He had made the wrong decision and was sending a lot of good soldiers to their deaths. Just as the messenger was about to repeat the command from Jarwe, Hawthorne called the cavalry back. The messenger returned to the transport ground without waiting for a response. It was clear that his job was done and Hawthorne had no further use for him.

"Third rank! Move through the cavalry and prepare to march forward. Second rank!" Hawthorne increased his voice even though it wasn't necessary. "Prepare to retreat when the orglin are all dead. Defend the giants, but do not attack them."

Hawthorne figured that their blades would be dull from fighting the orglin and could not risk them attacking the giants. Hawthorne called out the new tactics, hoping that it wouldn't distract the second rank still fighting the orglin.

The soldiers at the front of the line were too busy to take any notice of Hawthorne. If there were any important messages for them then it would come from their field-commanders. It wasn't until they had finished killing the last of the orglin before they realised the new horror that had only just begun.

The soldiers facing the giants did their best to slow their advance, but weary from their strenuous attack with the orglin along with their dulled swords, it made the task almost impossible. More than one soldier fell to the mighty cudgel or was torn apart by the fierce whips. The third line made their way forward as fast as they could.

The soldiers of the second rank made their retreat allowing the third rank to move into position. The giants, having a relatively easy time with those from the second rank, kept up their assault. They weren't expecting such a quick and brutal attack from the third. Thousands of soldiers encircled the six giants, but only two or three attacked at any one time. Whenever the giants would swing at the soldiers in front of them, another slashed at their calves from behind.

Hawthorne watched the various battles intently, looking up every now and then to see if anything else was coming through the gateway. Each time he saw nothing his heart filled with hope.

Each time a soldier fell to the great cudgels the giants received more and more slashes to their legs. Eventually the giants started to fall, one by one. Once they were on the ground there was little they could do to stop the soldiers from stabbing at them with their swords and soon enough they all lay motionless.

The soldiers looked around to see what else there was to fight and when they realised there was nothing more a cheer of victory arose from the battlefield.

"I can't believe it's over." Hawthorne gasped, almost too afraid to speak. "There's nothing more coming through. We've won!" His voice rose, if ever so slightly, as the realisation washed over him.

"Don't relax too much," Drake's voice was grave as he stared at the gateway.

"What do you mean? Nothing is coming through," Hawthorne sounded confused as the cheering continued.

"Don't you think this has been far too easy?" Drake asked the question that had been running through his head. "The orglin has hardly put a dint in our ranks and we haven't even used the cavalry yet."

"So what do you think is going to happen?"

Before Drake had a chance to answer his question, a loud crack resonated throughout the battlefield. At first Hawthorne thought it was a burst of thunder, but when he saw the gateway start to crumble he knew what it was. Within a few seconds the gateway had completely disappeared and what waited for them on the other side sent a shiver down their spines.

Another gateway had been opened behind the first one and looked as though it was almost twice the size. Standing in front of it was a group of the strangest creatures he had ever seen. They had the bodies of a giant cat, about the same size of that of a horse, but with shorter cat-like legs. Their heads resembled giant rats with larger rat-like teeth protruding from their mouths. The other significant feature was their dragon-like tails with an arrowhead point at the end.

"What in the name of the Gods are they?" Hawthorne gasped.

"They are basilisks," Drake sounded just as breathless. He had heard of them, but had thought them purely to be legend. None had walked the Seven Kingdoms for well over a thousand years. Drake had no idea where the Evil One had found them, but there was no doubting what they were.

Hawthorne had studied many books on the mythical creatures of legend, but he had never come across a basilisk. If he was not staring at them then he would not have believed they existed. He had no idea what to do. He had no idea how to fight a basilisk or what commands to give his soldiers.

"What do we do?" Hawthorne voiced his concerns.

As the words came out of his mouth a loud, bloodcurdling scream came from the battlefield. Hawthorne shivered and felt the hairs stand upright on his arms and the back of his neck. The soldiers shrunk back from the noise, but still held their ground. Until they were told otherwise they would stay where they were and meet the enemy head on, although they hoped for the order to retreat.

Before Hawthorne had a chance to voice a command the basilisks started their charge. He still had no idea what he was going to do. He had no idea how to attack the evil creatures.

"I think it's time to bring in the cavalry," Drake suggested, although he really had no idea if it was the best plan. "Tell them to be wary though. A basilisk can't spit an acid from its tail that can eat through solid steel. They will have only a few seconds to remove whatever piece of armour has been struck before the acid will start eating into their flesh."

The screams coming from the battlefield only proved his point as the basilisks joined the fray. More than one soldier, thinking his armour would protect him from the green liquid, found out that it was not the case. Once the acid had eaten through the armour and touched the skin there was nothing anyone could do. Those touched by the acid screamed out in pain. When the pain became too much they simply dropped to the ground, still screaming, before finally slipping into the warm embrace of death. Some rolled around for over a minute before they were finally taken.

"It's time for you to lead," Drake burst out when still no command came.

"Cavalry, to the front!" The cavalry was still at the front of the line from before, but Hawthorne couldn't take his eyes from the battlefield to check. "Ready your charge!" he spoke as if in a dream.

The soldiers fought bravely against the basilisks. After the initial shock and the advice given from Hawthorne to avoid the green acid, the infantry was starting to make a battle of it. They closed their ranks to make it difficult for the basilisks to attack in large numbers, leaving themselves enough room to move out of the way from any acid attack. Despite the regrouping effort of the infantry there was little they could do against the ferocious attack of the basilisks. Hawthorne could only hope the cavalry would be more successful.

Hawthorne ordered the cavalry in and commanded the third rank to do its best to withdraw. The retreat was not as easy as it had been with the orglin. The basilisks were quick on their feet and were only concerned with killing the creatures in front of them. As the soldiers tried to retreat, the basilisks pushed hard.

For the first time Drake noticed that the rain had hit the battlefield and was starting to increase in intensity. There seemed little point in holding onto the spell and he could feel that the others wizards had released theirs. It would be impossible and pointless for him to try and hold the storm back by himself. He could already feel the strain starting to get to him.

The cavalry did their best to make their way through the retreating soldiers. With every soldier safely on the other side at least one had fallen to the advancing basilisks. Hawthorne could only stand and watch and hope the cavalry would have a better time of it.

Although the arrival of the horses and riders seemed to confuse the basilisks it was not Hawthorne had been expecting. He looked up at the gateway and the basilisks still dashed through. If it was anything like the hordes of orglin, Hawthorne didn't think they had a chance to win, at least not without help.

"Is there something you can do?" Hawthorne asked.

Drake had already been thinking about the best plan of attack. He knew there was no point in trying to close the gateway, but he knew he could help.

Without answering, Drake released his spell. The rain behind the main battlefront started to change colour. Some of the drops became a solid pale blue with swirling colours of red, yellow, orange and purple. When the rain hit the basilisks it had the same effect as the green acid coming from their tails. The skin started to smoke, then bubble as the acid rain took its toll. The creatures screeched again, this time in pain, as they were slowly dissolved.

Although the acid rain was sporadic, Drake made sure he kept a safe distance from the advancing cavalry. He had no real control over which drops would become acidic and which ones wouldn't and he didn't want to risk killing any soldiers. As much as he would have liked to change all the rain to acid and kill all of the basilisks in one attack he knew that wasn't possible, At least each basilisk he killed was one less to attack the cavalry.

Faxon felt the adrenaline rushing through his body as he rode at a walk towards the battlefront. He wanted nothing, like his fellow cavalryman, than to kick the flanks of his horse and change in, but like the others he had to contain himself. To charge in would only prove to kill the retreating soldiers.

As soon as they were through the infantry the battle began. Faxon had positioned himself so that he would be among the first to embattle the basilisks. The evil creatures fought with a ferocity that matched their appearance. If it hadn't been for his son's warning he wouldn't have worried about dodging the green liquid from the creatures' tails. It was almost the first attack he came up against and he quickly shifted in the saddle so the acid wouldn't hit him.

With sword in hand Faxon went on the attack. His war-horse had been in battle more than once and despite that it had been over a year since the king had ridden him, he knew exactly what his rider wanted. The basilisk fought with tail, teeth and claws. The war-horse was just a part of the battle as Faxon was. If the horse wasn't prepared for an attack it would be quickly scratched and bitten to death.

Faxon used his shield to block any attack from the powerful tail, almost being knocked from his horse on more than one occasion. As soon as the basilisk attacked with its head, Faxon knew it was time to strike. Its teeth were razor sharp, but not enough to penetrate his thick armour. Faxon used this to his advantage, letting the beast strike at him before hacking at its neck. The skin was a lot thinner than that of the orglin and the giants and Faxon found, if he put enough strength into the attack, he could sever the head clean off.

As the attack continued Faxon drove further and further into the group of basilisks until he noticed that the rain had changed colour and the basilisks were starting to... melt. It was a strange sight to behold as was the pungent smell of searing fur and flesh. The distraction was enough for Faxon to take his eyes from the approaching basilisks. One saw its chance to attack and shot a stream of green acid in his direction.

Faxon only saw the stream at the last moment and raised his shield to take the blow. His shield blocked most of the acid, but some splattered on his breastplate and down onto his horse. Quickly he threw his shield to the ground and with his free hand grabbed a small dagger and cut away his armour before the acid had a chance to seep into his skin.

Unfortunately there was nothing he could do for his war-house. It held its ground for as long as it could, but as the armour came away from Faxon it reared on its back legs in pain. Faxon, without a grip on its bridle, was thrown from his saddle and crashed onto the ground.

He knew his ribs had been broken as he staggered to his feet. His horse lay dead three paces away and the basilisks were already starting to close in. He looked around, but there was no sign of the other cavalry. He knew he was going to die, he had known that when he made the decision to join the final battle.

The basilisks slowed their advance, curious at what the creature was going to do with the small weapon in his hand. Faxon made a swipe with the dagger to show his intentions with no real hope in making a strike.

The basilisks remained out of striking distance and for a moment Faxon thought he might just survive, but then he felt a sharp, pointed tail slice through his stomach. Blood spurted from his mouth as his legs collapsed, but the tail kept him upright. He looked up at the sky and for a moment he thought he saw the sun shine through before his eyes closed for the last time.

Hawthorne was transfixed on the battlefield. He couldn't tell which side was truly winning. Even with the help from Drake it seemed as though the basilisks had the stronger numbers. Just when he was about to give up he looked at the gateway and realised that the last of the basilisks had come through. Not only that, but there were no more horrors following them. Hope returned to his heart as he watched the basilisks fall, either by sword or acid rain. Either way they were dying faster than the cavalry.

When the last of the basilisks fell Hawthorne let out a deep breath that he had no idea he was holding. It was over; the final battle was finally over. He was about to let out a yell of relief when he looked at Drake.

The wizard had released his spell and was doing his best to remain on his feet. The spell had taken more from him than he had expected, but it was over.

"Is that it?" Hawthorne asked, barely daring to speak.

"I sure hope so," Drake replied, dropping to his knees.

The soldiers weren't going to wait. When they realised the basilisks were all dead they let out a cheer of joy. As far as they were concerned the final battle was over. When the gateway didn't instantly come crashing down the cheer intensified. Hawthorne wanted to cry out in joy, but he just couldn't bring himself to. He had a bad feeling and that wasn't a good sign.

Suddenly that rain stopped and the sun shone down on the battlefield. Before Hawthorne could take it as a good sign a loud crack boomed throughout the battlefield and the second gateway shattered into a million pieces. As soon as the shards hit the ground they disappeared.

What was standing on the other side almost knocked Hawthorne to the ground with shock. A field of evil creatures, many more than they had fought so far, stood in front of a third gateway.

Even from the distance Drake knew who was standing at the front of the army. The Dark Knight Morgoz had a wry grin on his face. It was as if he knew they had won and Drake had to admit he was feeling the same way. There was no way they could defeat the army before them with the remaining soldiers they had left and he certainly didn't have the energy to fight another battle.

"What do we do know?" Hawthorne finally voiced the question, but Drake had no answer for him.

Before Hawthorne could re-ask the question a loud screech came from the west. He couldn't image what new horror the Evil One had in store for them. If he could open his mouth and speak he would have ordered the army to attack, but he didn't have the heart. All that was waiting for them was death and nothing he could do would change that.

Chapter 30: Into the Nothing

Alaric opened his eyes, although he knew he wasn't really opening anything. The space around him was completely black, as he expected it to be. There would be time for change, but that would come later. It had been a long time, or at least it seemed like a long time, since he had been there. The nothingness around him felt somewhat calming' it was the first time he had felt at peace for as long as he could remember.

"Where are we?" Nyrra's voice sounded afraid. His voice resonated around Alaric. It was nowhere and everywhere at the same time.

"We are nowhere," Alaric replied, his voice calm. "And we are everywhere. This is the Nothing."

"Nothing? What are you talking about," the fear remained in his voice.

Alaric let out and audible sigh. He really thought his enemy would have known about the place they were in. On the other hand he had time to kill and there was really nothing else to do in the Nothing. Neither of them could kill each other in the Nothing, as they weren't really there. That thought made Alaric smile, or at least think he was smiling.

"This is the place where worlds wait to be born. We are on the edge of a new world. Soon there will be an intense explosion and then this space will be filled with planets, stars, moons and a myriad of creatures to roam them," Alaric explained.

Alaric could sense the panic in Nyrra, but couldn't work out why. There was nothing that could harm them in the Nothing. If nothing else, time was on their side, not that time really existed where they were.

"If there is going to be an explosion here then maybe we should leave?" Nyrra suggested.

"The Universe will come when it comes, but we are in no danger here. For now we exist outside of everything. Or you might say we don't exist at all." He added the last as a slight.

"What do you mean we don't exist?" Nyrra's voice was filled with horror.

Alaric knew he wouldn't take it so well. The big bad Evil One was acting like a scared little child. He wished he could just stay there forever and keep the Seven Kingdoms safe, but that just wasn't how things were meant to play out. Sooner or later Nyrra would work out how to leave and then they would be back to square one. There was no telling how long they would be there. Time passed differently. For every second they were in the Nothing it could be a year in the Seven Kingdoms. Alaric knew that would not be the case if he left when he was suppose to, but if they tried to stay longer there was no telling what would happen. They could even return years before they left. The thought would have made his head ache if he had a head in the Nothing.

"We are here and we are not here. We are nowhere and we are everywhere," Alaric continued. Although his words were nonsense it was the best he could explain things.

"Why have you brought us here?" Nyrra's voice sounded calmer.

That was the question Alaric had been waiting for and was surprised that it had taken so long. He had to admit the first time he had travelled to the Nothing it had taken him aback, but that was a different time and a different Nothing.

"You gave me the courtesy of offering me amnesty and I am here to do the same. Since you didn't like my first offer of the Northern Wasteland I thought I would suggest a more suitable one," Alaric started.

Nyrra started laughing. It seemed he had recovered from his initial fright. That would make it easier for Alaric. He had expected such a reaction and that was exactly what he wanted. It was much easier to control the situation if his opponent did as expected.

"Amnesty? What amnesty could you possibly offer me? I will win the final battle. It has been written and it shall be done. No! There is nothing you can offer me that will make me change my mind," Nyrra replied, confidence dripping from his words.

Again Alaric expected such a response. So far he had given nothing to Nyrra to make him change his mind. But things had only just started. Alaric had much more to offer him.

"You see, or you may not see, that we are on the edge of the birth of a new world. A world that is raw and untouched. This world will need a ruler. You could be that ruler. You could be here from the very start. No one would know any better. You could make it whatever you wanted," Alaric offered.

Alaric could sense that Nyrra was thinking over his offer. In the Nothing he could sense things much clearer. He didn't know exactly what Nyrra was thinking, but he knew exactly what he was feeling. He thought with a little more practice he could read Nyrra's mind as simply as if he had voiced it himself.

It was a good offer on face value and Nyrra had to take it seriously. In the end it was total control he wanted in the Seven Kingdoms, but starting out as supreme ruler, a God even, would be so much better. Just before he was about to agree Nyrra sensed something wasn't right. Like Alaric, Nyrra was starting to sense what Alaric was feeling and he knew the man was holding something back.

What Alaric had neglected to tell Nyrra was that there would be no sentient life forms on the new world or anywhere in the new universe. At best there would be water and plant life for Nyrra to destroy, but that would only last so long.

"What aren't you telling me?" Nyrra asked, the confidence slipping from his voice.

"There is nothing that you need to know." Alaric knew he was starting to lose him, but he wasn't going to be honest. All he needed to do was keep his concerns deep inside and not let Nyrra sense them. "This is a genuine offer. You have lived with mistrust for so long you no longer know true honesty."

Nyrra felt the tension leave. Alaric believed in his words and there could be no doubting his intention. Despite the offer Nyrra was still not sure. On face value it seemed like a great deal, but he still felt as though something was amiss. Alaric quickly picked up on his change of emotion and didn't wait for him to respond.

"If you think about it there could be no better offer. If you return to the Seven Kingdoms there is a good chance, even though you don't want to believe it, that you will fail. I am much stronger than you are now and I will not be beaten. This is your last chance."

To accentuate the threat Alaric pushed out with his anger. Whether it was true or not, Alaric needed to make Nyrra believe it. It was another nuance of the Nothing that the stronger will could prevail over a weaker one. He knew that Nyrra would never accept his offer on face value, but if he pushed his will then there was a chance he could change his mind.

Nyrra felt the pressure and strength coming from Alaric and started to think it was the right thing to do. At first he had been unsure, but that was now a distant memory. Alaric's words suddenly made sense. It would be nice to be the ruler of a new world.

Alaric felt the shift in Nyrra and pushed harder with his will. If he could convince Nyrra to stay then the final battle would be over. Before Alaric could speak again he let that thought enter his mind and suddenly it washed over Nyrra.

"You are trying to dupe me and it won't work," Nyrra said. "I don't know what you are keeping from me, but I will not stay here. It's time for you to take me back to *Crenallous*. It is there that this battle shall be decided. When that is done I might just come back here to rule this new world of yours," sarcasm returned to his voice. His confidence had returned.

"That is not possible," Alaric returned. "There is no telling what time it will be in the new world when you find a way to return. The only chance you have of being a God is if you remain here."

Nyrra thought for a moment. Again the idea sounded like something he should agree to, but then another thought entered his mind and he knew it was never an option.

Alaric cursed himself for letting his true feelings seep through. In the Nothing it didn't take much for things to change. Even as that thought passed through his mind he could feel the grip on Nyrra slipping. His enemy had regained control and he didn't think there would be anything he could do to get it back.

"I will give you one more chance to remain here. The birth of this world is moments away and I must be gone before it starts," Alaric offered.

"I will not be duped!" Nyrra's words boomed throughout the Nothing and Alaric knew it was time to leave. Nyrra was starting to gain the advantage and he knew just how dangerous that could be.

"Very well. Let the final battle truly begin."

Alaric's words were the last thing in the Nothing before life suddenly burst into being. At the centre of the new universe was a small, blue planet. Although there were no sentient life forms, as Alaric had predicted, neither was there life at the birth of the Seven Kingdoms' universe.

***

Alena looked around the cavern in shock when Alaric and Nyrra suddenly disappeared. It was not at all what she had been expecting. Although the morning was still young, she thought the battle would have already begun. Although she had no idea what was happening in Avalon, deep down she knew it was true.

Marina, who was standing a dozen paces away, had the same look of shock on her face. At first she thought Nyrra had won and he must have taken Alaric somewhere to kill him, but when he didn't return instantly she knew she was wrong. She was sure that Nyrra would have told her of his plan to leave the cavern. If she could trust no one else she could trust he whom they all called the Evil One.

It didn't take Marina long to compose herself. There were still enemies about and she didn't want them to know she was surprised. Her powers had come into their own since she had held the Sapphire stone, powers she had no idea she possessed, and she was more than capable of defending herself against Alena. It was the other two that she had to be careful of. It seemed that even Nyrra couldn't kill them and that meant they were to be feared.

"Where have they gone?" Alena finally asked, to no one in particular.

Asgard turned to Esgard and raised an eyebrow. Esgard just returned his look with a blank expression. No one was expecting the two to disappear.

"What is it?" Alena asked when there was no response. She could tell something was amiss and she didn't care if Marina heard. "You know something."

"That's just the problem," Asgard replied. "We don't know anything."

"This wasn't supposed to happen," Esgard added.

"What are you talking about?" Marina sneered. "Everything has been written, including the ending. Nyrra will be victorious and you will all die."

Asgard looked at Marina as if seeing her for the first time. At first her words upset him, as if she knew something he didn't, but then he realised she was just trying to irritate him. It was obvious that she too had no idea where they had gone.

"You are nothing but a slave to the Evil One's urges," Asgard replied. "You were once a Princess of the Seven Kingdoms, but now you are nothing but a slattern. Even if there was a chance for Nyrra to win he would not take you with him. You will die with the rest of us."

Marina started laughing. Although she doubted she was strong enough to defeat the two enigmas, she wasn't about to back down. At best she was playing for time. Nyrra would be back soon enough and all she had to do was stay alive.

In the short time she had spent with Nyrra he had helped her to unlock her powers. Most sorcerers took years of training to truly use their power, but Nyrra had shown her in less than a week. Until she knew exactly what she was up against she was going to keep things to herself. Nyrra had not told her they would be there and she doubted he knew they would be. That in itself was very disturbing. All she had been told was that she would have to kill the she-elf and that's exactly what she was going to do. She would just have to wait for the right time.

There was something about Marina that didn't sit right with Asgard. He had known her for only a short time as Bern and even then he knew there was something different about her. Without warning a burst of light shot towards Marina. Asgard had decided that it would safer to dispose of their problem than to try and fix it. There was too much at stake to take any risks.

Marina placed a magical shield up in front of her at the last moment. The light splashed into the barrier, sizzled and then disappeared. She had not been expecting an attack, but she had been prepared for one ever since they had arrived in the cavern. If she had been a moment slower the light would have completely consumed her.

It seemed as though the talking was over and it was time to attack. Marina still didn't have confidence in her abilities, but there seemed to be little choice. She knew there was no point in attacking the two unknown and she should focus all her attention on Alena. If she could distract the other two enough she might just get her chance to fulfil her side of the bargain with Nyrra.

"What are you doing?" Esgard asked, her voice filled with shock.

"She is here to kill us, what do you want me to do, sit back and let it happen?" Asgard snapped.

"It's not our place and you know that," Esgard replied with just as much venom in her voice.

Marina was busying herself making a spell when she overheard Esgard's words. At first they didn't make any sense, but she quickly understood their meaning.

"There have been many things that I thought were not our place, but I was quickly proven wrong. There is nothing about this that makes any sense," Asgard and Esgard seemed to forget about Marina as they continued their argument. "All I know is what I see before me."

"You have been with these people for too long," Esgard pushed. "They have clouded your mind. You know what we have been sent here to do so we must get on with it."

Both Alena and Marina wished they would stop being so cryptic. Neither of them knew who they really were and their words came dangerously close to revealing more than they wanted.

It was the perfect opportunity for Marina. The two mystery people were deep in conversatoin and wouldn't take any notice of her attack. Not only that, but it seemed as though Alena was so engrossed in their conversation that she didn't seem to realise Marina was even there. When Nyrra returned he would be so pleased. Her role in the final battle was also written in the *Dark Prophecy*, but the result was never told. Her victory would ensure the victory of the Great Lord.

Marina basked in the evil surrounding her as she slowly drew in the energy required for the spell. There seemed to be plenty of time and she didn't want to risk anyone knowing what she was doing. There was little doubt in her mind that a sneak attack was the only way she would succeed.

The cavern turned slightly darker, like a cloud passing over the sun, when Marina prepared to release her spell. If the others weren't so engrossed in their argument they would have known something bad was about to happen. When Marina released her spell a blue light shot out towards Alena. No one had a chance to react as the light sped towards its target.

All Alena could do was stand and watch as her doom approached. The light was half an inch from striking when it suddenly blinked out of existence. She had closed her eyes right before impact and it took her a few seconds to realise she was still alive. At first she looked towards Asgard and Esgard, but neither of them looked like they knew what had happened.

"Impossible!" Marina exclaimed.

"Did you really think I would let you kill her?" Alaric's voice came from behind. Marina spun around and all eyes moved to him.

No one had noticed his return, but they figured it had not been long. When they had overcome their initial shock they realised that Nyrra was not with him. For a moment they thought Alaric had defeated the Evil

One, but when there was a crackle of electricity and Nyrra reappeared they knew it wasn't true.

"Where have you been?" Alena gasped. She wanted to run across the cavern and embrace him, but she couldn't bring her legs to move.

"I have been fulfilling my role in the prophecy," Alaric replied.

He stood between Marina and Nyrra. It was the most precarious position for him to be in. If both Marina and Nyrra decided to attack, he would have a battle on two fronts. Despite his situation he didn't seem at all concerned and his strength helped the other three to relax, if ever so slightly.

Nyrra started laughing when he heard Alaric's comment, although there was something in his tone that made the others not quite believe in his mirth. There was no guessing where they had been, but if Alena was to have a guess she would say that Alaric had won. He seemed more confident than before and there was something nervous about the way Nyrra was standing.

"You have fulfilled nothing," Nyrra tried his best to regain his former malice, but they could still hear some uncertainty in his tone. "All you managed to do is waste time, but that is over now. It is time for the final battle to begin."

"Not yet," Alaric turned to face him. His voice was icy cold and sent shivers down everyone's spines. "The time is soon, but it is not now."

Nyrra knew Alaric was right, but that didn't make things any easier for him. When he arrived at the Cauldron Mountain he was full of confidence. There was no doubt in his mind that things would play out in his favour. In a matter of what seemed to be only minutes, but had seemed like days, things had changed. Alaric was stronger than he had had given him credit for and that in itself was dangerous. At any point in time Alaric could have killed him in the Nothing, or just simply left him there. Nyrra had no idea why he had brought him back, but he knew he had to be careful. If Alaric said it wasn't the time to attack than Nyrra would wait.

"What are you doing?" Marina hissed. "It's time to strike. Kill him, kill him now!"

Nyrra looked past Alaric and saw Marina, as if for the first time. He had brought her along to kill the she-elf and she couldn't even do that. He wondered if there was any point in keeping her around. Once he had won the final battle he didn't need her anymore and would enjoy roasting her over a hot fire, but didn't want to rush things. There were still games he had yet to play and he would need her for at least one of them.

"Be quiet now Marina," Alaric said. "I did have feelings for you once." He wasn't sure why he told her that, but he felt it was the right thing to do. "I find it hard to believe you have changed so much in such a short space of time." Although Alaric looked at Marina his senses were fixed on Nyrra. If he made any move to attack then he would know about it.

"You lost the right to tell me what to do when you betrayed me," Marina wasn't about to back down. If Nyrra wasn't going to stand up to the Cursed One then she would. The final battle was too important and she wasn't about to lose. It was the only way she would get Her back. "I will not bow down before you. I will see that you are dead before this day is out, even if he won't do it for himself."

"Mind yourself," Nyrra barked, taking his attention away from Alaric. "You are here at my bidding and can quite easily disappear."

The blood had already risen in her body and she was not going to be derided by anyone. Even though the Sapphire stone was locked safely away in Alaric's chest Marina could feel her presence. With every passing moment she could feel her connection growing stronger and she knew she had to get it back. With the stone in her possession she could destroy Alaric and Nyrra. Then she would be the rightful ruler of the Seven Kingdoms.

Her face felt flushed, but it remained its pale white colour. Alaric watched her closely and knew there was going to be an attack soon. He could feel her drawing in the evil energy which surrounded them. Although he had to be careful of Nyrra, he knew the he wouldn't attack until the time was right. No matter how much he wanted to win he had to abide by the prophecy.

Marina released the spell with all the rage she held inside her. A rush of blue light streamed towards Alaric. It's size was almost enough to completely block his view of her. Even though she was trying to kill him he had to admit he was impressed with what she had created.

Esgard looked at Asgard with an unasked question of whether they should help. The spell wasn't too complex and it would be easy enough for either of them to block it. Asgard simply shook his head. It wasn't their time to get involved. He felt that they had already revealed too much and now that Alaric had returned they had to wait.

The light shot towards Alaric, but just like the one that would have killed Alena it disappeared before striking. A gasp went around the cavern when it happened, but not because the spell had failed. No one really thought the spell would kill Alaric, but it was powerful enough that they should have been able to feel him create his defence, but there was nothing. Even Nyrra was surprised.

Alena suddenly moved into action. When Marina and the others were distracted she knew it was her time to strike.

Everyone was so focused on Alaric that no one, except Alaric himself, noticed the movement from her. Silently she drew her sword and then as swiftly as she could, moved up behind Marina. Even when the sword passed through her stomach the princess didn't realise what was happening. Never in her mind did she think that Alena would kill her and definitely not with a simple sword strike.

Slowly Marina dropped to her knees as blood spurted from the wound. As Alena withdrew her sword the look on Marina's face suddenly changed from anger to complete surprise. At no point did she think anyone would kill her, let along the she-elf. As she looked up at Alaric he thought he saw regret on her face.

If Alaric had any emotion left to give he knew he would have felt sad at her loss, but feelings were something long gone to him. All that mattered was winning the final battle and securing the safety of the Seven Kingdoms. As Marina's eyes finally closed, a feeling of relief washed over him.

"Now the final battle can begin!"

Chapter 31: Darshival Battle

Lord Richmond sat on his horse and stared out into the darkness. Before long it would be filled with soldiers and evil creatures fighting for the survival, or death, of everyone. When he first started out from Bellarome, with his life-long friend Tancred, he never really thought he would make it to the final battle. They had been part of a secret society bound to *The Prophecy of the Stone.* Although he could not be completely sure it seemed as though he was the only one left alive. He knew of no others, but it was a secret society and he didn't know everyone in the order.

He missed Tancred and wished his old friend was with him, but despite that he was proud of all he had accomplished. As much as he thought he was going to be in the Cauldron Mountain with Alaric, that wasn't the case. Although he couldn't be sure he knew Alaric had made it to the Mountain and would soon be fighting the Evil One.

Richmond took a deep breath and savoured the fresh, cool morning air. There was a soft smell of damp grass and he knew that wouldn't last long. Soon the cruel scent of death would fill the air. If things went bad then there would only be so many clean breaths he had left and he wanted to savour at least one of them.

As the light started to crest the horizon he heard the sound of footsteps approach from behind. He didn't need to turn around to know it was Ulman. The stalwart wizard had told him he would meet him on the hill when the sun rose and he wasn't a second late. He carried his large claymore in his arms, opposed to it sheathed on his back.

"Do you think the final battle is about to start?" Richmond asked when he saw the sword in the wizard's hands.

"Oh, this?" Ulman didn't even realise he had drawn it. "It's just something I do when I'm nervous." After answering he sheathed his sword. "I doubt I will get a chance to use my sword today," he sounded disappointed at the fact.

Richmond had to admit he was glad he wasn't going to be fighting. If he had to draw his sword then the battle had already been lost and it really would make no difference to the outcome. It was not through cowardice. He had dreamed of fighting in the final battle for a long time, but it was his lot to lead the Darshivallian Army. He didn't know why he had been chosen. There were many more qualified soldiers who could have lead them, but he knew it was right.

Richmond returned his gaze to the battlefield before he heard the sound of more footsteps. It was General Sorrell, the man Richmond had thought should lead the army, but it seemed the man would take the battlefield instead. In the end it would probably be better for someone of Sorrell's stature to be leading from the battlefront.

"Good morning general!" Richmond greeted him without taking his eyes from the battlefield.

"Good morning, Lord Richmond," Sorrell replied. "The army is assembled and ready for your orders, sir!"

Richmond knew the time was approaching and he needed to make a decision on how to organise the army. If he knew what the Evil One was going to throw at them, it would have made his decision much easier.

"Are you sure you don't know what evil creatures the Evil One has prepared for us?" Richmond asked Ulman again.

"For the last time," Ulman sounded annoyed "I do not know what is coming. The prophecies have never told us what would be waiting for us in Avalon." That was true despite Ulman's limited reading of them. "If I knew what was coming do you not think I would have told you already? It makes no sense for me to keep it to myself."

Richmond knew he was right, but he needed to ask the question regardless. The only option he had left was to guess what to do. If he had a better understanding of what evil creatures the Evil One had available to him, then he might have been able to plan. He had studied the creatures of legend when he was younger, but there was no way to tell what was fact and what was fiction.

"Bring the first rank of infantry and the longbowmen to the front. Have the cavalry ready next and then the last two ranks of infantry and the shortbowmen," Richmond ordered. He had no idea why he had made the decision, but it seemed as though it was the right one. He could only put it down to the prophecy telling him what to do and that made him feel better.

"Do you want me with the first line?" Sorrell asked, his voice strangely hopeful.

Richmond thought on the question. There were many great leaders in the Darshival army, but none where in the same league as General Sorrell. As much as Richmond would like him on the frontline he needed to reserve his greatest commander.

"I think it would be best if you remained with the cavalry," Richmond replied.

Sorrell saluted and returned to give the commands. If he was disappointed with Richmond's decision he didn't show it. Richmond breathed a sigh of relief. He really wasn't used to leading an army and dealing with a seasoned general like Sorrell made him nervous. His attitude made things a lot easier.

"Don't worry about him," Ulman reassured him. "He is a consummate soldier. Even if he doesn't agree with your command if you issue it he will obey it. He knows his life is nothing compared to that of the army and if you asked to storm the battlefield by himself he would do so without question or regret."

Richmond had to admit Ulman's words gave him strength. He now knew it was time to address the army. They would want to hear uplifting words from their leader.

"Today is the day of the final battle," Richmond boomed, forgetting that Ulman's spell would make his voice carry. "We are Darshivallian soldiers!" he kept his voice high and it was returned by a cheer from the crowd. "We did not come here to fail. We came here to tell the Evil One that he has no place south of the wasteland. He may think he will be victorious today, but we will show him otherwise." His words brought another cheer from the soldiers. "We will show him what it means to be... Darshivallian!" The end of his speech brought an even louder cheer. It was not the first speech he had made, but he had decided from the start to keep it short. There was no telling when Nyrra's army would arrive and he didn't want to be in the middle of his speech when they did.

When Richmond had finished his speech Sorrell returned to speak with him. "A rousing speech my lord," he congratulated. "Do you have any idea when this battle might begin?"

Richmond moved his attention back to the battlefield to see if there was any indication. What he saw were dark storm clouds gathering in the distance. He didn't think that was a good sign of things to come. It was never fun fighting a battle in the rain.

"If those clouds are anything to go by I would be guessing that things are about to start any minute now," Richmond replied.

Sorrell stared out onto the battlefield, but there was still no sign of any army. He doubted the battle would start anytime soon. "It will take a good hour if not more for the battle to start once we see the enemy on the horizon. At this rate I would be surprised if we start before the midday meal," Sorrell actually sounded disappointed.

"I don't think they will be marching to Avalon," Unwin said. "At a guess I would imagine they would be coming by gateway or some other form of magical transportation."

"What about those clouds?" Sorrell asked. The clouds had moved a lot closer. He didn't know much about magic, but he did know a lot about the weather. "They are moving at an unnatural pace."

Unwin glanced at them, more following Sorrell's hand than with any intention to examine them. When he saw the distance they had travelled, he knew something wasn't right. It only took him a moment to realise what was happening and when he did he called for a messenger. The storm clouds now covered the full length of the battlefield and it would take more strength than Ulman alone to stop it.

"Tell the other wizards that we need to stop that storm," Ulman explained. He thought of explaining what he was going to do, but he doubted the messenger would remember everything. Also he knew the others would know what to do.

As if to answer his own reasoning, another messenger replaced the one who had just left. He had the same message that he had given the others. It seemed that he wasn't the only one to come to the realisation. Ulman didn't waste any time in creating the spell to keep the storm at bay.

As soon as Ulman had created the spell Richmond felt a sudden electricity in the air. At first he thought it was the spell, not that he should have been able to feel it, that Ulman had created, but he knew he was wrong when he saw a strip of brilliant light appear on the battlefield. Before Richmond could react, the light flashed across the sky and created a massive gateway. The gateway bubbled and popped a grotesque deep red and purple. It looked like something from his worst nightmare before it slowly started to coalesce.

"I guess that answers that question," Sorrell said.

Richmond looked at his subordinate before returning his attention to the battlefield as orglin stormed through the gateway. The final battle had started at long last and suddenly Richmond wished he still had hours, if not days, to wait.

"Do you want to send in the cavalry?" Sorrell asked. "We should be able to overrun them with no problems"

Richmond waited for a moment. What Sorrell said made sense and he really should be listening to the man's advice, but something deep inside him said that it wasn't the right decision. He didn't know why, but he was sure it was the prophecy telling him what to do.

"We need to save the horses for later," Richmond explained. "Archers to the front and fire at will. Infantry get ready to charge in," he commanded.

Sorrell saluted before returning to the army. Even if he didn't agree with Richmond's command he did nothing to show it. Although he wasn't going to attack until it was time for the cavalry to move forward, he still wanted to be there to assist them.

The longbow knew the command was for them and the shortbow was to remain behind. As soon as the orglin came close, they unleashed their first volley. By the time the arrows would reach the ground the orglin would be within range. They would only get two or three shots in before the infantry would have to engage with the enemy.

Richmond watched the arrows arc in the air and held his breath. Even when he had given the order, he didn't really think the arrows would hit their target. Whoever had created the storm had a great deal of power. Richmond thought they would be more than capable of stopping them. Ulman also watched with bated breath. If there was someone to stop the arrows he knew there was nothing he could do about it. The spell he used with the other wizards to keep the storm at bay would stop him from creating another spell with any great speed.

As the arrows fell and hit their targets Richmond and Ulman let out a sigh of relief at the same time. Both men noticed what the other had done, but neither wanted to bring attention to it. They were just grateful that the orglin were starting to fall. It looked as though the final battle was starting off in their favour.

When the arrows stopped, the infantry increased their march to a run. They wanted to hit the orglin with the same force. The light armour would protect the soldiers, and although it was not as thick as some of the other armies, it would be enough to keep the orglin claws and teeth at bay.

The two armies collided with a loud bang. The orglin threw themselves against the soldiers, which in turn put all their weight behind their charge. The orglin were only concerned about death and feeding and had no thoughts for their own safety. The soldiers, in stark contrast, were concerned with both the death of the orglin and their own lives.

Once Sorrell was satisfied the infantry knew what it had to do he returned to his horse. Even though he had wanted to charge in with the first rank of infantry, he had to admit he felt much more comfortable on horseback. He knew he would have his time soon enough. For a long time he had not believed in the prophecy, but he could no longer deny it. He knew if he had taken the battlefield with the infantry then it would have meant the destruction of them all.

The infantry fought with the same ferocity as the orglin, only they were much more controlled. They used sword, shield and superior weight to their advantage. The orglin had only planned for a massacre and couldn't change their tactics when the soldiers started cutting them down.

Hope filled Richmond's heart as he watched the battle unfold. For every solider that was brought down at least another hundred orglin were slain. Even as the orglin continued to storm though the gateway, Richmond thought they would be successful and wouldn't even need to use another rank of infantry.

Richmond quickly came to realise that he was wrong as the battle wore on. The soldiers at the front of the rank who continued to push into the swarm of orglin, were starting to lose the keenness of their swords. The thick hides of the evil creatures were dulling their blades quicker than anyone had expected. Even sword against sword wouldn't blunt their steel so quickly.

He looked over to where Sorrell was seated on his horse and even from the distance he could see the concern on the general's face. If Sorrell had been in charge of the army Richmond had little doubt that he would have swapped ranks already and would have saved many lives.

"Second rank!" Richmond boomed. "Move forward. First rank start your retreat. Archers give them some cover fire!" Richmond was grateful for Ulman's spell. The speed in which he could relay messages to the front line would save many lives. Especially if he was slow in realising what to do.

The soldiers at the front of the line slowly started to move backwards. It was the command they had been waiting for, although with the intensity of the orglin advance they knew it was going to be difficult.

The archers moved forward, ready to rain down some arrows and hopefully give the soldiers a chance to retreat.

What happened next shocked everyone. As the soldiers made their way over the piles of dead, the advancing orglin suddenly stopped. They jumped on the bodies and started to feed. The sight was enough to make more than one retreating soldier lose the contents of his stomach. The archers looked around at each other, not sure exactly what to do. The feasting orglin were out of range, but they would also be sitting targets if they advanced beyond their set line.

Richmond suddenly burst out laughing as he watched the horror unfold before him. Ulman was taken aback. Mirth was not the reaction he felt was appropriate for the situation. He quickly dampened his spell before the entire army heard Richmond's boisterous laughter.

"What is so funny?" Ulman finally asked when he finished.

"Just the way things are unfolding. I though the Evil One would send a well maintained and professional army at us, but it seems as though he is just throwing out the dregs. If the other armies are having it this easy we'll be done in time for the midday meal."

Ulman sniggered softly for a moment. Despite the severity of the situation he had to admit it was funny. The moment of levity helped Ulman to relax, if only for a moment. He didn't know if he was ever going to laugh again and appreciated Richmond's candour.

"Archers!" Richmond boomed. "Move up. Second rank! Hold your line!"

There was no point with the second rank joining the battle whilst the orglin were feeding. The respite would be a greater advantage to the Darshivallian army than to the orglin. The archers would be able to kill a number of orglin whilst the second rank moved into position. Although the sight was sickening, it gave them time to ready themselves for the onslaught.

Richmond watched the feeding and wished only that they had more arrows. For every orglin that fell to an archer a dozen more piled on to try and feed. The sight was disgusting, but exhilarating at the same time. If they had more arrows Richmond thought he could end the final battle without losing another soldier's life. Soon enough the feeding frenzy would be over and the real battle would recommence.

The archers had run out of arrows well before the orglin had finished feeding. With nothing left to do they slowly made their way back to the campsite. Without any arrows there was little they could do to help. They all carried a short sword, but very few were proficient in swordsmanship. It would only be a last resort if they were sent out to fight and the battle would already be lost.

Although the soldiers didn't need the order to advance. Richmond gave it anyway. When the orglin had cleared all the dead bodies, leaving only armour and a few spare bones, the soldiers started their charge. Just like the first charge, the two armies met with a loud crash.

The orglin that had just fed were slow and sluggish to attack. After they had feasted their motivation had vanished. If it wasn't for the densely packed orglin pushing up from behind they would have turned around and made for home. Instead they were easy practice for the second rank to start their attack.

The second rank of soldiers continued where the first had left off. They slashed and hacked at the oncoming orglin and killed at will. Richmond thought the final battle would soon be over, then he looked up and saw wave after wave of orglin continue to race through the gateway. Even at the rate the soldiers were killing them they would soon be overrun.

"Is there anything you can do to close that gateway?" Richmond asked. "If we don't find a way then all is lost."

Unwin looked towards the gateway and not for the first time. The very same thought had crossed his mind, but there was no solution. If he had time to study a gateway he was sure he could find the answer, but there was no time for that. Alaric had told them and trained them to create a gateway, but he'd said nothing about closing one not of their own making. That in itself gave him hope. If he needed to close the gateway he was sure Alaric would have told them how. The final battle needed to play out the way the prophecy wanted and it seemed it didn't want the gateways closed.

"There is nothing I can do to close it, I'm sorry," Ulman replied, not wanting to go into his full reasoning. "And besides, if I close it I'm sure someone else will just reopen it."

Richmond had to admit Ulman was right. It had been a nice thought, but it would never have worked. The Evil One needed to be defeated utterly for the threat to the Seven Kingdoms to be over forever. That thought renewed his vigour.

"Third rank!" Richmond boomed. "Ready to advance."

He wasn't going to leave anything to chance. The first rank had gone to the smithies to have their swords either sharpened or replaced. He wanted them assembled and ready to march before the second rank returned

Just as Richmond was about to give the command for the third rank to relieve the second, he looked up at the gateway. For the first time he could see the ground of Avalon between the gateway and the ever storming orglin. For a moment he thought the battle was nearly over until he saw five gigantic creatures lumber through. In one hand they held a mighty cudgel and in the other a cruel whip, which they used to push the orglin forward.

"What in the name of God Kings are they?" Richmond gasped. They did look familiar, like something he had seen in a book.

"They are giants," Ulman replied with just as much awe in his voice. "I thought they were long extinct."

"Cavalry!" Richmond choked out the words. He wasn't sure what he was going to do against such massive creatures, but he figured the cavalry would be on a better standing. "Move..."

General Sorrell looked out onto the battlefield and clenched his teeth. It had been the moment he had been waiting for, but the sight of the giants did nothing for his motivation. Even on horseback he would be at least two feet shorter than them. The sudden shock of the gigantic creatures threatened his resolve, but that was quickly replaced by adrenaline and he was ready to make his charge. If it was to be his last attack he was going to make it count.

Before Richmond could finish his command a messenger came running from the transport ground. Richmond wanted to dismiss him and continue his command. The messenger couldn't have come at a worse time.

"What do you want!" he barked uncontrollably.

"General Jarwe wanted me to tell you not to send in the cavalry," the messenger started. "The giants are powerful, but slow. If you send in the cavalry they will all be crushed."

"Then we are beaten?" Richmond sounded confused.

"They are powerful, but they are also slow. You need to use your infantry. They need to use slash-and-move tactics to bring them down."

The messenger waited for Richmond to question him further, but the lord just returned his attention to the battlefield. The line of orglin was starting to thin and it wouldn't be long before they were all dead. If he didn't make a command soon the second rank would be fighting the giants with dull blades and he didn't think they would last very long.

"Cavalry, hold your ground. Third rank! To the front of the line." He then recalled the instructions relayed to him from Jarwe. All he could do was trust the general knew what he was doing.

"Jarwe is right," Ulman said when Richmond had finished. "I should have remembered this when I first saw them. Many armies have lost all their cavalry in the past fighting against giants."

Richmond couldn't take his eyes from the battlefield to acknowledge Ulman's apology. Nothing had followed the giants through the gateway and from the look of the desolation on the other side there was nothing more to follow. A slight hope filled Richmond's heart. There was a very good chance that the final battle was nearly over and there had to be enough soldiers left to kill the five giants.

Even knowing what they were faced with, the soldiers of the third rank marched onto the battlefield without a care for their own safety. They had watched the other two ranks fight bravely against the orglin and wanted their chance to fight in the final battle. As they approached the giants that all changed. From the distance they didn't look so opposing, but up close was a different matter. The creatures loomed over them with thick muscles all over their bodies. Even with the instructions from Richmond they had no idea how they were going to defeat them.

The infantry were tentative when they reached the giants. On the march they had all intentions of following Richmond's order, but it was a different story when they were standing in front of the mighty creatures. One by one the soldiers were easily crushed by the cudgels or slashed by the cruel whips. Richmond watched on in horror as no one was listening to his command. It would only be a matter of time before the giants made their way through the third rank unless something changed.

"I think you need to do something," Ulman voiced the obvious.

Richmond barked his command again and Ulman's spell carried it across the battlefield. There was no doubting his tone. He meant every word and thankfully he saw the soldiers listen to his command.

The soldiers worked in twos and threes to slash at the flanks of the giants. At first the large beasts didn't realise the change in tactics and focused on the soldiers in front of them.

Finally, after what seemed like hours to Richmond, one of the giants came crashing to the ground. Even from such a distance he could hear the loud thud. He cringed at the sound, but kept his eyes firmly fixed on the battle. As soon as the giant hit the ground a group of soldiers jumped on top of it and started stabbing with their swords. At first the blades didn't want to penetrate, but the soldiers used all their strength and they finally found their mark.

After the first giant fell it didn't take long before the others met their destiny. Too many men had lost their lives, Richmond thought, but it was done. The giants were dead and it was time to move onto the next threat.

When Richmond looked up towards the gateway it confirmed what he had seen before. Nothing had followed the giants through. It took Richmond a moment to realise what it meant and it wasn't until there was a cry of victory from the battlefield that he let himself believe.

"It's over," Richmond gasped, hardly able to speak at all. "Nothing more is coming through. It's finally over," his voice was still breathless.

"I don't think so," Ulman's voice was grave. "This was too easy. The final battle of legend would not be finished so easily."

"Easily? I'm not sure I would consider that battle to be easy. Bloody, desperate and hard fought maybe, but not easy," Richmond snapped.

"I didn't mean any offen..." before Ulman could finish there came a loud crack from the battlefield.

Even if Ulman had finished what he was about to say Richmond would not have heard it anyway. As he looked towards the gateway he saw it suddenly shatter into a million pieces before falling to the ground and disappearing. What was waiting for them on the other side sent a shiver down his spine.

Strange creatures about twice the size of the largest lizard Richmond had ever seen in books, with large bat-like wings stood before them. They had a sharp pointed tail and a serpents head with razor sharp teeth and a forked tongue.

"Dragons! Infant dragons?" He couldn't believe the words as they came out of his mouth. "I thought that were all dead except for the great black Khan himself."

"They are not dragons." For a moment Richmond was relieved. "They are wyverns," Ulman explained.

"What in the name of the Gods is a wyvern?" Richmond asked, transfixed on the new horror before him.

"They are a distant relative of the dragon. It seems that the Evil One had been hiding them in the wasteland. He is pulling out all the stops."

Richmond wanted to ask what Ulman meant by his last comment, but there were more important matters. For the moment the wyvern seemed happy to stay where they were, but that wouldn't remain for long. He had no idea what to he could do against them. The creatures had wings and could fly. Whatever he sent after them they could just fly over and attack them from behind or attack their campsite itself.

"Send in the cavalry," Ulman suggested.

"Is there any point?" Richmond asked. "Won't the wyvern just fly over them?"

"Their wings are not as strong as their larger relatives. They can fly, but not very high and not for very long. Again they can breathe fire, but nothing as hot or as far as a dragon. Don't get me wrong, they will be the toughest enemy we have ever faced, but they are still able to be killed. One thing they can do that dragon's can't is blow ice. Males blow fire and females blow ice. If you are too close when she does you will be frozen solid, but you do need to be very close."

Ulman's words did little to reassure Richmond, but there was nothing for it. If he didn't make the command soon then the third rank would soon be overrun. If he didn't think the cavalry had a chance against them, he knew the infantry had even less.

"Cavalry to the front. Archers, move in behind," Richmond thought the shortbow would be of some use when the wyvern took the skies. "Third rank start your retreat!" Richmond was grateful again for the spell that carried his voice to all the troops.

As soon as he had finished, the air was filled with hundreds of screeches from the wyvern. The sound made Richmond feel sick in the stomach and almost knocked him to the ground. The horses also reacted and whether by choice or by fear the cavalry moved into a gallop making the third rank's retreat even more dangerous. Realising their danger the field-marshals ordered the soldiers to turn and attack.

Richmond watched the infantry turn and wanted to bark his command again, but he knew they were right. Marching towards charging cavalry would kill most of them before they reached the campsite. Their only chance of survival was to turn and face the wyvern.

As soon as the soldiers had turned around, the wyvern started their advance. At first they moved on their short legs with vicious talons on the end of their feet. They started off very slowly, almost comically, but the further they moved the quicker their pace became.

Just when the soldiers were about to engage, the front rows of wyvern took to the air. The soldiers at the front of the line twisted and turned to see where they were going, causing the soldiers behind to go crashing into them. The wyvern coming through the gateway didn't take to the air. They stayed on the ground to attack the fallen soldiers.

The wyvern were airborne made for the approaching cavalry. The cavalry managed to pull their horses back to a canter and then to a walk. Sorrell was at the front of the line and doing his best to command, but he had no idea what they were up against and he had no idea how they were going to win.

The wyvern could only fly at a maximum of six feet above the heads of the cavalry. From that distance the soldiers couldn't kill them, but then the wyvern couldn't kill the soldiers either. The soldiers on horseback reined their mounts to a halt when the creatures started flying over their heads. For a moment they thought the wyvern were heading straight for the campsite, but they swooped down to attack.

As Ulman had said, the male wyvern breathed fire down towards their prey and the females blew ice. Any solider and horse caught in either were either instantly engulfed in fire or frozen to death. Sorrell regained his senses with just enough time to move out of the way from a spray of fire from above. As the beast flew past, Sorrell slashed out at the soft underbelly of the creature. To his surprise his sword passed through its skin and its gizzards fell out. The wyvern crashed to the ground, dead.

The first attack from the wyvern was deadly. Many soldiers and horses lay charred on the ground or frozen solid. Their shields were useless against the onslaught. After their first attack the wyvern landed. They neither had the strength to fly nor the fuel to breathe more fire or ice.

The wyvern were about the same size as the horses making the attack from horseback a lot easier. Sorrell didn't know how Richmond knew to leave the cavalry until the wyvern arrived, but it was a masterstroke.

General Sorrell soon learned that it wasn't going to be as easy to kill the wyvern on the ground as he had hoped. The flesh on the underbelly was very soft, but they had scale-like plate steel on their backs and up their necks. Although the creatures were slow to move their legs, their necks and tails whipped around with surprising speed. More than one horse fell to their snapping jaws.

The wyvern charged in towards the soldiers as they were picking themselves up off the ground. Before the soldiers at the front of the line could steady themselves, the wyvern were upon them. The only thing that saved most of their lives was their armour. The wyvern on the ground tried to snap the soldiers in half with their razor sharp teeth, but they weren't strong enough to penetrate the soldiers' armour.

After the initial shock the soldiers chopped down on the creatures' necks. The thick scales that protected the wyvern's backs were a lot smaller on their necks. Even so it still took two or three attempts before they could break the surface.

Sorrell hacked left and right with his sword. The wyvern snapped at him from both sides as his horse danced out of any danger. He knew if he rode a lesser horse he would already be dead. Some of the other cavalrymen were not so lucky.

By the time the shortbow archers reached the cavalry there was little they could do. The hardened scales protected the wyvern from the arrows. If they took to the air again then they could penetrate their soft underbelly, but it didn't look like they were going to. The only real place the archers could attack the wyvern was in the eyes and that would be nearly impossible in the heat of battle. They had just as much chance of hitting the horses or soldiers as they were of killing a wyvern. Without the order to retreat they would remain on the battlefield, but they made sure they were out of harm's way. If the wyvern turned on them then there wouldn't be much they could do to defend themselves.

Richmond watched both battles and although the infantry seemed to be faring better than the cavalry, he didn't think either would survive.

"Is there anything you can do to help?" Richmond asked, more hopeful than anything else.

Ulman was watching the battle closely. At first he hoped the soldiers would be able to dispatch the wyvern, but he quickly realised they couldn't. To make matters worse the storm had caught up with the battlefront. It seemed as though the spell to hold back the storm was also a losing battle. One by one he felt the other wizards let go of the spell and he knew keeping it himself would be a waste of time. As soon as he let the spell go the rain started to beat down.

"Let me see what I can do," Ulman said.

There was little room between the two combatants. Ideally Ulman would have created a spell to destroy groups of wyvern at a time, but he would also kill soldiers if he did. Individually creating spells would drain his energy even more, but there was no choice.

Sorrell found he could tempt the wyvern into snapping at his exposed legs if he kicked out. When he quickly retracted the bait he was able to chop down on the creatures' necks. The tactic seemed to be the best way to kill the wyvern and the other soldiers followed his lead.

Ulman concentrated hard as he started his spell. With the base of the spell made, he would be able to unleash his death amongst the wyvern. Dark purple bolts of electricity shot down from the sky. As soon as it touched one of the creatures it exploded into pieces. The soldiers and horses nearby were covered with blood and other body parts. What Ulman had not factored on was the hardened scales which acted as a lethal projectile. The scales killed men, horses and wyvern alike.

"Keep going," Richmond said after Ulman stopped the spell.

"What? I can't keep killing the soldiers!"

"If you don't the wyvern will win and they will all be dead soon enough. Try and focus your attacks as close to the gateway as you can. That should stem the flow of wyvern and decrease the risk to our soldiers," Richmond suggested.

Ulman silently cursed himself for not thinking of the solution first. There was still enough room between the gateway and the van to cast his spells.

With renewed vigour Ulman lashed out with his spell. The battlefield resonated with the sound of thunder as the purple lightning crackled down with lethal accuracy. With each exploding wyvern another five or six were killed from the shrapnel.

For the first time since the wyvern had taken the battlefield, Richmond dared to hope that they were going to win. Ulman's spell was killing the wyvern almost as soon as they entered through the gateway. Some were killed even before they made it through, giving relief to the soldiers at the front of the line.

Slowly the cavalry seemed to be getting the best of them. It was lucky the third rank had not made it back to the campsite. They were able to hold back the wyvern coming through the gateway. Once they were used to the battle, and with their superior numbers, they were quickly able to kill all the wyvern around them.

Soon enough the last of the winged creatures scuttled through the gateway. It was the first time since the first gateway had collapsed that Richmond actually believed they were going to win the final battle. He couldn't bring himself to dare to hope, but the thought was still in the back of his mind.

With all the nearby wyvern dead, the cavalry, still under the command of General Sorrell, moved forward to help the infantry. The soldiers on the ground had neither given ground nor gained any, but they had also not given the wyvern enough room take to the air. If they had, the soldiers would have quickly been eliminated.

Sorrell led the charge, careful to avoid trampling any of the soldiers on foot and the wyvern were quickly overrun by the double attack. Sorrell pushed forward until all the creatures were dead. When he finally looked up he was face-to-face with the gateway. On the other side was the desolation of the Northern Wasteland, but there were no more creatures waiting.

From his vantage point Richmond could also see there was nothing more on the other side of the gateway. He held his breath as he waited for the gateway to collapse. When nearly a minute had passed and the gateway remained, he let out his breath.

"I think that might be it," Richmond whispered.

To echo Richmond's words, Sorrell let out a cheer of success when he realised there was nothing more coming through. The cheers were echoed around the battlefield by the other soldiers and when the first and second rank realised what was happening they also cried out in elation.

Suddenly the rain stopped and the sun returned to the sky. At first Richmond thought it was a good sign, but when he heard a deafening crack his heart sank. Like the first gateway the second suddenly shattered into a million pieces.

What was standing on the other side almost knocked Richmond to the ground in shock. Just when he had thought the final battle was over, it seemed that worse was still yet to come. A gateway twice the size as the last one stood on the other side of the battlefield. A sea of evil creatures of which Richmond could only recognise about half, stood waiting for the order to attack.

Ulman took a step forward when he saw a lone figure standing in front of the new army. Instantly he recognised it as the Dark Knight Argoz. Although he couldn't be sure it didn't look like Argoz had been involved in creating the storm spell. If that was the case there was nothing Ulman could do. It took all his remaining strength to stay on his feet. Another spell would drain him completely before he even had a chance to cast it.

"What can we do against this?" Richmond asked.

"Pray," Ulman replied, his voice weak.

Before Richmond had a chance to say anything else there came a loud screech from the west. Whatever it was Richmond didn't think it sounded friendly. Even if the soldiers had been fresh, there was no chance they could defeat the Evil One's army. The final battle was over, and it was not going to end well for the Alliance.

Chapter 32: The Final Battle Begins

Marina lay dead on the floor. Alaric had not taken a second glance at her since Alena had killed her. He was too focused on Nyrra, as he should be. Alena, on the other hand, couldn't take her eyes from her. She knew that Alaric had had feelings for her not too long ago. Although he hadn't spoken about his time with Marina, she knew they had been close.

It wasn't the death of Marina that worried Alena. She was trying to kill them all and would have gladly done so. It was the nonchalant manner in which he had taken her death. That thought should have made her feel better, but instead it sent a shiver down her spine.

"Don't worry," the soft voice came. She had not noticed the strange couple, Asgard and Esgard, move next to her. "He knows what he's doing. We have to have faith that he will win."

Her words didn't make Alena feel any better, but there was nothing else she could do. The final battle was to be fought between Alaric and Nyrra and them alone. She hoped either Asgard or Esgard would do something to help, but she knew they could not. Whatever they were there to do it would be revealed soon enough.

If Alaric had been more focused on Marina he would have missed the look on Nyrra's face when she had died. It certainly couldn't be called sorrow or even remorse, but there had definitely been something there. Although Alaric couldn't be completely sure he thought he had just won a small battle. Whatever Nyrra had planned for Marina, he didn't think it had been achieved. That in itself was a pleasant thought.

"I must admit I didn't see that coming," Nyrra was the first to speak. His voice remained hard, yet there was an edge that didn't sound right. "Now it is time for you and me. You have delayed this long enough."

Nyrra now wore a deep red cloak with a scarlet shirt and pants. He pushed back the left side of his cloak and revealed a slender sword, similar to Alaric's elven blade, but with a nasty looking jagged edge. He tapped the hilt with his right hand, but Alaric knew that wasn't the real threat. With his left hand Nyrra reached into his right breast pocket, trying his best to avoid anyone noticing, before he retrieved the Ruby stone.

Alaric remained where he was. He looked as calm as if he was about to go for a stroll on a warm spring evening. Alena could hardly believe it. She wasn't currently the target of the Evil One and she was already shaking uncontrollably. Even if she wanted to run for her life she didn't think her legs would work. She had never been more afraid in her life and yet she felt at peace.

Slowly a large wooden chest materialised next to Alaric. It floated gently in the air next to his left hip. Everyone knew what was inside. Alaric had been finding the other six *Stones of Power* around the Seven Kingdoms.

Each stone was inset into an artefact, unlike the Ruby stone. At one point in time each of the stones had been possessed and used by one of the rulers of each of the kingdoms. Even Avalon had a ruler a long time ago.

"Choose your weapon," Nyrra sneered.

The lid of the chest swung open without Alaric touching it. Slowly the six artefacts floated, one by one. First came the Jade dagger. The stone glowed softly, if not aggressively. Next came the Sapphire ring. The stone glowed dimly as if it was in mourning. The Topaz sceptre followed shortly after. It glowed brighter than the others, as if it was excited at the prospect of things to come. The next to come was the Opal crown. The colours in the stone swirled and glowed softly and could almost be described as quiet. The Emerald bracelet followed quickly behind and the green light burned with excitement. The last to rise from the chest, and the slowest, was the Onyx necklace. It was the only stone that didn't glow at all, but instead moved until the gold chain was hanging around Alaric's neck. Once it was in place it started to pulsate gently, as if it was content.

"I should have known you would have chosen the Onyx stone to fight me with. Even so it won't do you any good. I was always much stronger than my brother of black and today will be no different." Nyrra refrained from laughing, but it was clear he wanted to.

Alaric only just heard what his opponent had said. His head was filled with persistent voices all repeating the same statement. 'Kill him! Kill him! Kill him! Kill him!'

"If you would be quiet that's exactly what I'm trying to do," Alaric spoke with his mind's voice.

The voices suddenly silenced. They had been so used to being ignored that they didn't know what to say when Alaric finally agreed with them. It was the moment they had been waiting for.

"What are you talking about?" Alaric asked when his head was quiet. "I will be using all the stones to destroy you."

Nyrra burst out laughing. "That I would like to see. Not even you have the power to use all six stones at once, but by all means I wouldn't want to stop you from killing yourself."

Esgard let out a soft gasp as the other five artefacts attached themselves to Alaric. The crown placed itself softly on his head. The dagger found a light sheath on the right of Alaric's belt with the sceptre settling on the left. The ring slid itself onto Alaric's right index finger and the bracelet onto his left wrist.

Both Esgard and Asgard had to silently agree with what Nyrra had said. They knew if anyone tried to use even two of the stones at any one time they would be consumed by their power. They couldn't believe that Alaric was going to attempt such a feat, but they had to trust that he knew what he was doing.

Nyrra couldn't believe what he was seeing. The stones would completely drain Alaric of his energy before they even started. Sweat appeared on Alaric's brow and for a moment he looked unsteady on his feet. It was something that had never been attempted before and Nyrra was more than happy that it was happening during the final battle.

"Ready when you are," Alaric said as he remained perfectly still. Throughout the entire charade he had not moved. If everyone didn't know better they would have thought someone else had placed the artefacts on him.

Nyrra wasn't sure what to do. With the display from Alaric he had expected him to attack first. He could feel the heat of the Ruby stone in his hand as its glow intensified. It could only be described as angry. If Nyrra wasn't keen to attack, the Ruby stone definitely was.

It didn't take Nyrra long to realise if he didn't attack then nothing was going to happen. He couldn't work out what Alaric was doing, but if he was happy to wait then it couldn't be a good thing.

"It is time to strike!" the voice hissed inside his mind.

Nyrra smiled. The voice was right. It was time to strike.

The cavern suddenly darkened as Nyrra prepared his attack. Still Alaric remained where he was. If it wasn't for the gentle rise and fall of his chest Alena would have thought he'd been turned into a statue. She couldn't believe that he did nothing to defend himself. She could certainly understand his attitude against Marina, but not against the Evil One himself.

Suddenly a thick beam of red light shot from Nyrra. The beam was six feet high and three feet wide. Even if it looked like Alaric was ready to leap out of the way Alena didn't think it would be possible for him to avoid the light.

The beam moved at incredible speed and yet it seemed like slow motion. The light made it a foot away from Alaric before it hit a barrier of multicoloured light. Instead of disappearing like everyone thought it would, it was suddenly blocked and it continued to push forward. As it did the intensity of the Ruby stone increased casting an eerie red glow throughout the cavern.

Strangely enough Alaric remained completely still as if he wasn't even concerned about the attack, Alena thought he should be showing signs of strain. Defending against Nyrra's attack with the aid of the Ruby stone could not be easy. Even the sweat that had appeared on his brow had disappeared. A smile crossed Alena's face as she realised it had just been a ruse to give Nyrra a false sense of confidence.

Nyrra and the stone strained to break through Alaric's defences. It was obvious by the different colours in his barrier that he was utilising all the stones in his possession. No matter what Nyrra tried there was nothing he could do to get his deadly red light through. Eventually he gave up, although the Ruby stone tried for a few more seconds before the light blinked out of existence.

"Did you really think a simple trick like that was going to be enough to kill me?" Alaric's voice was level, but everyone heard the sarcasm. "I would have thought better from the man everyone fears. If that is the best you can do then this will be all over with very soon."

Whether it was through his own rage or that of the stone Nyrra grew red in the face. It had not been an easy spell to create, but Alaric's words hit their mark. Nyrra's fury bubbled inside him and he didn't care if his next spell brought the entire mountain down on top of them.

Alaric remained calm. He knew exactly what he had done and he knew Nyrra was planning an even stronger attack. It was true that the Ruby stone had the greatest amount of power of all the stones, but Alaric knew he could harness all six in his defence. It would take a miracle for Nyrra to break through.

This time small beams of light shot at Alaric from all around the cavern. Despite the random nature of the attacks the three standing vigil did not have to move. None of the beams came close. No one knew if it was Nyrra who was focusing his attacks on Alaric or if Alaric was diverting the attacks towards himself. Either way the three were grateful for their protection.

Again the red light couldn't make it within a foot of the Chosen One. Each time it looked as though it was going to strike him, it hit a piece of coloured force field. All the time Alaric remained where he was. If he was suffering at all from the attack there was no outward sign. No matter how many beams of light or how hard Nyrra pushed them into the barrier, nothing would get through. The cavern started to tremble with the effort until he finally stopped.

Nyrra let out a deep breath before sucking in an even deeper one. It was clear that he was starting to feel the strain of the spells he had created. The Ruby stone continued to glow with an angry intensity. The six stones arrayed around Alaric remained calm in their gentle glowing.

When it was clear that Nyrra wasn't going to continue his attack, Alaric stepped forward. It was the first time he had really moved since the battle had started. Alena was the only one who noticed two distinct footprints in the stone floor from where he had been standing. It was the only indication that he had put any effort into his defence.

Alaric shook his head before he started talking. "It seems as though I will have to finish this," again there was no emotion to his tone. "I know you can attack, but let's see if you can defend."

Alaric struck out with his first attack without warning. A rock the size of Nyrra's head suddenly appeared three paces behind him. Before anyone knew what was happening, the rock hurled itself at Nyrra. Only at the last minute did it explode in a brilliant red light. If Nyrra was surprised at the attack he didn't show it. The Onyx stone shone brightly for a second before it calmed itself.

It was no surprise to Alaric that Nyrra was able to block his first attack. He was already planning his second when the rock was travelling towards its target. A funnel of water appeared in front of him, swirling with an intensity that Alena wouldn't have thought possible. Droplets of water, as sharp as razors, whipped toward the Evil One. The speed of the attack would have sliced even the fastest of opponents, but again it was stopped before it reached him. The water bounced off Nyrra without touching him, cascading to the ground in a shower of red.

That was enough for Alaric to begin with. He could see the strain on Nyrra's face. The attack had taken something from his opponent and that could only be a good thing. The battle of the stones was always going to be tough. Even working with the extra five he had no real advantage against Nyrra and the Ruby stone. Alaric remembered the last time he was in the cavern. He had been chosen to destroy the Ruby stone, not that he thought it was actually possible. If that had been the case, and he had been successful, then the final battle would already be over.

"It is time to destroy him!" the voice came inside Nyrra's head, dripping with malice.

"He is stronger than I thought," Nyrra responded. "I don't know what you want me to do."

"I have been with him before. He is not that strong," the voice was filled with contempt.

"That was a long time ago. He has changed. We need to be careful."

"He has grown strong? More like you have grown weak. If you don't have the power to defeat him then give me control."

Nyrra's mind voice went silent. He wanted to think on the offer, but he knew the voice in his head would know exactly what he was thinking. There was nothing for it. He knew he couldn't defeat Alaric. The man had grown much stronger than he had thought, but Nyrra wasn't going to concede the final battle. He was prophesised to win and that's exactly what he was going to do.

"Very well, do what you have to," Nyrra conceded.

Nyrra felt himself fade into the back of his mind. His initial reaction was to fight the feeling, but he knew he had no choice. It would be a struggle to regain control of his body, but it was a risk he was willing to take. If he didn't then he was dead anyway, so he had nothing to lose. All he could do was remain in the back of his mind and watch the final battle through someone else's eyes.

As soon as the Ruby stone had taken control of Nyrra's body he was surrounded by a soft red glow. Only Alaric truly understood what was happening. Ever since he had started gathering the stones they had all tried to gain control of him. On certain occasions he had almost given in, but he knew once he did he would never get it back. He also knew that Nyrra had to be desperate to give control to the Ruby stone.

"I didn't think this day would come," the words came from Nyrra, but the voice was not his. There was a subtle echo in the words and the voice was deeper."Now it is time for you to pay."

The stones around Alaric intensified their glow at the sound of the Ruby stone and the voices inside his head started again. After seeing the Ruby stone take control of Nyrra they all wanted control of Alaric. They all claimed they could help him win, but Alaric pushed them aside. He needed their help, but not their control.

"I was wondering who I would actually be fighting. Throughout all the prophecies and all the information I've been able to gather that is the one answer I was unable to find."

"What is he talking about?" Alena dared to ask the question.

Suddenly it dawned on Asgard what was happening. At first he had thought Nyrra was about to unleash a spell that would bring the mountain top down upon them, but after Alaric's words he knew what was happening. It had been the moment he had been waiting for. It was the reason why he and Esgard had come to be.

"This is it!" he said, as if Esgard had not already realised.

"What is it?" Alena asked.

"I think you should go to the back of the cavern," Esgard warned. "You don't want to get in the way."

Alena had no idea what she was talking about, but the tone in her voice forced Alena into action. She was surprised that her legs even worked as she slowly backed away from the battle.

"There is nothing my brothers and sisters can do to save you. This was always my world and it was only a matter of time before I returned to claim it. Now that I have control of this body and the power within, there is nothing that can stop me."

Alaric remained calm. As much as he didn't know exactly what was about to happen he did have an indication. He couldn't plan for every eventuality, but he had narrowed them down to the most likely. The Ruby stone taking over Nyrra's body had been one of them.

"Let's see what you can do, that he couldn't!"

The Ruby stone didn't waste any more time with inane banter. Its first attack looked similar to those from Nyrra, but the beam of light was opaque and not translucent. A cylinder of red light, six inches in diameter and three feet long, shot towards Alaric. Like with all the other attacks it stopped a foot before reaching him. This time it was stopped by a light green screen. When the cylinder struck the barrier it made the sound like a thunderclap which resonated around the cavern. Alaric was pushed backwards a couple of inches by the force of the impact.

The red light tried in vain to push through the barrier and as it did, splinters of red fell to the floor. With each passing moment the green barrier started to shrink. As it did, the glow of the Emerald stone started to lose its intensity. It was obvious tht if the barrier disappeared before the cylinder of red then Alaric would be consumed.

"Now?" asked Esgard.

"Not yet," replied Asgard.

Alena could hardly watch as the cylinder and the barrier diminished at the same time. At the rate they were both deteriorating she had no idea which was going to disappear first. Sweat appeared on Alaric's brow and this time it wasn't for show. Even with the aid of the Emerald stone the strain was becoming apparent. Just when she thought Alaric had the better of Nyrra it seemed as though the tables had turned.

"Now!" Asgard's voice was firm.

Alena wasn't sure what they were planning on doing, but the tone in Asgard's voice made her feel better. Even though the battle between the red light and the green barrier wasn't over both lights suddenly disappeared. The look on Nyrra's face showed that he wasn't expecting such a result. The emerald stone stopped glowing and lost all of its colour. It looked nothing more than a small crystal.

As Alena watched Nyrra she saw a figure appear behind him against the wall of the cavern. It glowed a soft green and looked to be the shape of a woman. As much as she wanted to ask what it was she didn't want to distract anyone, or draw attention to herself. The final battle was in full swing and she was quite happy to stand back and watch.

The Ruby stone, using Nyrra's body, looked around the cavern in contempt. He had not finished his attack and wondered who had stopped it. He saw Asgard and Esgard, but didn't seem to recognise who they were.

Despite the failure of the first attack he readied his second and another red cylinder of light shot out. This one was only five inches in diameter, but still three feet long. Deep crimson ripples pulsated along its outside as it shot towards Alaric. Just like the first cylinder it was stopped by a sudden barrier, this time a deep blue. The Sapphire stone in the ring on Alaric's finger intensified its glow.

This time the cylinder became narrow instead of shorter as it tried to drill its way through the blue barrier. Sparks of red light fell to the floor as the Ruby stone tried its best to break through. The strain was even more evident on Alaric's face as he tried to hold the Ruby stone at bay. The one true advantage he had over Nyrra was that he was still in control. The Ruby stone would burn Nyrra's body out if it thought he had a chance to finish off Alaric.

Alena couldn't be sure, but it looked as though the sapphire barrier was fading quicker than the emerald had. The first battle had seemed so close until it finished. Alena was worried that this time the Ruby stone was going to win.

Just as it looked as though the barrier was about to collapse on itself, both it and the cylinder disappeared. Alena let out a breath of relief when she realised that Alaric had not been struck.

A blue figure, that also looked to be female, appeared behind Nyrra. Again the stone didn't seem to notice what had happened. Deep inside his mind Nyrra knew something was wrong. The Ruby stone was too focused on trying to kill Alaric that it wasn't truly aware of its surroundings. He tried to call out, but the stone wasn't listening. It was too busy preparing its next attack.

It didn't take long for Ruby to fire another red cylinder at Alaric. As with the last attack it was slightly narrower, but this time it was also slightly shorter. Alena thought it was a sign that Nyrra was losing his strength. She had not worked out that the Ruby stone had taken control and thought Nyrra was the one doing the fighting.

The cylinder was stopped by another green force field, this one a little darker in shade than the first. The Jade stone, inset in the dagger, shone brighter than it ever had. The strain was again evident on Alaric's face. What Alena had not noticed was the soft glow of the Topaz stone in-between attacks, healing Alaric of his stress.

Alena was sure the red light was whittling away the green barrier quicker than it had the blue one before it. She wished there was something she could do to help, but she knew that was impossible. If she came close to the battle then Nyrra would kill her, there was no doubt in her mind. She had to wonder why she was even there. She had done nothing and was just a liability.

Except for the red glow, Alena thought Nyrra looked as calm and as fresh as when the battle started. At the start it looked like Alaric was beating Nyrra, but now it seemed it was the other way around. She didn't know how much longer he could keep defending.

Like the first two attacks, the third ended just before the cylinder of light managed to penetrate the barrier. Again Alena let out a deep breath of relief. For the moment they were all still alive. It couldn't be much longer before the final battle was over. All she could do was hope that Alaric knew what he was doing. Only three stones remained with any colour left in them.

Another female figure in green appeared behind Nyrra. If the Ruby stone had been paying more attention it would have noticed, but the next attack came almost as soon as the last one had finished. The red cylinder of light was again slightly narrower and slightly shorter than the last one. Just before the light hit Alaric it stuck a light blue barricade with swirling colours.

This time Alena knew the light would destroy the barrier before it was destroyed itself. She had no idea what had stopped the other attacks, but if it didn't work again then Alaric would be hit. She didn't know if the light would kill him outright, but it wouldn't do him any good.

Alaric's legs started to shake as he strained to keep the barrier up. Even with the help of the Opal stone it was still a demanding effort. He didn't need to hold out for much longer. Everything was going to plan, but he wasn't sure he was going to make it. Each time the Topaz stone healed him the end result became less and less. He had hardly started the battle again when he thought he was about to collapse.

Just before the barrier was about to disappear from the attack both it and the cylinder of light vanished again. Sweat poured down Alena's face with the stress. Each time Nyrra attacked, she thought it would be the final one. She had no idea what was happening, but she was thankful he was still alive. She could only hope that Alaric was about the go on the attack as another figure, this time male, appeared beside the others. It was a light blue colour with swirls of green, red, yellow, orange and purple throughout. The colour in the Opal stone faded away until only a simple clear crystal remained.

For a moment Alaric thought he was going to drop to his knees, but the Topaz stone shone again and filled him with strength. He knew time was running short and he steeled himself for the next attack.

The cylinder was shorter and narrower yet again and yet it had lost none of its potency. Before it could strike, a yellow barrier was created. Alaric seemed to strengthen his stance with the appearance of the new barrier and the Topaz stone glowed brighter than all the others before it. Not only was it controlling the barrier it was also healing Alaric of his strains.

With the added pressure of healing Alaric the Topaz stone wasn't able to assist as much with the barrier. The direct result was that it diminished much quicker than the others. The cylinder, despite being half the size of the original, was quickly eating away at the yellow barrier. There was no chance it would hold up against the burrowing light. Just as Alena thought Alaric was about to be left open to attack, the barrier and the light blinked out of existence.

The Ruby stone, through Nyrra, let out a scream of anguish. It had thrown everything at Alaric and the man was still alive. It could feel the body of Nyrra tiring, but he knew he had one more attack left in him. If he burnt out the body in destroying the enemy then that would be an acceptable risk.

Nyrra's voice in the depth of his own mind screamed. He knew something was wrong and not just that his body was fading. Alaric was doing something, or something was being done for him. He could sense something behind them, but he couldn't see through his own eyes. Regardless of what he could or couldn't see he knew something was wrong and he needed the Ruby stone to listen to him. His yells fell on deaf ears. The Ruby stone was in a rage and could only focus on killing Alaric.

Alaric panted for breath. The Topaz stone was gone and all that remained at the top of the sceptre was a plain crystal. There was nothing left to ease him of his pain. The only stone left in its original state was the Onyx stone hanging around his neck. The stone pulsated softly, waiting for instructions.

The attack came again without warning. The ruby red cylinder was now only an inch in diameter and three feet in length. It shot towards Alaric like a bolt from a crossbow. At the last moment another barrier, this time as black as pitch, appeared in front of Alaric.

"Now!" Esgard said.

"What?" Asgard replied. "Do you know what will happen?"

"You know it is meant to be. We always knew this is the way things had to end, it's just that we didn't want to believe it."

Asgard knew she was right, but that didn't make it any easier on him. He had shared the body of Alaric's best friend and he still held onto some of those emotions. Despite his feelings he knew Esgard was right and there was no time to second guess her.

Alena let out a scream, the first sound she had made since the battle had started, when the deep black barrier suddenly disappeared. For the first time the cylinder didn't disappear with the barrier and Alaric was left defenceless. For a moment it was suspended in time, but then it shot through Alaric's stomach, disappearing upon exiting. Alaric dropped to his knees.

The entire cavern went silent before a burst of laughter came from the Ruby stone. "It's over. I've won." The voices of Ruby and Nyrra spoke at the same time.

Chapter 33: Castalia Battle

Captain Elyas stood at the front of the army and stared out into the darkness. Despite his protests, he had been told to move into position. The place where he stood was where he was to command the army. He didn't have a problem with commanding them, the problem was that the rest of the army had not arrived. Minerva had transported the dwarven army to the battlefield, but since then there had been no sign of her. Hulkan had told him he thought there was some kind of trouble, but when Elyas pushed him for more information he couldn't provide any. Without the full army Elyas didn't think they would last long against the Evil One. He wanted to wait until Minerva arrived, but he had been forced into position.

There was nothing else he could do. His heart was filled with terror. There was no telling when the final battle was going to begin and if the rest of the army wasn't there they would surely fail. He couldn't understand what had gone wrong. As far as he knew the High Chancellor was supporting the final battle and that should have been enough. There was no reason why the rest of the Castalial army shouldn't been in Avalon like all the others.

Elyas had managed to split his soldiers into two ranks, although they were not full ranks. There were another four ranks due to pass through a gateway with Minerva, along with two more ranks of archers, one long and one short. Unlike the other kingdoms, Castalia didn't have any cavalry. Some of their commanders rode horses, but that was it.

Even without horses their superior numbers made them the greatest force in the Alliance and that was why they had been chosen to take the centre position. Although they didn't know what the Evil One was going to throw at them, they all agreed that the middle was the key point of the battle. That would have all been well and good if the entire army was there and not still in Castalia.

As the grey of dawn gave a dull light Elyas heard the sounds of footsteps behind him. For a moment he thought it was Minerva and he couldn't bring himself to turn around. Deep down he knew it was one of his sub-commanders looking for instruction.

"General Elyas!" Elyas recognised the voice of Corporal Horace.

He didn't think he would ever get used to being called general. He had been a captain for as long as he could remember and was quite happy with his lot in life. Everyone had decided if he was going to be leading the army then he should be a general. It made perfect sense, despite his objections. Elyas still felt he could be an effective leader with captain as his title, but they had all disagreed. In the end there was nothing he could do except to accept the promotion.

"How are the soldiers, corporal?" Elyas asked without taking his eyes from the battlefield.

"Nervous to say the least," Horace replied. "Have you heard any news on the rest of the army?"

"Nothing," Elyas replied. "We have to trust that Minerva knows what she's doing and will be here in time." His words were more to reassure himself than Horace.

"Maybe if you gave some orders that might reassure them?"

Elyas had no doubts that would reassure his soldiers, but he had no idea what orders to give. No one had told him what they would be up against, which made it impossible to plan their own attack. He didn't know what he could say that would appease the worried soldiers, but Horace was right, he had to do something.

"Have the first rank line up ready to march. Keep the second rank close. If, or should I say when, Minerva arrives with the rest of the army we can move the second rank straight into battle." Elyas was happy with his command. If Minerva didn't show up then it wouldn't matter what he said, they would soon all be dead.

"Very good sir, I will see it done," Horace saluted before leaving.

Elyas felt a little better with Horace's reaction to his order. He didn't know if it was the right choice, but there seemed little else he could do. Until Minerva arrived his choices were limited. He let out a sigh and then looked around quickly to see if anyone had heard it, but everyone else was busy and no one nearby.

When the army had moved into place Elyas knew it was time to address them. It had been agreed that all the leaders should make a rousing speech to the soldiers before the final battle began.

The speeches would be made shortly after sunrise to ensure there would be time before the Evil One's army arrived. Elyas didn't need to look to the east to know the sun had already crested the horizon.

Elyas turned around and made his way to the small platform that had been erected in front of the army. In the end it wasn't really necessary, but when they made it they assumed the entire army would be present.

Unlike the other six leaders Elyas didn't have anyone to help project his voice throughout the army. Luckily there were only two ranks present and most of the soldiers would be able to hear him.

"Soldiers of Castalia!" Elyas started his speech and the soldiers were suddenly silenced. "There is a reason why we have been placed in the middle of the Alliance and it's not because of our superior numbers... It's because of our superior skill in battle!" A raucous cheer came from the soldiers. "The Evil One will be here soon and he will expect us to run in fear, but we will not do that." A resounding 'no' was shouted back at him.

"The Evil One will be expecting an easy battle, but that will not be the case." The soldiers barked back another 'no'.

"We are here to fight for all the Seven Kingdoms and everyone who lives within. Are we going to let the Evil One win and subjugate us all?" An even louder 'no' was heard.

"Then we will stand and fight and at the end of this day we shall be victorious." Another cheer came from the soldiers. "Whatever the Evil One throws at us we will stand strong. We fight for all that is good and we shall not fail!" The end of his speech brought an even louder cheer as he made his way down from the platform. He had done all that he could to raise the spirits of the army. Only time would tell if his words were true.

As he looked back out over the battlefield he noticed dark storm clouds in the distance. Although they were far away, he didn't think it boded well for the battle. Fighting in the rain was bad enough, but it looked as though there was a torrential storm on its way. He wished there was a way to stop it, but there was nothing he could do.

Before he had a chance to look around he heard the voice of a messenger, which made him jump.

"General, where is Minerva?" the messenger sounded confused.

"She has not arrived yet!" Elyas sounded annoyed.

"When will she be here?"

"We haven't heard from her. Is there something I can help you with? I don't know if you realise, but the final battle is about to start and I need to concentrate."

"Ah, yes, sorry. When Minerva gets here General Jarwe said that the approaching storm isn't natural. She will need to add her strength to the spell the other wizards are about to create."

Elyas nodded his acceptance and then waved the messenger away. There was nothing else he could do. He needed to focus on what was ahead, not that he knew what that was.

Suddenly the hair stood up on the back of his neck. A sudden electricity filled the air and he knew it wasn't from the coming storm. Something was about to happen. Deep down, one way or another, he knew the final battle was about to start.

Elyas watched the battlefield closely as a strip of light appeared in the distance. Before he had a chance react, it ripped across the sky creating the largest gateway he had ever seen. It spanned further than the width of the army and it was clear the Evil One was expecting the full Castalial army. If the Evil One's army came through the entire gateway there was a good chance Elyas' soldiers would be outflanked if he only sent in the first rank. His heart sank. It seemed they had already lost and the battle had yet to begin.

A sea of orglin rushed through the gateway. There was no more time to think. The new general had to make his first real decision.

"First rank!" he boomed at the top of his voice. "Charge!"

As soon as they heard the command the soldiers rushed into action. They could see the orglin racing towards them and they knew exactly what they had to do. Elyas could only hope the soldiers could protect their flanks and prevent the orglin from getting past.

The two armies crashed together in a miasma of carnage. It didn't take long for Elyas to realise that the oncoming orglin had no intention of trying to use the flanks to bypass the first rank of soldiers. The evil creatures were bent on destruction and just wanted to attack.

Horace made sure he was in the first rank of soldiers to storm the battlefield. He had no intention of waiting back with the other commanders. The first rank needed a battlefield commander and he had taken the job. The final battle was about to start and he wasn't going to be left behind. He charged out at the front of the army. If he was going to die then it would be at the head of the battle.

As the battle continued Elyas relaxed a little. The soldiers were having a relatively easy time with the orglin, but he knew it wouldn't last long. Castalia would soon have issues with their swords becoming dull. Unlike some of the other commanders, Elyas could see it coming. He had studied the Evil One's armies as a cadet and remembered the issues they'd had in the past fighting orglin.

The only problem was that he had a serious lack of numbers. It was not a problem Elyas thought he would have. They were positioned in the middle of the army due to their size, but without the rest of his ranks he commanded the least. It would only be a matter of time before the orglin overran them, but until then Elyas was not about to give in.

"Second rank!" Elyas boomed. "Ready to march." Before he could give them the command, he needed a flag bearer to relay his orders. Elyas was the only commander who had kept his flag bearers in the army. Without the aid of magic he would need to use semaphore to relay his commands.

"Order the first rank to start their retreat and allow the second rank room to pass by."

The messenger left quickly to relay the information to the flag bearers. As soon as the message reached the soldiers Horace called for a slow retreat. His sword was covered in thick, oily, black blood making each orglin harder and harder to kill. He made sure he was at the front of the line as the soldiers started to make their way back to the campsite.

As he backed through the sea of dead bodies, the approaching orglin stopped their advance and started feasting on the dead. At first he was sickened, but when he realised they were no longer being pursued, he was able to relax slightly. The feeding orglin were actually going to give them a chance to retreat. Normally retreating was the most dangerous part of a pitched battle, but this time there would be no casualties.

The second rank moved up past the first, but under Horace's command they didn't engage the creatures. Elyas would have made the command himself, but there was no semaphore signing for 'hold back until the enemy has finished feeding'. There was no point in engaging the orglin whilst they were busy feeding and anything that gave Minerva more time was a good thing.

Elyas had no preconceptions that they could defeat the Evil One with just two ranks. Even at the rate the orglin were diminishing it still looked as though they would have enough to defeat the soldiers. By the time the second rank's swords had dulled sufficiently to call a retreat, not even half the first rank's swords would be sharpened. Even with the spare swords not all the soldiers could return to the battlefield.

Elyas could hardly believe what he was seeing. The orglin piled on top of each other to get to the juicy meat below. Flesh and bones flew in the air and armour was tossed aside so they could get to the meaty goodness inside. If he was somewhere else he would have let the contents of his stomach fly from his mouth, but that wouldn't set a good example for the rest of the army.

After what seemed like hours, the orglin had finished their gorging and the battle recommenced. "Charge!" Elyas shouted, but no one heard him, not that they needed to. When the orglin started moving forward so did the soldiers and the battle continued with the same ferocity as when it had started.

"Have you heard anything from Minerva?" Elyas jumped as the voice of Horace came from behind.

"Sorry, corporal I didn't hear you approach," Elyas said, not taking his eyes from the carnage.

Horace repeated his question without acknowledging his apology. There was little time for formalities.

"There has been no sign of Minerva. I fear that if she arrives now it may already be too late. The second rank can only last for so long before it needs to return."

"Don't give up hope general," Horace tried to reassure him. "The soldiers will be ready to march back on the battlefield when the second rank needs reinforcing. With a little luck the orglin will stop to feed again."

There seemed no reason why they wouldn't. The evil creatures seemed more concerned with feeding than with fighting. All they wanted to do was try and tear into the flesh of the soldiers. As much as their teeth and claws were razor sharp they weren't strong enough to pierce the tempered steel armour. Only a stray claw through the facial gap in their helmets or an attack to arms or legs would bring them down.

"I'm sure you will know if and when they arrive," Elyas returned. "There is not much more we can do until then. Ready yourself for your next attack and pray that Minerva doesn't take much longer."

Horace saluted Elyas, even though his back was to him, before returning to the army. He had to admit that Elyas was right. If Minerva didn't arrive soon then all would be lost. If one army failed then the entire Alliance would fail. Of all the armies comprised of the Alliance he would have thought that Castalia have been the strongest.

Horace did his best to reassemble the first rank of soldiers. With some still changing swords and some waiting in the smithies it was a difficult task. Regardless of how many men he had he would be ready to march when the time came. Nothing would stop the enemy from advancing, except stopping to feed, and that was exactly what they had to do. To the last man Horace would push forward.

"Messenger!" Elyas called.

A messenger ran up from the transport ground. Originally they had been designed to relay messages throughout the seven armies, but since Minerva had not arrived Elyas needed to use them for himself.

"Tell Horace to lead his soldiers onto the battlefield to help the second rank."

"But..."

"There is no time. Tell the remaining soldiers to stay in the camp, for now," Elyas barked his command.

The messenger didn't understand the order, but he knew better than to question him twice. He had been a messenger long enough to know that he didn't need to understand the reasoning. As soon as he was sure Elyas was finished he raced off to relay the message.

When the runner was gone Elyas put his right hand up to his head. He heard the words coming from his mouth, but he had no idea where they had come from. His head swam and for a moment and he thought he was going to faint. When his senses returned he thought about rescinding the order, but the soldiers had already started moving into action. For whatever reason he had made the command he could only hope it was the right one.

Before Elyas had a chance to make any further decisions he heard the sound of footsteps approach. The sound was a surprise and he spun around quickly. At first he thought it was a messenger, but when he saw who it was he instantly dropped to his knees.

"Arise general, this is no time for prostration."

"Yes, your holiness," Elyas rose to his feet, but he still kept his head down.

"This is the final battle, there is no need for this. Simply call me Tiberius," the High Chancellor's voice was level.

"Of course, but what are you doing here?" Elyas asked.

"A very good question, but one for another time. For now I am here to take control of the army."

"I shall return to the army then and take the battlefield?"

"Not just yet. You're going to want to see this," Tiberius smiled.

Elyas looked out onto the battlefield. The soldiers available from the first rank had met up with the second. For the first time the army looked like a complete unit, but that wasn't going to last for much longer. Their swords would soon dull and the orglin would overrun them. Elyas didn't know what he was thinking when he sent in the soldiers from the first rank. All he had accomplished was sealing their fate.

"Soldiers, start your retreat!" Tiberius kept his voice level, but it still managed to carry to all to soldiers on the battlefield.

Horace, when he had a moment spare, looked around in shock. He had no idea where the command had come from and no idea what its maker was planning. There were no soldiers to replace the ones fighting. They would have a small respite when the orglin fed, but then they would be overrun. There would be nothing they could do to keep the creatures out of their camp. Despite his concerns he did as commanded and started the retreat.

Like the first retreat the orglin stopped to feast and didn't bother chasing down the fleeing soldiers. If they had they might have been ready for what was to come. As the soldiers were half way back to the campsite a gateway opened. Soldiers poured through onto the battlefield and charged towards the feeding orglin. The returning soldiers were so surprised they stopped where they were and some nearly turned and ran. When they realised it was a friendly army coming to relieve them they continued their retreat.

A full rank of soldiers raced through the gateway from Castalia onto the battlefield. When the last of the soldiers passed through, the gateway disappeared. The next shock was what was behind the gateway. Another full rank of soldiers stood ready to march.

"Move up!" Tiberius commanded.

Elyas had no idea what had just happened. His head was swimming. All of sudden they had been about to be overrun by orglin and then the tide of the battle had changed. The soldiers charging forward didn't wait for the orglin to finish feeding. The evil creatures at the front of the battle were taken by surprise and were killed instantly. It wasn't until all the feeding orglin were dead before the battle truly recommenced.

Suddenly Elyas realised there was something else standing with them. He had heard no footsteps and even the presence seemed to have arrived out of nowhere. When he saw it was Minerva and not the Evil One himself he visibly relaxed

"Thank the Gods you have arrived," Elyas said, taking his eyes from the battlefield for the first time.

"I am sorry I am late, but it was necessary. It seems the prophecy works in mysterious ways. I would say that I arrived just in time," Minerva replied.

Elyas shook away her casual response and asked the question he had been asking himself all morning. "What took you so long? All the others arrived either yesterday or throughout the night?"

"There will be time for stories later," Minerva brushed aside the question with the skill of a master wizard. "By the looks of things that storm is not natural. I think my brothers and sisters could use some assistance in holding it at bay."

As much as Elyas wanted answers he had to admit that Minerva was right. There would be time for answers after the final battle was over. If they lost then it really wouldn't matter and Minerva could take her secret to the grave.

"What do you want me to do?" Elyas asked. Since the High Chancellor had taken over command of the army he wasn't sure what he should do.

"For the moment you can stay there," Minerva replied. "There will be time for you to join the army shortly."

Again Elyas wanted to ask what her words meant, but he knew he wouldn't get a response. He doubted he would ever get an answer. He just had to trust that she knew what she was talking about. He had to admit that he always knew he would take part in the battle but he knew the time was not yet right.

With the arrival of the third and fourth rank of soldiers the battle certainly looked more manageable. Even with the orglin still coming through the gateway he thought they would easily win. There were still three more ranks of soldiers waiting in Castalia and Minerva just had to move them across to Avalon.

After what seemed like a lifetime Tiberius called the third rank to retreat and the fourth to relieve it. Again the orglin stopped to feed on the ever growing pile of dead bodies. There were a lot more orglin than men, but the dead concerned Elyas. There seemed to be a never ending supply of orglin and even at their rate of death they would still outlast the army.

After the third and fourth rank had swapped over, Minerva created a gateway to send the soldiers of the third rank behind the campsite. They would also need to use the smithy before they were ready to fight again and she didn't want them getting mixed up. When that gateway was gone Elyas saw that Minerva had brought across the fifth rank of soldiers. It was all starting to make sense to him, but he was still concerned with the never ending supply of evil.

"Is there anything else you can do about that gateway?" Elyas asked. "We have been fighting for hours and the flow of orglin hasn't faltered."

Minerva looked at the gateway and simply shook her head. There was nothing she could do to close it and she needed to conserve her strength. She didn't know what was still to come, but she had a feeling she would be needed again before it was over.

Elyas opened his mouth to speak, but Tiberius spoke first. "There is nothing we can do to close the gateway. Even if it was possible I'm sure whoever opened it in the first place would just do so again." The High Chancellor's words made sense, but they still did little to appease the newly made general.

At first he didn't want to relinquish control of the army, but as the minutes passed he wanted nothing more than to join the soldiers on the battlefield. Standing and watching had become too frustrating, but he still knew the time wasn't right.

"There!" The High Chancellor pointed to the gateway. "The orglin have stopped and we still have two more ranks of soldiers waiting in Castalia. The final battle is about to conclude."

"Don't be so sure," Minerva warned.

"What in the name of the God Kings are those?" Elyas asked with awe as a dozen gigantic creatures ambled after the orglin.

Like the giants on the other battlefields the ones approaching carried a cudgel in one hand and a cruel leather whip in the other. They lashed out at any orglin that didn't want to rush forward. The twelve giants had managed to whip the entire army of orglin into a frenzy.

"They are giants," Minerva spoke with a sombre tone that didn't nothing to reassure Elyas. "I would never have thought I would see one again," she almost sounded excited.

"I think you might want to ready the fifth rank," Elyas suggested as Tiberius stared blankly at the new arrivals.

"Ah, yes, of course," he stumbled back to reality. "Fifth rank! Start your approach."

The fifth rank started to march onto the battlefield. Since Tiberius hadn't called for the fourth rank to retreat they knew to contain their advance. That last thing they wanted to do was reach the battlefront before the leading rank was ready to leave. They could also see the giants coming up from behind and were in no hurry to engage them.

"What are we going to do against them?" Tiberius asked. Even at the distance he could see that they would be too large for a man to fight. He didn't even think a group of men would be able to bring them down.

Before Minerva had a chance to answer a messenger ran up from the transport ground. "There is a message from General Jarwe." He didn't wait to be asked to speak. "The giants are mighty creatures, but they are slow. You need to use slash and run tactics to bring them down. Don't try and fight them head on." The messenger didn't wait for a response before returning to the others.

When the fourth rank was almost finished with the orglin Tiberius called for their retreat. He also relayed the information from Jarwe to the soldiers. Elyas was glad Minerva had arrived. The spell she used had definitely revolutionised the battle.

Despite the new information on how to fight the giants it was a different story when they were face to face. The first soldiers were smashed by the cudgels or slashed by the whips. It wasn't until the soldiers started to work together before they looked like they could possibly bring one down.

The soldiers in front of the giants, mainly there as a distraction, were in the most danger. Those running in, slashing at the legs and then quickly moving out again were only getting killed from glancing blows. It was more bad luck than anything else.

Elyas could hardly watch the battle. Even with the soldiers slashing at the giants' legs it didn't look like they were going to be brought down. The thick skin of the giants was harder to penetrate than that of the orglin, but eventually one dropped to its knees. Blood spurted from a gash on the back of its leg. The giant dropped his whip to steady itself, but it was still able to swing out with its cudgel. It managed to kill another three soldiers before it was finally brought down and killed.

After the death of the first giant the others slowly started to drop. Although Elyas estimated the giants had caused more fatalities that the orglin, there were still plenty of soldiers left alive. All in all the final battle had not been as bad as Elyas had thought.

When the last of the giants fell a cheer of victory arose from the soldiers. It was only at that point did Elyas realise nothing more was coming through the gateway. His heart lifted as he felt the final battle might be over, but deep down he knew that wasn't true. He still had a part to play on the battlefield.

"We've done it!" the High Chancellor cried out. "It's over!"

"Not yet," echoed Minerva and Elyas at the same time.

Before Tiberius had a chance to ask what they meant a loud crack resonated around the battlefield. The soldiers were suddenly silenced by the sound and all eyes turned towards the gateway. Slowly cracks appeared in its surface until it shattered into a million pieces. The shards of gateway splintered on the ground before disappearing altogether.

Like the other six armies, the Castalial solders saw an even more terrifying army on the other side, standing in front of an even larger gateway.

"What in the name of God Kings created those," Tiberius gasped.

Elyas looked out in horror. What stood in front of them was a mass of giant spiders and scorpions. It was like something out of a nightmare and Elyas had to pinch himself to make sure he wasn't dreaming. When he realised he wasn't, his heart raced even faster. Despite his fear he knew it was time for him to join the battlefield.

"I will take my leave," Elyas said. "I will take the lead of the next rank, but I ask one favour."

"What is that?" Tiberius raised an eyebrow at the question.

"As soon as we take the battlefield send in the last rank. We will need all our soldiers to defeat these creatures."

Elyas didn't wait for a response from the High Chancellor. He knew, deep down, even if he hadn't said anything Tiberius would have sent them in. He would need every fresh soldier if he was going to defeat Nyrra's army.

Tiberius looked at Minerva, but she was too busy concentrating on the storm. The clouds had rolled ever closer to the battlefront and she knew it wouldn't be much longer before there was nothing she could do to hold it at bay.

As soon as Elyas left to join the rank, there came a sickening screech from the battlefield. The giant spiders and scorpions began their advance. At first the soldiers didn't know what to do. The shock of the new arrivals had them stunned, but only for a moment. Even without command the soldiers pushed forward.

The two armies hit each other with a yell from one side and a screech from the other. Unlike the orglin the spiders and scorpions were able to penetrate the soldiers' armour. The spiders had sharp fangs that could pierce through the metal and inject a lethal dose of venom. The scorpions had a razor sharp tail and vice like pincers that could not only penetrate the armour, but could also cut the soldiers in two. The soldiers fought hard, but for every evil creature they felled at least a dozen soldiers lay dead. Not only that but the storm clouds had reached them and the rain started to fall.

The High Chancellor waited for Elyas to settle himself at the fore of the next rank before he give the command for the fifth rank to retreat and the sixth to charge forward. By the time Elyas made the battlefield, half the soldiers from the fifth rank had been slain, either by the giants or their new enemy.

"Bring on the last rank," Tiberius said to Minerva.

Minerva only just heard the words as she could feel the other wizards releasing their spells to hold back to storm. There was nothing she could do by herself and slowly she did the same. When the spell had been released she opened the gateway to Castalia and allowed the last rank of soldiers to join the battlefield.

With the extra soldiers Elyas stormed the battlefield. He instructed three soldiers to fight, with two in reserve if one fell. The system seemed to be working and slowly the spiders and the scorpions began to fall, but like the orglin their numbers didn't seem to diminish as more and more came running through the gateway.

"Is there anything you can do to help?" Tiberius was almost too afraid to ask the question.

Minerva had been watching the battle closely. The spiders and the scorpions fought with a ferocity that Minerva had not thought possible. The soldiers fought valiantly, but they were no match for their enemy. The spiders' bodies resembled that of a small horse and their legs made them able to stand over the men. The scorpions were just as large, if not larger. If Minerva didn't do something to help then she was afraid the soldiers would eventually be defeated.

"Just give me some room," Minerva said as she threw her arms out in front of herself.

Tiberius felt the air around him whirl as Minerva prepared her spell. The hairs on the back of his arms stood on end and he felt a tingle in the back of his neck. He knew whatever she was preparing was very powerful.

The ground rumbled as Minerva released her spell. The air behind the main battlefront swirled around until a waterspout appeared from the ground to the sky. Minerva was using the storm against the enemy. More waterspouts picked up spiders and scorpions and tossed them into the air. The droplets of rain, whipped into a frenzy, were as sharp as razors and ripped through the unfortunate creatures.

Elyas battled in the midst of the action. Working in groups seemed to be the best way to take down the creatures. One would do their best to avoid getting killed whilst the other two would try and hack the legs off, one at time. The spiders were easier to take down whereas the scorpions could use their tails to attack those on its flanks.

With the attacks from front and behind, it looked as though the battle had turned. The waterspouts relieved the soldiers as only half the enemy could get through from the gateway. With the battlefield thinning out of enemies, Elyas found they could fight in fours and fives, giving them a greater chance of survival.

Slowly the numbers of arachnids on the battlefield started to dwindle. As Minerva let her spell go they could see that there was a decent gap between the back of the arachnids and the gateway. It seemed as though they had managed to survive the onslaught. With nothing more coming through, the final battle would soon be over.

Elyas' intensity didn't stop until he turned around and realised there were no more creatures for him to kill. When he looked towards the gateway he saw that there was nothing more coming through. Suddenly the storm clouds parted and the sun shone down. Finally Elyas let out a cheer of success that was quickly echoed around him.

"That's it!" Tiberius couldn't believe the words as they left his mouth. "We've done it. The final battle is over."

Minerva was about to add her voice to the celebrations when a sudden feeling of horror came over her. She couldn't place what it meant, but she knew the final battle wasn't over. Whatever the Evil One had waiting for them, it sent shivers down her spine.

It didn't take long before another deafening crack could be heard from the battlefield. Slowly at first the gateway started to crack before it shattered to the ground before disappearing altogether.

What was standing on the other side was nothing at all what Minerva had been expecting. She knew when she heard the crack there would be another army waiting for them, but the mass of evil creatures was unfathomable. If they thought they had already fought the bulk of Nyrra's army they were all sadly mistaken.

Amongst the sea of orglin were all the other creatures the seven armies had battled. There were golems, basilisks, giants, giant spiders and scorpions by the dozens. It was the army they were expecting to face at the start of the battle, not the end. No matter what they did there was little chance they would survive what could only be called a massacre.

"What are we going to do against that?" Tiberius asked.

"Fight!" was all Minerva could respond.

Before Tiberius could give the order to attack there came a loud screech from the west. He didn't know what beast could make such a noise, but he didn't think it sounded friendly. For right or for wrong the final battle was about to end and Tiberius didn't think he would be around to see the day out.

Chapter 34: The Final Battle is Over

Jarwe stood atop the raised platform that had been built for him to watch and command all the armies of the Alliance. It stood only four paces high and was positioned behind the Castalial campsite. Under normal circumstances he wouldn't have been able to see anything, but the wizards had created a way for him to see all seven armies whenever he wanted.

The sun had yet to rise and even with the torches around him he couldn't see anything. There were seven plates of glass, two feet high by four feet wide, laid out in front of him. Each piece of glass showed him a view of each of the individual battlefields.

When he had first heard of the trick he didn't believe it would work, but after they showed him, he was convinced. The glass had been prepared before they had left Remidia, but would not work until they were put in place the day before. When Jarwe stood atop the platform and looked into the glasses he could see the empty battlefields. It was the most amazing thing he had ever seen and wished he'd had such a tool in other battles he had commanded.

As the sun started to crest the horizon Jarwe heard the sound of footsteps coming up the platform stairs behind him. He didn't need to look around to know it was Sorrell's advisor Wojtek. As much as he wanted to help his general it had been decided that he was best suited to remain with Jarwe.

"Have you eaten anything general?" Wojtek asked.

"I don't think I will be eating until the battle is over, or at least once we have won the final battle. If we lose then I doubt I will be overly concerned with food," Jarwe replied.

"Be that as it may there is no telling how long it will take before the final battle starts and I notice you didn't eat anything for the evening meal," Wojtek pushed.

Jarwe turned around and saw a platter of food in Wojtek's arms. It was filled with breads, cheeses and dried meats and he had to admit it did look appetising. He had not been hungry before he could see and smell the food. It was typical for Jarwe not to eat before a battle, but it seemed as though he was about to break tradition.

"I will eat something if you would join me. I believe that you have also not eaten for some time," Jarwe returned.

There was a small table and chairs at the back of the platform. Originally it had been designed to hold any war plans, but since they had no idea what they were up against it was not required. In the end it was perfect for them to share their morning meal.

Wojtek didn't feel like eating, but after his speech towards Jarwe he didn't think he could refuse. The two men sat down to eat as if they were in peacetime. Jarwe had to admit he was grateful for the distraction. Until the final battle there was little he could do. All the commanders were in place and there was nothing else he could do to help them.

"What do you think the Evil One will throw at us?" Wojtek asked, making casual conversation as they ate.

"I'm sure we will see his orglin," Jarwe said as he wiped the corner of his mouth. "They do seem to be his wretched creature of choice. Outside of that I have no idea."

"Do you think we can win?" it was the question Wojtek truly wanted to ask.

"Of course we can," Jarwe sounded surprised. "If we didn't believe that then what are we even doing here. Now I admit that we are against the wall and the odds are against us, but I won't admit that to anyone but you. I have to have faith that we are doing the right thing and we can succeed."

Wojtek simply nodded his agreement, although he didn't really look like he believed it. Of course he wouldn't mention his concerns to anyone else. Morale was a big part of any army and he wouldn't do anything to jeopardise it. He would only reveal his true fears to Jarwe.

"Don't fear my friend," Jarwe continued. "I didn't travel this far just to lose. At the end of the day we shall be victorious."

Strangely enough Jarwe's words seemed to reassure his new advisor. It never ceased to amaze Wojtek how easily Jarwe could settle his nerves. There could be no doubt that he was a great man and deserved the right to lead the Alliance into the final battle.

"What do you want me to do?" Wojtek asked.

"You can stay here and keep me company," Jarwe smiled. "I don't want to be living through the final battle by myself."

Although it had never been discussed, Wojtek had assumed that would be the case since he hadn't been assimilated into the Darshivallian army. As much as he would have liked to be with Sorrell he knew his place was with Jarwe.

Suddenly Jarwe looked up from where he was seated as if someone had said his name. Wojtek looked around nervously but couldn't locate what had caused his reaction. At first he was worried, but as Jarwe slowly stood and walked to his viewing glasses his nerves settled.

"Has it started?" Wojtek asked excitedly as he rose himself.

"Not yet," Jarwe looked up at the sky as he spoke. "There is something wrong though," he mused as he watched the dark storm clouds in the distance. "I don't think those clouds are natural."

"How can you tell? They look fine to me."

"They are moving too fast," Jarwe's tone was suddenly filled with panic. "Get me seven messengers."

Wojtek recognised the tone in his voice. Whatever Jarwe had seen it needed to be relayed to the commanders on the battlefield. He returned shortly after with seven messengers from the transport ground, set up not too far behind the platform.

"That storm is not natural. It is speeding towards us brought on by the Evil One, or some of his agents. We need to impede its progress. Tell the seven wizards that they must pool their resources and keep it at bay. Now go!"

The messengers didn't need to be told twice. They heard the urgency in their general's voice and raced off to relay his commands to the others.

"This is it!" Jarwe stated. "The final battle is about to begin."

It wasn't long after his words before the glasses laid out in front of him became a hive of activity. Wojtek left him for a moment to see if there was anything to report from the messengers. There was little he could do to help and Jarwe was focused on the ensuing battles in front of him.

When Wojtek returned he had a grave expression on his face. If Jarwe could pull his eyes away from the panels he would have known instantly that something was wrong. At first Wojtek didn't know if he should interrupt the general, but then he decided the information was too important to wait.

"I'm sorry to interrupt you, but we have some disturbing news." He paused for a moment, but when it was clear Jarwe wasn't going to acknowledge him he continued. "Minerva has not arrived from Castalia. She brought the dwarven army yesterday, but has not been heard from since. The Castalial army only has two ranks of soldiers."

"That makes more sense. It looked as though they were light on men," Jarwe didn't sound concerned.

"I thought you would be more worried," Wojtek wasn't going to let it pass.

"And what would you have me do?" Jarwe kept his eyes on the glass.

Wojtek opened his mouth, but then stopped. Jarwe was right. There was nothing they could do. It was too late to divert soldiers from one of the other armies and it would only prove to weaken the flanks. The only way to see what was happening in Castalia was to pull one of the other wizards away from the battlefield and that could be just as destructive. Wojtek remembered one of his first lessons as a child. 'Don't try and change what you cannot hope to fix.'

"I guess you're right," Wojtek replied, almost too softly for Jarwe to hear.

Jarwe ignored the comment and returned to watching the battles take place. Wojtek moved up beside his commander so he could also witness them. Even from as far away from the battlefield as they were, Wojtek thought he could smell the blood of the dead and dying soldiers.

The battles continued until finally the flow of orglin stopped. What followed made Wojtek feel weak at the knees. He could only hope that the glass screens were distorting the image, but he knew that wasn't the case. He was also unprepared for what the soldiers were about to face once the orglin had all been destroyed.

"They are giants," Jarwe said, as much for his own benefit as anyone else. He needed to say it aloud for himself to believe what his eyes clearly saw.

"What? I thought they had been extinct for over a century."

"We all did, but it seems that isn't the case," Jarwe replied. As well as seeing the battlefield, Jarwe had the chance to listen to what the different commanders were saying. When he heard some of the orders he realised the mistake some were making. "I need the messengers again."

Wojtek jumped into action. He didn't know what Jarwe was thinking, but it didn't really matter. If he needed the messengers than that's what he would get.

With all seven messengers lined up, Jarwe finally took his eyes from the looking glasses. "Let the seven commanders know that they need to send in more infantry to attack the giants. If they use cavalry then they will lose more soldiers than necessary. They need to use slash and run tactics to bring down the giants. Only when they are on the ground will they be able to be killed." Jarwe almost felt sad with his command. The giants had once been peaceful creatures roaming the Seven Kingdoms before their lives were twisted by the Evil One. He didn't think they deserved to be completely eliminated, but it seemed they had no other option.

Jarwe quickly returned to his screens to make sure his orders had been obeyed. There was little doubt anyone would go against him. Soldiers were still dying, but he knew his tactics would keep that number to a minimum.

When all the giants had fallen a cheer resonated around the seven battlefields. The soldiers thought the battle was over and for a moment Wojtek felt the same, but Jarwe didn't change his countenance. As much as he hoped the final battle was over, he knew there was more to come. All he could do was wait for the Evil One to reveal his next trick.

Almost as one the gateways in front of the cheering soldiers let out a loud crack and then shattered to the ground. Wojtek jumped at the sudden noise, but Jarwe didn't seem at all perturbed.

When Wojtek contained himself and returned his gaze to the glasses he couldn't believe what he saw. An entirely new army appeared on all seven screens. It seemed that the orglin was just a teaser for the main event.

"How are we going to survive this?" Wojtek sounded defeated. If it was up to him, and it was an option then he would have conceded defeat and surrendered.

"We have good men in charge and we still have the wizards. All we can do now is watch and wait," Jarwe replied. His voice was as stalwart as ever.

Jarwe was right. There was little they could do. What he had already done might have been enough to save the final battle, but only time would tell. It was up to the soldiers to do the rest.

Wojtek could hardly watch, but he couldn't take his eyes from the screens as the men and evil creatures were slaughtered. It was the most gruesome battle he had ever seen, even the most gruesome of all time. It was the final battle and a battle of such magnitude deserved no other title. Finally when the fighting was over he couldn't believe it was the Alliance that still stood.

"Is that it?" he could hardly bring the words to leave his mouth.

"I don't know. It might be," Jarwe hoped although he knew there was still more to come.

Before long the gateways came crumbling down again revealing a new horror. Jarwe looked from one screen to the next and saw a Dark Knight standing in front of each army. Finally it sunk in that this was truly the Evil One's army. Everything else had just been to test the resolve of the Alliance, only Jarwe didn't think the soldiers had much left in them. They had fought bravely, but they could not possibly surmount the odds stacked against them. Before Jarwe could truly give up he heard a loud screech from the west.

"What is this new hell?" Wojtek gasped.

"This is either our salvation or our doom, only time will tell!"

***

The black barrier disappeared and the cylinder of light passed through Alaric's stomach. Alena let out a scream of horror as Alaric sunk to his knees. Blood trickled from his wound and pooled onto the ground around him. Alena couldn't believe it, the Evil One had won. She wanted to run to his side, but her legs wouldn't move, no matter how hard she tried.

The glowing figure of Nyrra and the Ruby stone couldn't believe what they saw. Even though they were trying to kill Alaric they never truly believed it would happen. A sickly laugh came out of Nyrra's throat as the Ruby stone controlled body took a step forward.

Before it could take another step closer Esgard and Asgard moved between them. The Ruby stone looked upon them through Nyrra's eyes as if seeing them for the first time. For a moment he didn't realise who they were, but the recognition crossed its face.

"So you are here?" Ruby asked.

"It was foretold. This is why we came into being and this is what we were destined to do," Esgard said.

"And you have failed. How long have you waited for this moment and you have failed." An evil grin crossed Nyrra's face.

"Turn around and tell us that was have failed," Asgard said.

The evil grin quickly dropped from his face. For the first time Ruby felt the presence of the six figures standing behind him. The last thing he wanted to do was turn around, but he knew he had no choice. Staying where he was would do nothing to aid his cause.

"No, it cannot be," Nyrra's voice was strained.

"It is time for you to come home, brother," the words were echoed by six strange voices.

Nyrra's body tried to move away from the figures, but his feet were rooted to the floor. No matter what Ruby did he couldn't move the body. It could hear Nyrra whimpering somewhere in the corner of his mind, but that was the least of his concerns.

"What are you doing?" Ruby's voice came from Nyrra.

"It is time. We have been gone for too long. We can't be complete without you brother," all six voices spoke as one.

"No!" Ruby cried out. "I am not done here. This is my world. I will stay and rule it."

"It is time," this time Asgard spoke. "You have all been here too long. It is time for you to go home now. Stop fighting. There is nothing you can do to stay."

A red figure started being pulled from Nyrra's body. It was clear that it still wanted to stay, but the force was too strong. Nyrra stumbled forward as the red figure was pulled out and positioned with the other six.

Nyrra's consciousness rushed back to the fore and he collapsed to the ground. The Ruby stone hadn't drained him completely, but it would take time before he could even stand again. All he could do was breathe and look out at the scene before him.

Alaric was on his knees, holding onto his stomach trying desperately to keep the blood from pouring out. Suddenly the memory of the battle returned to Nyrra. He had won. The last attack had hit its mark and Alaric was soon to die. The final battle was over and he had won. It took a great effort, but a smile crossed his face.

"I wouldn't be so sure if I was you," Asgard looked down over Nyrra and smiled an evil smile. "It is all over for you Nyrra. Your reign of terror is at an end."

"I know you now, you and your partner. I know you can't kill me and your saviour is nearly dead. I might be exhausted now, but soon enough

I will regain my strength. When that is done I will bring a nightmare down on your Seven Kingdoms, no matter what happens in Avalon," Nyrra coughed and laughed in unison.

"You are forgetting one person," Esgard couldn't hide her grin.

Alena stumbled forward as her legs suddenly worked again. Her first reaction was to rush to Alaric's side, but something stopped her. Deep down she knew there was something else she needed to do. Despite the scene in front her she knew the final battle was not yet over.

"You asked why you were here," Esgard spoke to Alena. "This is why. You must kill Nyrra and end this."

Alena fingered the hilt of her sword. She had almost forgotten it was there, but now it felt as heavy as a rock. She didn't think she had the strength to draw it, but she knew it was silliness.

"What can I do?" Alena asked. "I am not strong enough to kill the Evil One."

It was a legitimate response, but it was the only option they had. Normally they would agree with her, but in his current state a newborn baby could best him for strength.

"If ever you were to trust anyone now is the time," Asgard spoke gently. "This is why you were brought here. This is your part to play in the final battle."

Alena knew he was right. She had questioned why Alaric had brought her to the Cauldron Mountain and she could not dispute the answer. If it was her job to finish the final battle, kill Nyrra and save the Seven Kingdoms, then that's what she would do.

As she walked across to where Nyrra lay it felt as though her legs were working for the first time. Despite the assurance the danger was over she could still feel her nerves were on edge. She thought at any moment Nyrra was going to jump to his feet. The closer she came, the slower she moved until she was finally standing over him.

Alena couldn't believe she was there. It was Alaric's job to kill Nyrra not hers. When she drew her blade the sound of steel sliding across its scabbard echoed around the cavern. As she raised the blade above her head she jumped and squeaked as something gripped her ankle.

"Think about what you are doing," Nyrra's voice was weak. Sweat poured down his pale face with the strain of keeping his grip. "Your saviour is dying and there is no saving him. You will be left alone. We were always supposed to end up together. Search deep inside yourself and you will know it to be true."

"What about Marina?" Nyrra's touch made her skin crawl, but she still couldn't bring herself to kill him.

"She was nothing. She was never anything. She was a means to an end. It had always been you."

"Don't listen to him," Esgard warned.

"He is just playing for time. Every moment that passes he gains more energy," Asgard added.

Alena knew they were right. Before Nyrra had a chance to speak again she brought her sword down, point first, into his chest. Blood spurted from the wound and then his mouth. Under normal circumstances Nyrra would have been able to heal himself before any lasting damage was done, but in his weakened state there was nothing he could do. He coughed once, spitting blood on the ground, as he felt the life force draining from him.

With the last life left in him Nyrra looked past Alena to where Alaric was still on his knees. His face had turned pale and sweat poured down his body. It would only be a matter of minutes before he died. For a moment hope filled his heart. If Alaric was going to die then he had to live. The final battle needed a victor and if it wasn't going to be Alaric then it had to be him. That was the last thought that ran through his mind.

Alena released her sword and stumbled backwards. It was finally over. The Seven Kingdoms were finally safe. Relief washed over her and nearly knocked her from her feet before she remembered Alaric. She composed herself and rushed to his side.

"Alaric!" Tears rolled down her cheek.

"It's finally over," his voice was calm. "Don't cry!" Alaric brushed away the tears from Alena's cheeks, leaving smears of blood instead. It was the first time for a long time he had shown her any affection and it made the tears flow even faster.

"You're going to be alright? Nyrra is dead!" Alena sobbed.

"My time is done," Alaric replied, taking Alena in his arms.

"No, you can't die," Alena was openly crying now. "I love you. We were supposed to leave here together. That was what I was fighting for."

"My job was to see the Seven Kingdoms safe from the Evil One and that is what I've done. There is no place for me here anymore. Deep down I always knew that I was never leaving this mountain," Alaric explained.

Alena looked up at his face. The sweat had gone and the colour had returned. For a moment she thought he was getting better, but then she realised the end was all the sooner. Without thinking she reached up and kissed his lips. She drew away sharply when she realised that he was already dead.

"Did it have to be this way?" Asgard asked no one in particular.

"You know it could have ended no other way," Esgard replied.

Asgard knew she was right. Although they had no idea before the battle finished, when it was over it all made sense. He turned his attention to the seven glowing figures at the far side of the room and instantly dropped to one knee.

"Arise!" the yellow figure said as it stepped forward. "You have served us well. It now time for us to leave."

Asgard stood and looked up at the figures. One by one they slowly disappeared. The sight made both Asgard and Esgard smile. It had been a long time coming, but they had finally finished their tasks.

"Who or what were they?" Alena asked. She had stopped crying, but looked as though she could start again at any moment. She let Alaric's body rest on the ground and stood.

"They are the seven God Kings," Asgard said.

"What?" Alena sounded shocked. "How can that be possible?"

It was the seven wizards, who were servants to the God Kings, who created the stones. They looked then like they do now," Asgard pointed to the dead body of Alaric and the simple crystals which now lay scattered around him. "It was those wizards who used the stones to imprison the God Kings and thus imbibing them with their power."

Alena couldn't believe what she was hearing.

"So where do you two come into it?" she asked.

"We are the followers of the God Kings, some might call us demi-gods, but I really don't like that term. We are who we are and nothing else," Asgard continued.

It didn't really give Alena much information, but she seemed satisfied with the answer.

"So what do we do now?"

"It's time to go. We will take you back to Avalon and then our time here is truly over," Esgard said.

"What about Alaric?" She couldn't bring herself to look down at him. If she did she would break out crying again.

"He has already left," Asgard replied.

Alena looked down and all that remained were the seven clear, crystal stones. She had no idea what had happened to Alaric, but she could only hope he was at peace. Whatever had changed in him to make him so hard had seemingly disappeared with his impending doom.

"What about these?" Alena pointed at the stones.

"I think we should do what Alaric originally came here to do. Toss them into the fire and be done with them," Asgard suggested. "And then we shall leave."

At first Alena didn't want to touch them, but when she did she realised they had lost all their power. To look at them they were just innate stones, but they still had the power to trap the God Kings again if they fell into the wrong hands.

Alena slowly walked to the crack in the middle of the floor with the stones in her arms. For a moment she wasn't sure it was the right thing to do as she stared into the fiery pit. Taking a deep breath she dropped the stones into the fire below.

"It's time to go!" Esgard said as the mountain started to rumble and the three disappeared.

***

The screech caused everyone on the southern end of the battlefield to stop and stare to the west. Nyrra's army didn't seem concerned with the sudden noise, but they made no move to attack. Jarwe first looked to the west, but then returned to his magical screens. All seven panels moved their views to the western side of the battlefield. Whatever new horror was coming was going to affect what happened next.

As Jarwe stared into the screen a huge winged animal appeared. He had seen such creatures in books when he was younger, but he never thought he would live to see a dragon in real life. A figure sat on the gigantic creature's back as it flew towards the battlefield.

All the soldiers stood and watched the sky. Until they were given instructions on what to do they weren't going anywhere. The new army was too great for them to surmount and they could only hope the approaching creature was coming to help and not hinder them.

With a loud whoop of its wings the dragon swooped down to attack. One more shriek indicated its intention. Jarwe held his breath as he waited to see what would come.

A stream of fire exhaled from the dragon's mouth. Only the soldiers on the battlefield could truly see its intended victims. Jarwe let his breath out when he saw the first of the Dark Knights being consumed in flame. There was no time for any reaction. Even as the dragon swept across the front of the Evil One's army none of the Dark Knights could avoid their utter destruction. With the end of the Dark Knights the gateway simply blinked out of existence.

Jarwe couldn't believe what he saw happen next. Without their masters to keep them under control, the sea of creatures suddenly turned on themselves. A spray of orglin flew into the air as one of the giants swung its mighty cudgel. A screech came from one of the wyvern as it snapped at a giant spider. Golems and minotaurs swung mighty arms at each other. It was complete mayhem.

The soldiers didn't know what to think as they watched the Evil One's army implode. There didn't seem to be any reason to remain on the battlefield, but they would not return to the campsite before they were ordered to.

All the commanders and wizards watched on in shock as Khan and his rider swooped in for another attack. The fire burned through the evil creatures with impunity. Even the stone golems could not resist the flames. In all their wildest dreams they couldn't imagine such a result. If things didn't change, the final battle would be over, for real.

"Have the soldiers return to camp," Jarwe said to Wojtek as he watched the carnage on screen. "It looks like the creatures are too busy killing each other than attacking us. I think out part in the final battle is over."

As much as Wojtek wanted to watch the battle he did what Jarwe requested. It did seem as though things were over and the soldiers were no longer needed. The last thing he saw before he left the platform was Khan doing another sweep across the opposing army. If the creatures didn't kill themselves it seemed Khan would do the job for them.

The battle was more ferociously fought than any of the pitched battles with the Alliance. Jarwe still couldn't believe what he was watching. Even with Khan scorching rows upon rows of the vile creatures, he still thought if they turned on the Alliance they would have the numbers to win. That could happen at any moment, but as the battle continued it seemed as though it wouldn't be the case. They had no intention of storming across the battlefield and fighting.

In less than an hour the Alliance had gone from certain destruction to absolute victory as Khan made his last swoop over the enemy. When he finished at the western end of the battlefield no more of Nyrra's evil creatures remained. Even their carcases had been completely incinerated. If it wasn't for the scorched earth and the Alliance Army to the south, no one would have known the final battle had been fought in that field in Avalon.

Silence passed over battlefield and encampments. On face value it seemed as though the final battle was over, but they had been there twice already. No one had the heart to even breathe the words.

"The war is over!" Jarwe called out and his voice carried throughout the battlefield.

Not only was the final battle over, but the war with Evil One's minions was complete. Everyone suddenly looked to the west as they heard a loud explosion. The top of the Cauldron Mountain flew into the air amidst fire and lava. It was a sign that the battle between Alaric and Nyrra was also complete.

Chapter 35: A Deep Breath

Jarwe stood in the middle of the battlefield with the seven commanders and seven wizards. They stood on a patch grass that had somehow missed being scorched by Khan. The dragon had disappeared to the west, but they all knew he would return. No one had spoken once they all arrived. There was only one question they all wanted to ask, but no one could bring themselves to ask it. It was Jarwe who broke the silence.

"Do you think Alaric has defeated the Evil One?" he asked everyone.

"I hope so," Eldred was the first to reply.

"I think so," Minerva said.

"I agree, I think we would know if he has lost," Gwydion added his voice.

Jarwe smiled and nodded. He had to believe they were right. It could not have ended like it did if Alaric's had lost. If Nyrra was the victor then they would all be dead. He couldn't imagine Nyrra would have let his entire army be destroyed in such a manner.

A great beating of wings broke Jarwe's reverie. Everyone looked to the west and saw Khan approaching. From the distance no one had been able to recognise the figure on his back, but as the great dragon approached they could see it was a serpentant. It wasn't until Khan landed did they recognise Viper.

"Greetings to you all," Viper spoke when he was standing on the ground. Khan turned away, obviously not interested in the conversation. There was a smug expression on Viper's face. When no one returned his greeting he continued. "I would have thought a thank you was in order."

"What are you doing here?" Eldred finally asked.

"I told you I was on your side. It's quite sad that you never believed me."

"What about the others?" Eldred had had the most contact with Viper and everyone seemed happy to let him do the talking.

"Do you think Khan would have come if they weren't on board? It took all seven of us to convince the last of the great dragons to join us and on your side. He was quite happy to see you all destroyed, but in the end we convinced him of the right decision." Viper stopped and looked around. "I see there is someone missing. Where is Alaric?"

"We haven't seen him since he left for *Crenallous*. We have no idea what happened," Eldred replied.

"I think we can all agree that Nyrra is dead," Viper sounded pleased with his revelation. "If he was alive then he would be here by now. The mountain has exploded and that signals the end."

"Then by that theory shouldn't Alaric be here?" Hadar asked, not liking the flow of information.

"My daughter was with them as well," Orric said, his voice thick with concern.

"Speculation is going to get us nowhere," Gwydion spoke calmly. "We need to focus on what we can do."

They all knew he was right. There were only enough supplies to keep the army fed for another day at most. With the final battle and their new mode of transportation they hadn't brought many supplies with them.

"I guess it's time to start moving back to our own kingdoms," Hawthorne suggested.

The seven wizards all looked at each other with exasperated expressions on their faces. It had been a long few days and they were all exhausted. Some of them were surprised they were still standing. They wouldn't be able to create another gateway until they had all eaten and rested.

"I think we shall plan on leaving in the morning," Ulman's gruff voice belied his fatigue. "I don't think we'll be much good to anyone before them."

"Of course, I should have thought..." Hawthorne back peddled.

"It's alright. It's been a long couple of days for all of us. I think you all need to get your soldiers to make camp. We will leave in the morning," Althea offered.

"What are you going to do?" Eldred asked Viper.

"We are going to continue the search for our queen. With Nyrra dead there is nothing holding us back. We believe she is trapped somewhere in the Northern Wasteland. It can be the only place," Viper explained. "Khan will be coming with us."

The great dragon turned around at the mention of his name. "There is nothing left for me here," his voice was a deep rumble. "I will leave your Seven Kingdoms and look for a comfortable place to live out my life."

Their words brought a feeling of relief amongst the group. As much as Viper and Khan had helped them in the final battle they all know just how evil they could both be. If the serpentants and the last of great dragons were to leave, then the Seven Kingdoms would be much safer.

"I guess we'll be off then," Viper said when it was clear the conversation was over. "The next time we meet I will be leading an army across the border with the queen by my side." Viper winked at the group before mounting Khan and flying away.

The beating of the great beasts wings nearly knocked some of them off their feet. No one knew what to make of Viper's veiled threat, whether it was serious or a joke. Even if the wizards were strong enough to cast a spell there was little they could do against Khan. They might have been able to kill Viper, but that would have been the last thing they would do and it wasn't worth the risk. If the serpentants returned one day they would just have to be ready.

***

Alena wiped a tear from her eye as the three of them suddenly appeared in the main campsite of the Alliance. She still couldn't believe what she had witnessed. The Evil One was dead, but so was Alaric. The final battle was over, but it should not have ended in such a way. In none of the prophecies was it ever told that they would both die.

"Where are the others?" Alena asked.

Before anyone could answer they heard the beating wings of Khan as he flew overhead before turning to the north. Alena didn't think that was a good sign. The dragon had always been renowned for following Nyrra. She couldn't imagine what it was doing on the battlefield or why it was seemingly leaving. It was just one more reason why she needed to speak with the others.

"They are returning from the battlefield. They will be gathering in the command tent before returning to their own armies. In the morning they will leave for their respective homes," Asgard said.

"Then let's go. There's no point staying here. I am sure the command tent is being filled with food and drink. I don't know about you, but I am ravenous," Alena took a step forward, but stopped again when the other two didn't move.

"This is the end of the line for us. Our job here is done and it is time for us to move on," Esgard almost sounded sad.

"Yes, it is a glorious day. The Evil One is dead and the God Kings are free. There is nothing left for us here," Asgard almost sounded happy.

"Where will you go?" Alena sounded shocked.

"I don't know," Asgard replied.

"Wherever the wind takes us I guess," Esgard replied.

The two kept looking at each and then they slowly faded away. Alena wasn't sure exactly what had happened, but it seemed to be a day for that. Although she didn't really know either of them she felt sad at their departure. Suddenly she realised she was standing all alone and she could feel the tears welling up inside. Despite the sadness she felt it was a glorious day and she needed to celebrate. The Evil One had finally been destroyed and the Seven Kingdoms were safe. As much as her home, Elhjem, had been destroyed they could easily rebuild it. Soon enough it would be bigger and better than before.

Without another thought Alena made her way to the command tent. When she arrived she found it was a hive of activity. All the commanders and wizards had returned from the battlefield and were seated around the large war table. Places had been left for Bern, Alaric and Alena if and when they were to return. A number of functionaries moved around with plates and glasses, setting the table for the feast that was being prepared. Everyone had a mug of ale or a goblet of wine to celebrate the victory. When they saw Alena at the entrance to the tent everyone went quiet.

Alena just stood and looked at everyone. Like them, she didn't know what to say. They could all tell by the expression on her face that something was wrong. When her sight came to rest on her father's face a tear rolled down her cheek. She steeled herself before continuing into the tent. Still no one knew what to say. It was obvious that Alaric and Bern weren't with her.

"How are you my daughter?" Orric finally asked.

Alena moved to spare seat next to her father and sat down. She wanted nothing more than bury her head in his chest and weeping uncontrollably, but it was not the time. She had information that they all needed. There would be time to mourn later.

"I am fine thank you," Alena started. After taking a deep breath she recalled as much of what happened in the cavern inside Crenallous as she could. She didn't know everything and even repeating what she did know didn't really make sense. In the end there was relief and sadness as she concluded her story.

"So it is truly over?" Jarwe asked.

"I believe it is," Alena replied.

"Of course it is!" Hadar boomed. "Now it's time to celebrate."

There was nothing more that needed to be said as the food started to arrive. The soldiers had been told to relax and enjoy themselves. The final battle was over. There would be celebrations when they returned home, but for the moment they could wallow in their victory.

The commanders stayed late into the night. The festivities continued even with the fatigue of the day. The alcohol kept flowing and there was no threat of it stopping in the morning as the festivities continued. The wizards left early. Their fatigue was much greater and once they had eaten they retired to their tents. They didn't have the energy to create a gateway to their island so they could sleep in their own beds.

It was late in the night and the candles in the tent had almost burned out when Jarwe finally stood. All the other commanders had long since retired. Despite the fact they didn't have any battles to fight in the morning there was still work to be done. Jarwe wanted to remain behind and enjoy the silence. A soft wind blew outside the tent and that was the only sound he could hear. It was like the world had just taken a deep breath of relief. The Seven Kingdoms were finally safe.

Epilogue: Going Home

Alaric floated over the Seven Kingdoms. If he had lips he would have smiled at what he saw, but he was just a floating consciousness. He no longer had any need for his body, which was a good thing since it no longer existed.

He looked down on Avalon. Seven large gateways had been created for the armies to return to their homes. The final battle was over and the armies of the Seven Kingdoms had been victorious. If only they could work together forever it would make the world a better place, but that would be asking too much. Alaric knew there would be wars between the different Kingdoms in the future, but nothing that would threaten the lives of everyone.

He focused on the Darshivallian army first. Lord Richmond had been his companion since he had left Crenallous the first time. He remembered Richmond and his friend and advisor Tancred, who had originally thought he was a follower of the Evil One. That thought would have made him laugh if he had vocal chords to make the sound or a mouth to let it out.

Richmond had offered to tell King Unwin about the death of his daughter, but Sorrell had said he had done enough. It was time for Richmond to return to Bellarome and reclaim his rightful place as lord. General Sorrell said he would take to job of telling Unwin, although they had all agreed to change the story. They didn't think Unwin needed to know his daughter had changed sides and had become a follower of the Evil One. They had agreed to tell King Unwin that the princess died trying to save Alaric and was caught in the cross-fire. Everyone who really knew what happened in Crenallous had agreed that was the story they would tell.

Alaric watched his friend and companion return home with the soldiers from Bellarome. A lot had changed since Richmond had left, but his return marked a new age in the city.

Richmond sat back in his sitting room. It had been a long time since he had been able to relax in his own home. Even when he had returned to gather more soldiers for the Alliance he didn't get to spend any time in his apartment. He took a deep breath in through his nose. He couldn't believe it still smelt the same. It reminded him of better times and the good times to come.

Suddenly a wave of sadness washed over him as he thought of his life-long friend. There had been little time to grieve for Tancred when he died. With the final battle over, his sorrow washed over him, but his grief wouldn't last long. With news of the victory reaching King Unwin he had declared a week long celebration throughout the kingdom. It wouldn't be long before the city was packed with people celebrating their victory.

There was much for Richmond to do, not only for the celebrations, but also for the recovery of the city. It had been a long time since he had left and there was a lot of paperwork for him to attend to. As much as it was tedious work he was looking forward to it. It was much better than trekking around the Seven Kingdoms with death waiting around every corner. He wouldn't have given it up for the world, but he would never like to do it again.

For the moment he relaxed back in his chair. There would be more time for rest later, but he was going to make the most of it while he could. The sight made Alaric feel happy. He was glad Richmond looked content.

Alaric let his conscious vision float over the Kingdom of Entero. Queen Oriana sat on her throne and looked out over the throng of functionaries and politicians before her. The army had started to return through the gateway and word had reached the castle that the final battle had been won, but that wasn't what Oriana was concerned about.

All the queen cared about was the return of Duke Xarles. The duke had been the leader behind her liberation when she was under the thrall of a Dark Knight. Even the thought of those times sent shivers down her spine. It was a time of her life that she wished she could forget. But the bonus was seeing Xarles for who he was. It was all she could do to stop from biting her fingernails as people came and went.

Alaric would have laughed if he could, but from happiness not humour. It was cute to see the queen in such a state, but he was glad no one else noticed. She had been through a lot, more than any of other rulers and she deserved a little happiness. He knew something that she didn't. Xarles felt the same as she did.

Since his death he had noticed he could do a few things that he couldn't before. One was he could sense what people were feeling, even if they didn't truly know it themselves.

Oriana jumped up from her throne when Xarles finally arrived. He was dirty from coming straight from the battlefield to the castle, but she didn't mind. She had already decided that she was going to marry him and make him the new Prince of Jarrat.

Xarles' eyes went straight to the queen as if there was no one else in the room. If anyone had tried to talk to him he wouldn't have heard them. If there was room for her to move she would have stepped down from her dais and rushed to meet him. The waiting was infuriating.

As soon as Xarles made the dais he bowed low. All the way to the throne his intentions were to take her in his arm and kiss her passionately, but when he reached her he couldn't bring himself to. If he was wrong then it would mean his own death, although he would prefer to die if it meant just one kiss from the woman he loved.

Oriana's head was pounding as her man approached and it almost stopped when he first looked up at her and then bent to pay homage. She did not care for formalities, but she couldn't fault him. Without thinking of the consequences she stepped down from her dais and gently lifted Xarles up by the shoulders. The entire throne room went quiet, but all Oriana could hear and see was the man standing before her. Without a second thought she leaned in for a kiss. Xarles moved backwards briefly before sweeping her up in his arms and kissing her on the lips. Alaric knew it was the start of a long and beautiful relationship.

Alaric let his consciousness drift across to where both the men of Castalia and the dwarves of the Western Dwarf Guild were making their way back home. It was by far the largest of the gateways created and they would be the last to leave Avalon.

The High Chancellor had taken his rightful place back in the Grand Cathedral. Alaric was quite happy with the new leader and they still had the most powerful army in the Seven Kingdoms. The last High Chancellor had been greedy and selfish. All he cared about were the diamonds being mined underneath the city and the riches they gave him. He was cruel and mean and Tiberius would serve as a much better leader.

He sat in his private chambers reflecting on what had happened. There had been so many followers of the Evil One in positions of power that he doubted he had rooted them all out, not that they had anyone to follow anymore. Even though the battle was finally over in Avalon, he never truly believed Nyrra would be gone.

There would be celebrations starting in the morning. It seemed like it was only yesterday that they were celebrating his coronation, but the end of evil deserved recognition. It was his turn to rule and he would do it well. He would make sure everyone prospered and he would not allow the oppression of his predecessor.

Alaric let the vision change to that of the guild. The dwarves had already made their way back being a small component of the army.

Brac had returned to the guild as a victorious leader. He claimed Hulkan had died bravely on the battlefield and with his dying words had returned command of the guild to Brac.

Hulkan's father, Ilar, didn't believe a word he said, but unless he could find someone to refute the story there was nothing he could do. He was sad his son was dead, but he was proud that he had died defending the Seven Kingdoms. Even if Brac lied about being given command he couldn't take that away from Hulkan or his memory.

Alaric knew otherwise as he looked down on them, but there was nothing he could do about it either. Brac wasn't truly an evil dwarf, he was just ambitious and sometimes that could outweigh logic. Even if Alaric could do something about the situation he wasn't sure he would. Brac would be a fair leader and that's all that really mattered.

The dwarves had suffered great loses on the battlefield, but like the others it would be a time to celebrate and not to mourn. There would be time to grieve when the celebrations were over. The dwarves would hold their own festivities away from the Castalial people. They had a lot to be proud of and they didn't want to get lost in other people's celebrations.

When Alaric was happy with what he saw he moved himself to the Cloumid Mountain range. Dorn had returned home at the head of the rest of the dwarven army. It had been a long time since he truly been home. He didn't consider the short visit to gain more soldiers truly a return. He was never going to be home until the final battle was over.

King Ashnar was glad to see the dwarves return. Even though he had feared and attack, there had been none. Dorn had been right and that was enough to welcome him back to the mountain and reinstate his position within the council. He would be given a village of his own to rule.

Alaric was glad that things were working out for his old companion. Although he hadn't had much to do with the dwarves they had taken his best friend, Bern, under their wing and looked after him when he wasn't able to. He knew they'd had a strong relationship and that meant something to Alaric.

He didn't stay long under the mountain. He knew his time was growing short. As much as he wanted to stay and watch over the Seven Kingdoms he knew he was needed elsewhere.

Since the death of his last incarnation his memories had flooded back to him. He had lived so many lives and had experienced so many different worlds. He thought he knew a lot as Alaric, but it didn't even touch the surface.

He moved across to Hondin Lel where Duke Hadar was moving his men back home. Alaric had liked the large man ever since they had met at his estate. He had helped them rescue Alena from Viper and Count Kerwin. There was something very genuine about him.

It had taken days for Hadar to make the ride home from Lel Dinion. As much as he wanted Althea to create a number of gateways throughout the kingdom, she had insisted that she could only create one to the capital. He had to admit the final battle had been a great drain on her and in the end he was just grateful she was doing anything to assist them.

Hadar rode home at the front of a small group of soldiers. He had tried to find his sons in Avalon and then in Lel Dinion, but there was no sign of them. It didn't necessarily mean they were dead, but he didn't think it was a good sign. It wasn't until he returned home did he find them both still alive.

They had been the first sub-commanders back through the gateway with soldiers from the west of Hondin Lel. They didn't remain in the city long as everyone was keen to return to see their loved ones. Hadar had promised that he would organise festivals for those who couldn't or wouldn't remain in the city.

As much as Hadar had wanted to return home straight away, King Lisle had insisted that he remain in the capital at least for one day of the celebrations. Despite his desire to return home to see his wife he couldn't refuse the king.

Again Alaric would have smiled, if he had lips, at the sight of Hadar casually relaxing around the dining table with his family as they shared the evening meal. If nothing else that was what Alaric had been fighting for. If he could have stayed for a moment longer he would have basked in their simple happiness, but it was time to move on.

His next trip brought him to the capital of Remidia. On his journey he passed over his old home of Arsiliac, which had been destroyed by the Evil One. Those who had survived the massacre had already started to rebuild the village. Alaric was glad that it wasn't going to be left to rot. He wished he could help, but that wasn't his job anymore.

He found Hawthorne sitting in his private apartment, tears rolling down his cheek. The festivals had just started in Remidel, but Hawthorne didn't feel like celebrating. Word had just reached him that his father, King Faxon, had taken the battlefield in Avalon. At first Hawthorne was proud that his father hadn't remained behind like most of the other leaders, but that quickly changed when he heard about his death. The body had been scorched with the rest of the bodies. If it hadn't been for a soldier who had seen Faxon fall, then no one would have known of the king's fate.

It would take weeks, if not months for the list of all the dead to be worked out. For the moment the celebrations were more important. There would be time for everyone to mourn when the festivities were over. Hawthorne would only have a short time for his grief before he would need to be seen. The celebrations wouldn't be complete without a visit from the royal family. He and his mother would make an appearance and would keep the king's death a secret until the celebrations were over. In the meantime they would just say he was too sick to go outside. It was a thin excuse, but the citizens would be too busy celebrating to think any more about it.

Hawthorne was king, or would be soon enough. When he was being tortured by the Dark Knight Dargoz he never thought he would see the day. As much as he always dreamed of one day being king he didn't think it would happen in such circumstances. Now that the day had come he wished it never had.

Alaric knew Hawthorne was the right man to lead Remidia into the new age of the Seven Kingdoms. Faxon had sacrificed his life, not only for his people, but for his kingdom. He knew deep down that there was no longer a place for him on the throne of Remidia. He knew as he passed through the gateway to Avalon he wouldn't be returning. If he had a chance he would have written a letter, but he was already on his horse when the realisation came to him.

There was nothing more for Alaric to see. His home kingdom was in great hands. His corporeal form drifted away to the elven home of *Nordligträ* in the Northern Forest. The occupants had almost been completely annihilated by a horde of orglin sent to kill the *Tree of Life.*

It was quickly agreed that the elves, under the leadership of Kilean had been given permission to return 'home'. They had been shunned for a long time, but in the end it was mutually beneficial. Alaric was pleased. It had been a long time ago when Kilean's father had taken a group of elves south and they had been completely shunned by those who remained.

Palen and Kilean both felt a wave of relief wash over them when the agreement had been made. If it was ever to happen, now was the best time. The elves were too busy celebrating the end of the final battle to care about old rivalries.

Alaric had been nervous about looking down over *Nordligträ.* It was the one place he didn't think would have settled down so quickly. He looked down at the elves dancing on the forest floor while music was being played. As much as he wanted to stay and watch he had one more place to visit before he left.

His last visit was the one he had been dreading. Elhjem had been destroyed by the Evil One and had been left in ruin, but that was the last thing on his mind. He both wanted and didn't want to see Alena once more before he left.

Before the final battle he had steeled his emotions and pushed them aside. There was no room for his feelings with Alena in his battle with Nyrra. It was the hardest thing he ever had to do. All he wanted was to hold her tight and make sure everything was alright.

The elves had been back from the battlefield for a week and already the village was starting to look better. The filth of the Evil One had disappeared with his death, leaving only the rubble from the destroyed buildings.

Makeshift houses had been built while they worked on something more permanent. They were the only ones who didn't, or at least hadn't had time, to celebrate their victory in Avalon. No one really seemed to care and Alaric didn't at all feel sorry for them. They had a job to do and the final battle wouldn't truly be over for them until they had restored their home.

It wasn't the elves, busy at work, that Alaric came to see. There was only one he really cared about and when it came time to see her he had paused. It would be the last time he would ever see her. Of all the lives he had lived and all the memories he contained he had never loved someone like he had loved Alena. Their time together had been so short and now he wasn't sure he was ready to say goodbye.

In the end he knew his time was growing shorter and shorter and if he wanted to see her one last time it would have to be now. Alaric let his conscious float down into the makeshift house of Orric. His daughter was curled up on a bedroll softly weeping. The sight would have broken Alaric's heart, if he had one.

Suddenly Alena sat up and looked around. It was as if she could sense his presence, but he knew that was impossible. No one could know he was there. He wasn't really there.

Even with her tear stained face Alaric thought she was the most beautiful creature he had ever seen. If he had lips nothing would have stopped him from kissing hers and yet there was nothing he could do. The only option left to him was to watch her loveliness. If he could have stayed in that moment for eternity he would be forever happy, but as he felt himself slowly fade away he knew that would never happen. A smile crossed Alena's face as he finally disappeared. It was last image he would ever have of her.

Alena looked up and said "Goodbye!"

The End

www.ingramcontent.com/pod-product-compliance
Lightning Source LLC
Chambersburg PA
CBHW020925020726
47495CB00002B/347

* 9 7 8 0 9 9 5 3 5 2 4 0 7 *